西游记

REVISED EDITION *Volume I*

The Journey to the West

Translated and Edited by Anthony C. Yu

The University of Chicago Press *Chicago & London*

Anthony C. Yu is the Carl Darling Buck Distinguished Service Professor Emeritus in the Humanities and Professor Emeritus of Religion and Literature in the Divinity School; also in the Departments of Comparative Literature, East Asian Languages and Civilizations, and English Language and Literature, and the Committee on Social Thought. His scholarly work focuses on comparative study of both literary and religious traditions.

Publication of this volume was made possible by a grant from the Chiang Ching-kuo Foundation for International Scholarly Exchange (USA).

The University of Chicago Press, Chicago 60637
The University of Chicago Press, Ltd., London
© 2012 by The University of Chicago
All rights reserved. Published 2012.
Printed in the United States of America

21 20 19 18 17 16 15 14 13 12   1 2 3 4 5

ISBN-13: 978-0-226-97131-5 (cloth)
ISBN-13: 978-0-226-97132-2 (paper)
ISBN-13: 978-0-226-97140-7 (e-book)
ISBN-10: 0-226-97131-7 (cloth)
ISBN-10: 0-226-97132-5 (paper)

Library of Congress Cataloging-in-Publication Data

Wu, Cheng'en, ca. 1500–ca. 1582, author.
  [Xi you ji. English. 2012]
  The journey to the West / translated and edited by Anthony C. Yu. — Revised edition.
      pages ; cm
  Summary: The story of Xuanzang, the monk who went from China to India in quest of Buddhist scriptures.
  Includes bibliographical references and index.
  ISBN: 978-0-226-97131-5 (v. 1: cloth : alkaline paper) — ISBN: 0-226-97131-7 (v. 1. : cloth : alkaline paper) — ISBN: 978-0-226-97132-2 (v. 1 : pbk. : alkaline paper) — ISBN: 0-226-97132-5 (v. 1 : pbk. : alkaline paper) — ISBN: 978-0-226-97140-7 (v. 1 : e-book) (print) — ISBN: 978-0-226-97133-9 (v. 2: cloth : alkaline paper) — ISBN: 0-226-97133-3 (v. 2 : cloth : alkaline paper) — ISBN: 978-0-226-97134-6 (v. 2 : paperback : alkaline paper) — ISBN: 0-226-97134-1 (v. 2 : paperback : alkaline paper) — ISBN: 978-0-226-97141-4 (v. 2 : e-book) (print) — ISBN: 978-0-226-97136-0 (v. 3 : cloth : alkaline paper) — ISBN: 0-226-97136-8 (v. 3 : cloth : alkaline paper) — ISBN: 978-0-226-97137-7 (v. 3 : paperback : alkaline paper) — ISBN: 0-226-97137-6 (v. 3 : paperback : alkaline paper) — ISBN: 978-0-226-97142-1 (v. 3 : e-book) (print) — ISBN: 978-0-226-97138-4 (v. 4 : cloth : alkaline paper) — ISBN: 0-226-97138-4 (v. 4 : cloth : alkaline paper) — ISBN: 978-0-226-97139-1 (v. 4 : paperback : alkaline paper) — ISBN: 978-0-226-97143-8 (v. 4 : e-book) 1. Xuanzang, ca. 596–664—Fiction. I. Yu, Anthony C., 1938–, translator, editor. II. Title.
  PL2697.H75E5 2012
  895.1'346—dc23

                                    2012002836

♾ This paper meets the requirements of ANSI/NISO Z39.48-1992 (Permanence of Paper).

FOR *Priscilla & Christopher*

上士聞道，勤而行之。
中士聞道，若存若亡。
下士聞道，大笑之；不笑，不足以為道。

(Daodejing 41)

The superior student who hears about
the Way practices it diligently.
The middling student who hears about
the Way now keeps it and now loses it.
The inferior student who hears about
the Way laughs at it loudly;
If he did not laugh, it would have
fallen short of the Way.

Die Sprache drükt niemals etwas
vollständig aus, sondern hebt nur
ein ihr hervorstechend scheinen-
des Merkmal hervor.

FRIEDRICH NIETZSCHE,
"Darstellung der Antiken Rhetorik"

Language never expresses something
fully, but only highlights some
significant characteristic feature.

Contents

Preface to the Revised Edition

A twofold purpose motivated my decision in 1969 to attempt a plenary English translation of *The Journey to the West*. On the matter of literary form, I wanted my version to rectify the distorted picture provided by Arthur Waley's justly popular abridgment (i.e., *Monkey, Folk Novel of China by Wu Ch'êng-ên*), which regrettably excised all poetic segments and cut out or revised prose passages at will. I felt strongly that it was high time that a classic Chinese novel like the one in question, though of extraordinary length and complexity, should be read in its entirety and not in bits and pieces. On the matter of the novel's understanding and critical interpretation, I wanted to redress an imbalance of emphasis championed by Dr. Hu Shi, who provided the Waley volume with the following observation: "[F]reed from all kinds of allegorical interpretations by Buddhist, Taoist, and Confucianist commentators, *Monkey* is simply a book of good humor, profound nonsense, good-natured satire, and delightful entertainment" (*Monkey*, p. 5). Many other Chinese scholars for most of the twentieth century shared this view. My own encounter with the text since childhood, under the kind and skillful tutelage of my late grandfather, who used the novel as a textbook for teaching me Chinese during the years of the Sino-Japanese war, had long convinced me that this work was nothing if not one of the world's most finely wrought literary allegories. The past four decades of studying, translating, and teaching it at the University of Chicago have also made me a happy witness to new directions in its scholarly research and interpretation. The persistent efforts of Japanese, European, American, and Chinese scholars—in diaspora and on the mainland during the last two decades—have joined to enlarge dramatically our understanding of the text's sources and religious context, especially those belonging to the Daoist religion since the late Tang.

Completed in 1983, the first full-length English translation of the novel spawned its own ironies. No sooner had all four volumes appeared than friends and colleagues far and near protested their unwieldy length, for general readers and for classroom usage. After years of resistance to pleas for a shorter edition, I decided, when approaching retirement in 2005, that an abridged version was indeed needed for classroom and readers' needs. The proposed text of about thirty-five chapters would (1) convert the old Wade-Giles system of romanization to the now globally accepted Hanyu

Pinyin system for all Chinese names, locales, and terms; (2) remove most scholarly footnotes and all Chinese texts; (3) provide a new and very brief introduction for general readers; and (4) include minor corrections of rhetoric and vocabulary where needed. The one-volume edition, *The Monkey and the Monk, An Abridgment of* The Journey to the West, was published in 2006 by the University of Chicago Press.

Production of this abridged version, paradoxically, made me realize further the endless effort of literary translation, in some ways analogous to a performer's varied readings of a familiar music score. The linguistic signs or musical notations remain the same, but the understanding of them may greatly alter. On the matter of tempo alone, a comparison of Glenn Gould's recordings of J. S. Bach's "The Complete Goldberg Variations" in 1955 and 1981 yields illuminating differences. My abridgment in every aspect (shorter introduction, simplified notes, emendations) certainly betokens awareness and assumptions of new knowledge. The first full-length edition, in turn, now displays quite a few pockets of datedness. I resolved that I would devote my new-found "leisure" in retirement to attempt a major and complete overhaul of the first edition. The principal objectives, consistent with, but not entirely identical to, those of the abridged volume, would be to (1) convert the entire romanization system to Pinyin; (2) restore and update or augment, where necessary, all scholarly annotations; (3) provide a major restatement of the introduction that, apart from providing basic information about the novel, would study the most important new scholarship on literary issues, religious traditions (especially on identified sources in the Buddhist and Daoist Canons and in extracanonical materials), and modes of interpretation; and (4) correct or emend both prose and poetic segments of the translation to make semantics and prosody more concise. Because the five pilgrims in the novel, like characters in fiction of another language (e.g., Russian), have multiple names, I have made uniform the way I translate them. Formal names and surnames are romanized (e.g., Chen Xuanzang, Sun Wukong). Informal names or nicknames become direct translations (e.g., Pilgrim for the Chinese "Xingzhe" [disciple or acolyte], Eight Rules for "Bajie," a change in the perjorative title for Monkey from the romanized "Bimawen" to "BanHorsePlague").[1] My hope is that this revised version, like volumes of the Arden Shakespeare, Third Series, or Dorothy L. Sayer's *The Divine Comedy*, will last for some time as a teaching edition.

The timely award of an Emeriti Fellowship by the Mellon Foundation in 2006 provided immense encouragement and assistance for the initial stage of technical work (scanning the four volumes and rendering the two thousand-plus pages in free text format), purchase of needed equipment and materials, and some travel to different libraries and centers. Professor

Martha Roth (dean of humanities at the University of Chicago) and Professor Richard Rosengarten (dean of the divinity school at the University of Chicago) have given generous help from the beginning, facilitating expert and unfailing computer support from two units of the university. I am grateful as well to the University of Chicago Press for its receptiveness to my proposal for a revised edition.

Dr. Yuan Zhou, curator of Regenstein Library's East Asian collections, and his able staff members William Alspaugh, Eizaburo Okuizumi, and Qian Xiaowen, have worked tirelessly to acquire needed materials far and near. As in the past, the encyclopedic bibliographical expertise of Dr. Tailoi Ma, director of Princeton University's East Asian Library and the Gest Collection, continues to furnish trusted guidance. Professor Lai Chi-Tim of the Chinese University of Hong Kong gave invaluable help to my ongoing labor by installing personally, during one of his visits, all available databases of Daoist scriptures into my computer. Professor Richard G. Wang (University of Florida) and Professor Yang Li (Shanghai University) provided diligent collaboration in tracking and identifying comprehensively the Daoist sources for both poetry and prose cited in the novel. Professor Nicholas Koss (Fu-jen University, Taiwan), Professor Qiancheng Li (Louisiana State University), and Professor Ping Shao (Davidson College) have showered me with their generous gifts of scholarly publications—of their own and of others—that are crucial for my research.

In early 2009, my wife and I were privileged to make our first visit to Australia where I served for a fortnight as Visiting Fellow at The China Institute of Australia National University. I wish I could name every one of the faculty and student colleagues whose extraordinary kindness and hospitality made that journey indelibly memorable. The constraint of space notwithstanding, I must register lasting gratitude to the faculty members of ANU College of Asia and the Pacific—Geremie Barmé, Duncan Campbell, John Markham, Benjamin Penny, and Richard Rigby—who offered constant friendship and intellectual stimulation, especially for my continuing work of translation and revision. Nathan Woolley, doctoral candidate at the college and executive assistant of the institute, attended to our every need. The generosity of John Minford, a friend and kindred spirit of more than three decades in things literary, linguistic, and (discovered during this visit to Australia) musical, made the entire journey possible. His and his wife Rachel's hospitality not only helped erase the strain of great distance between Canberra and Chicago, but it also allowed us to enjoy several cherished meetings with Professor Liu Ts'un-yan before his passing a few months later. My indebtedness to Professor Liu's scholarship should be apparent in the introduction and the notes studding this translation.

The final draft of the new, long introduction has benefited enormously from the sort of attentive and astute reading that one may expect only from true and generous friends, and this was bestowed by Professor Zhou Yiqun (Stanford University), Professor Nathan Sivin (emeritus, University of Pennsylvania), and Dr. Xu Dongfeng (now of Emory University). Their criticisms, corrections, and suggested emendations have vastly improved the manuscript. Remaining faults and errors are entirely my own. As I reach this phase of my project, my one sadness comes from the realization that all readers of the revised edition will no longer enjoy the rare art of the late Wen-ching Tsien (Mrs. T. H. Tsien), whose peerless Chinese calligraphy ornamented many pages of the original four volumes.

Portions of a recent essay, "The Formation of Fiction in *The Journey to the West*," *Asia Major*, third series, XXI/1 (2008): 15–44, were used in different parts of the introduction by permission.

When I began work on the translation long ago, it was an early and ready decision to dedicate the first volume to my wife and our only son. After more than four decades, it is both privilege and pleasure to renew the dedication.

Anthony C. Yu
Chicago, 2011

Preface to the First Edition

Though *The Journey to the West* is one of the most popular works of fiction in China since its first publication in the late sixteenth century, and though it has been studied extensively in recent years by both Oriental and Western scholars (notably Hu Shih, Lu Hsün, Chêng Chên-to, Ogawa Tamaki, Ōta Tatsuo, C. T. Hsia, Liu Ts'un-yan, Sawada Mizuho, and Glen Dudbridge), a fully translated text has never been available to Western readers, notwithstanding the appearance in 1959 of what is reputed to be a complete Russian edition.[1] Two early versions in English (Timothy Richard, *A Mission to Heaven*, 1913, and Helen M. Hayes, *The Buddhist Pilgrim's Progress*, 1930) were no more than brief paraphrases and adaptations. The French brought out in 1957 a two-volume edition which presented a fairly comprehensive account of the prose passages, but it left much of the poetry virtually untouched.[2] It was, moreover, riddled with errors and mistranslations. In 1964, George Theiner translated into English a Czech edition which was also greatly abridged.[3] This leaves us finally with the justly famous and widely read version of Arthur Waley, published in 1943 under the misleading title *Monkey, Folk Novel of China*.[4] Waley's work is vastly superior to the others in style and diction, if not always in accuracy, but unfortunately it, too, is a severely truncated and highly selective rendition.

Of the one hundred chapters in the narrative, Waley has chosen to translate only chapters 1-15, 18-19, 22, 37-39, 44-49, and 98-100, which means that he has included less than one-third of the original. Even in this attenuated form, however, Waley's version further deviates from the original by having left out large portions of certain chapters (e.g., 10 and 19). What is most regrettable is that Waley, despite his immense gift for, and magnificent achievements in, the translation of Chinese verse, has elected to ignore the many poems—some 750 of them—that are structured in the narrative. Not only is the fundamental literary form of the work thereby distorted, but also much of the narrative vigor and descriptive power of its language which have attracted generations of Chinese readers is lost. The basic reason for my endeavor here, in the first volume of what is hoped to be a four-volume unabridged edition in English, is simply the need for a version which will provide the reader with as faithful an image as possible of this, one of the four or five lasting monuments of traditional Chinese fiction.

My dependence on modern scholarship devoted to this work is apparent everywhere in both the introduction and the translation itself. I have stressed, however, in my discussion of the work those narrative devices and structural elements which have received comparatively little attention from recent commentators. For, in addition to being a work of comedy and satire masterfully wrought, *The Journey to the West* appears to embody elements of serious allegory derived from Chinese religious syncretism which any critical interpretation of it can ill afford to ignore.

A small portion of the introduction first appeared as "Heroic Verse and Heroic Mission: Dimensions of the Epic in the *Hsi-yu chi*," *Journal of Asian Studies* 31 (1972): 879–97, while another segment was written as part of an essay, "Religion and Allegory in the *Hsi-yu chi*," for *Persuasion: Critical Essays on Chinese Literature,* edited by Joseph S. M. Lau and Leo Lee (in preparation).

The commitment to so large an undertaking can hardly be kept without the encouragement and support of friends both at the University of Chicago and elsewhere. It has been my good fortune since my arrival at Chicago to have had Nathan Scott as a teacher and a colleague. He is an unfailing and illuminating guide in the area of literary theory and theological criticism, and my gratitude for the sustaining friendship of Professor Scott and his wife for more than a decade cannot be expressed in a few words. From the beginning, Dean Joseph Kitagawa of the University of Chicago's Divinity School has not only urged me to attempt this translation, but has also faithfully provided thoughtful assistance which has enabled me to carry forward, without too great disruption, each phase of research and writing in the face of equally demanding academic and administrative responsibilities. To Herlee Creel, Elder Olson, Mircea Eliade, Frank Reynolds, James Redfield (all of Chicago), C. T. Hsia (Columbia University), Joseph Lau (University of Wisconsin), and Giles Gunn (University of North Carolina at Chapel Hill), I must say that the warmth of their friendship and their enthusiasm for the project have been a constant source of strength and inspiration. David Roy has generously placed his superb library and his vast knowledge of Chinese literature at my disposal; the many discussions with him have saved me from several serious errors. David Grene has taught me, more by example than by precept, a good deal about the art of translation. Portions of this volume have also been read by D. C. Lau (University of London) and Nathan Sivin (MIT); their searching criticisms and suggestions, along with those of an anonymous reader, have decisively improved the manuscript.

I am indebted also to Philip Kuhn and Najita Tetsuo, past and present directors of the Far Eastern Language and Area Center at the University, for making available the needed funds at various stages of research. A grant by the Leopold Schepp Foundation of New York in the summer of 1973 enabled me to visit Japan and Taiwan to study the early editions of the narrative. The gracious hospitality and stimulating conversations provided by Kubo Noritada (Tōyō Bunka Kenkyūjo), Nakamura Kyoko (University of Tokyo), Tanaka Kenji (Jinbun Kagak'u Kenkyūjo), and Abe Masao (Nara University) made my stay in Japan unforgettable, though it was all too brief.

My thanks are due, too, to T. H. Tsien and his able staff at the Far Eastern Library of the University of Chicago (Tai Wen-pei, Robert Petersen, Ma Tai-loi, Ho Hoi-lap, and Kenneth Tanaka), who have offered me every assistance in the acquisition of materials and in the investigation of texts, and to Mrs. T. H. Tsien, whose elegant calligraphy has graced the pages of this edition. Araki Michio, doctoral candidate at the Divinity School and my sometime research assistant, has been invaluable in helping me read Japanese scholarship. Edmund Rowan, doctoral candidate at the Department of Far Eastern Languages and Civilizations, has proofread the entire typescript with meticulous care and discerning criticisms. No brief statement is adequate to indicate the selfless and painstaking labor of Mrs. Donna Guido and Miss Susan Hopkins in the preparation of the manuscript. Finally, I owe the successful completion of this first volume above all else to my wife and my young son. For their affectionate exhortations, for their unswerving devotion to the translation, and for their cheerful forbearance toward long stretches of obsessive work, the dedication betokens only a fraction of my gratitude.

Abbreviations

Antecedents	Glen Dudbridge, *The "Hsi-yu chi": A Study of Antecedents to the Sixteenth-Century Chinese Novel* (Cambridge, 1970)
Bodde	Derk Bodde, *Festivals in Classical China* (Princeton and Hong Kong, 1975)
BPZ	*Baopuzi* 抱朴子, Neipian and Waipian. SBBY
BSOAS	*Bulletin of the School of Oriental and African Studies*
Campany	Robert Ford Campany, *To Live as Long as Heaven and Earth: A Translation and Study of Ge Hong's "Traditions of Divine Transcendents"* (Berkeley, 2002)
CATCL	*The Columbia Anthology of Traditional Chinese Literature*, ed. Victor Mair (New York, 1994)
CHC	*The Cambridge History of China*, eds. Denis Twitchett and John K. Fairbank (15 vols. in multiple book-length parts. Cambridge and New York, 1978–2009)
CHCL	*The Columbia History of Chinese Literature*, ed. Victor Mair (New York, 2001)
CJ	Anthony C. Yu, *Comparative Journeys: Essays on Literature and Religion East and West* (New York, 2008)
CLEAR	*Chinese Literature: Essays Articles Reviews*
CQ	*China Quarterly*
DH	*Daoism Handbook*, ed. Livia Kohn (Leiden, 2000)
DHBWJ	*Dunhuang bianwenji* 敦煌變文集, ed. Wang Zhongmin 王重民 (2 vols., Beijing, 1957)
DJDCD	*Daojiao da cidian* 道教大辭典, ed. Li Shuhuan 李叔還 (Taipei, 1981)
DJWHCD	*Daojiao wenhua cidian* 道教文化辞典, ed. Zhang Zhizhe 张志哲 (Shanghai, 1994)
DZ	*Zhengtong Daozang* 正統道藏 (36 vols. Reprinted by Wenwu, 1988). Second set of numbers in JW citations refers to volume and page number.
ET	*The Encyclopedia of Taoism*, ed. Fabrizio Pregadio (2 vols., London and New York, 2008)
FSZ	*Da Tang Da Ci'ensi Sanzang fashi zhuan* 大唐大慈恩三藏法師傳, comp. Huili 慧立 and Yancong 彥悰. T 50, #2053. Text cited is that printed in SZZSHB.

1592	*Xinke chuxiang guanban dazi Xiyouji* 新刻出像官板大字西游記, ed. Huayang dongtian zhuren 華陽洞天主人. Fasc. rpr. of Jinling Shidetang edition (1592) in *Guben xiaoshuo jicheng* 古本小說集成, vols. 499-502 (Shanghai, 1990)
FXDCD	*Foxue da cidian* 佛學大辭典, comp. and ed., Ding Fubao 丁福保 (fasc. rpr. of 1922 ed. Beijing, 1988)
HFTWJ	Liu Ts'un-yan [Cunren] 柳存仁, *Hefengtang wenji* 和風堂文集 (3 vols., Shanghai, 1991)
HJAS	*Harvard Journal of Asiatic Studies*
HR	*History of Religions*
Herrmann	Albert Hermann, *An Historical Atlas of China*, new ed. (Chicago, 1966)
Hu Shi (1923)	Hu Shi 胡適, "*Xiyouji* kaozheng 西游記考證," in *Hu Shi wencun* 胡適文存 (4 vols., Hong Kong, 1962), 2: 354-99
Hucker	Charles O. Hucker, *A Dictionary of Official Titles in Imperial China* (Stanford, 1985)
IC	*The Indiana Companion to Traditional Chinese Literature*, ed. and comp. William H. Nienhauser Jr. (Bloomington, IN, 1986)
Isobe	Isobe Akira 磯部彰, *Saiyūki keiseishi no kenkyū* 西游記形成史の研究 (Tokyo, 1993)
j	*juan* 卷
JA	*Journal asiatique*
JAOS	*Journal of the American Oriental Society*
JAS	*Journal of Asian Studies*
JCR	*Journal of Chinese Religions*
JMDJCD	*Jianming Daojiao cidian* 簡明道教辭典, comp. and ed., Huang Haide et al., 黃海德 (Chengdu, 1991)
JW	*The Journey to the West* (Refers only to the four-volume translation of *Xiyouji* by Anthony C. Yu published by the University of Chicago Press, 1977-1983, of which the present volume is the first of four in a complete revised edition.)
Lévy	André Lévy, trad., *Wu Cheng'en, La Pérégrination vers l'Ouest*, Bibliothèque de la Pléiade (2 vols., Paris, 1991)
Li	*Li Angang Piping Xiyouji* 李安纲批评西游记 (2 vols., Beijing, 2004)
Little	Stephen Little with Shawn Eichman, *Daoism and the Arts of China* (Art Institute of Chicago, in association with University of California Press, 2000)
LSYYJK	*Lishi yuyan yanjiusuo jikan* 歷史語言研究所集刊

LWJ	"*Xiyouji*" *yanjiu lunwenji* 西游記研究論文集 (Beijing, 1957)
MDHYCH	Gu Zhichuan 顾之川, *Mingdai Hanyu cihui yanjiu* 明代汉语词汇研究 (Kaifeng, Henan, 2000)
Monkey	*Monkey: Folk Novel of China by Wu Ch'eng-en*, trans. Arthur Waley (London, 1943)
Ōta	Ōta Tatsuo 太田辰夫, *Saiyūki no kenkyū* 西游記の研究 (Tokyo, 1984)
Plaks	Andrew H. Plaks, *The Four Masterworks of the Ming Novel* (Princeton, 1987)
Porkert	Manfred Porkert, *The Theoretical Foundations of Chinese Medicine: Systems of Correspondence* (Cambridge, MA, 1974)
QSC	*Quan Songci* 全宋詞, ed. Tang Guizhang 唐圭璋 (5 vols., 1965; rpr. Tainan, 1975)
QTS	*Quan Tangshi* 全唐詩 (12 vols., 1966; rpr. Tainan, 1974)
Saiyūki	*Saiyūki* 西游記, trans. Ōta Tatsuo 太田辰夫 and Torii Hisayasu 鳥居久靖. Chūgoku koten bungaku taikei 中國古典文學大系, 31-32 (2 vols., Tokyo, 1971)
SBBY	Sibu beiyao 四部備要
SBCK	Sibu congkan 四部叢刊
SCC	Joseph Needham et al., *Science and Civilisation in China* (7 vols. in 27 book-length parts. Cambridge, 1954)
Schafer	Edward H. Schafer, *Pacing the Void: T'ang Approaches to the Stars* (Berkeley, Los Angeles, and London, 1977)
SCTH	*Sancai tuhui* 三才圖會 (1609 edition)
Soothill	*A Dictionary of Chinese Buddhist Terms*, comp. William Edward Soothill and Lewis Hodus (rpr. 1934 ed. by London: Kegan Paul, Trench, Trubner. Taipei, 1970)
SSJZS	*Shisanjing zhushu* 十三經注疏 (2 vols., Beijing, 1977)
SZZSHB	*Tang Xuanzang Sanzang zhuanshi huibian* 唐玄奘三藏傳史彙編, ed. Master Guangzhong 光中 (Taipei, 1988)
T	*Taishō shinshū dai-zōkyō* 大正新脩大藏經, eds. Takakusu Junijirō 高楠順次郎 and Watanabe Kaikyoku 渡邊海旭 (85 vols., Tokyo, 1934)
TC	*The Taoist Canon: A Historical Companion to the "Daozang"*, eds. Kristofer Schipper and Franciscus Verellen (3 vols., Chicago, 2004)
TP	*T'oung Pao*
TPGJ	*Taiping guangji* 太平廣記, comp. and ed. Li Fang 李昉 (5 vols., rpr. Tainan, 1975)
TPYL	*Taiping yulan* 太平御覽, comp. and ed. Li Fang (4 vols., Beijing, 1960)

Unschuld	Paul U. Unschuld, trans. and annotated, *Nan-Ching: The Classic of Difficult Issues* (Berkeley, Los Angeles, and London, 1986)
Veith	Ilza Veith, trans., *The Yellow Emperor's Classic of Internal Medicine*, new ed. (Berkeley, Los Angeles, and London, 1972)
WCESWJ	*Wu Cheng'en shiwenji* 吳承恩詩文集, ed. Liu Xiuye 劉修業 (Shanghai, 1958).
XMGZ	*Xingming guizhi* 性命圭旨, authorship attributed to an advanced student of one Yin Zhenren 尹真人, in *Zangwai Daoshu* 藏外道書 (36 vols., Chengdu, 1992-1994), 9: 506-95. For JW, I also consult a modern critical edition published in Taipei, 2005, with a comprehensive and learned set of annotations by Fu Fengying 傅鳳英. The citation from this particular edition will be denominated as XMGZ-Taipei.
XYJ	Wu Cheng'en 吳承恩, *Xiyouji* 西游記 (Beijing: Zuojia chubanshe, 1954). Abbreviation refers only to this edition.
XYJCD	*Xiyouji cidian* 西游記辞典, comp. and ed. Zeng Shangyan 曾上炎 (Zhengzhou, Henan, 1994)
XYJTY	Zheng Mingli 鄭明娳, *Xiyouji tanyuan* 西游記探源 (2 vols., 1982; rpr. Taipei, 2003)
XYJYJZL	*Xiyouji yanjiu zhiliao* 西游记研究资料, ed. Liu Yinbo 刘荫柏 (Shanghai, 1982)
XYJZLHB	"*Xiyouji*" *zhiliao huibian* 《西游记》资料汇编 (Zhongzhou, Henan, 1983)
YYZZ	*Youyang zazu* 酉陽雜俎 (SBCK edition)
ZYZ	*Zhongyao zhi* 中藥誌 (4 vols., Beijing, 1959-1961).
Yang	Yang Fengshi 楊逢時, *Zhongguo zhengtong Daojiao da cidian* 中國正統道教大辭典 (2 vols., Taipei, 1989-1992)
Yü	Chün-fang Yü, *Kuan-yin: The Chinese Transformation of Avalokiteśvara* (New York, 2001)
ZHDJDCD	*Zhonghua Daojiao da cidian* 中華道教大辭典, ed. Hu Fuchen 胡孚琛 et al. (Beijing, 1995)
Zhou	Zhou Wei 周緯, *Zhongguo bingqishi gao* 中國兵器史稿 (Beijing, 1957)

Citations from all Standard Histories, unless otherwise indicated, are taken from the Kaiming edition of *Ershiwushi* 二十五史 (9 vols.,1934; rpr. Taipei, 1959). Citations of text with traditional or simplified characters follow format of publications consulted.

Introduction

I HISTORICAL AND LITERARY ANTECEDENTS

The story of the late-Ming novel *Xiyouji* 西游記 (*The Journey to the West*) is loosely based on the famous pilgrimage of Xuanzang 玄奘 (596?–664), the monk who went from China to India in quest of Buddhist scriptures. He was not the first to have undertaken such a long and hazardous journey. According to a modern scholar's tabulations,[1] at least fifty-four named clerics before him, beginning with Zhu Shixing 朱士行 in 260 CE, had traveled westward both for advanced studies and to fetch sacred writings, though not all of them had reached the land of their faith. After Xuanzang, there were another fifty or so pilgrims who made the journey, the last of whom was the monk Wukong 悟空, who stayed in India for forty years and returned in the year 789.[2] Xuanzang's journey, therefore, was part of the wider movement of seeking the Dharma in the West, which spanned nearly five centuries. His extraordinary achievements and his personality, neither of which this novel attempts to depict literally, became part of the permanent legacy of Chinese Buddhism. He was, by most accounts, one of the best-known and most revered Buddhist monks.

Born probably in the year 596 in the province of Henan 河南,[3] in Tang-era Chenliu county 陳留 of Luozhou 洛州 (now Goushi county 緱氏縣), Xuanzang, whose secular surname was Chen 陳 and given name Wei 褘, is described by his biographers as having come from a family of fairly prominent officials. His grandfather Chen Kang 陳康 was erudite (professor more or less) in the School for the Sons of the State (*guozi boshi* 國子博士), a moderately high rank. Xuanzang's father Chen Hui 陳惠 mastered the classics early and loved to affect the appearance of a Confucian scholar. Xuanzang himself was reputed to have been a precocious child. When he was but eight years old and reciting the *Classic of Filial Piety* before his father, the young boy suddenly leapt to his feet to tidy his clothes. As the reason for his abrupt action, the youth declared: "Master Zeng [one of Confucius's disciples] heard his teacher's voice and rose from his mat. How could Xuanzang sit still when he hears his father's teachings?"[4] Despite this alleged practice of received virtue, the death of his father two years later and the influence of an elder brother who was a Buddhist monk already (Chen Su 陳素, religious name, Zhangjie 長捷) might have led to his joining the monastic community in the eastern Tang capital of Luoyang at age thirteen. Even at this time he had developed a deep interest in the study of

Buddhist scriptures, and he later journeyed with his brother to the western capital of Chang'an 長安 (today's Xi'an 西安) to continue his studies with that city's eminent clerics.

Xuanzang grew up in a period of tremendous social and intellectual ferment in Chinese history. Yang Jian 楊堅 (r. 581-604), the founding emperor of the Sui dynasty, came to power in 581, and though the dynasty itself lasted less than forty years (581-618), its accomplishments, in Arthur Wright's words, were

> prodigious and its effects on the later history of China were far-reaching. It represented one of those critical periods in Chinese history . . . when decisions made and measures taken wrought a sharp break in institutional development in the fabric of social and political life. The Sui reunified China politically after nearly three hundred years of disunion; it reorganized and unified economic life; it made great strides in the re-establishment of cultural homogeneity throughout an area where subcultures had proliferated for over three centuries. Its legacy of political and economic institutions, of codified law and governmental procedures, of a new concept of empire, laid the foundations for the great age of Tang which followed.[5]

It was also a time marked by the revival of religious traditions, for Sui Wendi (Yang Jian) actively sought the support and sanction of all three religions—Confucianism, Daoism, and Buddhism—to consolidate his empire, thus reversing the persecutory policies of some of his predecessors in the Northern Zhou dynasty and providing exemplary actions for the early Tang emperors in the next dynasty.[6] Though he might lack some of the personal piety of a previous Buddhist emperor such as Liang Wudi (r. 502-49), Wendi himself was unquestionably a devout believer whose imperial patronage gave to the Buddhist community the kind of support, security, and stimulus for growth not unlike that received by the Christian church under Constantine. This Chinese emperor began a comprehensive program of constructing stūpas and enshrining sacred relics in emulation of the Indian monarch Aśoka. He also established various assemblies of priests to propagate the faith and study groups to promote sound doctrines. Even allowing for some exaggerations in the Buddhist sources, it was apparent that Buddhism, by the end of the Sui dynasty, had enjoyed remarkable growth, as evidenced by the vast increase of converts, clerics, and temples throughout the land.

That Xuanzang himself at an early age was very much caught up in the intellectual activities spreading through his religious community at this time could perhaps best be seen in the kind of training he received as a young acolyte. His biographers mentioned specifically that after he first entered the Pure Land Monastery in Luoyang, he studied with abandon-

ment the *Niepan jing* 涅盤經 (*Nirvāṇa Sūtra*) and the *She dasheng lun* 攝
大乘論 (*Mahāyāna-saṁparigraha śāstra*) with two tutors (FSZ, *j* 1). These
two works are significant to the extent that they may shed light on part
of the doctrinal controversy continuing for some three centuries in Chinese Buddhism. A major Mahāyāna text, the *Nirvāṇa Sūtra*, was translated
three times: first by Faxian in collaboration with Buddha-bhadra, then by
Dharmakshema of Bei Liang in 421, and again by a group of southern Chinese Buddhists led by Huiyan (363-443) in the Yuanjia era (424-453). Its
widespread appeal, particularly in the south, and its repeated discussions
can readily be attributed to the emphasis on a more inclusive concept of
enlightenment and salvation. According to Kenneth Ch'en, the Buddhists
until this time had been taught that there is no self in nirvāṇa. In this sūtra,
however, they are told that the Buddha possesses an immortal self, and that
the final state of nirvāṇa is one of bliss and purity enjoyed by the eternal
self. *Saṁsāra* is thus a pilgrimage leading to the final goal of union with
the Buddha, and this salvation is guaranteed by the fact that all living beings possess the Buddha-nature. All living beings from the beginning of
life participated in the Buddha's eternal existence, and thereby dignity is
granted them as children of the Buddha.[7]

On the other hand, the śāstra, though also a Mahāyānist text, belongs to
the Yogācāra school of Indian idealism, and it stresses what may be called
a more elitist view of salvation.[8] In the biography, Xuanzang is depicted as
not only a specially able exponent of this text, but also as deeply vexed by
the question of whether all men, or only part of humanity, could attain Buddhahood. It was to resolve this particular question as well as other textual
and doctrinal perplexities that he decided to make what would become the
famous pilgrimage to India. Years later, when he was touring the land of the
faith, he prayed before a famous image of Guanyin (Avalokiteśvara) on his
way to Bengal, and his three petitions were: to have a safe and easy journey
back to China, to be reborn in Lord Maitreya's palace as a result of the knowledge he gained, and to be personally assured that he would become a Buddha
since the holy teachings claimed that not all men had the Buddha-nature.[9]

As he studied with various masters in China during his youth, Xuanzang became convinced that unless the encyclopedic *Yogā-cārya-bhūmi
śāstra* (*Yujia shidi lun* 瑜伽師地論), the foundational text of this school of
Buddhism, became available, the other idealistic texts could not be properly understood. He resolved to go to India, but the application made by
him and other Buddhist companions to the imperial court for permission
to travel was refused. "At this time," declares his official biography, "the
state's governance was new and its frontiers did not reach far. The people
were prohibited from going to foreign domains." The second emperor of
the Tang dynasty, Taizong 太宗 (r. 627-649), had just assumed his title, but

this man had usurped the throne by ambushing and murdering his two brothers and possibly even his own father, incidents unmistakably recalled in the novelistic episode on the emperor's tour of the underworld (chapter 11).[10] Because the slain brothers were stationed near the western frontier, loyal troops likely became restive when news of their commanders' death had reached them. The court's refusal to permit free passage to the western territories was thus understandable and received immediate and unquestioned obedience by Xuanzang's companions. Xuanzang, however, was of a different cast of mind. Emboldened by an auspicious dream in which he saw himself crossing a vast ocean treading on sprouting lotus leaves and uplifted to the peak of the sacred Sumeru Mountain by a powerful breeze, the young priest defied the imperial prohibition and set out, probably late in 627, by joining in secret a merchant caravan. This one exercise of personal religious commitment had, in fact, rendered the youthful pilgrim guilty of high treason, liable to immediate execution if caught by the authorities, but the transgressive and highly dangerous border crossing to exit Tang territory was successful.[11]

Sustaining appalling obstacles and hardships, Xuanzang traversed Turfan, Darashar, Tashkent, Samarkand, Bactria, Kapisa, and Kashmir, until he finally reached the Magadha Kingdom of mid-India (now Bodhgaya) around 631. Here he studied with the aged Silabhadra (Jiexian 戒賢) in the great Nālandā Monastery for five years—in three different periods separating his wide travels throughout the land of his faith. He visited many sacred sites, and, according to his biographers, expounded the Dharma before kings, priests, and laymen. Heretics and brigands alike were converted by his preaching, and scholastics were defeated in debates with him. To honor him, Indian Buddhists bestowed on him the titles Mahāyāna-deva (摩訶耶那提婆, the Celestial Being of the Great Vehicle) and Mokṣa-deva (木叉提婆, a Celestial Being of Deliverance). After sixteen years, in 643, he began his homeward trek, taking the wise precaution while en route in Turfan the following year of requesting in writing an imperial pardon for leaving China without permission.[12] Readily absolved by Taizong, who often owed his own rise to power to the decisive support of Buddhists on several occasions, Xuanzang arrived at the capital, Chang'an, in the first month of 645, bearing some 657 items (bu) of Buddhist scriptures. The emperor was away in the eastern capital, Luoyang, preparing for his campaign against Koguryŏ (the modern Korea).

In the following month, Xuanzang proceeded to Luoyang, where emperor and pilgrim finally met. More interested in "the rulers, the climate, the products, and the customs in the land of India to the west of the Snowy Peaks" (FSZ, j 6) than in the fine points of doctrinal development, Taizong was profoundly impressed by the priest's vast knowledge of foreign cultures and peoples. The emperor's appointive offer was declined; instead, Xuanzang declared his resolve to devote his life to the translation of sūtras and śāstras. The monk was first installed in the Hongfu Monastery 弘福 and subsequently in the Ci'en Monastery 慈恩 of Chang'an, the latter edifice having been built by the crown prince (later, emperor Gaozong) in memory of his mother. Supported by continuous royal favors and a large staff of some of the most able Buddhist clerics of the empire, Xuanzang spent the next nineteen years of his life translating and writing. By the time he died in 664, at the age of about seventy, he had completed translations of seventy-five scriptures in 1,347 scroll-volumes (*juan*), including the lengthy *Yogācārya-bhūmi śāstra* for which Taizong wrote in commendation the famous *Shengjiao xu* 聖教序 (Preface to the Holy Religion). Among Xuanzang's own writings, his *Cheng weishi lun* 成唯識論 (Treatise on the Establishment of the Consciousness-Only System) and the *Da Tang Xiyuji* 大唐西域記 (The Record of the Great Tang's Western Territories) were the best known, the first being an elaborate and subtle exposition of the *Trimsika* by Vasubandhu and a synthesis of its ten commentaries, and the latter a descriptive and anecdotal travelogue sometimes called the first Chinese work of geography dictated to the disciple Bianji 辯機 (d. 649).

This brief sketch of Xuanzang and account of his life, as told by his biographers, have much of the engaging blend of facts and fantasies, of myth and history, out of which fictions are made. There should be no surprise, therefore, that his exploits were soon incorporated into the biographical sections (*liezhuan*) of such a standard dynastic history as the *Jiu Tangshu* 舊唐書, although even this brief entry of no more than 362 characters was excised later by the poet-official and ardent Confucian Ouyang Xiu 歐陽修 (1007-72) in the *Xin Tangshu* 新唐書, his authorized revision of canonical history.[13] Despite this early instance of political censorship, the story of Xuanzang's life was celebrated repeatedly by both classical and demotic literary writings. Visual and iconographic depictions of this specific but imagined pilgrimage also could be found on wall murals and relief sculptures of varying geographical sites (some found on or near the northwestern silk route, while others in the southeastern coastal region), the earliest ones possibly dating to the late Tang.[14] Yet, it must be pointed out that the Xuanzang story—as finally told in the hundred-chapter narrative published in 1592 and titled *Xiyouji* (literally, the Record of the Westward Journey) of which the present work is a complete translation—and the historical Xuanzang have only the most tenuous relation. In nearly a millennium of evolution, the story of Tang Sanzang (Tripitaka, the honorific name of Xuanzang to commemorate his acquisition of Buddhist scriptures) and his journey to the West has been told by both pen and mouth and through a variety of literary forms which have included the short poetic tale, the drama, and finally the fully developed narrative using both prose and verse. In this long process of development, the theme of the pilgrimage for scriptures is never muted, but added to this basic constituent of the story are numerous features which have more in common with folktales, legends, religious lore, and creative fiction than with history. The account of a courageous monk's undertaking, motivated by profound religious zeal and commitment in defiance of imperial proscription, is actually displaced and eventually transformed into a tale of supernatural deeds and fantastic adventures, of mythic beings and animal spirits, of fearsome battles with monsters and miraculous deliverances from dreadful calamities. How all this came about is a study in itself, but a pioneering effort had been undertaken by Glen Dudbridge in his authoritative *The* Hsi-yu chi: *A Study of Antecedents to the Sixteenth-Century Chinese Novel*.[15] Supplemented by later scholarship written in Chinese and other languages, I shall review briefly only the most important literary versions of the westward journey prior to the late Ming narrative before proceeding to discuss the cultural materials specific to the hundred-chapter novel.

Between the time of the historical Xuanzang and the first literary version of his journey for which we have solid documentary evidence, there are a few scattered indications that fragments of the pilgrim's story and exploits were working their way already into late Tang poetry and anecdotal writings. In the biography, the monk is represented as having a special fondness for the *Heart Sūtra* (the *Prajñāpāramitāhṛdaya*), a very short text which he himself later translated, for it was by reciting it and by calling upon Guanyin that he found deliverance from dying of thirst and from hallucinations in the desert (FSZ, j 1).[16] By the time of the *Taiping guangji* 太平廣記, the encyclopedic anthology of anecdotes and miscellaneous tales compiled in 976-83, the brief account of Xuanzang contained therein already included the motif of the pilgrim's special relation with the sūtra. There we are told that an old monk, his face covered with sores and his body with pus and blood, was the one who had transmitted this sūtra to the pilgrim, for whom, "when he recited it, the mountains and the streams became traversable, and the roads were made plain and passable; tigers and leopards vanished from sight; demons and spirits disappeared. He thus reached the land of Buddha" (TPGJ, j 92, 10: 606). During the next century, Ouyang Xiu recalled drinking one night at the Shouling Monastery 壽靈 寺 in Yangzhou. He was told by an old monk there that when the place was used as a traveling palace by the Later Zhou emperor Shizong (r. 954-59), all the murals were destroyed except an exquisite one on one wall that depicted the story of Xuanzang's journey in quest of the scriptures.[17]

These two references, while clearly pointing to popular interest in the story, provide us with scant information on how this story has been told.

The first representation of a distinctive tale with certain characteristic figures and episodes appears, as Dudbridge puts it, "almost without warning." Two texts preserved in Japanese collections, which contain minor linguistic discrepancies but which recount essentially the same story, have been dated by most scholars as products of the thirteenth century: *Xindiao Da Tang Sanzang Fashi qujingji* 新雕大唐三藏法師取經記 (The Newly Printed Record of the Procurement of Scriptures by the Master of the Law, Tripitaka, of the Great Tang) and the *Da Tang Sanzang qujing shihua* 大唐三藏取經詩話 (The Poetic Tale of the Procurement of Scriptures by Tripitaka of the Great Tang). Originally belonging to the monastery Kōzanji 高山寺 northwest of Kyoto, these texts finally gained public attention upon their publication earlier in the twentieth century.[18]

As some of the earliest examples of printed popular fiction in China, the texts have deservedly attracted widespread scholarly interest and scrutiny, even though they in no way can be considered the "blueprint" for emplotting the hundred-chapter novel published some four centuries later.[19] As far as we know at present, they may have been the first to depict Xuanzang's pilgrimage as fiction, inaugurating the imaginative elaboration of the Tripitaka legend. The brief poetic tale of seventeen sections (with section 1 missing in both texts), narrated by prose interlaced with verse written mostly in the form of the heptasyllabic quatrain or *jueju* 絕句, tells of Xuanzang's journey through such mythic and fantastic regions as the palace of Mahābrahmā Devarāja, the Long Pit and the Great Serpent Range, the Nine Dragon Pool, the kingdoms of Guizimu, Women, Poluo, and Utpala Flowers, and the Pool of Wangmu (Queen Mother of the West) before his arrival in India. After procuring some 5,048 *juan* of Buddhist scriptures, Xuanzang returns to the Xianglin Monastery, where he is taught the *Heart Sūtra* by the Dīpaṁkara Buddha. On his way back to the region of Shaanxi, the pilgrim avenges the crime of a stepmother's murder of her son by splitting open a large fish and restoring the child to life. When he reaches the capital, the priest is met by the emperor and given the title "Master Tripitaka," after which the pilgrim and his companions are conveyed by celestial vehicles to Heaven.

A primitive version of the *Xiyouji* story hardly to be compared with the scope and complexity of the hundred-chapter narrative, the poetic tale nonetheless vindicates its importance by introducing a number of themes or episodes expanded and developed in subsequent literary treatments of the same story. These themes may be summarized as follows:

1. The Monkey Disciple or Acolyte (Skt. *ācārin, hou xingzhe* 猴行者) as protector and guide of Xuanzang (section 2 and passim) who gains the title Great Sage (Dasheng 大聖) at the end (section 17).

2. The gifts of the Mahābrahmā Devarāja: an invisible hat, a golden-ringed priestly staff, and an almsbowl (section 2; cf. JW, chapters 8 and 12, for the gifts to Xuanzang from Buddha and from the emperor).

3. The snow-white skeleton (section 6; cf. JW, chapters 27-31, the Cadaver Monster? or chapter 50).

4. Monkey's defeat of the White Tiger spirit through invasion of its belly (section 6; cf. JW, chapters 59, 75, and 82, for similar feats of Monkey).

5. The Deep-Sand God as possible ancestor of Sha Monk of the Ming narrative (section 8; JW, chapter 22).[20]

6. The Kingdom of Guizimu 鬼子母 (section 9; cf. scene 12 of the twenty-four-act drama also titled *Xiyouji*, and chapter 42 of JW).[21]

7. The Kingdom of Women, where Mañjuśrī and Samantabhadra appear as temptresses (section 10; cf. JW, chapters 23, 53-54).

8. The reference to Monkey's theft of immortal peaches and his capture by Wangmu (section 11; cf. JW, chapter 5).

9. The reference to the ginseng fruit and its childlike features (section 11; cf. JW, chapters 24-26).

Among the themes which appeared in the Song poetic tale, the introduction of a Monkey acolyte or disciple as the human pilgrim's lasting companion surely ranks as a highly significant one. Disguised as a white-robed scholar that Xuanzang met on the way, this simian figure anticipates in some ways the powerful, resourceful, and heroic Sun Wukong of XYJ. The place that Monkey claims to be his home is mentioned in exactly the same manner again in the much later twenty-four-scene drama version of the story (the Purple-Cloud Cave of the Flower-Fruit Mountain), while XYJ retains only the name of the mountain and bestows a new name (Water Curtain) to the cave dwelling. Throughout the tale, he is presented as both a past delinquent and a dedicated guardian who will deliver Xuanzang from his preordained afflictions during the pilgrimage.

In the biography of the historical monk, he was not accompanied on his journey by any supernatural beings, let alone animal figures. The tantalizingly cryptic reference ("Procurement of scriptures one owes to a monkey acolyte 取經煩猴行者") in a line of poetry by the Song poet, Liu Kezhuang 劉克莊 (1187-1269) on Buddhists and Daoists, gives an early hint of the animal figure's association with a scripture pilgrimage, but it neither explains the reason of this association nor identifies Xuanzang as the pilgrim.[22] The carved monkey figure located at the Kaiyuan si 開元寺 of Quanzhou 泉州 (Zayton), completed some time in 1237, is also, according to the description of G. Ecke and P. Demiéville,[23] identified by that temple tradition as Sun Wukong, though the depiction differs significantly from the novelistic figure's clothing and weapons.[24] Neither of these "sources," however, really explains how a popular religious folk hero such as Xuanzang has come to acquire this animal attendant, who gains steadily in popularity in subsequent literary accounts until finally, in the hundred-chapter narrative, he almost completely overshadows his master.

It is to the search for the possible origin of this fascinating figure and the reasons for his associations with, and prominence within, the Tripitaka legend that Dudbridge devotes all of his investigation in the second half of his study. The literary works which he examines in detail range from early prose tales of a white ape figure (the *Tang Baiyuan zhuan* 唐白猿傳 and the vernacular mid-Ming short story *Chen Xunjian Meiling shiqiji* 陳巡檢梅嶺 失妻記),[25] to Ming dramas such as the *Erlang shen suo Qitian Dasheng* 二 郎神鎖齊天大聖, *Erlang shen zuishe suomojing* 二郎神醉射鎖魔鏡, *Menglie Nezha san bianhua* 猛烈那吒三變化, *Guankou Erlang zhan jianjiao* 灌口二 郎斬健蛟, and the *Longji shan yeyuan ting jing* 龍濟山野猿聽經.[26] None of these works, however, can be shown decisively to be a "source" for the derivation of the later full-length novel. As Dudbridge sees the matter, the essential role of the white ape emerging from the tales under consideration is one of abductor and seducer of women, a characteristic foreign to the Monkey of the *Xiyouji*. In his opinion, "Tripitaka's disciple commits crimes which are mischievous and irreverent, but the white ape is from first to last a monstrous creature which has to be eliminated. The two acquire superficial points of similarity when popular treatments of the respective traditions, in each case of Ming date, coincide in certain details of nomenclature."[27] That might well have been the case, or it might have been that there were two related traditions concerning the monkey figure: one which emphasizes the monkey as a demon, evil spirit, and recreant in need of suppression by the warrior god Erlang or Naṭa as in the *Qitian Dasheng* plays, and one which portrays the monkey as capable of performing religious deeds as in the *tingjing* accounts. Both strands of the tradition might in turn feed into the evolving *Xiyouji* cycle of stories.[28]

In addition to these literary texts, the figure of Wuzhiqi 無知祁, the water fiend, has provided many scholars with a prototype of Sun Wukong, mainly because he, too, was a monster whose delinquent behavior led to his imprisonment beneath a mountain, first by the legendary King Yu, the conqueror of the primeval flood in China, and then again by Guanyin.[29] However, Dudbridge points out that such a theory involves the identification of Sun Wukong as originally a water demon and his early association with the Erlang cult of Sichuan, neither of which assumptions finds apparent support in the Kōzanji text.[30] It may be added that Wuzhiqi, though certainly known to the novel's author (he was referred to in chapter 66 as the Water Ape Great Sage [Shuiyuan dasheng 水猿大聖]), has been kept quite distinct from the monkey hero. One of Sun Wukong's specific weaknesses consistently emphasized in XYJ is that he loses much of his power and adroitness once he enters water (e.g., chapter 22). On the other hand, the novelistic simian hero's one most positive association with water also links him distantly to Wuzhiqi, because the mighty iron rod that has become part of Sun Wukong's trademark identity since chapter 3 is originally a divine ruler by which King Yu fixed the proper depths of rivers and seas when subduing the flood.

If indigenous materials prove insufficient to establish with any certainty the origin of the monkey hero, does it imply that one must follow Hu Shi's provocative conjectures and look for a prototype in alien literature?[31] An affirmative answer to this question seems inviting, since the universally popular Hanumat adventures in the *Rāmāyaṇa* (hereafter R)[32] story might have found their way into China through centuries of mercantile and religious traffic with India. Furthermore, the composition attributed to Vālmīki is known to have reached the Dunhuang texts in the form of Tibetan and Khotanese manuscripts. Subsequent research by both Chinese and European scholars, whom Dudbridge follows, has opined that early works of Chinese popular literature, whether in narrative or dramatic form, seem to contain no more than fragmentary and modified traces of the R epic in known Buddhist writings. Wu Xiaoling, who has canvassed a number of probable allusions to various episodes and incidents of R in extant Chinese Buddhist scriptures, has also argued for the improbability of the XYJ author having seen any of these.[33] The often noted similarities between Hanumat and the Monkey of the narrative (courage and prowess in battle, extraordinary magic powers that include rapid aerial flights and transformations, the use of an iron rod as a weapon, and the tendency to attack their enemies by gaining entrance into their bellies) perhaps point to a "fund of shared motifs,"[34] but Dudbridge's cautious suggestion is that well-attested evidence of the intervening stages was lacking to establish influence or derivation.

More recent scholarship, however, has steadily recognized that that "fund of shared motifs," a rather large one, cannot be so easily ignored either. First, interesting textual and geographical details from other sources may indicate the convergence of Chinese and Indian motifs "in a body of monkey lore" surrounding the Hangzhou monastery, Lingyin Si 靈隱寺, because they tell of resident monks who, like their non-Chinese counterparts, at one time raised monkeys. Monkeys reared in the Lingyin Monastery are said to have the surname Sun, using exactly the same pun on homophones of the graph *sun* (i.e., 孫 and 猻) as in the novel (chapter 1) with respect to the pilgrim's eldest disciple, while monkeys brought up in India's Spirit Vulture Mountain are said to have memorized and been able to recite the Triśaraṇa 三歸依 formula of taking refuge in the Buddha, the

Dharma, and the Saṅgha. The stories not only reinforce and perpetuate the striking theme of pious simians listening to scriptural exposition (猿聽經) favored and celebrated by Chinese literati and painters on account of the white gibbon's "monogramous family life, his solitary habits," and mournful cries that evoke and elicit weeping, but even more significantly, but they also specifically associate the Lingyin Mountain with the attributed abode of Buddha in India, the Spirit Garuḍa Peak 靈鷲峰 (Sk. Gṛdhra-kūṭa).[35] What is important about this group of legend and story is its exaltation of monkeys and the varying species such as gibbons, macaques, chimpanzees, and apes—along with other creatures like lions, peacocks, elephants, bears, bulls, and fishes—as beings capable of responding to Buddhist evangelistic speech and action by which the animals may even find enlightenment. This Chinese "religious" monkey fashioned in narrative, poetic, dramatic, and visual representation may be magically potent, mischievous, and even transgressive, but it need not be a figure so confirmed in evil that he is always to be extirpated. Most noteworthily, the sentient creature's depicted action irrefutably constitutes one fundamental element of Indian religiosity encompassing both Hinduism and Buddhism, in which a huge variety of known animals and mythical beasts has been pressed into ritual service to the gods.[36] Such a tendency might also have found demonstrable adaptation in the Daoist pantheon and the fiction thereof.[37] By contrast, the dominant Chinese cultrual tradition's simian lore may preserve some references to monkey-like creatures able to communicate in human speech, but there is no known account of a monkey attending a lecture on the *Classic of Filial Piety* or the Confucian Four Books.[38] Indeed, the ritual theory articulated by state-sponsored Confucianism was perfectly clear on what distinguished human beings from animals: "A parrot can speak, but it does not cease being a bird; an ape can speak, but it does not cease being a beast. If now a human being does not observe ritual, is this person's mind not beastly even if endowed with the ability of speech? For only animals do not observe ritual" (*Liji* 禮記, chapter 1 in SSJZS 1: 1231).

The carved monkey figure of Quanzhou's Buddhist temple, the different versions of the violent and rebellious ape in the Wuzhiqi myth and other dramatic accounts, the numerous textual representations of monkey fiends or demons that that are worshipped as malevolent cult dieties in need of religious exorcism,[39] and the legend of the Lingyin Temple's pious simians have lent weight to Dudbridge's own previous suggestion for associating an early (by late Northern or early Southern Song) development of the XYJ story tradition with China's southeastern coastal region, in parts belonging to the modern Fujian province.[40] He cites as evidence a story from the Song collectanea of largely "tales of the anomalous (*zhiguai xiaoshuo* 志怪小說)," the *Yijianzhi* 夷堅志 by Hong Mai 洪邁 (1123–1202),

that relates how a Monkey King 猴王, whose cultic worship inflicted fever and frenzy upon the populace, was brought to submission and also deliverance by the Buddhist elder Zongyan 宗演 through his recitation in Sanskrit "the *dhāranī* of the All-Compassionate (大悲咒)."[41] Both Dudbridge and Isobe Akira's subsequent discussion on additional textual sources of this tale and a couple of other similar stories seem to have emphasized the linkage to XYJ tradition primarily through the figure of a Monkey King.[42] As I read the tale, however, what is most striking are the means and meaning of salvific pacification, since in the full-length novel, a recitation of *dhāranī* (spells, *zhou* 咒) is joined to the three fillets Buddha gave to Guanyin as weapons for compelling conversion (XYJ, chapter 8). For activating the three fillets, Buddha transmitted to Guanyin three fictionalized and punning spells (*dhāranī, zhou*) named "the Golden, the Constrictive, and the Prohibitive 金, 緊, 禁," and these fillets and spells would be used eventually by both Xuanzang and Guanyin on Sun Wukong (chapter 14), the Bear Monster (chapters 16-17), and the Red Boy (chapters 40-42) to induce submission to Buddhism.

According to the novel, all three of these characters are deviant animalistic creatures who nonetheless find authentic religious deliverance. (The Red Boy of the novel had a Bull Monster for a father and a female demon for a mother. Both parents at the end of the episode also repented and went off to attain "the right fruit" through religious self-cultivation.) What is even more interesting is that the monkey figure's taming by his fillet and the pain inflicted by the recited *dhāranī*, as all readers of the novel must remember, literally traverses almost the entire length of the narrative, from chapter 14 until Sun Wukong himself attains apotheosis in Buddhahood in chapter 100. This protracted allegory of arduous religious discipline leading to eventual enlightenment, I would argue, may well have been rhetorically anticipated, if not actually inspired, in part by the *gātha* 偈 (prosodically, a heptasyllabic quatrain) uttered by the Buddhist Zongyan to instruct his penitent monkey. The third poetic line of Hong Mai's story—"You must believe your own mind is originally the Buddha 須信自心元是佛"—not only asserts at once a didactic thesis rehearsed continuously in the later Ming novel, but it also accords with a doctrinal emphasis much debated in Chan (Zen 禪) Buddhism (i.e., on the Buddha-nature as self or mind) and enthusiastically embraced by subsequent Quanzhen (全真) Daoism that appeared around 1170 and drew considerably on Chan.[43] Texts from both traditions, in turn, pervasively shape and color the language of the full-length novel. Hong Mai's story resonates directly with the late Ming novel because a short tale of two score sentences and a long narrative of roughly 600,000 characters both purport to reveal through their plots why and how a Monkey King, already endowed with supernal powers, would still need to attain Buddhahood.

In terms of chronology, Hong Mai's line, in fact, directly echoes the first line of a poetic composition by Zhang Boduan 張伯端 (982/4?-1082), styled Ziyang Zhenren 紫陽真人, who was the reputed founder of the southern lineage 南宗 of the Quanzhen Order. Zhang's poetic composition titled "Ode to 'This Mind is Buddha' 『即心是佛』頌" begins with the line, "The Buddha is Mind and the Mind is Buddha 佛即心兮心即佛,"[44] which the XYJ author/redactor significantly appropriated for a slightly modified ode that prefaces chapter 14 of the novel. That fictional episode detailing Sun Wukong's final submission to Buddhism and his formal enlistment in the scripture pilgrimage just as significantly has been capped by the titular couplet: "Mind Monkey returns to the Right. / The Six Robbers vanish from sight 心猿歸正, 六賊無蹤." Because Zongyan's instruction in Hong Mai's story is directed to a monkey and not a human being, one need but recall the first two lines of the commentarial verse at the height of Sun Wukong's brawl in Heaven (JW, chapter 7; XYJ, p. 70) to perceive the concordant meaning of mind and monkey threading the linguistic fabric of all three texts to render them pieces cut from the same doctrinal cloth: "An ape's body of Dao weds the human mind. / Mind is a monkey—this meaning's profound 猿猴道體配人心, 心即猿猴意思深."

Dudbridge's monograph of 1970 praised Wu Xiaoling for showing "with admirable thoroughness that the Buddhist canon, which represents China's greatest single import from India, carries no more than fragmentary and modified traces of the *Rāmāyaṇa* story and its leading figures, whether in rapid summaries or in passing allusions. These give no grounds for an assumption that the story was generally current in China."[45] Less than a decade after this verdict, Ji Xianlin, who would produce eventually another Chinese translation of the Indian epic, came to the exact opposite conclusion when he canvassed the same Buddhist canon, because he became convinced that the minutely episodic fragments of the epic pervading the sacred texts in Chinese were "egregiously abundant 多的出奇."[46] After all, much of the huge Buddhist canon, even if not yet enshrined in the magnitude of its final form, had already circulated in Chinese society for at least a thousand years by the time of the 1592 novel. Currency of the Indian epic might not have existed as a discrete textual entity, like the *Chronicles of the Three Kingdoms* 三國志 of official historiography that prefigured its much later fictional counterpart, *The Three Kingdoms* 三國演義, but one can hardly assert that bits and pieces of allusions to the epic were unknown to the Chinese public. Building on Ji's specific labor on the Indian epic, no less than a massive body of evidence indicating the profusion and adaptation of Indian materials—motifs and themes in addition to specific linguistic echoes and textual citations—in traditional Chinese literary writings and sacred scriptures, Victor Mair's 1989 essay might have settled a lengthy scholarly debate by demonstrating that such materials indeed pile up parallels between the characters of Hanumat and Sun Wukong.[47] Even more compellingly and appropriately, his study suggests—to this reader at least—that the evolution of the novelistic monkey character was mediated through the lengthiest and most voluminous process of textual translation and cultural exchange the world has ever known and the impact that process had on Chinese writings and other cultural artifacts. Our current knowledge of both process and impact is widening but far from complete. Moreover, the particular relations between Hanumat and Sun Wukong were complicated by the transmission of a story and its summation or allusion in the diverse media of text or oral telling.[48]

It is the merit of Mair's essay to show in copious detail how references to the Indian epic had existed in Buddhist scriptures not just for Chinese readership but also for that of other lands. In the course of an expanding eastward journey, fragments, episodes, motifs, and themes of the Rāma story had found their way into a huge area of Central, Northeast, and Southeast Asia, including Tocharistan, Khotan, Tibet, Southeast Asia, and Japan, apart from China. To mention just a few examples, the forty-sixth story in the *Liudu ji jing* 六度集經, speciously named "Jātaka of an Unnamed King" (*Anāmaka-rāja-jātaka*), is actually a Chinese translation of the *Ṣaṭ-pāramitā-saṃgraha-sūtra* [?] by one Seng Hui 僧會 in as early as 251.[49] Moreover, it paraphrases the entire epic story in Chinese: "we have Rāma's exile, Sītā's abduction by Rāvaṇa, the duel of Rāvaṇa with Jaṭāyus, the battle between Sugrīva and Vālin, the construction of a bridge to Laṅkā, Hanumat's curing of the fallen soldiers, Hanumat's rescue of Sītā, and a variant of Sītā's ordeal by fire (*agni-pariṣā*)."[50] Complementing this text is the *Shi shewang yuan* 十奢王緣 (Tale of Causal Origins Concerning King Ten Luxuries), translated in 472 by Kiṃkārya in collaboration with the Chinese cleric Tanyao 曇曜.[51] It again presents numerous crucial incidents and episodes of the Indian epic. Finally, the historical Xuanzang himself could not have been ignorant of the poem, because his own "rendition of the *Mahāvibhāṣā* commentary 阿毘達摩大毘婆沙論" specifically considers the long epic's 12,000 *ślokas* as all having been designed to elucidate the twin themes of Rāvaṇa's abduction of Princess Sītā and her rescue by Rāma.[52]

When the novel and the epic are juxtaposed, *Journey* (chapters 68–71) and *Rāmāyaṇa* contain astonishing and sustained parallels in plot construction and description of characters. The comparable features include the anguish caused by the abducted loss of a spouse (Rāma's grief for Sītā; the King of the Scarlet-Purple Kingdom for his queen consort); the misery of the female prisoners as depicted in facial dejection, unkempt and dirty clothing, disheveled hairdo, absence of make-up, jewelry, and ornaments, and constant weeping (XYJ chapter 70, vs. R V. 13: 18–33); and devising tokens of recognition (rings and bracelets) by the different monkey figures to establish the kidnapped female's identity. When the novel's Bodhisattva Guanyin providentially explains the separation and reunion of the royal couple, she discloses the human king's one past offense while hunting when his arrow accidentally wounded the Bodhisattva Great King Peacock. As another study astutely observes, "the motif of the hunter who becomes separated from someone he loves as a result of karmic retribution runs rampant through Indian literature," and part of the XYJ story here thus recalls not just the *Rāmāyaṇa* but also similar notions of "desire, yearning, and separation" surfacing from the very beginning of the even longer epic *Mahābhārata*.[53]

We may perhaps never be able to resolve the question of Sun Wukong's origin to every reader's satisfaction, but every reader with a vested interest in this topic seems also all too eager in choosing far-fetched details that would intimate heroic "personality (*xingge* 性格)" and ferocious "form or appearance (*xingxiang* 形象)" to fund, allegedly, the progressive literary development of Monkey's depiction or any random aspect associated with the evolving story of Xuanzang's pilgrimage. These details favored by sundry Chinese (e.g., Zheng Mingli) and Japanese (e.g., Uchida Michio, Isobe Akira, Nakano Miyoko) scholars on the ape are usually preserved in selected texts of the Buddhist canon and, as such, are no more or less "historical" than the textualized representation of a Fujian cult figure in story or ethnography. In any study of literary derivation or influence, even the existence of a cult for a particular mythical figure—whether Odysseus or Sun Wukong—cannot take priority over linguistic and textual comparison. Nor can such study ignore how the eventual composition appropriated the source materials—whether in discernible chunks or minute fragments, whether in strict fidelity to borrowed language or with unfettered freedom and creativity in its modification. We shall see, as we move through this introduction, that one cannot fully understand the full-length XYJ without appreciating its Indian and Buddhist as well as its native roots.

If the genealogy of Sun Wukong remains controversial, we have at least three other texts of major import between the Kōzanji version and the hundred-chapter narrative of the sixteenth century, texts which undoubtedly contributed to the formation of the latter. First, there is a passage of a little less than 1,100 characters which is preserved in the scant surviving remnants of the *Yongle dadian* 永樂大典 (the encyclopedic collection compiled in 1403–08 under commission of the Ming emperor Chengzu 成祖). This passage constitutes a remarkable parallel to portions of chapter 9 in the hundred-chapter narrative (chapter 10 in the 1592 XYJ).[54] Though the episodes concerning Tripitaka's genealogy and public debut receive much fuller treatment in the later work, the essential sequences (i.e., the conversations between a fisherman named Zhang Shao and a woodcutter named Li Ding, the transgressions of the Dragon King and his conviction by the fortune-teller Yuan Shoucheng, and the dream execution of the dragon by the prime minister Wei Zheng [580–643] in the midst of a chess game with the emperor Taizong) and certain sentences and phrases (e.g., the Dragon King's address to the emperor: "Your majesty is the true dragon, whereas I am only a false dragon") are nearly identical in both accounts. What is of greater interest here is that the *Yongle dadian* extract is listed under an old source named *Xiyouji*, which may well have existed as a kind of *Urtext* for all the dramatic and narrative works that are to follow. This text, unfortunately, is now lost, and the lack of information on authorship, texts, and publisher prohibits any conclusion other than the existence of a document or documents by such a name two centuries before the circulation of the full-length novel.

Such a conclusion may certainly find further support in the *Pak t'ongsa ŏnhae* (in Chinese, the *Pu tongshi yanjie* 朴通事諺解), a Korean reader in colloquial Chinese first printed probably some time in the mid-fifteenth century, though the surviving version now preserved in the Kyu-chang-kak collection of the Seoul University library has a preface which dates from 1677. This manual contains an account of Tripitaka's experience in the *Che-chi Guo* 車遲國 (the Cart-Slow Kingdom of chapters 44–46 in the novel), and, more significantly, "the picture of ordinary people going out to buy popular stories in a book [which] confirms that a *Xiyouji* was among those available."[55] There are, moreover, a number of references to mythic regions and to various demons and gods (including Zhu Bajie 猪八戒 [translated in the present edition as Zhu Eight Rules], appointed Janitor of the Altars at the end of the journey) which find echoes in subsequent dramatic and narrative accounts.[56] There is too little external evidence to allow reconstructing a lost text, but internal analysis of this document, as Dudbridge aptly observes, presents "evidence as a trend . . . that the *Xiyouji* story, now well known in published form, was progressively assuming an accepted and less variable form."[57]

That form was finally established by the dramatic versions of the story, of which fortunately we possess at least one more or less complete sample among the six known stage works supposedly devoted to the XYJ theme. This is the twenty-four-scene *zaju* titled *Xiyouji* 西游記, which was discovered in Japan and first reprinted there in 1927–1928.[58] The play was initially thought to be the lost work of the same title by the Yuan playwright, Wu Changling 吳昌齡. The ascription, however, has been conclusively repudiated by Sun Kaidi, though Sun's own thesis that the play was written by Yang Jingxian 楊景賢 (alternatively Jingyan 景言) has been challenged also.[59] Whoever the author was, the play is of crucial importance, not only because of its unique length when compared with other dramas of the genre, but also because of its content. It represents the fullest embodiment of the major themes and figures of the XYJ story prior to the hundred-chapter novel.

Acts 1–4 present at length the adventures of Xuanzang's parents as well as the abandonment and rescue of the young priest and his revenge of his father's murderers. Subsequent acts dramatize the royal commission of Xuanzang to procure scriptures, the provision of a dragon-horse and guardian deities by Guanyin for the scripture pilgrim, the mischievous adventures of the monkey hero Sun Xingzhe, and his subsequent submission to Tripitaka as the monk's disciple and protector. The figure Zhu Bajie is also given extensive coverage (acts 13–16). In this regard, the play is unique not only because Naṭa and not Erlang subdues the monkey (unlike the case of the other *Qitian dasheng* plays), but also because Erlang has to capture Zhu Bajie who, in Zhu's own words, fears no one except the deity's small hound. Readers of the hundred-chapter XYJ will readily recognize these themes when they reappear in the transformed context of the developed narrative. In the case of Sun and Zhu's relations to the divine figures, they may also perceive how the genius of the late Ming author has adapted his "source" to the logic of his massive masterpiece.

II   TEXT AND AUTHORSHIP

If the antecedents to the sixteenth-century narrative are numerous and complex, the vast family of texts and the different versions of *The Journey to the West* itself, both abridged and unabridged, and the controversial puzzle of who might have been the author or final redactor of the 1592 publication present no less formidable areas of investigation to the serious student of this work. We are fortunate once again to have the scholarship of Glen Dudbridge,[60] whose earlier informative examinations of the narrative's textual history and related issues will be supplemented by more recent discussions.

The principal part of the critical controversy surrounding the genesis of *The Journey to the West* as a developed novel has to do with the relation of the hundred-chapter version to two shorter versions. One of these is the *Sanzang chushen quanzhuan* 三藏出身全傳 (The Complete Account of Sanzang's Career), commonly known as the Yang version because its putative author is Yang Zhihe 楊志和, probably a contemporary of many Fujian publishers at the end of the sixteenth century but about whom little additional information is available. The work, preserved at Oxford's Bodleian Library and dated by Dudbridge to no later than 1633, may well be the earliest copy. Its forty "chapter-like units"[61] came together with the *Dongyouji* (Journey to the East), the *Nanyouji* (Journey to the South), and the *Beiyouji* (Journey to the North), three tales of comparable length which recount the directional voyages of various figures in myth and legend. This group became familiar in a later Qing printing known as the *Siyouji zhuan* 四游記傳 (The Recorded Accounts of The Four Journeys) or *Siyou quanzhuan* 四游全傳. Though the earliest extant reprint dates from 1730, its printing format points back to a date almost a century earlier.

The other brief version of the *Xiyouji* is titled the *Tang Sanzang Xiyou shini (=e) zhuan* 唐三藏西游釋尼(=厄)傳 (The Chronicle of Deliverances in Tripitaka Tang's Journey to the West), commonly known as the Zhu version after its compiler, Zhu Dingchen 朱鼎臣 of Canton. The extant version similar in length to the Yang version is preserved in Taiwan, Japan, and the Library of Congress, but all three copies lack title page and table of contents. The best guess places publication at about 1595 or slightly later.[62] The Zhu text has a distinctive long chapter on the "Chen Guangrui 陳光蕊 story," which tells of Xuanzang's birth (he was sent to his mother as a prenatal gift by one or another celestial deities) and early adventures linked to the catastrophes that befall his parents. Abandoned at birth by an abducted and then widowed mother, the infant drifted on a river until a Buddhist monk rescued him. Upon reaching adulthood, Xuanzang avenged his father's murder and his mother's disgrace at the hands of a pirate. That story, modified, appears also as chapter 9 first in an abridged Qing edition of the XYJ bearing the name of *Xiyou zhengdao shu* 西游證道書 (A Book for the Illumination of *Dao* by the Westward Journey), compiled by Huang Taihong 黃太鴻 and Wang Xiangxu 汪象旭 and dated by Dudbridge to around 1662.[63] The chapter, however, is missing in the earliest full-length version published in 1592, exactly seven decades earlier, by the Nanjing publishing house named Shidetang 世德堂 (The Hall of Generational Virtue) and in several other editions almost immediately following which are based on this text.[64] Since the title of the Zhu text is also explicitly named in the heptasyllabic regulated poem which opens the hundred-chapter novel (see the present translation's chapter 1, where I have rendered its last line as: "Read *The Tale of Woes Dispelled on Journey West*"), the critical controversy centers on which version is the earliest.

Though scholars in the past have advocated the temporal priority of either the Yang or the Zhu version, Dudbridge seems to me to have clearly established the supremacy of the 1592 Shidetang text which, in his judgment, "promises to stand as close to the original as any that survives."[65] Four decades after this declaration that in itself also already possessed another four decades of antecedent disputation, we have little new data or compelling interpretation that would significantly modify, let alone overturn, his verdict. The debate over textual priority, in the words of Andrew Plaks, had "seesawed back and forth,"[66] going through all three such possible options as (1) 1592, Zhu version, Yang version; (2) Zhu version, Yang version, 1592; and (3) Yang version, 1592, and Zhu version, but no combination has won consensus as the best. Perhaps it should be remarked, parenthetically, that for the Chinese tradition, textual criticism is also a venerable practice that harks back to high antiquity. Generally, however, there are no criteria on which Chinese critics agree for determining what linguistic phenomena are verifiable signs of changes that amount to deliberate abbreviation, abridgment, or expansion.

Texts as late as vernacular Chinese fiction require attention to a new set of social and material issues. Thus even the valuable work done by the late Liu Ts'un-yan, Zheng Mingli, Li Shiren, and others reveals a predilection to construe from word usages or modifications (abbreviation or lengthening of syntax, reduction, addition, or change of vocabulary, correction, or corruption of accepted prosodic convention) what passes as sufficient evidence of self-conscious abridgment or fullness of expression. They seldom consider targeted readership and its reading habits, competence in literacy assumed for publishers, printers, and even typesetters, and market conditions of both publishing houses and consumers correlated with time and urban conditions of production. That is why they often assume that a text is entirely the product of a single creative intelligence. More recent scholarship in textual criticism and in the sociology of print culture in China and Europe, however, has steadily advanced the view that a published text is formed by competing social forces and processes, even if a single author was responsible for its genesis.[67] A work like *The Journey to the West* astounds and delights through its bountiful perfection as a finished novel, but the analysis of its formative history and intertextual lineage, fragments and citations from many sources, and commentarial insertions created or appropriated for direct structuring into the novel will add to our wonderment at the diverse and even conflicting features thus embodied. The novel, in sum, represents a complex discursive heterology not disposed to easy assimilation or classification.

After the People's Republic of China was founded, the first standard modern critical edition, on which the present translation is based, was published by Beijing's Zuojia chubanshe 作家出版社 in 1954, using the 1592 edition as a primary "basic 底本" text, with minor but requisite corrections, clarifications, and collations established by comparison with six other abridged and unabridged editions of *The Journey to the West* brought out in the Qing period.[68] When compared with its numerous literary antecedents, the 1592 hundred-chapter novel may be seen at once as a culmination of a long and many-faceted tradition as well as a creative synthesis and expansion of all the major figures and themes associated with the story of Xuanzang's westward journey. Though the narrative far surpasses any of the previous dramatic or narrative accounts in scope and length, the author/redactor also reveals a remarkably firm sense of structure and an extraordinary capacity for organizing disparate materials in the presentation of his massive tale. Certain details related to the development of plot and characters evince thoughtful planning, preparation, and execution. The basic outline of the narrative, as we have it in the modern edition, may be divided into the following five sections:

1. (Chapters 1-7): The birth of Sun Wukong, his acquisition of immortality and magic powers under the tutelage of Patriarch Subhodi, his invasion and disturbance of Heaven, and his final subjugation by Buddha under the Mountain of Five Phases. Despite the elements of supernatural fantasy and magic crowding all the episodes of the segment, the note sounded in the narrated experience emphasizes consistently how the monkey figure is acquiring "the way of the human being."

2. (Chapter 8): The Heavenly Council in which Buddha declares his intention to impart the Buddhist canon to the Chinese, the journey of Guanyin to the land of the East to find the appropriate scripture pilgrim, and her encounters with all of Xuanzang's future disciples foreshadowing the lengthy pilgrimage in reverse direction.

3. (Chapters 9-12): The background and birth of Xuanzang, his vengeance of his father's murderers, Wei Zheng's execution of the Jing River Dragon, the journey of Tang Taizong to the underworld, his convening of the Mass for the Dead, and the epiphany of Guanyin leading to the commission of Xuanzang as the scripture pilgrim.

4. (Chapters 13-97): The journey itself, developed primarily through a long series of captures and releases of the pilgrims by monsters, demons, animal spirits, and gods in disguise which form the bulk of the eighty-one ordeals (*nan* 難) preordained for the human pilgrim, Xuanzang.

5. (Chapters 98-100): The successful completion of the journey, the audience with Buddha, the return with scriptures to Chang'an for an audience with the Tang emperor Taizong, and the pilgrims' final canonization by Buddha in the Western Paradise.

This book completely translates the modern edition of 1954, a collated text and not a pristine duplication of the 1592 edition. Therefore, I have not followed Dudbridge's advice or the editorial practice of some of the more recent critical Chinese editions to exclude chapter 9. For reasons stated elsewhere, I am persuaded that the "Chen Guangrui story" is essential to the plot of the *Xiyouji* as a whole, even though it was not part of the hundred-chapter novel's earliest known version.[69]

Despite the popularity which this narrative has apparently enjoyed since its publication, the identity of its author, as in the case of such other major works of Chinese fiction as the *Jinpingmei* (The Plum in the Golden Vase) and the *Fengshen yanyi*, remains unclear. In his preface to the Shidetang edition, Chen Yuanzhi 陳元之 emphasized that neither he, nor the Huayang Dongtian Zhuren 華陽洞天主人 (Master of the Huanyang Grotto-Heaven) who checked this edition, nor Tang Guanglu 唐光祿,[70] the publisher who "requested the preface" from Chen, knew who the author was. Indeed, all the known individuals who had anything to do with published editions of *The Journey to the West* in the Ming dynasty were silent on this point. Several writers in the Qing period, however, had already suggested that Wu Cheng'en 吳承恩 (ca. 1500-1582) created the narrative. But it was not until after the essay of 1923 by Hu Shi that scholars widely accepted this theory. Wu, a native of the Shanyang 山陽 district in the prefecture of Huai'an 淮安 (the modern Jiangsu 江蘇), was never more than a minor official during his lifetime, having been selected as a Tribute Student 歲貢生 in 1544, and achieved a certain reputation as a poet and humorous writer. Modern studies of Wu include an edition of his collected writings and a thorough reconstruction of his life and career.[71]

The ascription of *The Journey to the West* to Wu is based primarily on an entry in the *Yiwenzhi* 藝文志 (Bibliography of Books and Documents) section of the *Gazetteer of Huai'an Prefecture* 淮安府志, compiled in the Ming Tianqi 天啟 reign period (1621-27), whereafter Wu's name are listed the following works:

Sheyangji 射陽集, 4 ce 冊, ——*juan* 卷; preface to *Chunqiu liezhuan* 春秋列傳序; *Xiyouji* 西游記.[72]

An additional reference may be found in the *Qianqingtang shumu* 千頃堂書目, a private Catalogue of the Thousand-Acre Hall completed at the end of the seventeenth century,[73] in which the title *Xiyouji* is again printed after the name of Wu Cheng'en. The entry, however, is included within the section on "Geography" (輿地論), in the division of "Histories" (史).

Further listings noted by Hu Shi include the *Huai'an Gazetteer* and the *Shanyang District Gazetteer* 山陽縣志, compiled during the Kangxi 康熙 (1662-1722) and Tongzhi 同治 (1862-74) reigns of the Qing.[74] Of the several writers in this dynasty who affirmed Wu to be the author of the *Xiyouji*, the two most frequently cited are Wu Yujin 吳玉搢 (1698-1773) and Ding Yan 丁晏 (1794-1875), a noted textual scholar of the classics. In the *Shan-*

yang zhiyi 山陽志遺 (Supplement to the Shanyang Gazetteer), Wu Yujin has the following observation that merits a full quotation:

The Old Gazetteer of the Tianqi [1621-27] period listed the Master [i.e., Wu Cheng'en] as the ranking writer of recent years whose works had been collected. He was said to be "a man of exceptional intelligence and many talents who read most widely; able to compose poetry and prose at a stroke of the brush, he also excelled in humor and satire 復善諧謔. The several kinds of anecdotal records (*zaji* 雜記幾種) he produced brought him resounding fame at the time." I did not know at first what sort of books the anecdotal records were until I read the *Huaixian wenmu* 淮賢文目 (Catalog of Writings by Huai Regional Worthies [i.e., *j* 19, 3 b]), where it was recorded that *Xiyouji* was authored by the Master. I have discovered that *Xiyouji*, the old title of which was *The Book for the Illumination of Dao*, is so named because its content was thought to be consonant with the Great Principle of the Golden Elixir 金丹大旨. Yu Daoyuan 虞道園 [i.e., Yu Ji 虞集, 1272-1348] of the Yuan dynasty had written a preface, in which he claimed that this book was written by the Changchun Daoist Adept with the surname of Qiu [i.e., Qiu Chuji 邱處機, 1148-1227] at the beginning of the Yuan period. The regional gazetteer, however, claims that it was by the hand of the Master. Since the Tianqi period is not far removed from the time of the Master [Wu Cheng'en died ca. 1582 and the Tianqi reign began in 1621], that statement must have had some basis 其言必有所本. It might have meant to indicate that Changchun first composed this account 初有此記, and when it reached the Master later, he made it into a work of popular fiction (literally, a popular exposition of a [different or fictive] meaning) 至先生乃為之通俗演義, much as *The Records of the Three Kingdoms* 三國志 had originated from Chen Shou 陳壽 (d. 297), but the fiction (*yanyi* 演義) goes by the name of Luo Guanzhong 羅貫中 (1315/18-1400?) to whom the Ming novel (oldest complete printed edition dating to 1522) was attributed.[75] The fact that the book [i.e., XYJ] contains a great number of expressions peculiar to our local dialects should undoubtedly render it a product of someone from the Huai district.[76]

All the points made in this passage by Wu, living a century later than the full-length novel's first publication, are still topics of debate today. They include: descriptions of the putative author's gifts and witty predilections; attributed authorship to Wu Cheng'en of a work titled XYJ; Wu Yujin's professed familiarity with the Qing edition of *Xiyou zhengdao shu* containing the Yuan scholar Yu Ji's preface to XYJ and its asserted linkage with the religious ideas of the Yuan Quanzhen Patriarch, Qiu Chuji; the suggested use of the *Records of The Three Kingdoms* as the source in relation to Luo Guanzhong's later novel as an analogy for positing an earlier version of the XYJ authored by Qiu Chuji that eventually became in Wu Cheng'en's hands the hundred-chapter work of 1592; and the abundance of local idioms and diction of the Huai region found in the novel. Not one of these topics has been settled.

Take the criterion of the use of local idioms and dialects, for example. Although the novel's annotations of each critical edition subsequent to the 1954 version have benefited from further research and clarification, such editorial labor has also made clear that the range of vernacular features exceeds that defined by the Huai'an area alone.[77] Even if only the idioms of a single region were deployed consistently, that itself again cannot assume the illogical inference that the author or redactor had to be also someone from that region. The abundance of Shandong linguistic features in texts like *Outlaws from the Marshes* or *Plum in the Golden Vase* cannot of itself prove that a Shandongese wrote it any more than the excellence of the prose in *Under Western Eyes* would furnish conclusive proof that Joseph Conrad was a native writer of English.

Since the appearance of Hu Shi's essay, Wu Cheng'en's authorship has been widely accepted by scholars everywhere. This thesis was challenged by Glen Dudbridge, who in turn followed the arguments advanced by Tanaka Iwao. Essentially, the objection of Tanaka includes the additional following points:

1. The title *Xiyouji* listed in the *Huai'an Gazetteer* cannot be positively identified with the hundred-chapter narrative.

2. There is no known precedent in Chinese literary history for equating anecdotal records (*zaji*) with works of fiction.

3. Wu Cheng'en's reputed excellence in humorous compositions is not positive evidence of authorship.

4. None of the known persons associated with the first publication of the hundred-chapter version had any idea who the author was.

5. The famous iconoclast and literary critic Li Zhi 李贄 (styled, Zhuowu 卓吾 1527–1602), credited with having edited such major works of literature as the *Shuihuzhuan*, the *Xixiangji*, and possibly the *Xiyouji* with a full-blown commentary attached, made no mention of Wu Cheng'en's authorship even in that last work (which is disputed).[78]

The last of Tanaka's five reasons for doubting the authorship of Wu Cheng'en is ostensibly the most cogent, since Li's alleged activities relative to his editing of *The Journey to the West* could not have occurred more than twenty years after Wu's death. If Wu's fame was as widespread as the *Huai'an Gazetteer* had claimed, why did Li seem to be completely ignorant of it, especially when his annotations of the narrative in many places clearly reflect his admiration for its anonymous author?[79]

There can be more than one answer to this question. Tanaka's inference—that silence is ignorance, and that Li's ignorance further casts doubt on Wu's putative achievements—is only one among several possibilities. It is merely an argument ex silentio, for Li at no point made the specific assertion that Wu was not the author. Moreover, if Wu Cheng'en was known to be fond of befriending some of the Seven Masters of Later Times[80]—the group of literary theorists and writers of late Ming who championed the imitation of the classics—one wonders if Li Zhi would be inclined to suspect Wu's hand in XYJ, or, even if he had known Wu to be the author, to credit him publicly with the authorship. Li himself, we must remember, was the declared foe and staunch critic of this literary movement, and his own imprisonment and eventual suicide were caused in no small way by his stubborn iconoclasm in views both political and literary.[81] On the other hand, the fact that Li was indeed silent should caution the critic from too hasty an acceptance of Wu's authorship.

The authenticity of the commentarial remarks in this edition attributed to Li Zhi, in fact, has been questioned repeatedly, and most scholars today retain the skepticism already voiced in the Qing. Nonetheless, the importance of the remarks themselves, usually appearing in "end-of-chapter overall commentary 回末總批," ought not again to be dismissed easily, because their content—consistently sardonic and witty enough to recall aspects of Li's rhetoric and style—hardly hews to the line of later criticism that tends to exalt either Neo-Confucianism or Quanzhen Daoism, a conscientiously syncretistic blend of Chan Buddhist and Daoist ideas advocated by the lineage. Without thoroughly studying the Li edition, comparing it with his other fictional and dramatic commentaries along with later Ming-Qing editions of XYJ, the issue of authenticity cannot be settled.

With regard to the reputation of Wu Cheng'en as a humorist, it is certainly true that that characteristic alone cannot establish Wu as the author. Nor, of course, should this trait be ignored, since the narrative is rich comedy and satire. Another equally significant aspect of Wu's character which may link him to *The Journey to the West* is his self-declared predilection for the marvelous, the exotic, and the supramundane in literature. In the *Yudingzhi xu* 禹鼎志序, a preface to a group of stories, now lost, which he wrote on one of the legendary sage kings of Chinese antiquity, Wu said:

> I was very fond of strange stories when I was a child. In my village-school days, I used to buy stealthily popular novels and historical recitals. Fearing that my father and my teacher might punish me for this and rob me of these treasures, I carefully hid them in secret places where I could enjoy them unmolested. As I grew older, my love for strange stories became even stronger, and I learned of things stranger than what I had read in my childhood.

When I was in my thirties, my memory was full of these stories accumulated through years of eager seeking. I have always admired such writers of the Tang Dynasty as Tuan Ch'êng-shih [Duan Chengshi 段成式, author of the *Youyang zazu* 酉陽雜俎] and Niu Sheng-ju [Niu Sengru 牛僧儒, author of the *Xuanguai lu* 玄怪錄], who wrote short stories so excellent in portrayal of men and description of things. I often had the ambition to write a book (of stories) which might be compared with theirs. But I was too lazy to write, and as my laziness persisted, I gradually forgot most of the stories which I had learned. Now only these few stories, less than a score, have survived and have so successfully battled against my laziness that they are at last written down. Hence this Book of Monsters. I have sometimes laughingly said to myself that it is not I who have found these ghosts and monsters, but they, the monstrosities themselves, which have found me! . . . Although my book is called a book of monsters [literally, *zhiguai* 志怪], it is not devoted to provide illumination for ghosts: it also records the strange things of the human world and sometimes conveys a little bit of moral lesson.[82]

That the author of the hundred-chapter novel could have been familiar with the contents of the *Youyang zazu* may be seen from the references to the Three Worms in chapter 15 and Wu Gang 吳剛 in chapter 22. The book thus mentioned, however, is more than simply an anthology of fabulous tales of the ninth-century Tang era. Duan Chengshi (c. 800–863), in the words of the late Edward H. Schafer, an authority on Tang manifold culture both native and imported, was a "bibliophile, word-fancier, and collector of curiosa," and the book Duan compiled and wrote

collected data on every subject, especially information that was outside the realm of common knowledge—such as the use of wooden traps to catch elephants in some foreign land, knowledge that he picked up from a Cantonese physician who had it from a foreign ship captain. Indeed, he sought new knowledge far outside the walls of his library and was noted for his rather scandalous consorting with vagabonds, maid-servants, and foreigners, and even counted "Romans" (Anatolians? Syrians?) and Indians among his informants. Much of the data he collected in this way was linguistic, and it would not be an exaggeration to characterize him as a pioneering field linguist. He also reported on foreign scripts and book-styles; he knew imported incenses and perfumes, such as gum guggul, ambergris, and balm of Gilead—as well as their commercial names in exotic languages—and the names and characteristics of foreign medicinal herbs and garden flowers. He collected reports on the unseen or supernal worlds from persons who claimed expert knowledge of such places; . . . But he was no mere recorder: he often voices his own doubts about the reliability of reports he has received and sometimes goes to considerable pains to check their accuracy with supposed witnesses. For this and other reasons the *Yu-yang tsa-tsu* is no mere mindless collectanea—it has very much the personal stamp of its author, an open-minded book-lover not bound by books.[83]

Schafer's meticulous description of the Tang anthology ironically casts further doubt on Wu's authorship of XYJ, for not many of the elements mentioned, or even allusions to or verbal echoes of them, have turned up in XYJ. The novel itself does not bear up Wu's professed fondness for Duan's title. The near-century-long debate on the authorship of this Chinese masterpiece has yet to resolve this fundamental problem. Given the magnitude, length, and complexity of the hundred-chapter novel, thorough examination and analysis of what might have been the materials alluded to and, even more important, made use of by the actual text itself become the indispensable task of any serious interpreter of a literary document like XYJ. The nature and sources (to the extent that they are discoverable) of the document's language and rhetoric provide the nonnegotiable basis for a considered judgment on what that document is about. The results of such labor should then be compared and correlated with the characteristics and discernible features of any known writings of a person nominated for putative authorship. How this fundamental problem has been treated in the history of XYJ's reception, however, clearly reveals the difference dividing premodern readers and the early twentieth-century scholars like Hu Shi and Lu Xun. Whereas the Qing readers were fascinated by much of the content and allegorical rhetoric of the novel's text, the modern scholars seemed far more eager to find a person as the likely authorial candidate. Before the end of this section of this introduction, therefore, it is necessary to take up briefly the novel's reception by two of its premodern readers (the second one admittedly putative and controversial) before one can entertain the question (in the last two parts of the introduction) of whether the novel's aim and message coincide with Wu Cheng'en's description of his now lost book of stories written to record "the strange things of the human world and sometimes and . . . a little bit of moral lesson."

The earliest moral lesson that has surfaced in XYJ, as far as the readers are concerned, has to be that articulated in the preface of the Shidetang edition by one Chen Yuanzhi. According to him,

> We do not know who wrote the book, *Journey to the West*. Some claimed that it originated from the domain of a prince's household; others, from the likes of the "Eight Squires (八公之徒)";[84] still others, that a prince himself created it. When I look at its meaning, it appears to be a champion of reckless humor, a composition of overflowing chatter. There used to be a preface [? 舊有序],[85] but it did not record the name of its author. Could it be on account of the possible offense caused by such vulgar language? Its narration takes

up monkey, a monkey that is taken to be the spirit of the heart-and-mind (心之神). The horse: the horse is taken to be the galloping of the will (意之馳). The name Bajie: eight is the number of things prohibited, so that it can be taken as the wood phase of the liver's pneumatic energy (肝氣之木). Sand: flowing sand, that is to be taken as the water phase of the kidney's pneumatic energy (腎氣之水). As for Tripitaka [Sanzang 三藏, originally the Buddhist nomenclature for the triple canon and also an honorary title conferred on the scripture pilgrim of both history and this novel], it refers to the three storages that hoard viscerally (using 藏 [articulated as cang when used as a verb] to pun on simultaneously zang 藏, treasury, storehouse, and 臟, the viscera) the spirit, the sound, and the pneumatic energy that [would enable one to become] the lord of a citadel (郭郭之主). Demons: demons are taken as the barriers (zhang 障, Skt., māra) of the mouth, the ears, the nose, the tongue, the body, the will, the fears, the contradictions, and the fantasies. That is the reason why demons are born of the mind, and they are also subdued by the mind. That is the reason for subduing the mind in order to subdue demons, and for subduing demons to return to principle. Returning to principle is to revert back to the primal beginning (太初), which is the mind without anything more to be subdued. This indeed is how the Dao is accomplished and plainly allegorized in this book (其書直寓言者哉)![86]

This passage (of only a few sentences in the original Chinese) conveys what sort of impression the reading of the novelistic text had made on this author of a preface written for the earliest known edition of the hundred-chapter novel. The esoteric terminologies coming into view are first of all consistent with a communal milieu for the formation of a text like XYJ, if the "eight squires" indeed allude to some group like the one mentioned by Ge Hong and King Huainan. The latter himself, as we have pointed out in note 84, was no stranger to cultic ritualists or their writings and practices. In addition, Chen Yuanzhi ends the section not merely with a blunt use of the term "allegory," but also provides unmistakable clues as to what sort of an allegory the book purports to have fashioned by noting some of its constitutive diction and themes.

The five pilgrims as the novel's central figures, for example, are transformed in Chen's reading at once into multiple metaphors: not only the monkey and the horse are already identified as "The Monkey of the Mind and the Horse of the Will 心猿意馬," a pair of figurative terms that populate countless texts of both Buddhism and Daoism, but also the delinquent Pig, given the religious nickname Bajie 八戒 [Eight Rules or Prohibitions] at his conversion in the novel, is furthered troped as "the wood phase of the liver's pneumatic energy." Chen's interpretation, in fact, highlights the chain of metaphoric correlation of bodily or somatic features and ingredients with cosmological processes (e.g., wood and water, two of the Five Phases or *wuxing* 五行) pervading the universe and microcosmically the whole of the human body. As will be shown in further detail in part IV of this introduction, such a use of correlation specifically invokes and validates the language and technique of physiological or internal alchemy (*neidan* 內丹) advocated and practiced by many of the Quanzhen adepts. The allusion to the mental genesis of "demons 魔" and their "subduing or suppression 攝" also by the mind (*xin*) replicates the doctrinal emphasis of Chan Buddhism and its adaptation by Quanzhen discourse that, in line with the tenets of Daoist writings at large, envisages gods and demons residing in one's body. The third point about Chen's preface, moreover, directly anticipates Wu Yujin's observation cited earlier, for both pieces of writing mutually strengthen the novel's essential linkage to Quanzhen Daoism by referring to a preface attributed to Yu Ji, a document unique to the 1662 edition of the novel titled *Xiyou zhengdaoshu* that also identifies the Yuan Daoist and alchemist Qiu Chuji, alias (style or *hao*) Changchun Zhenren, as the XYJ's author. Qiu, after all, was the second disciple of Wang Chongyang, the founding patriarch of the Quanzhen Order.

Yu Ji of this second preface of the novel, printed some seventy years later than the known first edition, was an erudite scholar flourishing in 1272-1348. His composition claims that he was given the manuscript by the Daoist Purple Jade 紫瓊道人, who further claimed that it was written by the Perfected Lord Qiu Changchun 邱長春真君. Upon reading it, says Yu,

> I saw that what the book records are the events of acquiring scriptures by Xuanzang, the Tang Master of the Law. Now scripture acquisition did not begin in the Tang, for it existed since the eras of the Han to the Liang, but the activities by Xuanzang of the Tang were the most illustrious. His endurance of a long and dangerous journey and his experiences of immense difficulty, thoroughly recounted in Emperor Taizong's "Preface to the Holy Religion," require no further rehearsal by posterity. As I personally perceive the Perfected Lord's purpose, what is said may regard Xuanzang, but its meaning does not concern Xuanzang. Scripture acquisition is recorded, but the intent is actually not about acquiring scripture, for [that event] is borrowed only to indicate or symbolize (*yu* 喻) the Great Way (*da Dao* 大道). Monkey, horse, metal, and wood are the *yin-yang* aspects of our body; ghost, goblin, monster, and demon are also the demonic hindrances (*mozhang* 魔障) of our human life. Although the book is exceedingly strange, expending undoubtedly several hundred thousand words [an astonishingly accurate word count], but its general importance may be stated in one sentence: it is only about the retrieving or releasing one's mind (收放心而已). For whether we folks act like demons and become Buddha are all dependent on this mind.

Released, this mind becomes the erroneous mind. When the erroneous mind is aroused, it can become so demonic that there is no place that its movement and transformation cannot reach. An example of this is when the Mind Monkey calls himself a king, a sage, to disturb greatly the Celestial Palace. When this mind is retrieved, it will be the true mind, and once the true mind appears, it can extinguish demons. Similarly, there is no place that its movement and transformation cannot reach. An example of this is when the Mind Monkey subdue[s] monsters and bind[s] fiends so as to illumine the Buddha's fruit.[87]

As can be seen readily from the citation, Yu's reading of the novel plainly complements the emphasis of Chen Yuanzhi. The thrust of the entire novel, according to Yu, is about the control and liberation of the mind, an interpretation that accords with Chan Buddhism—especially its so-called Southern Lineage (南宗)—and the entire Quanzhen tradition from its founding patriarchs of the Song-Yuan era to the Qing and present-day communities. Despite the putative author's scholarly reputation, Yu Ji's preface is controversial, as the novel's critics past and present have severe doubts about its authenticity. They ask why it did not turn up until seven decades later in a Qing printed edition of the novel. Many surmise that it might have been a forged document inserted into the Qing edition. If the authorship of the preface is questionable, Yu's account of how he learned of the Quanzhen patriarch Qiu Chuji as the author of XYJ is thus also suspect.

On the other hand, the historical Yu Ji was active in the Daoist communities of his time, counting among his friends quite a few members of the major lineages of Daoism (Quanzhen, Zhengyi, Maoshan, and Zhendadao Jiao). As Liu Ts'un-yan has shown, Yu Ji also wrote a discerning and knowledgeable preface to a group of miscellaneous writings (some prose, poems, and ritual texts) titled *Minghe yuyin* 鳴鶴餘音 (The crying crane's lingering sounds) now preserved in DZ 744–45. The collection actually was compiled by an itinerant Daoist named Peng Zhizhong 彭致中, but one section in the collection details Yu Ji's friendship and happy exchanges of poems with one Feng Zunshi 馮尊師 (Honored Master Feng), about whose activities Yu wrote the preface.[88]

Yu Ji's allegation of the Yuan Daoist Qiu Chuji as the original author of XYJ has met also stiff resistance. What complicates matters is the fact that, as noted previously, the Qing scholar Wu Yujin in "The Supplement to the Shanyang Gazetteer" has also credited Qiu with a book of exactly the same name of *Xiyouji*, or literally in its full form, The Record of the Westward Journey by the Perfected Man of Enduring Spring, *Changchun zhenren Xiyouji* 長春真人西游記. This book, however, is no help at all to solve the mystery of the novel's origin, since readers will discover at once that it concerns topics of travel and geography. With a preface that addresses Qiu as "Father Teacher, *fushi* 父師," the book actually narrates at one point the circumstance of Qiu's death. For these reasons, most scholars firmly regard the book's author as likely one of Qiu's principal disciples, Li Zhichang 李志常, who purported to record Qiu's lengthy and arduous journey in 1221–1224 from Beijing to Genghis Khan's court in Karakorum in the Mongol heartland. Past seventy years old then, Qiu led some eighteen of his disciples on this visit.[89] Despite the different nature of this XYJ, as Andrew Plaks points out, there is one other reference found in Qiu's corpora that attributes to the patriarch one more work by the same name so as to "reveal the true scriptures in the Western Heaven 西游記, 邱祖傳, 指示真經在西天."[90] As any reader of Qiu's gathered religious writings in both prose and poetry will readily testify, all of his writings are about the ritual precepts and practices of Quanzhen Daoism. In sum, Qiu's association with the novel XYJ as we know it in the Shidetang version, precisely because of the novelistic use of identifiable rhetoric and terminologies from religious sources, cannot be dismissed out of hand.

Finally, one strong argument against a Yuan origin of the novel ostensibly stems from a different kind of textual evidence, not the massive presence of religious topoi and rhetoric, but the novel's use of official and bureaucratic titles that began only in the Ming. If Qiu were granted the novel's authorship, so this argument goes, how could a Yuan verbal artifact employ nomenclatures not known until centuries later? Against this seemingly irrefutable thesis, contemporary readers loyal to the Yuan and Quanzhen *Sitz-im-Leben* for the text's initial production have countered with the argument that the hundred-chapter novel, though its essential form and content emerged in the Yuan, might have been modified in subsequent production. Later editions of the Ming also seem to display here and there the titles of officials that were in use only in the Qing. Are we then to assume a Qing authorship for the Ming novel?[91]

In summary, this vexing dispute over the novel's authorship, similar to that on the priority of its textual versions, has also seesawed back and forth for nearly a century without resolution. We now know that there exist several texts from the Yuan to the Ming with the name "The Record of the Westward Journey or *Xiyouji*." The extant Yuan text is not a novel at all, but its firm association with Qiu Chuji, a Yuan Daoist and the second patriarch of the Quanzhen lineage, prods us to wonder whether Qiu had connection to some other texts with the same or a similar name, now lost, that recount the evolving story about Xuanzang's pilgrimage. Apart from a fully formed drama of twenty-four scenes also titled XYJ, a local prefectural gazetteer credits a minor late Ming official with a book or composition by the name of XYJ, but there is no information on what sort of a work that is. Most Chinese scholars in the early decades of the twentieth century since Hu Shi have embraced Wu Cheng'en as the most likely author of the first printed, full-length version of the novel. In more recent decades, doubts about Wu's authorship are heard with increasing frequency, and much of this "revisionist" critique of Hu's thesis arises from readers' escalating attention to the actual linguistic content and rhetorical affinities of the fiction text that are difficult to reconcile or harmonize with the content in Wu Cheng'en's known writings.[92]

This last problem has persuaded two of the most astute scholars of traditional Chinese fiction outside of China to withhold full support for Wu's authorship. After a comprehensive survey on aspects of the novel manifestly related to Quanzhen Daoism, the late Professor Liu Ts'un-yan of Australia, though constrained to deny the novel's initial authorship to Qiu Chuji, nonetheless plainly asserted the "high possibility" of a Quanzhen version of the narrative existing prior to the 1592 edition, written by someone belonging to that same religious community "撰寫者自己是全真教中人."[93] He does not rule out a Ming date for the author or final redactor, but he is less certain about late-Ming literati's familiarity with some of the subtle and hidden allusions in Quenzhen writings, an estimation that may not be entirely accurate. In his equally long and erudite chapter on this novel, probing with special acuity its religious and philosophical rhetoric, Professor Andrew Plaks of the United States has entertained "a remote possibility" of "a prototype" for the novel as "a Yuan (or even a late Sung) composition," but his chapter's final thesis considers the novel, exemplified by the Shidetang and other editions, to be "essentially a product of the sixteenth-century intellectual milieu."[94] The conclusion reached by these two specialists may indicate scholarly open-mindedness or cautious equivocation that, paradoxically, may further validate the insight of someone like Wu Yujin cited earlier. To argue for a possible Yuan prototype or some version of XYJ that eventually was brought to its completed form in the 1592 printed version by a nameless author or final redactor—is this not analogous indeed to that Qing reader's interesting use of the transformation of official history (that is, the Three Kingdoms) into fiction by different hands of author and redactors to gloss his understanding of the formative process for the hundred-chapter *Xiyouji*?

III THE USES AND SOURCES OF POETRY

Unlike any typical Western work of fiction since the Renaissance, *The Journey to the West* is made up of prose heavily interlaced with verse of many varieties and lengths. Incorporation of poetry into prose narration is not, of course, unique to Chinese vernacular fiction. For distant Western parallels, one may point to the early satiric fragments of Menippus, the later *Consolation of Philosophy* by Boethius, a work like *Aucassin and Nicolette,* and the writings of Bunyan and Rabelais. In Chinese literature, however, this form of writing has enjoyed more sophisticated and artful cultivation, for the use of poetry to serve specific literary functions is already a characteristic of Tang fiction and drama.[95] In such narrative works as the *Yingying-zhuan* 鶯鶯傳 and the *Songyue jianü* 嵩岳嫁女, poems advance the action by revealing the emotional conditions of the characters, or serve as set pieces of dramatic dialogue, a feature that later dramatic literature develops extensively. The growing popularity of Buddhist literatures and the development of religious prosimetric writings called transformational texts (*bianwen* 變文) further motivated the employment of narrative, descriptive, and didactic verse in prose fiction.

No reader of the *Dazhidu lun* 大智度論 or the *Vimalakīrti-nirdeśa sūtra,* to pick two examples at random, can fail to perceive that characteristic which Maurice Winternitz has called "an old form of Buddhist composition": namely, that of "expressing an idea first in prose and then garbing it in verse, or [of] commencing the presentation of a doctrine in prose and then continuing it in verse."[96] Nor can that reader fail to notice, when he or she turns from the Buddhist canon to the transformational texts, how the addition of poetry to summarize or develop the prose has become one of the defining features of this popular form of writing.

Since the discovery of these *bianwen* texts in the caves of Dunhuang in 1899, their historical basis is well known. Dating from the eighth and ninth centuries, many of the texts took as their subject the *Leben und Treiben* of Buddhist saints and heroes, though many other secular stories dealt with persons and events from Chinese legend or history as well. The origin of the religious *bianwen* has been traced to the evangelism of Buddhist monks, who sought to accommodate their more abstruse doctrines to a popular audience through storytelling, a practice for which the Buddha himself might be said to have provided the exemplary precedent.[97] Not incomparable to some of the patristic and medieval epic paraphrases of biblical themes in the West (e.g., the *Libri Evangeliorum IV* of Juvencus, the *Carmen Paschale* of Sedulius, the anonymous but massive Old Saxon *Heliand,* and the *De Vita et Gestis Christi* of Jacobus Bonus), these *bianwen* consisted of imaginative elaborations and expansions of individual episodes in a Buddhist sūtra, with events and persons freely altered or added. Alternating between short sections of semiliterary prose and lengthier sections composed mainly of the penta- or heptasyllabic poetic line, the *bianwen* may amplify a relatively short unit (about one or two hundred characters) of the *Saddharma-puṇḍarīka sūtra* or the *Vimala-kīrti-nirdeśa sūtra* into a narrative of several thousand characters in length.[98] In all probability, these stories were first sung or chanted during temple festivals, and, to judge from observations made in the *Gaoseng zhuan* 高僧傳 (Biographies of Eminent Monks, compiled by Huijiao 慧皎, 497–554 CE), popular reaction to the presentations, especially those describing the agonies of hell, could be extremely emotional.[99]

The popularity and success of the Buddhist *bianwen* may be seen in the widespread emulation of its form by subsequent authors of secular topics drawn from both history and folklore. The mixture of poetry and prose in narration as a distinctive mode of composition thus made its mark permanently on Chinese literary history, exerting enormous influence on the development of popular drama and the practice of storytelling from then on. The indebtedness of Chinese colloquial fiction to these art forms in turn has been a familiar theme of modern scholarship. Scholars who have studied the formal characteristics of the dramatic and narrative literature in medieval China have noted such poetic functions as commentary, moral judgment, exemplum, and summary.[100] By the time of the Ming-Qing novelists, the combination of verse and prose in narration had evolved into a highly flexible medium. In the exploitation of this technique, few writers could rival the author of *The Journey to the West* in creative skill, keen observational power, vivid vocabulary, and sure command of a wide variety of poetic forms.

One of the unusual features shared by the four or five monumental classics of traditional Chinese fiction is, interestingly, the differentiated and peculiar use of poetry. In the *The Three Kingdoms*, for example, a small number of poems selected from mostly known but unidentified historical poets provide mainly choric commentary on characters and incidents, thereby, in fact, validating once more one of the most significant functions of the traditional literati lyric—that of singing about history or *yongshi* 詠史. In *The Plum in the Golden Vase*, on the other hand, "the lyrics of actual popular songs . . . and a complex mosaic of borrowed language, comprising proverbial sayings, catch phrases, stock epithets and couplets and quotations from early poetry and song, and formulaic language of all kinds inherited from the literary tale" are brilliantly and massively deployed to express "the spoken or unspoken thoughts of the characters."[101] In the Qing novel *The Story of the Stone* (or *Hongloumeng*, Dream of the Red Chamber), the lyrics—all composed by the author, as far as we know—function primarily to reveal the subjectivity and development of the protagonists and to act occasionally as a futile though deeply moving critique of a decadent Confucian morality.

The Journey to the West's very many poems are mostly original.[102] They excel in formal varieties and assume a large share of the narrative responsibility. At every opportunity, the author eagerly displays his poetic skills by weaving into the fabric of his tale a poem of the style of the *jueju* 絕句 (a rhymed quatrain of penta- or heptasyllabic lines with fixed tonal pattern), or of the *lüshi* 律詩 (an eight-line rhymed poem with lines of the same length and one fixed tonal pattern), or of the *pailü* 排律 (a long poem using a single rhyme scheme for virtuosic effect, with the middle parallel couplets often constructed like those of a *lüshi* serially extended), or of the *ci* 詞 (generally, a short, rhymed lyric of irregular meter and of two parts or sections, with one or more patterns of different tones or pitches), or of the *fu* 賦 (the rhyme-prose or rhapsody, rhymed or unrhymed). Running the length of the first chapter alone, which tells of Monkey's birth and his life up to the time when he was given the name Wukong, are no fewer than seventeen poems exemplifying nearly all the forms just mentioned. Though it is not at all apparent in the widely read, abridged translation by Arthur Waley (pp. 11-12), there is a poem depicting the monkey's frolic "under the shade of some pine trees," and another *lüshi* sketches the curtainlike waterfall immediately after its discovery by the monkeys.

A comprehensive study of the narrative's poetry would require a separate monograph much lengthier than this introduction. Here I can only point out some of the most important functions of the verse in the narrative: it describes scenery, battles, seasons, and living beings both human and nonhuman; it presents dialogues; and it provides commentary on the action and the characters. Poems in the last category make frequent use of religious themes and rhetoric as well as allegorical devices. I shall study some of these in the final section.

It is not without reason that the author of XYJ has been ranked by C. T. Hsia as "one of the most skilled descriptive poets in all Chinese literature,"[103] for much of the descriptive verse in this narrative is marked by extraordinary realism, vivid delineation, and vivacious humor. Though it may be impossible to duplicate the terse rhythm of the three-syllabic line with end rhymes used in the poem portraying the frolic of the monkeys (chapter 1), I have attempted to catch something of its characteristic vigor in my translation.

> *Swinging from branches to branches*
> *Searching for flowers and fruits;*
> *They played two games or three*
> *With pebbles and with pellets.* [see 1: 102].

Another example of this type of poetic sketch may be taken from chapter 89, where we have the following poem on a butterfly.

> *A pair of gossamer wings,*
> *Twin feelers of silvery shade:*

It flies so swiftly in the wind,
And dances slowly in the sun.
With nimble speed passing over walls and streams,
It blithely with the fragrant catkins flirts;
Its airy frame loves most the scent of fresh flowers,
Where its graceful form unfolds with greatest ease.

A third example of the poet's descriptive power may be taken from chapter 20, where Tripitaka is asked to depict a violent gust that the pilgrims encounter on their way. "Look at this wind!" he said.

Augustly it blows in a blusterous key,
An immense force leaving the jade-green sky.
It passes the ridge, just hear the trees roar.
It moves in the wood, just see the poles quake. [see 1: 399].

These three poems are but brief illustrations of the author's superb poetic eye and his uncanny ability to capture in a few lines the essential qualities of his subject. That subject may be a mosquito (chapter 16), a bee (chapter 55), a bat (chapter 65), a moth (chapter 84), an ant (chapter 86), a rabbit (chapter 95), or one of the numerous monsters with whom Tripitaka's disciples must engage in combat, the battle itself, or the scenery of the different regions through which the pilgrims must pass. But what the reader meets again and again in these poems is an enthralling spectacle of exquisite details. Indeed, if judged by some of the traditional norms of Chinese lyric poetry, most of the poems of *The Journey to the West* might be considered inferior products because of their graphic and, occasionally, unadorned diction. The language is often too explicit, too direct, too bold, to be evocative or suggestive. They do not seek that quality of metaphorical elusiveness which most Chinese lyric poets cherish and seek to inculcate in their verse.

What is scorned by tradition, however, may turn out to be a poetic trait of special merit in XYJ. For what the author has sought to express in these poems is hardly the kind of lyricism suffused with symbolic imageries so characteristic of the earlier poetry of reclusion, nor is he attempting to achieve the subtle fusion of human emotion and nature that many of the Tang and Song poets aimed for. Most of all, he is not trying to enlist the service of the lyrical tradition to realize the ancient ideal of "expressing serious intent or aspiration (*shi yan zhi*)." None of these descriptive poems bears profound moral ideas or weighty philosophical substances. Often they lack "weight and solidity," in the words of one critic,[104] but that is precisely because they are not meant to be read as independent poetic entities. Their complete integration into the narrative as a whole is what gives them their "epic" force.

Divorced from their contexts, the lengthy similes of Homer or Vergil are no more impressive than the balladic lines of "Chevy Chase."

Through the many poems of scenic depiction, what the author of XYJ seeks to convey to us seems to be the overpowering immediacy of nature, with all its fullness and richly contrasting variety, as the main characters in the narrative experience it. To give us this sense of munificence in the natural order, the verse frequently uses what may be called delayed amplification. In the first chapter, where the Flower-Fruit Mountain (the birthplace of Sun Wukong) is introduced, part of the testimonial *fu* poem reads:

> *Its majesty commands the wide ocean;*
> *Its splendor rules the jasper sea;*
> *Its majesty commands the wide ocean*
> *When, like silver mountains, the tide sweeps fishes into caves;*
> *Its splendor rules the jasper sea*
> *When snowlike billows send forth serpents from the deep.* [see 1: 100-1].

When the monkeys, the subjects of Sun Wukong, later enjoy a feast, the delicacies include

> *Golden balls and pearly pellets;*
> *Red ripeness and yellow plumpness.*
> *Golden balls and pearly pellets are the cherries,*
> *Their colors truly luscious.*
> *Red ripeness and yellow plumpness are the plums,*
> *Their taste—a fragrant tartness.*

Again, the setting we are made to see of the abode of the Bear Monster in chapter 17 is a cave which is surrounded by

> *Mist and smoke abundant,*
> *Cypress and pine umbrageous.*
> *Mist and smoke abundant, their hues surround the door;*
> *Cypress and pine umbrageous, their green entwines the gate.*

In these lines of poetry, repetition is the apparent means by which the poet partially overcomes the limitations inherent in his medium: the extreme economy of construction and the tendency toward conventional diction. One does not need to read much classic Chinese verse to recognize that poets use phrases such as "wide ocean (汪洋)," "snowlike billows (雪浪)," "red ripeness (紅綻)," "yellow plumpness (黃肥)," and "cypress and pine umbrageous (松柏森森)" so regularly that they are formulaic. In this regard, most of the novel's scenic poems show little interest in moving beyond traditional descriptive vocabularies and metaphors. The extensive employment of *wuxing* (Five Phases) and alchemical terminologies in most of the commentarial poems, though exceptional, has antecedents in many of the minor poets from the Tang on who were religious adepts. What the author has done in the narrative that merits our attention is the way he breaks up into separate lines the phrases that *ordinarily* would be joined together. Instead of simply stating "Cypress and pine umbrageous, their green entwines the gate," he first mentions the cypresses and the bamboos before proceeding to their appearance and condition. This procedure retards the movement of the poetic line by giving a more leisurely pace to a metrical rhythm that is normally terse and rapid. The repetitions compel our attention and serve to enhance the amplitude of the poetic utterance. Cumulatively these poems impress us with the encyclopedic range of the poet's interest and the fineness of his vision, for there is hardly anything that is too mundane or too exotic for his scrutiny. Foodstuff of all kinds, household utensils, birds, animals, and insects, plants and flowers of sundry varieties, the beings of heaven and hell—all proceed unhurriedly before us in their colorful and manifold plenitude, and we are also given a profound sense of "God's plenty."

The poems are equally effective in transcribing for us the sense of time passing, the ever recurring pattern of seasonal change.[105] Though the length of Tripitaka's journey in the narrative has been purposefully changed by its author from the historical Xuanzang's nearly seventeen years to fourteen, the aim is not to minimize the arduous duration of Tripitaka's undertaking. On the contrary, many details are present in the narrative to emphasize the temporal span of the journey. Not only do the pilgrims themselves repeatedly talk about distance and time (cf. XYJ, chapter 24, p. 270; chapter 80, p. 911; chapter 86, pp. 986-87; chapter 88, p. 1000; chapter 91, p. 1029; chapter 92, p. 1039; chapter 93, p. 1055), but the narrator also stresses the vast span of the pilgrimage by means of frequent poetic descriptions of seasonal alterations. Soon after Sun Wukong's submission to the scripture pilgrim, the narrative in chapter 14 reads:

> Tripitaka rode his horse, with Pilgrim [i.e., Wukong] leading the way; they journeyed by day and rested by night, taking food and drink according to their needs. Soon it was early winter. You see
>
> *Frost blighted maples and the wizened trees;*
> *Few verdant pine and cypress still on the ridge.* [see 1: 313].

In chapter 18, however, this is the contrasting scene we have after Sun Wukong has recovered a lost cassock.

> As Pilgrim led the way forward, it was the happiest time of spring. You see
>
> *The horse making light tracks on grassy turfs;*
> *Gold threads of willow swaying with fresh dew.* [see 1: 368].

These and similar poetic passages (cf. XYJ, chapter 20, p. 223; chapter 23, p. 256; chapter 56, pp. 643-44) are not intended merely for conveying to us the sense and beauty of seasonal change. More important, such accounts of the seasons, in themselves no more than familiar literary exercises in the Chinese lyric tradition, are designed to help the readers grasp the effects on those who must take time to reach a distant goal. Constantly exposed to the whims of nature, the pilgrims are the ones who must, as the Chinese put it, "feed on wind and rest on dew (餐風宿露)," who must be "capped by the moon and cloaked by the stars (戴月被星)." Just as the cycles of ordeals and adversities accentuate the suffering of Tripitaka and his disciples, so even the ostensibly charming and innocuous shifts of the seasons add to the hardships ("The strong, cold wind / Tears at the sleeve! / How does one bear this chilly might of night?") encountered on the way. In this manner, time is both spatialized and physicalized, its effect thus reinforcing our impression of how immense is the journey to the West.

Their compelling descriptive power notwithstanding, these poems are sometimes, paradoxically, devoid of local color and impression. This is especially true of those designed to depict a place. Invariably the verse refers to precipitous cliffs and exotic flowers, to buildings of carved beam and verdant forests of pines and bamboos, to the cries of cranes and phoenixes, and to the congregation of rare and mythic animals. The poems, to be sure, vary in content and syntax, but if the author did not specify the location, it would be impossible to distinguish between the birthplace of Sun Wukong (Flower-Fruit Moutain) in chapter 1, the Black Wind Mountain in chapter 17, the Spirit Mountain (*Lingshan*) which is Buddha's abode, in chapters 52 and 98, or the counterfeit *Lingshan* in chapter 65, where the pilgrims meet one of their most formidable adversaries.

This perplexing fusion of the particular and the typical is what enables the entire narrative to be imbued with a kind of epic grandeur, energy, and expansiveness. In his thoughtful essay "The Realistic and Lyric Elements in the Chinese Medieval Story," Jaroslav Průšek has suggested that the prose and poetic portions of the *bianwen* and the *huaben* constitute two levels of representing reality. Recalling how Balzac found it praiseworthy that Sir Walter Scott impregnated the novel "with the spirit of olden times, combined in it drama and dialogue, portrait, landscape and description, introduced into it fantasy and truth—elements typical of the epic [as a genre that, strictly speaking, was unknown in Chinese literary history]—and placed poetry in closest intimacy with the most ordinary speech," Průšek thinks that the lyrical poetical insertions into the realistic prose segments of the Chinese story "form—possibly quite unintentionally—a kind of second plane to the actual story, raise it—even though it be unconsciously—to the demonstrations of a certain philosophical conception of the world."[106]

While Průšek's observation, to some extent, can be applied to *The Journey to the West*, it does not quite isolate the particular virtue of the work. Its poetic insertions are neither "interludes" nor "interruptions"; they are, rather, integral parts of the total narrative. Not unlike some of the great landscape paintings of the Song and the Yuan periods, in which a thousand details subsist in a delicate union of concreteness and ideality, the poetry here at once heightens and elevates by pointing simultaneously to the concreteness of a certain site and to its mysterious and elemental character. Most important, the lyric impulse is always placed at the service of the epic; the descriptions do not call attention to themselves as poetic entities in their own right but, rather, constantly strengthen the elan and verve of the story. As Erich Auerbach has written so perceptively of *The Divine Comedy*, "the vivid descriptions of landscape in which the great poem abounds are never autonomous or purely lyrical; true, they appeal directly to the reader's emotions, they arouse delight or horror; but the feelings awakened by the landscape are not allowed to seep away like vague romantic dreams, but forcefully recapitulated, for the landscape is nothing other than the appropriate scene or metaphorical symbol of human destiny."[107] Similarly, the mountains, the monasteries, the monsters, the deities, the rivers and plains, and the seasons in *The Journey to the West* are significant only in relation to the fate of the pilgrims. The appearance of any locality can be either menacing or tutelary precisely because it forebodes danger or shelter for Tripitaka and his companions. So too, the accounts of the glorious epiphany of Guanyin in chapter 12 and of the fearful visages of the Green-Hair Lion, the Yellow-Tusk Elephant, and the Garuda Monster in chapter 75 achieve their greatest impact only when the reader knows they can assist or impede the pilgrims' progress.

To stress the central importance of such experience and its influence on the quality of the poetry is not to overlook verbal humor, another often-praised aspect of the narrative. One of the best examples of narrative realism masterfully blended with comic irony may be found in chapter 67, where an elder of a village is seeking Monkey's aid to rid the people of a python monster.

> "Oldie," said Pilgrim [JW's translation of *xingzhe* 行者 (disciple or acolyte), the nickname of Xuanzang gave to Sun Wukong], "the monster-spirit is not hard to catch. It is hard *only* because the families in this region are not united in their efforts." "How did you reach this conclusion?" asked the old man.
>
> "For three years," Pilgrim replied, " this monster-spirit has been a menace, taking the lives of countless creatures. If each family here were to donate an ounce of silver, I should think that five hundred families would yield at

least five hundred ounces. With that amount of money, you could hire an exorcist anywhere who would be able to catch the fiend for you. Why did you permit him to torture you for these three years?"

"If you bring up the subject of spending money," said the old man, "I'm embarrassed to death! Which one of our families did not disburse indeed three or five ounces of silver? The year before last we found a monk from the south side of this mountain and invited him to come. But he didn't succeed." "How did that monk go about catching the monster?" asked Pilgrim.

The old man said:

"That man of the Saṅgha,
He had on a kasāya,
He first quoted the Peacock;
He then chanted the Lotus.
Burned incense in an urn;
Grasped with his hand a bell.
As he thus sang and chanted,
He aroused the very fiend.
Astride the clouds and the wind,
He came to our village.
The monk fought with the fiend—
In truth some tall tale to tell!
One stroke brought forth a punch,
One stroke delivered a scratch.
The monk tried hard to respond:
In response his hair was gone!
In a while the fiend had won
And gone back to mist and smoke.
(Mere dried scabs being sunned!)[108]
We drew near to take a look:
The bald head was smashed like a watermelon!"

The language of this passage may certainly bring to mind such works in the West as the Homeric *Batrachomyomachia* (Battle of the Frogs and Mice) and Pope's *The Rape of the Lock*. But what is noteworthy is how the XYJ author adds his own characteristic brand of wit at the expense of religion, for two lines of this particular poem poke fun at the Buddhist priest battling the python monster: "The monk tried hard to respond: / In response his hair was gone." The word "respond" alludes to the Buddhist doctrine of mutual union, the correspondence of mind with mental data dependent on five kinds of correspondence common to both: the senses, reason, process, object, and time. Formally, this is called "the Law of Response or *xiangying fa*

相應法," but the last graph of the doctrinal phrase can in the vernacular mean simply method or power. The polysemia of the word elicits from our author the apt and hilarious pun on Buddhist law and power with the homonym "hair, *fa* 髮" that at once predicts the monk's miserable defeat. Such witty construction notwithstanding, this is no mere episode of the mock heroic in *The Journey to the West* because its context remains most serious. Despite the scene's relaxed, comic tone, the ordeal facing Pilgrim and his companion, Bajie, is not illusory. Shortly thereafter they will again have to battle a real and dangerous opponent in the figure of the monster, which is another part of the ordeal preordained for the pilgrims.

This deliberate harnessing of the poetic elements to augment the narrative force may be detected also in many of the poetic speeches of the narrative. The technique of advancing the action through poetic dialogues is no doubt inherited directly from the colloquial short stories and popular dramas of earlier periods, but it has now become a highly flexible and effective device. Most of these speeches are spoken as challenges to battle or descriptions of weapons, for which the author of XYJ exploits the longer form of the *pailü* with utmost virtuosity. The challenges to battle are usually delivered immediately before the character engages in actual combat. They provide occasions for the speaker not only to indulge in polemical humor and to provoke his adversary, but also frequently to reminisce, to recount his own history. Thus, when Bajie demands from Sha Wujing his name and surname before the battle in chapter 22, this is the reply he receives:

> My spirit was strong since the time of birth.
> I had made a tour of the whole wide world,
> Where my fame as a hero became well known—
> A gallant type for all to emulate. [see 1: 424].

Though this speech of poetic declamation by Sha Wujing, or any of those by other characters in the narrative (cf. chapters 19, 52, 70, 85, 86), is not comparable in length to, say, the tales of Odysseus, it serves a similar function, common to most heroic tales, of filling in the background of a hero's life, just as "Homer makes Nestor boast of his lost youth or Phoenix tell of his lurid past."[109]

Finally, the last major function of the verse in XYJ concerns the provision of authorial commentary, in the form of prefatory synopsis of narrative meaning for a chapter, doctrinal exposition attributed to different characters, and allegorical interpretation of characters and incidents in the narrative. In chapter 19, to cite our first example, Monkey, after a fierce battle and a little requisite disclosure of his identity along with his membership in the scripture pilgrimage community, brought to submission the piglike, deliquent Daoist Marshal of Heavenly Reeds. As the two of them traveled back to greet their master in the Gao Village, the narrator broke into the following regulated poem:

> Strong is metal's nature to vanquish wood:
> Mind Monkey has the Wood Dragon subdued.
> With metal and wood both obedient as one,
> All their love and virtue will grow and show.
> One guest and one host there's nothing between;
> Three matings, three unions—there's great mystery!
> Nature and feelings gladly fused as Last and First:
> Both will surely be enlightened in the West.

Readers of premodern Chinese fiction know that countless persons— usually but not only male—would band together for martial, religious, or even literary reasons. In their association or society, fraternal or sorosistic order, they address each other in kinship terms like "brothers" and "sisters," as they would likely do even in real life. Readers of this novel will realize that after chapter 19, when a third member of the pilgrimage is found in the figure of Zhu Bajie, the Pig, a little society of this nature has been formed, one that seems no different at all from similar collectivities emerging in the opening chapters of the novel *Three Kingdoms* at the Peaches Garden or that of the 108 outlaws by the Marshes of Mount Liang. Even premodern readers of Chinese fiction, however, may not have been prepared to understand the poem cited, in which strange terms and puzzling connections describe the new relationship between Xuanzang's monkey disciple (already an odd and wholly unhistorical companion) and a renegade Daoist deity, now half-human and half-pig.

Such a narrative tack persists throughout the lengthy story. When the pilgrims finally arrive near their long-sought destination, the Thunderclap Monastery that is Buddha's abode in chapter 98—when, in sum, all five of the entourage in a most imaginatively narrated episode have succeeded in casting off the "shell" of their physical form during their perilous crossing of the Cloud-Transcending Stream—the narrator again intrudes with this enigmatic quatrain:

> Delivered from their mortal flesh and bone,
> A primal spirit of mutual love has grown.
> Their work done, they become Buddhas this day,
> Free of their former six-six senses's sway.

It requires no keen perception to notice that metaphors again abound in these four lines of verse, but what sort of allegory are they attempting to create for us readers? Is this also part of how "the book plainly allegorizes the Dao's perfection 此其以為道之成耳, 此其書直寓言者," to quote again Chen Yuanzhi's words in a portion of the first printed edition's preface cited in part II of this introduction? Some answer to such questions will occupy our analysis in part IV of this introduction. The present section of the introduction will end with a comprehensive listing of identifiable sources, cited in whole or in part, verbatim or modified, from Daoist texts that are canonical or noncanonical. Most of these quotations or paraphrastic allusions are poems or revised parts thereof, but there are several prose passages as well. The text of XYJ presents us with at least twenty such citations as follows:

1. Chapter 2, p. 16: The long poem uttered by the Patriarch Subodhi as an oral formula to instruct Sun Wukong at night on the secrets of internal alchemy. The poem was quoted verbatim in Fu Qinjia 傅勤家, *Zhongguo Daojiao shi* 中國道教史 (Taiwan, 1975, reprint of Shanghai, 1937), p. 131. Fu did not indicate whether the novel XYJ was, in fact, the source of the poem or whether it was used both in the novel and elsewhere. He simply stated that the piece was used by those "in the cultivation of the Way in posterity" to explain certain passages and terminologies in the *Huang-ting neijing jing* 黃庭內景經, DZ 331 (Eastern Jin, 317–420 CE), and in the *Qianque leishu* 潛確類書 (ed. Chen Renxi 陳仁錫, printed in 1631–1633 and officially banned book of 120 *j*).

2. Chapter 7, p. 70: A quatrain celebrating Sun Wukong's iron rod begins with the line, "One beam of light supernal fills the supreme void." It is a slightly altered quotation of a poetic line by the patriarch Ma Danyang 馬丹陽 (1131–1183 CE) of the northern lineage of the Quanzhen Order and the first disciple of the founder, Wang Chongyang. See the "Jianxing song 見性誦," in *Dongxuan jinyu ji* 洞玄金玉集, from DZ 1149, 25: 590.

3. Chapter 8, p. 78: Prefatorial verse in the form of a lyric, to the tune of "Su Wu in Slow Pace 蘇武慢." With alteration of only the last three lines, it is a full citation of a lyric to the same tune by one Feng Zunshi 馮尊師, in *Minghe yuyin* 鳴鶴餘音, from DZ 1100, 24: 262–63.

4. Chapter 11, p. 115: Prefatorial verse that begins with the line, "A hundred years pass by like flowing streams 百歲光陰似水流." The heptasyllabic regulated poem actually is a poetic paraphrase and partial adaptation of a prose "Shengtang wen 昇堂文 (Proclamation upon the ascension of the Main Hall, a ritual text)," by one Qin Zhenren 秦真人, in *Minghe yuyin*, DZ 1100, 24: 308–09.

5. Chapter 12, p. 133: The text for the deliverance of the orphaned souls drafted by Xuanzang for the emperor to approve before the start of the Grand Mass of Land and Water. The entire prose portion that begins

with the sentence, "The supreme virtue is vast and endless, for Buddhism is founded upon Nirvāṇa 至德渺茫, 禪 [likely a generic use of the term Chan] 宗寂滅," is a reworking of the opening segment of another "Shengtang wen" by Feng Zunshi, in *Minghe yuyin*, 24: 308. The text also is collected in the *Dongyuan ji* 洞淵集, DZ 1063, 23: 875, as "Shengtang shizhong 昇堂示眾 (Ascending the Hall to instruct the multitude)," but here there is no indication of author.

6. Chapter 14, p. 153: The prefatorial poem beginning with the line, "The Buddha is Mind and the Mind is Buddha 佛即心兮心即佛." As indicated in part I of this introduction, this piece directly reworks an ode by Zhang Boduan (982/4?–1082), reputed founder of the southern lineage of the Quanzhen Order. See the *Wuzhen pian* 悟真篇, gathered in the collection, *Xiuzhen shishu* 修真十書 in DZ 263, 4: 746.

7. Chapter 20, p. 223: Near the end of the pentasyllabic prefatorial verse, there are the following two lines. "When both Bull and Man disappear [with Bull used here as a metonym of Buddha], / the jade-green sky is bright and clear 人牛不見時, 碧天光皎潔." These directly allude to the following lines by Tan Chuduan 譚處端 that end a lyric to the tune of "Thinking Perpetually of the Immortals, Changsi xian 長思仙": "Sedge slippers go back; / The little calf follows. / The bright moon high up shines on an ancient dike, / When both Bull and Man disappear 芒兒歸, 牛兒隨, 明月高空照古堤, 人牛不見時." See *Shuiyun ji* 水雲集, in DZ 1160, 25: 862.

8. Chapter 29, p. 326: The prefatorial verse is a lyric to the tune of "Moon Over the West River, Xijiang yue 西江月" that is a near-verbatim quotation of another lyric to the same tune by Zhang Boduan. See the *Xiuzhen shishu Wuzhen pian* in DZ 263, 4: 748.

9. Chapter 36, p. 420: This episode narrates the human pilgrim receiving instructions (both serious and comical) on how to harness somatic ingredients for internal alchemy from his three disciples while enjoying bright moonlight. The poem first uttered by Sun Wukong—"After the moon's First Quarter and before the Last; / The physic tastes balanced, energy's form is whole. / Return with the picking and refine it in the stove [i.e., one's body cavity] 前弦之後後弦前, 藥味平平氣象全, 採得歸來爐裏鍛"—quotes the first three lines of a quatrain by Zhang Boduan again from the *Xiuzhen shishu Wuzhen pian*, in DZ 263, 4:730. The poem is further commented line by line by one Wang Qingsheng 王慶升 in *Yuanqing zhiming pian* 爰清子至命篇, in DZ 1089, 24: 196. The last line of Zhang's poem reads: "When refined, nurse it warmly like cooking something fresh 鍛成溫養似烹鮮." That line is changed in the novel to read: "Determination's fruit is the Western Heaven 志心功果即西天."

10. Chapter 38, p. 439: A long poem describing a plantain tree begins with the line, "A type of spirit root most sightly 一種靈苗秀." It seems to be a modified version of a line of a lyric to the tune of "Residential Sounds Lamenting Pleasure's Lateness, Yusheng henhuan chi 寓聲恨歡遲" from *Changchun Zhenren Xiyouji* 長春真人西游記 in which Qiu Chuji wrote about some crysanthemums presented to him by a Daoist congregation on the day of Double Ninth: "A type of spirit root, its frame and nature special 一種靈苗體性殊," in DZ 1429, 34:497. Some of the same diction and syntax appear in another poem by Qiu, this time the first line of a heptasyllabic regulated poem on cranes—"A type of spirit fowl, its frame and nature lofty 一種靈禽體性殊"—from his *Panxi ji* 磻溪集, in DZ 1159, 25: 813.

11. Chapter 50, p. 574: The prefatorial verse, to the tune of "A Southern Branch, Nankezi 南柯子," is a near-verbatim citation of another lyric to the same tune, with minor changes of diction. The source is from Ma Danyang's lyric titled, "A Gift for Various Daoist Friends," in *Jianwu ji* 漸悟集, from DZ 1142, 25: 467–68.

12. Chapter 53, p. 609: The prefatorial verse, a lyric to the tune of "Moon Over the West River" is a near-verbatim citation of another lyric to the same tune, with only minor changes of diction. The source is from Zhang Boduan's lyric (#11) in *Xiuzhen shishu Wuzhen pian*, in DZ 263, 4: 743.

13. Chapter 64, p. 734: At the Shrine of Sylvan Immortals, Tripitaka held a discussion of poetry with four tree spirits and also a debate on Buddhism and Daoism. Part of the monk's exposition of his faith that begins with the observation, "Chan is quiescence, and the Law is salvation 禪者, 靜也, 法者, 度也," cites actually words from another "Shengtang wen" by Feng Zunshi. The XYJ text reads:

The wondrous ways of ultimate virtue, vast and boundless, can neither be seen nor heard. It can, however, extinguish the six organs of sense and the six kinds of perception. Thus perfect wisdom has neither birth nor death, neither want nor excess; it encompasses both form and emptiness, and it reveals the non-reality of both sages and common people.

To seek perfection you must know the mallet and tongs of Primal Origin;
To intuit the Real you must know Śākyamuni's technique.
Exploit the power of mindlessness;
Tread till you crush Nirvāṇa.

The Daoist text reads:

Now the ultimate Way is vast and boundless, and the wondrous Way can neither be seen nor heard. . . . Action, cessation, and no-action fuse to become unmixed purity. Then you may sweep away all sentient beings and play amidst the Bodhi. Without death or life, there is neither excess nor indebtedness. The holy and the secular are at your bidding, and you encompass both form and emptiness. . . .

Let loose Primal Beginning's tong and mallet,
And cut short Śākyamuni's technique.
Exploit the the power of mindlessness;
Tread till you crush Nirvāṇa (DZ 1100, 24: 308).

14. Chapter 64, p. 735: As the conversation went on between Tripitaka and the four tree spirits, the tone of the last four became discernibly more polemical against the monk's professed faith. Thus Cloud-Brushing Dean 拂雲叟 remarked:

Instead of consulting the Liezi,
You hold fast to your Sanskrit.
Now the Dao
Was originally established in China.
Instead, you seek in the West illumination.
Your're wasting your straw sandals!
I wonder what it is that you are after?
A stone lion must have gouged out your heart!
Wild foxes' saliva has filled your bone marrow!
You forget your origin to practice Chan,
Vainly seeking the Buddha's fruit.
Yours are like the prickly riddles of our Bramble Ridge,
Like its tangled enigmas.
For such a superior man,
Could there be deliverance?
How could this kind of model
Transmit an authentic imprint?
You must examine your present features,
For quiescence itself has life.
A bottomless bamboo basket will bail water;
A rootless iron tree will bring forth flowers.
Plant your feet firmly on the Linbao summit:
You'll return to attend Maitreya's assembly.

From the same Daoist text by Feng Zunshi we read:

Without consulting the Liezi
You cling fast to Sanskrit.

You were established in China,
But you sought from the West illumination.
Wasting in vain your straw sandals,
What are you looking for?
A stone lion has gouged out your heart;
Wild foxes' saliva filled your bone marrow.
With desire you practice Chan
And hope to bear Buddha's fruit.
With such bramble riddles
You dare to deceive man?
For such a superior man
Could there be deliverance? . . .
Seek to exalt the life of your lot,
Examine your present features,
For quiescence itself has life.
A bottomless basket bails water;
A rootless iron tree blossoms.
Of this form of a model
How could one transmit an imprint? . . .
Before the Lingbao summit
Who could gain a foothold? (DZ 1100, 24: 308)

15. Chapter 65, p. 744: At the Small Thunderclap Temple where Tripitaka blindly prostrated himself to worship a specious Buddha, with
the result that the entire band of pilgrims were captured, the narrative breaks into a commentarial poem. The heptasyllabic regulated
verse begins with the line, "The green-eyed monkey knew both false
and real 碧眼猢兒認假真," which reworks actually another couple of
lines from the same "Shengtang wen" by Feng Zunshi. They are: "With
words all without flavor [an allusion to *Zhuangzi* 2] / Hoot back the
green-eyed barbarian monk 炎炎言下, 叱回碧眼胡僧." See DZ 1100,
24: 308.

16. Chapter 78, pp. 896–97: At the court of the Bhikṣu Kingdom, Tripitaka
was again forced to discuss his faith when he was asked by the ruler
whether "a monk is able to transcend death, whether submission to
Buddha can bring a person longevity." Tripitaka thus replied:

For the person who's a monk,
All causal relations have been abolished;
And to him who understands reality,
All things are but emptiness. . . .
When you, plain and simple, reduce your desire,

You will with ease an endless life acquire.
為僧者, 萬緣都罷; 了性者, 諸法皆空....
素素純純寡愛欲, 自然享壽永無窮.

This lengthy disquisition of his understanding of Buddhism is actually composed of selected lines and phrases from a "Rhymeprose on the Ground of the Mind, Xindi fu 心地賦," by one Sanyu Zhenren 三于真人 in *Minghe yuyin*, DZ 1100, 24: 305. The assembled piece reads:

Earthly affairs without end
In our view are all empty.
If you are taught in the Gate of Mystery,
You must work on the ground of the mind.
"Great wisdom displays no effort" [a citation from *Zhuangzi* 2]
Within the realm of contentment;
True basis is all silent
And carefree in Nirvāṇa....
With six senses pure a thousand seeds [i.e., the Ālyavijñāna or seed-store of consciousness] *die;*
With the Three Realms empty a hundred points [i.e., of beginning] *are curbed.*
Sight, hearing, knowledge, and feeling
Are the causes of barriers for the Way....
If you wish to persevere in learning the Way,
You must understand the mind:
A cleansed mind's illumined by one single light;
An occupied mind's attacked by all phenomena....
You already know all phenomena are empty,
And all causes [i.e., the pratyaya or conditional causality] *are for naught.*
To work merit and labor in sitting
Only fit the Way's wild ones;
Dispensing alms and spreading kindness
Are only virtue's duplicity.
Great cunning seems stupid;
Still one knows no action in every affair;
A good scheme is not planned,
For one must on every count let go.
Only let your mind be unmoved
And all your doings will perfect themselves....
Know then all things are empty
And all senses must be banished.
世事無窮, 觀來盡空. 既向玄門受教, 便於心地下功. 大智閑閑, 澹泊在不生之內; 真機默默, 逍遙於寂滅之中.... 六根淨而千種滅; 三

界空而百端治. 見聞知覺, 是障道之元因.... 若乃堅成學道, 須當
了心. 心淨則孤明獨照; 心存則萬境皆侵.... 行功打坐, 乃道之狂.
步惠施恩, 即德之詐. 大巧若拙, 還知事事無為. 善計非籌, 直要頭
頭放下. 但使一心不動, 萬行自全.... 是知物物皆空, 塵塵總棄.

17. Chapter 78, p. 897: The ruler in this chapter, however, is under the
spell of his father-in-law (*guozhang* 國丈), who happens to have been a
white deer, a pet of the South Pole Star God. Escaping from its celestial
realm, the deer went to the court of the Bhikṣu Kingdom, assuming the
human form of a Daoist. Hearing Tripitaka's exposition of his "Buddhist" faith, the deer spirit advanced his scornful rebuttal:

You have no idea that I,
Who seek immortality,
Possess the hardiest of bones;
Who comprehend the Way,
Am most intelligent in spirit.
I carry basket and gourd to visit friends in the mountain;
I gather a hundred herbs to help people in the world.
Divine flowers I pick to make a hat;
Fragrant orchids I pluck to form a mat.
I sing to clapping of hands
And rest on clouds after I dance.
Explaining the principles of Dao,
I exalt the true teachings of Laozi;
Dispensing amulets and water,
I rid the human world of monstrous miasmas.
I rob Heaven and Earth of their energies
And pluck from the sun and moon their essences.
Yin and yang activated, the elixir gels;
Fire and Water harmonized, the embryo's formed.
When the yin of Two Eights recedes,
It's both dim and blurry;
When the yang of Three Nines expands,
It's both dark and obscure.
In accord with the four seasons I gather herbs;
By nine cyclic turns my elixir's perfected.
Astride the blue phoenix,
I ascend the purple mansion;
Mounting the white crane,
I reach the capital of jade,
Where I join all Heaven's luminaries
In zealous display of the wondrous Way.

Could this be compared with the quiescence of your Buddhism,
The dark divinity of your tranquillity?
The stinking corpse bequeathed by Nirvāṇa
That can never leave the mortal dust?
Among the Three Religions mine's the highest mystery.
Dao alone is noble since the dawn of history!

The Daoist's speech again is a pastiche of sentences from a "Rhymeprose on Honoring the Way, Zundao fu 尊道賦," by the Song emperor Renzong (1040–1063). This remarkable tribute begins with the lines— "Among the Three Religions, / Only the Way should be most honored. / Above [its followers] do not pay homage to the Son of Heaven; / Below they do not consult the lords and officials 三教之內, 惟道至尊. 上不朝於天子; 下不謁於公卿." And the long piece ends with the same exalted assessment: "Compared with the Confucian religion's high ranks and illustrious posts, / Such wealth and nobility are only floating clouds. / Compared with the Buddhist religion's extinction as ecstasy, / How could they escape the worldly dust? / As we examine the Three Religions, / Only the Way should be most honored 比儒教分官高職顯, 富貴浮雲. 比釋教分寂滅為樂, 豈脫凡塵? 朕觀三教, 惟道至尊" (*Minghe yuyin*, in DZ 1100, 24: 305).

18. Chapter 87, p. 988: The prefatorial lyric to the tune of "Su Wu in Slow Pace" [actually only half a poem] is another near-verbatim citation of a lyric to the same tune (#7) by Feng Zunshi, *Minghe yuyin*, in DZ 1100, 24: 263. The poem begins: "The Great Way's deep and mysterious— / How it waxes and wanes, / Once told, will astonish both gods and spirits 大道幽深, 如何消息, 說破鬼神驚駭."

19. Chapter 91, p. 1028: With modest alterations of rhetoric, the prefatorial heptasyllabic regulated poem quotes from Ma Danyang's lyric to the tune of "Auspicious Partridge, Rui zhegu 瑞鷓鴣," in "Jianwu ji." See DZ 1100, 25: 475.

20. Chapter 96, p. 1080: Prefatorial lyric to the tune of "Moon Over the West River" is a near-verbatim citation, with only minor changes of diction, of another lyric to the same tune by Zhang Boduan from his "Wuzhen pian." See *Xiuzhen shishu*, in DZ 263, 4: 748.

21. Chapter 99, p. 1117: A verse in which the narrator comments when the tutelary deities on order of Guanyin drop the pilgrims on their second homeward journey from the sky, the last of the eighty-one ordeals preordained for the Tang Monk. The heptasyllabic poem ends with the two lines: "In the ancient wondrous mix of *Kinship of the Three*, / elixir won't gel if there's slight errancy 古來妙合參同契毫髮差殊不結丹."

The last line is a verbatim citation of a quatrain (poem #27) of Zhang's in the "Wuzhen pian," DZ 263, 4: 729.

IV THE MONK, THE MONKEY, AND THE FICTION OF ALLEGORY

In an essay on *The Journey to the West* published in a volume titled *Sibu gudian xiaoshuo pinglun* (Criticism of Four Classic Novels) during the Great Proletarian Cultural Revolution, a committee on literature at the Normal University of Shanghai nearly thirty years ago attempted to pinpoint the distinctive feature of this work: "In the first place, what distinguishes the *Xiyouji* from most other fiction of antiquity is that it is a novel of the supra-mundane."[110] Few readers will dispute that such may be the prima facie character of this epic narrative on Buddhist pilgrimage. It is surprising that, until the last two decades, few critics have made serious investigation into the significance of the supramundane, the mythic, and, indeed, the religious themes and rhetoric that pervade the entire work. This may be a reaction to the emphases of the editors and compilers of previous centuries who, from the moment of the work's public appearance, regarded it as a work of profound allegory. Chen Yuanzhi's preface to the 1592 edition of the novel that we have briefly discussed took the lead. Lu Xun's pioneering and highly influential short history of Chinese novels devotes three chapters to what he labels "Novels of Gods and Demons (*shenmo xiaoshuo* 神魔 小說)," but he did not press further and use textual analysis to explain why many of the same gods and demons take on different meanings in different works of fiction.[111]

In what may be the most widely read and most often reprinted abridgment of the work, the *Xiyou zhenquan* 西游真詮 (The True Explanation of the Westward Journey), its early Qing editor Chen Shibin 陳士斌 (in his preface to the novel dated 1696) has also developed the most thoroughgoing allegorical interpretation through the use of alchemical, *yinyang*, and *Yijing* (*Classic of Change*) lore. Likely following the occasional examples provided by the original author himself (cf. the prefatory poem of chapter 26), Chen uses the speculative but popular eccentricities of ideography to interpret the Cave of the Three Stars and Slanting Moon (the abode of the Patriarch Subodhi where Sun Wukong attained his vast magic powers at the first stage of his enlightenment) as meaning the mind or the heart (*xin* 心). The Chinese graph as reproduced here is composed of a crescentlike long stroke surrounded above by three short dot-like strokes.[112] This attempt by Chen and others to interpret the narrative as a detailed treatise of internal alchemy might have led another Qing editor, half a century later, to take a different tack. In his unabridged hundred-chapter *Xinshuo Xiyouji* (The

Journey to the West, Newly Interpreted) of 1749, Zhang Shushen declared in the section entitled "*Xiyouji* zongpi 西游記總批 (Overall Comments on *The Journey to the West*)" that "the book *Xiyou* has been designated by the ancients as a book meant to illuminate the *Dao* [a pointed dig at the 1662 edition titled *Xiyou zhengdao shu*, with the Daoist-leaning preface attributed to Yu Ji discussed in part II of this introduction], by which it originally means the *Dao* of the sages, the worthies, and the Confucians (儒 *Ru*). To consider it an illumination of the *Dao* of immortals and Buddhism would be a mistake, indeed."[113] From a point of view clearly unsympathetic to the popular movement of Three-Religions-Joining-As-One (*sanjiao heyi* 三教合一, a possibly millennium-old notion to be discussed later), Zhang defended the story of the quest for Buddhist scriptures as an allegory of the classic Confucian doctrines on the illustration of virtue (*mingde* 明德) and the rectification of the mind (*zhengxin* 正心), ignoring the repeated and complex elaborations of *zhengxin* in Chan Buddhism also for at least a thousand years prior to his time.

To oppose this tendency to treat the narrative as a manual for Buddhist, Daoist, or Confucian self-cultivation, Hu Shi emphatically declared in his essay of 1923 that the author intended neither subtle language nor profound meaning. Wu Cheng'en's overriding purpose in writing the narrative, according to Hu, was simply to air his satiric view of life and the world.[114] For this modern Chinese philosopher and literary historian, *The Journey to the West* is above all a marvelous comic work, as Hu says in the foreword to Arthur Waley's abridged translation, "a book of . . . profound nonsense."[115] Hu's evaluation of the work of *Xiyouji*'s premodern compilers and commentators was severe:

> *Xiyouji* for these several centuries has been ruined by countless Daoists, monks, and Confucians. The Daoists said, this book is a volume of wonderous formulas for the golden elixir. The monks said, this book is about the method of mind cultivation in the Gate of Chan. The Confucians said, this book is one on the principles of rectifying the mind and rendering sincere the will. These interpretations are the great adversaries of *Xiyouji*.[116]

How influential this view of Hu has been may be seen in the echoing remarks of Lu Xun, another giant of early modern Chinese letters:

> Though its author was a student of Confucius, this book actually arose from playfulness and not from discussion of *Dao*. That is why only platitudes like the mutual birth and conquest cycles of the Five Phases are seen occasionally in the entire book, which is especially not learned in Buddhism.[117]

The influence of Hu is also seen in countless other writers and commentators. Perhaps the extreme position along this line is represented by the verdict of Tanaka Kenji and Arai Ken, who have asserted that, unlike other traditional tales of the supernatural in China, this late Ming narrative neither is accompanied by the shadow of religion and superstition nor emphasizes the karmic principle of reward and retribution. Rather, the world of *Xiyouji* manifests what Miki Katsumi has said of it in his *Saiyūki Oboegaki*: "human liberation from mystery and progress from the medieval world to the spirit of modernity."[118]

Not all modern students of this work, however, subscribe to such an astonishing view of its nature. While fully acknowledging the wealth of comedy and satire in the novel, C. T. Hsia pointedly challenged Hu's judgment when he observed that "the phrase 'profound nonsense' . . . concedes the necessity for philosophical or allegorical interpretation."[119] Since the time of this assertion, many scholars around the globe have not merely conceded such necessity, but they have also probed and mined deeply the vast supply of textual sources funding and fertilizing the composition of the hundred-chapter narrative. Although there is no consensus on whether the entire story represents a fully developed and self-consistent allegory (similar to, say, Dante's *Commedia* or Spenser's *Faerie Queene*), Chinese, Japanese, European, and American academicians have exerted a noteworthy, even if not concerted, effort to reverse the critical tendencies dominant in the early republican period. My intention here is only to exploit this massive scholarship to highlight what requires further investigation if we are to appreciate the novel as a work of full-blown fiction.[120] These features, linguistically and thematically interrelated, concern (1) the monk and the transformed depiction of both pilgrim and pilgrimage, (2) the monkey and his significance in the journey, and (3) the fiction of religious allegory.

The Monk and the Transformed Depiction of Both Pilgrim and Pilgrimage

Part I of this introduction pointed out that the historical Xuanzang's motivation to undertake his protracted and precarious journey to fetch scriptures from India was entirely a matter of personal faith. A young religious zealot, he defied the law of the state against going abroad. The *Account of Conduct* (行狀), composed by his disciple Mingxiang 冥祥 probably in 664 CE and thus the earliest biography of the priest serving as official obituary, relates the incident of a nameless barbarian (*hu* 胡人) hired to assist the pilgrim slip past undetected the five signal-fire ramparts strung out beyond the Jade Gate Pass (玉門關).

> In the middle of the night [while they were resting by a riverbank], the barbarian arose and walked toward the Master of the Law with a drawn blade, intent on killing him. Whereupon the Master of the Law rose up and began

immediately to recite the name of Buddha and a sūtra. The barbarian sat down, only to stand up once more after a little while, saying to the priest: "According to the Law of the State (國家法), it is a most serious crime to go to a foreign state for personal reasons (私向外國, 罪名極重). When you pass through the road beneath those five signal fires, you will be caught for certain. Wherever you are arrested, you will be a dead man (一處被擒即死人)! Since your disciple still has family obligations, how could I take this on myself? Imperial law cannot be breached. Allow me to go back with the Master."

The Master of the Law replied, "Xuanzang can only die facing the West, but I vow I shall not return East and live. If my patron cannot do this, he is free to turn back. Let Xuanzang proceed by himself."[121]

For a priest "vowing to tour the region of the West so as to inquire about the perplexities [of his faith] 法師.... 乃誓遊西方以問所惑" (FSZ 1 in SZZSHB, p. 7), the act of embarking on his journey was indisputably treasonous and illegal. For him as a Tang subject and an ethnic Han to be reminded by a "barbarian" of both the nature and risk of his illicit action also conveyed immense irony, but this part of the historical record clearly exerted no impact on the long and complex process of *fictionalization* transforming monk Xuanzang's character and the meaning of his pilgrimage. Nowhere is this transformation more apparent than at the very beginning of a *different narrative* of the story begun in the Song poetic tale. When the account proceeds after the lost chapter 1 segment, it starts with the monkey figure's appearance as a "white-robed scholar" asking the human pilgrim whether he was going to the Western Heaven to acquire scriptures. The monk's reply betokens a sudden and potent emergence of fiction with these words: "Your humble monk has received this imperial commission: because the living multitudes in the Land of the East have not yet possessed the Buddhist religion, I thus must acquire scriptures 貧僧奉敕,為東土眾生未有佛教, 是取經也." This assertion about his appointed task is repeated with expanded words in chapter 15 when he was queried by Buddhist monks in India about his journey: "I received from the Tang emperor a decreed commission [奉唐帝詔敕] because the living multitudes in the Land of the East have not possessed the Buddhist religion. Thus my special reason for rushing to your country to beg for the Great Vehicle."[122] The addition of a single adjective (decreed) to the graph for command or commission (*chi*) has the unmistakable force of documentary authorization.

Modern scholars have recognized this episode's importance mainly because it initiates the narrative association of the fictive Xuanzang with the monkey acolyte (*hou xingzhe*) that, over the next several centuries, would reach its climactic figure towering over the hundred-chapter novel of 1592.

By contrast, virtually no study has paid attention to the human pilgrim's brief re-mark and its implications in which the seeds of an immense fiction are sown by two patently false claims: that the Buddhist religion has yet to reach China at the time of the pilgrimage and that his journey is undertaken by imperial authoriza-tion. As far as I know, neither the literary and material antecedents of the novel nor the scholarship devoted to their study have offered any plausible explanation for the first lie. That erroneous assertion about Buddhism's entry into China might have been a popular invention of either ignorance or fantasy, caused perhaps by the desire to inflate Xuanzang's stature fur-ther by eliding his scripture acquisition with the introduction of the reli-gion into the country. Concerning the second claim by the Tang Monk in the poetic tale, there are many details studding the long, formative history of the XYJ fiction to emphasize that the monk's relationship with the em-peror and his court *before* leaving China is an indispensable feature. Not-ing some of these details may help us understand better the story finalized in the 1592 version.

As I pointed out in the beginning of this introduction, Chen Xuan-zang was a native of central western China. Apart from his nearly seven-teen years abroad, he never left that region. In the account of the legend-ary Xuanzang evolving through dramatic, novelistic, and possibly religious texts (e.g., the various *baojuan* 寶卷 and *shanshu* 善書 appearing in the Ming), however, we encounter a protagonist of different pedigree and situ-ated in a vastly different geographical setting. This account tells of a pater-nal lineage originating from Haizhou 海州, in Hongnong county 弘農縣. It relocates Xuangzang and his family all the way to modern Jiangsu 江蘇 province.[123] It ties the first eighteen years of Xuanzang's life and its vicissi-tudes to the coastal region of southeastern China, as told by the twenty-four scene drama and the controversial chapter 9 absent from the 1592 edition. Xuanzang, the infant abandoned by his mother on a river, was rescued and reared by a Buddhist abbot of Gold Mountain 金山,[124] who eventually helped the former avenge parental wrongs. As told also in the drama with the same name of XYJ, Buddhist "providence" personified in the goddess Guanyin crucially shapes events so that they lead eventually to the Tang emperor's selecting Xuanzang as the scripture-seeker.[125] All versions of the hundred-chapter XYJ displace the intensely personal zeal of a plebian priest by the new motivations undergirding his enormous enterprise: Bud-dha's compassionate wisdom in offering scriptures as a salvific gift to the unenlightened, sinful Chinese in the Land of the East counterpoints the fictive pilgrim's religious devotion and his loyalty to the emperor. Perhaps building from Guanyin's speech in the drama, the all-important chapter 8 of the novel locates the true and foundational motivation for the scripture enterprise squarely in Buddha's prescient and transcendent wisdom to which Guanyin, the Tang emperor, the human candidate for the pilgrimage, and his four disciples obediently responded.

In the controversial chapter 9 of the novel, the story becomes one about the social status and eminence of Xuanzang's immediate family—father as incomparable scholar who took first honors (or *zhuangyuan*) in the civil service examination and was rewarded by marriage to a prime minister's daughter—and how that connection helped the orphaned priest avenge his parents and meet eventually the emperor who would choose him as the scripture pilgrim. Even in the 1592 Shidetang edition which omits this chapter, a long biographical poem (XYJ, p. 131; JW 1: 275) and the prose narration in chapter 12 display the following stable ingredients: the pilgrim's prenatal identity as the Buddha's disciple, the Elder Gold Cicada; his exile to the human world for inattentiveness during a lecture by Buddha; his father's success and marriage to the high minister Yin Kaishan's daughter; the father's subsequent murder by a pirate; Xuanzang's ordeal at birth on a river leading to his nickname, Child River Float, and his rescue by the Abbot of Gold Mountain Monastery; his reunion with his mother and paternal grandmother; his success in avenging his father; his father's revivification; and the emperor's eventual selection of Xuanzang as the scripture pilgrim. Taken as a whole, they form the consistent elements of a story complex exploiting certain features of the Jātaka tales (闍多伽: e.g., stories on prior and present incarnations of Buddhas and bodhisattvas) and of morality books (e.g., Xuanzang's restoring his grandmother's eyesight by saliva and tongue-licking, an example of "moving Heaven by filial feelings 孝感動天"). In this regard, whether the problematic chapter 9 is authentic or not is a moot question, because all the Ming and Qing full-length editions of the novel known to us, with or without this chapter, include all of these fictional details and make them germane to the pilgrim's person and experience.

The question that a critical reader at this point must raise is *why*: why must the novel make central use of such a popular Xuanzong story, so at odds with known history? If for millennia historiography ruled as "the supreme narrative model in [premodern] China" to which all other literary genres respect and emulate,[126] why does the hundred-chapter XYJ fashion its human protagonist in a manner that would surely try—as it has, indeed, down to the present day—the patience of his historically aware readers? It is too easy to answer that ingredients gathered from Jātaka tales and morality books provided more entertainment for readers. As I interpret the story, a cardinally important element that hitherto has been ignored or dismissed is that the fiction links the human pilgrim and the Tang court even before the pilgrimage. That linkage—most false but also most true—has profound implications for shaping the meaning of both the human pilgrim's character and his mission.

The pilgrim's father and his marital family, as the novelistic adaptation of the legend makes clear, had been well known to Tang Taizong even *before* disaster struck, and so the adult Xuanzang's attempt at vengeance eighteen years later received ready assistance from the court. Ostensibly a device for elevating the social status of the pilgrim, such thematic details are even more plausible markers of karmic affinity. Intent on keeping his promise to hold a Grand Mass of Land Water after his death and tour of the Underworld, the emperor Taizong, when presented with Xuanzang's suggested candidacy, "thought silently for a long time and said, 'Can Xuanzang be the son of Grand Secretary Chen Guangrui?'" (XYJ, p. 132; JW 1: 276). The ruler's recognition and Guanyin's epiphany immediately following thus provide the foundation of the long novel: this momentous enterprise of seeking scriptures could not have been due merely to the piety of a little-known individual, let alone the lawless zeal of a defiant cleric. Its transcendent origin is the mind of the Buddhist Patriarch himself, but the immense journey requires the equal partnership of a supreme human ruler on earth.

Such an emphasis, deriving from the Song poetic tale's two short allusions to the Tang Monk's "imperial mission," has made it impossible—and perhaps even irrelevant—to reconcile known historical chronology of Xuanzang with the legend's chronotope, the fictive time scheme required by the Chen Guangrui story.[127] Despite that textual contradiction, no reader of the full-length novel can miss how deeply in Xuanzang's consciousness is imprinted the magnitude of the imperial favor and charge bestowed on him. In sharp contrast to the historical figure's initial defiance of the ban on travel, the fictive priest—promoted to be the emperor's bond-brother in return for his willingness to seek the scriptures—said to the ruler: "Your Majesty, what ability and what virtue does your poor monk possess that he should merit such affection from your Heavenly Grace? I shall not spare myself in this journey, but I shall proceed with all diligence until I reach the Western Heaven. If I did not attain my goal or the true scriptures, I would not dare return to our land even if I were to die. May I fall into eternal perdition in Hell" (JW 1: 290).

Whereas the historical pilgrim, upon his successful return to China with the scriptures, felt compelled to seek imperial pardon for "braving to transgress the authoritative statutes and departing for India on one's own authority" through both written memorial and direct oral petition (FSZ 6), the fictive priest would be welcomed by a faithful ruler, who had a Scripture-Anticipation Tower (望經樓) built to await his envoy for eleven more years (chapter 100). This portrait of the pilgrimage's imperial sponsorship, intervention (most notably in the travel rescript bearing the imperial seal administered by the emperor himself),[128] and reception helps explain why the fictive priest considered his religious mission to be his obligation to his lord and state. The mission's success fulfilled equally his vows to Buddha and to a human emperor. At the beginning of chapter 13, the lead-in poem thus launches the priest's journey: "The rich Tang ruler issued a decree / Deputing Xuanzang to seek the source of Zen 大有唐王降敕封 / 欽差玄奘問禪宗."

The fact that the fictive pilgrim was sent on his way by the highest human authority also changes fundamentally Xuanzang's identity and its mode of disclosure. In sharp contrast to the historical figure who, deciding to defy the court's proscription to travel to the western frontier, "dared not show himself in public but rested during the day and journeyed only at night 不敢公出, 乃晝伏夜行" (FSZ 1, in SZZSHB, p. 9), the novelistic Xuanzang did not hesitate to tell the first stranger he met that he was an imperial envoy sent by the Tang emperor to seek scriptures from Buddha in the Western Heaven (XYJ, chapter 13, p. 147; JW 1: 299). Throughout the priest's journey, the bold and unwavering announcement of this august mission by both master and disciples became a refrain to every conceivable audience—divine, demonic, or human—much as the imperial travel rescript authorizing his undertaking would be signed and stamped with royal seals of all the states and kingdoms the pilgrims visited as proof of their gaining permitted passage (chapter 100). The "Shengjiao xu 聖教序 (Preface to the Holy Religion)" bestowed by the historical Taizong on the repatriated Xuanzang, transcribed nearly verbatim in chapter 100 of the novel, declared unambiguously that the dangerous journey was the monk's solitary expedition (承危遠邁, 策杖孤征). In that ex post facto encomium bequeathed to a cleric newly pardoned for a seventeen-year old crime against the state,[129] not even the emperor could claim credit for authorizing or assisting the project in any manner. On the other hand, the invented rescript, in poignant irony, would not allow the readers ever to forget that imperial charge and enablement were as much needed as the assistance of the gods.

Throughout the novel's lengthy course, there are quite a few occasions on which Xuanzang, expressing undying loyalism to his emperor, frets about his inability to fulfill the decreed wish of his human lord 旨意 as much as the dreaded failure to reach and see Buddha. Fearing that an illness might prove fatal during the episode of the Sea-Pacifying Monastery in chapter 81, a tearful Tripitaka would write a poem that he wants Monkey to take back to the Tang court, to inform his Sage Lord 聖君 of his precarious health and request another pilgrim be sent to take his place. Captured by a leopard monster in chapter 85, Tripitaka explains to a fellow prisoner that "If I lose my life here, would that not have dashed the expectation of the emperor and the high hopes of his ministers? 今若喪命, 可不盼殺那君王, 辜負那臣子?" When told by his interlocutor, a stereotypical woodcutter who is the sole supporter of an old widowed mother (cf. the one who spoke to Monkey in chapter 1), the priest breaks into loud wailing, crying:

How pitiful! How pitiful!

If mountain rustics still long for their kin,
This poor monk's been trained to chant sūtras in vain.

To serve the ruler or to serve one's parents follows the same principle: you live by the kindness of your parents, as I do by the kindness of my ruler 山人尚有思親意, / 空教貧僧會念經. 事君事親, 皆同一理: 你為親恩, 我為君恩 (XYJ, p. 975).

I should remind the novel's readers that there was no justification, and no possibility, for the historical Xuanzang to utter words such as these on his secret pilgrimage to India, or even after his return to his native land and being favored with imperial patronage for the rest of his life. When the historical Tang emperor bid the honored priest accept an imperial appointment soon after his homecoming, the cleric declined with forthright boldness: "Xuanzang during his youth had already entered the Gate of the Black Robes and received in submission the Way of Buddha. The ultimate principle of mystery is what I practice, and I have not heeded [full force of "hearing" in Buddhist rhetoric] the Confucian religion 玄奘少踐緇門, 服膺佛道, 玄宗是習, 孔教未聞" (FSZ 6, in SZZSHB, p. 133). Even as the rhetoric of courtly propriety, this statement reported in historiography directly contradicts the emotional outburst in the novelistic episode cited earlier.

The sentiments finding expression in the novel, on the other hand, fall squarely within the most familiar discourse of historical Confucian teachings. They justly echo his parting address to his monastic community at the Temple of Great Blessings 洪福寺 on the eve of his journey: "I have already made a great vow and a profound promise that, if I do not acquire the true scriptures, I shall fall into eternal perdition in Hell. Since I have received such grace and favor from the monarch, I have no alternative but to requite my country to the limit of loyalty 我已發了弘誓大願, 不取真經, 永墮沉淪地獄. 大底是受王恩寵, 不得不盡忠以報國耳" (XYJ 1: 141; JW 1: 290). That remark, in turn, even more pointedly repeats a similar confession spoken by the Xuanzang of the twenty-four-scene *zaju*: "Honored viewers, attend to the single statement by this lowly monk: a subject must reach the limit of loyalty, much as a son must reach the limit of filial piety. There is no other means of requital than the perfection of both loy-

alty and filial piety 眾官, 聽小僧一句言語: 為臣盡忠, 為子盡孝, 忠孝兩
全, 餘無所報" (Act 5, in *Zaju Xiyouji*, 2: 648). Words such as these may seem
hackneyed and platitudinous to modern ears, but they faithfully portray
the fictional Xuanzang. Built consistently on the tradition of antecedent
legend, but with important innovative additions apparently supplied by
the Shidetang author, Xuanzang's characterization in the novel seems to fit
preponderantly a stereotype—the traditional scholar-official or the "undiluted Confucian 醇儒."[130]

If the full-length novel presumes the ideology of the unity of the Three
Religions (三教歸一, 三教合一) for both its content and genetic context,
who among the five fictive pilgrims is more appropriate than the human
monk to embody fully political loyalism and filial piety, especially when all
four of the other disciples imperfectly partake of human culture and lineage? The historical Xuanzang was unquestionably a hero of religion, turning his back on family and court in his youth to face appalling dangers, and
without doubt a master of literary Sinitic and of scriptural styles shaped by
difficult encounters with Indic languages. His biography, compiled by two
disciples and touched with hagiography, duly recorded serial visitations to
various states of Central Asia and India beset by encounters with gods and
demons, physical perils and privations, triumphal religious proselytism,
and royal hospitality in many locales. Nonetheless, could a historically impeccable version of this character have amused and entertained the multi-
farious sixteenth-century reading public?

The novelistic figure is timid, ethically fastidious, occasionally dog-
matic, heedful of slander, and prone to partiality—like typical male leads
in Ming drama and vernacular fiction—but nevertheless filial and politically loyal. Most interestingly, although this pilgrim, consistent with his
vocational vow of celibacy, resists sexual temptations in all circumstances
(chapters 24, 54–55, 82–83), he is also so fond of poetry that he discusses
poetics with tree monster-spirits (chapter 64) and composes quatrains in
a region near India (chapter 94). Perhaps in parody of filial piety blended
with the religious notion of reverting to the source and origin 反本還原
extolled in both Daoism and Buddhism, the narrative shows him to be
so attached to his mother (when he is not thinking about the emperor)
that one ordeal as he nears his goal reenacts the fated marriage of his parents—the chance selection of the father by an embroidered ball his mother
throws (chapters 93–95). In this episode on the Kingdom of India, where to
the Tang Monk's chauvinistic eyes the clothing, utensils, manner of speech,
and behavior of the people completely resemble those of the Great Tang
(XYJ, chapter 93, p. 1056), the pilgrim's persistent invocation of maternal
experience also justly invites Monkey's teasing about his master's "longing for the past 慕古之意" (XYJ, chapter 94, p. 1062). Such a person, dwell-

ing in the religiously syncretistic world of the full-length novel, seems a fit representative of Confucianism, at least as the vast populace imagines it.

Fit representative or not, however, the novel's human pilgrim is no *chunru* or "undiluted Confucian." Since the story is about a cleric named Xuanzang in the Tang, the pilgrim is unalterably adulterated: he has to be a Buddhist monk, a man who has taken "holy orders," as it were, from a foreign religion and, in principle, could declare only conditional allegiance to the stipulated authority claimed by such canonical Confucian institutions as the state and the family. Even as a Buddhist monk, moreover, the fictional Xuanzang's character is significantly at odds with what we know of the historical figure. As part I of this introduction has sketched out briefly, the real Xuanzang had entered a Pure Land monastery as a zealot in his early teens. Devoting his entire life to the study of some of the most advanced and difficult doctrines of his faith, he undertook a long, perilous pilgrimage and acquired many texts that lie at the foundations of the Buddhist tradition called *Faxiang zong* 法相宗, or the Dharmalakṣaṇa (Characteristics of the Dharmas), also known as "The Consciousness-Only Lineage 唯識宗." The translation of these texts upon his return to China and his own doctrinal writings and commentaries became lasting accomplishments. His lineage was also called *Ci'en zong* 慈恩宗 after the emperor installed him at the temple of the same name. The principal doctrine distinguishing this particular school of Buddhism, with its emphasis on extreme idealism, may be summed up in the assertion by one of its two ancient founders, Vasubandhu (b. ca 400 CE): "All this world is ideation only." As elucidated by a modern scholar, "it claims that the external world is but a fabrication of our consciousness, that the external world does not exist, that the internal ideation presents an appearance as if it were an outer world. The entire external world is therefore an illusion."[131]

So briefly stated, the Faxiang teachings may superficially resonate with many doctrines of other Buddhist lineages, including Chan (Zen). The tradition spent centuries struggling with such daunting issues as the role of imagination in our acquisition of knowledge, the mutual dependence of causes and conditions for certain temporal phenomena and our sensual apprehension of them, and the attainment of perfect knowledge puncturing the impermanence veiling all things.[132] Nonetheless, unlike the novel's Xuanzang, the historical monk based his entire career upon unwavering trust in the efficacy of language. Neither Xuanzang and his immediate disciples nor their foreign predecessors ever questioned the roles of mind, thought, and linguistic signs in the arduous quest for ultimate reality or truth. In sum, they did not dismiss human language as an illusory phenomenon; on the contrary, they were unreserved in their commitment to writing, including translation, as trustworthy communication. This commitment betokens also the unambiguous recognition of intellectual work enshrined in language—therefore, supremely in literacy—as a religious necessity. Such dedication to intense labor on abstruse and taxing philosophical issues may have even led to the decline of the lineage not long after the demise of Xuanzang and the circle of his immediate disciples.

The Xuanzang story complex seems to belong to a different form of Buddhism. In note 125, I mentioned that the preincarnate name bestowed on the monk in the dramatic version seems to identify him with Vairocana Buddha, and, if such a reading is correct, would immediately establish the human cleric's linkage to Chan Buddhism. Certain formal and thematic ties can be detected several centuries earlier in the Song poetic tale. During their travel beyond the "Incense Mountain Temple 香山寺," for example, the Monkey disciple told the priest that although they had reached "the Country of Snakes . . . , none of the snakes here are vicious, because they all possess the Buddha nature" (*Shihua*, p. 7; cf. CHCL, p. 1185)—a notion central to Chan doctrines.[133] In chapter 2 of the poetic tale, no sooner had the monkey acolyte officially joined the pilgrimage when the chapter formally ended with a dialogue in verse, spoken by both the monkey and by the human pilgrim (*Shihua*, p. 2). In chapter 8 (title lacking) where the pilgrims met up with the Deep Sand God, three quatrains spoken by the god, the monkey, and the priest also ended the episode (*Shihua*, p. 17). Because the narrative is punctuated constantly by brief snippets of poetry, some of which are no more than crude doggerels, modern Chinese scholars tend to regard the poetic tale as a form of *huaben* storytelling that began in late Tang and flourished in the Song within the general history of vernacular fiction's development. To the extent, however, that the verse segments of this particular poetic tale often articulate an explicitly doctrinal or evangelistic message from one character to another, the form is remarkably similar to the Chan *Platform Sūtra*, the only text acknowledged historically as that tradition's scripture. Didactic priestly instructions and professions of either ignorance or enlightenment in response to them in this text are almost always couched in verse or the *gāthā*.[134]

One of the famous protagonists dramatized in the scriptural text is the patriarch Huineng 慧能, alternately 惠能 (638–713), whose conspicuous talent was his percipience despite illiteracy (*Tanjing*, chapter 1, p. 18; *Platform Scripture*, section 8, p. 39). The narrative depiction does not merely dwell on his inability to read or write; even more pointedly, it emphasizes his uncanny ability to intuit and apprehend the meaning of anything read to him. When the patriarch conversed with a nun in a later episode,

the nun said, "If you can't even recognize words, how could you understand the meaning?" The master said, "The wondrous principles of the various Buddhas are not dependent on language 諸佛妙理, 非關文字." (*Tanjing*, chapter 7, p. 132)

In Huineng's dismissive view of language, writing has worth only for accommodating human inadequacies. Accordingly,

> all scriptures and writings, both the Great Vehicle and the Small Vehicle, and the twelve sections of the scripture [i.e., the total Buddhist canon] are provided for men. It is because man possesses the nature of wisdom that these were instituted. If there were no men in the world, there would naturally not be any dharmas. We know, therefore, that dharmas exist because of man and that there are all these scriptures because there are people to preach them.
>
> The reason is that among men some are wise and others are stupid. The stupid are inferior, whereas the wise are superior. The deluded consult the wise and the wise explain the Law to the stupid and enable them to understand and to open up their minds. (*Platform Scripture*, section 30, p. 79)

Such a view of language underlines the fundamental paradox of Chan: exalting a goal of enlightenment (whether gradual or immediate) attainable through mental and spiritual intuition (with or without the aid of phenomena or dharma as either material or symbolic medium—in other words, an enigmatic utterance, an act like a slap or a punch, and an object like a mummified corpse or a skull),[135] the tradition nonetheless depends on language—in both sermons and writings—to articulate, record, and transmit the patriarchal sayings (*yulu* 語錄) and deeds.

The Monkey and His Significance in the Journey

We shall now see in greater detail how the paradoxes of Chan are directly germane to the reading of our 1592 novel. A principal part of the fictional transformation of the priest Xuanzang, as the previous section has pointed out, lies in establishing the pilgrim's intimate relationship with the emperor prior to the journey, so that the journey becomes an imperial commission. In the novel's crucial scene of the priest's selection as the scripture seeker, a long poem recalls Xuanzang's history that summarizes the controversial chapter 9 supplemented by fragments of similar content in scene 1 of the dramatic version. The narrative elaborates further:

> So that very day the multitude [of officials] selected the priest Xuanzang, a man who had been a monk since childhood, who maintained a vegetarian diet, and who had received the commandments the moment he left his mother's womb.... [He] had no love for glory or wealth, being dedicated wholly to the pursuit of nirvāṇa. Their investigations revealed that he had

an excellent family background and the highest moral character. Not one of the thousands of classics and sūtras he had failed to master; none of the Buddhist chants and hymns was unknown to him. [When this candidate was brought into the emperor's presence], Taizong was delighted, saying to him, "You are truly a monk of great virtue and possessing the mind of Chan." (XYJ, chapter 12, pp. 131-32; JW 1: 276)

This eulogy of Xuanzang's character and learning echoes an eloquent declamation in the drama XYJ by the Chan Master Danxia [Cinnabar Aura] 丹霞禪師, Abbot of Gold Mountain, who had rescued the abandoned infant from death in the river. "Since infancy I have brought in Child River Float. At seven, he could read and write; at fifteen, there was no work of scripture that he did not know. He commands comprehensive understanding of our lineage's principle of nature and vitality. This old monk, therefore, gave him the religious name of Xuanzang. Now Xuan means the mysterious, and Zang means great [in the sense of powerful]. His name thus indicates that he can apprehend greatly the fine points of mystery" (Zaju, 2: 639-10).

The description of young Xuanzang's erudition and intellectual prowesss validates, at least partially, Lu Xun's charge that the authors of the novel and the drama were ignorant of Buddhist learning. The ideals of Chan are not erected upon the mastery of "a thousand classics and ten thousand canons." Despite that eulogy of the legendary Tripitaka, neither the drama nor the novel offers us a priest who lives up to that formulaic encomium. What is more interesting is the appearance of the word Chan in both texts used to describe both Xuanzang's rescuer and the pilgrim himself. One might argue that even before Ming times, people used the word to stand for Buddhism in a general sense, but "Master of Chan" was never indiscriminately used. Moreover, the words of the abbot giving his own interpretation of Xuanzang as a name directly suggest a correlation with Chan Buddhism as integrated with Quanzhen conceptualities, notably "inner nature" and "life" or "vitality" (xingming).

The depiction of the novelistic Xuanzang surely and constantly associates him and his entourage with Chan. Revealing examples can readily be found in both narrative content and such titular couplets as "Tripitaka does not forget his origin; / The Four Sages test the Chan Mind" (chapter 24); "The Child's tricky transformations confuse the Chan Mind; / Ape, Horse, Spatula, and Wood Mother—all are lost" (chapter 40); "The Chan Lord, taking food, has demonic conception; / Yellow Dame brings water to dissolve perverse pregnancy" (chapter 53); "Rescuing Tuoluo, Chan Nature is secure; / Escaping defilement, the Mind of Dao is pure" (chapter 67); "Mind Monkey envies Wood Mother; / The demon lord plots to devour Chan" (chapter 85); and "Chan, reaching Jade-Flower, convenes an assembly; / Mind Monkey, Wood, and Earth take in disciples" (chapter 88). This sort of explicit labeling can be misleading, because the fictive Xuanzang also lacks virtues cherished by the Chan tradition. Throughout the lengthy journey, he is so dull of mind and impoverished in perception that he never seems able to learn from his experience of all the means and media—the cycles of captivity and release staged by gods and demons— "providentially" sent his way for his enlightenment.

We may briefly consider this central and protracted irony by starting from the story's end, when the pilgrims succeed in reaching Buddha's abode in India and receiving the first gift of the long-sought scriptures. The volumes thus bestowed, however, were blank. When Tripitaka discovered the truth on their homeward journey,

> [he] heaved big sighs and said, "Our people in the Land of the East simply have no luck! What good is it to take back a wordless, empty volume like this? How could I possibly face the Tang emperor? The crime of mocking one's ruler is greater than one punishable by execution!" (XYJ, chapter 98, p. 1111)

Only after Monkey's encouragement did the five pilgrims turn back to beg Buddha once again for scriptures with words.

"The true scriptures without words (*wuzi zhenjing* 無字真經)" often appear in other popular writings, fictional and nonfictional. The novel uses them to mock "the monks of the Land of the East as being too blind and stupid to recognize" (in the words of the Buddha Dīpaṃkara in XYJ, chapter 98, p. 1110) their true worth. This situation may also echo the Chan view of language. Within the novel's structure, nonetheless, Tripitaka's lament only accentuates again his forgetfulness no less than his blindness. A little earlier, he already had received an anticipatory lesson, so to speak, from his eldest and most percipient disciple Sun Wukong. The biography of the historical pilgrim has made clear that he was especially fond of reciting the name of the Bodhisattva Guanyin coupled with the tersely brief *Heart Sūtra*, the transmission of which he had received in Sichuan from a sickly man covered with sores and pus. At the time when he was crossing the Sand River on his exit from China, he found that the scripture would dispel "various vicious demons, strange apparitions, and weird beings" that not even the invocation of Guanyin's name alone could exorcise (FSZ, chapter 1 in SZZSHB, p. 12).

Although the novel attributes instead the sūtra's transmission to the Crow's Nest Chan Master (the name may be another significant allusion), the narrative maintains the human monk's attachment to the sūtra. Hence the irony of the following episode when Tripitaka again wonders out loud how much longer the journey will take.

> "Master," said Pilgrim, "could it be that you have quite forgotten again the *Heart Sūtra* . . . ?"
>
> Tripitaka said, "That *Prajñā-pāramitā* is like a cassock or an almsbowl that accompanies my very body. Since that Crow's Nest Chan Master taught it to me, has there been a day that I didn't recite it? . . . I could recite the piece backward! How could I have forgotten it?"
>
> "Master, you may be able to recite it," said Pilgrim, "but you haven't begged that Chan Master for its proper interpretation."
>
> "Ape-head!" snapped Tripitaka. "How dare you say that I don't know its interpretation! Do you?"
>
> "Yes, I know its interpretation!" replied Pilgrim. After that exchange, neither Tripitaka nor Pilgrim uttered another word, [thereby inviting raucous teasing from the other two disciples, Zhu Eight Rules and Sha Monk, that Monkey was no seminarian and knew nothing of scriptural interpretation. Then the master spoke].
>
> "Wuneng and Wujing," said Tripitaka, "stop this claptrap! Wukong made his interpretation in a speechless language. That's true interpretation." (XYJ, chapter 93, pp. 1050-51)

The colloquy here makes apparent that Tripitaka "got it right," so to speak, after his Monkey disciple provided an appropriately symbolic medium of wordlessness to remind his master not to chatter and complain endlessly and still reciting a scripture that powerfully affirms the vacuity of all phenomena and all sense perceptions (see JW, chapter 19, for a full citation of the sūtra as translated by the historical Xuanzang).

As another example of Chan motifs in XYJ, an even earlier episode anticipated this part of the story, when master and disciple take up another discussion of the sūtra. In chapter 43 (XYJ, p. 494) when on their journey the sound of rushing water as usual alarmed the human pilgrim, Monkey had to give him another lesson on what it meant to transcend sensory turmoil:

> Old Master, . . . you have quite forgotten again the *Heart Sūtra*. . . . You have forgotten the sentence about "no eye, ear, nose, tongue, body, or mind." Those of us monks who have left our own family should see no form with our eyes, should hear no sound with our ears, should smell no smell with our noses, should taste no taste with our tongues; our bodies should have no knowledge of heat or cold, and our minds should gather no vain thoughts. This is called the extermination of the Six Robbers.

Sun Wukong, in fact, is reminding his master of events in chapter 14 immediately after he was released from the Mountain of Five Phases to make submission to Tripitaka, when his slaying of six brigands with his rod becomes a literalized narration of the lesson expounded here.

The conversation between master and disciple indicates that the human monk was still slow to learn how to control his bodily senses through his mind. The narrative later provides a similar dialogue in which the disciple teaches the master (XYJ, chapter 85, p. 966). When Tripitaka complained that the sight of "a precipitous mountain with violent vapors and savage clouds soaring up" had unsettled him, Monkey accused him of again forgetting the scripture. Rebuking further the master's denial, his disciple said that even with the knowledge of the sūtra, Tripitaka would need to recall this *gāthā*:

> Seek not afar for Buddha on Spirit Mount;
> Mount Spirit dwells only inside your mind.
> There's in each man a Spirit Mount stūpa:
> Beneath this stūpa you must be refined.

"Disciple," said Tripitaka, "you think I don't know this? According to these four lines, the lesson of all scriptures concerns only the cultivation of the mind."

"Of course, that goes without saying," said Pilgrim. "For when the mind is pure, it shines forth as a solitary lamp, and when the mind is secure, the entire phenomenal world becomes clarified. The tiniest error, however, makes for the way to slothfulness, and then you'll never succeed even in ten thousand years. Maintain your vigilance with the utmost sincerity, and Thunderclap will be right before your eyes. But when you afflict yourself like that with fears and troubled thoughts, then the Great Way and, indeed, Thunderclap seem far away."

This passage is probably one of the most significant ones in the entire narrative for several reasons: it enables the educated reader to see (1) that the journey to the West is not just a physical trek but symbolizes something else; (2) that the sum of scriptural doctrine unanimously affirmed by master and disciple concerns the cultivation of mind; and (3) that the author, through his invented character, has no reservation in advancing patent religious syncretism in his fiction by adding a poetic commentary that, formally speaking, is quite alien to the Buddhist sūtra.

It is no accident that the pilgrimage, as many readers have remarked, gradually and surely acquires a highly symbolic, even allegorical, meaning in the novel. Whereas the biographical accounts of the historical monk all tend to dwell on the literal variety of places and kingdoms the pilgrim visited, the novel progressively renders the journey as one of paradoxical doubleness: great distance and immediate traversal. As early as when he first joined the pilgrimage, Sun Wukong gave his human master a succinct lecture about the journey's meaning:

> You can walk from the time of your youth till the time you grow old, and after that, till you become youthful again; and even after going through such a cycle a thousand times, you may still find it difficult to reach the place where you want to go to. But when you perceive, by the resoluteness of your will, the Buddha-nature in all things, and when every one of your thoughts goes back to its very source in your memory, that will be the time you arrive at the Spirit Mountain 只要你見性志誠, 念念回首處, 即是靈山. (XYJ, chapter 24, p. 270)

What is even more astonishing about this affirmation of "sudden enlightenment" redolent of one of Chan's key doctrines is the setting of Monkey's little lecture. After all, the *Platform Sūtra* asserts repeatedly, "To see the Western Region takes only an instant 見西方只在刹那" (*Tanjing*, chapter 3, p. 78). Immediately before Sun Wukong spoke, Sha Monk asked him just how far it was to Thunderclap Temple, the abode of Buddha. Monkey's reply was: "One hundred and eight thousand miles 十萬八千里." As any reader will remember, this is the distance covered by the magic of one cloud somersault that Monkey had learned from Patriarch Subodhi in chapter 2 (XYJ, p. 18). That was why he could boast to his fellow disciple, the Pig Eight Rules Zhu, when they were stranded at the Flowing-Sand River (chapter 22, p. 249), that if it were only he who had to journey to see Buddha, all he had to do was "to nod his head twice and stretch his waist once." The great distance would be covered in an instant. Is there any particular significance to the number of miles? Here is the answer from the *Platform Scripture* (section 35, p. 91–92):

> If the mind is absolutely pure, the Western Region is not far away. But if one's mind is not pure, it will be difficult to go and be born there through reciting the name of the Buddha. If one has removed the Ten Evils, he will have traveled a hundred thousand miles, and if one is free from the Eight Perversions, he will have traveled eight thousand miles. (see also the *Tanjing*, chapter 3, p. 77)

Monkey's use of a quatrain as a *gāthā* to amplify the meaning of both mind cultivation and the journey's symbolic distance, however, does not, as far as we know, stem directly from a Chan Buddhist source. It derives from a noncanonical Daoist text that integrates certain Chan concepts and terms with Quanzhen doctrines. Completely subscribing to the hermeneutical principles practiced by those advocating the unity of the Three Religions, the book titled *Xingming guizhi* (Talismanic Directives to the Cultivation of Nature and Vitality) "is a comprehensive *neidan* [internal or physiological alchemy] text dating from the Ming period."[136] In the section on "Nourishing the Fundamental Origin 涵養本原," we read the following:

> The Confucians call it "Spirit Terrace" [or Estrade]; the Daoists call it "Spirit Pass": and the Buddhists call it "Spirit Mountain." The Three Religions belong to the same Dharma Gate, and all [their doctrines] are not beyond this one aperture to spiritual enlightenment. The Buddhist Religion says: "Seek not afar for Buddha on Spirit Mount; . . . / Beneath this stūpa you must be refined" 儒曰靈臺, 道曰靈關, 釋曰靈山, 三教同一法門, 總不外此靈明一竅. 釋教曰, 佛在靈山莫遠求 / 靈山只在汝心頭 / 人人有個靈山塔 / 好向靈山塔下修. (XMGZ 9: 532; XMGZ-Taipei, pp. 146-47)

Neither the novel XYJ nor this Daoist treatise identifies the source of this poem or which one of our texts might have been quoting the other. Nevertheless, such evidence indicates our novel is steeped in a cultural milieu that affirms the Three Religions as belonging to the same fold in practice and belief.

That impression, in turn, should enable us to see as well why the novel has provided its human protagonist, for all his reputed learning in Buddhism and habitual rehearsal of Confucian pieties, a monkey-tutor who, as many readers (including Mao Zedong) would argue, is the true hero of the novel. Although Tripitaka might be able to declare in chapter 85 that "the lesson of all scriptures [presumably including those he was still seeking] concerns only the cultivation of the mind," it is the novel's author who gave him a disciple and companion that incarnates mind itself. The figure of Sun Wukong, as conceived and developed throughout the book, brilliantly embodies the venerable idiom, "the monkey of the mind."

It is no accident that a narrative ostensibly devoted to Xuanzang's pilgrimage would begin with seven chapters focused solely on an imagined figure, a capacious structural feature found *only* in the 1592 novel. This part of the story concerns a different quest: "the sprouting of [Monkey's] religious inclination 道心開發" in chapter 1 that leads to his search for the Way 訪道 and its eventual acquisition 得道. When he succeeds in the first stage of learning the secret of realized immortality from the Patriarch Subhodi, the narration's emphasis (chapter 2) at first seems to accentuate his superhuman powers and physical transformation: "I left weighed down by bones of mortal stock. / The Dao attained makes light both body and frame" (XYJ, chapter 1, p. 20; JW 1: 125). At the height of his battle in Heaven, however, the couplet opening one of the three commentarial verses in chapter 7 I cited earlier refines and deepens the polysemia of the Monkey figure: "An ape's body of Dao weds the human mind. / Mind is a monkey—this meaning's profound 猿猴道體配人心 / 心即猿猴意思深" (XYJ, chapter 1, p. 79; JW 1: 190). Because the Monkey of the Mind was a stock idiom common to Buddhist and Daoist usage long before the novel appeared, most readers past and present have passed over the puns and metaphors in these lines without exploring further how skillfully this seemingly trite appellation has acquired new meaning in the entire work.

The narrative context of this poem is when Monkey will soon face the comic but disastrous wager with Buddha himself, who addresses his insolent opponent as "only a monkey who happened to become a spirit, ... merely a beast who has just attained human form in this incarnation" (XYJ, chapter 7, pp. 81–82; JW 1: 193), or, as he tags him elsewhere, a bogus immortal (yaoxian 妖仙). In the religio-magical cosmos presumed by the full-length novel, the attainment of magical or transcendent powers (de Dao) is open to both humans and such nonhumans as plants, animals, rocks, and mountains, or fans, swords, and lutes. But the process also entails a form of hierarchy more consonant with conventional Confucian values: for nonhumans, the goal of their first stage must be the acquisition of human speech, manners, and other characteristics of human culture. That was what Monkey learned in chapter 1, whereas the giant white turtle of chapter 49 acquired speech but not human form (or he would have shed his shell), and the giant python monster of chapter 67 could not even speak. We might well ask whether the Monkey of the first seven chapters has truly attained unity with the human heart-and-mind on his initiation at the Mountain of Heart and Mind, or only with his submission to Tripitaka, in the episode titled "The Monkey of the Mind Returns to the Right 心猿歸正" (chapter 14). In any case, Monkey's experience in the cave and his receipt from Subhodi of the secrets of alchemy and immortality ought not to be slighted, because the names of the mountain and the cave complement his first conversation with the patriarch.

"What is your family name [xing 姓]?" The Monkey King again replied, "I have no nature [xing 性]. If a man rebukes me, I am not offended; if he hits me, I am not angered. . . . My whole life's without ill temper." "I'm not speaking of your temper," the Patriarch said, "I'm asking after the name of your parents." "I have no parents either," said the Monkey King. ". . . I recall there used to be an immortal stone on the Flower-Fruit Mountain. I was born in the year when it split open."

When the Patriarch heard this, he was secretly pleased . . . and said, "though your features are not the most attractive, you do resemble a pignolia-eating monkey (husun 猢猻). This gives me the idea of taking a surname for you from your appearance. I intended to call you the name 'Hu 猢.' Now, if I drop the animal radical from this word, what's left is a compound made up of the two characters, *gu* 古 and *yue* 月. *Gu* means aged and *yue* means female, but an aged female cannot reproduce.

Therefore it is better to give you the surname of 'Sun.' If I drop the animal radical from this word, what we have left is the compound of *zi* 子 and *xi* 系. *Zi* means a boy and *xi* means a baby, and that name exactly accords with the Doctrine of the Baby Boy. So your surname will be 'Sun 孫.'"

When the Monkey King heard this, he was filled with delight. "Splendid! Splendid!" he cried, kowtowing. "At last I know my name" . . . . Laughing, the Patriarch [also] said, "You will hence be given the religious name Wake-to-the-Void (*Wukong*)." (XYJ, chapter 1, pp. 11-12; JW 1: 114-15)

This name Wukong (Wake-to-the-Void, 悟空) brings quickly to mind such concepts as *śūnya*, *śūnyatā*, and *māyā* in Buddhism, which point to the emptiness, the vacuity, and the unreality of all things and all physical phenomena. These are, in fact, cardinal doctrines of the Yogācāra school of which the historical Xuanzang himself, as we have seen, is an able exponent. It is not without reason, therefore, that when the fictive Tripitaka first learns of Monkey's name in chapter 14, he exclaims with pleasure, "It exactly fits the emphasis of our lineage."

The person who made the observation, we also know, is not the historical Xuanzang, and one could justly question at this point whether "our lineage" refers to the Faxiang or Consciousness-Only variety or another tradition infiltrated hugely by Chan and Quanzhen notions. The earlier chitchat between Subhodi and his student with all that punning amidst etymological and anagrammatic analysis of a few Chinese graphs may sound almost vaudevillian. But to a reader alert to both context and the thin veil of allegory, the cave's name and this small episode add up to an important slogan endlessly proclaimed by both Chan Buddhism and Quanzhen Daoism: the attainment of Buddhahood or enlightenment depends on one's "illiminating the mind and seeing one's own nature [as Buddha's and hence one's own original nature], *mingxin jianxing* 明心見性." Hence the key Chan Buddhist scripture declares: "Each should view one's mind so that each should see one's own nature. . . . If one understands one's own nature, the very moment of awakening would make one arrive [in] the land of Buddha 各自觀心, 自見本性. . . . 若識自性一悟即至佛地" (*Tanjing*, chapter 2, p. 39). This is the lesson of the novel that the powerful recalcitrant ape tries to teach his master.

To understand the relationship between Xuanzang and his simian disciple is already to follow the insight of readers from the Ming to contemporary scholars that one principal subject of the novel, as summarized by even Tripitaka himself, irrefutably focuses on the cultivation of heart-and-mind, a subject that has been prevalent in the discourse of philosophical elites like the Neo-Confucians from Song to Ming and in the idioms and jargons of pedestrian morality advocates and even popular entertainers. The pithiness of this abstract term of cultivation, however, may prevent us from seeing the multiplicity of its meaning that finds such ingenious deployment in the novel. Although Xuanzang before the pilgrimage (chapter 13) can already assert that "when the mind is active, all kinds of māra come into existence; when the mind is extinguished, all kinds of māra will be extinguished 心生, 種種魔生; 心滅, 種種魔滅" (XYJ, p. 143; JW 1: 294), his experience throughout the journey reveals that such a declaration for him at the time seems no more than a rote paraphrase of similar ideas in many Buddhist writings (e.g., "心生即種種法生, 心滅即種種法滅"), especially those associated with the Chan sect.[137] For him—and the readers as well—to learn the full implications of such a doctrine will require the journey's eighty-one ordeals no less than Tripitaka's unquestioned unanimity with his mind-monkey, at once his teacher and his disciple. Tripitaka must let the mind of Monkey become his mind so that he may "wake to the void." Without this transformative union and vision, he will regard a monster like the Red Boy as a good person (chapters 40-42) and see the specious Thunderclap Monastery as the real one (chapters 65-67).

This central paradox, as it finds narrative exposition and enactment in the novel, thus perforce departs from the kind of syncretic idealism of a Neo-Confucian Wang Shouren 王守仁 (Yangming 陽明, 1472-1529). Although that Ming philosopher admits that "the lessons of Chan and of the Sages are all about cultivating to the limit of one's heart-and-mind 禪之學與聖人之學, 皆求其盡其心也," and that Confucianism differs from Chan Buddhism only with a hair's breadth ("相去毫厘矣"), Wang's patently Mencian diction nevertheless clings to a traditional critique of Buddhism for "ignoring canonical human relations, abandoning affairs and things [of the world] . . . , and fostering selfishness and self-benefit 外人倫, 遺事物. . . . 起於自私自利."[138] By contrast, the novel's unapologetic religious orientation now seeks to unite Buddhist and Confucian precepts in a markedly different manner. The fictive Xuanzang is first presented as someone with impeccable credentials of a loyal subject and filial son, but even though he has not ignored human relations, he must still learn the truth adumbrated in chapter 14's prefatorial poem—"The Mind is the Buddha and the Buddha is Mind 佛即心兮心即佛"[139]—a chapter ending dramatically with Monkey's thunderous clamor that his Master has arrived at last to set him free. Reading through the novel's entire length, it is plain that what the fictive Xuanzang must learn is to hold fast constantly to the doctrines of the loftiest idealism or mentalism enshrined in the *Heart Sūtra* (chapters 32 and 85). Even more painfully, he—and the readers, too—must realize, through the seemingly violent but repeated episodes of eliminating the Six Robbers (chapters 14 and 56), that the cherished, inviolable Law of the monk's faith (the Buddhist commandment not to take life) is itself contradictory. For this imperative as such is also fundamentally empty and thus requires noetic transcendence in the very process of self-cultivation.

The Heart-and-Mind that must be consulted and utilized thus dialectically needs also to be controlled or harnessed 管制, as every reader who encounters the Tight-Fillet episodes would realize. Moreover, Monkey's own experience as the Tang Monk's disciple mirrors his master's experience, one constituted by a series of imprisonment and release, harmonious integration and disastrous dissolution, epitomized in the idiom, "to subdue or release the Monkey of the Mind 收放心猿," a phrase that echoes the alleged dicta on the novel by the Yuan scholar Yu Ji discussed in part II of this introduction: that the book "is all about the retrieval or release of one's mind." The Monkey of the Mind, *xinyuan*, may well be read as a pun on *xinyuan* 心願, or mental wish. Both the metaphoric name itself and the need to control the mind have filled the discourses of both Buddhism and Quanzhen Daoism.[140] Most importantly, physical pain and mental anguish persistently accompany the human pilgrim no less than his devoted disciple on this journey. In this sense, the enlistment of a monkey acolyte as the most appropriate guardian and guide for the human monks *cannot be adequately explained alone by reference to literary antecedents*. The profoundly creative author of the hundred-chapter novel has transmuted a banal idiom into the unprecedented and unrivalled character Sun Wukong. The language and emplotment of the narrative more than once suggest that the monkey is a part of Tripitaka himself.[141] This kind of symbolic or allegorical union of two figures, objects, or even two bodily parts or organs may certainly find suggestive precedent in both Chan and Daoist writings. In the words of a contemporary scholar,

> 'Taming the Horse of the Mind', an allegory of spiritual discipline, has a number of avatars in Chinese religious culture. An example in the *Daozang* is found in the 'Three Essentials for the Cultivation of the Perfection According to the Superior Vehicle' by Gao Daokuan (1195–1277), a Quanzhen master in the lineage of the twelfth-century patriarch Ma Danyang.... [It] likens the disciplining of the mind (*xin*) and of human nature (*xing*) to the training of a horse. The allegory was current in Quanzhen Daoism and constituted a variant of the Training of the Buffalo in Chan Buddhism and of the Bridling of the Horse of the will (*yima*), the latter popularised in the novel *Journey to the West*. In Quanzhen-inspired Yuan poetic drama (*zaju*),

the horse appears, in the manner of the Inner Alchemical metaphors . . . , as an anatomical personification of the Daoist Yellow Court (*huangting*), i.e. the central organ of the heart or mind (*xin*).[142]

"Popularised" in our novel, indeed, but Professor Verellen could have added the other animal, monkey, to the horse. In another Yuan play authored by Fan Zi'an 范子安, "Chen Jiqing wushang zhuyezhou 陳季卿誤上 竹葉舟 (Chen Jiqing boarded by mistake the bamboo-leaf boat)," the character Lü Dongbin sings the following lines:

> *I don't pick any strange seedlings or exotic herbs,*
> *Nor do I wear treasured script and numinous talisman.*
> *I only need to nurse this spirit till it's pure like water,*
> *To smelt my bone marrow till it's like cheese,*
> *All day long tying up tight the Monkey of the Mind and the Horse of the Will*
>   *to a post* 也不採甚麼奇苗異草, / 也不佩甚麼寶篆靈符, / 只要養的
>   這精神似水, / 煉的這骨髓如酥, / 常日把那心猿意馬牢拴拄.[143]

The aria for the famous transcendent here, like the collected lyrics attributed to the "historical" Lü in QSC 5: 3858–60, is shifting the emphasis of alchemical self-cultivation by external aids to internal discipline of body and mind.

A Chan- or Quanzhen-inspired novel like XYJ was not written necessarily as a work of religious proselytism. Some contemporary Chinese scholars argued that it is, but whether we should accept this thesis without qualification is another matter. Before we end this section on the Monkey, I want to discuss other textual examples of how religious idioms feed and facilitate fictive representation, a topic that, for me, is far more interesting and important. Because both Chan and Quanzhen discourses have focused on the difficult paradox of at once consulting and disregarding the power of *xin*, the heart-and-mind generating the nearly irresistible drives of emotion and intellect, the novel's depiction of Sun Wukong's character, on more than one occasion, is similarly double-sided. Not simply a demotic hero and instinctual political rebel, as many Chinese critics have tended to read him, Sun personifies a crucial part of the human being essential for the pilgrimage's success, but also demanding constant restraint.

When the internal contradiction of the Mind/Heart's cultivation seems to reach an insoluble aporia, because mindlessness and mindfulness are both necessary and dispensable, the faculty of Mind/Heart can literally split into two identical entities of two minds or double-mindedness (*erxin*, 二心) that, according to the brilliant allegory of chapters 56, 57, and 58, only Buddha's transcendent wisdom can overcome.[144] In this exciting and hilarious episode when Sun Wukong battled his own inseparable mirror image throughout the cosmos till they reached the Western Heaven, Buddha's words to calm a startled assembly attending the Patriarch's lecture expose the nature of the avatars: "You are all of one mind, but take a look at Two Minds (*erxin*) in conflict arriving here" (XYJ, chapter 58, p. 672). The swift and violent slaying of the Sixth-Ear Macaque named for Monkey's double thus enacts literally two lines of a commentarial poem in the same chapter 58, preceding even Buddha's clarification (XYJ, p. 671): "If one has two minds, disasters he'll breed / . . . The Gate of Chan must learn the No Mind Spell 人有二心生禍災 / . . . . 禪門須學無心訣."[145]

An earlier episode (chapter 17) gives another brilliant twist of narration to the truth of this formula, when Tripitaka's cassock, a gift of Buddha through the Tang emperor, was stolen by a bear monster. Sun Wukong asks the Bodhisattva Guanyin, who came to the pilgrims' assistance, to change into the form of the monster to gain access to the real one, whom they both plan to attack.

> Immediately the Bodhisattva exercised her great mercy and boundless power. With her infinite capacity for transformation, her mind moved in perfect accord with her will, and her will with her body: in one blurry instant, she changed into the form of the immortal Lingxuzi [one of the monsters]. . . . When Pilgrim saw the transformation, he cried, "Marvelous, Marvelous! Is the monster the Bodhisattva, or is the Bodhisattva the monster?" The Bodhisattva smiled and said, "Wukong, the Bodhisattva and the monster, they both exist in a single thought (*yinian* 一念). Considered in terms of their origin, they are all nothing [or nonexistent] (若論本來, 皆屬無有)." (XYJ, chapter 17, p. 201; JW 1: p. 000)

That a Bodhisattva Guanyin and a monster are progeny of one and the same thought counters Tripitaka's paraphrase of a cardinal Buddhist doctrine: "when the mind is active [*xinsheng* 心生, literally, when the mind is born or grows], all kinds of māra [i.e., demons or demonic barriers] come into existence; when the mind is extinguished, all kinds of māra will be extinguished" (XYJ, chapter 13, p. 143; see also note 137). The active mind (*xinsheng, xindong*) is thus when the heart/mind is in motion or movement, a state that both Buddhists and Daoists would dearly like to arrest or avoid. Even those outside such religious traditions, Chinese from the ancient Mencius to the modern Chairman Mao Zedong, with countless elites and commoners throughout history, have cherished and sought the unmoved mind (*budongxin* 不動心).[146] The fiction of Guanyin's transformation in chapter 17, however, points to an ironic reversal because it depicts presumably the good that "one thought" can generate: by moving her mind and her will, says the novel, the Bodhisattva as monster will eventually bring the monster to submit. The XYJ author's utilization of the potent philosophical religion of mind or mentalism shared by Chan and Quanzhen lineages is thus not merely repetitive but also subtly faceted. Even the powerful and apparently real figure of the Bull Monster King narratively exists—like the macaque of Monkey's double—only as another Sun Wukong, perhaps even as a repressed other. Unexpectedly, Monkey himself declaims this striking equation (chapter 61): "Bull King was in fact from Mind Monkey changed. / Now's the best time for us to reach the source 牛王本是猿猴變, 今番正好會源流" (JW 3: 174; XYJ, p. 701). Since certain Buddhist doctrines assert that the enlightened mind renders as all phenomena (*zhongzhong fa* 種種法, the Dharma as myriad things that have entity and bear their own attributes) undifferentiable and thus unreal, we can argue that, conversely, the linguistic proliferation of such vivid unreality as realistic phenomena defines this novel's incomparable achievement in fiction. In the final analysis, is it not the creative writer's mind in motion that ushers into existence the myriad demons and gods—and much else—in this fiction? Every being inhabiting the novelistic universe may be subject to the ideal of the unmoved mind so loudly proclaimed throughout, but the artist who has created this universe cannot do so without his or her mind's arousal, motion, and growth. Guanyin's instruction to Monkey may have answered her interlocutor's immediate query with perfect doctrinal correctness, but it sounds to me like a most perceptive definition of fiction as well: "Considered in terms of their origin, they are all nothing."

The Fiction of Religious Allegory

The biographical account of Xuanzang's pilgrimage does not record that he was accompanied from beginning to end by disciples, companions, or even a beast of burden. The poetic tale of the Song that started the Tripitaka legend mentions repeatedly that the pilgrim's entourage had seven persons, including the converted monkey acolyte. For the full-length novel of 1592, the total number of the pilgrims is perhaps significantly fixed at five, with the human master attended by four disciples, one of which is a dragon-horse. This numerical structure of the pilgrims may betoken a design of multiple signification.

First, the enterprise of scripture-seeking by means of a protracted and perilous journey has become a corporate endeavor, not simply the triumphant accomplishment of one courageous and long-suffering zealot. Not only is the fictional Tripitaka in constant need of his disciples, but the author also just as regularly alters and diminishes his human protagonist to indicate *why* he needs them. Readers past and present have protested the foolishness, the cowardice, the obtuseness, and a host of other weaknesses bedeviling this Tripitaka's character, but such a delineation is necessary if the disciples' presence is not to be superfluous. Throughout the novel, Tripitaka persists in his own delusions and illusions, appositely winning the epithet bestowed on him by both Sun Wukong and the narrator that he is of "fleshly eyes and mortal stock 肉眼凡胎."

When, in chapter 22, the pilgrims are stranded on the eastern shore of the Flowing-Sand River, Wukong and Wuneng debate how to help Tripitaka across the river.

> "You have no idea," says Pilgrim, who seldom resists boasting a little of his own ability, "about the capacity of my cloud somersault, which with one leap can cover a hundred and eight thousand miles. . . ." "Elder Brother," says Eight Rules, "if it's so easy, all you need to do is to carry Master on your back: nod your head, stretch your waist, and jump across. . . ." To which Pilgrim, after some reflection, responds: "But it is required of Master to go through all these strange territories before he finds deliverance from the sea of sorrows; hence even one step turns out to be difficult." (JW 1: 427-28)

These remarks by the two disciples point up the fundamental truth concerning Tripitaka's pilgrimage: for all the supernatural forces coming to aid or harm him, Tripitaka must journey to the West as a human mortal. Just as he is conditioned by his physical limitations, and the thousand hills and ten thousand waters cannot be circumvented, so he is also subject to intellectual errors, emotional delusions, and moral shortcomings. His dependence on his followers, especially Sun Wukong, is therefore utterly necessary.

Second, what renders all three disciples of the mortal monk so powerful, however, is the fact that each of them is able to bring something unusual to assist the human master. The first sign of potency, appositely, seems to be an external instrument, appearing as the magic weapons that each of them possesses, which, in the course of the narrative, become extensions of their characters. The device is also manifestly literary, because the famous warriors of Chinese history and fiction are nearly always identified by some peculiar weapons of their own. Guan Yu 關羽 (160-219) has his Scimitar of the Green Dragon and Crescent Moon and Lü Bu 呂布 (d. 198) has his Halberd of Square Sky in *The Three Kingdoms*; "Black Cyclone" Li Kui 李逵 has his pair of battle-axes in the *Outlaws of the Marshes*. The list of fighters with their particular weapons, magical or otherwise, is almost endless in the *Investiture of the Gods*. Few such instruments of war, however, receive the kind of eulogistic and meticulous treatment accorded the rod of Pilgrim, the muckrake of Eight Rules, and the priestly staff of Sha Monk in *The Journey to the West*. Prior to their battle in chapter 19, when Pilgrim asked Eight Rules whether his rake is used "to plough the fields or plant vegetables for the Gao family [his secular in-laws]," his reply, again in the form of a long *pailü* poem, draws heavily on mythological allusions to emphasize the celestial splendor of his weapon. "Just listen to my recital!" he says: "This is divine ice steel greatly refined, / Polished so highly that it glows and shines" [see p. 382]. A little later, in chapter 22, when Sha Wujing is in turn questioned by Eight Rules about his weapon, this is part of his reply: "It's called the treasure staff good for crushing fiends, / Forever placed in Divine Mists to rout the ogres" [see p. 428].

Needless to say, the iron rod of Wukong himself, the most famous weapon in the entire narrative, is also the mightiest of all; its origin is traced supposedly to its first use by the legendary King Yu, the conqueror of the Flood in China. This piece of iron, tipped with gold at both ends, is employed by Yu to fix the depths of the rivers and the oceans (chapters 3 and 88), after which it is stored in the deepest part of the Eastern Ocean until Monkey acquires it. On a few occasions, Wukong's rod is referred to as peculiarly fitting for his apish personality, perhaps a sardonic reference to the monkeys playing with sticks or poles in vaudeville shows in traditional China,[147] much as the Pig's muckrake humorously reminds us of his owner's swinish nature and farming talents. But Monkey's rod throughout the narrative is also that indispensable instrument by which he overcomes the demons and ogres crowding the pilgrims's journey. As he says in the panegyric on his weapon in chapter 88: "It can everywhere the Tiger tame and the Dragon subdue; / It can everyplace the monster exorcise and the demon smelt." Since the phrases, "tame the Tiger and subdue the Dragon," "exorcise the monster and smelt the demon," can refer, metaphorically, to the alchemical action within the body as well,[148] the magic rod becomes also an implement of the self-cultivation practiced by its master. For this reason, when it is the turn of the three disciples of Tripitaka to make disciples themselves in chapter 88, they teach martial arts (*wuyi* 武藝) to the three human princes of the Jade-Flower Kingdom. The weapons they instruct them to use are identical to those of the pilgrims, but only after the princes' mortal frames have been transformed by the immortal breath of Sun Wukong can they carry a rod, a rake, and a staff of immense weight, but still less heavy than the original weapons. Even more significantly, their linkage to Daoism is already made in the novel, for when the weapons of the pilgrims are stolen, the closing poetic commentary in chapter 88 declares: "Dao can't be left for a moment; / What can be left is not the Dao. / When weapons divine are stolen, / The seekers have labored in vain." Because the poem's first two lines quote verbatim the opening sentences of the *Doctrine of the Mean*, one of the four canonical texts of classical Confucianism now appropriated by another tradition, divine weapons (*shenbing*) have become metaphors for the cultivation of Dao, not the Confucian kind but the one sought and practiced vigilantly by the Daoist seekers 參修者.

The three disciples' weapons symbolizing their success in the first stage of their quest for immortality serve to mark them as adepts in the mysteries of longevity. Witness the lengthy *pailü* poems spoken by Zhu Wuneng in chapter 19 and by Sha Wujing in chapter 22. What these poems describe is the process of internal alchemy that texts of the *Daoist Canon* have discussed with endless variations, and which contemporary scholars have studied increasingly.[149] The process offers to the practititoner, among other things, longevity, health, magical powers, and ascent to Heaven in broad daylight at its successful completion. That which Zhu Wuneng has been able to attain, despite his early indolence and sloth, is also the achievement of both Wukong and Sha Wujing, who are, by their own testimonies (cf. XYJ, chapter 17, pp. 192-93; chapter 52, pp. 600-601; chapter 63, p. 721; chapter 70, pp. 795-96; chapter 71, pp. 811-12; chapter 86, p. 980; chapter 94, pp. 1060-61, for Wukong; chapter 22, pp. 247-48, and chapter 94, p. 1061, for Wujing) and by evidence in the narrative, more earnest in the practice of religion. They thus qualify as the human monk's guardians on a physical journey fraught with peril.

Third, the religious attainment of the disciples also highlights their paradoxical status in the story. Monkey, as we recall, an animal literally created by Heaven and Earth, learned part of the secrets of Daoist immortality. Sha Monk's antecedent might have ultimately derived from the historical Xuanzang's biographical account of his experience at the River of Flowing Sand. The author of the Song poetic tale (in a fragment of section 8) modified and amalgamated it with the story of the Deep-Sand God 深沙神.[150] According to Sha's own poetic autobiography recited in chapter 22, he was born a human, but his determination to "learn of the Dao 學道" through cultivation brought success and celestial appointment in the Daoist pantheon as the Curtain-Raising Captain before the Jade Emperor's throne. Similarly, Zhu Eight Rules, as he confessed to Monkey in chapter 19's autobiographical poem, led a foolish and slothful existence until he was converted by "a true transcendent 真仙" to the austere teachings of Quanzhen alchemy. His ascent to Heaven was rewarded also with an appointment of the Daoist Court as the Marshal of Heavenly Reeds 天蓬元帥, a naval commander. Finally, the white horse that carried Tripitaka faithfully to India was originally a dragon prince. All the disciples in their previous lives already were deities, but for some form of major transgressions (Monkey for his revolt against Heaven and repeated acts of theft and violence, the Pig for trying to rape the Goddess of the Moon when he was drunk, Sha Monk for breach of imperial etiquette by breaking a crystal wine goblet, and the dragon for setting fire to his father's palace), they were arrested and exiled to Earth to suffer and to atone for their crimes. To round out the character of the group of the five pilgrims, we learn as well from chapter 12's poetic biography of the human pilgrim that he shares exactly the same fate as his disciples: "Gold Cicada was his former divine name. / As heedless he was of the Buddha's talk, / He had to suffer in this world of dust, / To fall in the net by being born a man" (XYJ, p. 131; JW 1: 275). Different antecedent versions of the journey story in literary history might have provided different and even conflicting textual and personal details for these five pilgrims, but the full-length novel enjoys the distinction of bestowing on this community a particular, powerful bond of purposive commonality: for prior crimes and misdeeds, the five of them must suffer and join together on a piacular pilgrimage, the successful completion of which restores and elevates their transcendent status. In this conception of the pilgrims as a unified community, the elements of progressive incarnation favored by Buddhist Jātaka tales are joined seamlessly to the Daoist theme of the "banished immortal 謫仙" and his or her redemption.[151] The religious ideals and actions mandated for the pilgrims no less than their rewards represent the syncretistic fruits promised by Quanzhen Buddho-Daoism.

It may be asked at this point what sort of merit the disciples do succeed in making during their lengthy journey. The most obvious answer to this question must be, of course, their success in overcoming the marauding hordes of demons and monsters along the way which seek to harm the pilgrim monk. Thus when Eight Rules kills the Tiger Vanguard in chapter 20, he is congratulated by both the narrator (in verse) and by Wukong for achieving his first merit. But to consider the worth of the disciples to reside solely in their protection of the Tang Monk, however demanding such a responsibility may be, is to miss the more profound meaning. The later sections of the novel unmistakably indicate that the narrative does not merely focus on what sort of personal, or even imperial, rewards the action of the pilgrims will bring with their successful journey. There are also insistent rehearsals of how the excesses, the heroic energies, and the representative individualism of a Sun Wukong (restless intelligence, resourcefulness, impetuosity) or a Zhu Eight Rules (appetites for food and sex, sloth) are transformed and used to benefit countless people along the way.

It is remarkable how many episodes of encounters with ogres and demons end, not only in their defeat or in Tripitaka's deliverance, but also in a kingdom restored, a lost child recovered, an estranged family reunited, and a Flame-Throwing Mountain extinguished so that travel and agriculture may resume. The conquest of the monsters is not simply a victory for the heavenly powers or a restoration of an individual ascetic's psychic or mental equilibrium; the reestablishment of human social order is just as crucial because it comes as a result of the defeat of the chthonic, antinomian forces resident in the demonic world. That even the rather shallow and insensitive Tripitaka begins to appreciate the character of Monkey and the frequency with which he has performed eleemosynary service of great magnitude is what we see at the beginning of chapter 88, after that disciple has brought rain to a region suffering from intense drought. "As he rode, the Tang monk said to Pilgrim: 'Worthy disciple! Your virtuous fruit this time even surpasses your achievement when you rescued those infants at the Bhikṣu Kingdom. It's entirely your merit!'" (XYJ, p. 998).

To understand the meaning of the journey as involving atonement and redemption for all five pilgrims is also to recognize the salvific implications of all Three Religions in the novel. Confucianism, insisting on unyielding loyalism to state, parents, and familial patriarchs even in the face of death, has long canonized officials and plebians after death for their meritorious virtue. The rites authorized by the state mark these persons as transcendent beings worthy to receive worship and regular sacrifice. Some of the teachings of Buddhism conflated with Daoism (such as the need to purge harmful desires) are similarly acknowledged. Buddha and his divine followers do constitute part of the entire celestial hierarchy (the rest are popular and Daoist divinities of both native and foreign origins), and in this sense the Buddhist pantheon may seem, in Arthur Wright's words, "a victim of its own adaptability."[152] There are nonetheless some subtle differentiations in the narrative concerning the three groups of deities. Whereas the bureaucratic pretension and incompetence of all three become frequent targets of the author's biting satire, the wisdom and compassion of Buddha—and, to a slightly lesser degree, of Guanyin—are characteristics the other deities (including the Jade Emperor) do not share.

Because of the immense appeal of Sun Wukong's character, many modern critics, especially those who favor a political interpretation of the narrative,[153] have found it difficult to accept Monkey's subjugation in chapter 7, let alone the use of the golden fillet later as an instrument of discipline to inflict unbearable pain whenever he is recalcitrant. Monkey's "conversion" for them becomes a basic flaw in the narrative. After his release from the Five Phases Mountain in chapter 14, his portrayal as a faithful guardian of the cowardly and ineffectual Buddhist pilgrim seems to contradict the magnificent heroic character whose defiance and love of independence we have come to cherish and admire in the first seven chapters.

Such a view fails to do justice to the complexity of the narrative. If the journey signifies for the pilgrims a new beginning, as we have argued, a freely given opportunity for self-rectification, it also becomes a gradual process of merit-making that complements and magnifies the theme of Buddha's mercy. This motif recurs in the narrative. A conspicuous example is when the dragon joins the pilgrimage in chapter 15 after Guanyin brings it to submission at the Eagle Grief Stream, transforming it to a horse for the use of the human pilgrim and promising "the true fruit of a golden body" when it achieves the proper merit. Monkey eventually turns recalcitrant again, complaining to the goddess that "the road to the West is so treacherous! If I have to accompany this ordinary monk, when will I ever get there? If I have to endure all these miseries, I may well lose my life. What sort of merit do you think I'll achieve?" (JW 1: 328). Guanyin's response to this outburst is not only a further promise that she would always come to Pilgrim's aid, but also the gift of three more magic hairs "with life-saving power" that she implants on the back of Monkey's head, thereby winning his just gratitude for her acting as "the Bodhisattva of Great Mercy and Compassion." By her words of encouragement and her additional gift of magic power to Monkey, which will indeed prove to be life-saving in a later crisis (chapter 70), the Bodhisattva Guanyin is consistent with a long tradition that venerates Avalokiteśvara for enlightening and delivering her followers from all kinds of perils and pains.[154]

Fourth, the common fate of the pilgrims not only serves to emphasize the pilgrimage as communal enterprise, but their very number facilitates the proliferation of allegory because they multiply the possibility of signs. This advantage does not mean that the disciples themselves are consciously playing multiple roles because their characters and their names signify many things in the discourse of internal alchemy. To give a parallel but not far-fetched example, the Beatrice of Dante's *Commedia* may symbolize a "historical" young lady, a devout Christian believer and thus also a figuration of the Church as the Bride of Christ, and a type of Mary, the Mother of Christ who would be elevated eventually to the position of coredemptrix in Roman Catholic theology. But in the poem itself, Beatrice the imagined character simply acts as a human person providentially ordained to appear after her death in a vision to the mortal poet-pilgrim; her words and actions do not imply her full awareness that she personifies all those other roles. The multiple allegorical meanings of her person are troped to the readers only through the poet's inventive language.

This is exactly what happens also with respect to the Chinese novel, for it frequently designates the three disciples of Tripitaka by the terminology of Five Phases (*wuxing* 五行) and of alchemy. A quick glance at some of the titular couplets will make such usages apparent (emphasis mine).

Chapter 32:

On the Level-Top Mountain the Sentinel brings a message;
At the Lotus-Flower Cave the *Wood Mother* meets disaster.

Chapter 40:

The *Baby's* playful form disturbs the Mind of Chan;
Ape, Horse, *Spatula*,[155] and *Wood Mother* all [fight] in vain.

Chapter 47

> The Sage Monk is blocked by night at the Passing-to-Heaven River;
> In compassion *Metal* and *Wood* rescue a little child.

Chapter 53

> Eating and drinking, the Chan Lord is demonically conceived;
> The *Yellow Dame* carries water to abort the weird child.

It is impossible to correlate all five members of the pilgrimage with the many traditional orders of the Five Evolutive Phases—cosmogonic, mutual production, mutual conquest, and "modern"[156]—in a satisfying way, but the associations of Wukong, Wuneng, and Wujing are consistent. Monkey is invariably identified with metal or gold (*jin* 金), and he is frequently referred to as *jingong* 金公 or *jinweng* 金翁 (the Lord or Squire of Gold or Metal). According to the notes following chapter 22 of the 1954 Beijing edition, the reason is threefold: first, in spagyrical literature, lead (*qian* 鉛)—one of the two or three most important ingredients in alchemy—is given the name of Lord or Squire of Gold, from the belief that true lead is born from the Celestial Stem (*tiangan* 天干) of *Geng* 庚. Not surprisingly, the corresponding metal to the stem is either metal or gold. Moreover, the Branches of the Earth (*dizhi* 地支), which with the Celestial Stems combine to form the Chinese sexagenary cycle, are so arranged that the combination of *shenyou* 申酉 directly matches the combination of *gengshen* 庚申 in the celestial system. Because the symbolical animal of the horary character *shen* 申 is a monkey, the correlation is thus made complete. By the same process of reasoning, Zhu Wuneng is given the name Wood Mother (*mumu* 木母) in the narrative, for it is a term used by alchemists to designate mercury (*gong* 汞). True mercury is supposed to have been born from the horary character of *hai* 亥, for which the symbolical animal is a boar or a pig.[157] As for Sha Wujing, he is almost always linked to the earth, bearing at times the name Earth Mother (*tumu* 土母), at times the name Yellow Dame (*huangpo* 黃婆), and at times the name Spatula. Since in the literature of internal alchemy the five phases are further correlated with the pneumatic vitality (*qi* 氣) of the five viscera, these three disciples of Tripitaka are thereby made symbols of the interior elements ascribed to the human body. According to the *Neidan huanyuan jue* 內丹還原訣 (Formula for the Internal Elixir reverting to the Origin), for example, metal or gold is correlated with the secretion of the lungs, earth or Yellow Dame points to the liquid or secretion of the spleen, and wood corresponds to the pneumatic vitality of the liver.[158] Such a schematization thus provides the narrator of XYJ with a complex system of correspondences by which he may account for, and comment on, the experience and action of the pilgrims.

When Wukong first brings Wuneng to submission and leads him back to see Tripitaka, the narrator, as we have seen at the end of part III of this introduction, presents a testimonial regulated poem to comment on the action. We should further observe in this poem that the emphasis is placed upon the peaceful relation that exists—and should exist—between Wukong and Wuneng, just as the ideal state of the body sought by those engaging in the process of self-cultivation is one characterized by the harmonious balance of the pneumatic vitalities. This is the reason why somatic or physiological elements are still affirmed in the linguistic subconscious as the verities of social relations, so that adepts still wrote of them as "ruler and subject," "husband and wife," "friends," and "host and guest." It is for this same reason, therefore, that when the pilgrims reach one of the lowest points in their journey—the occasion of Wukong's first banishment, when Tripitaka believes the Pig's slander—the narrator comments in chapter 30:

> *The Horse of the Will and the Ape of the Mind are all dispersed;*
> *The Metal Squire and the Wood Mother are scattered both;*
> *Yellow Dame is wounded, from everyone divorced;*
> *With reason and right so divided, what can be achieved?*

Throughout the long tale, the ubiquitous but unobtrusive voice of the narrator in fact provides a running, reflexive commentary—usually through interpolated verse of many varieties and the brief prose introductions to new episodes—and gently reminds the reader of allegory's presence even within the fun-filled and lively depictions of cosmic battles, fantastic beings, bizarre experiences, and extraordinary feats of mental and physical bravura. To craft a story radically different from a synopsis of secular canonical or Buddhist history, the author has manipulated idioms and terms from selected writings in both the Buddhist and the Daoist canons. Constructing an intricate story with multiple lines of signification and at the same time providing its own commentary reflects the discursive predilection of the "Three Religions as One" movement to which I have referred to several times. By the late Ming, it had gained widespread adherence throughout the populace.[159] As frequently articulated in fiction and fiction commentaries of the Ming-Qing periods, the movement's syncretic discourse was truly a hermeneutics of fusion or integration, wherein the widely disparate concepts and categories of traditional Confucianism, Daoism, and Buddhism were deliberately harmonized and unified as mutually interpretive terms. That this discourse was intimately known to our novel's author could be seen in lines of poetry describing a lecture by Subhodi (chapter 2), the master who first transmitted to the Monkey King the secrets of immortality and other magic powers. The content and method of his lecture are revealing: "The doctrines of three vehicles he subtly rehearsed / . . . .

For a while he lectured on Dao; / For a while he spoke on Chan— / To harmonize the Three Parties was a natural thing 妙演三乘教,... / 說一會道, 講一會禪, 三家配合本如然" (XYJ, chapter 2, p. 13; JW 1:116).

Scholars usually take the Three Parties (*sanjia*, literally Three Lineages but often translated also as Schools) to be another standard name of the three religious traditions, but in the novel's context, even such a seemingly innocuous nomenclature takes on special significance. In the *Xingming guizhi* to which I have alluded earlier, there is an illustration of a seated adept cultivating physiological alchemy (*neidan*) with the label, "Diagram of the Three Parties meeting each other 三家相見圖." It bears in its upper left corner the inscription, "Spermal essence, pneumatic vitality, and spirit are fused by me into one entity 精氣神由我合成一個." A triangle of three circles is drawn across the center of his abdomen bearing the labels of the three (see fig. 1).[160]

This chapter in the novel is when Monkey acquires his first lessons in the spagyrical arts. The first poetic formula Subhodi communicated to him aloud (*koujue* 口訣) contains the line "All power resides in the semen, the breath, and the spirit (*jing, qi, shen*)." Its syncretic implications are noteworthy. Indeed, the text of the XMGZ seems to have provided the most illuminating exegesis for both its own diagram and the formula imparted to Monkey by Subhodi:

Collecting the Three to return to the One is based on emptiness and quiescence. Empty the mind, and spirit will unite with the nature; quiet the body, and spermal essence and emotion will become quiescent. When intention reaches Great Concentration [*dading*, a Buddhist term], then the three origins fuse to become one. When emotion unites with the nature, it is called the pairing of Metal and Wood [because emotion correlates with metal and nature correlates with wood]; when spermal essence unites with spirit, it is called the intercourse of Fire and Water [because dragon as spirit correlates with water, while spermal essence as tiger correlates with fire]; when intention reaches Great Concentration, the Five Phases are complete. However, the transformation of spermal essence into pneumatic vitality stems from the body not being moved; the transformation of pneumatic vitality into spirit stems from the mind not being moved; and the self-transformation of spirit into emptiness comes about because intention is unmoved.... When body, mind, and intention fuse together, then the Three Parties meet each other to create the Baby Boy 攝三歸一, 在乎虛靜. 虛其心, 則神與性合; 靜其身, 則精與情寂; 意大定, 則三元混一. 情合性謂之金木併, 精合神謂之水火交, 意大定謂之五行全. 然而精化為氣者, 由身之不動也. 氣化為神者, 由心之不動也. 神化為虛者, 由意之不動也.... 身心意合, 則三家相見結嬰兒也. (XMGZ-Taipei, p. 115)

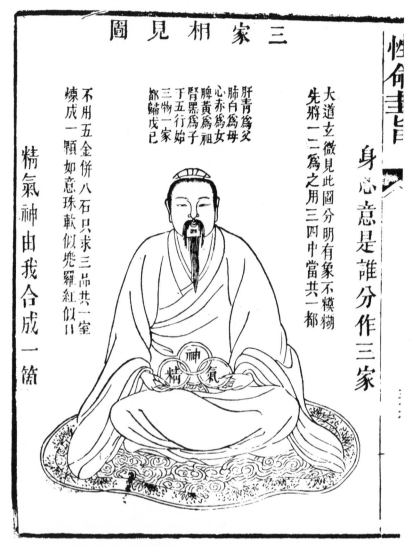

三家相見圖

大道玄微見此圖分明有象不模糊
先將一二爲之用三四中當共一都

身忘意是誰分作三家

性命圭旨

肝青爲父
肺白爲母
心赤爲女
脾黃爲祖
腎黑爲子
下五行始
三物一家
都歸戊己

不用五金併八石只求三品共一室
煉成一顆如意珠軟似塊羅紅似[]

精氣神由我合成一箇

FIG. 1 Diagram of "The Three Parties Meeting"

The Baby Boy is none other than the "holy embryo or *shengtai* 聖胎," the avatar of the realized state of immortality in the adept's body. It also explains why Subhodi says in chapter 1 that the name he gives to Monkey "exactly accords with the fundamental doctrine of the Baby Boy 正合嬰兒 之本論."

Lest this "Baby" talk seems wildly esoteric, another visual example is given here to illustrate the amazing inconographic syncretism documented in modern scholarship (see fig. 2).

FIG. 2 Image of a Buddha with a smiling baby boy (from SCC V/5: 62). This kind of icon is not an isolated specimen, but according to Needham's documentation, many Buddhas and arhats are made or fashioned with the additional head of a baby lodged in their abdomens. See additional photographs in SCC V/5: 81, 83, 84, and 90.

These material images, in turn, elucidate the comic episode in chapters 53 and 54 of the novel, when by accident Tripitaka and the Pig drink some water from a stream named Mother-and-Child River 子母河 bordering the Women Kingdom of Western Liang. The geographical sources for this kingdom may have derived from texts associated with Xuanzang (e.g., the *Da Tang Xiyuji*, *j* 11, and the *FSZ*, *j* 4) and those of canonical history, but the narrative focuses satirically on the mistakes of the pilgrims in relieving their thirst, for the water makes both of the males pregnant. Appositely, the titular couplets label their experience as "demonic conception 鬼孕 and perverse pregnancy 邪胎" that only the magic water of Abortion Stream 落胎泉 can dissolve. When Monkey and Sha Monk return with the hard-won liquid to rectify their companions' errors, the commentarial poem celebrates in explicit alchemical rhetoric:

> *In vain the form of Baby Boy's conceived;*
> *Earth Mother* [i.e., Sha Monk] *with ease has merit achieved.*
> *Heresy pushed down, right faith's on track,*
> *The lord of the mind* [i.e., Monkey], *all smiles, now comes back.* (XYJ, chapter 53, p. 618)

In an even more decisive indication of such syncretism, Buddha proclaims at the novel's beginning (chapter 8) that in his possession were "the scriptures for the cultivation of immortality, the gate to ultimate virtue 修真之經, 正善之門." Repeated more expansively at the end (chapter 98), he calls the scriptures "not only . . . the numinous mirror of our faith, but actually the source of the Three Religions 雖為我門之龜鑑, 實乃三教之源流." Such a line of affirmation would surely astonish orthodox Buddhists, but for the serious student of the novel, what is even more astonishing is not just this asserted unity of the three religions vis-à-vis the Buddhist canon. It is the wide-ranging utilization of diverse source materials for the ingenious making of fiction that stamps the novel's literary originality. The chapters of the Cart Slow Kingdom 車遲國 (44–46) may serve as a convenient and final example.

This episode has to do with Monkey and three Daoist fiends engaging in a series of contests to determine which party has greater power to produce rain for drought relief. The most memorable detail is probably the hilarious account of how Monkey made the Daoists drink his and his two companions' urine as holy water. For more politically minded readers, the Daoists' slander that led to the ruler's bitter persecution of the Buddhists by elevating the Daoists in his court may well recall some such episodes in the history of China.[161] After he had exterminated the animal spirits and enlightened the king and his subjects, Monkey's parting admonition to the ruler (chapter 47) is that he should never "believe in false doctrines" which, in the context of the episode, decidedly means the belief in Daoism to the exclusion of the other two religions. "I hope," says Monkey pointedly, "you will honor the unity of the Three Religions: revere the monks, revere also the Daoists, and take care to nurture the talented. Your kingdom, I assure you, will be secure forever" (XYJ, pp. 540-41). The peaceful coexistence of religions, in sum, is the best policy for social stability and a lasting state. That form of coexistence is already taking shape within this community of scripture-seekers.

At its most basic level of a miracle tale, moreover, the Cart-Slow episode also reveals an obvious affinity with similar stories of agon in magic found in religious texts like the Tanakh. Consider the parallel with Moses' duel with ancient Egypt's magicians and sorcerers in the Exodus story (Exodus 7-10) or the Hebrew prophet Elijah's contest with the priests and prophets of Ba'al (I Kings, 18). As I have pointed out in a previous essay, however, the XYJ story may have first developed also from Buddhist hagiographic sources:[162] the life and activities of the Indian monk Amoghavajra (Bukong 不空) reputed to have helped introduce Tibetan Buddhism to the Tang court during the reigns of Xuanzong (712-56), Suzong 肅宗 (r. 756-63), and Daizong 代宗 (r. 63-79). Highly honored during his long career under these emperors, during which time he also engaged in magic contests with a Daoist named Luo Gongyuan 羅公遠, at his life's end he was made a *guoshi* 國師 (Preceptor of State), a title that also belongs to the three Daoist monsters in XYJ. In Bukong's biography, both emperor Xuanzong and Daizong had requested the monk to pray for rain to relieve severe drought.[163]

The three Daoist priests in the novel, we recall, are actually a tiger, a white deer, and a mountain goat, but their names and original natures, interestingly enough, may have come directly from writings on internal alchemy found in the Daoist canon. A large number of texts devoted to various and variant discussions of the physiological alchemist's quest for longevity has presented a fairly consistent description of how he must reverse the downward bodily flow of spermal essence, pneumatic vitality, and spirit and force these primary vitalities up again along a path in the spine to the top of his head. These elements, so galvanized in the cultivation process called "returning the essence to replenish the brain, *huanjing bunao* 還精補腦",[164] are to be visualized as the cargo transported by an ox or buffalo cart 牛車, a deer cart 鹿車, and a goat cart 羊車, quite often also referred to as Three River-Carts or River-Chariots 三河車 (see fig. 3).[165]

The *neidan* process that circulates the three kinds of *qi* within the body is first named Little Celestial Cycle 小周天, which is correlated with the diurnal cycle of twelve [Chinese] hours. It then leads to a complementary, second-stage process named Great Celestial Cycle 大周天 that is correlated

LES TROIS CHARIOTS

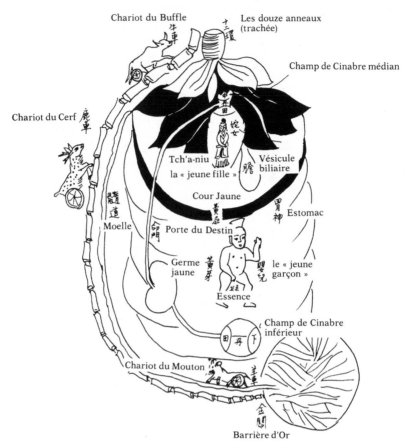

Chariot du Buffle

牛車

十二環

Les douze anneaux
(trachée)

Champ de Cinabre médian

Chariot du Cerf 鹿車

牛田

蛇女

Tch'a-niu
la « jeune fille »

膽

Vésicule
biliaire

Cour Jaune

黃庭

髓道

Moelle

命門

胃神

Estomac

Porte du Destin

Germe
jaune

黃芽

嬰兒

le « jeune
garçon »

生主

Essence

Champ de Cinabre
inférieur

丹田下

Chariot du Mouton

羊車

金閒

Barrière d'Or

Dessin d'après un tableau de Yen-lo tseu
dans le *Sieou-tchen chechou* (k. 18).

FIG. 3 The Three Chariots (*sanche*) as Alchemical Transport. The original diagram
is found in "Zhazhu jiejing 雜著捷徑," collected in *Xiuzhen shishu* 修真十書, DZ 263,
4: 690; the clarified and enlarged diagram is taken from Farzee Baldrian-Hussein,
Procédés secrets du Joyau magique, p. 173, where the Chariot du Buffle, du Cerf, and
du Mouton are French translations of the Chariot of Buffalo, of Deer, and of Goat,
respectively.

with the annual cycle of 365 days, conducted along two *qi* circulation tracts,
the superintendent (*du* 督) tract that runs up the back of the body and the
conception (*ren* 任) that runs up its front.[166] According to two contemporary scholars, both processes may underlie episodic allegories that form
chapters 32–66, and chapters 67–83, respectively.[167]

If the names of the carts give clues about two of the three Great Immortals in the novel (Deer-Strength and Goat-Strength), how should we understand the name of the fictive kingdom Chechi (Cart Slow)? The last word, *chi* 遲, apparently has the common sense of slowness or tardiness 遲慢, and the whole name may well refer to the pace of the alchemist's arduous effort of cultivation 煉功, an effort described by Wang Chongyang as "using the three carts to transport [the cargo] up to the Kunlun Peak [the cranial crown] 用三車搬運上昆侖頂."[168] Among the countless examples that echo this remark, one says: "The Mysterious Pearl flies to top Mount Kunlun; / Day or night the River-Carts do not stop at all 玄珠飛趁昆侖去, 晝 夜河車不暫停" (XMGZ-Taipei, p. 325). Or as a modern lexicographer has described the action: "Drawing out the lead and adding mercury, one ferries the great drug beyond the passes. All the way it is like a cart in a river's water, going upstream against the currents, until [it] is sent back to the Yellow Court 抽鉛添汞, 運大藥過關, 一路如河中車水, 逆流而上, 然後送歸黃 庭也."[169] If we puzzle over the topographic metaphor of *guan* 關, we need only consult Wang's explanation: "When the three carts move, . . . they pass the Celestial Pass to go past the lower Double Passes of *Shen* and *Yu*, two anastomotic loci. The Double Pass is the spine ridge 三車行時, . . . 過天關, 過下雙關腎俞二穴, . . . 雙關, 夾脊是也."[170]

With those key depictions, the narration of XYJ's chapter 44 suddenly takes on meaning beyond matter-of-fact realism: "Pilgrim lowered his cloud gradually to take a closer look. Aha! The cart was loaded with bricks, tiles, . . . and the like. The ridge was exceedingly tall, and leading up to it was a small, spine-like path flanked by two vertical passes, with walls like two giant cliffs. How could the cart be dragged up there 行者漸漸按下雲頭來看處, 呀! 那 車子裝的都是磚瓦...之類. 灘頭上坡阪最高; 又有一道夾脊小路, 兩座大 關, 關下路都是直立壁陡之崖, 那車兒怎麼曳得上去?" (XYJ, p. 406).

After Monkey had slain the two Daoists who were party to the persecution of the monks, he walked up to the sandy beach and, "exerting his magic power, yanked the cart through the two passes and up the spine ridge before picking it up and smashing it to pieces 使個神通, 將車兒曳過雙關, 穿過夾脊, 提起來摔得粉碎." Apart from the sociopolitical theme that is prominent in this entire episode, it is impossible to overlook the allegory when we consider both the novelistic narrative and the technical Daoist terms and figures of speech so pervasively employed.

There is one more final twist on this emergence of allegorical language appropriated from Daoist texts that has escaped critical attention. Daoists themselves display sophisticated awareness when they resort to the figures of topography and laboratory to depict the materials and methods of outer or inner alchemy. With admirable succinctness, the twelfth-century text

FIG. 4 The Double Passes (*shuang guan*). This diagram is reproduced from TC 2: 717. The Chinese inscription of two graphs to the left reads *piyu* 譬喻, often translated as "metaphor" but literally, the term can mean analogous symbolism.[171]

Jindan zhizhi 金丹直指 by Zhou Wusuo 周無所 declares that "the furnace and the reaction-vessel will be likened to by means of a human body 爐鼎以身譬者, and the drugs will be symbolized by the precious substances of bodily organs 藥物以心中之寶喻之."[172]

The diagram of the human body cavity as topography referred to in

Schipper and Verellen's *The Taoist Canon* (TC) cited earlier carries the label "analogous illustration or symbolism, *piyu* 譬喻." The crucial term in this context is, of course, the word *pi*, meaning to inform (*gao* 告), to liken, to compare, to illustrate, or to suppose, and it is often translated as a simile or metaphor in modern usages. Historically, the word has played a sustained and hugely important role in Chinese linguistics and language philosophy, ranging from being one of the six foundational principles of the Chinese graph (e.g., *qupi* 取譬) formulated by the ancient lexicologist Xu Shen (fl. 100 CE), through interaction with medieval Buddhism to assume the translated name of analogy or *Avadāna*—the eighth of the twelve divisions of the Mahāyana canon—to appearing in numerous titles on rhetoric by Chinese authors secular or religious, and finally, to even theological treatises on analogy by early modern Jesuit missionaries in China.[173] One unnoticed example of this word's munificent suggestiveness across the centuries occurs at the very beginning of the 1754 version of *The Story of the Stone*: "*Story of the Stone* is what likens itself to what the Stone had recorded as events 石頭記是自譬石頭所記之事也."[174] The intriguing implications of so pithy an assertion of metaphorical representation for understanding fiction in China have yet to be fathomed.

Finally, we are prepared to see how religion and literature converge in the making of the journey's fiction, all without a trace of didacticism or proselytism. The fiction of XYJ is built upon a fundamental irony: it not only freely altered the historical account of a Buddhist cleric's ineradicable acts of devotion to his faith but also transformed its meaning by means of linguistic signs massively appropriated from other religious traditions.[175] This act of fiction-making is analogous to scouring Islamic concepts and terms from the Koran to make a new Milton's *Paradise Lost* or Dante's *Commedia*! The wonder is that the Chinese novel has stitched so seamlessly a fabric of three religions that remained in tension (and occasionally in serious conflict) with one another down through history. The company of five pilgrims, on the other hand, does not merely become a harmonious community at the end; throughout the narrative, it also evolves steadily into different aspects of a single person in his development toward some form of psychic and physiological integration.

In a previous essay, I had observed how the five pilgrims as some aspects of the human self interacting and traveling within a physical body might "conjure up the rather bizarre image" similar to "the diminished figures of Issac Asimov's *Fantastic Voyage* coursing through the bloodstream."[176] I hardly expected in 1982 that my little comparison would have been anticipated four centuries ago by these words of a precious scroll text, the *Qingyuan Miaodao Xiansheng Zhenjun Yiliao Zhenren huguo youmin zhongxiao Erlang Baojuan* 清源妙道顯聖一了真人護國佑民忠孝二郎寶卷:

[The pilgrims] *Walking forward,*
Dash toward Thunder-Clap.
Persons and horse make up these five monks.
The Tang Monk follows the Horse of the Will,
While Mind Monkey is our Sun Wukong.
Zhu Eight Rules—
Essence, breath, and spirit;
Sha Monk, the xue *vessels [xuemai 血脈],*[177] *course through the whole*
  body. . . .
Analogic words of the Tang Monk will never leave his person 望前走, 奔雷
  音, 連人帶馬五眾僧. 唐僧隨著意馬走, 心猿就是孫悟空. 豬八戒, 精
  氣神; 沙僧血脈遍身通. . . . 唐僧譬語不離身.[178]

As the scripture-seeking story evolves from the Song to the Ming, the
trend becomes stronger to interpret the pilgrims and their experience as
imagistic embodiment, enactment, and synthesis of philosophical and religious abstractions that also exist as mutual glosses. Not only might the
XYJ author be a Confucian scholar, as Lu Xun has observed, but the principal human protagonist in Tripitaka must also be even more of one who
is at the same time on his way to becoming a Daoist adept and an enlightened Buddhist priest, much as the Monkey of the Mind will progressively
become Tripitaka's own true mind even when the disciple figure at the end
will be transformed into a realized immortal (*zhenxian*), acquiring simultaneously the title, Buddha Victorious in Strife.

The hundred-chapter novel's hermeneutics of deliberate integration
has sparked and sustained authorial creativity to imagine, in the most
ingenious and unprecedented ways, the malleable fluidity of linguistic
meaning. This is the sign of the greatest allegorical literature, for fiction is
literally generated by the figuration of language. The late literary compara-
tivist Paul de Man has written on the "allegorical dimension" as constitut-
ing "the real depth of literary insight" in "the work of all genuine writers"
by citing the famous lines from "Le Cygne" in *Les fluers du mal*, by French
modernist poet Charles Baudelaire,[179]

[N]*ew palaces and scaffoldings, new blocks,*
Old suburbs, all become for me an allegory.

Such lines expressive of the "poetic state of mind" in Western writings,
however, may bear an even truer semblance to "the inner landscape" described and celebrated in Daoist writings. According to Kristofer Schipper,
the eminent authority on Daoism, "'the body is a country' . . . with mountains and rivers, ponds, forests, paths and barriers, a whole landscape laid
out with dwellings, palaces, towers, walls, and gates sheltering a vast popu-

lation."[180] Schipper's words, of course, are based on the striking series of similes drawn by the Daoist Ge Hong of early medieval times:

> Thus the body of a person is the image of a state: the locales of chest and abdomen are like palaces and halls; the order of the four limbs is like the settings of suburbs; the separation into bones and joints is like the hundred officials. Spirit is similar to a ruler, blood is similar to subjects, and the pneumatic vitality is similar to the people. Therefore, if one knows how to govern the body, one will know how to govern a state 故一人之身, 一國之象也. 胸腹之位, 猶宮室也. 四肢之列, 猶郊境也. 骨節之分, 猶百官也. 神猶君也. 血猶臣也. 氣猶民也. 故知治身則能治國也.[181]

In view of this predilection for analogy found in Daoist discourse, the novel's tendency may seem to surpass even its religious sources on the multiplication of metaphors: for if the Daoist visualization (neiguan 內觀) of the human body's interior can come to expression only in allegorical language as the Kunlun Peak 昆侖頂, the Mount of Jade Capital 玉京山, the Mansion of Blue Tenuity 青虛府, the City of Purple Gold 紫金城, and so forth,[182] the art of *The Journey to the West* is to make sport of such allegory by making more allegory. After all, Daoist writings abundantly exploit this practice of seemingly unbridled extension of signs. One example can be found in the XMGZ-Taipei, p. 340:

> Thus [an authority] says, "One thing divides into two, and one can know the things's two names." But the elixir scriptures dare not leak out the names of these two things. That is why there are many types of cunning symbols—a myriad words and a thousand names—innumerable indeed. Take, for example, when one speaks of the nature of one's head, the metaphor may be mercury, dragon, fire, root, sun, soul, the li-trigram [☲], the qian-trigram [☰], the ji-celestial stem, heaven, ruler, emptiness, hare, nothingness, lord, floating, vermilion, an island rising from the sea, a fair girl, and Mount Kunlun 故.... 云: 『一物分為二, 能知二者名』. 這二者之名, 丹經不敢漏洩; 巧喻多端, 萬字千名, 不可勝計. 如論頂中之性者, 喻之曰: 汞也, 龍也, 火也, 根也, 日也, 魂也, 離也, 乾也, 己也, 天也, 君也, 虛也, 兔也, 無也, 主也, 浮也, 朱砂也, 浮桑也, 妊女也, 昆侖也.

Such an antinomian view of referentiality may outrage Confucians insistent on the rectification of names, but it may also gladden the heart of even a jaded contemporary poststructuralist. According to the German thinker Walter Benjamin, the figurative descriptions in metaphor and allegory indicate "precisely the non-being of what [they] represent."[183] Benjamin's judgment is validated by our Chinese novel's persistent and pervasive practice that allegorizes further its own selected language and diction to produce plots, characters, events, experiences, and reflexive commentaries of literary fiction. Thus the "double passes (*shuangguan*)" and "interlocking ridge (*jiaji*)" envisaged in the Daoist spinal column generated an intricate tale of bitter contests between Buddhists and Daoists, revealing the difficulties and dangers of error in both method and material confronting the self-cultivating alchemist. The chain of signs in the series of association and correlation can be nearly endless, as lengthy and magnificent as the imagined pilgrimage from China to India to fetch scriptures.

For more than a couple of generations of Chinese critics, Lu Xun's classification of the *Xiyouji* as the chef-d'oeuvre among the novels of gods and demons (*shenmo xiaoshuo*) had served as a normative designation, to which the first professional translator of this novel into English, Arthur Waley, had also added his own understanding:

> [T]he idea that the hierarchy in Heaven is a replica of government on earth is an accepted one in China. Here as so often the Chinese let the cat out of the bag, where other countries leave us guessing. It has often enough been put forward as a theory that a people's gods are the replica of its earthly rulers. In most cases the derivation is obscure. But in Chinese popular belief there is no ambiguity. Heaven is simply the whole bureaucratic system transferred bodily to the empyrean.[184]

To this reasonable but somewhat simplistic affirmation of Durkheimian collectivity, Hamlet's words on Shakespeare's stage sound a needed caveat: "There are more things in heaven and earth, Horatio, / Than are dreamt of in our philosophy." As this analysis of parts of the novel hopes to make clear, passage between earth and the empyrean flows through a course of two-way traffic. Another cat escaping from our Chinese bag reveals that the celestial and the cosmic—indeed, the divine and the demonic—may be transferred just as readily back to the firmly terrestrial, to the somatic aspects of the body and the intensely human self.

"The Bodhisattva and the monster," to recall Guanyin's words to her monkey disciple in chapter 17 of the novel, "both exist in a single thought. Considered in terms of their origin, they are all nothing." "Nothing will come of nothing," rages King Lear famously to his hapless Cordelia, but Shakespeare, their creator, knows differently when he "gives to airy nothing / A local habitation and a name" (A Midsummer-Night's Dream 5.1. 16-17). So does a contemporary novelist when she asserts that "the triumph over nothingness that art represents is assured of a future beyond even our ability to imagine. We acclaim the marvelous in ourselves."[185] Such triumph, too, finds magnificent representation in the enduring art of *The Journey to the West*.

西游记

ONE

The divine root conceives, its source revealed;
Mind and nature nurtured, the Great Dao is born.

The poem says:

> *Ere Chaos's divide, with Heav'n and Earth a mess,*
> *No human appeared in this murkiness.*
> *When Pan Gu broke the nebula apart,*[1]
> *The dense and pure defined, did clearing start.*
> *Enfold all life supreme humaneness would*
> *And teach all things how become good they should.*
> *To know cyclic time's work, if that's your quest,*
> *Read* Tale of Woes Dispelled on Journey West.[2]

We heard that, in the order of Heaven and Earth, a single period consisted of 129,600 years. Dividing this period into twelve epochs were the twelve stems of Zi, Chou, Yin, Mao, Chen, Si, Wu, Wei, Shen, Yu, Xu, and Hai, with each epoch having 10,800 years. Considered as the horary circle, the sequence would be thus: the first sign of dawn appears in the hour of Zi, while at Chou the cock crows; daybreak occurs at Yin, and the sun rises at Mao; Chen comes after breakfast, and by Si everything is planned; at Wu the sun arrives at its meridian, and it declines westward by Wei; the evening meal comes during the hour of Shen, and the sun sinks completely at Yu; twilight sets in at Xu, and people rest by the hour of Hai. This sequence may also be understood macrocosmically. At the end of the epoch of Xu, Heaven and Earth were obscure and all things were indistinct. With the passing of 5,400 years, the beginning of Hai was the epoch of darkness. This moment was named Chaos, because there were neither human beings nor the two spheres. After another 5,400 years Hai ended, and as the creative force began to work after great perseverance, the epoch of Zi drew near and again brought gradual development. Shao Kangjie[3] said:

> *When to the middle of Zi winter moved,*
> *No change by Heaven's mind had been approved.*
> *The male principle had but barely stirred,*
> *But the birth of all things was still deferred.*

At this point, the firmament first acquired its foundation. With another 5,400 years came the Zi epoch; the ethereal and the light rose up to form the four phenomena of the sun, the moon, the stars, and the Heavenly bodies. Hence it is said, the Heaven was created at Zi. This epoch came to its end in another 5,400 years, and the sky began to harden as the Chou epoch approached. The *Classic of Change* said:

Great was the male principle;
Supreme, the female!
They made all things,
In obedience to Heaven.

At this point, the Earth became solidified. In another 5,400 years after the arrival of the Chou epoch, the heavy and the turbid condensed below and formed the five elements of water, fire, mountain, stone, and earth. Hence it is said, the Earth was created at Chou. With the passing of another 5,400 years, the Chou epoch came to its end and all things began to grow at the beginning of the Yin epoch. The *Book of Calendar* said:

The Heavenly aura descended;
The earthly aura rose up.
Heaven and Earth copulated,
And all things were born.

At this point, Heaven and Earth were bright and fair; the yin had intercourse with the yang. In another 5,400 years, during the Yin epoch, humans, beasts, and fowls came into being, and thus the so-called three forces of Heaven, Earth, and Man were established. Hence it is said, man was born at Yin.

Following Pan Gu's construction of the universe, the rule of the Three August Ones, and the ordering of the relations by the Five Thearchs,[4] the world was divided into four great continents. They were: the East Pūrvavideha Continent, the West Aparagodānīya Continent, the South Jambūdvīpa Continent, and the North Uttarakuru Continent. This book is solely concerned with the East Pūrvavideha Continent.[5]

Beyond the ocean there was a country named Aolai. It was near a great ocean, in the midst of which was located the famous Flower-Fruit Mountain. This mountain, which constituted the chief range of the Ten Islets and formed the origin of the Three Islands,[6] came into being after the creation of the world. As a testimonial to its magnificence, there is the following poetic rhapsody:

Its majesty commands the wide ocean;
Its splendor rules the jasper sea;
Its majesty commands the wide ocean
When, like silver mountains, the tide sweeps fishes into caves;
Its splendor rules the jasper sea

When snowlike billows send forth serpents from the deep.
On the southwest side pile up tall plateaus;
From the Eastern Sea arise soaring peaks.
There are crimson ridges and portentous rocks,
Precipitous cliffs and prodigious peaks.
Atop the crimson ridges
Phoenixes sing in pairs:
Before precipitous cliffs
The unicorn singly rests.
At the summit is heard the cry of golden pheasants;
In and out of stony caves are seen the strides of dragons:
In the forest are long-lived deer and immortal foxes.
On the trees are divine fowls and black cranes.
Strange grass and flowers never wither:
Green pines and cypresses always keep their spring.
Immortal peaches are ever fruit-bearing;
Lofty bamboos often detain the clouds.
Within a single gorge the creeping vines are dense;
The grass color of meadows all around is fresh.
This is indeed the pillar of Heaven, where a hundred rivers meet—
The Earth's great axis, in ten thousand kalpas unchanged.

There was on top of that very mountain an immortal stone, which measured thirty-six feet and five inches in height and twenty-four feet in circumference. The height of thirty-six feet and five inches corresponded to the three hundred and sixty-five cyclical degrees, while the circumference of twenty-four feet corresponded to the twenty-four solar terms of the calendar.[7] On the stone were also nine perforations and eight holes, which corresponded to the Palaces of the Nine Constellations and the Eight Trigrams. Though it lacked the shade of trees on all sides, it was set off by epidendrums on the left and right. Since the creation of the world, it had been nourished for a long period by the seeds of Heaven and Earth and by the essences of the sun and the moon, until, quickened by divine inspiration, it became pregnant with a divine embryo. One day, it split open, giving birth to a stone egg about the size of a playing ball. Exposed to the wind, it was transformed into a stone monkey endowed with fully developed features and limbs. Having learned at once to climb and run, this monkey also bowed to the four quarters, while two beams of golden light flashed from his eyes to reach even the Palace of the Polestar. The light disturbed the Great Benevolent Sage of Heaven, the Celestial Jade Emperor of the Most Venerable Deva, who, attended by his divine ministers, was sitting in the Cloud Palace of the Golden Arches, in the Treasure Hall of the

Divine Mists. Upon seeing the glimmer of the golden beams, he ordered Thousand-Mile Eye and Fair-Wind Ear to open the South Heaven Gate and to look out. At this command the two captains went out to the gate, and, having looked intently and listened clearly, they returned presently to report, "Your subjects, obeying your command to locate the beams, discovered that they came from the Flower-Fruit Mountain at the border of the small Aolai Country, which lies to the east of the East Pūrvavideha Continent. On this mountain is an immortal stone that has given birth to an egg. Exposed to the wind, it has been transformed into a monkey, who, when bowing to the four quarters, has flashed from his eyes those golden beams that reached the Palace of the Polestar. Now that he is taking some food and drink, the light is about to grow dim." With compassionate mercy the Jade Emperor declared, "These creatures from the world below are born of the essences of Heaven and Earth, and they need not surprise us."

That monkey in the mountain was able to walk, run, and leap about; he fed on grass and shrubs, drank from the brooks and streams, gathered mountain flowers, and searched out fruits from trees. He made his companions the tiger and the lizard, the wolf and the leopard; he befriended the civet and the deer, and he called the gibbon and the baboon his kin. At night he slept beneath stony ridges, and in the morning he sauntered about the caves and the peaks. Truly,

> In the mountain there is no passing of time;
> The cold recedes, but one knows not the year.[8]

One very hot morning, he was playing with a group of monkeys under the shade of some pine trees to escape the heat. Look at them, each amusing himself in his own way by

> Swinging from branches to branches,
> Searching for flowers and fruits;
> They played two games or three
> With pebbles and with pellets;
> They circled sandy pits;
> They built rare pagodas;
> They chased the dragonflies;
> They ran down small lizards;
> Bowing low to the sky,
> They worshiped Bodhisattvas;
> They pulled the creeping vines;
> They plaited mats with grass;
> They searched to catch the louse
> That they bit or sqeezed to death;

They dressed their furry coats;
They scraped their fingernails;
Those leaning leaned;
Those rubbing rubbed;
Those pushing pushed;
Those pressing pressed;
Those pulling pulled;
Those tugging tugged.
Beneath the pine forest and free to play,
They washed themselves in the green-water stream.

So, after the monkeys had frolicked for a while, they went to bathe in the mountain stream and saw that its currents bounced and splashed like tumbling melons. As the old saying goes,

Fowls have their fowl speech,
And beasts have their beast language.

The monkeys said to each other, "We don't know where this water comes from. Since we have nothing to do today, let us follow the stream up to its source to have some fun." With a shriek of joy, they dragged along males and females, calling out to brothers and sisters, and scrambled up the mountain alongside the stream. Reaching its source, they found a great waterfall. What they saw was

A column of white rainbows rising,
A thousand yards of snow-caps flying.
The sea wind blows but cannot sever
What a river moon lights up forever.
Its cold breath divides the green glades;
Its branches wet the verdant shades.
This torrent named a waterfall
Seems like a curtain hanging tall.

All the monkeys clapped their hands in acclaim: "Marvelous water! Marvelous water! So this waterfall is distantly connected with the stream at the base of the mountain, and flows directly out, even to the great ocean." They said also, "If any of us had the ability to penetrate the curtain and find out where the water comes from without hurting himself, we would honor him as king." They gave the call three times, when suddenly the stone monkey leaped out from the crowd. He answered the challenge with a loud voice, "I'll go in! I'll go in!" What a monkey! For

Today his fame will spread wide.
His fortune the time does provide.

He's fated to live in this place,
Sent by a king to god's palace.

Look at him! He closed his eyes, crouched low, and with one leap he jumped straight through the waterfall. Opening his eyes at once and raising his head to look around, he saw that there was neither water nor waves inside, only a gleaming, shining bridge. He paused to collect himself and looked more carefully again: it was a bridge made of sheet iron. The water beneath it surged through a hole in the rock to reach the outside, filling in all the space under the arch. With bent body he climbed on the bridge, looking about as he walked, and discovered a beautiful place that seemed to be some kind of residence. Then he saw

Fresh mosses piling up indigo,
White clouds like jade afloat,
And luminous sheens of mist and smoke;
Empty windows, quiet rooms,
And carved flowers growing smoothly on benches;
Stalactites suspended in milky caves;
Rare blossoms voluminous over the ground.
Pans and stoves near the wall show traces of fire;
Bottles and cups on the table contain leftovers.
The stone seats and beds were truly lovable;
The stone pots and bowls were more praiseworthy.
There were, furthermore, a stalk or two of tall bamboos,
And three or five sprigs of plum flowers.
With a few green pines always draped in rain,
This whole place indeed resembled a home.

After staring at the place for a long time, he jumped across the middle of the bridge and looked left and right. There in the middle was a stone tablet on which was inscribed in regular, large letters:

The Blessed Land of Flower-Fruit Mountain,
The Cave Heaven of Water-Curtain Cave.[9]

Beside himself with delight, the stone monkey quickly turned around to go back out and, closing his eyes and crouching again, leaped out of the water. "A great stroke of luck," he exclaimed with two loud guffaws, "a great stroke of luck!"

The other monkeys surrounded him and asked, "How is it inside? How deep is the water?" The stone monkey replied, "There isn't any water at all. There's a sheet iron bridge, and beyond it is a piece of Heaven-sent property."

"What do you mean that there's property in there?" asked the monkeys.

Laughing, the stone monkey said, "This water splashes through a hole in the rock and fills the space under the bridge. Beside the bridge there is a stone mansion with trees and flowers. Inside are stone ovens and stoves, stone pots and pans, stone beds and benches. A stone tablet in the middle has the inscription,

> The Blessed Land of the Flower-Fruit Mountain,
> The Cave Heaven of the Water-Curtain Cave.

This is truly the place for us to settle in. It is, moreover, very spacious inside and can hold thousands of the young and old. Let's all go live in there, and spare ourselves from being subject to the whims of Heaven. For we have in there

> A retreat from the wind,
> A shelter from the rain.
> You fear no frost or snow;
> You hear no thunderclap.
> Mist and smoke are brightened,
> Warmed by a holy light—
> The pines are evergreen:
> Rare flowers, daily new."

When the monkeys heard that, they were delighted, saying, "You go in first and lead the way." The stone monkey closed his eyes again, crouched low, and jumped inside. "All of you," he cried, "Follow me in! Follow me in!" The braver of the monkeys leaped in at once, but the more timid ones stuck out their heads and then drew them back, scratched their ears, rubbed their jaws, and chattered noisily. After milling around for some time, they too bounded inside. Jumping across the bridge, they were all soon snatching dishes, clutching bowls, or fighting for stoves and beds—shoving and pushing things hither and thither. Befitting their stubbornly prankish nature, the monkeys could not keep still for a moment and stopped only when they were utterly exhausted.

The stone monkey then solemnly took a seat above and spoke to them: "Gentlemen! 'If a man lacks trustworthiness, it is difficult to know what he can accomplish!'[10] You yourselves promised just now that whoever could get in here and leave again without hurting himself would be honored as king. Now that I have come in and gone out, gone out and come in, and have found for all of you this Heavenly grotto in which you may reside securely and enjoy the privilege of raising a family, why don't you honor me as your king?" When the monkeys heard this, they all folded their hands on their breasts and obediently prostrated themselves. Each one of them then lined up according to rank and age, and, bowing reverently, they intoned, "Long live our great king!" From that moment, the stone monkey ascended the throne of kingship. He did away with the word "stone" in his name and assumed the title, Handsome Monkey King. There is a testimonial poem that says:

> Triple spring mated to beget all things.
> A divine stone quickened by the sun and moon
> Changed from egg to ape to reach the Great Way.
> Loanname and surname[11] matched elixir made.
> Formless inside he yields no image known;
> His outward guise coheres in action shown.
> In every age all persons will yield to him:
> Hailed a king, a sage, he is free to roam.

The Handsome Monkey King thus led a flock of gibbons and baboons, some of whom were appointed by him as his officers and ministers. They toured the Flower-Fruit Mountain in the morning, and they lived in the Water-Curtain Cave by night. Living in concord and sympathy, they did not mingle with bird or beast but enjoyed their independence in perfect happiness. For such were their activities:

> In the spring they gathered flowers for food and drink.
> In the summer they went in quest of fruits for sustenance.
> In the autumn they amassed taros and chestnuts to ward off time.
> In the winter they searched for yellow-sperms[12] to live out the year.

The Handsome Monkey King had enjoyed this insouciant existence for three or four hundred years when one day, while feasting with the rest of the monkeys, he suddenly grew sad and shed a few tears. Alarmed, the monkeys surrounding him bowed down and asked, "What is disturbing the Great King?" The Monkey King replied, "Though I am very happy at the moment, I am a little concerned about the future. Hence I'm distressed." The monkeys all laughed and said, "The Great King indeed does not know contentment! Here we daily have a banquet on an immortal mountain in a blessed land, in an ancient cave on a divine continent. We are not subject to the unicorn or the phoenix, nor are we governed by the rulers of mankind. Such independence and comfort are immeasurable blessings. Why, then, does he worry about the future?" The Monkey King said, "Though we are not subject to the laws of man today, nor need we be threatened by the rule of any bird or beast, old age and physical decay in the future will disclose the secret sovereignty of Yama, King of the Underworld. If we die, shall we not have lived in vain, not being able to rank forever among the Heavenly beings?"

When the monkeys heard this, they all covered their faces and wept mournfully, each one troubled by his own impermanence. But look! From among the ranks a bareback monkey suddenly leaped forth and cried aloud, "If the Great King is so farsighted, it may well indicate the sprouting of his religious inclination. There are, among the five major divisions of all living creatures,[13] only three species that are not subject to Yama, King of the Underworld." The Monkey King said, "Do you know who they are?" The monkey said, "They are the Buddhas, the immortals, and the holy sages; these three alone can avoid the Wheel of Transmigration as well as the process of birth and destruction, and live as long as Heaven and Earth, the mountains and the streams." "Where do they live?" asked the Monkey King. The monkey said, "They do not live beyond the world of the Jambūdvīpa, for they dwell within ancient caves on immortal mountains." When the Monkey King heard this, he was filled with delight, saying, "Tomorrow I shall take leave of you all and go down the mountain. Even if I have to wander with the clouds to the corners of the sea or journey to the distant edges of Heaven, I intend to find these three kinds of people. I will learn from them how to be young forever and escape the calamity inflicted by King Yama."

> Lo, this utterance at once led him
> To leap free of the Transmigration Net,
> And be the Great Sage, Equal to Heaven.

All the monkeys clapped their hands in acclamation, saying, "Wonderful! Wonderful! Tomorrow we shall scour the mountain ranges to gather plenty of fruits, so that we may send the Great King off with a great banquet."

Next day the monkeys duly went to gather immortal peaches, to pick rare fruits, to dig out mountain herbs, and to chop yellow-sperms. They brought in an orderly manner every variety of orchids and epidendrums, exotic plants and strange flowers. They set out the stone chairs and stone tables, covering the tables with immortal wines and food. Look at the

> Golden balls and pearly pellets,
> Red ripeness and yellow plumpness.
> Golden balls and pearly pellets are the cherries,
> Their colors truly luscious.
> Red ripeness and yellow plumpness are the plums,
> Their taste—a fragrant tartness.
> Fresh lungans
> Of sweet pulps and thin skins.
> Fiery lychees
> Of small pits and red sacks.

Green fruits of the Pyrus are presented by the branches.
The loquats yellow with buds are held with their leaves.
Pears like rabbit heads and dates like chicken hearts
Dispel your thirst, your sorrow, and the effects of wine.
Fragrant peaches and soft almonds
Are sweet as the elixir of life:
Crisply fresh plums and strawberries
Are sour like cheese and buttermilk.
Red pulps and black seeds compose the ripe watermelons.
Four cloves of yellow rind enfold the big persimmons.
When the pomegranates are split wide,
Cinnabar grains glisten like specks of ruby:
When the chestnuts are cracked open,
Their tough brawns are hard like cornelian.
Walnut and silver almonds fare well with tea.
Coconuts and grapes may be pressed into wine.
Hazelnuts, yews, and crabapples overfill the dishes.
Kumquats, sugarcanes, tangerines, and oranges crowd the tables.
Sweet yams are baked,
Yellow-sperms overboiled,
The tubers minced with seeds of waterlily,
And soup in stone pots simmers on a gentle fire.
Mankind may boast its delicious dainties,
But what can best the pleasure of mountain monkeys.

The monkeys honored the Monkey King with the seat at the head of the table, while they sat below according to their age and rank. They drank for a whole day, each of the monkeys taking a turn to go forward and present the Monkey King with wine, flowers, and fruits. The next day the Monkey King rose early and gave the instruction, "Little ones, cut me some pine-wood and make me a raft. Then find me a bamboo for the pole, and gather some fruits and the like. I'm about to leave." When all was ready, he got onto the raft by himself. Pushing off with all his might, he drifted out toward the great ocean and, taking advantage of the wind, set sail for the border of South Jambūdvīpa Continent. Here is the consequence of this journey:

The Heaven-born monkey, strong in magic might,
He left the mount and rode the raft to catch fair wind:
He drifted across the sea to seek immortals' way,
Determined in heart and mind to achieve great things.
It's his lot, his portion, to quit earthly zeals:
Calm and carefree, he'll face a lofty sage.

He'd meet, I think, a true, discerning friend:
The source disclosed, all dharma will be known.

It was indeed his fortune that, after he boarded the wooden raft, a strong southeast wind (which lasted for days) sent him to the northwestern coast, the border of the South Jambūdvīpa Continent. He took the pole to test the water, and, finding it shallow one day, he abandoned the raft and jumped ashore. On the beach there were people fishing, hunting wild geese, digging clams, and draining salt. He approached them and, making a weird face and some strange antics, he scared them into dropping their baskets and nets and scattering in all directions. One of them could not run and was caught by the Monkey King, who stripped him of his clothes and put them on himself, aping the way humans wore them. With a swagger he walked through counties and prefectures, imitating human speech and human manners in the marketplaces. He rested by night and dined in the morning, but he was bent on finding the way of the Buddhas, immortals, and holy sages, on discovering the formula for eternal youth. He saw, however, that the people of the world were all seekers after profit and fame; there was not one who showed concern for his appointed end. This is their condition:

When will end this quest for fortune and fame,
This tyrant of early rising and retiring late?
Riding on mules they long for noble steeds;
By now prime ministers, they hope to be kings.
For food and raiment they suffer stress and strain,
Never fearing Yama's call to reckoning.
Seeking wealth and power to give to sons of sons,
There's not one ever willing to turn back.

The Monkey King searched diligently for the way of immortality, but he had no chance of meeting it. Going through big cities and visiting small towns, he unwittingly spent eight or nine years on the South Jambūdvīpa Continent before he suddenly came upon the Great Western Ocean. He thought that there would certainly be immortals living beyond the ocean; so, having built himself a raft like the previous one, he once again drifted across the Western Ocean until he reached the West Aparagodānīya Continent. After landing, he searched for a long time, when all at once he came upon a tall and beautiful mountain with thick forests at its base. Since he was afraid neither of wolves and lizards nor of tigers and leopards, he went straight to the top to look around. It was indeed a magnificent mountain:

A thousand peaks stand like rows of spears,
Like ten thousand cubits of screen widespread.

The sun's beams lightly enclose the azure mist;
In darkening rain, the mount's color turns cool and green.
Dry creepers entwine old trees;
Ancient fords edge secluded paths.
Rare flowers and luxuriant grass.
Tall bamboos and lofty pines.
Tall bamboos and lofty pines
For ten thousand years grow green in this blessed land.
Rare flowers and luxuriant grass
In all seasons bloom as in the Isles of the Blest.
The calls of birds hidden are near.
The sounds of streams rushing are clear.
Deep inside deep canyons the orchids interweave.
On every ridge and crag sprout lichens and mosses.
Rising and falling, the ranges show a fine dragon's pulse.[14]
Here in reclusion must an eminent man reside.

As he was looking about, he suddenly heard the sound of a man speaking deep within the woods. Hurriedly he dashed into the forest and cocked his ear to listen. It was someone singing, and the song went thus:

I watch chess games, my ax handle's rotted.[15]
I chop at wood, zheng zheng the sound.
I walk slowly by the cloud's fringe at the valley's entrance.
Selling my firewood to buy some wine,
I am happy and laugh without restraint.
When the path is frosted in autumn's height,
I face the moon, my pillow the pine root.
Sleeping till dawn
I find my familiar woods.
I climb the plateaus and scale the peaks
To cut dry creepers with my ax.

When I gather enough to make a load,
I stroll singing through the marketplace
And trade it for three pints of rice,
With nary the slightest bickering
Over a price so modest.
Plots and schemes I do not know;
Without vainglory or attaint
My life's prolonged in simplicity.
Those I meet,
If not immortals, would be Daoists,
Seated quietly to expound the Yellow Court.

When the Handsome Monkey King heard this, he was filled with delight, saying, "So the immortals are hiding in this place." He leaped at once into the forest. Looking again carefully, he found a woodcutter chopping firewood with his ax. The man he saw was very strangely attired.

> On his head he wore a wide splint hat
> Of seed-leaves freshly cast from new bamboos.
> On his body he wore a cloth garment
> Of gauze woven from the native cotton.
> Around his waist he tied a winding sash
> Of silk spun from an old silkworm.
> On his feet he had a pair of straw sandals,
> With laces rolled from withered sedge.
> In his hands he held a fine steel ax;
> A sturdy rope coiled round and round his load.
> In breaking pines or chopping trees
> Where's the man to equal him?

The Monkey King drew near and called out: "Reverend immortal! Your disciple raises his hands." The woodcutter was so flustered that he dropped his ax as he turned to return the salutation. "Blasphemy! Blasphemy!" he said. "I, a foolish fellow with hardly enough clothes or food! How can I bear the title of immortal?" The Monkey King said, "If you are not an immortal, how is it that you speak his language?" The woodcutter asked, "What did I say that sounded like the language of an immortal?" The Monkey King explained, "When I came just now to the forest's edge, I heard you singing, 'Those I meet, if not immortals, would be Daoists, seated quietly to expound the *Yellow Court*.' The *Yellow Court* contains the perfected words of the Way and Virtue. What can you be but an immortal?"

Laughing, the woodcutter said, "I can tell you this much: the tune of that lyric is named 'A Court Full of Blossoms,' and it was taught to me by an immortal, a neighbor of mine. He saw that I had to struggle to make a living and that my days were full of worries, so he told me to recite the poem whenever I was troubled. This, he said, would both comfort me and rid me of my difficulties. It happened that I was anxious about something just now, so I sang the song. It didn't occur to me that I would be overheard."

The Monkey King said, "If you are a neighbor of the immortal, why don't you follow him in the cultivation of the Way? Wouldn't it be nice to learn from him the formula for eternal youth?" The woodcutter replied, "My lot has been a hard one all my life. When I was young, I was indebted to my parents' nurture until I was eight or nine. As soon as I began to have some understanding of human affairs, my father unfortunately died, and my mother remained a widow. I had no brothers or sisters, so there was no alternative but for me alone to support and care for my mother. Now that my mother is growing old, all the more I dare not leave her. Moreover, my fields are rather barren and desolate, and we haven't enough food or clothing. I can't do more than chop two bundles of firewood to take to the market in exchange for a few pennies to buy a few pints of rice. I cook that myself, serving it to my mother with the tea that I make. That's why I can't practice austerities."

The Monkey King said, "According to what you have said, you are indeed a gentleman of filial piety, and you will certainly be rewarded in the future. I hope, however, that you will show me the way to the immortal's abode, so that I may reverently call upon him." "It's not far," the woodcutter said. "This mountain is called the Mountain of Mind and Heart, and in it is the Cave of Slanting Moon and Three Stars. Inside the cave is an immortal by the name of the Patriarch Subodhi, who has already sent out innumerable disciples. Even now there are thirty or forty persons who are practicing austerities with him. Follow this narrow path and travel south for about seven or eight miles, and you will come to his home." Grabbing the woodcutter, the Monkey King said, "Honored brother, go with me. If I receive any benefit, I will not forget the favor of your guidance." "What a boneheaded fellow you are!" the woodcutter said. "I have just finished telling you these things, and you still don't understand. If I go with you, won't I be neglecting my livelihood? And who will take care of my mother? I must chop my firewood. You go on by yourself!"

When the Monkey King heard this, he had to take his leave. Emerging from the deep forest, he found the path and went past the slope of a hill. After he had traveled seven or eight miles, a cave dwelling indeed came into sight. He stood up straight to take a better look at this splendid place, and this was what he saw:

> Mist and smoke in diffusive brilliance,
> Flashing lights from the sun and moon,
> A thousand stalks of old cypress,
> Ten thousand stems of tall bamboo.
> A thousand stalks of old cypress
> Draped in rain half fill the air with tender green;
> Ten thousand stems of tall bamboo
> Held in smoke will paint the glen chartreuse.
> Strange flowers spread brocades before the door.
> Jadelike grass emits fragrance beside the bridge.
> On ridges protruding grow moist green lichens;
> On hanging cliffs cling the long blue mosses.
> The cries of immortal cranes are often heard.

Once in a while a phoenix soars overhead.
When the cranes cry,
Their sounds reach through the marsh to the distant sky.
When the phoenix soars up,
Its plume with five bright colors embroiders the clouds.
Black apes and white deer may come or hide;
Gold lions and jade elephants may leave or bide.
Look with care at this blessed, holy place:
It has the true semblance of Paradise.

He noticed that the door of the cave was tightly shut; all was quiet, and there was no sign of any human inhabitant. He turned around and suddenly perceived, at the top of the cliff, a stone slab approximately eight feet wide and over thirty feet tall. On it was written in large letters:

The Mountain of Mind and Heart;
The Cave of Slanting Moon and Three Stars.

Immensely pleased, the Handsome Monkey King exclaimed, "People here are truly honest. This mountain and this cave really do exist!" He stared at the place for a long time but dared not knock. Instead, he jumped onto the branch of a pine tree, picked a few pine seeds and ate them, and began to play.

After a moment he heard the door of the cave open with a squeak, and an immortal youth walked out. His bearing was exceedingly graceful; his features were highly refined. This was certainly no ordinary young mortal, for he had

His hair bound with two cords of silk,
A wide robe with two sleeves of wind.
His body and face seemed most distinct,
For visage and mind were both detached.
Long a stranger to all worldly things
He was the mountain's ageless boy.
Untainted even with a speck of dust,
He feared no havoc by the seasons wrought.

After coming through the door, the boy shouted, "Who is causing disturbance here?" With a bound the Monkey King leaped down from the tree, and went up to him bowing. "Immortal boy," he said, "I am a seeker of the way of immortality. I would never dare cause any disturbance." With a chuckle, the immortal youth asked, "Are you a seeker of the Way?" "I am indeed," answered the Monkey King. "My master at the house," the boy said, "has just left his couch to give a lecture on the platform. Before even announcing his theme, however, he told me to go out and open the door, saying, 'There is someone outside who wants to practice austerities. You may go and receive him.' It must be you, I suppose." The Monkey King said, smiling, "It is I, most assuredly!" "Follow me in then," said the boy. With solemnity the Monkey King set his clothes in order and followed the boy into the depths of the cave. They passed rows and rows of lofty towers and huge alcoves, of pearly chambers and carved arches. After walking through innumerable quiet chambers and empty studios, they finally reached the base of the green jade platform. Patriarch Subodhi was seen seated solemnly on the platform, with thirty lesser immortals standing below in rows. He was truly

> An immortal of great ken and purest mien,
> Master Subodhi, whose wondrous form of the West
> Had no end or birth by work of the Double Three.[16]
> His whole spirit and breath were with mercy filled.
> Empty, spontaneous, it could change at will,
> His Buddha-nature able to do all things.
> The same age as Heaven had his majestic frame.
> Fully tried and enlightened was this grand priest.

As soon as the Handsome Monkey King saw him, he prostrated himself and kowtowed times without number, saying, "Master! Master! I, your pupil, pay you my sincere homage." The Patriarch said, "Where do you come from? Let's hear you state clearly your name and country before you kowtow again." The Monkey King said, "Your pupil came from the Water-Curtain Cave of the Flower-Fruit Mountain, in the Aolai Country of the East Pūrvavideha Continent."

"Chase him out of here!" the Patriarch shouted. "He is nothing but a liar and a fabricator of falsehood. How can he possibly be interested in attaining enlightenment?" The Monkey King hastened to kowtow unceasingly and to say, "Your pupil's word is an honest one, without any deceit." The Patriarch said, "If you are telling the truth, how is it that you mention the East Pūrvavideha Continent? Separating that place and mine are two great oceans and the entire region of the South Jambūdvīpa Continent. How could you possibly get here?" Again kowtowing, the Monkey King said, "Your pupil drifted across the oceans and trudged through many regions for more than ten years before finding this place." The Patriarch said, "If you have come on a long journey in many stages, I'll let that pass. What is your surname (xing)?"[17] The Monkey King again replied, "I have no temper (xing). If a man rebukes me, I am not offended; if he hits me, I am not angered. In fact, I simply repay him with a ceremonial greeting and that's all. My whole life's without ill temper." "I'm not speaking of your temper," the Patriarch said. "I'm asking after the name of your parents." "I have no parents either," said the Monkey King. The Patriarch said, "If you have no parents, you must have been born from a tree." "Not from a tree," said the Monkey King, "but from a rock. I recall that there used to be an immortal stone on the Flower-Fruit Mountain. I was born the year the stone split open."

When the Patriarch heard this, he was secretly pleased, and said, "Well, evidently you have been created by Heaven and Earth. Get up and show me how you walk." Snapping erect, the Monkey King scurried around a couple of times. The Patriarch laughed and said, "Though your features are not the most attractive, you do resemble a pignolia-eating monkey (*husun*). This gives me the idea of taking a surname for you from your appearance. I intended to call you by the name *Hu*. If I drop the animal radical from this word, what's left is a compound made up of the two characters, *gu* and *yue*. *Gu* means aged and *yue* means female, but an aged female cannot reproduce. Therefore, it is better to give you the surname of *Sun*. If I drop the animal radical from this word, what we have left is the compound of *zi* and *xi*. *Zi* means a boy and *xi* means a baby, and that name exactly accords with the fundamental Doctrine of the Baby Boy. So your surname will be 'Sun.'"

When the Monkey King heard this, he was filled with delight. "Splendid! Splendid!" he cried, kowtowing, "At last I know my surname. May the master be even more gracious! Since I have received the surname, let me be given also a personal name, so that it may facilitate your calling and commanding me." The Patriarch said, "Within my tradition are twelve characters that have been used to name the pupils according to their divisions. You are one who belongs to the tenth generation." "Which twelve characters are they?" asked the Monkey King. The Patriarch replied, "They are: wide (*guang*), great (*da*), wise (*zhi*), intelligence (*hui*), true (*zhen*), conforming (*ru*), nature (*xing*), sea (*hai*), sharp (*ying*), wake-to (*wu*), complete (*yuan*), and awakening (*jue*). Your rank falls precisely on the word 'wake-to' (*wu*). You will hence be given the religious name 'Wake-to-the-Void' (*wukong*). All right?" "Splendid! Splendid!" said the Monkey King, laughing. "Henceforth I shall be called Sun Wukong." So it was that,

> At nebula's parting he had no name.
> Smashing stubborn void needs Wake-to-the-Void.

We do not know what fruit of Daoist cultivation he succeeded in attaining afterward; let's listen to the explanation in the next chapter.

TWO

Fully awoke to Bodhi's wondrous truths;
He cuts off Māra, returns to the root, and joins
*   Primal Spirit.*[1]

Now we were speaking of the Handsome Monkey King, who, having received his name, jumped about joyfully and went forward to give Subodhi his grateful salutation. The Patriarch then ordered the congregation to lead Sun Wukong outdoors and to teach him how to sprinkle water on the ground and dust, and how to speak and move with proper courtesy. The company of immortals obediently went outside with Wukong, who then bowed to his fellow students. They prepared thereafter a place in the corridor where he might sleep. Next morning he began to learn from his schoolmates the arts of language and etiquette. He discussed with them the scriptures and the doctrines; he practiced calligraphy and burned incense. Such was his daily routine. In more leisurely moments he would be sweeping the grounds or hoeing the garden, planting flowers or pruning trees, gathering firewood or lighting fires, fetching water or carrying drinks. He did not lack for whatever he needed, and thus he lived in the cave without realizing that six or seven years had slipped by. One day the Patriarch ascended the platform and took his high seat. Calling together all the immortals, he began to lecture on a great doctrine. He spoke

> *With words so florid and eloquent*
> *That gold lotus sprang up from the ground.*
> *The doctrine of three vehicles he subtly rehearsed,*[2]
> *Including even the laws' minutest tittle.*
> *The yak's-tail*[3] *waved slowly and spouted elegance:*
> *His thunderous voice moved e'en the Ninth Heaven.*
> *For a while he lectured on Dao;*
> *For a while he spoke on Chan—*
> *To harmonize the Three Parties*[4] *is a natural thing.*
> *One word's elucidation filled with truth*
> *Points to the birthless showing nature's mystery.*

Wukong, who was standing there and listening, was so pleased with the talk that he scratched his ear and rubbed his jaw. Grinning from ear to ear, he could not refrain from dancing on all fours! Suddenly the Patriarch saw this and called out to him, "Why are you madly jumping and dancing in the ranks and not listening to my lecture?" Wukong said, "Your pupil was devoutly listening to the lecture. But when I heard such wonderful things from my reverend master, I couldn't contain myself for joy and started to leap and prance about quite unconsciously. May the master forgive my sins!"

"Let me ask you," said the Patriarch, "if you comprehend these wonderful things, do you know how long you have been in this cave?" Wukong said, "Your pupil is basically feeble-minded and does not know the number of seasons. I only remember that whenever the fire burned out in the stove, I would go to the back of the mountain to gather firewood. Finding a mountainful of fine peach trees there, I have eaten my fill of peaches seven times." The Patriarch said, "That mountain is named the Ripe Peach Mountain. If you have eaten your fill seven times, I suppose it must have been seven years. What kind of Daoist art would you like to learn from me?" Wukong said, "I am dependent on the admonition of my honored teacher. Your pupil would gladly learn whatever has a smidgen of Daoist flavor."

The Patriarch said, "Within the tradition of Dao, there are three hundred and sixty heteronomous divisions, all the practices of which may result in Illumination. I don't know which division you would like to follow." "I am dependent on the will of my honored teacher," said Wukong. "Your pupil is wholeheartedly obedient." "How would it be," said the Patriarch, "if I taught you the practice of the Method division?" Wukong asked, "How would you explain the practice of the Method division?" "The practice of the Method division," said the Patriarch, "consists of summoning immortals and working the planchette, of divination by manipulating yarrow stalks, and of learning the secrets of pursuing good and avoiding evil." "Can this sort of practice lead to immortality?" asked Wukong. "Impossible! Impossible!" said the Patriarch. "I won't learn it then," Wukong said.

"How would it be," said the Patriarch again, "if I taught you the practice of the Schools division?" "What is the meaning of the Schools division?" asked Wukong. "The Schools division," the Patriarch said, "includes the Confucians, the Buddhists, the Daoists, the Dualists, the Mohists, and the Physicians. They read scriptures or recite prayers; they interview priests or conjure up saints and the like." "Can this sort of practice lead to immortality?" asked Wukong. The Patriarch said, "If immortality is what you desire, this practice is like setting a pillar inside a wall." Wukong said, "Master, I'm a simple fellow and I don't know the idioms of the marketplace. What's setting a pillar inside a wall?" The Patriarch said, "When people build houses and want them to be sturdy, they place a pillar as a prop inside the wall. But someday the big mansion will decay, and the pillar too will rot." "What you're saying then," Wukong said, "is that it is not long-lasting. I'm not going to learn this."

The Patriarch said, "How would it be if I taught you the practice of the Silence division?" "What's the aim of the Silence division?" Wukong asked.

"To cultivate fasting and abstinence," said the Patriarch, "quiescence and inactivity, meditation and the art of cross-legged sitting, restraint of language, and a vegetarian diet. There are also the practices of yoga, exercises standing or prostrate, entrance into complete stillness, contemplation in solitary confinement, and the like." "Can these activities," asked Wukong, "bring about immortality?" "They are no better than the unfired bricks on the kiln," said the Patriarch. Wukong laughed and said, "Master indeed loves to beat about the bush! Haven't I just told you that I don't know these idioms of the marketplace? What do you mean by the unfired bricks on the kiln?" The Patriarch replied, "The tiles and the bricks on the kiln may have been molded into shape, but if they have not been refined by water and fire, a heavy rain will one day make them crumble." "So this too lacks permanence," said Wukong. "I don't want to learn it."

The Patriarch said, "How would it be if I taught you the practice of the Action division?" "What's it like in the Action division?" Wukong asked. "Plenty of activities," said the Patriarch, "such as gathering the yin to nourish the yang, bending the bow and treading the arrow, and rubbing the navel to pass breath. There are also experimentation with alchemical formulas, burning rushes and forging cauldrons, taking red lead, making autumn stone, and drinking bride's milk and the like."[5] "Can such bring about long life?" asked Wukong. "To obtain immortality from such activities," said the Patriarch, "is also like scooping the moon from the water." "There you go again, Master!" cried Wukong. "What do you mean by scooping the moon from the water?" The Patriarch said, "When the moon is high in the sky, its reflection is in the water. Although it is visible therein, you cannot scoop it out or catch hold of it, for it is but an illusion." "I won't learn that either!" said Wukong.

When the Patriarch heard this, he uttered a cry and jumped down from the high platform. He pointed the ruler he held in his hands at Wukong and said to him: "What a mischievous monkey you are! You won't learn this and you won't learn that! Just what is it that you are waiting for?" Moving forward, he hit Wukong three times on the head. Then he folded his arms behind his back and walked inside, closing the main doors behind him and leaving the congregation stranded outside. Those who were listening to the lecture were so terrified that everyone began to berate Wukong. "You reckless ape!" they cried, "you're utterly without manners! The master was prepared to teach you magic secrets. Why weren't you willing to learn? Why did you have to argue with him instead? Now you have offended him, and who knows when he'll come out again?" At that moment they all resented him and despised and ridiculed him. But Wukong was not angered in the least and only replied with a broad grin. For the Monkey King, in fact, had already solved secretly, as it were, the riddle in the pot; he therefore did not quarrel with the other people but patiently held his tongue. He reasoned that the master, by hitting him three times, was telling him to prepare himself for the third watch; and by folding his arms behind his back, walking inside, and closing the main doors, was telling him to enter by the back door so that he might receive instruction in secret.

Wukong spent the rest of the day happily with the other pupils in front of the Divine Cave of the Three Stars, eagerly waiting for the night. When evening arrived, he immediately retired with all the others, pretending to be asleep by closing his eyes, breathing evenly, and remaining completely still. Since there was no watchman in the mountain to beat the watch or call the hour, he could not tell what time it was. He could only rely on his own calculations by counting the breaths he inhaled and exhaled. Approximately at the hour of Zi,[6] he arose very quietly and put on his clothes. Stealthily opening the front door, he slipped away from the crowd and walked outside. Lifting his head, he saw

The bright moon and the cool, clear dew,
Though in each corner not one speck of dust.
Sheltered fowls roosted in the woods;
A brook flowed gently from its source.
Darting fireflies dispersed the gloom.
Wild geese spread word columns through the clouds.
Precisely it was the third-watch hour—
Time to seek the Way whole and true.

You see him following the familiar path back to the rear entrance, where he discovered that the door was, indeed, ajar. Wukong said happily, "The reverend master truly intended to give me instruction. That's why the door was left open." He reached the door in a few large strides and entered sideways. Walking up to the Patriarch's bed, he found him asleep with his body curled up, facing the wall. Wukong dared not disturb him; instead, he knelt before his bed. After a little while, the Patriarch awoke. Stretching his legs, he recited to himself:

"Hard! Hard! Hard!
The Way is most obscure!
Deem not the gold elixir a common thing.
Without a perfect man's transmiting a subtle rune,
You'd have vain words, worn mouth, and tongue waxed dry!"

"Master," Wukong responded at once. "Your pupil has been kneeling here and waiting on you for a long time." When the Patriarch heard Wukong's voice, he rose and put on his clothes. "You mischievous monkey!" he exclaimed, sitting down cross-legged, "Why aren't you sleeping in front? What are you doing back here at my place?" Wukong replied, "Before the platform and the congregation yesterday, the master gave the order that your pupil, at the hour of the third watch, should come here through the rear entrance in order that he might be instructed. I was therefore bold enough to come directly to the master's bed."

When the Patriarch heard this, he was terribly pleased, thinking to himself, "This fellow is indeed an offspring of Heaven and Earth. If not, how could he solve so readily the riddle in my pot!" "There is no third party here save your pupil," Wukong said. "May the master be exceedingly merciful and impart to me the way of long life. I shall never forget this gracious favor." "Since you have solved the riddle in the pot," said the Patriarch, "it is an indication that you are destined to learn, and I am glad to teach you. Come closer and listen carefully. I will impart to you the wondrous way of long life." Wukong kowtowed to express his gratitude, washed his ears, and listened most attentively, kneeling before the bed. The Patriarch said:

"This bold, secret saying that's wondrous and true:
Spare, nurse nature and life—there's nothing else.
All power resides in the semen, breath, and spirit;
Store these securely lest there be a leak.
Lest there be a leak!
Keep within the body!
Heed my teaching and the Way itself will thrive.
Hold fast oral formulas so useful and keen
To purge concupiscence, to reach pure cool;
To pure cool
Where the light is bright.
You'll face the elixir platform, enjoying the moon.[7]
The moon holds the jade rabbit, the sun, the crow;[8]
The tortoise and snake are now tightly entwined.[9]
Tightly entwined,
Nature and life are strong.
You can plant gold lotus e'en in the midst of flames.
Squeeze the Five Phases jointly, use them back and forth—[10]
When that's done, be a Buddha or immortal at will!"

At that moment, the very origin was disclosed to Wukong, whose mind became spiritualized as blessedness came to him. He carefully committed to memory all the oral formulas. After kowtowing to thank the Patriarch, he left by the rear entrance. As he went out, he saw that

The eastern sky began to pale with light,
But golden beams shone on the Westward Way.

Following the same path, he returned to the front door, pushed it open quietly, and went inside. He sat up in his sleeping place and purposely rustled
the bed and the covers, crying, "It's light! It's light! Get up!" All the other
people were still sleeping and did not know that Wukong had received a
good thing. He played the fool that day after getting up, but he persisted in
what he had learned secretly by doing breathing exercises before the hour
of Zi and after the hour of Wu.[11]

Three years went by swiftly, and the Patriarch again mounted his throne
to lecture to the multitude. He discussed the scholastic deliberations and
parables, and he discoursed on the integument of external conduct. Suddenly he asked, "Where's Wukong?" Wukong drew near and knelt down.
"Your pupil's here," he said. "What sort of art have you been practicing
lately?" the Patriarch asked. "Recently," Wukong said, "your pupil has begun to apprehend the nature of all things and my foundational knowledge
has become firmly established." "If you have penetrated to the dharma nature to apprehend the origin," said the Patriarch, "you have, in fact, entered
into the divine substance. You need, however, to guard against the danger of
three calamities." When Wukong heard this, he thought for a long time and
said, "The words of the master must be erroneous. I have frequently heard
that when one is learned in the Way and excels in virtue, he will enjoy the
same age as Heaven; fire and water cannot harm him and every kind of disease will vanish. How can there be this danger of three calamities?"

"What you have learned," said the Patriarch, "is no ordinary magic:
you have stolen the creative powers of Heaven and Earth and invaded the
dark mysteries of the sun and moon. Your success in perfecting the elixir
is something that the gods and the demons cannot countenance. Though
your appearance will be preserved and your age lengthened, after five hundred years Heaven will send down the calamity of thunder to strike you.
Hence you must be intelligent and wise enough to avoid it ahead of time.
If you can escape it, your age will indeed equal that of Heaven; if not, your
life will thus be finished. After another five hundred years Heaven will
send down the calamity of fire to burn you. That fire is neither natural
nor common fire; its name is the Fire of Yin, and it arises from within the
soles of your feet to reach even the cavity of your heart, reducing your entrails to ashes and your limbs to utter ruin. The arduous labor of a millennium will then have been made completely superfluous. After another
five hundred years the calamity of wind will be sent to blow at you. It is not
the wind from the north, south, east, or west; nor is it one of the winds of

four seasons; nor is it the wind of flowers, willows, pines, and bamboos. It is called the Mighty Wind, and it enters from the top of the skull into the body, passes through the midriff, and penetrates the nine apertures.[12] The bones and the flesh will be dissolved and the body itself will disintegrate. You must therefore avoid all three calamities."

When Wukong heard this, his hairs stood on end, and, kowtowing reverently, he said, "I beg the master to be merciful and impart to me the method to avoid the three calamities. To the very end, I shall never forget your gracious favor." The Patriarch said, "It is not, in fact, difficult, except that I cannot teach you because you are somewhat different from other people." "I have a round head pointing to Heaven," said Wukong, "and square feet walking on Earth. Similarly, I have nine apertures and four limbs, entrails and cavities. In what way am I different from other people?" The Patriarch said, "Though you resemble a man, you have much less jowl." The monkey, you see, has an angular face with hollow cheeks and a pointed mouth. Stretching his hand to feel himself, Wukong laughed and said, "The master does not know how to balance matters! Though I have much less jowl than human beings, I have my pouch, which may certainly be considered a compensation."

"Very well, then," said the Patriarch, "what method of escape would you like to learn? There is the Art of the Heavenly Ladle, which numbers thirty-six transformations, and there is the Art of the Earthly Multitude, which numbers seventy-two transformations." Wukong said, "Your pupil is always eager to catch more fishes, so I'll learn the Art of the Earthly Multitude." "In that case," said the Patriarch, "come up here, and I'll pass on the oral formulas to you." He then whispered something into his ear, though we do not know what sort of wondrous secrets he spoke of. But this Monkey King was someone who, knowing one thing, could understand a hundred! He immediately learned the oral formulas and, after working at them and practicing them himself, he mastered all seventy-two transformations.

One day when the Patriarch and the various pupils were admiring the evening view in front of the Three Stars Cave, the master asked, "Wukong, has that matter been perfected?" Wukong said, "Thanks to the profound kindness of the master, your pupil has indeed attained perfection; I now can ascend like mist into the air and fly." The Patriarch said, "Let me see you try to fly." Wishing to display his ability, Wukong leaped fifty or sixty feet into the air, pulling himself up with a somersault. He trod on the clouds for about the time of a meal and traveled a distance of no more than three miles before dropping down again to stand before the Patriarch. "Master," he said, his hands folded in front of him, "this is flying by cloud-soaring." Laughing, the Patriarch said, "This can't be called cloud-soaring! It's more like cloud-crawling! The old saying goes, 'The immortal tours the North

Sea in the morning and reaches Cangwu by night.' If it takes you half a day to go less than three miles, it can't even be considered cloud-crawling."

"What do you mean," asked Wukong, "by saying, 'The immortal tours the North Sea in the morning and reaches Cangwu by night'?" The Patriarch said, "Those who are capable of cloud-soaring may start from the North Sea in the morning, journey through the East Sea, the West Sea, the South Sea, and return again to Cangwu. Cangwu refers to Lingling in the North Sea. It can be called true cloud-soaring only when you can traverse all four seas in one day." "That's truly difficult!" said Wukong, "truly difficult!" "Nothing in the world is difficult," said the Patriarch; "only the mind makes it so." When Wukong heard these words, he kowtowed reverently and implored the Patriarch, "Master, if you do perform a service for someone, you must do it thoroughly. May you be most merciful and impart to me also this technique of cloud-soaring. I would never dare forget your gracious favor." The Patriarch said, "When the various immortals want to soar on the clouds, they all rise by stamping their feet. But you're not like them. When I saw you leave just now, you had to pull yourself up by jumping. What I'll do now is to teach you the cloud-somersault in accordance with your form." Wukong again prostrated himself and pleaded with him, and the Patriarch gave him an oral formula, saying,

"Make the magic sign, recite the spell, clench your fist tightly, shake your body, and when you jump up, one somersault will carry you one hundred and eight thousand miles." When the other people heard this, they all giggled and said, "Lucky Wukong! If he learns this little trick, he can become a dispatcher for someone to deliver documents or carry circulars. He'll be able to make a living anywhere!"

The sky now began to darken, and the master went back to the cave dwelling with his pupils. Throughout the night, however, Wukong practiced ardently and mastered the technique of cloud-somersault. From then on, he had complete freedom, blissfully enjoying his state of long life.

One day early in the summer, the disciples were gathered under the pine trees for fellowship and discussion. They said to him, "Wukong, what sort of merit did you accumulate in another incarnation that led the master to whisper in your ear, the other day, the method of avoiding the three calamities? Have you learned everything?" "I won't conceal this from my various elder brothers," Wukong said, laughing. "Owing to the master's instruction in the first place and my diligence day and night in the second, I have fully mastered the several matters!" "Let's take advantage of the moment," one of the pupils said. "You try to put on a performance and we'll watch." When Wukong heard this, his spirit was aroused and he was most eager to display his powers. "I invite the various elder brothers to give me a subject," he said. "What do you want me to change into?" "Why not a pine tree?" they said. Wukong made the magic sign and recited the spell; with one shake of his body he changed himself into a pine tree. Truly it was

> *Thickly held in smoke through all four seasons,*
> *Its chaste fair form soars straight to the clouds.*
> *With not the least likeness to the impish monkey,*
> *It's all frost-tried and snow-tested branches.*

When the multitude saw this, they clapped their hands and roared with laughter, everyone crying, "Marvelous monkey! Marvelous monkey!" They did not realize that all this uproar had disturbed the Patriarch, who came running out of the door, dragging his staff. "Who is creating this bedlam here?" he demanded. At his voice the pupils immediately collected themselves, set their clothes in order, and came forward. Wukong also changed back into his true form, and, slipping into the crowd, he said, "For your information, Reverend Master, we are having fellowship and discussion here. There is no one from outside causing any disturbance." "You were all yelling and screaming," said the Patriarch angrily, "and were behaving in a manner totally unbecoming to those practicing cultivation. Don't you know that those in the cultivation of Dao resist

> *Opening their mouths lest they waste their breath and spirit,*
> *Or moving their tongues lest they provoke arguments?*

Why are you all laughing noisily here?" "We dare not conceal this from the master," the crowd said. "Just now we were having fun with Wukong, who was giving us a performance of transformation. We told him to change into a pine tree, and he did indeed become a pine tree! Your pupils were all applauding him and our voices disturbed the reverend teacher. We beg his forgiveness."

"Go away, all of you," the Patriarch said. "You, Wukong, come over here! I ask you what sort of exhibition were you putting on, changing into a pine tree? This ability you now possess, is it just for showing off to people? Suppose you saw someone with this ability. Wouldn't you ask him at once how he acquired it? So when others see that you are in possession of it, they'll come begging. If you're afraid to refuse them, you will give away the secret; if you don't, they may hurt you. You are actually placing your life in grave jeopardy." "I beseech the master to forgive me," Wukong said, kowtowing. "I won't condemn you," said the Patriarch, "but you must leave this place." When Wukong heard this, tears fell from his eyes. "Where am I to go, Teacher?" he asked. "From wherever you came," the Patriarch said, "you should go back there." "I came from the East Pūrvavideha Continent," Wukong said, his memory jolted by the Patriarch, "from the Water-Curtain

Cave of the Flower-Fruit Mountain in the Aolai Country." "Go back there quickly and save your life," the Patriarch said. "You cannot possibly remain here!" "Allow me to inform my esteemed teacher," said Wukong, properly penitent, "I have been away from home for twenty years, and I certainly long to see my subjects and followers of bygone days again. But I keep thinking that my master's profound kindness to me has not yet been repaid. I, therefore, dare not leave." "There's nothing to be repaid," said the Patriarch. "See that you don't get into trouble and involve me: that's all I ask."

Seeing that there was no other alternative, Wukong had to bow to the Patriarch and take leave of the congregation. "Once you leave," the Patriarch said, "you're bound to end up evildoing. I don't care what kind of villainy and violence you engage in, but I forbid you ever to mention that you are my disciple. For if you but utter half the word, I'll know about it; you can be assured, wretched monkey, that you'll be skinned alive. I will break all your bones and banish your soul to the Place of Ninefold Darkness, from which you will not be released even after ten thousand afflictions!" "I will never dare mention my master," said Wukong. "I'll say that I've learned this all by myself." Having thanked the Patriarch, Wukong turned away, made the magic sign, pulled himself up, and performed the cloud-somersault. He headed straight toward the East Pūrvavideha, and in less than an hour he could already see the Flower-Fruit Mountain and the Water-Curtain Cave. Rejoicing secretly, the Handsome Monkey King said to himself:

"I left weighed down by bones of mortal stock.
The Dao attained makes light both body and frame.
'Tis this world's pity that none firmly resolves
To learn such mystery that by itself is plain.
'Twas hard to cross the seas in former time.
Returning this day, I travel with ease.
Words of farewell still echo in my ears.
I ne'er hope to see so soon the eastern depths!"

Wukong lowered the direction of his cloud and landed squarely on the Flower-Fruit Mountain. He was trying to find his way when he heard the call of cranes and the cry of monkeys; the call of cranes reverberated in the Heavens, and the cry of monkeys moved his spirit with sadness. "Little ones," he called out, "I have returned!" From the crannies of the cliff, from the flowers and bushes, and from the woods and trees, monkeys great and small leaped out by the tens of thousands and surrounded the Handsome Monkey King. They all kowtowed and cried, "Great King! What laxity of mind! Why did you go away for such a long time and leave us here longing for your return like someone hungering and thirsting? Recently, we have been brutally abused by a monster, who wanted to rob us of our Water-Curtain Cave. Out of sheer desperation, we fought hard with him. And yet all this time, that fellow has plundered many of our possessions, kidnapped a number of our young ones, and given us many restless days and nights watching over our property. How fortunate that our great king has returned! If the great king had stayed away another year or so, we and the entire mountain cave would have belonged to someone else!"

Hearing this, Wukong was filled with anger. "What sort of a monster is this," he cried, "that behaves in such a lawless manner? Tell me in detail and I will find him to exact vengeance." "Be informed, Great King," the monkeys said, kowtowing, "that the fellow calls himself the Monstrous King of Havoc, and he lives north of here." Wukong asked, "From here to his place, how great is the distance?" The monkeys replied, "He comes like the cloud and leaves like the mist, like the wind and the rain, like lightning and thunder. We don't know how great the distance is." "In that case," said Wukong, "go and play for a while and don't be afraid. Let me go and find him."

Dear Monkey King! He leaped up with a bound and somersaulted all the way northward until he saw a tall and rugged mountain. What a mountain!

Its penlike peak stands erect;
Its winding streams flow unfathomed and deep.
Its penlike peak, standing erect, cuts through the air;
Its winding streams, unfathomed and deep, reach diverse sites on earth.
On two ridges flowers rival trees in exotic charm;
At various spots pines match bamboos in green.
The dragon on the left
Seems docile and tame;
The tiger on the right
Seems gentle and meek.
Iron oxen[13]
On occasion are seen plowing.
Gold-coin flowers are frequently planted.
Rare fowls make melodious songs;
The phoenix stands facing the sun.
Rocks worn smooth and shiny
By water placid and bright
Appear by turns grotesque, bizarre, and fierce.
In countless numbers are the world's famous mountains
Where flowers bloom and wither; they flourish and die.
What place resembles this long-lasting scene
Wholly untouched by the four seasons and eight epochs?[14]

This is, in the Three Regions,[15] *the Mount of Northern Spring,*
The Water-Belly Cave, nourished by the Five Phases.[16]

The Handsome Monkey King was silently viewing the scenery when he heard someone speaking. He went down the mountain to find who it was, and he discovered the Water-Belly Cave at the foot of a steep cliff. Several imps who were dancing in front of the cave saw Wukong and began to run away. "Stop!" cried Wukong. "You can use the words of your mouth to communicate the thoughts of my mind. I am the lord of the Water-Curtain Cave in the Flower-Fruit Mountain south of here. Your Monstrous King of Havoc, or whatever he's called, has repeatedly bullied my young ones, and I have found my way here with the specific purpose of settling matters with him."

Hearing this, the imps darted into the cave and cried out, "Great King, a disastrous thing has happened!" "What sort of disaster?" asked the Monstrous King. "Outside the cave," said the imps, "there is a monkey who calls himself the lord of the Water-Curtain Cave in the Flower-Fruit Mountain. He says that you have repeatedly bullied his young ones and that he has come to settle matters with you." Laughing, the Monstrous King said, "I have often heard those monkeys say that they have a great king who has left the family to practice self-cultivation. He must have come back. How is he dressed, and what kind of weapon does he have?" "He doesn't have any kind of weapon," the imps said. "He is bare-headed, wears a red robe with a yellow sash, and has a pair of black boots on. He looks like neither a monk nor a layman, neither a Daoist nor an immortal. He is out there making demands with naked hands and empty fists." When the Monstrous King heard this, he ordered, "Get me my armor and my weapon." These were immediately brought out by the imps, and the Monstrous King put on his breastplate and helmet, grasped his scimitar, and walked out of the cave with his followers. "Who is the lord of the Water-Curtain Cave?" he cried with a loud voice. Quickly opening wide his eyes to take a look, Wukong saw that the Monstrous King

Wore on his head a black gold helmet
Which gleamed in the sun;
And on his body a dark silk robe
Which swayed in the wind;
Lower he had on a black iron vest
Tied tightly with leather straps;
His feet were shod in finely carved boots,
Grand as those of warriors great.
Ten spans—the width of his waist;
Thirty feet—the height of his frame;

He held in his hands a sword;
Its blade was fine and bright.
His name: the Monster of Havoc
Of most fearsome form and look.

"You have such big eyes, reckless monster, but you can't even see old Monkey!" the Monkey King shouted. When the Monstrous King saw him, he laughed and said, "You're not four feet tall, nor are you thirty years old; you don't even have weapons in your hands. How dare you be so insolent, looking for me to settle accounts?" "You reckless monster!" cried Wukong. "You are blind indeed! You think I'm small, not knowing that it's hardly difficult for me to become taller; you think I'm without weapon, but my two hands can drag the moon down from the edge of Heaven. Don't be afraid; just have a taste of old Monkey's fist!" He leaped into the air and aimed a blow smack at the monster's face. Parrying the blow with his hand, the Monstrous King said, "You are such a midget and I'm so tall; you want to use your fist but I have my scimitar. If I were to kill you with it, I would be a laughingstock. Let me put down my scimitar, and we'll see how well you can box." "Well said, fine fellow," replied Wukong. "Come on!"

The Monstrous King shifted his position and struck out. Wukong closed in on him, hurtling himself into the engagement. The two of them pummeled and kicked, struggling and colliding with each other. It is easy to miss on a long reach, but a short punch is firm and reliable. Wukong jabbed the Monstrous King in the short ribs, hit him on his chest, and gave him such heavy punishment with a few sharp blows that the monster stepped aside, picked up his huge scimitar, aimed it straight at Wukong's head, and slashed at him. Wukong dodged, and the blow narrowly missed him. Seeing that his opponent was growing fiercer, Wukong now used the method called the Body beyond the Body. Plucking a handful of hairs from his own body and throwing them into his mouth, he chewed them to tiny pieces and then spat them into the air. "Change!" he cried, and they changed at once into two or three hundred little monkeys encircling the combatants on all sides. For you see, when someone acquires the body of an immortal, he can project his spirit, change his form, and perform all kinds of wonders. Since the Monkey King had become accomplished in the Way, every one of the eighty-four thousand hairs on his body could change into whatever shape or substance he desired. The little monkeys he had just created were so keen of eye and so swift of movement that they could be wounded by neither sword nor spear. Look at them! Skipping and jumping, they rushed at the Monstrous King and surrounded him, some hugging, some pulling, some crawling in between his legs, some tugging at his feet. They kicked and punched; they yanked at his hair and poked at his eyes; they pinched his nose and tried to sweep him completely off his feet, until they tangled themselves into confusion.

Meanwhile Wukong succeeded in snatching the scimitar, pushed through the throng of little monkeys, and brought the scimitar down squarely onto the monster's skull, cleaving it in two. He and the rest of the monkeys then fought their way into the cave and slaughtered all the imps, young and old. With a shake, he collected his hair back onto his body, but there were some monkeys that did not return to him. They were the little monkeys kidnaped by the Monstrous King from the Water-Curtain Cave.

"Why are you here?" asked Wukong. The thirty or fifty of them all said tearfully, "After the Great King went away to seek the way of immortality, the monster menaced us for two whole years and finally carried us off to this place. Don't these utensils belong to our cave? These stone pots and bowls were all taken by the creature." "If these are our belongings," said Wukong, "move them out of here." He then set fire to the Water-Belly Cave and reduced it to ashes. "All of you," he said to them, "follow me home." "Great King," the monkeys said, "when we came here, all we felt was wind rushing past us, and we seemed to float through the air until we arrived here. We don't know the way. How can we go back to our home?" Wukong said, "That's a magic trick of his. But there's no difficulty! Now I know not only one thing but a hundred! I'm familiar with that trick too. Close your eyes, all of you, and don't be afraid."

Dear Monkey King. He recited a spell, rode for a while on a fierce wind, and then lowered the direction of the cloud. "Little ones," he cried, "open your eyes!" The monkeys felt solid ground beneath their feet and recognized their home territory. In great delight, every one of them ran back to the cave along the familiar roads and crowded in together with those waiting in the cave. They then lined up according to age and rank and paid tribute to the Monkey King. Wine and fruits were laid out for the welcome banquet. When asked how he had subdued the monster and rescued the young ones, Wukong presented a detailed rehearsal, and the monkeys broke into unending applause. "Where did you go, Great King?" they cried. "We never expected that you would acquire such skills!"

"The year I left you all," Wukong said, "I drifted with the waves across the Great Eastern Ocean and reached the West Aparagodānīya Continent. I then arrived at the South Jambūdvīpa Continent, where I learned human ways, wearing this garment and these shoes. I swaggered along with the clouds for eight or nine years, but I had yet to learn the Great Art. I then crossed the Great Western Ocean and reached the West Aparagodānīya Continent.[17] After searching for a long time, I had the good fortune to discover an old Patriarch, who imparted to me the formula for enjoying the same age as Heaven, the secret of immortality." "Such luck is hard to meet even after ten thousand afflictions!" the monkeys said, all congratulating him. "Little ones," Wukong said, laughing again, "another delight is that our entire family now has a name."

"What is the name of the great king?"

"My surname is Sun," replied Wukong, "and my religious name is Wu-kong." When the monkeys heard this, they all clapped their hands and shouted happily, "If the great king is Elder Sun, then we are all Junior Suns, Suns the Third, small Suns, tiny Suns—the Sun Family, the Sun Nation, and the Sun Cave!" So they all came and honored Elder Sun with large and small bowls of coconut and grape wine, of divine flowers and fruits. It was indeed one big happy family! Lo,

> *The surname is one, the self's returned to its source.*
> *This glory awaits—a name recorded in Heaven!*

We do not know what the result was and how Wukong would fare in this realm; let's listen to the explanation in the next chapter.

THREE

Four Seas and a Thousand Mountains all bow to submit;
From Ninefold Darkness ten species' names are removed.[1]

Now we were speaking of the Handsome Monkey King's triumphant return to his home country. After slaying the Monstrous King of Havoc and wresting from him his huge scimitar, he practiced daily with the little monkeys the art of war, teaching them how to sharpen bamboos for making spears, file wood for making swords, arrange flags and banners, go on patrol, advance or retreat, and pitch camp. For a long time he played thus with them. Suddenly he grew quiet and sat down, thinking out loud to himself, "The game we are playing here may turn out to be something quite serious. Suppose we disturb the rulers of humans or of fowls and beasts, and they become offended; suppose they say that these military exercises of ours are subversive, and raise an army to destroy us. How can we meet them with our bamboo spears and wooden swords? We must have sharp swords and fine halberds. But what can be done at this moment?" When the monkeys heard this, they were all alarmed. "The great king's observation is very sound," they said, "but where can we obtain these things?" As they were speaking, four older monkeys came forward, two female monkeys with red buttocks and two bareback gibbons. Coming to the front, they said, "Great King, to be furnished with sharp-edged weapons is a very simple matter." "How is it simple?" asked Wukong. The four monkeys replied, "East of our mountain, across two hundred miles of water, is the boundary of the Aolai Country. In that country there is a king who has numberless men and soldiers in his city, and there are bound to be all kinds of metalworks there. If the great king goes there, he can either buy weapons or have them made. Then you can teach us how to use them for the protection of our mountain, and this will be the stratagem for assuring ourselves of perpetuity." When Wukong heard this, he was filled with delight. "Play here, all of you," he said. "Let me make a trip."

Dear Monkey King! He quickly performed his cloud somersault and crossed the two hundred miles of water in no time. On the other side he did indeed discover a city with broad streets and huge marketplaces, countless houses and numerous arches. Under the clear sky and bright sun, people were coming and going constantly. Wukong thought to himself, "There must be ready-made weapons around here. But going down there to buy a few pieces from them is not as good a bargain as acquiring them by magic." He therefore made the magic sign and recited a spell. Facing the ground on the southwest, he took a deep breath and then blew it out. At once it became a mighty wind, hurtling pebbles and rocks through the air. It was truly terrifying:

Thick clouds in vast formation moved o'er the world;
Black fog and dusky vapor darkened the Earth;
Waves churned in seas and rivers, affrighting fishes and crabs;
Boughs broke in mountain forests, wolves and tigers taking flight.
Traders and merchants were gone from stores and shops.
No single man was seen at sundry marts and malls.
The king retreated to his chamber from the royal court.
Officials, martial and civil, returned to their homes.
This wind toppled Buddha's throne of a thousand years
And shook to its foundations the Five-Phoenix Tower.

The wind arose and separated the king from his subjects in the Aolai Country. Throughout the various boulevards and marketplaces, every family bolted the doors and windows and no one dared go outside. Wukong then lowered the direction of his cloud and rushed straight through the imperial gate. He found his way to the armory, knocked open the doors, and saw that there were countless weapons inside. Scimitars, spears, swords, halberds, battle-axes, scythes, whips, rakes, drumsticks, drums, bows, arrows, forks, and lances—every kind was available. Highly pleased, Wukong said to himself, "How many pieces can I possibly carry by myself? I'd better use the magic of body division to transport them." Dear Monkey King! He plucked a handful of hairs, chewed them to pieces in his mouth, and spat them out. Reciting the spell, he cried, "Change!" They changed into thousands of little monkeys, who snatched and grabbed the weapons. Those that were stronger took six or seven pieces, the weaker ones two or three pieces, and together they emptied out the armory. Wukong then mounted the cloud and performed the magic of displacement by calling up a great wind, which carried all the little monkeys back to their home.

We tell you now about the various monkeys, both great and small, who were playing outside the cave of the Flower-Fruit Mountain. They suddenly heard the sound of wind and saw in midair a huge horde of monkeys approaching, the sight of which made them all flee in terror and hide. In a moment, Wukong lowered his cloud and, shaking himself, collected the pieces of hair back onto his body. All the weapons were piled in front of the mountain. "Little ones," he shouted, "come and receive your weapons!" The monkeys looked and saw Wukong standing alone on level ground. They came running to kowtow and ask what had happened. Wukong then recounted to them how he had made use of the mighty wind to transport the weapons. After expressing their gratitude, the monkeys all went to grab at the scimitars and snatch at the swords, to wield the axes and scramble for spears, to stretch the bows and mount the arrows. Shouting and screaming, they played all day long.

The following day, they marched in formation as usual. Assembling the monkeys, Wukong found that there were forty-seven thousand of them. This assembly greatly impressed all the wild beasts of the mountain— wolves, insects, tigers, leopards, mouse deer, fallow deer, river deer, foxes, wild cats, badgers, lions, elephants, apes, bears, antelopes, boars, musk-oxen, chamois, green one-horn buffaloes, wild hares, and giant mastiffs. Led by the various demon kings of no fewer than seventy-two caves, they all came to pay homage to the Monkey King. Henceforth they brought annual tributes and answered the roll call made every season. Some of them joined in the maneuvers; others supplied provisions in accordance with their rank. In an orderly fashion, they made the entire Flower-Fruit Mountain as strong as an iron bucket or a city of metal. The various demon kings also presented metal drums, colored banners, and helmets. The hurly-burly of marching and drilling went on day after day.

While the Handsome Monkey King was enjoying all this, he suddenly said to the multitude, "You all have become adept with the bow and arrow and proficient in the use of weapons. But this scimitar of mine is truly cumbersome, not at all to my liking. What can I do?" The four elder monkeys came forward and memorialized, "The great king is a divine sage, and therefore it is not fit for him to use an earthly weapon. We do not know, however, whether the great king is able to take a journey through water?" "Since I have known the Way," said Wukong, "I have the ability of seventy-two transformations. The cloud somersault has unlimited power. I am familiar with the magic of body concealment and the magic of displacement. I can find my way to Heaven or I can enter the Earth. I can walk past the sun and the moon without casting a shadow, and I can penetrate stone and metal without hindrance. Water cannot drown me, nor fire burn me. Is there any place I can't go to?" "It's a good thing that the great king possesses such powers," said the four monkeys, "for the water below this sheet iron bridge of ours flows directly into the Dragon Palace of the Eastern Ocean. If you are willing to go down there, Great King, you will find the old Dragon King, from whom you may request some kind of weapon. Won't that be to your liking?" Hearing this, Wukong said with delight, "Let me make the trip!"

Dear Monkey King! He jumped to the bridgehead and employed the magic of water restriction. Making the magic sign with his fingers, he leaped into the waves, which parted for him, and he followed the waterway straight to the bottom of the Eastern Ocean. As he was walking, he suddenly ran into a yakṣa[2] on patrol, who stopped him with the question, "What divine sage is this who comes pushing through the water? Speak plainly so that I can announce your arrival." Wukong said, "I am the Heaven-born sage Sun Wukong of the Flower-Fruit Mountain, a near neighbor of your old Dragon King. How is it that you don't recognize me?" When the yakṣa heard this, he hurried back to the Water-Crystal Palace to report. "Great King," he said, "there is outside a Heaven-born sage of the Flower-Fruit Mountain named Sun Wukong. He claims that he is a near neighbor of yours, and he is about to arrive at the palace." Aoguang, the Dragon King of the Eastern Ocean, arose immediately; accompanied by dragon sons and grandsons, shrimp soldiers and crab generals, he came out for the reception. "High Immortal," he said, "please come in!" They went into the palace for proper introduction, and after offering Wukong the honored seat and tea, the king asked, "When did the high immortal become accomplished in the Way, and what kind of divine magic did he receive?" Wukong said, "Since the time of my birth, I have left the family to practice self-cultivation. I have now acquired a birthless and deathless body. Recently I have been teaching my children how to protect our mountain cave, but unfortunately I am without an appropriate weapon. I have heard that my noble neighbor, who has long enjoyed living in this green-jade palace and its shell portals, must have many divine weapons to spare. I came specifically to ask for one of them."

When the Dragon King heard this, he could hardly refuse. So he ordered a perch commander to bring out a long-handled scimitar, and presented it to his visitor. "Old Monkey doesn't know how to use a scimitar," said Wukong. "I beg you to give me something else." The Dragon King then commanded a whiting lieutenant together with an eel porter to carry out a nine-pronged fork. Jumping down from his seat, Wukong took hold of it and tried a few thrusts. He put it down, saying, "Light! Much too light! And it doesn't suit my hand. I beg you to give me another one." "High Immortal," said the Dragon King, laughing, "won't you even take a closer look? This fork weighs three thousand six hundred pounds." "It doesn't suit my hand," Wukong said, "it doesn't suit my hand!" The Dragon King was becoming rather fearful; he ordered a bream admiral and a carp brigadier to carry out a giant halberd, weighing seven thousand two hundred pounds. When he saw this, Wukong ran forward and took hold of it. He tried a few thrusts and parries and then stuck it in the ground, saying, "It's still light! Much too light!" The old Dragon King was completely unnerved. "High Immortal," he said, "there's no weapon in my palace heavier than this halberd." Laughing, Wukong said, "As the old saying goes, 'Who worries about the Dragon King's lacking treasures!' Go and look some more, and if you find something I like, I'll offer you a good price." "There really aren't any more here," said the Dragon King.

As they were speaking, the dragon mother and her daughter slipped out and said, "Great King, we can see that this is definitely not a sage with meager abilities. Inside our ocean treasury is that piece of rare magic iron by which the depth of the Heavenly River[3] is fixed. These past few days the iron has been glowing with a strange and lovely light. Could this be a sign that it should be taken out to meet this sage?" "That," said the Dragon King, "was the measure with which the Great Yu[4] fixed the depths of rivers and oceans when he conquered the Flood. It's a piece of magic iron, but of what use could it be to him?" "Let's not be concerned with whether he could find any use for it," said the dragon mother. "Let's give it to him, and he can do whatever he wants with it. The important thing is to get him out of this palace!" The old Dragon King agreed and told Wukong the whole story. "Take it out and let me see it," said Wukong. Waving his hands, the Dragon King said, "We can't move it! We can't even lift it! The high immortal must go there himself to take a look." "Where is it?" asked Wukong. "Take me there."

The Dragon King accordingly led him to the center of the ocean treasury, where all at once they saw a thousand shafts of golden light. Pointing to the spot, the Dragon King said, "That's it—the thing that is glowing." Wukong girded up his clothes and went forward to touch it: it was an iron rod more than twenty feet long and as thick as a barrel. Using all his might, he lifted it with both hands, saying, "It's a little too long and too thick. It would be more serviceable if it were somewhat shorter and thinner." Hardly had he finished speaking when the treasure shrunk a few feet in length and became a layer thinner. "Smaller still would be even better," said Wukong, giving it another bounce in his hands. Again the treasure became smaller. Highly pleased, Wukong took it out of the ocean treasury to examine it. He found a golden hoop at each end, with solid black iron in between. Immediately adjacent to one of the hoops was the inscription, "The Compliant Golden-Hooped Rod. Weight: thirteen thousand five hundred pounds." He thought to himself in secret delight, "This treasure, I suppose, must be most compliant with one's wishes." As he walked, he was deliberating in his mind and murmuring to himself, bouncing the rod in his hands, "Shorter and thinner still would be marvelous!" By the time he took it outside, the rod was no more than twenty feet in length and had the thickness of a rice bowl.

See how he displayed his power now! He wielded the rod to make lunges and passes, engaging in mock combat all the way back to the Water-Crystal Palace. The old Dragon King was so terrified that he shook with fear, and the dragon princes were all panic-stricken. Sea-turtles and tortoises drew in their necks; fishes, shrimps, and crabs all hid themselves. Wukong held the treasure in his hands and sat in the Water-Crystal Palace. Laughing, he said to the Dragon King, "I am indebted to my good neighbor for his profound kindness." "Please don't mention it," said the Dragon King. "This piece of iron is very useful," said Wukong, "but I have one further state-ment to make." "What sort of statement does the high immortal wish to make?" asked the Dragon King. Wukong said, "Had there been no such iron, I would have let the matter drop. Now that I have it in my hands, I can see that I am wearing the wrong kind of clothes to go with it. What am I to do? If you have any martial apparel, you might as well give me some too. I would thank you most heartily." "This, I confess, is not in my posses-sion," said the Dragon King. Wukong said, "A solitary guest will not disturb two hosts. Even if you claim that you don't have any, I shall never walk out of this door." "Let the high immortal take the trouble of going to another ocean," said the Dragon King. "He might turn up something there." "To visit three homes is not as convenient as sitting in one," said Wukong, "I beg you to give me one outfit." "I really don't have one," said the Dragon King, "for if I did, I would have presented it to you."

"Is that so?" said Wukong. "Let me try the iron on you!"

"High Immortal," the Dragon King said nervously, "don't ever raise your hand! Don't ever raise your hand! Let me see whether my brothers have any and we'll try to give you one." "Where are your honored brothers?" asked Wukong. "They are," said the Dragon King, "Aoqin, Dragon King of the Southern Ocean; Aoshun, Dragon King of the Northern Ocean; and Ao-run, Dragon King of the Western Ocean." "Old Monkey is not going to their places," said Wukong. "For as the common saying goes, 'Three in bond can't compete with two in hand.' I'm merely requesting that you find something casual here and give it to me. That's all." "There's no need for the high im-mortal to go anywhere," said the Dragon King. "I have in my palace an iron drum and a golden bell. Whenever there is any emergency, we beat the drum and strike the bell and my brothers are here shortly." "In that case," said Wukong, "go beat the drum and strike the bell." The turtle general went at once to strike the bell, while the tortoise marshal came to beat the drum.

Soon after the drum and the bell had sounded, the Dragon Kings of the Three Oceans got the message and arrived promptly, all congregating in the outer courtyard. "Elder Brother," said Aoqin, "what emergency made you beat the drum and strike the bell?" "Good Brother," answered the old Dragon, "it's a long story! We have here a certain Heaven-born sage from the Flower-Fruit Mountain, who came here and claimed to be my near neighbor. He subsequently demanded a weapon; the steel fork I presented he deemed too small, and the halberd I offered too light. Finally he himself took that piece of rare, divine iron by which the depth of the Heavenly River was fixed and used it for mock combat. He is now sitting in the palace and also de-manding some sort of battle dress. We have none of that here. So we sounded the drum and the bell to invite you all to come. If you happen to have some such outfit, please give it to him so that I can send him out of this door!"

When Aoqin heard this, he was outraged. "Let us brothers call our army together," he said, "and arrest him. What's wrong with that?" "Don't talk about arresting him!" the old Dragon said, "don't talk about arresting him! That piece of iron—a small stroke with it is deadly and a light tap is fatal! The slightest touch will crack the skin and a small rap will injure the muscles!" Aorun, the Dragon King of the Western Ocean, said, "Second elder brother should not raise his hand against him. Let us rather assemble an outfit for him and get him out of this place. We can then present a formal complaint to Heaven, and Heaven will send its own punishment."

"You are right," said Aoshun, the Dragon King of the Northern Ocean, "I have here a pair of cloud-treading shoes the color of lotus root." Aorun, the Dragon King of the Western Ocean said, "I brought along a cuirass of chain-mail made of yellow gold." "And I have a cap with erect phoenix plumes, made of red gold," said Aoqin, the Dragon King of the Southern Ocean. The old Dragon King was delighted and brought them into the Water-Crystal Palace to present the gifts. Wukong duly put on the gold cap, the gold cuirass, and cloud-treading shoes, and, wielding his compliant rod, he fought his way out in mock combat, yelling to the dragons, "Sorry to have bothered you!" The Dragon Kings of the Four Oceans were outraged, and they consulted together about filing a formal complaint, of which we make no mention here.

Look at that Monkey King! He opened up the waterway and went straight back to the head of the sheet iron bridge. The four old monkeys were leading the other monkeys and waiting beside the bridge. They suddenly beheld Wukong leaping out of the waves: there was not a drop of water on his body as he walked onto the bridge, all radiant and golden. The various monkeys were so astonished that they all knelt down, crying, "Great King, what marvels! What marvels!" Beaming broadly, Wukong ascended his high throne and set up the iron rod right in the center. Not knowing any better, the monkeys all came and tried to pick the treasure up. It was rather like a dragonfly attempting to shake an ironwood tree: they could not budge it an inch! Biting their fingers and sticking out their tongues, every one of them said, "O Father, it's so heavy! How did you ever manage to bring it here?" Wukong walked up to the rod, stretched forth his hands, and picked it up. Laughing, he said to them, "Everything has its owner. This treasure has presided in the ocean treasury for who knows how many thousands of years, and it just happened to glow recently. The Dragon King only recognized it as a piece of black iron, though it is also said to be the divine rarity which fixed the bottom of the Heavenly River. All those fellows together could not lift or move it, and they asked me to take it myself. At first, this treasure was more than twenty feet long and as thick as a barrel. After I struck it once and expressed my feeling that it was too large, it grew smaller. I wanted it smaller still, and again it grew smaller. For a third time I commanded it, and it grew smaller still! When I looked at it in the light, it had on it the inscription, 'The Compliant Golden-Hooped Rod. Weight: thirteen thousand five hundred pounds.' Stand aside, all of you. Let me ask it to go through some more transformations."

He held the treasure in his hands and called out, "Smaller, smaller, smaller!" and at once it shrank to the size of a tiny embroidery needle, small enough to be hidden inside the ear. Awestruck, the monkeys cried, "Great King! Take it out and play with it some more." The Monkey King took it out from his ear and placed it on his palm. "Bigger, bigger, bigger!" he shouted, and again it grew to the thickness of a barrel and more than twenty feet long. He became so delighted playing with it that he jumped onto the bridge and walked out of the cave. Grasping the treasure in his hands, he began to perform the magic of cosmic imitation. Bending over, he cried, "Grow!" and at once grew to be ten thousand feet tall, with a head like the Tai Mountain and a chest like a rugged peak, eyes like lightning and a mouth like a blood bowl, and teeth like swords and halberds. The rod in his hands was of such a size that its top reached the thirty-third Heaven and its bottom the eighteenth layer of Hell. Tigers, leopards, wolves, and crawling creatures, all the monsters of the mountain and the demon kings of the seventy-two caves, were so terrified that they kowtowed and paid homage to the Monkey King in fear and trembling. Presently he revoked his magical appearance and changed the treasure back into a tiny embroidery needle stored in his ear. He returned to the cave dwelling, but the demon kings of the various caves were still frightened, and they continued to come to pay their respects.

At this time, the banners were unfurled, the drums sounded, and the brass gongs struck loudly. A great banquet of a hundred delicacies was given, and the cups were filled to overflowing with the fruit of the vines and the juices of the coconut. They drank and feasted for a long time, and they engaged in military exercises as before. The Monkey King made the four old monkeys mighty commanders of his troops by appointing the two female monkeys with red buttocks as marshals Ma and Liu, and the two bareback gibbons as generals Beng and Ba. The four mighty commanders, moreover, were entrusted with all matters concerning fortification, pitching camps, reward, and punishment. Having settled all this, the Monkey King felt completely at ease to soar on the clouds and ride the mist, to tour the four seas and disport himself in a thousand mountains. Displaying his martial skill, he made extensive visits to various heroes and warriors; performing his magic, he made many good friends. At this time, moreover, he entered into fraternal alliance with six other monarchs: the Bull Monster King, the Dragon Monster King, the Garuda Monster King, the Giant Lynx

King, the Macaque King, and the Orangutan King. Together with the Handsome Monkey King, they formed a fraternal order of seven. Day after day they discussed civil and military arts, exchanged wine cups and goblets, sang and danced to songs and strings. They gathered in the morning and parted in the evening; there was not a single pleasure that they overlooked, covering a distance of ten thousand miles as if it were but the span of their own courtyard. As the saying has it,

One nod of the head goes farther than three thousand miles;
One twist of the torso covers more than eight hundred.

One day, the four mighty commanders had been told to prepare a great banquet in their own cave, and the six kings were invited to the feast. They killed cows and slaughtered horses; they sacrificed to Heaven and Earth. The various imps were ordered to dance and sing, and they all drank until they were thoroughly drunk. After sending the six kings off, Wukong also rewarded the leaders great and small with gifts. Reclining in the shade of pine trees near the sheet iron bridge, he fell asleep in a moment. The four mighty commanders led the crowd to form a protective circle around him, not daring to raise their voices. In his sleep the Handsome Monkey King saw two men approach with a summons with the three characters "Sun Wukong" written on it. They walked up to him and, without a word, tied him up with a rope and dragged him off. The soul of the Handsome Monkey King was reeling from side to side. They reached the edge of a city. The Monkey King was gradually coming to himself, when he lifted up his head and suddenly saw above the city an iron sign bearing in large letters the three words "Region of Darkness." The Handsome Monkey King at once became fully conscious. "The Region of Darkness is the abode of Yama, King of Death," he said. "Why am I here?" "Your age in the World of Life has come to an end," the two men said. "The two of us were given this summons to arrest you." When the Monkey King heard this, he said, "I, old Monkey himself, have transcended the Three Regions and the Five Phases;[5] hence I am no longer under Yama's jurisdiction. Why is he so confused that he wants to arrest me?" The two summoners paid scant attention. Yanking and pulling, they were determined to haul him inside. Growing angry, the Monkey King whipped out his treasure. One wave of it turned it into the thickness of a rice bowl; he raised his hands once, and the two summoners were reduced to hash. He untied the rope, freed his hands, and fought his way into the city, wielding the rod. Bull-headed demons hid in terror, and horse-faced demons fled in every direction. A band of ghost soldiers ran up to the Palace of Darkness, crying, "Great Kings! Disaster! Disaster! Outside there's a hairy-faced thunder god fighting his way in!"

Their report alarmed the Ten Kings of the Underworld so much that they quickly straightened out their attire and went out to see what was happening. Discovering a fierce and angry figure, they lined up according to their ranks and greeted him with loud voices: "High Immortal, tell us your name. High Immortal, tell us your name." "I am the Heaven-born sage Sun Wukong from the Water-Curtain Cave in the Flower-Fruit Mountain," said the Monkey King, "what kind of officials are you?" "We are the Emperors of Darkness," answered the Ten Kings, bowing, "the Ten Kings of the Underworld." "Tell me each of your names at once," said Wukong, "or I'll give you a drubbing."

The Ten Kings said, "We are: King Qinguang, King of the Beginning River, King of the Song Emperor, King of Avenging Ministers, King Yama, King of Equal Ranks, King of the Tai Mountain, King of City Markets, King of the Complete Change, and King of the Turning Wheel."[6]

"Since you have all ascended the thrones of kingship," said Wukong, "you should be intelligent beings, responsible in rewards and punishments. Why are you so ignorant of good and evil? Old Monkey has acquired the Dao and attained immortality. I enjoy the same age as Heaven, and I have transcended the Three Regions and leapt clear of the Five Phases. Why, then, did you send men to arrest me?"

"High Immortal," said the Ten Kings, "let your anger subside. There are many people in this world with the same name and surname. Couldn't the summoners have made a mistake?" "Nonsense! Nonsense!" said Wukong. "The proverb says, 'Officials err, clerks err, but the summoner never errs!' Quick, bring out your register of births and deaths, and let me have a look."

When the Ten Kings heard this, they invited him to go into the palace to see for himself. Holding his compliant rod, Wukong went straight up to the Palace of Darkness and, facing south, sat down in the middle. The Ten Kings immediately had the judge in charge of the records bring out his books for examination. The judge, who did not dare tarry, hastened into a side room and brought out five or six books of documents and the ledgers on the ten species of living beings. He went through them one by one—short-haired creatures, furry creatures, winged creatures, crawling creatures, and scaly creatures—but he did not find his name. He then proceeded to the file on monkeys. You see, though this monkey resembled a human being, he was not listed under the names of men; though he resembled the short-haired creatures, he did not dwell in their kingdoms; though he resembled other animals, he was not subject to the unicorn; and though he resembled flying creatures, he was not governed by the phoenix. He had, therefore, a separate ledger, which Wukong examined himself. Under the heading "Soul 1350" he found the name Sun Wukong recorded, with the description: "Heaven-born Stone Monkey. Age: three hundred and forty-two years. A good end."

Wukong said, "I really don't remember my age. All I want is to erase my name. Bring me a brush." The judge hurriedly fetched the brush and soaked it in heavy ink. Wukong took the ledger on monkeys and crossed out all the names he could find in it. Throwing down the ledger, he said, "That ends the account! That ends the account! Now I'm truly not your subject." Brandishing his rod, he fought his way out of the Region of Darkness. The Ten Kings did not dare approach him. They went instead to the Green Cloud Palace to consult the Bodhisattva King Kṣitigarbha and made plans to report the incident to Heaven, which does not concern us for the moment.

While our Monkey King was fighting his way out of the city, he was suddenly caught in a clump of grass and stumbled. Waking up with a start, he realized that it was all a dream. As he was stretching himself, he heard the four mighty commanders and the various monkeys crying with a loud voice, "Great King! How much wine did you imbibe? You've slept all night long. Aren't you awake yet?" "Sleeping is nothing to get excited about," said Wukong, "but I dreamed that two men came to arrest me, and I didn't perceive their intention until they brought me to the outskirts of the Region of Darkness. Showing my power, I protested right up to the Palace of Darkness and argued with the Ten Kings. I went through our ledger of births and deaths and crossed out all our names. Those fellows have no hold over us now." The various monkeys all kowtowed to express their gratitude. From that time onward there were many mountain monkeys who did not grow old, for their names were not registered in the Underworld. When the Handsome Monkey King finished his account of what had happened, the four mighty commanders reported the story to the demon kings of various caves, who all came to tender their congratulations. Only a few days had passed when the six sworn brothers also came to congratulate him, all of them delighted about the cancellation of the names. We shall not elaborate here on their joyful gathering.

We shall turn instead to the Great Benevolent Sage of Heaven, the Celestial Jade Emperor of the Most Venerable Deva, who was holding court one day in the Treasure Hall of Divine Mists, the Cloud Palace of Golden Arches. The divine ministers, civil and military, were just gathering for the morning session when suddenly the Daoist immortal Qiu Hongzhi[7] announced, "Your Majesty, outside the Translucent Palace, Aoguang, the Dragon King of the Eastern Ocean, is awaiting your command to present a memorial to the Throne." The Jade Emperor gave the order to have him brought forth, and Aoguang was led into the Hall of Divine Mists. After he had paid his respects, a divine page boy in charge of documents received the memorial, and the Jade Emperor read it from the beginning. The memorial said:

From the lowly water region of the Eastern Ocean at the East Pūrvavideha Continent, the small dragon subject, Aoguang, humbly informs the Wise Lord of Heaven, the Most Eminent High God and Ruler, that a bogus immortal, Sun Wukong, born of the Flower-Fruit Mountain and resident of the Water-Curtain Cave, has recently abused your small dragon, gaining a seat in his water home by force. He demanded a weapon, employing power and intimidation; he asked for martial attire, unleashing violence and threats. He terrorized my water kinsmen, and scattered turtles and tortoises. The Dragon of the Southern Ocean trembled; the Dragon of the Western Ocean was filled with horror; the Dragon of the Northern Ocean drew back his head to surrender; and your subject Aoguang flexed his body to do obeisance. We presented him with the divine treasure of an iron rod and the gold cap with phoenix plumes; giving him also a chain-mail cuirass and cloud-treading shoes, we sent him off courteously. But even then he was bent on displaying his martial prowess and magical powers, and all he could say to us was "Sorry to have bothered you!" We are indeed no match for him, nor are we able to subdue him. Your subject therefore presents this petition and humbly begs for imperial justice. We earnestly beseech you to dispatch the Heavenly host and capture this monster, so that tranquility may be restored to the oceans and prosperity to the Lower Region. Thus we present this memorial.

When the Holy Emperor had finished reading, he gave the command: "Let the Dragon God return to the ocean. We shall send our generals to arrest the culprit." The old Dragon King gratefully touched his forehead to the ground and left. From below the Immortal Elder Ge, the Celestial Master,[8] also brought forth the report. "Your Majesty, the Minister of Darkness, King Qinguang, supported by the Bodhisattva King Kṣitigarbha, Pope of the Underworld, has arrived to present his memorial." The jade girl in charge of communication came from the side to receive this document, which the Jade Emperor also read from the beginning. The memorial said:

The Region of Darkness is the nether region proper to Earth. As Heaven is for gods and Earth for ghosts, so life and death proceed in cyclic succession. Fowls are born and animals die; male and female, they multiply. Births and transformations, the male begotten of the procreative female—such is the order of Nature, and it cannot be changed. But now appears Sun Wukong, a Heaven-born baneful monkey from the Water-Curtain Cave in the Flower-Fruit Mountain, who practices evil and violence, and resists our proper summons. Exercising magic powers, he utterly defeated the ghostly messengers of Ninefold Darkness; exploiting brute force, he terrorized the Ten Merciful Kings. He caused great confusion in the Palace of Darkness; he abrogated by force the Register of Names, so that the category of monkeys is now beyond control, and inordinately long life is given to the simian family. The wheel of transmigration is stopped, for birth and death are eliminated in each kind of monkey. Your poor monk therefore risks offending your Heavenly authority in presenting this memorial. We humbly beg you to send forth your divine army and subdue this monster, to the end that life and death may once more be regulated and the Underworld rendered perpetually secure. Respectfully we present this memorial.

When the Jade Emperor had finished reading, he again gave a command: "Let the Lord of Darkness return to the Underworld. We shall send our generals to arrest this culprit." King Qinguang also touched his head to the ground gratefully and left.

The Great Heavenly Deva called together his various immortal subjects, both civil and military, and asked, "When was this baneful monkey born, and in which generation did he begin his career? How is it that he has become so powerfully accomplished in the Way?" Scarcely had he finished speaking when, from the ranks, Thousand-Mile Eye and Fair-Wind Ear stepped forward. "This monkey," they said, "is the Heaven-born stone monkey of three hundred years ago. At that time he did not seem to amount to much, and we do not know where he acquired the knowledge of self-cultivation these last few years and became an immortal. Now he knows how to subdue dragons and tame tigers,[9] and thus he is able to annul by force the Register of Death." "Which one of you divine generals," asked the Jade Emperor, "wishes to go down there to subdue him?"

Scarcely had he finished speaking when the Long-Life Spirit of the Planet Venus came forward from the ranks and prostrated himself. "Highest and Holiest," he said, "within the three regions, all creatures endowed with the nine apertures can, through exercise, become immortals. It is not surprising that this monkey, with a body nurtured by Heaven and Earth, a frame born of the sun and moon, should achieve immortality, seeing that his head points to Heaven and his feet walk on Earth, and that he feeds on the dew and the mist. Now that he has the power to subdue dragons and tame tigers, how is he different from a human being? Your subject therefore makes so bold as to ask Your Majesty to remember the compassionate grace of Creation and issue a decree of pacification. Let him be summoned to the Upper Region and given some kind of official duties. His name will be recorded in the Register and we can control him here. If he is receptive to the Heavenly decree, he will be rewarded and promoted hereafter; but if he is disobedient to your command, we shall arrest him forthwith. Such an action will spare us a military expedition in the first place, and, in the second, permit us to receive into our midst another immortal in an orderly manner."

The Jade Emperor was highly pleased with this statement, and he said, "We shall follow the counsel of our minister." He then ordered the Star

Spirit of Songs and Letters to compose the decree, and delegated the Gold Star of Venus to be the viceroy of peace. Having received the decree, the Gold Star went out of the South Heaven Gate, lowered the direction of his hallowed cloud, and headed straight for the Flower-Fruit Mountain and the Water-Curtain Cave. He said to the various little monkeys, "I am the Heavenly messenger sent from above. I have with me an imperial decree to invite your great king to go to the Upper Region. Report this to him quickly!" The monkeys outside the cave passed the word along one by one until it reached the depth of the cave. "Great King," one of the monkeys said, "there's an old man outside bearing a document on his back. He says that he is a messenger sent from Heaven, and he has an imperial decree of invitation for you." Upon hearing this, the Handsome Monkey King was exceedingly pleased. "These last two days," he said, "I was just thinking about taking a little trip to Heaven, and the heavenly messenger has already come to invite me!" The Monkey King quickly straightened out his attire and went to the door for the reception. The Gold Star came into the center of the cave and stood still with his face toward the south. "I am the Gold Star of Venus from the West," he said. "I came down to Earth, bearing the imperial decree of pacification from the Jade Emperor, and invite you to go to Heaven to receive an immortal appointment." Laughing, Wukong said, "I am most grateful for the Old Star's visit." He then gave the order: "Little ones, prepare a banquet to entertain our guest." The Gold Star said, "As a bearer of imperial decree, I cannot remain here long. I must ask the Great King to go with me at once. After your glorious promotion, we shall have many occasions to converse at our leisure." "We are honored by your presence," said Wukong; "I am sorry that you have to leave with empty hands!" He then called the four mighty commanders together for this admonition: "Be diligent in teaching and drilling the young ones. Let me go up to Heaven to take a look and to see whether I can have you all brought up there too to live with me." The four mighty commanders indicated their obedience. This Monkey King mounted the cloud with the Gold Star and rose up into the sky. Truly

> He ascends the high rank of immortals from the sky;
> His name's enrolled in cloud columns and treasure scrolls.

We do not know what sort of rank or appointment he received; let's listen to the explanation in the next chapter.

FOUR

Appointed a BanHorse, could he be content? Named Equal to Heaven, he's still not appeased.

The Gold Star of Venus left the depths of the cave dwelling with the Handsome Monkey King, and together they rose by mounting the clouds. But the cloud somersault of Wukong, you see, is no common magic; its speed is tremendous. Soon he left the Gold Star far behind and arrived first at the South Heaven Gate. He was about to dismount from the cloud and go in when the Devarāja Virūḍhaka leading Pang, Liu, Kou, Bi, Deng, Xin, Zhang, and Tao, the various divine heroes, barred the way with spears, scimitars, swords, and halberds and refused him entrance. The Monkey King said, "What a deceitful fellow that Gold Star is! If old Monkey has been invited here, why have these people been ordered to use their swords and spears to bar my entrance?" He was protesting loudly when the Gold Star arrived in haste. "Old man," said Wukong angrily to his face, "why did you deceive me? You told me that I was invited by the Jade Emperor's decree of pacification. Why then did you get these people to block the Heaven Gate and prevent my entering?" "Let the Great King calm down," the Gold Star said, laughing. "Since you have never been to the Hall of Heaven before, nor have you been given a name, you are quite unknown to the various heavenly guardians. How can they let you in on their own authority? Once you have seen the Heavenly Deva, received an appointment, and had your name listed in the Immortal Register, you can go in and out as you please. Who would then obstruct your way?" "If that's how it is," said Wukong, "it's all right. But I'm not going in by myself." "Then go in with me," said the Gold Star, pulling him by the hand.

As they approached the gate, the Gold Star called out loudly, "Guardians of the Heaven Gate, lieutenants great and small, make way! This person is an immortal from the Region Below, whom I have summoned by the imperial decree of the Jade Emperor." The Devarāja Virūḍhaka and the various divine heroes immediately lowered their weapons and stepped aside, and the Monkey King finally believed what he had been told. He walked slowly inside with the Gold Star and looked around. For it was truly

His first ascent to the Region Above,
His sudden entrance into the Hall of Heaven,
Where ten thousand shafts of golden light whirled as a coral rainbow,
And a thousand layers of hallowed air diffused mist of purple.

Look at that South Heaven Gate!
Its deep shades of green
From glazed tiles were made;
Its radiant battlements
Adorned with treasure jade.
On two sides were posted scores of celestial sentinels,
Each of whom, standing tall beside the pillars,
Carried bows and clutched banners.
All around were sundry divine beings in golden armor,
Each of them holding halberds and whips,
Or wielding scimitars and swords.
Impressive may be the outer court;
Overwhelming is the sight within!
In the inner halls stood several huge pillars
Circled by red-whiskered dragons whose golden scales gleamed in the sun.
There were, moreover, a few long bridges;
Above them crimson-headed phoenixes circled with soaring plumes of
     many hues.
Bright mist shimmered in the light of the sky.
Green fog descending obscured the stars.
Thirty-three Heavenly mansions were found up here,
With names like the Scattered Cloud, the Vaiśrvaṇa, the Pāncavidyā, the
     Suyāma, the Nirmāṇarati . . .[1]
On the roof of every mansion the ridge held a stately golden beast.
There were also the seventy-two treasure halls,
With names like the Morning Assembly, the Transcendent Void, the Precious
     Light, the Heavenly King, the Divine Minister . . .
In every hall beneath the pillars stood rows of jade unicorn.
On the Platform of Canopus,[2]
There were flowers unfading in a thousand millennia;
Beside the oven for refining herbs,
There were exotic grasses growing green for ten thousand years.
He went before the Tower of Homage to the Sage,
Where he saw robes of royal purple gauze
Brilliant as stars refulgent,
Caps the shape of hibiscus,
Resplendent with gold and precious stones,
And pins of jade and shoes of pearl,
And purple sashes and golden ornaments.
When the golden bells swayed to their striking,
The memorial of the Three Judges[3] would cross the vermilion courtyard;
When the drums of Heaven were sounded,

Ten thousand sages of the royal audience would honor the Jade Emperor.
He went, too, to the Treasure Hall of Divine Mists
Where nails of gold penetrated frames of jade,
And colorful phoenixes danced atop scarlet doors.
Here were covered bridges and winding corridors
Displaying everywhere openwork carvings most elegant;
And eaves crowding together in layers three and four,
On each of which reared up phoenixes and dragons.
There was high above
A round dome big, bright, and brilliant—
Its shape, a huge gourd of purple gold,
Below which guardian goddesses hung out their fans
And jade maidens held up their immortal veils.
Ferocious were the sky marshals overseeing the court;
Dignified, the divine officials protecting the Throne.
There at the center, on a crystal platter,
Tablets of the Great Monad Elixir were heaped;
And rising out of the cornelian vases
Were several branches of twisting coral.
So it was that
Rare goods of every order were found in Heaven's Hall,
And nothing like them on Earth could ever be seen—
Those golden arches, silver coaches, and that Heavenly house,
Those coralline blooms and jasper plants with their buds of jade.
The jade rabbit passed the platform to adore the king.
The golden crow flew by to worship the sage.[4]
Blessed was the Monkey King coming to this Heavenly realm,
He who was not mired in the filthy soil of man.

The Gold Star of Venus led the Handsome Monkey King to the Treasure Hall of Divine Mists, and, without waiting for further announcement, they went into the imperial presence. While the Star prostrated himself, Wukong stood erect by him. Showing no respect, he cocked his ear only to listen to the report of the Gold Star. "According to your decree," said the Gold Star, "your subject has brought the bogus immortal." "Which one is the bogus immortal?" asked the Jade Emperor graciously. Only then did Wukong bow and reply, "None other than old Monkey!" Blanching with horror, the various divine officials said, "That wild ape! Already he has failed to prostrate himself before the Throne, and now he dares to come forward with such an insolent reply as 'None other than old Monkey'! He is worthy of death, worthy of death!" "That fellow Sun Wukong is a bogus immortal from the Region Below," announced the Jade Emperor, "and he has only recently acquired the form of a human being. We shall pardon him this time for his ignorance of court etiquette." "Thank you, Your Majesty," cried the various divine officials. Only then did the Monkey King bow deeply with folded hands and utter a cry of gratitude. The Jade Emperor then ordered the divine officials, both civil and military, to see what vacant appointment there might be for Sun Wukong to receive. From the side came the Star Spirit of Wuqu, who reported, "In every mansion and hall everywhere in the Palace of Heaven, there is no lack of ministers. Only at the imperial stables is a supervisor needed." "Let him be made a BanHorsePlague,"[5] proclaimed the Jade Emperor. The various subjects again shouted their thanks, but Monkey only bowed deeply and gave a loud whoop of gratitude. The Jade Emperor then sent the Star Spirit of Jupiter to accompany him to the stables.

The Monkey King went happily with the Star Spirit of Jupiter to the stables in order to assume his duties. After the Star Spirit had returned to his own mansion, the new officer gathered together the deputy and assistant supervisors, the accountants and stewards, and other officials both great and small and made thorough investigation of all the affairs of the stables. There were about a thousand celestial horses,[6] and they were all

Hualius and Chizhis
Lu'ers and Xianlis,
Consorts of Dragons and Purple Swallows,
Folded Wings and Suxiangs,
Juetis and Silver Hooves,
Yaoniaos and Flying Yellows.
Chestnuts and Faster-than-Arrows,
Red Hares and Speedier-than-Lights,
Leaping Lights and Vaulting Shadows,
Rising Fogs and Triumphant Yellows,
Wind Chasers and Distance Breakers.
Flying Pinions and Surging Airs,
Rushing Winds and Fiery Lightnings.
Copper Sparrows and Drifting Clouds,
Dragonlike piebalds and Tigerlike pintos,
Dust Quenchers and Purple Scales,
And Ferghanas[7] *from the Four Corners.*
Like the Eight Steeds and Nine Stallions
They have no rivals within a thousand miles!
Such are these fine horses.
Every one of which

Neighs like the wind and gallops like thunder to show a mighty spirit.
They tread the mist and mount the clouds with unflagging strength.

Our Monkey King went through the lists and made a thorough inspection of the horses. Within the imperial stables, the accountants were in charge of getting supplies; the stewards groomed and washed the horses, chopped hay, watered them, and prepared their food; and the deputies and assistants saw to the overall management. Never resting, the Bima oversaw the care of the horses, fussing with them by day and watching over them diligently by night. Those horses that wanted to sleep were stirred up and fed; those that wanted to gallop were caught and placed in the stalls. When the celestial horses saw him, they all behaved most properly and they were so well cared for that their flanks became swollen with fat.

More than half a month soon went by, and on one leisurely morning, the various department ministers gave a banquet to welcome and congratulate him. While they were drinking happily, the Monkey King suddenly put down his cup and asked: "What sort of rank is this BanHorsePlague of mine?" "The rank and the title are the same," they said. "But what ministerial grade is it?" "It does not have a grade," they said. "If it does not have a grade," said the Monkey King, "I suppose it must be the very highest." "Not at all," they replied, "it can only be called 'the unclassified'!" The Monkey King said, "What do you mean by 'the unclassified'?" "It is really the meanest level," they said. "This kind of minister is the lowest of the low ranks; hence he can only look after horses. Take the case of Your Honor, who, since your arrival, have been so diligent in discharging your duties. If the horses are fattened, you will only earn yourself a 'Fairly Good!' If they look at all thin, you will be roundly rebuked. And if they are seriously hurt or wounded, you will be prosecuted and fined."

When the Monkey King heard this, fire leaped up from his heart. "So that's the contempt they have for old Monkey!" he cried angrily, gnashing his teeth. "At the Flower-Fruit Mountain I was honored as king and patriarch. How dare they trick me into coming to look after horses for them, if horse tending is such a menial service, reserved only for the young and lowly? Is such treatment worthy of me? I'm quitting! I'm quitting! I'm leaving right now!" With a crash, he kicked over his official desk and took the treasure out of his ear. One wave of his hand and it had the thickness of a rice bowl. Delivering blows in all directions, he fought his way out of the imperial stables and went straight to the South Heaven Gate. The various celestial guardians, knowing that he had been officially appointed a Ban-HorsePlague, did not dare stop him and allowed him to fight his way out of the Heaven Gate.

In a moment, he lowered the direction of his cloud and returned to the Flower-Fruit Mountain. The four mighty commanders were seen drilling troops with the Monster Kings of various caves. "Little ones," this Monkey King cried in a loud voice, "old Monkey has returned!" The flock of monkeys all came to kowtow and received him into the depths of the cave dwelling. As the Monkey King ascended his throne, they busily prepared a banquet to welcome him. "Receive our congratulations, Great King," they said. "Having gone to the region above for more than ten years, you must be returning in success and glory." "I have been away for only half a month," said the Monkey King. "How can it be more than ten years?"

"Great King," said the various monkeys, "you are not aware of time and season when you are in Heaven. One day in Heaven above is equal to a year on Earth. May we ask the Great King what ministerial appointment he received?"

"Don't mention that! Don't mention that!" said the Monkey King, waving his hand. "It embarrasses me to death! That Jade Emperor does not know how to use talent. Seeing the features of old Monkey, he appointed me to something called the BanHorsePlague, which actually means taking care of horses for him. It's a job too low even to be classified! I didn't know this when I first assumed my duties, and so I managed to have some fun at the imperial stables. But when I asked my colleagues today, I discovered what a degraded position it was. I was so furious that I knocked over the banquet they were giving me and rejected the title. That's why I came back down." "Welcome back!" said the various monkeys, "welcome back! Our Great King can be the sovereign of this blessed cave dwelling with the greatest honor and happiness. Why should he go away to be someone's stable boy?" "Little ones," they cried, "send up the wine quickly and cheer up our Great King."

As they were drinking wine and conversing happily, someone came to report: "Great King, there are two one-horned demon kings outside who want to see you." "Show them in," said the Monkey King. The demon kings straightened out their attire, ran into the cave, and prostrated themselves. "Why did you want to see me?" asked the Handsome Monkey King. "We have long heard that the Great King is receptive to talents," said the demon kings, "but we had no reason to request your audience. Now we learn that our Great King has received a divine appointment and has returned in success and glory. We have come, therefore, to present the Great King with a red and yellow robe for his celebration. If you are not disdainful of the uncouth and the lowly and are willing to receive us plebeians, we shall serve you as dogs or as horses." Highly pleased, the Monkey King put on the red and yellow robe while the rest of them lined up joyfully and did homage. He then appointed the demon kings to be the Vanguard Commanders, Marshals of the Forward Regiments. After expressing their thanks, the demon kings asked again, "Since our Great King was in Heaven for a long time, may we ask what kind of appointment he received?" "The Jade Emperor belittles the talented," said the Monkey King. "He only made me something called the BanHorsePlague." Hearing this, the demon kings said again, "Great King has such divine powers! Why should you take care of horses for him? What is there to stop you from assuming the rank of the Great Sage, Equal to Heaven?" When the Monkey King heard these words, he could not conceal his delight, shouting repeatedly, "Bravo! Bravo!" "Make me a banner immediately," he ordered the four mighty commanders, "and inscribe on it in large letters, 'The Great Sage, Equal to Heaven.' Erect a pole to hang it on. From now on, address me only as the Great Sage, Equal to Heaven, and the title Great King will no longer be permitted. The Monster Kings of the various caves will also be informed so that it will be known to all." Of this we shall speak no further.

We now refer to the Jade Emperor, who held court the next day. The Celestial Master Zhang[8] was seen leading the deputy and the assistant of the imperial stables to come before the vermilion courtyard. "Your Majesty," they said, prostrating themselves, "the newly appointed BanHorsePlague, Sun Wukong, objected to his rank as being too low and left the Heavenly Palace yesterday in rebellion." Meanwhile, the Devarāja Virūḍhaka, leading the various celestial guardians from the South Heaven Gate, also made the report, "The BanHorsePlague for reasons unknown to us has walked out of the Heaven Gate." When the Jade Emperor heard this, he made the proclamation: "Let the two divine commanders and their followers return to their duties. We shall send forth celestial soldiers to capture this monster." From among the ranks, Devarāja Li,[9] who was the Pagoda Bearer, and his Third Prince Naṭa came forward and presented their request, saying, "Your Majesty, though your humble subjects are not gifted, we await your authorization to subdue this monster." Delighted, the Jade Emperor appointed Pagoda Bearer Devarāja Li Jing to be grand marshal for subduing the monster, and promoted Third Prince Naṭa to be the great deity in charge of the Three-Platform Assembly of the Saints. They were to lead an expeditionary force at once for the Region Below.

Devarāja Li and Naṭa kowtowed to take leave and went back to their own mansion. After reviewing the troops and their captains and lieutenants, they appointed Mighty-Spirit God to be Vanward Commander, the Fish-Belly General to bring up the rear, and the General of the Yakṣas to urge the troops on. In a moment they left by the South Heaven Gate and went straight to the Flower-Fruit Mountain. A level piece of land was selected for encampment, and the order was then given to the Mighty-Spirit God to provoke battle. Having received his order and having buckled and knotted his armor properly, the Mighty-Spirit God grasped his spreading-flower ax and came to the Water-Curtain Cave. There in front of the cave he saw a great mob of monsters, all of them wolves, insects, tigers, leopards, and the like; they were all jumping and growling, brandishing their swords and waving their spears.

"Damnable beasts!" shouted the Mighty-Spirit God. "Hurry and tell the BanHorsePlague that I, a great general from Heaven, have by the authorization of the Jade Emperor come to subdue him. Tell him to come out quickly and surrender, lest all of you be annihilated!" Running pell-mell into the cave, those monsters shouted the report, "Disaster! Disaster!" "What sort of disaster?" asked the Monkey King. "There's a celestial warrior outside," said the monsters, "who claims the title of an imperial envoy. He says he came by the holy decree of the Jade Emperor to subdue you, and he orders you to go out quickly and surrender, lest we lose our lives." Hearing this, the Monkey King commanded, "Get my battle dress!" He quickly donned his red gold cap, pulled on his yellow gold cuirass, slipped on his cloud-treading shoes, and seized the compliant golden-hooped rod. He led the crowd outside and set them up in battle formation. The Mighty-Spirit God opened wide his eyes and stared at this magnificent Monkey King:

> The gold cuirass worn on his body was brilliant and bright;
> The gold cap on his head also glistened in the light.
> In his hands was a staff, the golden-hooped rod,
> That well became the cloud-treading shoes on his feet.
> His eyes glowered strangely like burning stars.
> Hanging past his shoulders were two ears, forked and hard.
> His remarkable body knew many ways of change,
> And his voice resounded like bells and chimes.
> This BanHorsePlague with beaked mouth and gaping teeth
> Aimed high to be the Equal to Heaven Sage.

"Lawless ape," the Mighty-Spirit God roared powerfully, "do you recognize me?" When the Great Sage heard these words, he asked quickly, "What sort of dull-witted deity are you? Old Monkey has yet to meet you! State your name at once!" "Fraudulent simian," cried the Mighty-Spirit, "what do you mean, you don't recognize me? I am the Celestial General of Mighty-Spirit, the Vanward Commander and subordinate to Devarāja Li, the Pagoda Bearer, from the divine empyrean. I have come by the imperial decree of the Jade Emperor to receive your submission. Strip yourself of your apparel immediately and yield to the Heavenly grace, so that this mountainful of creatures can avoid execution. If you dare but utter half a 'No,' you will be reduced to powder in seconds!"

When the Monkey King heard those words, he was filled with anger.

"Reckless simpleton!" he cried. "Stop bragging and wagging your tongue! I would have killed you with one stroke of my rod, but then I would have no one to communicate my message. So, I'll spare your life for the moment. Go back to Heaven quickly and inform the Jade Emperor that he has no regard for talent. Old Monkey has unlimited abilities. Why did he ask me to mind horses for him? Take a good look at the words on this banner. If I am promoted according to its title, I will lay down my arms, and the cosmos will then be fair and tranquil. But if he does not agree to my demand, I'll fight my way up to the Treasure Hall of Divine Mists, and he won't even be able to sit on his dragon throne!" When the Mighty-Spirit God heard these words, he opened his eyes wide, facing the wind, and saw indeed a tall pole outside the cave. On the pole hung a banner bearing in large letters the words, "The Great Sage, Equal to Heaven."

The Mighty-Spirit God laughed scornfully three times and jeered, "Lawless ape! How fatuous can you be, and how arrogant! So you want to be the Great Sage, Equal to Heaven! Be good enough to take a bit of my ax first!" Aiming at his head, he hacked at him, but, being a knowledgeable fighter, the Monkey King was not unnerved. He met the blow at once with his golden-hooped rod, and this exciting battle was on.

> The rod was named Compliant;
> The ax was called Spreading Flower.
> The two of them, meeting suddenly,
> Did not yet know their weakness or strength;
> But ax and rod
> Clashed left and right.
> One concealed secret powers most wondrous;
> The other vaunted openly his vigor and might.
> They used magic—
> Blowing out cloud and puffing up fog;
> They stretched their hands,
> Splattering mud and spraying sand.
> The might of the celestial battler had its way:
> But the Monkey had boundless power of change.
> The rod uplifted—a dragon played in water;
> The ax arrived—a phoenix sliced through flowers.
> Mighty-Spirit, whose name spread through the world,
> In prowess truly could not match the other one.
> The Great Sage whirling lightly his iron staff
> Could numb the body with one blow on the head.

The Mighty-Spirit God could oppose him no longer and allowed the Monkey King to aim a mighty blow at his head, which he hastily sought to parry with his ax. With a crack the ax handle split in two, and Mighty-Spirit turned swiftly to flee for his life. "Imbecile! Imbecile!" laughed the Monkey King, "I've already spared you. Go and report my message at once!"

Back at the camp, the Mighty-Spirit God went straight to see the Pagoda Bearer Devarāja. Huffing and puffing, he knelt down saying, "The Ban-HorsePlague indeed has great magic powers! Your unworthy warrior cannot prevail against him. Defeated, I have come to beg your pardon." "This fellow has blunted our will to fight," said Devarāja Li angrily. "Take him out and have him executed!" From the side came Prince Naṭa, who said, bowing deeply, "Let your anger subside, Father King, and pardon for the moment the guilt of Mighty-Spirit. Permit your child to go into battle once, and we shall know the long and short of the matter." The Devarāja heeded the admonition and ordered Mighty-Spirit to go back to his camp and await trial.

This Prince Naṭa, properly armed, leaped from his camp and dashed to the Water-Curtain Cave. Wukong was just dismissing his troops when he saw Naṭa approaching fiercely. Dear Prince!

> *Two boyish tufts barely cover his skull.*
> *His flowing hair has yet to reach the shoulders.*
> *A rare mind, alert and intelligent.*
> *A noble frame, pure and elegant.*
> *He is indeed the unicorn son from Heaven above,*
> *Truly immortal as the phoenix of mist and smoke.*
> *This seed of dragon has by nature uncommon features.*
> *His tender age shows no relation to any worldly kin.*
> *He carries on his body six kinds of magic weapons.*
> *He flies, he leaps; he can change without restriction.*
> *Now by the golden-mouth proclamation of the Jade Emperor*
> *He is appointed to the Assembly: its name, the Three Platforms*[10]

Wukong drew near and asked, "Whose little brother are you, and what do you want, barging through my gate?" "Lawless monstrous monkey!" shouted Naṭa. "Don't you recognize me? I am Naṭa, third son of the Pagoda Bearer Devarāja. I am under the imperial commission of the Jade Emperor to come and arrest you." "Little prince," said Wukong laughing, "your baby teeth haven't even fallen out, and your natal hair is still damp! How dare you talk so big? I'm going to spare your life, and I won't fight you. Just take a look at the words on my banner and report them to the Jade Emperor above. Grant me this title, and you won't need to stir your forces. I will submit on my own. If you don't satisfy my cravings, I will surely fight my way up to the Treasure Hall of Divine Mists."

Lifting his head to look, Naṭa saw the words, "Great Sage, Equal to Heaven." "What great power does this monstrous monkey possess," said

Naṭa, "that he dares claim such a title? Fear not! Swallow my sword." "I'll just stand here quietly," said Wukong, "and you can take a few hacks at me with your sword." Young Naṭa grew angry. "Change!" he yelled loudly, and he changed at once into a fearsome person having three heads and six arms. In his hands he held six kinds of weapons: a monster-stabbing sword, a monster-cleaving scimitar, a monster-binding rope, a monster-taming club, an embroidered ball, and a fiery wheel. Brandishing these weapons, he mounted a frontal attack. "This little brother does know a few tricks!" said Wukong, somewhat alarmed by what he saw. "But don't be rash. Watch my magic!" Dear Great Sage! He shouted, "Change!" and he too transformed himself into a creature with three heads and six arms. One wave of the golden-hooped rod and it became three staffs, which were held with six hands. The conflict was truly earth-shaking and made the very mountains tremble. What a battle!

The six-armed Prince Naṭa.
The Heaven-born Handsome Stone Monkey King.
Meeting, each met his match
And found each to be from the same source.
One was consigned to come down to Earth.
The other in guile disturbed the universe.
The edge of the monster-stabbing sword was quick;
The keen, monster-cleaving scimitar alarmed demons and gods;
The monster-binding rope was like a flying snake;
The monster-taming club was like the head of a wolf;
The lightning-propelled fiery wheel was like darting flames;
Hither and thither the embroidered ball rotated.
The three compliant rods of the Great Sage
Protected the front and guarded the rear with care and skill.
A few rounds of bitter contest revealed no victor,
But the prince's mind would not so easily rest.
He ordered the six kinds of weapon to change
Into hundreds and thousands of millions, aiming for the head.
The Monkey King, undaunted, roared with laughter loud,
And wielded his iron rod with artful ease:
One turned to a thousand, a thousand to ten thousand,
Filling the sky as a swarm of dancing dragons,
And shocked the Monster Kings of sundry caves into shutting their doors.
Demons and monsters all over the mountain hid their heads.
The angry breath of divine soldiers was like oppressive clouds.
The golden-hooped iron rod whizzed like the wind.
On this side,

The battle cries of celestial fighters appalled everyone;
On that side,
The banner-waving of monkey monsters startled each person.
Growing fierce, the two parties both willed a test of strength.
We know not who was stronger and who weaker.

Each displaying his divine powers, the Third Prince and Wukong battled for thirty rounds. The six weapons of that prince changed into a thousand and ten thousand pieces; the golden-hooped rod of Sun Wukong into ten thousand and a thousand. They clashed like raindrops and meteors in the air, but victory or defeat was not yet determined. Wukong, however, proved to be the one swifter of eye and hand. Right in the midst of the confusion, he plucked a piece of hair and shouted, "Change!" It changed into a copy of him, also wielding a rod in its hands and deceiving Naṭa. His real person leaped behind Naṭa and struck his left shoulder with the rod. Naṭa, still performing his magic, heard the rod whizzing through the air and tried desperately to dodge it. Unable to move quickly enough, he took the blow and fled in pain. Breaking off his magic and gathering up his six weapons, he returned to his camp in defeat.

Standing in front of his battle line, Devarāja Li saw what was happening and was about to go to his son's assistance. The prince, however, came to him first and gasped, "Father King! The BanHorsePlague is truly powerful. Even your son of such magical strength is no match for him! He has wounded me in the shoulder." "If this fellow is so powerful," said the Devarāja, turning pale with fright, "how can we beat him?" The prince said, "In front of his cave he has set up a banner bearing the words, 'The Great Sage, Equal to Heaven.' By his own mouth he boastfully asserted that if the Jade Emperor appointed him to such a title, all troubles would cease. If he were not given this name, he would surely fight his way up to the Treasure Hall of Divine Mists!" "If that's the case," said the Devarāja, "let's not fight with him for the moment. Let us return to the region above and report these words. There will be time then for us to send for more celestial soldiers and take this fellow on all sides." The prince was in such pain that he could not do battle again; he therefore went back to Heaven with the Devarāja to report, of which we speak no further.

Look at that Monkey King returning to his mountain in triumph! The monster kings of seventy-two caves and the six sworn brothers all came to congratulate him, and they feasted jubilantly in the blessed cave dwelling. He then said to the six brothers, "If little brother is now called the Great Sage, Equal to Heaven, why don't all of you assume the title of Great Sage also?" "Our worthy brother's words are right!" shouted the Bull Monster King from their midst,[11] "I'm going to be called the Great Sage, Parallel with Heaven." "I shall be called the Great Sage, Covering the Ocean," said the Dragon Monster King. "I shall be called the Great Sage, United with Heaven," said the Garuda Monster King. "I shall be called the Great Sage, Mover of Mountains," said the Giant Lynx King. "I shall be called the Tell-tale Great Sage," said the Macaque King. "And I shall be called the God-Routing Great Sage," said the Orangutan King. At that moment, the seven Great Sages had complete freedom to do as they pleased and to call themselves whatever titles they liked. They had fun for a whole day and then dispersed.

Now we return to the Devarāja Li and the Third Prince, who, leading the other commanders, went straight to the Treasure Hall of Divine Mists to give this report: "By your holy decree your subjects led the expeditionary force down to the Region Below to subdue the baneful immortal, Sun Wukong. We had no idea of his enormous power, and we could not prevail against him. We beseech Your Majesty to give us reinforcements to wipe him out." "How powerful can we expect one baneful monkey to be," asked the Jade Emperor, "that reinforcements are needed?" "May Your Majesty pardon us from an offense worthy of death!" said the prince, drawing closer. "That baneful monkey wielded an iron rod; he defeated first the Mighty-Spirit God and then wounded the shoulder of your subject. Outside the door of his cave he set up a banner bearing the words, 'The Great Sage, Equal to Heaven.' He said that if he were given such a rank, he would lay down his arms and come to declare his allegiance. If not, he would fight his way up to the Treasure Hall of Divine Mists."

"How dare this baneful monkey be so insolent!" exclaimed the Jade Emperor, astonished by what he had heard. "We must order the generals to have him executed at once!" As he said this, the Gold Star of Venus came forward again from the ranks and said, "The baneful monkey knows how to make a speech, but he has no idea what's appropriate and what isn't. Even if reinforcements are sent to fight him, I don't think he can be subdued right away without taxing our forces. It would be better if Your Majesty were greatly to extend your mercy and proclaim yet another decree of pacification. Let him indeed be made the Great Sage, Equal to Heaven; he will be given an empty title, in short, rank without compensation." "What do you mean by rank without compensation?" said the Jade Emperor. The Gold Star said, "His name will be Great Sage, Equal to Heaven, but he will not be given any official duty or salary. We shall keep him here in Heaven so that we may put his perverse mind at rest and make him desist from his madness and arrogance. The universe will then be calm and the oceans tranquil again." Hearing these words, the Jade Emperor said, "We shall follow the counsels of our minister." He ordered the mandate to be made up and the Gold Star to bear it hence.

The Gold Star left through the South Heaven Gate once again and headed straight for the Flower-Fruit Mountain. Outside the Water-Curtain Cave things were quite different from the way they had been the previous time. He found the entire region filled with the awesome and bellicose presence of every conceivable kind of monster, each one of them clutching swords and spears, wielding scimitars and staffs. Growling and leaping about, they began to attack the Gold Star the moment they saw him. "You, chieftains, hear me," said the Gold Star, "let me trouble you to report this to your Great Sage. I am the Heavenly messenger sent by the Lord above, and I bear an imperial decree of invitation." The various monsters ran inside to report, "There is an old man outside who says that he is a Heavenly messenger from the region above, bearing a decree of invitation for you." "Welcome! Welcome!" said Wukong. "He must be that Gold Star of Venus who came here last time. Although it was a shabby position they gave me when he invited me up to the region above, I nevertheless made it to Heaven once and familiarized myself with the ins and outs of the celestial passages. He has come again this time undoubtedly with good intentions." He commanded the various chieftains to wave the banners and beat the drums, and to draw up the troops in receiving order. Leading the rest of the monkeys, the Great Sage donned his cap and his cuirass, over which he tossed the red and yellow robe, and slipped on the cloud shoes. He ran to the mouth of the cave, bowed courteously, and said in a loud voice, "Please come in, Old Star! Forgive me for not coming out to meet you."

The Gold Star strode forward and entered the cave. He stood facing south and declared, "Now I inform the Great Sage. Because the Great Sage has objected to the meanness of his previous appointment and removed himself from the imperial stables, the officials of that department, both great and small, reported the matter to the Jade Emperor. The proclamation of the Jade Emperor said at first, 'All appointed officials advance from lowly positions to exalted ones. Why should he object to that arrangement?' This led to the campaign against you by Devarāja Li and Naṭa. They were ignorant of the Great Sage's power and therefore suffered defeat. They reported back to Heaven that you had set up a banner that made known your desire to be the Great Sage, Equal to Heaven. The various martial officials still wanted to deny your request. It was this old man who, risking offense, pleaded the case of the Great Sage, so that he might be invited to receive a new appointment, and without the use of force. The Jade Emperor accepted my suggestion; hence I am here to invite you." "I caused you trouble last time," said Wukong, laughing, "and now I am again indebted to you for your kindness. Thank you! Thank you! But is there really such a rank as the Great Sage, Equal to Heaven, up there?" "I made certain that this title was approved," said the Gold Star, "before I dared come with the decree. If there is any mishap, let this old man be held responsible."

Wukong was highly pleased, but the Gold Star refused his earnest invitation to stay for a banquet. He therefore mounted the hallowed cloud with the Gold Star and went to the South Heaven Gate, where they were welcomed by the celestial generals and guardians with hands folded at their breasts. Going straight into the Treasure Hall of Divine Mists, the Gold Star prostrated himself and memorialized, "Your subject, by your decree, has summoned here BanHorsePlague Sun Wukong." "Have that Sun Wukong come forward," said the Jade Emperor. "I now proclaim you to be the Great Sage, Equal to Heaven, a position of the highest rank. But you must indulge no more in your preposterous behavior." Bowing deeply, the monkey uttered a great whoop of thanks. The Jade Emperor then ordered two building officials, Zhang and Lu, to erect the official residence of the Great Sage, Equal to Heaven, to the right of the Garden of Immortal Peaches. Inside the mansion, two departments were established, named "Peace and Quiet" and "Serene Spirit," both of which were full of attending officials. The Jade Emperor also ordered the Star Spirits of Five Poles[12] to accompany Wukong to assume his post. In addition, two bottles of imperial wine and ten clusters of golden flowers were bestowed on him, with the order that he must keep himself under control and make up his mind to indulge no more in preposterous behavior. The Monkey King obediently accepted the command and went that day with the Star Spirits to assume his post. He opened the bottles of wine and drank them all with his colleagues. After seeing the Star Spirits off to their own palaces, he settled down in complete contentment and delight to enjoy the pleasures of Heaven, without the slightest worry or care. Truly

> His name divine, forever recorded in the Long-Life Book
> And kept from falling into saṃsāra, will long be known.

We do not know what took place hereafter; let's listen to the explanation in the next chapter.

FIVE

Disrupting the Peach Festival, the Great Sage steals elixir;
With revolt in Heaven, many gods would seize the fiend.

Now we must tell you that the Great Sage, after all, was a monkey monster; in truth, he had no knowledge of his title or rank, nor did he care for the size of his salary. He did nothing but place his name on the Register. At his official residence he was cared for night and day by the attending officials of the two departments. His sole concern was to eat three meals a day and to sleep soundly at night. Having neither duties nor worries, he was free and content to tour the mansions and meet friends, to make new acquaintances and form new alliances at his leisure. When he met the Three Pure Ones,[1] he addressed them as "Your Reverence"; and when he ran into the Four Thearchs,[2] he would say, "Your Majesty." As for the Nine Luminaries,[3] the Generals of the Five Quarters, the Twenty-Eight Constellations,[4] the Four Devarājas,[5] the Twelve Horary Branches,[6] the Five Elders of the Five Regions,[7] the Star Spirits of the entire Heaven, and the numerous gods of the Milky Way,[8] he called them all brother and treated them in a fraternal manner. Today he toured the east, and tomorrow he wandered west. Going and coming on the clouds, he had no specific itinerary.

Early one morning, when the Jade Emperor was holding court, the Daoist immortal Xu Jingyang[9] stepped from the ranks and went forward to memorialize, kowtowing, "The Great Sage, Equal to Heaven, has no duties at present and merely dawdles away his time. He has become quite chummy with the various Stars and Constellations of Heaven, calling them his friends regardless of whether they are his superiors or subordinates, and I fear that his idleness may lead to roguery. It would be better to give him some assignment so that he will not grow mischievous." When the Jade Emperor heard these words, he sent for the Monkey King at once, who came amiably. "Your Majesty," he said, "what promotion or reward did you have in mind for old Monkey when you called him?" "We perceive," said the Jade Emperor, "that your life is quite indolent, since you have nothing to do, and we have decided therefore to give you an assignment. You will temporarily take care of the Garden of Immortal Peaches. Be careful and diligent, morning and evening." Delighted, the Great Sage bowed deeply and grunted his gratitude as he withdrew.

He could not restrain himself from rushing immediately into the Garden of Immortal Peaches to inspect the place. A local spirit from the garden stopped him and asked, "Where is the Great Sage going?" "I have been authorized by the Jade Emperor," said the Great Sage, "to look after the Garden of Immortal Peaches. I have come to conduct an inspection." The local spirit hurriedly saluted him and then called together all the stewards in charge of hoeing, watering, tending peaches, and cleaning and sweeping. They all came to kowtow to the Great Sage and led him inside. There he saw

Radiantly young and lovely,
On every trunk and limb—
Radiantly young and lovely blossoms filling the trees,
And fruits on every trunk and limb weighing down the stems.
The fruits, weighing down the stems, hang like balls of gilt:
The blossoms, filling the trees, form tufts of rouge.
Ever they bloom, and ever fruit-bearing, they ripen in a thousand years;
Not knowing winter or summer, they lengthen out to ten thousand years.
Those that first ripen glow like faces reddened with wine,
While those half-grown ones
Are stalk-held and green-skinned.
Encased in smoke their flesh retains their green,
But sunlight reveals their cinnabar grace.
Beneath the trees are rare flowers and exotic grass
Which colors, unfading in four seasons, remain the same.
The towers, the terraces, and the studios left and right
Rise so high into the air that often cloud covers are seen.
Not planted by the vulgar or the worldly of the Dark City,
They are grown and tended by the Queen Mother of the Jade Pool.[10]

The Great Sage enjoyed this sight for a long time and then asked the local spirit, "How many trees are there?" "There are three thousand six hundred," said the local spirit. "In the front are one thousand two hundred trees with little flowers and small fruits. These ripen once every three thousand years, and after one taste of them a man will become an immortal enlightened in the Way, with healthy limbs and a lightweight body. In the middle are one thousand two hundred trees of layered flowers and sweet fruits. They ripen once every six thousand years. If a man eats them, he will ascend to Heaven with the mist and never grow old. At the back are one thousand two hundred trees with fruits of purple veins and pale yellow pits. These ripen once every nine thousand years and, if eaten, will make a man's age equal to that of Heaven and Earth, the sun and the moon." Highly pleased by these words, the Great Sage that very day made thorough inspection of the trees and a listing of the arbors and pavilions before returning to his residence. From then on, he would go there to enjoy the scenery once every three or four days. He no longer consorted with his friends, nor did he take any more trips.

One day he saw that more than half of the peaches on the branches of the older trees had ripened, and he wanted very much to eat one and sample its novel taste. Closely followed, however, by the local spirit of the garden, the stewards, and the divine attendants of the Equal to Heaven Residence, he found it inconvenient to do so. He therefore devised a plan on the spur of the moment and said to them, "Why don't you all wait for me outside and let me rest a while in this arbor?" The various immortals withdrew accordingly. That Monkey King then took off his cap and robe and climbed up onto a big tree. He selected the large peaches that were thoroughly ripened and, plucking many of them, ate to his heart's content right on the branches. Only after he had his fill did he jump down from the tree. Pinning back his cap and donning his robe, he called for his train of followers to return to the residence. After two or three days, he used the same device to steal peaches to gratify himself once again.

One day the Lady Queen Mother decided to open wide her treasure chamber and to give a banquet for the Grand Festival of Immortal Peaches, which was to be held in the Palace of the Jasper Pool. She ordered the various Immortal Maidens—Red Gown, Blue Gown, White Gown, Black Gown, Purple Gown, Yellow Gown, and Green Gown—to go with their flower baskets to the Garden of Immortal Peaches and pick the fruits for the festival. The seven maidens went to the gate of the garden and found it guarded by the local spirit, the stewards, and the ministers from the two departments of the Equal to Heaven Residence. The girls approached them, saying, "We have been ordered by the Queen Mother to pick some peaches for our banquet." "Divine maidens," said the local spirit, "please wait a moment. This year is not quite the same as last year. The Jade Emperor has put in charge here the Great Sage, Equal to Heaven, and we must report to him before we are allowed to open the gate." "Where is the Great Sage?" asked the maidens. "He is in the garden," said the local spirit. "Because he is tired, he is sleeping alone in the arbor." "If that's the case," said the maidens, "let us go and find him, for we cannot be late." The local spirit went into the garden with them; they found their way to the arbor but saw no one. Only the cap and the robe were left in the arbor, but there was no person to be seen. The Great Sage, you see, had played for a while and eaten a number of peaches. He had then changed himself into a figure only two inches high and, perching on the branch of a large tree, had fallen asleep under the cover of thick leaves. "Since we came by imperial decree," said the Seven-Gown Immortal Maidens, "how can we return empty-handed, even though we cannot locate the Great Sage?" One of the divine officials said from the side, "Since the divine maidens have come by decree, they should wait no longer. Our Great Sage has a habit of wandering off somewhere, and he must have left the garden to meet his friends. Go and pick your peaches now, and we shall report the matter for you." The Immortal Maidens followed his suggestion and went into the grove to pick their peaches.

They gathered two basketfuls from the trees in front and filled three more baskets from the trees in the middle. When they went to the trees at the back of the grove, they found that the flowers were sparse and the fruits scanty. Only a few peaches with hairy stems and green skins were left, for the fact is that the Monkey King had eaten all the ripe ones. Looking this way and that, the Seven Immortal Maidens found on a branch pointing southward one single peach that was half white and half red. The Blue Gown Maiden pulled the branch down with her hand, and the Red Gown Maiden, after plucking the fruit, let the branch snap back up into its position. This was the very branch on which the transformed Great Sage was sleeping. Startled by her, the Great Sage revealed his true form and whipped out from his ear the golden-hooped rod. One wave and it had the thickness of a rice bowl. "From what region have you come, monsters," he cried, "that you have the gall to steal my peaches?" Terrified, the Seven Immortal Maidens knelt down together and pleaded, "Let the Great Sage calm himself! We are not monsters, but the Seven-Gown Immortal Maidens sent by the Lady Queen Mother to pluck the fruits needed for the Grand Festival of Immortal Peaches, when the treasure chamber is opened wide. We just came here and first saw the local spirit of the garden, who could not find the Great Sage. Fearing that we might be delayed in fulfilling the command of the Queen Mother, we did not wait for the Great Sage but proceeded to pluck the peaches. We beg you to forgive us."

When the Great Sage heard these words, his anger changed to delight. "Please arise, divine maidens," he said. "Who is invited to the banquet when the Queen Mother opens wide her treasure chamber?" "The last festival had its own set of rules," said the Immortal Maidens, "and those invited were: the Buddha, the Bodhisattvas, the holy monks, and the arhats of the Western Heaven; Kuan-yin from the South Pole; the Holy Emperor of Great Mercy of the East; the Immortals of Ten Continents and Three Islands; the Dark Spirit of the North Pole; the Great Immortal of the Yellow Horn from the Imperial Center. These were the Elders from the Five Quarters. In addition, there were the Star Spirits of the Five Poles, the Three Pure Ones, the Four Deva Kings, the Heavenly Deva of the Great Monad, and the rest from the Upper Eight Caves. From the Middle Eight Caves there were the Jade Emperor, the Nine Heroes, the Immortals of the Seas and Mountains; and from the Lower Eight Caves, there were the Pope of Darkness and the Terrestrial Immortals. The gods and devas, both great and small, of every palace and mansion, will be attending this happy Festival of the Immortal Peaches."

"Am I invited?" asked the Great Sage, laughing. "We haven't heard your name mentioned," said the Immortal Maidens. "I am the Great Sage, Equal to Heaven," said the Great Sage. "Why shouldn't I, old Monkey, be made an honored guest at the party?" "Well, we told you the rule for the last festival," said the Immortal Maidens, "but we do not know what will happen this time." "You are right," said the Great Sage, "and I don't blame you. You all just stand here and let old Monkey go and do a little detection to find out whether he's invited or not."

Dear Great Sage! He made a magic sign and recited a spell, saying to the various Immortal Maidens, "Stay! Stay! Stay!" This was the magic of immobilization, the effect of which was that the Seven-Gown Immortal Maidens all stood wide-eyed and transfixed beneath the peach trees. Leaping out of the garden, the Great Sage mounted his hallowed cloud and headed straight for the Jasper Pool. As he journeyed, he saw over there

> *A skyful of holy mist with sparkling light,*
> *And five-colored clouds passing ceaselessly.*[11]
> *The cries of white cranes pierced the ninefold Heav'n;*
> *Purple fungi bloomed through a thousand leaves.*
> *Right in this midst an immortal appeared*
> *With a natural, fair face and manner distinct.*
> *His spirit glowed like a dancing rainbow;*
> *A list of no birth or death hung from his waist.*
> *His name, the Great Immortal of Naked Feet:*[12]
> *Attending the Peaches Feast he'd lengthen his age.*

That Great Immortal of Naked Feet ran right into the Great Sage, who, his head bowed, was just devising a plan to deceive the real immortal. Since he wanted to go in secret to the festival, he asked, "Where is the Venerable Wisdom going?" The Great Immortal said, "On the kind invitation of the Queen Mother, I am going to the happy Festival of Immortal Peaches." "The Venerable Wisdom has not yet learned of what I'm about to say," said the Great Sage. "Because of the speed of my cloud somersault, the Jade Emperor has sent old Monkey out to all five thoroughfares to invite people to go first to the Hall of Perfect Light for a rehearsal of ceremonies before attending the banquet." Being a sincere and honest man, the Great Immortal took the lie for the truth, though he protested, "In years past we rehearsed right at the Jasper Pool and expressed our gratitude there. Why do we have to go to the Hall of Perfect Light for rehearsal this time before attending the banquet?" Nonetheless, he had no choice but to change the direction of his hallowed cloud and go straight to the hall.

Treading the cloud, the Great Sage recited a spell and, with one shake of his body, changed into the form of the Great Immortal of Naked Feet. It did not take him very long before he reached the treasure chamber. He stopped his cloud and walked softly inside. There he found

Swirling waves of ambrosial fragrance,
Dense layers of holy mist,
A jade terrace decked with ornaments,
A chamber full of the life force,
Ethereal shapes of the phoenix soaring and the argus rising,
And undulant forms of gold blossoms with stems of jade.
Set upon there were the Screen of Nine Phoenixes in Twilight,
The Beacon Mound of Eight Treasures and Purple Mist,
A table inlaid with five-color gold,
And a green jade pot of a thousand flowers.
On the tables were dragon livers and phoenix marrow,
Bear paws and the lips of apes.[13]
Most tempting was every one of the hundred delicacies,
And most succulent the hue of every kind of fruit and food.

Everything was laid out in an orderly fashion, but no deity had yet arrived for the feast. Our Great Sage could not make an end of staring at the scene when he suddenly felt the overpowering aroma of wine. Turning his head, he saw, in the long corridor to the right, several wine-making divine officials and grain-mashing stewards. They were giving directions to the few Daoists charged with carrying water and the boys who took care of the fire in washing out the barrels and scrubbing the jugs. For they had already finished making the wine, rich and mellow as the juices of jade. The Great Sage could not prevent the saliva from dripping out of the corner of his mouth, and he wanted to have a taste at once, except that the people were all standing there. He therefore resorted to magic. Plucking a few hairs, he threw them into his mouth and chewed them to pieces before spitting them out. He recited a spell and cried "Change!" They changed into many sleep-inducing insects, which landed on the people's faces. Look at them, how their hands grow weak, their heads droop, and their eyelids sink down. They dropped their activities, and all fell sound asleep. The Great Sage then took some of the rare delicacies and choicest dainties and ran into the corridor. Standing beside the jars and leaning on the barrels, he abandoned himself to drinking. After feasting for a long time, he became thoroughly drunk, but he turned this over in his mind, "Bad! Bad! In a little while, when the invited guests arrive, won't they be indignant with me? What will happen to me once I'm caught? I'd better go back home now and sleep it off!"

Dear Great Sage! Reeling from side to side, he stumbled along solely on the strength of wine, and in a moment he lost his way. It was not the Equal to Heaven Residence that he went to, but the Tushita Palace. The moment he saw it, he realized his mistake. "The Tushita Palace is at the uppermost of the thirty-three Heavens," he said, "the Griefless Heaven, which is the home of the Most High Laozi. How did I get here? No matter, I've always wanted to see this old man but have never found the opportunity. Now that it's on my way, I might as well pay him a visit." He straightened out his attire and pushed his way in, but Laozi was nowhere to be seen. In fact, there was not a trace of anyone. The fact of the matter was that Laozi, accompanied by the Aged Buddha Dīpaṁkara, was giving a lecture on the tall, three-storied Red Mound Elixir Platform. The various divine youths, commanders, and officials were all attending the lecture, standing on both sides of the platform. Searching around, our Great Sage went all the way to the alchemical room. He found no one but saw fire burning in an oven beside the hearth, and around the oven were five gourds in which finished elixir was stored. "This thing is the greatest treasure of immortals," said the Great Sage happily. "Since old Monkey has understood the Way and comprehended the mystery of the Internal's identity with the External, I have also wanted to produce some golden elixir on my own to benefit people. While I have been too busy at other times even to think about going home to enjoy myself, good fortune has met me at the door today and presented me with this! As long as Laozi is not around, I'll take a few tablets and try the taste of something new." He poured out the contents of all the gourds and ate them like fried beans.

In a moment, the effect of the elixir had dispelled that of the wine, and he again thought to himself, "Bad! Bad! I have brought on myself calamity greater than Heaven! If the Jade Emperor has knowledge of this, it'll be difficult to preserve my life! Go! Go! Go! I'll go back to the Region Below to be a king." He ran out of the Tushita Palace and, avoiding the former way, left by the West Heaven Gate, making himself invisible by the magic of body concealment. Lowering the direction of his cloud, he returned to the Flower-Fruit Mountain. There he was greeted by flashing banners and shining spears, for the four mighty commanders and the monster kings of seventy-two caves were engaging in a military exercise. "Little ones," the Great Sage called out loudly, "I have returned!" The monsters dropped their weapons and knelt down, saying, "Great Sage! What laxity of mind! You left us for so long, and did not even once visit us to see how we were doing." "It's not that long!" said the Great Sage. "It's not that long!" They walked as they talked, and went deep inside the cave dwelling. After sweeping the place clean and preparing a place for him to rest, and after kowtowing and doing homage, the four mighty commanders said, "The Great Sage has been living for over a century in Heaven. May we ask what appointment he actually received?"

"I recall that it's been but half a year," said the Great Sage, laughing. "How can you talk of a century?" "One day in Heaven," said the commanders, "is equal to one year on Earth." The Great Sage said, "I am glad to say that the Jade Emperor this time was more favorably disposed toward me, and he did indeed appoint me Great Sage, Equal to Heaven. An official residence was built for me, and two departments—Peace and Quiet, and Serene Spirit—were established, with bodyguards and attendants in each department. Later, when it was found that I carried no responsibility, I was asked to take care of the Garden of Immortal Peaches. Recently the Lady Queen Mother gave the Grand Festival of Immortal Peaches, but she did not invite me. Without waiting for her invitation, I went first to the Jasper Pool and secretly consumed the food and wine. Leaving that place, I staggered into the palace of Laozi and finished up all the elixir stored in five gourds. I was afraid that the Jade Emperor would be offended, and so I decided to walk out of the Heaven Gate."

The various monsters were delighted by these words, and they prepared a banquet of fruits and wine to welcome him. A stone bowl was filled with coconut wine and presented to the Great Sage, who took a mouthful and then exclaimed with a grimace, "It tastes awful! Just awful!" "The Great Sage," said Beng and Ba, the two commanders, "has grown accustomed to tasting divine wine and food in Heaven. Small wonder that coconut wine now seems hardly delectable. But the proverb says, 'Tasty or not, it's water from home!'" "And all of you are, 'related or not, people from home'!" said the Great Sage. "When I was enjoying myself this morning at the Jasper Pool, I saw many jars and jugs in the corridor full of the juices of jade, which you have never savored. Let me go back and steal a few bottles to bring down here. Just drink half a cup, and each one of you will live long without growing old." The various monkeys could not contain their delight. The Great Sage immediately left the cave and, with one somersault, went directly back to the Festival of Immortal Peaches, again using the magic of body concealment. As he entered the doorway of the Palace of the Jasper Pool, he saw that the wine makers, the grain mashers, the water carriers, and the fire tenders were still asleep and snoring. He took two large bottles, one under each arm, and carried two more in his hands. Reversing the direction of his cloud, he returned to the monkeys in the cave. They held their own Festival of Immortal Wine, with each one drinking a few cups, which incident we shall relate no further.

Now we tell you about the Seven-Gown Immortal Maidens, who did not find a release from the Great Sage's magic of immobilization until a whole day had gone by. Each one of them then took her flower basket and reported to the Queen Mother, saying, "We are delayed because the Great Sage, Equal to Heaven, imprisoned us with his magic." "How many baskets of immortal peaches have you gathered?" asked the Queen Mother. "Only two baskets of small peaches, and three of medium-sized peaches," said the Immortal Maidens, "for when we went to the back of the grove, there was not even half a large one left! We think the Great Sage must have eaten them all. As we went looking for him, he unexpectedly made his appearance and threatened us with violence and beating. He also questioned us about who had been invited to the banquet, and we gave him a thorough account of the last festival. It was then that he bound us with a spell, and we didn't know where he went. It was only a moment ago that we found release and so could come back here."

When the Queen Mother heard these words, she went immediately to the Jade Emperor and presented him with a full account of what had taken place. Before she finished speaking, the group of wine makers together with the various divine officials also came to report: "Someone unknown to us has vandalized the Festival of Immortal Peaches. The juice of jade, the eight dainties, and the hundred delicacies have all been stolen or eaten up." Four royal preceptors then came up to announce, "The Supreme Patriarch of Dao has arrived." The Jade Emperor went out with the Queen Mother to greet him. Having paid his respects to them, Laozi said, "There are, in the house of this old Daoist, some finished Golden Elixir of Nine Turns,[14] which are reserved for the use of Your Majesty during the next Grand Festival of Cinnabar. Strange to say, they have been stolen by some thief, and I have come specifically to make this known to Your Majesty." This report stunned the Jade Emperor. Presently the officials from the Equal to Heaven Residence came to announce, kowtowing, "The Great Sage Sun has not been discharging his duties of late. He went out yesterday and still has not yet returned. Moreover, we do not know where he went." These words gave the Jade Emperor added anxiety.

Next came the Great Immortal of Naked Feet, who prostrated himself and said, "Yesterday, in response to the Queen Mother's invitation, your subject was on his way to attend the festival when he met by chance the Great Sage, Equal to Heaven. The Sage said to your subject that Your Majesty had ordered him to send your subject first to the Hall of Perfect Light for a rehearsal of ceremonies before attending the banquet. Your subject followed his direction and duly went to the hall. But I did not see the dragon chariot and the phoenix carriage of Your Majesty, and therefore hastened to come here to wait upon you."

More astounded than ever, the Jade Emperor said, "This fellow now falsifies imperial decrees and deceives my worthy ministers! Let the Divine Minister of Detection quickly locate his whereabouts!" The minister received his order and left the palace to make a thorough investigation. After obtaining all the details, he returned presently to report, "The person who has so profoundly disturbed Heaven is none other than the Great Sage, Equal to Heaven." He then gave a repeated account of all the previous incidents, and the Jade Emperor was furious. He at once commanded the Four Great Devarājas to assist Devarāja Li and Prince Naṭa. Together, they called up the Twenty-Eight Constellations, the Nine Luminaries, the Twelve Horary Branches, the Fearless Guards of Five Quarters,[15] the Four Temporal Guardians,[16] the Stars of East and West, the Gods of North and South, the Deities of the Five Mountains and the Four Rivers,[17] the Star Spirits of the entire Heaven, and a hundred thousand celestial soldiers. They were ordered to set up eighteen sets of cosmic net, to journey to the Region Below, to encircle completely the Flower-Fruit Mountain, and to capture the rogue and bring him to justice. All the deities immediately alerted their troops and departed from the Heavenly Palace. As they left, this was the spectacle of the expedition:

Yellow with dust; the churning wind concealed the darkening sky:
Reddish with clay, the rising fog o'erlaid the dusky world.
Because an impish monkey insulted the Highest Lord,
The saints of all Heaven descended to this mortal Earth.
Those Four Great Devarājas,
Those Fearless Guards of Five Quarters—
Those Four Great Deva Kings made up the main command;
Those Fearless Guards of Five Quarters moved countless troops.
Li, the Pagoda Bearer, gave orders from the army's center,
With the fierce Naṭa as the captain of his vanward forces.
The Star of Rāhu, at the forefront, made the roll call;
The Star of Ketu, noble and tall, brought up the rear:
Sōma, the moon, displayed a spirit most eager;
Āditya, the sun, was all shining and radiant.
Heroes of special talents were the Stars of Five Phases.
The Nine Luminaries most relished a good battle.
The Horary Branches of Zi, Wu, Mao, and Yao—
They were all celestial guardians of titanic strength.
To the east and west, the Five Plagues[18] and the Five Mountains!
To the left and right, the Six Gods of Darkness and the Six Gods of Light!
Above and below, the Dragon Gods of the Four Rivers!
And in tightest formation, the Twenty-Eight Constellations![19]
Citrā, Svātī, Viśākhā, and Anurādhā were the captains.
Revatī, Aśvinī, Apabharaṇī, and Kṛttikā knew combat well.
Uttara-Aṣāḍhā, Abhijit, Śravaṇā, Śraviṣṭha, Pūrva-Proṣṭhapada, Uttara-
* Proṣṭhapada,*
Rohiṇī, Mūlabarhaṇī, Pūrva-Aṣāḍhā—every one an able star!

Punarvasu, Tiṣya, Aśleṣā, Meghā, Pūrva-Phalgunī, Uttara-Phalgunī,
  and Hastā—
All brandished swords and spears to show their power.
Stopping the cloud and lowering the mist they came to this mortal world
And pitched their tents before the Mountain of Flower and Fruit.

The poem says:

The Heav'n-born Monkey King who can change a lot
Steals wine and elixir to joy in his mountain lair.
Since he spoiled the Feast of the Immortal Peach,
A hundred thousand Heaven troops spread the net of God.

Devarāja Li now gave the order for the celestial soldiers to pitch their tents, and a cordon was drawn so tightly around the Flower-Fruit Mountain that not even water could escape! Moreover, eighteen sets of cosmic net were spread out above and below the region, and the Nine Luminaries were then ordered to go into battle. They led their troops and advanced to the cave, in front of which they found a troop of monkeys, both great and small, prancing about playfully. "Little monsters over there," cried one of the Star Spirits in a severe voice, "where is your Great Sage? We are Heavenly deities sent here from the Region Above to subdue your rebellious Great Sage. Tell him to come here quickly and surrender. If he but utters half a 'No,' all of you will be executed." Hastily the little monsters reported inside, "Great Sage, disaster! Disaster! Outside there are nine savage deities who claim that they are sent from the Region Above to subdue the Great Sage." Our Great Sage was just sharing the Heavenly wine with the four mighty commanders and the monster kings of seventy-two caves. Hearing this announcement, he said in a most nonchalant manner,

"If you have wine today, get drunk today;
Mind not the troubles in front of your door!"

Scarcely had he uttered this proverb when another group of imps came leaping and said, "Those nine savage gods are trying to provoke battle with foul words and nasty language." "Don't listen to them," said the Great Sage, laughing.

"Let us seek today's pleasure in poetry and wine,
And cease asking when we may achieve glory or fame."

Hardly had he finished speaking when still another flock of imps arrived to report, "Father, those nine savage gods have broken down the door, and are about to fight their way in!"

"These reckless, witless gods!" said the Great Sage angrily. "They really have no manners! I was not about to quarrel with them. Why are they abusing me to my face?" He gave the order for the One-Horn Demon King to lead the monster kings of seventy-two caves to battle, adding that old Monkey and the four mighty commanders would follow in the rear. The Demon King swiftly led his troops of ogres to go out to fight, but they were ambushed by the Nine Luminaries and pinned down right at the head of the sheet iron bridge.

At the height of the melee, the Great Sage arrived. "Make way!" he yelled, whipping out his iron rod. One wave of it and it was as thick as a rice bowl and about twelve feet long. The Great Sage plunged into battle, and none of the Nine Luminaries dared oppose him. In a moment, they were all beaten back. When they regrouped themselves again in battle formation, the Nine Luminaries stood still and said, "You senseless BanHorsePlague! You are guilty of the ten evils.[20] You first stole peaches and then wine, utterly disrupting the Grand Festival of Immortal Peaches. You also robbed Laozi of his immortal elixir, and then you had the gall to plunder the imperial winery for your personal enjoyment. Don't you realize that you have piled up sin upon sin?" "Indeed," said the Great Sage, "these several incidents did occur! But what do you intend to do now?" The Nine Luminaries said, "We received the golden decree of the Jade Emperor to lead our troops here to subdue you. Submit at once, and spare these creatures from being slaughtered. If not, we shall level this mountain and overturn this cave!" "How great is your magical power, silly gods," retorted the Great Sage angrily, "that you dare to mouth such foolhardy words? Don't go away! Have a taste of old Monkey's rod!" The Nine Luminaries mounted a joint attack, but the Handsome Monkey King was not in the least intimidated. He wielded his golden-hooped rod, parrying left and right, and fought the Nine Luminaries until they were thoroughly exhausted. Every one of them turned around and fled, his weapons trailing behind him. Running into the tent at the center of their army, they said to the Pagoda Bearer Devarāja, "That Monkey King is indeed an intrepid warrior! We cannot withstand him, and have returned defeated."

Devarāja Li then ordered the Four Great Devarājas and the Twenty-Eight Constellations to go out together to do battle. Without displaying the slightest panic, the Great Sage also ordered the One-Horn Demon King, the monster kings of seventy-two caves, and the four mighty commanders to range themselves in battle formation in front of the cave. Look at this all-out battle! It was truly terrifying with

The cold, soughing wind,
The dark, dreadful fog.
On one side, the colorful banners fluttered;

On the other, lances and halberds glimmered.
There were row upon row of shining helmets,
And coat upon coat of gleaming armor.
Row upon row of helmets shining in the sunlight
Resembled silver bells whose chimes echoed in the sky;
Coat upon coat of gleaming armor rising clifflike in layers
Seemed like glaciers crushing the earth.
The giant scimitars
Flew and flashed like lightning;
The mulberry-white spears,
Could pierce even mist and cloud!
The crosslike halberds
And tiger-eye lashes
Were arranged like thick rows of hemp;
The green swords of bronze
And four-sided shovels
Crowded together like trees in a dense forest.
Curved bows, crossbows, and stout arrows with eagle plumes,
Short staffs and snakelike lances—all could kill or maim.
That compliant rod, which the Great Sage owned,
Kept tossing and turning in this battle with gods.
They fought till the air was rid of birds flying by;
Wolves and tigers were driven from within the mount;
The planet was darkened by hurtling rocks and stones,
And the cosmos bedimmed by flying dust and dirt.
The clamor and clangor disturbed Heaven and Earth;
The scrap and scuffle alarmed both demons and gods.

Beginning with the battle formation at dawn, they fought until the sun sank down behind the western hills. The One-Horn Demon King and the monster kings of seventy-two caves were all taken captive by the forces of Heaven. Those who escaped were the four mighty commanders and the troop of monkeys, who hid themselves deep inside the Water-Curtain Cave. With his single rod, the Great Sage withstood in midair the Four Great Devarājas, Li the Pagoda Bearer, and Prince Naṭa, and battled with them for a long time. When he saw that evening was approaching, the Great Sage plucked a handful of hairs, threw them into his mouth, and chewed them to pieces. He spat them out, crying, "Change!" They changed at once into many thousands of Great Sages, each employing a golden-hooped rod! They beat back Prince Naṭa and defeated the Five Devarājas.

In triumph the Great Sage collected back his hairs and hurried back to his cave. Soon, at the head of the sheet iron bridge, he was met by the four mighty commanders leading the rest of the monkeys. As they kowtowed to receive him they cried three times, sobbing aloud, and then they laughed three times, hee-heeing and ho-hoing. The Great Sage said, "Why do you all laugh and cry when you see me?" "When we fought with the Deva Kings this morning," said the four mighty commanders, "the monster kings of seventy-two caves and the One-Horn Demon King were all taken captive by the gods. We were the only ones who managed to escape alive, and that is why we cried. Now we see that the Great Sage has returned unharmed and triumphant, and so we laugh as well."

"Victory and defeat," said the Great Sage, "are the common experiences of a soldier. The ancient proverb says,

> You may kill ten thousand of your enemies,
> But you will lose three thousand of your allies!

Moreover, those chieftains who have been captured are tigers and leopards, wolves and insects, badgers and foxes, and the like. Not a single member of our own kind has been hurt. Why then should we be disconsolate? Although our adversaries have been beaten back by my magic of body division, they are still encamped at the foot of our mountain. Let us be most vigilant, therefore, in our defense. Have a good meal, rest well, and conserve your energy. When morning comes, watch me perform a great magic and capture some of these generals from Heaven, so that our comrades may be avenged." The four mighty commanders drank a few bowls of coconut wine with the host of monkeys and went to sleep peacefully. We shall speak no more of them.

When those Four Devarājas retired their troops and stopped their fighting, each one of the Heavenly commanders came to report his accomplishment. There were those who had captured lions and elephants and those who had apprehended wolves, crawling creatures, and foxes. Not a single monkey monster, however, had been seized. The camp was then secured, a great tent was pitched, and those commanders with meritorious services were rewarded. The soldiers in charge of the cosmic nets were ordered to carry bells and were given passwords. They encircled the Flower-Fruit Mountain to await the great battle of the next day, and each soldier everywhere diligently kept his watch. So this is the situation:

> The fiendish monkey riots through Heaven and Earth,
> But the net spreads open, ready night and day.

We do not know what took place after the next morning; let's listen to the explanation in the next chapter.

SIX

Guanyin, attending the banquet, inquires into the cause;
The Little Sage, exerting his power, subdues the
  Great Sage.

For the moment we shall not tell you about the siege of the gods or the
Great Sage at rest. We speak instead of the Great Compassionate Deliverer,
the Efficacious Bodhisattva Guanyin from the Potalaka Mountain of the
South Sea.[1] Invited by the Lady Queen Mother to attend the Grand Festival
of Immortal Peaches, she arrived at the treasure chamber of the Jasper Pool
with her senior disciple, Hui'an. There they found the whole place desolate and the banquet tables in utter disarray. Although several members of
the Heavenly pantheon were present, none was seated. Instead, they were
all engaged in vigorous exchanges and discussions. After the Bodhisattva
had greeted the various deities, they told her what had occurred. "Since
there will be no festival," said the Bodhisattva, "nor any raising of cups,
all of you might as well come with this humble cleric to see the Jade Emperor." The gods followed her gladly, and they went to the entrance to the
Hall of Perfect Light. There the Bodhisattva was met by the Four Celestial
Masters and the Immortal of Naked Feet, who recounted how the celestial
soldiers, ordered by an enraged Jade Emperor to capture the monster, had
not yet returned. The Bodhisattva said, "I would like to have an audience
with the Jade Emperor. May I trouble one of you to announce my arrival?"
The Heavenly Preceptor Qiu Hongji went at once into the Treasure Hall of
Divine Mists and, having made his report, invited Guanyin to enter. Laozi
then took the upper seat with the Emperor, while the Lady Queen Mother
was in attendance behind the throne.

The Bodhisattva led the crowd inside. After paying homage to the Jade
Emperor, they also saluted Laozi and the Queen Mother. When each of them
was seated, she asked, "How is the Grand Festival of Immortal Peaches?"
"Every year when the festival has been given," said the Jade Emperor, "we
have thoroughly enjoyed ourselves. This year it has been completely ruined
by a baneful monkey, leaving us with nothing but an invitation to disap-
pointment." "Where did this baneful monkey come from?" asked the Bodhisattva. "He was born of a stone egg on top of the Flower-Fruit Mountain
of the Aolai Country of the East Pūrvavideha Continent," said the Jade Emperor. "At the moment of his birth, two beams of golden light flashed immediately from his eyes, reaching as far as the Palace of the Polestar. We
did not think much of that, but he later became a monster, subduing the
Dragon and taming the Tiger as well as eradicating his name from the Reg-

ister of Death. When the Dragon Kings and the Kings of the Underworld brought the matter to our attention, we wanted to capture him. The Star of Long Life, however, observed that all the beings of the three regions that possessed the nine apertures could attain immortality. We therefore decided to educate and nurture the talented monkey and summoned him to the Region Above. He was appointed to the post of Bimawen at the imperial stables, but, taking offense at the lowliness of his position, he left Heaven in rebellion. We then sent Devarāja Li and Prince Naṭa to ask for his submission by proclaiming a decree of pacification. He was brought again to the Region Above and was appointed the Great Sage, Equal to Heaven—a rank without compensation. Since he had nothing to do but to wander east and west, we feared that he might cause further trouble. So he was asked to look after the Garden of Immortal Peaches. But he broke the law and ate all the large peaches from the oldest trees. By then, the banquet was about to be given. As a person without salary he was, of course, not invited; nonetheless, he plotted to deceive the Immortal of Naked Feet and managed to sneak into the banquet by assuming the Immortal's appearance. He finished off all the divine wine and food, after which he also stole Laozi's elixir and took away a considerable quantity of imperial wine for the enjoyment of his mountain monkeys. Our mind has been sorely vexed by this, and we therefore sent a hundred thousand celestial soldiers with cosmic nets to capture him. We haven't yet received today's report on how the battle is faring."

When the Bodhisattva heard this, she said to Disciple Hui'an, "You must leave Heaven at once, go down to the Flower-Fruit Mountain, and inquire into the military situation. If the enemy is engaged, you can lend your assistance; in any event, you must bring back a factual report." The Disciple Hui'an straightened out his attire and mounted the cloud to leave the palace, an iron rod in his hand. When he arrived at the mountain, he found layers of cosmic net drawn tightly and sentries at every gate holding bells and shouting passwords. The encirclement of the mountain was indeed watertight! Hui'an stood still and called out, "Heavenly sentinels, may I trouble you to announce my arrival? I am Prince Mokṣa, second son of Devarāja Li, and I am also Hui'an, senior disciple of Guanyin of South Sea. I have come to inquire about the military situation."

The divine soldiers of the Five Mountains at once reported this beyond the gate. The constellations Aquarius, Pleiades, Hydra, and Scorpio then conveyed the message to the central tent. Devarāja Li issued a directorial flag, which ordered the cosmic nets to be opened and entrance permitted for the visitor. Day was just dawning in the east as Hui'an followed the flag inside and prostrated himself before the Four Great Devarājas and Devarāja Li.

After he had finished his greetings, Devarāja Li said, "My child, where have you come from?" "Your untutored son," said Hui'an, "accompanied the Bodhisattva to attend the Festival of Immortal Peaches. Seeing that the festival was desolate and the Jasper Pool laid waste, the Bodhisattva led the various deities and your untutored son to have an audience with the Jade Emperor. The Jade Emperor spoke at length about Father and King's expedition to the Region Below to subdue the baneful monkey. Since no report has returned for a whole day and neither victory nor defeat has been ascertained, the Bodhisattva ordered your untutored son to come here to find out how things stand." "We came here yesterday to set up the encampment," said Devarāja Li, "and the Nine Luminaries were sent to provoke battle. But this fellow made a grand display of his magical powers, and the Nine Luminaries all returned defeated. After that, I led the troops personally to confront him, and the fellow also brought his forces into formation. Our hundred thousand celestial soldiers fought with him until evening, when he retreated from the battle by using the magic of body division. When we recalled the troops and made our investigation, we found that we had captured some wolves, crawling creatures, tigers, leopards, and the like. But we did not even catch half a monkey monster! And today we have not yet gone into battle."

As he was saying all this, someone came from the gate of the camp to report, "That Great Sage, leading his band of monkey monsters, is shouting for battle outside." The Four Devarājas, Devarāja Li, and the prince at once made plans to bring out the troops, when Mokṣa said, "Father King, your untutored son was told by the Bodhisattva to come down here to acquire information. She also told me to give you assistance should there be actual combat. Though I am not very talented, I volunteer to go out now and see what kind of a Great Sage this is!" "Child," said the Devarāja, "since you have studied with the Bodhisattva for several years, you must, I suppose, have some powers! But do be careful!"

Dear prince! Grasping the iron rod with both hands, he tightened up his embroidered garment and leaped out of the gate. "Who is the Great Sage, Equal to Heaven?" he cried. Holding high his compliant rod, the Great Sage answered, "None other than old Monkey here! Who are you that you dare question me?" "I am Mokṣa, the second prince of Devarāja Li," said Mokssa. "At present I am also the disciple of Bodhisattva Guanyin, a defender of the faith before her treasure throne. And my religious name is Hui'an." "Why have you left your religious training at South Sea and come here to see me?" said the Great Sage. "I was sent by my master to inquire about the military situation," said Mokṣa. "Seeing what a nuisance you have made of yourself, I have come specifically to capture you." "You dare to talk so big?" said the Great Sage. "But don't run away! Have a taste of old Monkey's rod!" Mokṣa was not at all frightened and met his opponent squarely with his own iron rod. The two of them stood before the gate of the camp at mid-mountain, and what a magnificent battle they fought!

> Though one rod is pitted against another, the iron's quite different;
> Though this weapon couples with the other, the persons are not the same.
> This one's called the Great Sage, a wayward primordial god;
> The other is Guanyin's disciple, a true hero and proud.
> The all-iron rod has been pounded a thousand times,
> Made by Six Gods of Darkness and Six Gods of Light.
> The compliant rod sets the depth of Heaven's river,
> A thing divine ruling the oceans with magic might.
> The two of them in meeting have found their match;
> Back and forth they battle in endless rounds.
> From this one the rod of stealthy hands,
> Savage and fierce,
> Around the waist stabs and jabs swiftly as the wind;
> From the other the rod, doubling as a spear
> Driving and relentless,
> Lets up not a moment its parrying left and right.
> On this side the banners flare and flutter;
> On the other the war drums roll and rattle.
> Ten thousand celestial fighters circle round and round.
> The monkey monsters of a whole cave stand in rows and rows.
> Weird fog and dark cloud spread throughout the earth.
> The fume and smoke of battle reach even Heaven's Home.
> Yesterday's battle was something to behold.
> Still more violent is the contest today.
> Envy the truly able Monkey King:
> Mokṣa's beaten—he is fleeing for life!

Our Great Sage battled Hui'an for fifty or sixty rounds until the prince's arms and shoulders were sore and numb and he could fight no longer. After one final, futile swing of his weapon, he fled in defeat. The Great Sage then gathered together his monkey troops and stationed them securely outside the entrance of the cave. At the camp of the Devarāja, the celestial soldiers could be seen receiving the prince and making way for him to enter the gate. Panting and puffing, he ran in and gasped out to the Four Devarājas, Pagoda Bearer Li, and Naṭa, "That Great Sage! What an ace! Great indeed is his magical power! Your son cannot overcome him and has returned defeated." Shocked by the sight, Devarāja Li at once wrote a memorial to the Throne to request further assistance. The demon king Mahābāli and Prince Mokṣa were sent to Heaven to present the document.

Not daring to linger, the two of them crashed out of the cosmic nets and mounted the holy mist and hallowed cloud. In a moment they reached the Hall of Perfect Light and met the Four Celestial Masters, who led them into the Treasure Hall of Divine Mists to present their memorial. Hui'an also saluted the Bodhisattva, who asked him, "What have you found out about the situation?" "When I reached the Flower-Fruit Mountain by your order," said Hui'an, "I opened the cosmic nets by my call. Seeing my father, I told him of my master's intentions in sending me. Father King said, 'We fought a battle yesterday with that Monkey King but managed to take from him only tigers, leopards, lions, elephants, and the like. We did not catch a single one of his monkey monsters.' As we were talking, he again demanded battle. Your disciple used the iron rod to fight him for fifty or sixty rounds, but I could not prevail against him and returned to the camp defeated. Thus father had to send the demon king Mahābāli and your pupil to come here for help." The Bodhisattva bowed her head and pondered.

We now tell you about the Jade Emperor, who opened the memorial and found a message asking for assistance. "This is rather absurd!" he said laughing. "Is this monkey monster such a wizard that not even a hundred thousand soldiers from Heaven can vanquish him? Devarāja Li is again asking for help. What division of divine warriors can we send to assist him?" Hardly had he finished speaking when Guanyin folded her hands and said to him. "Your Majesty, let not your mind be troubled! This humble cleric will recommend a god who can capture the monkey." "Which one would you recommend?" said the Jade Emperor. "Your Majesty's nephew," said the Bodhisattva, "the Immortal Master of Illustrious Sagacity Erlang,[2] who is living at the mouth of the River of Libations in the Guan Prefecture and enjoying the incense and oblations offered to him from the Region Below. In former days he himself slew six monsters. Under his command are the Brothers of Plum Mountain and twelve hundred plant-headed deities, all possessing great magical powers. However, he will agree only to special assignments and will not obey any general summons. Your Majesty may want to send an edict transferring his troops to the scene of the battle and requesting his assistance. Our monster will surely be captured." When the Jade Emperor heard this, he immediately issued such an edict and ordered the demon king Mahābāli to present it.

Having received the edict, the demon king mounted a cloud and went straight to the mouth of the River of Libations. It took him less than half an hour to reach the temple of the Immortal Master. Immediately the demon magistrates guarding the doors made this report inside: "There is a messenger from Heaven outside who has arrived with an edict in his hand." Erlang and his brothers came out to receive the edict, which was read before burning incense. The edict said:

The Great Sage, Equal to Heaven, a monstrous monkey from the Flower-Fruit Mountain, is in revolt. At the Palace he stole peaches, wine, and elixir, and disrupted the Grand Festival of Immortal Peaches. A hundred thousand Heavenly soldiers with eighteen sets of cosmic nets were dispatched to surround the mountain and capture him, but victory has not yet been secured. We therefore make this special request of our worthy nephew and his sworn brothers to go to the Flower-Fruit Mountain and assist in destroying this monster. Following your success will be lofty elevation and abundant reward.

In great delight the Immortal Master said, "Let the messenger of Heaven go back. I will go at once to offer my assistance with drawn sword." The demon king went back to report, but we shall speak no further of that.

This Immortal Master called together the Six Brothers of Plum Mountain: they were Kang, Zhang, Yao, and Li, the four grand marshals, and Guo Shen and Zhi Jian, the two generals. As they congregated before the court, he said to them, "The Jade Emperor just now sent us to the Flower-Fruit Mountain to capture a monstrous monkey. Let's get going!" Delighted and willing, the brothers at once called out the divine soldiers under their command. With falcons mounted and dogs on leashes, with arrows ready and bows drawn, they left in a violent magic wind and crossed in a moment the great Eastern Ocean. As they landed on the Flower-Fruit Mountain, they saw their way blocked by dense layers of cosmic net. "Divine commanders guarding the cosmic nets, hear us," they shouted. "We are specially assigned by the Jade Emperor to capture the monstrous monkey. Open the gate of your camp quickly and let us through." The various deities conveyed the message to the inside, level by level. The Four Devarājas and Devarāja Li then came out to the gate of the camp to receive them. After they had exchanged greetings, there were questions about the military situation, and the Devarāja gave them a thorough briefing. "Now that I, the Little Sage, have come," said the Immortal Master, laughing, "he will have to engage in a contest of transformations with his adversary. You gentlemen make sure that the cosmic nets are tightly drawn on all sides, but leave the top uncovered. Let me try my hand in this contest. If I lose, you gentlemen need not come to my assistance, for my own brothers will be there to support me. If I win, you gentlemen will not be needed in tying him up either; my own brothers will take care of that. All I need is the Pagoda Bearer Devarāja to stand in midair with his imp-reflecting mirror. If the monster should be defeated, I fear that he may try to flee to a distant locality. Make sure that his image is clearly reflected in the mirror, so that we don't lose him." The Devarājas set themselves up in the four directions, while the heavenly soldiers all lined up according to their planned formations.

With himself as the seventh brother, the Immortal Master led the four grand marshals and the two generals out of the camp to provoke battle. The other warriors were ordered to defend their encampment with vigilance, and the plant-headed deities were ordered to have the falcons and dogs ready for battle. The Immortal Master went to the front of the Water-Curtain Cave, where he saw a troop of monkeys neatly positioned in an array that resembled a coiled dragon. At the center of the array was the banner bearing the words "The Great Sage, Equal to Heaven." "That audacious monster!" said the Immortal Master. "How dare he assume the rank 'Equal to Heaven'?" "There's no time for praise or blame," said the Six Brothers of Plum Mountain. "Let's challenge him at once!" When the little monkeys in front of the camp saw the Immortal Master, they ran quickly to make their report. Seizing his golden-hooped rod, straightening out his golden cuirass, slipping on his cloud-treading shoes, and pressing down his red-gold cap, the Monkey King leaped out of the camp. He opened his eyes wide to stare at the Immortal Master, whose features were remarkably refined and whose attire was most elegant. Truly, he was a man of

> Features most comely and most noble mien,
> With shoulder-reaching ears and shining eyes.
> His head wore the Three Mountains Phoenix cap,
> His body donned a pale yellow goose-down robe.
> Gold threaded boots matched coiling dragon socks.
> Eight flower-like emblems his jade belt adorned.[3]
> From his waist hung the crescent pellet bow.
> His hands held a lance of three points and two blades.
> Once he cleaved Peach Mountain to save his mother.
> His one pellet struck a tall tree's two phoenixes .
> Slaying eight fiends flung far his fame
> As bond brother midst Plum Mountain's Seven Saints.
> His lofty mind scorned being high Heaven's kin;
> His pride led him to dwell near Libations Stream.
> From Chi City here's the kind heroic sage:[4]
> Of boundless epiphanies, he's named Erlang.

When the Great Sage saw him, he lifted high his golden-hooped rod with gales of laughter and called out, "What little warrior are you and where do you come from, that you dare present yourself here to provoke battle?" "You must have eyes but no pupils," shouted the Immortal Master, "if you don't recognize me! I am the maternal nephew of the Jade Emperor, Erlang, the King of Illustrious Grace and Spirit by imperial appointment. I have received my order from above to arrest you, the rebellious Bimawen ape. Don't you know that your time has come?" "I remember," said the Great Sage, "that the sister of the Jade Emperor some years ago became enamored of the Region Below; she married a man by the name of Yang and had a son by him.[5] Are you that boy who was reputed to have cleaved open the Peach Mountain with his ax? I would like to rebuke you roundly, but I have no grudge against you. I can hit you with this rod of mine too, but I'd like to spare your life! A little boy like you, why don't you hurry back and ask your Four Great Devarājas to come out?" When the Immortal Master heard this, he grew very angry and shouted, "Reckless ape! Don't you dare be so insolent! Take a sample of my blade!" Swerving to dodge the blow, the Great Sage quickly raised his golden-hooped rod to engage his opponent. What a fine fight there was between the two of them:

> Erlang, the God of Illustrious Kindness,
> And the Great Sage, Equal to Heaven!
> This one, haughty and proud, defied the Handsome Monkey King.
> That one, not knowing his man, would crush all stalwart foes.
> Suddenly these two met,
> And both desired a match—
> They had never known which was the better man;
> Today they'd learn who's strong and who's weak!
> The iron rod seemed a flying dragon,
> And the lance divine a dancing phoenix:
> Left and right they struck,
> Attacking both front and back.
> The Plum Mountain Six Brothers' awesome presence filled one side,
> While the four generals, like Ma and Liu, took command on the other.
> All worked as one to wave flags and roll drums;
> All helped the fight by cheers while beating the gong.
> Two sharp weapons sought a chance to hurt,
> But thrusts and parries did not slack one whit.
> The golden-hooped rod, wonder of the sea,
> Could change and fly to snare a victory.
> A little lag and your life is over!
> A tiny error and your luck runs out!

The Immortal Master fought the Great Sage for more than three hundred rounds, but the result still could not be determined. The Immortal Master, therefore, summoned all his magical powers; with a shake, he made his body a hundred thousand feet tall. Holding with both hands the divine lance of three points and two blades like the peaks that cap the Hua Mountain, this green-faced, saber-toothed figure with scarlet hair aimed a violent blow at the head of the Great Sage. But the Great Sage also exerted his magical power and changed himself into a figure having the features and height of Erlang. He wielded a compliant golden-hooped rod that resembled the Heaven-supporting pillar on top of Mount Kunlun to oppose the god Erlang. This vision so terrified the marshals, Ma and Liu, that they could no longer wave the flags, and so appalled the generals, Beng and Ba, that they could use neither scimitar nor sword. On the side of Erlang, the Brothers Kang, Zhang, Yao, Li, Guo Shen, and Zhi Jian gave the order to the plant-headed deities to let loose the falcons and dogs and to advance upon those monkeys in front of the Water-Curtain Cave with mounted arrows and drawn bows. The charge, alas,

> Dispersed the four mighty commanders of monkey imps
> And captured two or three thousand numinous fiends!

Those monkeys dropped their spears and abandoned their armor, forsook their swords, and threw away their lances. They scattered in all directions— running, screaming, scuttling up the mountain, or scrambling back to the cave. It was as if a cat at night had stolen upon resting birds: they darted up as stars to fill the sky. The Brothers thus gained a complete victory, of which we shall speak no further.

Now we were telling you about the Immortal Master and the Great Sage, who had changed themselves into forms which imitated Heaven and Earth. As they were doing battle, the Great Sage suddenly perceived that the monkeys of his camp were put to rout, and his heart grew faint. He changed out of his magic form, turned around, and fled, dragging his rod behind him. When the Immortal Master saw that he was running away, he chased him with great strides, saying, "Where you going? Surrender now, and your life will be spared!" The Great Sage did not stop to fight anymore but ran as fast as he could. Near the cave's entrance, he ran right into Kang, Zhang, Yao, and Li, the four grand marshals, and Guo Shen and Zhi Jian, the two generals, who were at the head of an army blocking his way. "Lawless ape!" they cried, "where do you think you're going?" Quivering all over, the Great Sage squeezed his golden-hooped rod back into an embroidery needle and hid it in his ear. With a shake of his body, he changed himself into a small sparrow and flew to perch on top of a tree. In great agitation, the six Brothers searched all around but could not find him. "We've lost the monkey monster! We've lost the monkey monster!" they all cried.

As they were making all that clamor, the Immortal Master arrived and asked, "Brothers, where did you lose him in the chase?" "We just had him boxed in here," said the gods, "but he simply vanished." Scanning the place with his phoenix eye wide open,[6] Erlang at once discovered that the Great Sage had changed into a small sparrow perched on a tree. He changed out of his magic form and took off his pellet bow. With a shake of his body, he changed into a sparrow hawk with outstretched wings, ready to attack its prey. When the Great Sage saw this, he darted up with a flutter of his wings;

changing himself into a cormorant, he headed straight for the open sky. When Erlang saw this, he quickly shook his feathers and changed into a huge ocean crane, which could penetrate the clouds to strike with its bill. The Great Sage therefore lowered his direction, changed into a small fish, and dove into a stream with a splash. Erlang rushed to the edge of the water but could see no trace of him. He thought to himself, "This simian must have gone into the water and changed himself into a fish, a shrimp, or the like. I'll change again to catch him." He duly changed into a fish hawk and skimmed downstream over the waves. After a while, the fish into which the Great Sage had changed was swimming along with the current. Suddenly he saw a bird that looked like a green kite though its feathers were not entirely green, like an egret though it had small feathers, and like an old crane though its feet were not red. "That must be the transformed Erlang waiting for me," he thought to himself. He swiftly turned around and swam away after releasing a few bubbles. When Erlang saw this, he said, "The fish that released the bubbles looks like a carp though its tail is not red, like a perch though there are no patterns on its scales, like a snake fish though there are no stars on its head, like a bream though its gills have no bristles. Why does it move away the moment it sees me? It must be the transformed monkey himself!" He swooped toward the fish and snapped at it with his beak. The Great Sage shot out of the water and changed at once into a water snake; he swam toward shore and wriggled into the grass along the bank. When Erlang saw that he had snapped in vain and that a snake had darted away in the water with a splash, he knew that the Great Sage had changed again. Turning around quickly, he changed into a scarlet-topped gray crane, which extended its beak like sharp iron pincers to devour the snake. With a bounce, the snake changed again into a spotted bustard standing by itself rather stupidly amid the water pepper along the bank. When Erlang saw that the monkey had changed into such a vulgar creature—for the spotted bustard is the basest and most promiscuous of birds, mating indiscriminately with phoenixes, hawks, or crows—he refused to approach him. Changing back into his true form, he went and stretched his bow to the fullest. With one pellet he sent the bird hurtling.

The Great Sage took advantage of this opportunity, nonetheless. Rolling down the mountain slope, he squatted there to change again—this time into a little temple for the local spirit. His wide-open mouth became the entrance, his teeth the doors, his tongue the Bodhisattva, and his eyes the windows. Only his tail he found to be troublesome, so he stuck it up in the back and changed it into a flagpole. The Immortal Master chased him down the slope, but instead of the bustard he had hit he found only a little temple. He opened his phoenix eye quickly and looked at it carefully. Seeing the flagpole behind it, he laughed and said, "It's the ape! Now he's trying to deceive me again! I have seen plenty of temples before but never one with a flagpole behind it. This must be another of that animal's tricks. Why should I let him lure me inside where he can bite me once I've entered? First I'll smash the windows with my fist! Then I'll kick down the doors!"

The Great Sage heard this and said in dismay, "How vicious! The doors are my teeth and the windows my eyes. What am I going to do with my eyes smashed and my teeth knocked out?" Leaping up like a tiger, he disappeared again into the air. The Immortal Master was looking all around for him when the four grand marshals and the two generals arrived together. "Elder Brother," they said, "have you caught the Great Sage?" "A moment ago," said the Immortal Master laughing, "the monkey changed into a temple to trick me. I was about to smash the windows and kick down the doors when he vanished out of sight with a leap. It's all very strange! Very strange!" The Brothers were astonished, but they could find no trace of him in any direction.

"Brothers," said the Immortal Master, "keep a lookout down here. Let me go up there to find him." He swiftly mounted the clouds and rose up into the sky, where he saw Devarāja Li holding high the imp-reflecting mirror and standing on top of the clouds with Naṭa. "Devarāja," said the Immortal Master, "have you seen the Monkey King?" "He hasn't come up here," said the Devarāja, "I have been watching him in the mirror."

After telling them about the duel in magic and transformations and the captivity of the rest of the monkeys, the Immortal Master said, "He finally changed into a temple. Just as I was about to attack him, he got away." When Devarāja Li heard these words, he turned the imp-reflecting mirror all the way around once more and looked into it. "Immortal Master," he said, roaring with laughter. "Go quickly! Quickly! That monkey used his magic of body concealment to escape from the cordon and he's now heading for the mouth of your River of Libations."

We now tell you about the Great Sage, who had arrived at the mouth of the River of Libations. With a shake of his body, he changed into the form of Holy Father Erlang. Lowering the direction of his cloud, he went straight into the temple, and the demon magistrates could not tell that he was not the real Erlang. Every one of them, in fact, kowtowed to receive him. He sat down in the middle and began to examine the various offerings; the three kinds of sacrificial meat brought by Li Hu, the votive offering of Zhang Long, the petition for a son by Zhao Jia, and the request for healing by Qian Bing. As he was looking at these, someone made the report, "Another Holy Father has arrived!" The various demon magistrates went quickly to look and were terror-stricken, one and all. The Immortal Master asked, "Did a so-called Great Sage, Equal to Heaven, come here?" "We haven't seen any Great Sage," said the demon magistrates. "But another Holy Father is in there examining the offerings." The Immortal Master crashed through the door; seeing him, the Great Sage revealed his true form and said, "There's no need for the little boy to strive anymore! Sun is now the name of this temple!"

The Immortal Master lifted his divine lance of three points and two blades and struck, but the Monkey King with agile body was quick to move out of the way. He whipped out that embroidery needle of his, and with one wave caused it to take on the thickness of a rice bowl. Rushing forward, he engaged Erlang face to face. Starting at the door of the temple, the two combatants fought all the way back to the Flower-Fruit Mountain, treading on clouds and mists and shouting insults at each other. The Four Devarājas and their followers were so startled by their appearance that they stood guard with even greater vigilance, while the grand marshals joined the Immortal Master to surround the Handsome Monkey King. But we shall speak of them no more.

We tell you instead about the demon king Mahābāli, who, having requested the Immortal Master and his Six Brothers to lead their troops to subdue the monster, returned to the Region Above to make his report. Conversing with the Bodhisattva Guanyin, the Queen Mother, and the various divine officials in the Hall of Divine Mists, the Jade Emperor said, "If Erlang has already gone into battle, why has no further report come back today?" Folding her hands, Guanyin said, "Permit this humble cleric to invite Your Majesty and the Patriarch of Dao to go outside the South Heaven Gate, so that you may find out personally how things are faring." "That's a good suggestion," said the Jade Emperor. He at once sent for his imperial carriage and went with the Patriarch, Guanyin, the Queen Mother, and the various divine officials to the South Heaven Gate, where the cortege was met by celestial soldiers and guardians. They opened the gate and peered into the distance; there they saw cosmic nets on every side manned by celestial soldiers, Devarāja Li and Naṭa in midair holding high the imp-reflecting mirror, and the Immortal Master and his Brothers encircling the Great Sage in the middle and fighting fiercely. The Bodhisattva opened her mouth and addressed Laozi: "What do you think of Erlang, whom this humble cleric recommended? He is certainly powerful enough to have the Great Sage surrounded, if not yet captured. I shall now help him to achieve his victory and make certain that the enemy will be taken prisoner."

"What weapon will the Bodhisattva use," asked Laozi, "and how will you assist him?" "I shall throw down my immaculate vase that I use for holding my willow sprig," said the Bodhisattva. "When it hits that monkey, at least it will knock him over, even if it doesn't kill him. Erlang, the Little Sage, will then be able to capture him."

"That vase of yours," said Laozi, "is made of porcelain. It's all right if it hits him on the head. But if it crashed on the iron rod instead, won't it be shattered? You had better not raise your hands; let me help him win." The Bodhisattva said, "Do you have any weapon?"

"I do, indeed," said Laozi. He rolled up his sleeve and took down from his left arm an armlet, saying, "This is a weapon made of red steel, brought into existence during my preparation of elixir and fully charged with theurgical forces. It can be made to transform at will; indestructible by fire or water, it can entrap many things. It's called the diamond cutter or the diamond snare. The year when I crossed the Hangu Pass, I depended on it a great deal for the conversion of the barbarians, for it was practically my bodyguard night and day. Let me throw it down and hit him." After saying this, Laozi hurled the snare down from the Heaven Gate; it went tumbling down into the battlefield at the Flower-Fruit Mountain and landed smack on the Monkey King's head. The Monkey King was engaged in a bitter struggle with the Seven Sages and was completely unaware of this weapon, which had dropped from the sky and hit him on the crown of his head. No longer able to stand on his feet, he toppled over. He managed to scramble up again and was about to flee, when the Holy Father Erlang's small hound dashed forward and bit him in the calf. He was pulled down for the second time and lay on the ground cursing, "You brute! Why don't you go and do your master in, instead of coming to bite old Monkey?" Rolling over quickly, he tried to get up, but the Seven Sages all pounced on him and pinned him down. They bound him with ropes and punctured his breastbone with a knife, so that he could transform no further.

Laozi retrieved his diamond snare and requested the Jade Emperor to return to the Hall of Divine Mists with Guanyin, the Queen Mother, and the rest of the Immortals. Down below the Four Great Deva Kings and Devarāja Li all retired their troops, broke camp, and went forward to congratulate Erlang, saying, "This is indeed a magnificent accomplishment by the Little Sage!" "This has been the great blessing of the Heavenly Devas," said the Little Sage, "and the proper exercise of their divine authority. What have I accomplished?" The Brothers Kang, Zhang, Yao, and Li said, "Elder Brother need have no further discussion. Let us take this fellow up to the Jade Emperor to see what will be done with him." "Worthy Brothers," said the Immortal Master, "you may not have a personal audience with the Jade Emperor because you have not received any divine appointment. Let the celestial guardians take him into custody. I shall go with the Devarāja to the Region Above to make our report, while all of you make a thorough search of the mountain here. After you have cleaned it out, go back to the River of Libations. When I have our deeds recorded and received our rewards, I shall return to celebrate with you." The four grand marshals and the two generals followed his bidding. The Immortal Master then mounted the clouds with the rest of the deities, and they began their triumphal journey back to Heaven, singing songs of victory all the way. In a little while, they reached the outer court of the Hall of Perfect Light, and the Heavenly preceptor went forward to memorialize to the Throne, saying, "The Four Great Devarājas have captured the monstrous monkey, the Great Sage, Equal to Heaven. They await the command of Your Majesty." The Jade Emperor then gave the order that the demon king Mahābāli and the celestial guardians take the prisoner to the monster execution block, where he was to be cut to small pieces. Alas, this is what happens to

Fraud and impudence, now punished by the Law;
Heroics grand will fade in the briefest time!

We do not know what will become of the Monkey King; let's listen to the explanation in the next chapter.

SEVEN

From the Eight Trigrams Brazier the Great Sage escapes; Beneath the Five Phases Mountain, Mind Monkey is still.[1]

Fame and fortune,
All predestined;
One must ever shun a guileful heart.
Rectitude and truth,
The fruits of virtue grow both long and deep.
A little presumption brings on Heaven's wrath:
Though yet unseen, it will surely come in time.
Ask the Lord of the East[2] for why
Such pains and perils now appear:
Because pride has sought to scale the limits,
Ignoring hierarchy to flout the law.

We were telling you about the Great Sage, Equal to Heaven, who was taken by the celestial guardians to the monster execution block, where he was bound to the monster-subduing pillar. They then slashed him with a scimitar, hewed him with an ax, stabbed him with a spear, and hacked him with a sword, but they could not hurt his body in any way. Next, the Star Spirit of the South Pole ordered the various deities of the Fire Department to burn him with fire, but that, too, had little effect. The gods of the Thunder Department were then ordered to strike him with thunderbolts, but not a single one of his hairs was destroyed. The demon king Mahābāli and the others therefore went back to report to the Throne, saying, "Your Majesty, we don't know where this Great Sage has acquired such power to protect his body. Your subjects slashed him with a scimitar and hewed him with an ax; we also struck him with thunder and burned him with fire. Not a single one of his hairs was destroyed. What shall we do?"

When the Jade Emperor heard these words, he said, "What indeed can we do to a fellow like that, a creature of that sort?" Laozi then came forward and said, "That monkey ate the immortal peaches and drank the imperial wine. Moreover, he stole the divine elixir and ate five gourdfuls of it, both raw and cooked. All this was probably refined in his stomach by the Samādhi fire[3] to form a single solid mass. The union with his constitution gave him a diamond body, which cannot be quickly destroyed. It would be better, therefore, if this Daoist takes him away and places him in the Brazier of Eight Trigrams, where he will be smelted by high and low heat. When he is finally separated from my elixir, his body will certainly be reduced to ashes." When the Jade Emperor heard these words, he told the Six Gods of Darkness and the Six Gods of Light to release the prisoner and hand him over to Laozi, who left in obedience to the divine decree. Meanwhile, the illustrious Sage Erlang was rewarded with a hundred gold blossoms, a hundred bottles of imperial wine, a hundred pellets of elixir, together with rare treasures, lustrous pearls, and brocades, which he was told to share with his brothers. After expressing his gratitude, the Immortal Master returned to the mouth of the River of Libations, and for the time being we shall speak of him no further.

Arriving at the Tushita Palace, Laozi loosened the ropes on the Great Sage, pulled out the weapon from his breastbone, and pushed him into the Brazier of Eight Trigrams. He then ordered the Daoist who watched over the brazier and the page boy in charge of the fire to blow up a strong flame for the smelting process. The brazier, you see, was of eight compartments corresponding to the eight trigrams of Qian, Kan, Gen, Zhen, Xun, Li, Kun, and Dui. The Great Sage crawled into the space beneath the compartment that corresponded to the Xun trigram. Now Xun symbolizes wind; where there is wind, there is no fire. However, wind could churn up smoke, which at that moment reddened his eyes, giving them a permanently inflamed condition. Hence they were sometimes called Fiery Eyes and Diamond Pupils.

Truly time passed swiftly, and the forty-ninth day arrived imperceptibly.[4] The alchemical process of Laozi was perfected, and on that day he came to open the brazier to take out his elixir. The Great Sage at the time was covering his eyes with both hands, rubbing his face and shedding tears. He heard noises on top of the brazier and, opening his eyes, suddenly saw light. Unable to restrain himself, he leaped out of the brazier and kicked it over with a loud crash. He began to walk straight out of the room, while a group of startled fire tenders and guardians tried desperately to grab hold of him. Every one of them was overthrown; he was as wild as a white brow tiger in a fit, a one-horned dragon with a fever. Laozi rushed up to clutch at him, only to be greeted by such a violent shove that he fell head over heels while the Great Sage escaped. Whipping the compliant rod out from his ear, he waved it once in the wind and it had the thickness of a rice bowl. Holding it in his hands, without regard for good or ill, he once more careened through the Heavenly Palace, fighting so fiercely that the Nine Luminaries all shut themselves in and the Four Devarājas disappeared from sight. Dear Monkey Monster! Here is a testimonial poem for him. The poem says:

This cosmic being fully fused with nature's gifts
Passes with ease through ten thousand toils and tests.

Vast and motionless like the One Great Void,
Perfect, quiescent, he's named the Primal Depth.
Long refined in the brazier, he's no mercury or lead,[5]
Just the very immortal, living above all things.
Forever transforming, he changes still;
Three refuges and five commandments[6] *he all rejects.*

Here is another poem:

A spirit beam filling the supreme void—
That's how the rod behaves accordingly.
It lengthens or shortens as one would wish;
Upright or prone, it grows or shrinks at will.

And another:

An ape's body of Dao weds the human mind.
Mind is a monkey—this meaning's profound.
The Great Sage, Equal to Heaven, is no false thought.
How could the post of BanHorse justly show his gifts?
"Horse works with Monkey" means both Mind and Will
Need binding firmly. Don't seek them outside.
All things back to Nirvāṇa follow one truth—
To join Tathāgata beneath twin trees.[7]

This time our Monkey King had no respect for persons great or small; he lashed out this way and that with his iron rod, and not a single deity could withstand him. He fought all the way into the Hall of Perfect Light and was approaching the Hall of Divine Mists, where fortunately Numinous Officer Wang,[8] aide to the Immortal Master of Adjuvant Holiness, was on duty. He saw the Great Sage advancing recklessly and went forward to bar his way, holding high his golden whip. "Wanton monkey," he cried, "where are you going? I am here, so don't you dare be insolent!" The Great Sage did not wait for further utterance; he raised his rod and struck at once, while Numinous Officer met him also with brandished whip. The two of them charged into each other in front of the Hall of Divine Mists. What a fight that was between

A red-blooded patriot of ample fame,
And a Heaven's rebel with notorious name!
The saint and sinner gladly tangle close
So that two brave fighters can test their skills.
Though the rod is fierce
And the whip is fleet,
How can the upright and just one forbear?

This one is a supreme god of judgment with thunderous voice;
The other, the Great Sage, Equal to Heaven, a monstrous ape.
The golden whip and the iron rod used by the two
Are both divine weapons from the House of God.
At Divine Mists Treasure Hall they show their might today,
Each displaying his prowess winningly.
This one brashly seeks to take the Big Dipper Palace;
The other with all his strength defends the sacred realm.
In bitter strife relentless they show their power;
Moving back and forth, whip or rod has yet to score.

The two of them fought for some time, and neither victory nor defeat could yet be determined. The Immortal Master of Adjuvant Holiness, however, had already sent word to the Thunder Department, and thirty-six thunder deities were summoned to the scene. They surrounded the Great Sage and plunged into a fierce battle. The Great Sage was not in the least intimidated; wielding his compliant rod, he parried left and right and met his attackers to the front and to the rear. In a moment he saw that the scimitars, lances, swords, halberds, whips, maces, hammers, axes, gilt bludgeons, sickles, and spades of the thunder deities were coming thick and fast. So with one shake of his body he changed into a creature with six arms and three heads. One wave of the compliant rod and it turned into three; his six arms wielded the three rods like a spinning wheel, whirling and dancing in their midst. The various thunder deities could not approach him at all. Truly his form was

Tumbling round and round,
Bright and luminous;
A form everlasting, how imitated by men?
He cannot be burned by fire.
Can he ever be drowned in water?
A lustrous pearl of mani[9] he is indeed,
Immune to all the spears and the swords.
He could be good;
He could be bad;
Present good and evil he could do at will.
He'd be an immortal, a Buddha, if he's good;[10]
Wickedness would cloak him with hair and horn.
Endlessly changing he runs amok in Heaven,
Not to be seized by fighting lords or thunder gods.

At the time the various deities had the Great Sage surrounded, but they could not close in on him. All the hustle and bustle soon disturbed the Jade

Emperor, who at once sent the Wandering Minister of Inspection and the Immortal Master of Blessed Wings to go to the Western Region and invite the aged Buddha to come and subdue the monster.

The two sages received the decree and went straight to the Spirit Mountain. After they had greeted the Four Vajra-Buddhas and the Eight Bodhisattvas in front of the Treasure Temple of Thunderclap, they asked them to announce their arrival. The deities therefore went before the Treasure Lotus Platform and made their report. Tathāgata at once invited them to appear before him, and the two sages made obeisance to the Buddha three times before standing in attendance beneath the platform. Tathāgata asked, "What causes the Jade Emperor to trouble the two sages to come here?"

The two sages explained as follows: "Some time ago there was born on the Flower-Fruit Mountain a monkey who exercised his magic powers and gathered to himself a troop of monkeys to disturb the world. The Jade Emperor threw down a decree of pacification and appointed him a Bimawen, but he despised the lowliness of that position and left in rebellion. Devarāja Li and Prince Naṭa were sent to capture him, but they were unsuccessful, and another proclamation of amnesty was given to him. He was then made the Great Sage, Equal to Heaven, a rank without compensation. After a while he was given the temporary job of looking after the Garden of Immortal Peaches, where almost immediately he stole the peaches. He also went to the Jasper Pool and made off with the food and wine, devastating the Grand Festival. Half-drunk, he went secretly into the Tushita Palace, stole the elixir of Laozi, and then left the Celestial Palace in revolt. Again the Jade Emperor sent a hundred thousand Heavenly soldiers, but he was not to be subdued. Thereafter Guanyin sent for the Immortal Master Erlang and his sworn brothers, who fought and pursued him. Even then he knew many tricks of transformation, and only after he was hit by Laozi's diamond snare could Erlang finally capture him. Taken before the Throne, he was condemned to be executed; but, though slashed by a scimitar and hewn by an ax, burned by fire and struck by thunder, he was not hurt at all. After Laozi had received royal permission to take him away, he was refined by fire, and the brazier was not opened until the forty-ninth day. Immediately he jumped out of the Brazier of Eight Trigrams and beat back the celestial guardians. He penetrated into the Hall of Perfect Light and was approaching the Hall of Divine Mists when Numinous Officer Wang, aide to the Immortal Master of Adjuvant Holiness, met and fought with him bitterly. Thirty-six thunder generals were ordered to encircle him completely, but they could never get near him. The situation is desperate, and for this reason, the Jade Emperor sent a special request for you to defend the Throne."

When Tathāgata heard this, he said to the various bodhisattvas, "All of you remain steadfast here in the chief temple, and let no one relax his meditative posture. I have to go exorcise a demon and defend the Throne."

Tathāgata then called Ānanda and Kāśyapa, his two venerable disciples, to follow him. They left the Thunderclap Temple and arrived at the gate of the Hall of Divine Mists, where they were met by deafening shouts and yells. There the Great Sage was being beset by the thirty-six thunder deities. The Buddhist Patriarch gave the dharma-order: "Let the thunder deities lower their arms and break up their encirclement. Ask the Great Sage to come out here and let me ask him what sort of divine power he has." The various warriors retreated immediately, and the Great Sage also threw off his magical appearance. Changing back into his true form, he approached angrily and shouted with ill humor, "What region are you from, monk, that you dare stop the battle and question me?" Tathāgata laughed and said, "I am Śākyamuni, the Venerable One from the Western Region of Ultimate Bliss. I have heard just now about your audacity, your wildness, and your repeated acts of rebellion against Heaven. Where were you born, and in which year did you succeed in acquiring the Way? Why are you so violent and unruly?" The Great Sage said, "I was

> Born of Earth and Heaven, immortal divinely fused,
> An old monkey hailing from the Flower-Fruit Mount.
> I made my home in the Water-Curtain Cave;
> Seeking friend and teacher, I learned the Great Mystery.
> Perfected in the many arts of ageless life,
> I learned to change in ways boundless and vast.
> Too narrow the space I found on that mortal earth:
> I set my mind to live in the Green-jade Sky.
> In Divine Mists Hall none should long reside,
> For king may follow king in the reign of man.
> If might is honor, let them yield to me.
> He only is hero who dares to fight and win!"

When the Buddhist Patriarch heard these words, he laughed aloud in scorn. "A fellow like you," he said, "is only a monkey who happened to become a spirit. How dare you be so presumptuous as to want to seize the honored throne of the Exalted Jade Emperor? He began practicing religion when he was very young, and he has gone through the bitter experience of one thousand seven hundred and fifty kalpas, with each kalpa lasting a hundred and twenty-nine thousand six hundred years. Figure out yourself how many years it took him to rise to the enjoyment of his great and limitless position! You are merely a beast who has just attained human form in this incarnation. How dare you make such a boast? Blasphemy! This is sheer blasphemy, and it will surely shorten your allotted age. Repent while there's still time and cease your idle talk! Be wary that you don't encounter such peril that you will be cut down in an instant, and all your original gifts will be wasted."

"Even if the Jade Emperor has practiced religion from childhood," said the Great Sage, "he should not be allowed to remain here forever. The proverb says,

Many are the turns of kingship:
By next year the turn will be mine!

Tell him to move out at once and hand over the Celestial Palace to me. That'll be the end of the matter. If not, I shall continue to cause disturbances and there'll never be peace!" "Besides your immortality and your transformations," said the Buddhist Patriarch, "what other powers do you have that you dare to usurp this hallowed region of Heaven?" "I've plenty of them!" said the Great Sage. "Indeed, I know seventy-two transformations and a life that does not grow old through ten thousand kalpas. I know also how to cloud somersault, and one leap will take me one hundred and eight thousand miles. Why can't I sit on the Heavenly throne?"

The Buddhist Patriarch said, "Let me make a wager with you. If you have the ability to somersault clear of this right palm of mine, I shall consider you the winner. You need not raise your weapon in battle then, for I shall ask the Jade Emperor to go live with me in the West and let you have the Celestial Palace. If you cannot somersault out of my hand, you can go back to the Region Below and be a monster. Work through a few more kalpas before you return to cause more trouble."

When the Great Sage heard this, he said to himself, snickering, "What a fool this Tathāgata is! A single somersault of mine can carry old Monkey one hundred and eight thousand miles, yet his palm is not even one foot across. How could I possibly not jump clear of it?" He asked quickly, "You're certain that your decision will stand?" "Certainly it will," said Tathāgata. He stretched out his right hand, which was about the size of a lotus leaf. Our Great Sage put away his compliant rod and, summoning his power, leaped up and stood right in the center of the Patriarch's hand. He said simply, "I'm off!" and he was gone—all but invisible like a streak of light in the clouds. Training the eye of wisdom on him, the Buddhist Patriarch saw that the Monkey King was hurtling along relentlessly like a whirligig.

As the Great Sage advanced, he suddenly saw five flesh-pink pillars supporting a mass of green air. "This must be the end of the road," he said. "When I go back presently, Tathāgata will be my witness and I shall certainly take up residence in the Palace of Divine Mists." But he thought to himself, "Wait a moment! I'd better leave some kind of memento if I'm going to negotiate with Tathāgata." He plucked a hair and blew a mouthful of magic breath onto it, crying, "Change!" It changed into a writing brush with extra thick hair soaked in heavy ink. On the middle pillar he then wrote in large letters the following line: "The Great Sage, Equal to Heaven, has made a tour of this place." When he had finished writing, he retrieved his hair, and with a total lack of respect he left a bubbling pool of monkey urine at the base of the first pillar. He reversed his cloud somersault and went back to where he had started. Standing on Tathāgata's palm, he said, "I left, and now I'm back. Tell the Jade Emperor to give me the Celestial Palace."

"You pisshead ape!" scolded Tathāgata. "Since when did you ever leave the palm of my hand?" The Great Sage said, "You are just ignorant! I went to the edge of Heaven, and I found five flesh-pink pillars supporting a mass of green air. I left a memento there. Do you dare go with me to have a look at the place?" "No need to go there," said Tathāgata. "Just lower your head and take a look." When the Great Sage stared down with his fiery eyes and diamond pupils, he found written on the middle finger of the Buddhist Patriarch's right hand the sentence, "The Great Sage, Equal to Heaven, has made a tour of this place." A pungent whiff of monkey urine came from the fork between the thumb and the first finger. Astonished, the Great Sage said, "Could this really happen? Could this really happen? I wrote those words on the pillars supporting the sky. How is it that they now appear on his finger? Could it be that he is exercising the magic power of foreknowledge without divination? I won't believe it! I won't believe it! Let me go there once more!"

Dear Great Sage! Quickly he crouched and was about to jump up again, when the Buddhist Patriarch flipped his hand over and tossed the Monkey King out of the West Heaven Gate. The five fingers were transformed into the Five Phases of metal, wood, water, fire, and earth. They became, in fact, five connected mountains, named Five-Phases Mountain, which pinned him down with just enough pressure to keep him there. The thunder deities, Ānanda, and Kāśyapa all folded their hands and cried in acclamation:

Praise be to virtue! Praise be to virtue!

He learned to be human, born from an egg that year,
And aimed to reap the authentic Way's fruit.
He lived in a fine place by kalpas untouched.
One day he changed, expending vim and strength.
Craving high place, he flouted Heaven's reign,
Mocked saints and stole pills, breaking great relations.
Evil, full to the brim, now meets retribution.
We know not when he may find release.

After the Buddhist Patriarch Tathāgata had vanquished the monstrous monkey, he at once called Ānanda and Kāśyapa to return with him to the Western Paradise. At that moment, however, Tianpeng[11] and Tianyou, two celestial messengers, came running out of the Treasure Hall of Divine Mists and said, "We beg Tathāgata to wait a moment, please! Our Lord's grand carriage will arrive momentarily." When the Buddhist Patriarch heard these words, he turned around and waited with reverence. In a moment he did indeed see a chariot drawn by eight colorful phoenixes and covered by a canopy adorned with nine luminous jewels. The entire cortege was accompanied by the sound of wondrous songs and melodies, chanted by a vast celestial choir. Scattering precious blossoms and diffusing fragrant incense, it came up to the Buddha, and the Jade Emperor offered his thanks, saying, "We are truly indebted to your mighty dharma for vanquishing that monster. We beseech Tathāgata to remain for one brief day, so that we may invite the immortals to join us in giving you a banquet of thanks." Not daring to refuse, Tathāgata folded his hands to thank the Jade Emperor, saying, "Your old monk came here at your command, Most Honorable Deva. Of what power may I boast, really? I owe my success entirely to the excellent fortune of Your Majesty and the various deities. How can I be worthy of your thanks?" The Jade Emperor then ordered the various deities from the Thunder Department to send invitations abroad to the Three Pure Ones, the Four Ministers, the Five Elders, the Six Women Officials,[12] the Seven Stars, the Eight Poles, the Nine Luminaries, and the Ten Capitals. Together with a thousand immortals and ten thousand sages, they were to come to the thanksgiving banquet given for the Buddhist Patriarch. The Four Great Imperial Preceptors and the Divine Maidens of Nine Heavens were told to open wide the golden gates of the Jade Capital, the Treasure Palace of Primal Secret, and the Five Lodges of Penetrating Brightness. Tathāgata was asked to be seated high on the Numinous Terrace of Seven Treasures, and the rest of the deities were then seated according to rank and age before a banquet of dragon livers, phoenix marrow, juices of jade, and immortal peaches.

In a little while, the Jade-Pure Celestial Worthy of Commencement, the Highest-Pure Celestial Worthy of Numinous Treasure, the Great-Pure Celestial Worthy of Moral Virtue,[13] the Immortal Masters of Five Influences, the Star Spirits of Five Constellations, the Three Ministers, the Four Sages, the Nine Luminaries, the Left and Right Assistants, the Devarāja, and Prince Naṭa all marched in leading a train of flags and canopies in pairs. They were all holding rare treasures and lustrous pearls, fruits of longevity and exotic flowers to be presented to the Buddha. As they bowed before him, they said, "We are most grateful for the unfathomable power of Tathāgata, who has subdued the monstrous monkey. We are grateful, too, to the Most Honorable Deva, who is having this banquet and asked us to come here to offer our thanks. May we beseech Tathāgata to give this banquet a name?"

Responding to the petition of the various deities, Tathāgata said, "If a name is desired, let this be called 'The Great Banquet for Peace in Heaven.'" "What a magnificent name!" the various Immortals cried in unison. "Indeed, it shall be the Great Banquet for Peace in Heaven." When they finished speaking, they took their seats separately, and there was the pouring of wine and exchanging of cups, pinning of corsages[14] and playing of zithers. It was indeed a magnificent banquet, for which we have a testimonial poem. The poem says:

> That Immortal Peach Feast the ape disturbed
> Is topped by this Banquet for Peace in Heav'n.
> Dragon flags and phoenix carts glow in halos bright;
> Blazing signs and banners whirl in hallowed light.
> The tunes and songs divine are sweet and fair;
> Phoenix pipes and jade flutes both loudly play.
> Fragrant incense shrouds this assembly of saints.
> All the world's tranquil to praise the Holy Court.

As all of them were feasting merrily, the Lady Queen Mother also led a host of divine maidens and immortal singing girls to come before the Buddha, dancing with nimble feet. They bowed to him, and she said, "Our Festival of Immortal Peaches was ruined by that monstrous monkey. We are beholden to the mighty power of Tathāgata for the enchainment of this mischievous ape. In the celebration during this Great Banquet for Peace in Heaven, we have little to offer as a token of our thanks. Please accept, however, these few immortal peaches plucked from the large trees by our own hands." They were truly

> Half red, half green, and spouting aroma sweet,
> These luscious divine roots of ten thousand years.
> Pity those fruits planted at Wuling Spring![15]
> How could they match the marvels of Heaven's home:
> Those tender ones of purple veins so rare in the world,
> And those peerlessly sweet of pale yellow pits?
> They lengthen age, prolong life, and change your frame.
> He who's lucky to eat them will ne'er be the same.

After the Buddhist Patriarch had pressed together his hands to thank the Queen Mother, she ordered the immortal singing girls and the divine maidens to sing and dance. All the immortals at the banquet applauded enthusiastically. Truly there were

Whorls of Heavenly incense filling the seats,
And profuse array of divine petals and stems.
Jade capital and golden arches in what great splendor!
How priceless, too, the strange goods and rare treasures!
Every pair had the same age as Heaven.
Every set increased through ten thousand kalpas.
Mulberry fields or vast oceans, let them shift and change.
He who lives here has neither grief nor fear.

The Queen Mother commanded the immortal maidens to sing and dance, as wine cups and goblets clinked together steadily. After a little while, suddenly

A wondrous fragrance came to meet the nose,
Rousing Stars and Planets in that great hall.
The gods and the Buddha put down their cups.
Raising his head, each waited with his eyes.
There in the air appeared an aged man,
Holding a most luxuriant long-life plant.
His gourd had elixir often thousand years.
His book listed names twelve millennia old.
Sky and earth in his cave knew no constraint.
Sun and moon were perfected in his vase.[16]
He roamed the Four Seas in joy serene,
And made the Ten Islets[17] *his tranquil home.*
Getting drunk often at the Peaches Feast
He woke; the moon shone brightly as of old.
He had a long head, short frame, and large ears.
His name: Star of Long Life from South Pole.

After the Star of Long Life arrived and greeted the Jade Emperor, he also went up to thank Tathāgata, saying, "When I first heard that the baneful monkey was being led by Laozi to the Tushita Palace to be refined by alchemical fire, I thought peace was surely secured. I never suspected that he could still escape, and it was fortunate that Tathāgata in his goodness had subdued this monster. When I got word of the thanksgiving banquet, I came at once. I have no other gifts to present to you but these purple agaric, jasper plant, jade-green lotus root, and golden elixir." The poem says:

Jade-green lotus and golden drug are given to Śākya.
Like the sands of Ganges is the age of Tathāgata.
The brocade of the three wains is calm, eternal bliss.[18]
The nine-grade garland is a wholesome, endless life.[19]
The true master of the Mādhyamika School[20]

Dwells in the Heaven of both form and emptiness.[21]
The great earth and cosmos all call him Lord.
His sixteen-foot diamond frame's great in blessing and age.[22]

Tathāgata accepted the thanks cheerfully, and the Star of Long Life went to his seat. Again there was pouring of wine and exchanging of cups. The Great Immortal of Naked Feet also arrived. After prostrating himself before the Jade Emperor, he too went to thank the Buddhist Patriarch, saying, "I am profoundly grateful for your dharma, which subdued the baneful monkey. I have no other things to convey my respect but two magic pears and some lire dates, which I now present to you."

The poem says:

The Naked-Feet Immortal brought fragrant pears and dates
To give to Amitābha, whose count of years is long.
Firm as a hill is his Lotus Platform of Seven Treasures;
Brocadelike is his Flower Seat of Thousand Gold adorned.
No false speech is this—his age equals Heaven and Earth;
Nor is this a lie—his luck is great as the sea.
Blessing and long life reach in him their fullest scope,
Dwelling in that Western Region of calm, eternal bliss.

Tathāgata again thanked him and asked Ānanda and Kāśyapa to put away the gifts one by one before approaching the Jade Emperor to express his gratitude for the banquet. By now, everyone was somewhat tipsy. A Spirit Minister of Inspection then arrived to make the report, "The Great Sage is sticking out his head!" "No need to worry," said the Buddhist Patriarch. He took from his sleeve a tag on which were written in gold letters the words *Oṁ maṇi padme hūṁ*. Handing it over to Ānanda, he told him to stick it on the top of the mountain. This deva received the tag, took it out of the Heaven Gate, and stuck it tightly on a square piece of rock at the top of the Mountain of Five Phases. The mountain immediately struck root and grew together at the seams, though there was enough space for breathing and for the prisoner's hands to crawl out and move around a bit. Ānanda then returned to report, "The tag is tightly attached."

Tathāgata then took leave of the Jade Emperor and the deities, and went with the two devas out of the Heaven Gate. Moved by compassion, he recited a divine spell and called together a local spirit and the Fearless Guards of Five Quarters to stand watch over the Five-Phases Mountain. They were told to feed the prisoner with iron pellets when he was hungry and to give him melted copper to drink when he was thirsty. When the time of his chastisement was fulfilled, they were told, someone would be coming to deliver him. So it is that

The brash, baneful monkey in revolt against Heaven
Is brought to submission by Tathāgata.
He drinks melted copper to endure the seasons,
And feeds on iron pellets to pass the time.
Tried by this bitter misfortune sent from the Sky,
He's glad to be living, though in a piteous lot.
If this hero is allowed to struggle anew,
He'll serve Buddha in future and go to the West.

Another poem says:

Prideful of his power once the time was ripe,
He tamed dragon and tiger, flaunting wily might.
Stealing peaches and wine, he roamed Heaven's House.
He found trust and grace in the City of Jade.
He's now bound, for his evil's full to the brim.
By good stock[23] unfailing his breath will rise again.
If he's indeed to flee Tathāgata's hands,
He must await from Tang court the holy monk.

We do not know in what month or year hereafter the days of his penance will be fulfilled; let's listen to the explanation in the next chapter.

EIGHT

Our Buddha makes scriptures to impart ultimate bliss; Guanyin receives the decree to go up to Chang'an.[1]

Ask at meditation-pass
Why even countless queries
Would lead just to empty old age!
Shine bricks to make mirrors?
Hoard snow for foodstuff?[2]
How many youths are thus deceived;
A feather swallows the great ocean?
A mustard seed holds the Sumeru?[3]
Golden Dhūta is gently smiling.[4]
The enlightened transcends the ten stops[5] and three wains[6]
Sluggards must join the four beasts and six ways.[7]
Who can hear below the Thoughtless Cliff,
Beneath the Shadowless Tree,
The cuckoo's one call for the dawn of spring?
Roads at Caoxi, perilous;[8]
Clouds on Vulture's Peak, dense;[9]
Here an old friend's voice turns mute.
At a ten thousand-foot waterfall
Where a five-petal lotus unfolds,
Incense wraps an old temple's drapes.
In that hour,
Once you break through to the source,
The Dragon King's three jewels you'll see.[10]

The tune of this lyric is named "Su Wu at Slow Pace."[11]

We shall now tell you about our Sovereign Buddha Tathāgata, who took leave of the Jade Emperor and returned to the Treasure Monastery of Thunderclap. All the three thousand buddhas, the five hundred arhats, the eight diamond kings, and the countless bodhisattvas held temple pennants, embroidered canopies, rare treasures, and immortal flowers, forming an orderly array before the Spirit Mountain and beneath the two Śāla Trees to welcome him. Tathāgata stopped his hallowed cloud and said to them:

I have
With deepest prajñā[12]
Looked through the three realms.[13]

All fundamental nature
Will end in extinction
Like empty phenomena
Existing as nothing.
The wily ape's extirpation,
This, none can comprehend.
Name, birth, death, and origin
Of all forms appear thus.

When he had finished speaking, he beamed forth the śārī light,[14] which filled the air with forty-two white rainbows, connected end to end from north to south. Seeing this, the crowd bowed down and worshipped.

In a little while, Tathāgata gathered together the holy clouds and blessed fog, ascended the lotus platform of the highest rank, and sat down solemnly. Those three thousand buddhas, five hundred arhats, eight diamond kings, and four bodhisattvas folded their hands and drew near. After bowing down, they asked, "The one who caused disturbance in Heaven and ruined the Peach Festival, who was he?" "That fellow," said Tathāgata, "was a baneful monkey born in the Flower-Fruit Mountain. His wickedness was beyond all bounds and defied description. The divine warriors of the entire Heaven could not bring him to submission. Though Erlang caught him and Laozi tried to refine him with fire, they could not hurt him at all. When I arrived, he was just making an exhibition of his might and prowess in the midst of the thunder deities. When I stopped the fighting and asked about his antecedents, he said that he had magic powers, knowing how to transform himself and how to cloud somersault, which would carry him one hundred and eight thousand miles at a time. I made a wager with him to see whether he could leap clear of my hand. I then grabbed hold of him while my fingers changed into the Mountain of Five Phases, which had him firmly pinned down. The Jade Emperor opened wide the golden doors of the Jade Palace, invited me to sit at the head table, and gave a Banquet for Peace in Heaven to thank me. It was only a short while ago that I took leave of the throne to come back here." All were delighted by these words. After they had expressed their highest praise for the Buddha, they withdrew according to their ranks; they went back to their several duties and enjoyed the *bhūtatathatā*.[15] Truly it is the scene of

Holy mist encompassing Tianzhu,[16]
Rainbow light enclosing the Honored One,
Who is called the First in the West,
The King of the Formlessness School.[17]
Often black apes are seen presenting fruits.
Tailed-deer holding flowers in their mouths,

Blue phoenixes dancing,
Colorful birds singing,
The spirit tortoise boasting of his age,
And the divine crane picking agaric.
They enjoy in peace the Pure Land's Jetavana,[18]
The Dragon Palace, and worlds vast as Ganges' sands.
Every day the flowers bloom;
Every hour the fruits ripen.
They work silence to reach perfection.
They meditate to bear the right fruit.
They do not die nor are they born.
No growth is there, nor any decrease.
Mist and smoke wraithlike may come and go.
No seasons intrude, nor are years recalled.

The poem says:

To go or come is casual and free;
Of fear or sorrow there's not one degree.
Fields of Ultimate Bliss are flat and wide.
In this great world no four seasons abide.

As the Buddhist Patriarch lived in the Treasure Monastery of the Thunderclap in the Spirit Mountain, he called together one day the various buddhas, arhats, guardians, bodhisattvas, diamond kings, and mendicant monks and nuns and said to them, "We do not know how much time has passed here since I subdued the wily monkey and pacified Heaven, but I suppose at least half a millennium has gone by in the worldly realm. As this is the fifteenth day of the first month of autumn, I have prepared a treasure bowl filled with a hundred varieties of exotic flowers and a thousand kinds of rare fruit. I would like to share them with all of you in celebration of the Feast of the Ullambana Bowl.[19] How about it?" Every one of them folded his hands and paid obeisance to the Buddha three times to receive the festival. Tathāgata then ordered Ānanda to take the flowers and fruits from the treasure bowl, and Kāśyapa was asked to distribute them. All were thankful, and they presented poems to express their gratitude.

The poem of blessing says:

The star of blessing shines before Lokajyeṣṭha,[20]
Who enjoys blessing lasting and immense.
His blessing's boundless virtue endures as Earth.
His blessing's source is gladly linked to Heaven.
His blessing's fields, far planted, prosper each year.
His blessing's sea, huge and deep, is ever strong.

His blessing fills the world and all will be blessed.
May his blessing increase, endless and complete.

The poem of wealth says:

His wealth weighs a mountain where the phoenix sings.
His wealth trails the seasons to wish him long life.
He gains wealth in huge sums as his body health.
He joys in wealth abundant as the world in peace.
His wealth's reach equals Heaven is ever safe.
His wealth's name is sealike but even more pure.
His wealth's grace far-reaching is sought by all.
His wealth is boundless, enriching countless lands.

The poem of long life says:

The Star of Long Life gives gifts to Tathāgata,
From whom light of long life begins now to shine.
The long life fruits fill the bowls with hues divine.
The long life blooms, newly plucked, deck the lotus throne.
The long life verse, how elegant and finely wrought.
The long life songs are scored by gifted minds.
The long life's length matches the sun and moon's.
Long life, like sea and mountain, is twice as long!

After the bodhisattvas had presented their poems, they invited Tathāgata to disclose the origin and elucidate the source. Tathāgata gently opened his benevolent mouth to expound the great dharma and to proclaim the truth. He lectured on the wondrous doctrines of the three vehicles, the five skandhas,[21] and the *Śūraṅgamā Sūtra*. As he did so, celestial dragons were seen circling above and flowers descended like rain in abundance. It was truly thus:

The Chan mind shines bright like a thousand rivers' moon;
True nature's pure and great as an unclouded sky.

When Tathāgata had finished his lecture, he said to the congregation, "I have "watched the Four Great Continents, and the morality of their inhabitants varies from place to place. Those living on the East Pūrvavideha revere Heaven and Earth, and they are straightforward and peaceful. Those on the North Uttarakuru, though they love to destroy life, do so out of the necessity of making a livelihood. Moreover, they are rather dull of mind and lethargic in spirit, and they are not likely to do much harm. Those of our West Aparagodānīya are neither covetous nor prone to kill; they control their humor and temper their spirit. There is, to be sure, no illuminate

of the first order, but everyone is certain to attain longevity. Those who reside in the South Jambūdvīpa, however, are prone to practice lechery and
delight in evildoing, indulging in much slaughter and strife. Indeed, they
are all caught in the treacherous field of tongue and mouth, in the wicked
sea of slander and malice. However, I have three baskets of true scriptures
which can persuade man to do good." Upon hearing these words, the various bodhisattvas folded their hands and bowed down. "What are the three
baskets of authentic scriptures," they asked, "that Tathāgata possesses?"

Tathāgata said, "I have one collection of vinaya, which speaks of
Heaven; one collection of śāstras, which tells of the Earth; and one collection of sūtras, which redeems the damned. Altogether the three collections of scriptures contain thirty-five divisions written in fifteen thousand
one hundred forty-four scrolls. They are the scriptures for the cultivation
of immortality; they are the gate to ultimate virtue. I myself would like to
send these to the Land of the East; but the creatures in that region are so
stupid and so scornful of the truth that they ignore the weighty elements
of our Law and mock the true sect of Yoga. Somehow we need a person
with power to go to the Land of the East and find a virtuous believer. He
will be asked to experience the bitter travail of passing through a thousand
mountains and ten thousand waters to come here in quest of the authentic
scriptures, so that they may be forever implanted in the east to enlighten
the people. This will provide a source of blessings great as a mountain and
deep as the sea. Which one of you is willing to make such a trip?"

At that moment, the Bodhisattva Guanyin came near the lotus platform
and paid obeisance three times to the Buddha, saying, "Though your disciple is untalented, she is willing to go to the Land of the East to find a
scripture pilgrim." Lifting their heads to look, the various buddhas saw that
the Bodhisattva had

A mind perfected in the four virtues,[22]
A golden body filled with wisdom,
Fringes of dangling pearls and jade,
Scented bracelets set with lustrous treasures,
Dark hair piled smartly in a coiled-dragon bun,
And brocade sashes fluttering as phoenix quills.
Her green jade buttons
And white silk robe
Bathed in holy light;
Her velvet skirt
And golden cords
Wrapped by hallowed air.
With brows of new moon shape

And eyes like two bright stars,
Her jadelike face beams natural joy,
And her ruddy lips seem a flash of red.
Her immaculate vase overflows with nectar from year to year,
Holding sprigs of weeping willow green from age to age.
She disperses the eight woes;
She redeems the multitude;
She has great compassion;
Thus she rules the Tai Mountain
And lives at the South Sea.
She saves the poor, searching for their voices,
Ever heedful and solicitous,
Ever wise and efficacious.
Her orchid heart delights in green bamboos;
Her chaste nature loves the wisteria.
She is the merciful lord of the Potalaka Mountain,
The Living Guanyin from the Cave of Tidal Sound.

When Tathāgata saw her, he was most delighted and said to her, "No other person is qualified to make this journey. It must be the Honorable Guanyin of mighty magic powers—she's the one to do it!" "As your disciple departs for the east," said the Bodhisattva, "do you have any instructions?"

"As you travel," said Tathāgata, "you are to examine the way carefully. Do not journey high in the air, but remain at an altitude halfway between mist and cloud so that you can see the mountains and waters and remember the exact distance. You will then be able to instruct closely the scripture pilgrim. Since he may still find the journey difficult, I shall also give you five talismans." Ordering Ānanda and Kāśyapa to bring out an embroidered cassock and a nine-ring priestly staff, he said to the Bodhisattva, "You may give this cassock and this staff to the scripture pilgrim. If he is firm in his intention to come here, he may put on the cassock and it will protect him from falling back into the wheel of transmigration. When he holds the staff, it will keep him from meeting poison or harm." The Bodhisattva bowed low to receive the gifts. Tathāgata then took out also three fillets and handed them to the Bodhisattva, saying, "These treasures are called the tightening fillets, and though they are all alike, their uses are not the same. I have a separate spell for each of them: the Golden, the Constrictive, and the Prohibitive Spell. If you encounter on the way any monster who possesses great magic powers, you must persuade him to learn to be good and to follow the scripture pilgrim as his disciple. If he is disobedient, this fillet may be put on his head, and it will strike root the moment it comes into contact with the flesh. Recite the particular spell which belongs to the fillet and it will cause the head to swell and ache so painfully that he will think his brains are bursting. That will persuade him to come within our fold."

After the Bodhisattva had bowed to the Buddha and taken her leave, she called Disciple Hui'an to follow her. This Hui'an, you see, carried a huge iron rod that weighed a thousand pounds. He followed the Bodhisattva closely and served her as a powerful bodyguard. The Bodhisattva made the embroidered cassock into a bundle and placed it on his back; she hid the golden fillets, took up the priestly staff, and went down the Spirit Mountain. Lo, this one journey will result in

> A Buddha son returning to keep his primal vow.
> The Gold Cicada Elder will clasp the candana.[23]

The Bodhisattva went to the bottom of the hill, where she was received at the door of the Jade Perfection Daoist Abbey by the Great Immortal of Golden Head. The Bodhisattva was presented with tea, but she did not dare linger long, saying, "I have received the dharma-decree of Tathāgata to look for a scripture pilgrim in the Land of the East." The Great Immortal said, "When do you expect the scripture pilgrim to arrive?" "I'm not sure," said the Bodhisattva. "Perhaps in two or three years' time he'll be able to get here." So she took leave of the Great Immortal and traveled at an altitude halfway between cloud and mist in order that she might remember the way and the distance. We have a testimonial poem for her that says:

> A search through ten thousand miles—no need to say!
> To state who will be found is no easy thing.
> Has not seeking someone been just like this?
> What's been my whole life, was that a mere chance?
> We preach the Dao, our method turns foolish
> When saying meets no belief; we preach in vain.
> To find some percipient I'd yield liver and gall.
> There's affinity, I think, lying straight ahead.

As the mentor and her disciple journeyed, they suddenly came upon a large body of Weak Water, for this was the region of the Flowing Sand River.[24] "My disciple," said the Bodhisattva, "this place is difficult to cross. The scripture pilgrim will be of temporal bones and mortal stock. How will he be able to get across?" "Teacher," said Hui'an, "how wide do you suppose this river is?" The Bodhisattva stopped her cloud to take a look, and she saw that

> In the east it touches the sandy coast;
> In the west it joins the barbaric states;
> In the south it reaches even Wuyi;[25]

In the north it comes near the Tartars.
Its width is eight hundred miles,
And its length must measure many thousand more.
The water flows as if Earth is heaving its frame.
The current rises like a mountain rearing its back.
Outspread and immense;
Vast and interminable.
The sound of its towering billows reaches distant ears.
The raft of a god cannot come here,
Nor can a leaf of the lotus stay afloat.
Lifeless grass in the twilight drifts along the crooked banks.
Yellow clouds conceal the sun to darken the long dikes.
Where can one find the traffic of merchants?
Has there been ever a shelter for fishermen?
On the flat sand no wild geese descend;
From distant shores comes the crying of apes.
Only the red smartweed flowers know this scene,
Basking in the white duckweed's fragile scent.

The Bodhisattva was looking over the river when suddenly a loud splash was heard, and from the midst of the waves leaped an ugly and ferocious monster. He appeared to have

A green, though not too green,
And black, though not too black,
Face of gloomy complexion;
A long, though not too long,
And short, though not too short,
Sinewy body with naked feet.
His gleaming eyes
Shone like two lights beneath the stove.
His mouth, forked at the corners,
Was like a butcher's bloody bowl.
With teeth protruding like swords and knives,
And red hair all disheveled,
He bellowed once and it sounded like thunder,
While his legs sprinted like whirling wind.

Holding in his hands a priestly staff, that fiendish creature ran up the bank and tried to seize the Bodhisattva. He was opposed, however, by Hui'an, who wielded his iron rod, crying, "Stop!", but the fiendish creature raised his staff to meet him. So the two of them engaged in a fierce battle beside the Flowing Sand River, which was truly terrifying.

The iron rod of Mokṣa
Displays its power to defend the Law;
The monster-taming staff of the creature
Labors to show its heroic might.
Two silver pythons dance along the river's bank.
A pair of godlike monks charge each other on the shore.
This one plies his talents as the forceful lord of Flowing Sand.
That one, to attain great merit, protects Guanyin by strength.
This one churns up foam and stirs up waves.
That one belches fog and spits out wind.
The stirred-up foams and waves darken Heaven and Earth.
The spat-out fog and wind make dim both sun and moon.
The monster-taming staff of this one
Is like a white tiger emerging from the mountain;
The iron rod of that one
Is like a yellow dragon lying on the way.
When used by one,
This weapon spreads open the grass and finds the snake.
When let loose by the other,
That weapon knocks down the kite and splits the pine.
They fight until the darkness thickens
Save for the glittering stars,
And the fog looms up
To obscure both sky and land.
This one, long a dweller in the Weak Water, is uniquely fierce.
That one, newly leaving the Spirit Mountain, seeks his first win.

Back and forth along the river the two of them fought for twenty or thirty rounds without either prevailing, when the fiendish creature stilled the other's iron rod and asked, "What region do you come from, monk, that you dare oppose me?" "I'm the second son of the Pagoda Bearer Devarāja," said Mokṣa, "Mokṣa, Disciple Hui'an. I am serving as the guardian of my mentor, who is looking for a scripture pilgrim in the Land of the East. What kind of monster are you that you dare block our way?" "I remember," said the monster, suddenly recognizing his opponent, "that you used to follow the Guanyin of the South Sea and practice austerities there in the bamboo grove. How did you get to this place?" "Don't you realize," said Mokṣa, "that she is my mentor—the one over there on the shore?"

When the monster heard these words, he apologized repeatedly. Putting away his staff, he allowed Mokṣa to grasp him by the collar and lead him away. He lowered his head and bowed low to Guanyin, saying, "Bodhisattva, please forgive me and let me submit my explanation. I am no monster; rather, I am the Curtain-Raising General who waits upon the phoenix chariot of the Jade Emperor at the Divine Mists Hall. Because I carelessly broke a crystal cup at one of the Festivals of Immortal Peaches, the Jade Emperor gave me eight hundred lashes, banished me to the Region Below, and changed me into my present shape. Every seventh day he sends a flying sword to stab my breast and side more than a hundred times before it leaves me. Hence my present wretchedness! Moreover, the hunger and cold are unbearable, and I am driven every few days to come out of the waves and find a traveler for food. I certainly did not expect that my ignorance would today lead me to offend the great, merciful Bodhisattva."

"Because of your sin in Heaven," said the Bodhisattva, "you were banished. Yet the taking of life in your present manner surely is adding sin to sin. By the decree of Buddha, I am on my way to the Land of the East to find a scripture pilgrim. Why don't you come into my fold, take refuge in good works, and follow the scripture pilgrim as his disciple when he goes to the Western Heaven to ask Buddha for the scriptures? I'll order the flying sword to stop piercing you. At the time when you achieve merit, your sin will be expiated and you will be restored to your former position. How do you feel about that?" "I'm willing," said the monster, "to seek refuge in right action." He said also, "Bodhisattva, I have devoured countless human beings at this place. There have even been a number of scripture pilgrims here, and I ate all of them. The heads of those I devoured I threw into the Flowing Sand, and they sank to the bottom, for such is the nature of this water that not even goose down can float on it. But the skulls of the nine pilgrims floated on the water and would not sink. Regarding them as something unusual, I chained them together with a rope and played with them at my leisure. If this becomes known, I fear that no other scripture pilgrim will want to come this way. Won't it jeopardize my future?"

"Not come this way? How absurd!" said the Bodhisattva. "You may take the skulls and hang them round your neck. When the scripture pilgrim arrives, there will be a use for them." "If that's the case," said the monster, "I'm now willing to receive your instructions." The Bodhisattva then touched the top of his head and gave him the commandments.[26] The sand was taken to be a sign, and he was given the surname "Sha" and the religious name "Wujing,"[27] and that was how he entered the Gate of Sand.[28] After he had seen the Bodhisattva on her way, he washed his heart and purified himself; he never took life again but waited attentively for the arrival of the scripture pilgrim.

So the Bodhisattva parted with him and went with Mokṣa toward the Land of the East. They traveled for a long time and came upon a high mountain, which was covered by miasma so foul that they could not ascend it on foot. They were just about to mount the clouds and pass over it when a sudden blast of violent wind brought into view another monster of most ferocious appearance. Look at his

> Lips curled and twisted like dried lotus leaves;
> Ears like rush-leaf fans and hard, gleaming eyes;
> Gaping teeth as sharp as a fine steel file's;
> A long mouth wide open like a fire pot.
> A gold cap is fastened with bands by the cheek.
> Straps on his armor seem like scaleless snakes.
> He holds a rake—a dragon's outstretched claws;
> From his waist hangs a bow of half-moon shape.
> His awesome presence and his prideful mien
> Defy the deities and daunt the gods.

He rushed up toward the two travelers and, without regard for good or ill, lifted the rake and brought it down hard on the Bodhisattva. But he was met by Disciple Hui'an, who cried with a loud voice, "Reckless monster! Desist from this insolence! Look out for my rod!" "This monk," said the monster, "doesn't know any better! Look out for my rake!" The two of them clashed together at the foot of the mountain to discover who was to be the victor. It was a magnificent battle!

> The monster is fierce.
> Hui'an is powerful.
> The iron rod jabs at the heart;
> The muckrake swipes at the face.
> Spraying mud and splattering dust darken Heaven and Earth;
> Flying sand and hurling rocks scare demons and gods.
> The nine-teeth rake,
> All burnished,
> Loudly jingles with double rings;
> The single rod,
> Black throughout,
> Leaps and flies in both hands.
> This one is the prince of a Devarāja;
> That one is the spirit of a grand marshal.
> This one defends the faith at Potalaka;
> That one lives in a cave as a monster.
> Meeting this time they rush to fight,
> Not knowing who shall lose and who shall win.

At the very height of their battle, Guanyin threw down some lotus flowers from midair, separating the rod from the rake. Alarmed by what he saw, the fiendish creature asked, "What region are you from, monk, that you dare to play this 'flower-in-the-eye' trick on me?" "Cursed beast of fleshly eyes and mortal stock!" said Mokṣa. "I am the disciple of the Bodhisattva from South Sea, and these are lotus flowers thrown down by my mentor. Don't you recognize them?" "The Bodhisattva from South Sea?" asked the fiend. "Is she Guanyin who sweeps away the three calamities and rescues us from the eight disasters?" "Who else," said Mokṣa, "if not she?" The fiend threw away his muckrake, lowered his head, and bowed, saying, "Venerable brother! Where is the Bodhisattva? Please be so good as to introduce me to her." Mokṣa raised his head and pointed upward, saying, "Isn't she up there?" "Bodhisattva!" the fiend kowtowed toward her and cried with a loud voice, "Pardon my sin! Pardon my sin!"

Guanyin lowered the direction of her cloud and came to ask him, "What region are you from, wild boar who has become a spirit or old sow who has become a fiend, that you dare bar my way?" "I am neither a wild boar," said the fiend, "nor am I an old sow! I was originally the Marshal of the Heavenly Reeds in the Heavenly River.[29] Because I got drunk and dallied with the Goddess of the Moon,[30] the Jade Emperor had me beaten with a mallet two thousand times and banished me to the world of dust. My true spirit was seeking the proper home for my next incarnation when I lost my way, passed through the womb of an old sow, and ended up with a shape like this! Having bitten the sow to death and killed the rest of the litter, I took over this mountain ranch and passed my days eating people. Little did I expect to run into the Bodhisattva. Save me, I implore you! Save me!"

"What is the name of this mountain?" asked the Bodhisattva.

"It's called the Mountain of the Blessed Mound," said the fiendish creature, "and there is a cave in it by the name of Cloudy Paths. There was a Second Elder Sister Egg originally in the cave. She saw that I knew something of the martial art and therefore asked me to be the head of the family, following the so-called practice of 'standing backward in the door.'[31] After less than a year, she died, leaving me to enjoy the possession of her entire cave. I have spent many days and years at this place, but I know no means of supporting myself and I pass the time eating people. I implore the Bodhisattva to pardon my sin."

The Bodhisattva said, "There is an old saying:

If you want to have a future,
Don't act heedless of the future.

You have already transgressed in the Region Above, and yet you have not changed your violent ways but indulge in the taking of life. Don't you know that both crimes will be punished?"

"The future! The future!" said the fiend. "If I listen to you, I might as well feed on the wind! The proverb says,

If you follow the law of the court, you'll be beaten to death;
If you follow the law of Buddha, you'll be starved to death!

Let me go! Let me go! I would much prefer catching a few travelers and munching on the plump and juicy lady of the family. Why should I care about two crimes, three crimes, a thousand crimes, or ten thousand crimes?" "There is a saying," said the Bodhisattva,

A man with good intent
Will win Heaven's assent.

If you are willing to return to the fruits of truth, there will be means to sustain your body. There are five kinds of grain in this world and they all can relieve hunger. Why do you need to pass the time by devouring humans?"

When the fiend heard these words, he was like one who woke from a dream, and he said to the Bodhisattva, "I would very much like to follow the truth. But 'since I have offended Heaven, even my prayers are of little avail.'"³² "I have received the decree from Buddha to go to the Land of the East to find a scripture pilgrim," said the Bodhisattva. "You can follow him as his disciple and make a trip to the Western Heaven; your merit will cancel out your sins, and you will surely be delivered from your calamities." "I'm willing. I'm willing," promised the fiend with enthusiasm. The Bodhisattva then touched his head and gave him the instructions. Pointing to his body as a sign, she gave him the surname "Zhu" and the religious name "Wuneng."³³ From that moment on, he accepted the commandment to return to the real. He fasted and ate only a vegetable diet, abstaining from the five forbidden viands and the three undesirable foods³⁴ so as to wait single-mindedly for the scripture pilgrim.

The Bodhisattva and Mokṣa took leave of Wuneng and proceeded again halfway between cloud and mist. As they were journeying, they saw in midair a young dragon calling for help. The Bodhisattva drew near and asked, "What dragon are you, and why are you suffering here?" The dragon said, "I am the son of Aorun, Dragon King of the Western Ocean. Because I inadvertently set fire to the palace and burned some of the pearls therein, my father the king memorialized to the Court of Heaven and charged me with grave disobedience. The Jade Emperor hung me in the sky and gave me three hundred lashes, and I shall be executed in a few days. I beg the Bodhisattva to save me."

When Guanyin heard these words, she rushed with Mokṣa up to the South Heaven Gate. She was received by Qiu and Zhang, the two Celestial Masters, who asked her, "Where are you going?" "This humble cleric needs to have an audience with the Jade Emperor," said the Bodhisattva. The two Celestial Masters promptly made the report, and the Jade Emperor left the hall to receive her. After presenting her greetings, the Bodhisattva said, "By the decree of Buddha, this humble cleric is journeying to the Land of the East to find a scripture pilgrim. On the way I met a mischievous dragon hanging in the sky. I have come specially to beg you to spare his life and grant him to me. He can be a good means of transportation for the scripture pilgrim." When the Jade Emperor heard these words, he at once gave the decree of pardon, ordering the Heavenly sentinels to release the dragon to the Bodhisattva. The Bodhisattva thanked the Emperor, while the young dragon also kowtowed to the Bodhisattva to thank her for saving his life and pledged obedience to her command. The Bodhisattva then sent him to live in a deep mountain stream with the instruction that when the scripture pilgrim should arrive, he was to change into a white horse and go to the Western Heaven. The young dragon obeyed the order and hid himself, and we shall speak no more of him for the moment.

The Bodhisattva then led Mokṣa past the mountain, and they headed again toward the Land of the East. They had not traveled long before they suddenly came upon ten thousand shafts of golden light and a thousand layers of radiant vapor. "Teacher," said Mokṣa, "that luminous place must be the Mountain of Five Phases. I can see the tag of Tathāgata imprinted on it." "So, beneath this place," said the Bodhisattva, "is where the Great Sage, Equal to Heaven, who disturbed Heaven and the Festival of Immortal Peaches, is being imprisoned." "Yes, indeed," said Mokṣa. The mentor and her disciple ascended the mountain and looked at the tag, on which was inscribed the divine words *Oṁ mani padme hūṁ*. When the Bodhisattva saw this, she could not help sighing, and composed the following poem:

I rue the impish ape not heeding the Law,
Who let loose wild heroics in bygone years.
His mind puffed up, he wrecked the Peach Banquet
And boldly stole in Tushita Palace.
He found no worthy match in ten thousand troops;
Through Ninefold Heaven he displayed his power.
Imprisoned now by Sovereign Tathāgata,
When will he be free to show once more his might?

As mentor and disciple were speaking, they disturbed the Great Sage, who shouted from the base of the mountain, "Who is up there on the mountain composing verses to expose my faults?" When the Bodhisattva heard those words, she came down the mountain to take a look. There beneath the rocky ledges were the local spirit, the mountain god, and the Heavenly sentinels guarding the Great Sage. They all came and bowed to receive the Bodhisattva, leading her before the Great Sage. She looked and saw that he was pinned down in a kind of stone box: though he could speak, he could not move his body. "You whose name is Sun," said the Bodhisattva, "do you recognize me?"

The Great Sage opened wide his fiery eyes and diamond pupils and nodded. "How could I not recognize you?" he cried. "You are the Mighty Deliverer, the Great Compassionate Bodhisattva Guanyin from the Potalaka Mountain of the South Sea. Thank you, thank you for coming to see me! At this place every day is like a year, for not a single acquaintance has ever come to visit me. Where did you come from?"

"I have received the decree from Buddha," said the Bodhisattva, "to go to the Land of the East to find a scripture pilgrim. Since I was passing through here, I rested my steps briefly to see you."

"Tathāgata deceived me," said the Great Sage, "and imprisoned me beneath this mountain. For over five hundred years already I have not been able to move. I implore the Bodhisattva to show a little mercy and rescue old Monkey!" "Your sinful karma is very deep," said the Bodhisattva. "If I rescue you, I fear that you will again perpetrate violence, and that will be bad indeed." "Now I know the meaning of penitence," said the Great Sage. "So I entreat the Great Compassion to show me the proper path, for I am willing to practice cultivation." Truly it is that

> One wish born in the heart of man
> Is known throughout Heaven and Earth.
> If vice or virtue lacks reward,
> Unjust must be the universe.

When the Bodhisattva heard those words from the prisoner, she was filled with pleasure and said to the Great Sage, "The scripture says,

> When a good word is spoken,
> An answer will come from beyond a thousand miles;
> When an evil word is spoken,
> Opposition will hail from beyond a thousand miles.

If you have such a purpose, wait until I reach the Great Tang Nation in the Land of the East and find the scripture pilgrim. He will be told to come and rescue you, and you can follow him as a disciple. You shall keep the teachings and hold the rosary to enter our gate of Buddha, so that you may again cultivate the fruits of righteousness. Will you do that?" "I'm willing, I'm willing," said the Great Sage repeatedly.

"If you are indeed seeking the fruits of virtue," said the Bodhisattva, "let me give you a religious name." "I have one already," said the Great Sage, "and I'm called Sun Wukong." "There were two persons before you who came into our faith," said the delighted Bodhisattva, "and their names, too, are built on the word 'Wu.' Your name will agree with theirs perfectly, and that is splendid indeed. I need not give you any more instruction, for I must be going." So our Great Sage, with manifest nature and enlightened mind, returned to the Buddhist faith, while our Bodhisattva, with attention and diligence, sought the divine monk.

She left the place with Mokṣa and proceeded straight to the east; in a few days they reached Chang'an of the Great Tang Nation. Forsaking the mist and abandoning the cloud, mentor and disciple changed themselves into two wandering monks covered with scabby sores[35] and went into the city. It was already dusk. As they walked through one of the main streets, they saw a temple of the local spirit. They both went straight in, alarming the spirit and the demon guards, who recognized the Bodhisattva. They kowtowed to receive her, and the local spirit then ran quickly to report to the city's guardian deity, the god of the soil, and the spirits of various temples of Chang'an. When they learned that it was the Bodhisattva, they all came to pay homage, saying, "Bodhisattva, please pardon us for being tardy in our reception." "None of you," said the Bodhisattva, "should let a word of this leak out! I came here by the special decree of Buddha to look for a scripture pilgrim. I would like to stay just for a few days in one of your temples, and I shall depart when the true monk is found." The various deities went back to their own places, but they sent the local spirit off to the residence of the city's guardian deity so that the teacher and the disciple could remain incognito in the spirit's temple. We do not know what sort of scripture pilgrim was found. Let's listen to the explanation in the next chapter.

NINE

Chen Guangrui, going to his post, meets disaster; Monk River Float, avenging his parents, repays his roots.

We now tell you about the city of Chang'an in the great nation's Shaanxi Province, which was the place that kings and emperors from generation to generation had made their capital. Since the periods of Zhou, Qin, and Han,

> *Three counties of flowers bloomed like brocade,*
> *And eight rivers[1] flowed encircling the city.*

It was truly a land of great scenic beauty. At this time the emperor Taizong[2] of the Great Tang dynasty was on the throne, and the name of his reign was Zhenguan. He had been ruling now for thirteen years, and the cyclical name of the year was Jisi.[3] The whole land was at peace: people came bearing tributes from eight directions, and the inhabitants of the whole world called themselves his subjects.

One day Taizong ascended his throne and assembled his civil and military officials. After they had paid him homage, the prime minister Wei Zheng[4] left the ranks and came forward to memorialize to the Throne, saying, "Since the world now is at peace and tranquility reigns everywhere, we should follow the ancient custom and establish sites for civil examinations, so that we may invite worthy scholars to come here and select those talents who will best serve the work of administration and government." "Our worthy subject has voiced a sound principle in his memorial," said Taizong. He therefore issued a summons to be proclaimed throughout the empire: in every prefecture, county, and town, those who were learned in the Confucian classics, who could write with ease and lucidity, and who had passed the three sessions of examination,[5] regardless of whether they were soldiers or peasants, would be invited to go to Chang'an to take the imperial examination.

This summons reached the place Haizhou, where it was seen by a certain man named Chen E (with the courtesy name of Guangrui), who then went straight home to talk to his mother, whose maiden name was Zhang. "The court," he said, "has sent a yellow summons, declaring in these southern provinces that there will be examinations for the selection of the worthy and the talented. Your child wishes to try out at such an examination, for if I manage to acquire an appointment, or even half a post, I would become more of a credit to my parents, magnify our name, give my wife a title, benefit my son, and bring glory to this house of ours. Such is the aspiration of your son: I wish to tell my mother plainly before I leave." "My son," said she of the Zhang family, "an educated person 'learns when he is young, but leaves when he is grown.' You should indeed follow this maxim. But as you go to the examination, you must be careful on the way, and, when you have secured a post, come home quickly." So Guangrui gave instructions for his family page to pack his bags, took leave of his mother, and began his journey. When he reached Chang'an, the examination site had just been opened, and he went straight in. He took the preliminary tests, passed them, and went to the court examination, where in three sessions on administrative policy he took first place, receiving the title "zhuangyuan," the certificate of which was signed by the Tang emperor's own hand. As was the custom, he was led through the streets on horseback for three days.

The procession at one point passed by the house of the chief minister, Yin Kaishan, who had a daughter named Wenjiao, nicknamed Mantangjiao (A Hall of Loveliness). She was not yet married, and at this time she was just about to throw down an embroidered ball from high up on a festooned tower in order to select her spouse. It happened that Chen Guangrui was passing below the tower. When the young maiden saw Guangrui's outstanding appearance and knew that he was the recent zhuangyuan of the examinations, she was very pleased. She threw down the embroidered ball, which just happened to hit the black gauze hat of Guangrui. Immediately, lively music of pipes and flutes could be heard throughout the area as scores of maids and serving-girls ran down from the tower, took hold of the bridle of Guangrui's horse, and led him into the residence of the chief minister for the wedding. The chief minister and his wife at once came out of their chambers, called together the guests and the master of ceremonies, and gave the girl to Guangrui as his bride. Together, they bowed to Heaven and Earth; then husband and wife bowed to each other, before bowing to the father- and mother-in-law. The chief minister then gave a big banquet and everyone feasted merrily for a whole evening, after which the two of them walked hand in hand into the bridal chamber.

At the fifth watch early next morning, Taizong took his seat in the Treasure Hall of Golden Chimes as civil and military officials attended the court. Taizong asked, "What appointment should the new zhuangyuan receive?" The prime minister Wei Zheng said, "Your subject has discovered that within our territory there is a vacancy at Jiangzhou. I beg my Lord to grant him this post." Taizong at once made him governor of Jiangzhou and ordered him to leave without delay. After thanking the emperor and leaving the court, Guangrui went back to the house of the chief minister to inform his wife. He took leave of his father- and mother-in-law and proceeded with his wife to the new post at Jiangzhou.

As they left Chang'an and went on their journey, the season was late spring:

A soft wind blew to green the willows;
A fine rain spotted to redden the flowers.

As his home was on the way, Guangrui returned to his house where husband and wife bowed together to his mother, Lady Zhang. "Congratulations, my son," said she of the Zhang family, "you even came back with a wife!" "Your child," said Guangrui, "relied on the power of your blessing and was able to attain the undeserved honor of zhuangyuan. By imperial command I was making a tour of the streets when, as I passed by the mansion of Chief Minister Yin, I was hit by an embroidered ball. The chief minister kindly gave his daughter to your child to be his wife, and His Majesty appointed him governor of Jiangzhou. I have returned to take you with me to the post." She of the Zhang family was delighted and packed at once for the journey.

They had been on the road for a few days when they came to stay at the Inn of Ten Thousand Flowers, kept by a certain Liu Xiaoer. She of the Zhang family suddenly became ill and said to Guangrui, "I don't feel well at all. Let's rest here for a day or two before we journey again." Guangrui obeyed. Next morning there was a man outside the inn holding a golden carp for sale, which Guangrui bought for a string of coins. He was about to have it cooked for his mother when he saw that the carp was blinking its eyes vigorously. In astonishment, Guangrui said, "I have heard that when a fish or a snake blinks its eyes in this manner, that's the sure sign that it's not an ordinary creature!" He therefore asked the fisherman, "Where did you catch this fish?" "I caught it," said the fisherman, "from the river Hong, some fifteen miles from this district." Accordingly, Guangrui sent the live fish back to the river and returned to the inn to tell his mother about it. "It is a good deed to release living creatures from captivity," said she of the Zhang family. "I am very pleased." "We have stayed in this inn now for three days," said Guangrui. "The imperial command is an urgent one. Your child intends to leave tomorrow, but he would like to know whether mother has fully recovered." She of the Zhang family said, "I'm still not well, and the heat on the journey at this time of year, I fear, will only add to my illness. Why don't you rent a house for me to stay here temporarily and leave me an allowance? The two of you can proceed to your new post. By autumn, when it's cool, you can come fetch me." Guangrui discussed the matter with his wife; they duly rented a house for her and left some cash with her, after which they took leave and left.

They felt the fatigue of traveling, journeying by day and resting by night, and they soon came to the crossing of the Hong River, where two boatmen,

Liu Hong and Li Biao, took them into their boat. It happened that Guangrui was destined in his previous incarnation to meet this calamity, and so he had to come upon these fated enemies of his. After ordering the houseboy to put the luggage on the boat, Guangrui and his wife were just about to embark when Liu Hong noticed the beauty of Lady Yin, who had a face like a full moon, eyes like autumnal water, a small, cherrylike mouth, and a tiny, willowlike waist. Her features were striking enough to sink fishes and drop wild geese, and her complexion would cause the moon to hide and put the flowers to shame. Stirred at once to cruelty, he plotted with Li Biao; together they punted the boat to an isolated area and waited until the middle of the night. They killed the houseboy first, and then they beat Guangrui to death, pushing both bodies into the water. When the lady saw that they had killed her husband, she made a dive for the water, but Liu Hong threw his arms around her and caught her. "If you consent to my demand," he said, "everything will be all right. If you do not, this knife will cut you in two!" Unable to think of any better plan, the lady had to give her consent for the time being and yielded herself to Liu Hong. The thief took the boat to the south bank, where he turned the boat over to the care of Li Biao. He himself put on Guangrui's cap and robe, took his credentials, and proceeded with the lady to the post at Jiangzhou.

We should now tell you that the body of the houseboy killed by Liu Hong drifted away with the current. The body of Chen Guangrui, however, sank to the bottom of the water and stayed there. A yakṣa on patrol at the mouth of the Hong River saw it and rushed into the Dragon Palace. The Dragon King was just holding court when the yakṣa entered to report, saying, "A scholar has been beaten to death at the mouth of the Hong River by some unknown person, and his body is now lying at the bottom of the water." The Dragon King had the corpse brought in and laid before him. He took a careful look at it and said, "But this man was my benefactor! How could he have been murdered? As the common saying goes, 'Kindness should be paid by kindness.' I must save his life today so that I may repay the kindness of yesterday." He at once issued an official dispatch, sending a yakṣa to deliver it to the municipal deity and local spirit of Hongzhou, and asked for the soul of the scholar so that his life might be saved. The municipal deity and the local spirit in turn ordered the little demons to hand over the soul of Chen Guangrui to the yakṣa, who led the soul back to the Water Crystal Palace for an audience with the Dragon King.

"Scholar," asked the Dragon King, "what is your name? Where did you come from? Why did you come here, and for what reason were you beaten to death?" Guangrui saluted him and said, "This lowly student is named Chen E, and my courtesy name is Guangrui. I am from the Hongnong district of Haizhou. As the unworthy zhuangyuan of the recent session of examination, I was appointed by the court to be governor of Jiangzhou, and I was going to my post with my wife. When I took a boat at the river, I did not expect the boatman, Liu Hong, to covet my wife and plot against me. He beat me to death and tossed out my body. I beg the Great King to save me." Hearing these words, the Dragon King said, "So, that's it! Good sir, the golden carp that you released earlier was myself. You are my benefactor. You may be in dire difficulty at the moment, but is there any reason why I should not come to your assistance?" He therefore laid the body of Guangrui to one side, and put a preservative pearl in his mouth so that his body would not deteriorate but be reunited with his soul to avenge himself in the future. He also said, "Your true soul may remain temporarily in my Water Bureau as an officer." Guangrui kowtowed to thank him, and the Dragon King prepared a banquet to entertain him, but we shall say no more about that.

We now tell you that Lady Yin hated the bandit Liu so bitterly that she wished she could devour his flesh and sleep on his skin! But because she was with child and did not know whether it would be a boy or a girl, she had no alternative but to yield reluctantly to her captor. In a little while they arrived at Zhiangzhou; the clerks and the lictors all came to meet them, and all the subordinate officials gave a banquet for them at the governor's mansion. Liu Hong said, "Having come here, a student like me is utterly dependent on the support and assistance of you gentlemen." "Your Honor," replied the officials, "is first in the examinations and a major talent. You will, of course, regard your people as your children; your public declarations will be as simple as your settlement of litigation is fair. We subordinates are all dependent on your leadership, so why should you be unduly modest?" When the official banquet ended, the people all left.

Time passed by swiftly. One day, Liu Hong went far away on official business, while Lady Yin at the mansion was thinking of her mother-in-law and her husband and sighing in the garden pavilion. Suddenly she was seized by tremendous fatigue and sharp pains in her belly. Falling unconscious to the ground, she gave birth to a son. Presently she heard someone whispering in her ear: "Mantangjiao, listen carefully to what I have to say. I am the Star Spirit of South Pole, who sends you this son by the express command of the Bodhisattva Guanyin. One day his name will be known far and wide, for he is not to be compared with an ordinary mortal. But when the bandit Liu returns, he will surely try to harm the child, and you must take care to protect him. Your husband has been rescued by the Dragon King; in the future both of you will meet again even as son and mother will be reunited. A day will come when wrongs will be redressed and crimes punished. Remember my words! Wake up! Wake up!" The voice ceased and departed. The lady woke up and remembered every word; she clasped her son tightly to her but could devise no plan to protect him. Liu Hong then returned and wanted to have the child killed by drowning the moment he saw him. The lady said, "Today it's late already. Allow him to live till tomorrow and then have him thrown into the river."

It was fortunate that Liu Hong was called away by urgent business the next morning. The lady thought to herself: "If this child is here when that bandit returns, his life is finished! I might as well abandon him now to the river, and let life or death take its own course. Perhaps Heaven, taking pity on him, will send someone to his rescue and to have him cared for. Then we may have a chance to meet again." She was afraid, however, that future recognition would be difficult; so she bit her finger and wrote a letter with her blood, stating in detail the names of the parents, the family history, and the reason for the child's abandonment. She also bit off a little toe from the child's left foot to establish a mark of his identity. Taking one of her own inner garments she wrapped the child and took him out of the mansion when no one was watching. Fortunately the mansion was not far from the river. Reaching the bank, the lady burst into tears and wailed long and loud. She was about to toss the child into the river when she caught sight of a plank floating by the river bank. At once she prayed to Heaven, after which she placed the child on the plank and tied him securely to it with some rope. She fastened the letter written in blood to his chest, pushed the plank out into the water, and let it drift away. With tears in her eyes, the lady went back to the mansion, but we shall say no more of that.

Now we shall tell you about the boy on the plank, which floated with the current until it came to a standstill just beneath the Temple of Gold Mountain. The abbot of this temple was called Monk Faming. In the cultivation of perfection and comprehension of truth, he had attained already the wondrous secret of birthlessness. He was sitting in meditation when all at once he heard an infant crying. Moved by this, he went quickly down to the river to have a look, and discovered the baby lying there on a plank at the edge of the water. The abbot quickly lifted him out of the water. When he read the letter in blood fastened to his chest, he learned of the child's origin. He then gave him the baby name River Float[6] and arranged for someone to nurse and care for him, while he himself kept the letter written in blood safely hidden. Time passed by like an arrow, and the seasons like a weaver's shuttle; River Float soon reached his eighteenth year. The abbot had his hair shaved and asked him to join in the practice of austerities, giving him the religious name Xuanzang. Having had his head touched and having received the commandments, Xuanzang pursued the Way with great determination.

One day in late spring, the various monks gathered in the shade of pine trees were discussing the canons of Chan and debating the fine points of the mysteries. One feckless monk, who happened to have been completely outwitted by Xuanzang's questions, shouted angrily, "You damnable beast! You don't even know your own name, and you are ignorant of your own parents! Why are you still hanging around here playing tricks on people?" When Xuanzang heard such language of rebuke, he went into the temple and knelt before the master, saying with tears flowing from his eyes, "Though a human being born into this world receives his natural endowments from the forces of yin and yang and from the Five Phases, he is always nurtured by his parents. How can there be a person in this world who has no father or mother?" Repeatedly and piteously he begged for the names of his parents. The abbot said, "If you truly wish to seek your parents, you may follow me to my cell." Xuanzang duly followed him to his cell, where, from the top of a heavy crossbeam, the abbot took down a small box. Opening the box, he took out a letter written in blood and an inner garment and gave them to Xuanzang. Only after he had unfolded the letter and read it did Xuanzang learn the names of his parents and understand in detail the wrongs that had been done them.

When Xuanzang finished reading, he fell weeping to the floor, saying, "How can anyone be worthy to bear the name of man if he cannot avenge the wrongs done to his parents? For eighteen years, I have been ignorant of my true parents, and only this day have I learned that I have a mother! And yet, would I have even reached this day if my master had not saved me and cared for me? Permit your disciple to go seek my mother. Thereafter, I will rebuild this temple with an incense bowl on my head, and repay the profound kindness of my teacher." "If you desire to seek your mother," said the master, "you may take this letter in blood and the inner garment with you. Go as a mendicant monk to the private quarters at the governor's mansion of Jiangzhou. You will then be able to meet your mother."

Xuanzang followed the words of his master and went to Jiangzhou as a mendicant monk. It happened that Liu Hong was out on business, for Heaven had planned that mother and child should meet. Xuanzang went straight to the door of the private quarters of the governor's mansion to beg for alms. Lady Yin, you see, had had a dream the night before in which she saw a waning moon become full again. She thought to herself, "I have no news from my mother-in-law; my husband was murdered by this bandit; my son was thrown into the river. If by chance someone rescued him and had him cared for, he must be eighteen by now. Perhaps Heaven wished us to be reunited today. Who can tell?"

As she was pondering the matter in her heart, she suddenly heard someone reciting the scriptures outside her residence and crying repeatedly, "Alms! Alms!" At a convenient moment, the lady slipped out and asked him, "Where did you come from?" "Your poor monk," said Xuanzang, "is the disciple of Faming, abbot of the Temple of Gold Mountain." "So you are the disciple of the abbot of that temple?" she asked and invited him into the mansion and served him some vegetables and rice. Watching him closely, she noticed that in speech and manner he bore a remarkable resemblance to her husband. The lady sent her maid away and then asked, "Young master! Did you leave your family as a child or when you grew up? What are your given name and your surname? Do you have any parents?" "I did not leave my family when I was young," replied Xuanzang, "nor did I do so when I grew up. To tell you the truth, I have a wrong to avenge great as the sky, an enmity deep as the sea. My father was a murder victim, and my mother was taken by force. My master the abbot Faming told me to seek my mother in the governor's mansion of Jiangzhou."

"What is your mother's surname?" asked the lady. "My mother's surname is Yin," said Xuanzang, "and her given name is Wenjiao. My father's surname is Chen and his given name is Guangrui. My nickname is River Float, but my religious name is Xuanzang."

"I am Wenjiao," said the lady, "but what proof have you of your identity?" When Xuanzang heard that she was his mother, he fell to his knees and wept most grievously. "If my own mother doesn't believe me," he said, "you may see the proof in this letter written in blood and this inner garment." Wenjiao took them in her hands, and one look told her that they were the real things. Mother and child embraced each other and wept.

Lady Yin then cried, "My son, leave at once!" "For eighteen years I have not known my true parents," said Xuanzang, "and I've seen my mother for the first time only this morning. How could your son bear so swift a separation?" "My son," said the lady, "leave at once, as if you were on fire! If that bandit Liu returns, he will surely take your life. I shall pretend to be ill tomorrow and say that I must go to your temple and fulfill a vow I made in a previous year to donate a hundred pairs of monk shoes. At that time I shall have more to say to you." Xuanzang followed her bidding and bowed to take leave of her.

We were speaking of Lady Yin, who, having seen her son, was filled with both anxiety and joy. The next day, under the pretext of being sick, she lay on her bed and would take neither tea nor rice. Liu Hong returned to the mansion and questioned her. "When I was young," said Lady Yin, "I vowed to donate a hundred pairs of monk shoes. Five days ago, I dreamed that a monk demanded those shoes of me, holding a knife in his hand. From then on, I did not feel well." "Such a small matter!" said Liu Hong. "Why didn't you tell me earlier?" He at once went up to the governor's hall and gave the order to his stewards Wang and Li that a hundred families of the city were each to bring in a pair of monk shoes within five days. The families obeyed and completed their presentations. "Now that we have the shoes," said Lady Yin to Liu Hong, "what kind of temple do we have nearby that I can go to fulfill my vow?" Liu Hong said, "There is a Temple of Gold Mountain here in Jiangzhou as well as a Temple of Burned Mountain. You may go to whichever one you choose." "I have long heard," said the lady, "that the Temple of Gold Mountain is a very good one. I shall go there." Liu Hong at once gave the order to his stewards Wang and Li to prepare a boat. Lady Yin took a trusted companion with her and boarded the boat. The boatmen poled it away from the shore and headed for the Temple of Gold Mountain.

We now tell you about Xuanzang, who returned to the temple and told the abbot Faming what had happened. The next day, a young housemaid arrived to announce that her mistress was coming to the temple to fulfill a vow she had made. All the monks came out of the temple to receive her. The lady went straight inside to worship the Bodhisattva and to give a great vegetarian banquet. She ordered the housemaid to put the monk shoes and stockings in trays and have them brought into the main ceremonial hall. After the lady had again worshipped with extreme devoutness, she asked the abbot Faming to distribute the gifts to the various monks before they dispersed. When Xuanzang saw that all the monks had left and that there was no one else in the hall, he drew near and knelt down. The lady asked him to remove his shoes and stockings, and she saw that there was, indeed, a small toe missing from his left foot. Once again, the two of them embraced and wept. They also thanked the abbot for his kindness in fostering the youth.

Faming said, "I fear that the present meeting of mother and child may become known to that wily bandit. You must leave speedily so that you may avoid any harm." "My son," the lady said, "let me give you an incense ring. Go to Hongzhou, about fifteen hundred miles northwest of here, where you will find the Ten Thousand Flowers Inn. Earlier we left an aged woman there whose maiden name is Zhang and who is the true mother of your father. I have also written a letter for you to take to the capital of the Tang emperor. To the left of the Golden Palace is the house of Chief Minister Yin, who is the true father of your mother. Give my letter to your maternal grandfather, and ask him to request the Tang emperor to dispatch men and horses to have this bandit arrested and executed, so that your father may be avenged. Only then will you be able to rescue your old mother. I dare not linger now, for I fear that knave may be offended by my returning late." She went out of the temple, boarded the boat, and left.

Xuanzang returned weeping to the temple. He told his master everything and bowed to take leave of him immediately. Going straight to Hongzhou, he came to the Ten Thousand Flowers Inn and addressed the innkeeper, Liu Xiaoer, saying, "In a previous year there was an honored guest here by the name of Chen whose mother remained at your inn. How is she now?" "Originally," said Liu Xiaoer, "she stayed in my inn. Afterwards she went blind, and for three or four years did not pay me any rent. She now lives in a dilapidated potter's kiln near the Southern Gate, and every day she goes begging on the streets. Once that honored guest had left, he was gone for a long time, and even now there is no news of him whatever. I can't understand it."

When Xuanzang heard this, he went at once to the dilapidated potter's kiln at the Southern Gate and found his grandmother. The grandmother said, "Your voice sounds very much like that of my son Chen Guangrui." "I'm not Chen Guangrui," said Xuanzang, "but only his son! Lady Wenjiao is my mother." "Why didn't your father and mother come back?" asked the grandmother. "My father was beaten to death by bandits," said Xuanzang, "and one of them forced my mother to be his wife." "How did you know where to find me?" asked the grandmother. "It was my mother," answered Xuanzang, "who told me to seek my grandmother. There's a letter from mother here and there's also an incense ring."

The grandmother took the letter and the incense ring and wept without restraint. "For merit and reputation," she said, "my son came to this! I thought that he had turned his back on righteousness and had forgotten parental kindness. How should I know that he was murdered? Fortunately, Heaven remembered me at least in pity, and this day a grandson has come to seek me out."

"Grandmother," asked Xuanzang, "how did you go blind?" "Because I thought so often about your father," said the grandmother. "I waited for him daily, but he did not return. I wept until I was blind in both eyes." Xuanzang knelt down and prayed to Heaven, saying, "Have regard of Xuanzang who, at the age of eighteen, has not yet avenged the wrong done to his parents. By the command of my mother, I came this day to find my grandmother. If Heaven would take pity on my sincerity, grant that the eyes of my grandmother regain their sight." When he finished his petition, he licked the eyes of his grandmother with the tip of his tongue. In a moment, both eyes were licked open and they were as of old. When the grandmother saw the youthful monk, she said, "You're indeed my grandson! Why, you are just like my son Guangrui!" She felt both happy and sad. Xuanzang led his grandmother out of the kiln and went back to Liu Xiaoer's inn, where he rented a room for her to stay. He also gave her some money, saying, "In a little more than a month's time, I'll be back."

Taking leave of his grandmother, he went straight to the capital and found his way to the house of the chief minister Yin on the eastern street of the imperial city. He said to the porter, "This little monk is a kinsman who has come to visit the chief minister." The porter made the report to the chief minister, who replied, "I'm not related to any monk!" But his wife said, "I dreamed last night that my daughter Mantangjiao came home. Could it be that our son-in-law has sent us a letter?" The chief minister therefore had the little monk shown to the living room. When he saw the chief minister and his wife, he fell weeping to the floor. Taking a letter from within the folds of his robe, he handed it over to the chief minister. The chief minister opened it, read it from beginning to end, and wept without restraint. "Your Excellency, what is the matter?" asked his wife. "This monk," said the chief minister, "is our grandson. Our son-in-law, Chen Guangrui, was murdered by bandits, and Mantangjiao was made the wife of the murderer by force." When the wife heard this, she too wept inconsolably.

"Let our lady restrain her grief," said the chief minister. "Tomorrow morning I shall present a memorial to our Lord. I shall lead the troops myself to avenge our son-in-law." The next day, the chief minister went into court to present his memorial to the Tang emperor, which read:

> The son-in-law of your subject, the zhuangyuan Chen Guangrui, was proceeding to his post at Jiangzhou with members of his family. He was beaten to death by the boatman Liu Hong, who then took our daughter by force to be his wife. He pretended to be the son-in-law of your subject and usurped his post for many years. This is indeed a shocking and tragic incident. I beg Your Majesty to dispatch horses and men at once to exterminate the bandits.

The Tang emperor saw the memorial and became exceedingly angry. He immediately called up sixty thousand imperial soldiers and ordered the chief minister Yin to lead them forth. The chief minister took the decree and left the court to make the roll call for the troops at the barracks. They proceeded immediately toward Jiangzhou, journeying by day and resting by night, and they soon reached the place. Horses and men pitched camps on the north shore, and that very night, the chief minister summoned with golden tablets[7] the Subprefect and County Judge of Jiangzhou to his camp. He explained to the two of them the reason for the expedition and asked for their military assistance. They then crossed the river and, before the sky was light, had the mansion of Liu Hong completely surrounded. Liu Hong was still in his dreams when at the shot of a single cannon and the unisonous roll of drums, the soldiers broke into the private quarters of the mansion. Liu Hong was seized before he could offer any resistance. The chief minister had him and the rest of the prisoners bound and taken to the field of execution, while the rest of the soldiers pitched camp outside the city.

Taking a seat in the great hall of the mansion, the chief minister invited the lady to come out to meet him. She was about to do so but was overcome by shame at seeing her father again, and wanted to hang herself right there. Xuanzang learned of this and rushed inside to save his mother. Falling to his knees, he said to her, "Your son and his grandfather led the troops here to avenge father. The bandit has already been captured. Why does mother want to die now? If mother were dead, how could your son possibly remain alive?" The chief minister also went inside to offer his consolation. "I have heard," said the lady, "that a woman follows her spouse to the grave. My husband was murdered by this bandit, causing me dreadful grief. How could I yield so shamefully to the thief? The child I was carrying—that was my sole lease on life that helped me bear my humiliation! Now that my son is grown and my old father has led troops to avenge our wrong, I who am the daughter have little face left for my reunion. I can only die to repay my husband!"

"My child," said the chief minister, "you did not alter your virtue according to prosperity or adversity. You had no choice! How can this be regarded as shame?" Father and daughter embraced, weeping; Xuanzang also could not contain his emotion. Wiping away his tears, the chief minister said, "The two of you must sorrow no more. I have already captured the culprit, and I must now dispose of him." He got up and went to the execution site, and it happened that the Subprefect of Jiangzhou had also apprehended the pirate Li Biao, who was brought by sentinels to the same place. Highly pleased, the chief minister ordered Liu Hong and Li Biao to be flogged a hundred times with large canes. Each signed an affidavit, giving a thorough account of the murder of Chen Guangrui. First Li Biao was nailed to a wooden ass, and after it had been pushed to the marketplace, he was cut to pieces and his head exposed on a pole for all to see. Liu Hong was then taken to the crossing at the Hong River, to the exact spot where he had beaten Chen Guangrui to death. The chief minister, the lady, and Xuanzang all went to the bank of the river, and as libations they offered the heart and liver of Liu Hong, which had been gouged out from him live. Finally, an essay eulogizing the deceased was burned.

Facing the river the three persons wept without restraint, and their sobs were heard down below in the water region. A yakṣa patrolling the waters brought the essay in its spirit form to the Dragon King, who read it and at once sent a turtle marshal to fetch Guangrui. "Sir," said the king, "Congratulations! Congratulations! At this moment, your wife, your son, and your father-in-law are offering sacrifices to you at the bank of the river. I am now letting your soul go so that you may return to life. We are also presenting you with a pearl of wish fulfillment,[8] two rolling-pan pearls,[9] ten bales of mermaid silk,[10] and a jade belt with lustrous pearls. Today you will enjoy the reunion of husband and wife, mother and son." After Guangrui had given thanks repeatedly, the Dragon King ordered a yakṣa to escort his body to the mouth of the river and there to return his soul. The yakṣa followed the order and left.

We tell you now about Lady Yin, who, having wept for some time for her husband, would have killed herself again by plunging into the water if Xuanzang had not desperately held on to her. They were struggling pitifully when they saw a dead body floating toward the river bank. The lady hurriedly went forward to look at it. Recognizing it as her husband's body, she burst into even louder wailing. As the other people gathered around to look, they suddenly saw Guangrui unclasping his fists and stretching his legs. The entire body began to stir, and in a moment he clambered up to the bank and sat down, to the infinite amazement of everyone. Guangrui opened his eyes and saw Lady Yin, the chief minister Yin, his father-in-law, and a youthful monk, all weeping around him. "Why are you all here?" said Guangrui.

"It all began," said Lady Yin, "when you were beaten to death by bandits. Afterwards your unworthy wife gave birth to this son, who is fortunate enough to have been brought up by the abbot of the Gold Mountain Temple. The abbot sent him to meet me, and I told him to go seek his maternal grandfather. When father heard this, he made it known to the court and led troops here to arrest the bandits. Just now we took out the culprit's liver and heart live to offer to you as libations, but I would like to know how my husband's soul is able to return to give him life." Guangrui said, "That's all on account of our buying the golden carp, when you and I were staying at the Inn of Ten Thousand Flowers. I released that carp, not knowing that it was none other than the Dragon King of this place. When the bandits pushed me into the river afterward, he was the one who came to my rescue. Just now he was also the one who gave me back my soul as well as many precious gifts, which I have here with me. I never even knew that you had given birth to this boy, and I am grateful that my father-in-law has avenged me. Indeed, bitterness has passed and sweetness has come! What unsurpassable joy!"

When the various officials heard about this, they all came to tender their congratulations. The chief minister then ordered a great banquet to thank his subordinates, after which the troops and horses on the very same day began their march homeward. When they came to the Inn of Ten Thousand Flowers, the chief minister gave order to pitch camp. Guangrui went with Xuanzang to the Inn of Liu to seek the grandmother, who happened to have dreamed the night before that a withered tree had blossomed. Magpies behind her house were chattering incessantly as well. She thought to herself, "Could it be that my grandson is coming?" Before she had finished talking to herself, father and son arrived together. The youthful monk pointed to her and said, "Isn't this my grandmother?" When Guangrui saw his aged mother, he bowed in haste; mother and son embraced and wept without restraint for a while. After recounting to each other what had happened, they paid the innkeeper his bill and set out again for the capital. When they reached the chief minister's residence, Guangrui, his wife, and his mother all went to greet the chief minister's wife, who was overjoyed. She ordered her servants to prepare a huge banquet to celebrate the occasion. The chief minister said, "This banquet today may be named the Festival of Reunion, for truly our whole family is rejoicing."

Early the next morning, the Tang emperor held court, during which time the chief minister Yin left the ranks to give a careful report on what had taken place. He also recommended that a talent like Guangrui's be used in some important capacity. The Tang emperor approved the memorial, and ordered that Chen E be promoted to Subchancellor of the Grand Secretariat so that he could accompany the court and carry out its policies. Xuanzang, determined to follow the way of Zen, was sent to practice austerities at the Temple of Infinite Blessing. Some time after this, Lady Yin calmly committed suicide after all, and Xuanzang went back to the Gold Mountain Temple to repay the kindness of abbot Faming. We do not know how things went thereafter; let's listen to the explanation in the next chapter.

TEN

The Old Dragon King's foolish schemes transgress Heaven's decrees;
Prime Minister Wei's letter seeks help from an official of the dead.

For the time being, we shall make no mention of Guangrui serving in his post and Xuanzang practicing austerities. We tell you now about two worthies who lived on the banks of the river Jing outside the city of Chang'an: a fisherman by the name of Zhang Shao and a woodman by the name of Li Ding.[1] The two of them were scholars who had passed no official examination, mountain folks who knew how to read. One day in the city of Chang'an, after they had sold the wood on the one's back and the carp in the other's basket, they went into a small inn and drank until they were slightly tipsy. Each carrying a bottle, they followed the bank of the Jing River and walked slowly back.

"Brother Li," said Zhang Shao, "in my opinion those who strive for fame will lose their lives on account of fame; those who live in quest of fortune will perish because of riches; those who have titles sleep embracing a tiger; and those who receive official favors walk with snakes in their sleeves. When you think of it, their lives cannot compare with our carefree existence, close to the blue mountains and fair waters. We cherish poverty and pass our days without having to quarrel with fate."

"Brother Zhang," said Li Ding, "there's a great deal of truth in what you say. But your fair waters cannot match my blue mountains." "On the contrary," said Zhang Shao, "your blue mountains cannot match my fair waters, in testimony of which I offer a lyric[2] to the tune of 'Butterflies Enamored of Flowers' that says:

In a small boat o'er ten thousand miles of misty waves
I lean to the silent, single sail,
Circled by sounds of the mermaid-fish.
My mind cleansed, my care purged, here lacks wealth or fame;
Leisurely I pick stems of bulrushes and reeds.

Counting the seagulls is pleasure to be told!
At willowed banks and reeded bays
My wife and son join my joyous laugh.
I sleep most soundly as wind and wave recede;
No shame, no glory, nor any misery."

Li Ding said, "Your fair waters are not as good as my blue mountains. I also have as testimony a lyric poem to the tune of 'Butterflies Enamored of Flowers' that says:

> At a dense forest's pine-seeded corner
> I hear, wordless, the oriole—
> Its deft tongue's a tuneful pipe.
> Pale reds and bright greens announce the warmth of spring;
> Summer comes abruptly; so passes time.
>
> Then autumn arrives (for it's an easy change)
> With fragrant golden flowers
> Most worthy of our joy;
> And cold winter descends, swift as a finger snaps.
> Ruled by no one, I'm free in all four climes."

The fisherman said, "Your blue mountains are not as good as my fair waters, which offer me some fine things to enjoy. As testimony I have here a lyric to the tune of 'The Partridge Sky'":

> The fairyland cloud and water do suffice:
> Boat adrift, oars accumbent—this is my home.
> I split fishes live and cook green turtles;
> I steam purple crabs and boil red shrimps.
>
> Green reed-shoots,
> Water-plant sprouts;
> Better still the 'chicken heads,'[3] the walter caltrops,
> Lotus roots, old or young, the tender celery leaves,
> Arrowheads, white caltrops, and niaoying flowers."

The woodman said, "Your fair waters are not as good as my blue mountains, which offer me some fine things to enjoy. As testimony I too have a lyric to the tune of 'The Partridge Sky':

> On tall, craggy peaks that touch heaven's edge
> A grass house, a straw hut would make up my home.
> Cured fowls, smoked geese surpass turles or crabs;
> Hares, antelopes, and deer best fishes or shrimps.
>
> The scented chun leaves;
> The yellow lian sprouts;[4]
> Bamboo shoots and mountain tea are even better!
> Purple plums, red peaches, prunes and apricots ripe,
> Sweet pears, sour dates, and cassia flowers."

The fisherman said, "Your blue mountains are truly not as good as my fair waters. I have another lyric to the tune of 'The Heavenly Immortal':

One leaflike skiff goes where'er I choose to stay.
I fear not ten thousand folds of wave or mist.
I drop hooks and cast nets to catch fresh fish:
With no sauce or fat,
It's tastier yet.
Old wife and young son complete my home.

When fishes are plenty, I leave for Chang'an marts
And barter them for wine I drink till drunk.
A coir coat shrouds me, on autumnal stream I lie;
Snoring, asleep,
No fret or care—
I love not the glory or the pomp of man."

The woodman said, "Your fair waters are still not as good as my blue mountains. I too have a poem to the tune of 'The Heavenly Immortal':

A few straw houses built beneath a hill.
Pines, orchids, plums, bamboos—lovable all!
Passing groves, climbing mountains, I seek dried woods.
With none to chide,
I sell as I wish:
How much, how little, depends on my yield.

I use the cash to buy wine as I please.
Earthen crocks, clay flagons—both put me at ease.
Sodden with wine, in the pine shade I lie:
No anxious thoughts;
No gain or loss;
No care for this world's failure or success."

The fisherman said, "Brother Li, your moutain life is not as pleasing as my livelihood on the waters. As testimony, I have a lyric to the tune of 'Moon Over West River':

Red smartweeds's thick blooms glow in moonlight;[5]
Yellow rush-leaves tousled, wind-shaken.
The blue sky, clean and distant, in empty Chu River:
Drawing my lines, I stir a deep pool of stars.

In rank and file big fishes enter the net;
Teams of tiny perches swallow the hooks.

Their taste is special when they're caught and cooked.
My laughter presides over rivers and lakes."

The woodman says, "Brother Zhang, your life on the waters is not as pleasing as my livelihood in the mountains. As testimony, I also have a lyric to the tune of 'Moon Over West River':

Dead leaves, parched creepers choking the road;
Snapped poles, aged bamboos crowding the hill;
Dried tendrils and sedges in disheveled growth
I break and take; my ropes truss the load.

Willow trunks hollowed by insects,
Pine branches clipped off by wind,
I gather and stockpile, ready for winter's cold.
Change them for wine or cash as I wish."

The fisherman said, "Though your life in the mountains is not bad, it is still not as charming and graceful as mine is on the fair waters. As testimony, I have a lyric to the tune of 'Immortal by the River':

Falling tide moves my one boat away;
I rest my oars, my song comes with the night.
The coir coat, the waning moon—how charming they are!
No seagull darts up from fright
As rosy clouds spread through the sky.

I sleep without care at reeded isles,
Still snoozing when the sun is high.
I work after my own plans and desires.
Vassals in cold nights tending court,
Could theirs match my pleasure and peace?"

The woodman said, "The charm and grace of your fair waters cannot be compared with those of my blue mountains. I too have a testimony to the tune of 'Immortal by the River':

I walk autumn's frosty paths dragging my ax;
In night's cool I pole back my load,
Stranger still with temples stuck with flowers.
I push clouds to find my way out;
Moon-stuck I call open my gate.

Rustic wife and young son greet me with smiles;
On straw bed and wooden pillow I lie.

Steamed pears and cooked millet are soon prepared.
The urn's brew newly mellowed
Will add to my secret joys."

The fisherman said, "All these things in our poems have to do with our livelihood, the occupations with which we support ourselves. But your life not as good as those leisurely moments of mine, for which I have as testimony a regulated poem. The poem says:

Idly I watch the blue sky's white cranes fly.
My boat stops stream-side, my door's half-closed.
By the sail my son's taught to knot fishing threads;
Rowing stops, I join my wife to dry the nets.
My mind is still: thus I know the water's calm.
My self's secure: hence I feel the wind is light.
I freely don my green coir and bamboo hat:
That beats wearing a robe with purple sash.

The woodman said, "Your leisurely moments are not as good as mine, for which I also have a regulated poem as a testimony. The poem says:

Idly I watch billows of white clouds fly,
Or sit in my thatched hut's closed bamboo gates.
I open leisurely books to teach my son;
At times I face guests to play circling chess.[6]
My cane strolls with my songs through floral paths;
Aroused, I climb green mountains, lute in hand.
Straw sandals, hemp sashes, and coarse cloth quilts
All beat silk garments when your heart is free!"

Zhang Shao said, "Li Ding, the two of us indeed are

Lucky to have light songs to amuse us.
We don't need castanets or flasks of gold.[7]

But the poems we have recited thus far are occasional pieces, hardly anything unusual. Why don't we attempt a long poem in the linking-verse manner,[8] and see how fares the conversation between the fisherman and the woodman?"

Li Ding said, "That's a marvelous proposal, Brother Zhang! Please begin."

My boat rests on the green water's mist and wave.[9]
My home's deep in mountains and open plains.
I love the streams and bridges as spring tide swells;

I care for ridges veiled by the clouds of dawn.
My fresh carps from Longmen are often cooked;[10]
My dried woods, worm-rotted, are daily burnt.
Nets of many kinds will support my age.
Both pole and rope will see me to the end.
I lie in a skiff and watch wild geese fly;
I sprawl on grassy paths when wild swans cry.
I have no stake in fields of mouth and tongue;
Through seas of scandal I've not made my way.
Hung-dried by the stream my net's like brocade;
Polished new on rocks, my ax shows a fine blade.
Beneath autumn's moon I oft fish alone;
In spring hills all quiet I meet no one.
Fishes are changed for wine for me and wife to drink;
Firewood is used to buy a bottle for my son.
I sing and freely pour on my heart's desire;
In songs and sighs there's none to restrain me.
I call fellow boatmen to come as brothers;
With friends we join the codgers of the wilds.
We make rules, play games, and exchange the cups;
We break words, remake them, when we pass the mugs.
Cooked shrimps, boiled crabs are my daily feasts;
I'm daily fed by smoked fowls and fried ducks.
My unlettered wife makes tea languidly;
My mountain wife cooks rice most leisurely.
When dawn comes, I lift my staff to stir the waves;
At sunrise I pole my wood to cross big roads.
I don coir coat after rain to catch live carps;
Wind-blown I wield my ax to cut dried pines.
Hiding tracks to flee the world, I'm like a fool;
Blotting name and surname, I play deaf and dumb.

Zhang Shao said, "Brother Li, just now I presumed to take the lead and began with the first line of the poem. Why don't you begin this time and I shall follow you."

A rustic who feigns to be romantic;
An oldie taking pride in streams and lakes.
My lot is leisure, I seek laxity and ease.
Shunning talk and gossip, I love my peace.
In moonlit nights I sleep in safe straw huts;
When sky dims I'm draped with light coir cape.
I befriend with ardor both pines and plums;

I'm pleased to mingle with egrets and gulls.
My mind has no plans for fortune or fame;
My ears are deaf to the din of spear and drum.
At any time I'd pour my fragrant wine;
My day's three meals are soups of leafy greens.
My living rests on two bundles of wood;
My trade is my pole fit with hooks and lines.
I call our young son to sharpen my ax;
I tell my small rogue he should mend our nets.
Spring comes, I love to watch the willows green;
Warm days gladden the sight of rushes and reeds.
To flee summer's heat I plant new bamboos;
I pick young lotus to cool myself in June.
When Frost Descends the fatted fowls are slain;
By Double Ninth[11] I'd cook the roe-filled crabs.
I sleep deep in winter though the sun is high;
When the sky's tall and hazy, I'd not fry!
Throughout the year I roam free in the hills;
In all four climes I sail the lakes at will.
Gathering wood I own the immortals' feel;
Dropping my rod, I sport no worldly form.
My door's wild blossoms are fragrant and bright;
My stem's green water flows calm and serene.
Content, I seek not the Three Dukes' seats.[12]
Like a ten-mile city my nature's firm.
Cities, though tall, must resist a siege;
Dukes, though of high rank, must the summon heed.
Delight in hills and streams is truly rare.
Thank Heaven, thank Earth, let's thank the gods!

The two of them thus recited poems and songs and composed linking-verses. Arriving at the place where their ways parted, they bowed to take leave of each other. "Elder Brother Li," said Zhang Shao, "take care as you go on your way. When you climb the mountains, be wary of the tiger. If you were harmed, I would find, as the saying goes,

one friend missing on the street tomorrow."

When Li Ding heard these words, he grew very angry saying, "What a scoundrel you are! Good friends would even die for each other! But you, why do you say such unlucky things to me? If I'm to be harmed by a tiger, your boat will surely capsize in the river." "I'll never capsize my boat in the river," said Zhang Shao. Li Ding said, "As

There are unexpected storms in the sky
So there is sudden weal or woe with man.[13]

What makes you so sure that you won't have an accident?"

"Elder Brother Li," said Zhang Shao, "you say this because you have no idea what may befall you in your business, whereas I can predict what'll happen in my kind of business. And I assure you that I won't have any accident." "The kind of living you pick up on the waters," said Li Ding, "is an exceedingly treacherous business. You have to take chances all the time. How can you be so certain about your future?"

"Here's something you don't know about," said Zhang Shao. "In this city of Chang'an, there's a fortune teller who plies his trade on the West Gate Street. Every day I give him a golden carp as a present, and he consults the sticks in his sleeve for me. I follow his instructions when I lower my nets, and I've never missed in a hundred times. Today I went again to buy his prediction; he told me to set my nets at the east bend of the Jing River and to cast my line from the west bank. I know I'll come back with a fine catch of fishes and shrimps. When I go up to the city tomorrow, I'll sell my catch and buy some wine, and then I'll get together with you again, old brother." The two men then parted.

There is, however, a proverb: "What is said on the road is heard in the grass." For you see, it happened that a yakṣa on patrol in the Jing River overheard the part of the conversation about not having missed a hundred times. He dashed back to the Water Crystal Palace and hastily reported to the Dragon King, shouting, "Disaster! Disaster!" "What sort of disaster?" asked the Dragon King.

"Your subject," said the yakṣa, "was patrolling the river and overheard a conversation between a woodman and a fisherman. Before they parted, they said something terrible. According to the fisherman, there is a fortune teller on West Gate Street in the city of Chang'an who is most accurate in his calculations. Every day the fisherman gives him a carp, and he then consults the sticks in his sleeve, with the result that the fisherman has not missed once in a hundred times when he casts his line! If such accurate calculations continue, will not all our water kin be exterminated? Where will you find any more inhabitants for the watery region who will toss and leap in the waves to enhance the majesty of the Great King?"

The Dragon King became so angry that he wanted to take the sword and go at once up to Chang'an to slay the fortune teller. But his dragon sons and grandsons, the shrimp and crab ministers, the samli counselor, the perch Subdirector of the Minor Court, and the carp President of the Board of Civil Office all came from the side and said to him, "Let the Great King restrain his anger. The proverb says, 'Don't believe everything you hear.' If the Great King goes forth like this, the clouds will accompany you and the rains will follow you. We fear that the people of Chang'an will be terrified and Heaven will be offended. Since the Great King has the power to appear or disappear suddenly and to transform into many shapes and sizes, let him change into a scholar. Then go to the city of Chang'an and investigate the matter. If there is indeed such a person, you can slay him without delay; but if there is no such person, there is no need to harm innocent people." The Dragon King accepted their suggestion; he abandoned his sword and dismissed the clouds and the rains. Reaching the river bank, he shook his body and changed into a white-robed scholar, truly with

> *Features most virile,*
> *A stature towering;*
> *A stride most stately—*
> *So orderly and firm.*
> *His speech exalts Kong and Meng;*
> *His manner embodies Zhou and Wen.[14]*
> *He wears a silk robe of the color of jade;*
> *His casual head-wrap's shaped like the letter one.[15]*

Coming out of the water, the Dragon King strode to the West Gate Street in the city of Chang'an. There he found a noisy crowd surrounding someone who was saying in a lofty and self-assured manner, "Those born under the Dragon will follow their fate; those under the Tiger will collide with their physiognomies.[16] The branches Yin, Chen, Si, and Hai may be said to fit into the grand scheme, but I fear your birthday may clash with the Planet Jupiter." When the Dragon King heard this, he knew that he had come upon the fortune-teller's place. Walking up to it and pushing the people apart, he peered inside to see

> *Four walls of exquisite writings;*
> *A room full of brocaded paintings;*
> *Smoke unending from the treasure duck;[17]*
> *And such pure water in a porcelain vase.*
> *On both sides are mounted Wang Wei's paintings;*
> *High above his seat hangs the Guigu form.[18]*
> *The ink slab from Duanxi,[19]*
> *The golden smoke ink,*
> *Both match the great brush of frostiest hair;*
> *The crystal balls,*
> *Guo Pu's numbers,[20]*
> *Neatly face new classics of soothsaying.*
> *He knows the hexagrams well;*

He's mastered the eight trigrams;
He perceives the laws of Heaven and Earth;
He discerns the ways of demons and gods.
One tray before him fixes the cosmic hours;
His mind clearly orders all planets and stars.
Truly those things to come
And those things past
He beholds as in a mirror;
Which house will rise
And which will fall
He foresees like a god.
He knows evil and decrees the good;
He prescribes death and predicts life.
His pronouncements quicken the wind and rain;
His brush alarms both spirits and gods.
His shop sign has letters to declare his name;
This divine diviner, Yuan Shoucheng.

Who was this man? He was actually the uncle of Yuan Tiankang, president of the Imperial Board of Astronomy in the present dynasty. The
gentleman was truly a man of extraordinary appearance and elegant features; his name was known throughout the great country and his art was
considered the highest in Chang'an. The Dragon King went inside the door
and met the Master; after exchanging greetings, he was invited to take the
seat of honor while a boy served him tea. The Master asked, "What would
you like to know?" The Dragon King said, "Please forecast the weather." The
Master consulted his sticks and made his judgment:

Clouds hide the hilltop
And fog shrouds the tree.
The rain you'd divine
Tomorrow you'll see.

"At what hour will it rain tomorrow, and how much rain will there be?"
asked the Dragon King. "At the hour of the Dragon the clouds will gather,"
said the Master, "and thunder will be heard at the hour of the Serpent. Rain
will come at the hour of the Horse and reach its limit at the hour of the
Sheep.[21] There will be altogether three feet, three inches, and forty-eight
drops of rain." "You had better not be joking now," said the Dragon King,
laughing. "If it rains tomorrow and if it is in accordance with the time and
the amount you prophesied, I shall present you with fifty taels of gold as
my thanks. But if it does not rain, or if the amount and the hours are incorrect, I tell you truly that I shall come and break your front door to pieces

and tear down your shop sign. You will be chased out of Chang'an at once so that you may no longer seduce the multitude." "You may certainly do that," said the Master amiably. "Good-bye for now. Please come again tomorrow after the rain."

The Dragon King took leave and returned to his water residence. He was received by various aquatic deities, who asked, "How was the Great King's visit to the soothsayer?" "Yes, yes, yes," said the Dragon King, "there is indeed such a person, but he's a garrulous fortune-teller. I asked him when it would rain, and he said tomorrow; I asked him again about the time and the amount, and he told me that clouds would gather at the hour of the Dragon, thunder would be heard at the hour of the Serpent, and that rain would come at the hour of the Horse and would reach its limit at the hour of the Sheep. Altogether there would be three feet, three inches, and forty-eight drops of water. I made a wager with him: if it is as he said, I'll reward him with fifty taels of gold. If there is the slightest error, I'll break down his shop and chase him away, so that he will not be permitted to seduce the multitude at Chang'an." "The Great King is the supreme commander of the eight rivers," said the water kin, laughing, "the great Dragon Deity in charge of rain. Whether there is going to be rain or not, only the Great King knows that. How dare he speak so foolishly? That soothsayer is sure to lose!"

While the dragon sons and grandsons were laughing at the matter with the fish and crab officials, a voice was heard suddenly in midair announcing, "Dragon King of the Jing River, receive the imperial command." They raised their heads to look and saw a golden-robed guardian holding the decree of the Jade Emperor and heading straight for the water residence. The Dragon King hastily straightened out his attire and burned incense to receive the decree. After he made his delivery, the guardian rose into the air and left. The Dragon King opened the decree, which said:

> We bid the Eight-Rivers Prince
> To call up thunder and rain;
> Pour out tomorrow your grace
> To benefit Chang'an's race.

The instructions regarding the hours and the amount of rain written on the decree did not even differ in the slightest from the soothsayer's prediction. So overwhelmed was the Dragon King that his spirit left him and his soul fled, and only after awhile did he regain consciousness. He said to his water kinsmen, "There is indeed an intelligent creature in the world of dust! How well he comprehends the laws of Heaven and Earth! I'm bound to lose to him!"

"Let the Great King calm himself," said the samli counselor. "Is it so difficult to get the better of the fortune-teller? Your subject here has a little plan that will silence that fellow for good." When the Dragon King asked what the plan was, the counselor said, "If the rain tomorrow misses the timing and the amount specified by a mere fraction, it will mean that his prediction is not accurate. Won't you have won? What's there to stop you then from tearing up his shop sign and putting him on the road?" The Dragon King took his counsel and stopped worrying.

The next day he ordered the Duke of Wind, the Lord of Thunder, the Boy of Clouds, and the Mother of Lightning to go with him to the sky above Chang'an. He waited until the hour of the Serpent before spreading the clouds, the hour of the Horse before letting loose the thunder, the hour of the Sheep before releasing the rain, and only by the hour of the Monkey did the rain stop.[22] There were only three feet and forty drops of water, since the times were altered by an hour and the amount was changed by three inches and eight drops.

After the rain, the Dragon King dismissed his followers and came down from the clouds, transformed once again into a scholar dressed in white. He went to the West Gate Street and barged into Yuan Shoucheng's shop. Without a word of explanation, he began to smash the shop sign, the brushes, and the ink slab to pieces. The Master, however, sat on his chair and remained unmoved, so the Dragon King unhinged the door and threatened to hit him with it, crying, "You're nothing but a bogus prophet of good and evil, an imposter who deludes the minds of the people! Your predictions are incorrect; your words are patently false! What you told me about the time and quantity of today's rain was utterly inaccurate, and yet you dare sit so smugly and so high on your seat? Leave here at once before you are executed!" Still Yuan Shoucheng was not at all intimidated. He lifted up his head and laughed scornfully. "I'm not afraid!" he said. "Not in the least! I'm not guilty of death, but I fear that you have committed a mortal crime. You can fool other people, but you can't fool me! I recognize you, all right: you are not a white-robed scholar but the Dragon King of the Jing River. By altering the times and holding back the quantity of rain, you have disobeyed the decree of the Jade Emperor and transgressed the law of Heaven. On the dragon execution block you won't escape the knife! And here you are, railing at me!"

When the Dragon King heard these words, his heart trembled and his hair stood on end. He dropped the door quickly, tidied his clothes, and knelt before the Master saying, "I beg the Master not to take offense. My previous words were spoken in jest; little did I realize that my prank would turn out to be such a serious crime. Now I have indeed transgressed the law of Heaven. What am I to do? I beseech the Master to save me. If you won't, I'll never let you go!" "I can't save you," said Shoucheng, "I can only point out to you what may be a way of life." "I'm willing to be instructed," said the Dragon.

The Master said, "You are to be executed tomorrow by the human judge, Wei Zheng, at the third quarter past the hour of noon. If you want to preserve your life, you must go quickly to plead your case before the present emperor Tang Taizong, for Wei Zheng is the prime minister before his throne. If you can win the emperor's favor, you'll be spared." Hearing this, the Dragon took leave with tears in his eyes. Soon the red sun sank down and the moon arose. You see

> Smoke thickens on purple mountains as homing crows tire;
> Travelers on distant journeys head for inns;
> Young wild geese at fords rest on field and sand.
> The silver stream appears[23]
> To hasten the time float.[24]
> Lights fare in a lone village from dying fames:
> Wind sweeps the burner to clear Daoist yard of smoke
> As man fades away in the butterfly dream.[25]
> The moon moves floral shadows up the garden's rails.
> The stars are rife
> As water clocks strike;
> So swiftly the gloom deepens that it's midnight.

Our Dragon King of the Jing River did not even return to his water home; he waited in the air until it was about the hour of the Rat,[26] when he descended from the clouds and mists and came to the gate of the palace. At this time the Tang emperor was just having a dream about taking a walk outside the palace in the moonlight, beneath the shades of flowers. The Dragon suddenly assumed the form of a human being and went up to him. Kneeling, he cried out, "Your Majesty, save me, save me!" "Who are you?" asked Taizong. "We would be glad to save you." "Your Majesty is the true dragon," said the Dragon King, "but I am an accursed one. Because I have disobeyed the decree of Heaven, I am to be executed by a worthy subject of Your Majesty, the human judge Wei Zheng. I have therefore come here to plead with you to save me." "If Wei Zheng is to be the executioner," said Taizong, "we can certainly save you. You may leave and not worry." The Dragon King was delighted and left after expressing his gratitude.

We tell you now about Taizong, who, having awakened, was still turning over in his mind what he had dreamed. Soon it was three-fifths past the hour of the fifth watch, and Taizong held court for his ministers, both civil and martial. You see

> Smoke shrouding the phoenix arches;
> Incense clouding the dragon domes;
> Light shimmering as the silk screens move;

Clouds brushing the feather-trimmed flags;[27]
Rulers and lords harmonious as Yao and Shun;[28]
Rituals and music solemn as Han's and Zhou's.
The attendant lamps,
The court-maiden fans
Show their colors in pairs;
From peacock screens
And unicorn halls
Light radiates everywhere.
Three cheers for long life!
A wish for reign everlasting!
When a whip cracks three times,
The caps and robes will bow to the Crown.
Brilliant palatial blooms, endued by Heaven's scent;
Pliant bank willows, sung and praised by court music.
The screens of pearl,
The screens of jade,
Are drawn high by golden hooks:
The dragon-phoenix fan,
The mountain-river fan,[29]
Rest on top of the royal carriage.
The civil lords are noble and refined;
The martial lords, strong and valiant.
The imperial path divides the ranks:
The vermilion court aligns the grades.
The golden seal and purple sashes bearing the three signs[30]
Will last for millions of years as Heaven and Earth.

After the ministers had paid their homage, they all went back to standing in rows according to their rank. The Tang emperor opened his dragon eyes to look at them one by one: among the civil officials were Fang Xuanling, Du Ruhui, Xu Shizhi, Xu Jingzong, and Wang Guei; and among the military officials were Ma Sanbao, Duan Zhixian, Yin Kaishan, Cheng Yaojin, Liu Hongzhi, Hu Jingde, and Qin Shubao. Each one of them was standing there in a most solemn manner, but the prime minister Wei Zheng was not to be seen anywhere. The Tang emperor asked Xu Shizhi to come forward and said to him, "We had a strange dream last night: there was a man who paid homage to us, calling himself the Dragon King of the Jing River. He said that he had disobeyed the command of Heaven and was supposed to be executed by the human judge Wei Zheng. He implored us to save him, and we gave our consent. Today only Wei Zheng is absent from the ranks. Why is that?" "This dream may indeed come true," answered Shizhi, "and Wei

Zheng must be summoned to court immediately. Once he arrives, let Your Majesty keep him here for a whole day and not permit him to leave. After this day, the dragon in the dream will be saved." The Tang emperor was most delighted: he gave the order at once to have Wei Zheng summoned to court.

We speak now of prime minister Wei Zheng, who studied the movement of the stars and burned incense at his home that evening. He heard the cries of cranes in the air and saw there a Heavenly messenger holding the golden decree of the Jade Emperor, which ordered him to execute in his dream the old dragon of the Jing River at precisely the third quarter past the noon hour. Having thanked the Heavenly grace, our prime minister prepared himself in his residence by bathing himself and abstaining from food; he was also sharpening his magic sword and exercising his spirit, and therefore he did not attend court. He was terribly flustered when he saw the royal officer on duty arriving with the summons. Not daring, however, to disobey the emperor's command, he had to dress quickly and follow the summons into court, kowtowing and asking for pardon before the throne. The Tang emperor said, "We pardoned indeed our worthy subject."

At that time the various ministers had not yet retired from the court, and only after Wei Zheng's arrival was the curtain drawn up for the court's dismissal. Wei Zheng alone was asked to remain; he rode the golden carriage with the emperor to enter the chamber for relaxation, where he discussed with the emperor tactics for making the empire secure and other affairs of state. When it was just about midway between the hour of the Serpent and the hour of the Horse, the emperor asked the royal attendants to bring out a large chess set, saying, "We shall have a game with our worthy subject." The various concubines took out the chessboard and set it on the imperial table. After expressing his gratitude, Wei Zheng set out to play chess with the Tang emperor, both of them moving the pieces step by step into positions. It was completely in accordance with the instruction of the *Classic of Chess:*

The way of chess exalts discipline and caution; the most powerful pieces should remain in the center, the weakest ones at the flanks, and the less powerful ones at the corners. This is a familiar law of the chess player. The law says: "You should rather lose a piece than an advantage. When you strike on the left, you must guard your right; when you attack in the rear, you must watch your front. Only when you have a secure front will you also have a rear, and only if you have a secure rear will you maintain your front. The two ends cannot be separated, and yet both must remain flexible and not be encumbered. A broad formation should not be too loose, while a tight position should not be constricted. Rather than clinging on to save a single piece, it is better to sacrifice it in order to win; rather than moving without purpose, it is better to remain stationary in order to be self-supportive. When your adversary outnumbers you, your first concern is to survive; when you outnumber your adversary, you must strive to exploit your force. He who knows how to win will not prolong his fight; he who is a master of positions will not engage in direct combat; he who knows how to fight will not suffer defeat; and he who knows how to lose will not panic. For chess begins with proper engagement but ends in unexpected victory. If your enemy, even without being threatened, is bringing up his reinforcement, it is a sign of his intention to attack; if he deserts a small piece without trying to save it, he may be stalking a bigger piece. If he moves in a casual manner, he is a man without thoughts; response without thought is the way to defeat. The *Classic of Poetry* says:

Approach with extreme caution
As if facing a deep canyon.

Such is the meaning thereof.
The poem says:

The chessboard's the earth; the pieces are the sky;
The colors are light and dark as the whole universe.
When playing reaches that skillful, subtle stage,
Boast and laugh with the old Immortal of Chess.[31]

The two of them, emperor and subject, played chess until three quarters past the noon hour, but the game was not yet finished. Suddenly Wei Zheng put his head on the table and fell fast asleep. Taizong laughed and said, "Our worthy subject truly has worn himself out for the state and exhausted his strength on behalf of the empire. He has therefore fallen asleep in spite of himself." Taizong allowed him to sleep on and did not arouse him. In a little while, Wei Zheng awoke and prostrated himself on the ground saying, "Your subject deserves ten thousand deaths! Your subject deserves ten thousand deaths! Just now I lost consciousness for no reason at all. I beg Your Majesty's pardon for such insult against the emperor."

"What insult is there?" said Taizong. "Arise! Let us forget the old game and start a new one instead." Wei Zheng expressed his gratitude. As he put his hand on a piece, a loud clamor was heard outside the gate. It was occasioned by the ministers Qin Shubao and Xu Mougong, who arrived with a dragon head dripping with blood. Throwing it in front of the emperor, they said, "Your Majesty, we have seen seas turn shallow and rivers run dry, but a thing as strange as this we have never even heard of." Taizong arose with Wei Zheng and said, "Where did this thing come from?" "South of the Thousand-Step Corridor," replied Shubao and Mougong, "at the crossroads, this dragon head fell from the clouds. Your lowly subjects dare not withhold it from you."

In alarm, the Tang emperor asked Wei Zheng, "What's the meaning of this?" Turning to kowtow to him, Wei Zheng said, "This dragon was executed just now by your subject in his dream." When the Tang emperor heard this, he was seized with fear and said, "When our worthy minister was sleeping, I did not see any movement of body or limb, nor did I perceive any scimitar or sword. How could you have executed this dragon?" Wei Zheng replied, "My lord, although

My body was before my master,
I left Your Majesty in my dream;
My body before my master faced the unfinished game,
With dim eyes fully closed;
I left Your Majesty in my dream to ride the blessed cloud,
With spirit most eager and alert.
That dragon on the dragon execution block
Was bound up there by celestial hosts.
Your subject said,
'For breaking Heaven's law,
You are worthy of death.
Now by Heaven's command,
I end your wretched life.'
The dragon listened in grief;
Your subject bestirred his spirit;
The dragon listened in grief,
Retrieving claws and scales to await his death;
Your subject bestirred his spirit,
Lifting robe and taking step to hold high his blade.
With one loud crack the knife descended;
And thus the head of the dragon fell from the sky."

When Taizong heard these words, he was filled with both sadness and delight. The delight was caused by his pride in having a minister as good as Wei Zheng. If he had worthies of this kind in his court, he thought, need he worry about the security of his empire? He was saddened, however, by the fact that he had promised in his dream to save the dragon, and he had not anticipated that the creature would be killed in this manner. He had to force himself to give the order to Shubao that the dragon head be hung on display at the market, so that the populace of Chang'an might be informed. Meanwhile, he rewarded Wei Zheng, after which the various ministers dispersed.

That night he returned to his palace in deep depression, for he kept remembering the dragon in the dream crying and begging for his life. Little did he expect that the turn of events would be such that the dragon still could not escape calamity. Having thought about the matter for a long time, he became physically and mentally drained. At about the hour of the second watch, the sound of weeping was heard outside the door of the palace, and Taizong became even more fearful. He was sleeping fitfully when he saw our Dragon King of the Jing River holding his head dripping with blood in his hand, and crying in a loud voice: "Tang Taizong! Give me back my life! Give me back my life! Last night you were full of promises to save me. Why did you order a human judge in the daytime to have me executed? Come out, come out! I am going to argue this case with you before the King of the Underworld." He seized Taizong and would neither let go nor desist from his protestation. Taizong could not say a word; he could only struggle until perspiration covered his entire body. Just at the moment when it seemed that nothing could separate them, fragrant clouds and colorful mists appeared from the south. A Daoist priestess came forward and waved a willow twig. That headless dragon, still mourning and weeping, left at once toward the northwest. For you see, this was none other than the Bodhisattva Guanyin, who by the decree of Buddha was seeking a scripture pilgrim in the Land of the East. She was staying in the temple of the local spirit at the city of Chang'an when she heard in the night the weeping of demons and the crying of spirits. So she came specially to drive the accursed dragon away and to rescue the emperor. That dragon went directly to the court of the Underworld to file suit, of which we shall say no more.

We now tell you about Taizong, who, when he awoke, could only yell aloud, "Ghost! Ghost!" He so terrified the queens of three palaces, the concubines of six chambers, and the attending eunuchs that they remained sleepless for the entire night. Soon it was the fifth watch, and all the officials of the court, both civil and military, were waiting for an audience outside the gate. They waited until dawn, but the emperor did not appear, and every one of them became apprehensive and restless. Only after the sun was high in the sky did a proclamation come out saying, "We are not feeling too well. The ministers are excused from court." Five or six days went by swiftly, and the various officials became so anxious that they were about to enter the court without summons and inquire after the throne. Just then the queen mother gave the order to have the physician brought into the palace, and so the multitude waited at the gate of the court for some news. In a little while, the physician came out and he was questioned about the emperor's illness. "The pulse of His Majesty is irregular," said the physician, "for it is weak as well as rapid. He blabbers about seeing ghosts. I also perceive that there were ten movements and one rest, but there is no breath left in his viscera. I am afraid that he will pass away within seven days." When the various ministers heard this statement, they paled with fright.

In this state of alarm, they again heard that Taizong had summoned Xu Mougong, Huguo Gong, and Yuchi Gong to appear before him. The three ministers hurried into the auxiliary palace, where they prostrated themselves. Speaking somberly and with great effort, Taizong said, "My worthy subjects, since the age of nineteen I have been leading my army in expeditions to the four corners of the Earth. I have experienced much hardship throughout the years, but I have never encountered any kind of strange or weird thing. This day, however, I have seen ghosts!"

"When you established your empire," said Yuchi Gong, "you had to kill countless people. Why should you fear ghosts?" "You may not believe it," said Taizong, "but outside this bedroom of mine at night, there are bricks thrown and spirits screaming to a degree that is truly unmanageable. In the daytime it's not too bad, but it's intolerable at night!" "Let Your Majesty be relieved," said Shubao, "for this evening your subject and Jingde[32] will stand guard at the palace gate. We shall see what sort of ghostly business there is." Taizong agreed to the proposal, and Mougong and the other ministers retired after expressing their gratitude.

That evening the two ministers, in full battle dress and holding golden bludgeon and battle-ax, stood guard outside the palace gate. Dear generals! Look how they are attired:

> They wore on their heads bright glimmering golden helmets,
> And on their bodies cuirasses of dragon scales.
> Their jeweled breastplates glow like hallowed clouds:
> With lion knots tightly drawn,
> And silk sashes newly spun.
> This one had phoenix eyes facing the sky to frighten the stars:
> The other had brown eyes glowering like lightning and the shining moon.
> They were once warriors of the greatest merit;
> But now they've become
> For all time the guardians of the gates,
> In all ages the protectors of the home.[33]

The two generals stood beside the door for the entire night and did not see the slightest disturbance. That night Taizong rested peacefully in the palace; when morning came he summoned the two generals before him and thanked them profusely, saying, "Since falling ill, I haven't been able to sleep for days, and only last night did I manage to get some rest because of your presence. Let our worthy ministers retire now for some rest so that we may count on your protection once again at night." The two generals left after expressing their gratitude, and for the following two or three nights their standing guard brought continued peace. However, the royal appetite diminished and the illness became more severe. Taizong, moreover, could not bear to see the two generals overworked. So once again he called Shubao, Jingde, the ministers Du and Fang into the palace, saying to them, "Though I got some rest these past two days, I have imposed on the two generals the hardship of staying up all night. I wish to have portraits made of both of them by a skilled painter and have these pasted on the door, so that the two generals will be spared any further labor. How about it?" The various ministers obeyed; they selected two portrait painters, who made pictures of the two generals in their proper battle attire. The portraits were then mounted near the gate, and no incident occurred during the night.

So it was for two or three days, until the loud rattling of bricks and tiles was again heard at the rear gate of the palace. At dawn the emperor called together the various ministers, saying to them, "For the past few days there have been, happily, no incidents at the front of the palace, but last night the noises at the back door were such that they nearly frightened me to death." Mougong stepped forward and said, "The disturbances at the front door were driven off by Jingde and Shubao. If there is disturbance at the rear gate, then Wei Zheng ought to stand guard." Taizong approved the suggestion and ordered Wei Zheng to guard the rear door that night. Accepting the charge, Wei donned his full court regalia that evening; holding the sword with which he had slain the dragon, he stood at attention before the rear gate of the palace. What splendid heroic stature! Look how he is attired:

Green satin turban swaths his brow:
The silk robe's jade belt is waist-hung;
Windblown, craned-down sleeves fly like drifting snow.
He bests Lü and Shu's divine looks.[34]

His feet wear black boots most supple;
His hands hold a blade sharp and fierce.
With glaring eyes he stared at all four sides.
Which deviant god dares approach?[35]

A whole night went by and no ghost appeared. But though there were no incidents at either the front or the rear gate, the emperor's condition worsened. One day the queen mother sent for all the ministers to discuss funeral arrangements. Taizong himself also summoned Xu Mougong to his bedside to entrust to him the affairs of state, committing the crown prince to the minister's care as Liu Bei did to Zhuge Liang.[36] When he had finished speaking, he bathed and changed his garments, waiting for his time to come. Wei Zheng then stepped out from the side and tugged the royal garment with his hand, saying, "Let Your Majesty be relieved. Your subject knows something that will guarantee long life for Your Majesty."

"My illness," said Taizong, "has reached the irremediable stage; my life is in danger. How can you preserve it?" "Your subject has a letter here," said Wei, "which I submit to Your Majesty to take with you to Hell and give to the Judge of the Underworld, Jue."

"Who is Cui Jue?" asked Taizong.

"Cui Jue," said Wei, "was the subject of the deceased emperor, your father: at first he was the district magistrate of Cizhou, and subsequently he was promoted to vice president of the Board of Rites. When he was alive, he was an intimate friend and sworn brother of your subject. Now that he is dead, he has become a judge in the capital of the Underworld, having in his charge the chronicles of life and death in the region of darkness. He meets with me frequently, however, in my dreams. If you go there presently and hand this letter to him, he will certainly remember his obligation toward your lowly subject and allow Your Majesty to return here. Surely your soul will return to the human world, and your royal countenance will once more grace the capital." When Taizong heard these words, he took the letter in his hands and put it in his sleeve; with that, he closed his eyes and died. Those queens and concubines from three palaces and six chambers, the crown prince and the two rows of civil and military officials, all put on their mourning garb to mourn him, as the imperial coffin lay in state at the Hall of the White Tiger, but we shall say no more about that. We do not know how the soul of Taizong came back; let's listen to the explanation in the next chapter.

ELEVEN

Having toured the Underworld, Taizong returns to life; Having presented melons and fruits, Liu Quan marries again.

The poem says:[1]

> A hundred years pass by like flowing streams;
> Like froth and foam a lifetime's work now seems.
> Yesterday faces had a peach's glow;
> Today the temples float up flakes of snow.
> Termites disband—illusion then you'll learn![2]
> Cuckoos call[3] gravely for your early return.
> Secret good works will always life prolong.
> Virtue's not needy for Heav'n's care is strong.

We now tell you about Taizong, whose soul drifted out of the Tower of Five Phoenixes. Everything was blurred and indistinct. It seemed to him that a company of imperial guardsmen was inviting him to a hunting party, to which Taizong gladly gave his consent and went off with them. They had journeyed for a long time when suddenly all the men and horses vanished from sight. He was left alone, walking the deserted fields and desolate plains. As he anxiously tried to find his way back, he heard someone from beyond calling in a loud voice: "Great Tang Emperor, come over here! Come over here!" Taizong heard this and looked up. He saw that the man had

> A black gauze cap on his head;
> Rhinoceros horns around his waist.[4]
> His head's black gauze hat dangled pliant bands:
> His waist's rhino horns displayed plates of gold.
> He held an ivory plaque sheathed in hallowed mist;
> He wore a silk robe circled by holy light.
> His feet put on a pair of white-soled boots
> For treading cloud and climbing fog;
> He grasped by his heart a book of life and death,
> Which determined one's fate.
> His hair, luxuriant, flew above his ears:
> His beard fluttered and danced around his jaws.
> He was once a prime minister of Tang:
> Now he judged cases to serve Yama King.

Taizong walked toward him, and the man, kneeling at the side of the road, said to him, "Your Majesty, please pardon your subject for neglecting to meet you at a greater distance." "Who are you," asked Taizong, "and for what reason did you come to meet me?" The man said, "Half a month ago, your lowly subject met in the Halls of Darkness the Dragon Ghost of the Jing River, who was filing suit against Your Majesty for having him executed after promising to save him. So the great king Qinguang of the first chamber immediately sent demon messengers to arrest you and bring you to trial before the Three Tribunes. Your subject learned of this and therefore came here to receive you. I did not expect to come late today, and I beg you to forgive me."

"What is your name," said Taizong, "and what is your rank?" "When your lowly subject was alive," said that man, "he served on Earth before the previous emperor as the district magistrate of Cizhou. Afterwards I was appointed vice president of the Board of Rites. My surname is Cui and my given name is Jue. In the Region of Darkness I hold a judgeship in the Capital of Death." Taizong was very glad; he went forward and held out his royal hands to raise the man up, saying, "I am sorry to have inconvenienced you. Wei Zheng, who serves before my throne, has a letter for you. I'm glad that we have a chance to meet here." The judge expressed his gratitude and asked where the letter was. Taizong took it out of his sleeve and handed it over to Cui Jue, who received it, bowing, and then opened it and read:

> Your unworthily beloved brother Wei Zheng sends with bowed head this letter to the Great Judge, my sworn brother the Honorable Mr. Cui. I recall our former goodly society, and both your voice and your countenance seem to be present with me. Several years have hastened by since I last heard your lofty discourse. I could only prepare a few vegetables and fruits to offer to you as sacrifices during the festive times of the year, though I do not know whether you have enjoyed them or not. I am grateful, however, that you have not forgotten me, and that you have revealed to me in my dreams that you, my elder brother, have ascended to an even higher office. Unfortunately, the worlds of Light and Darkness are separated by a gulf wide as the Heavens, so that we cannot meet face to face. The reason that I am writing you now is the sudden demise of my emperor, the accomplished Taizong, whose case, I suppose, will be reviewed by the Three Tribunes, so that he will certainly be given the opportunity to meet you. I earnestly beseech you to remember our friendship while you were living and grant me the small favor of allowing His Majesty to return to life. This will be a very great favor to me, for which I thank you once more.

After reading the letter, the judge said with great delight, "The execution of the old dragon the other day by the human judge Wei is already known to your subject, who greatly admires him for this deed. I am, moreover, indebted to him for looking after my children. Since he has written such a letter now, Your Majesty need have no further concern. Your lowly subject will make certain that you will be returned to life, to ascend once more your throne of jade." Taizong thanked him.

As the two of them were speaking, they saw in the distance two young boys in blue robes holding banners and flags and calling out, "The King of the Underworld has an invitation for you." Taizong went forward with Judge Cui and the two boys. He suddenly saw a huge city, and on a large plaque above the city gate was the inscription in gold letters, "The Region of Darkness, The Gate of Spirits." Waving the banners, the blue robes led Taizong into the city. As they walked along, they saw at the side of the street the emperor's predecessor Li Yuan, his elder brother Jiancheng, and his deceased brother Yuanji, who came toward them, shouting, "Here comes Shimin![5] Here comes Shimin!" The brothers clutched at Taizong and began beating him and threatening vengeance. Having no place to dodge, the emperor fell into their clutch; and only when Judge Cui called a blue-faced, hook-tusked demon to drive them away could he escape and continue his journey.

They had traveled no more than a few miles when they arrived at a towering edifice with green tiles. This building was truly magnificent. You see

Lightly ten thousand folds of colored mists pile high;
Dimly a thousand strands of crimson brume appear.
Heads of wild beasts rear up from the eaves aglow.
Pairs of lambent roof tiles rise in tiers of five.
Rows of red-gold nails bore deeply into doors;
Crosswise, slabs of white jade make up the rails.
Windows near the lights release morning smoke.
The screens, the curtains, flash like fiery bolts.
High-rising towers reach to the azure sky.
Criss-crossing hallways join the treasure rooms.
Fragrance from beast-shaped tripods line royal robes;
Scarlet silk lanterns brighten the portals' leaves.
On the left, hordes of fierce Bull-heads stand;
On the right, gruesome Horse-faces line up.
Gold placards turn to greet the ghosts of the dead;
White silk descends to lead the deceased souls.
It bears this name: The Central Gate of Hell,
The Darkness Hall of the Princes of Hades.

As Taizong was looking at the place, there came from within the tinkling of girdle jade, the mysterious fragrance of divine incense, and two pairs of torch candles followed by the Ten Kings of the Underworld coming down the steps. The Ten Kings were: King Qinguang, King of the Beginning River, King of the Song Emperor, King of Avenging Ministers, King Yama, King of Equal Ranks, King of the Tai Mountain, King of City Markets, King of Complete Change, and King of the Turning Wheel. Coming out of the Treasure Hall of Darkness, they bowed to receive Taizong, who, feigning modesty, declined to lead the way. The Ten Kings said, "Your Majesty is the emperor of men in the World of Light, whereas we are but the kings of spirits in the World of Darkness. Such are indeed our appointed stations, so why should you defer to us?" "I'm afraid that I have offended all of you," said Taizong, "so how can I dare to speak of observing the etiquette of ghosts and men, of Light and Darkness?" Only after much protestation did Taizong proceed into the Hall of Darkness. After he had greeted the Ten Kings properly, they sat down according to the places assigned to hosts and guests.

After a little while, King Qinguang folded his hands in front of him and came forward, saying, "The Dragon Spirit of the Jing River accuses Your Majesty of having him slain after promising to save him. Why?" "I did promise him that nothing would happen," said Taizong, "when the old dragon appealed to me in my dream at night. He was guilty, you know, and was condemned to be executed by the human judge Wei Zheng. It was to save him that I invited Wei Zheng to play chess with me, not anticipating that Wei Zheng could have performed the execution in his dream! That was indeed a miraculous stratagem devised by the human judge, and, after all, the dragon was also guilty of a mortal offense. I fail to see how I am to blame." When the Ten Kings heard these words, they replied, bowing, "Even before that dragon was born, it was already written on the Book of Death held by the Star of South Pole that he should be slain by a human judge. We have known this all along, but the dragon lodged his complaint here and insisted that Your Majesty be brought down so that his case might be reviewed by the Three Tribunes. We have already sent him on his way to his next incarnation through the Wheel of Transmigration. We regret, however, that we have caused Your Majesty the inconvenience of this journey, and we beg your pardon for pressing you to come here."

When they had finished speaking, they ordered the judge in charge of the Books of Life and Death to bring out the records quickly so that they could ascertain what the allotted time of the emperor was to be. Judge Cui went at once to his chamber and examined, one by one, the ages preordained for all the kings in the world that were inscribed in the books. Startled when he saw that the Great Tang Emperor Taizong of the South Jambūdvīpa Continent was destined to die in the thirteenth year of the period Zhenguan, he quickly dipped his big brush in thick ink and added two strokes[6] before presenting the book. The Ten Kings took one look and saw that "thirty-three years" was written beneath the name Taizong. They asked in alarm, "How long has it been since Your Majesty was enthroned?" "It has been thirteen years," said Taizong. "Your Majesty need have no worry," said King Yama, "for you still have twenty years of life. Now that your case has been clearly reviewed, we can send you back to the World of Light." When Taizong heard this, he bowed to express his gratitude as the Ten Kings ordered Judge Cui and Grand Marshal Chu to accompany him back to life.

Taizong walked out of the Hall of Darkness and asked, saluting the Ten Kings once again, "What's going to happen to those living in my palace?" "Everyone will be safe," said the Ten Kings, "except your younger sister. It appears that she will not live long." "When I return to the World of Light," said Taizong, bowing again to thank them, "I have very little that I can present you as a token of my gratitude. Perhaps I can send you some melons or other kinds of fruit?" Delighted, the Ten Kings said, "We have eastern and western melons here, but we lack southern melons."[7] "The moment I get back," said Taizong, "I shall send you some." They bowed to each other with hands folded, and parted.

The marshal took the lead, holding a flag for guiding souls, while Judge Cui followed behind to protect Taizong. They walked out of the Region of Darkness, and Taizong saw that it was not the same road. He asked the judge, "Are we going on the wrong way?" "No," said the judge, "for this is how it is in the Region of Darkness: there is a way for you to come, but there is no way out. Now we must send Your Majesty off from the region of the Wheel of Transmigration, so that you can make a tour of Hell as well as be sent on your way to reincarnation." Taizong had little alternative but to follow their lead.

They had gone only a few miles when they came upon a tall mountain. Dark clouds touched the ground around it, and black mists shrouded the sky. "Mr. Cui," said Taizong, "what mountain is this?" The judge said, "It's the Mountain of Perpetual Shade in the Region of Darkness." "How can we go there?" asked Taizong fearfully. "Your Majesty need not worry," said the judge, "for your subjects are here to guide you." Shaking and quaking, Taizong followed the two of them and ascended the slope. He raised his head to look around and saw that

Its shape was both craggy and curvate,
And its form was even more tortuous.
Rugged like the Shu peaks;[8]
Tall like the Lu summits;
It was not a famed mountain in the World of Light,
But a treacherous place in the Region of Darkness.
Thickets of thorns sheltered monsters;

Tiers of stone ridges harbored demons.
No sound of fowl or beast came to one's ears;
Only ghosts or griffins walked before one's eyes.
The howling cold wind;
The endless black mist—
The howling cold wind was the huffing of infernal hosts;
The endless black mist was the puffing of demonic troops.
There was no scenic splendor though one looked high and low;
All was desolation when one stared left and right.
At that place there were mountains
And peaks,
And summits,
And caves,
And streams;
Only no grass grew on the mountains;
No peaks punctured the sky;
No travelers scaled the summits;
No caves ever harbored the clouds;
No water flowed in the streams.
They were all specters on the shores,
And bogies beneath the cliffs.
The phantoms huddled in the caves,
And lost souls hid on stream-floors.
All around the mountain,
Bull-heads and Horse-faces wildly clamored;
Half hidden and half in sight,
Hungry ghosts and needy souls often wept.
The judge in quest of souls,
In haste and fury delivered his summons;
The guard who chased the spirits,
Snorted and shouted to present his papers.
The Swift of Foot:
A boiling cyclone!
The Soul Snatcher:
A spreading dark mist!

Had he not trusted in the judge's protection, Taizong would have never made it across this Mountain of Perpetual Shade.

As they proceeded, they came to a place where there were many halls and chambers; everywhere they turned, melancholy cries blasted their ears and grotesque sights struck terror in their hearts. "What is this place?" asked Taizong again. "The Eighteenfold Hell behind the Mountain of Perpetual Shade," said the judge. "What is that?" said Taizong. The judge replied, "Listen to what I have to say:

The Hell of the Rack,
The Hell of Gloomy Guilt,
The Hell of the Fiery Pit:
All such sorrow,
All such desolation,
Are caused by a thousand sins committed in the life before;
They all come to suffer after they die.
The Hell of Hades,
The Hell of Tongue-Pulling,
The Hell of Skin-Shredding:
All those weeping and wailing,
All those pining and mourning,
Await the traitors, the rebels, and the Heaven baiters;
He of Buddha-mouth and serpent-heart will end up here.
The Hell of Grinding,
The Hell of Pounding,
The Hell of Crushing;
With frayed skin and torn flesh,
Gaping mouths and grinding teeth,
These are they who cheat and lie to work injustice,
Who fawn and flatter to deceive.
The Hell of Ice,
The Hell of Mutilation,
The Hell of Evisceration:
With grimy face and matted hair,
Knitted brow and doleful look,
These are they who fleece the simple with weights unjust,
And so bring ruin upon themselves.
The Hell of Boiling Oil,
The Hell of Grim Darkness,
The Hell of the Sword Mountain:
They shake and quake;
They sorrow and pine:
For oppressing the righteous by violence and fraud
They now must cower in their lonely pain.
The Hell of the Pool of Blood,
The Hell of Avīci.[9]
The Hell of Scales and Weights:
All the skins peeled and bones exposed,

The limbs cut and the tendons severed,
Are caused by murder stemming from greed,
The taking of life of both humans and beasts.
Their fall has no reversal in a thousand years—
Eternal perdition without release.
Each is firmly bound and tightly tied,
Shackled by both ropes and cords.
The slightest move brings on the Red-hair demons,
The Black-face demons,
With long spears and sharp swords;
The Bull-head demons,
The Horse-face demons,
With iron spikes and bronze gavels,
They strike till faces contort and blood flows down,
But cries to Earth and Heaven find no response.
So it is that man ought not his own conscience betray,
For gods have knowledge, who could get away?
Thus vice and virtue will at last be paid:
It differs only in coming soon or late."

When Taizong heard these words, he was terror-stricken. They went on for a little while and came upon a group of demon soldiers, each holding banners and flags and kneeling beside the road. "The Guards of the Bridges have come to receive you," they said. The judge ordered them to make way and proceeded to lead Taizong across a golden bridge. Looking to one side, Taizong saw another silver bridge, on which there were several travelers who seemed to be persons of principle and rectitude, justice and honesty. They too were led by banners and flags. On the other side was another bridge, with icy wind churning around it and bloody waves seething below. The continuous sound of weeping and wailing could be heard. "What is the name of that bridge?" asked Taizong. "Your Majesty," said the judge, "it is the No-Option Bridge. When you reach the World of Light, you must have this recorded for posterity. For below the bridge there is nothing but

A vast body of surging water;
A strait and treacherous path;
Like bales of raw silk flowing down the Long River,
Or the Pit of Fire floating up to Earth,
This cold air, oppressive, this bone-piercing chill;
This foul stench both irksome and nauseous.
The waves roll and swirl;
No boat comes or goes to ferry men across;
With naked feet and tangled hair

Those moving here and there are all damned spirits.
The bridge is a few miles long
But only three spans wide.
Its height measures a hundred feet;
Below, a thousand fathoms deep.
On top are no railways for hands to hold;
Beneath you have man-seizing savage fiends
Who, bound by cangues and locks,
Fight to flee No-Option's parlous path.
Look at those ferocious guardians beside the bridge
And those damned souls in the river—how truly wretched!
On branches and twigs
Clothes of green, red, yellow, and purple silk hang;
Below the precipice
Strumpets crouch for having abused their own in-laws.
Iron dogs and brass serpents will strive to feed on them.
Their fall's eternal—there is no way out."

The poem says:

Ghosts are heard wailing; demons often cry
As waves of blood rise ten thousand feet high.
Horse-faces and Bull-heads by countless scores
This No-Option Bridge grimly fortify.

While Taizong and his guides were speaking, the several Guardians of the Bridge went back to their station. Terrified by his vision, Taizong could only nod his head in silent horror. He followed the judge and the grand marshal across the malicious water of the No-Option River and the bitter Realm of the Bloody Bowl. Soon they arrived at the City of the Dead, where clamoring voices were heard proclaiming distinctly, "Li Shimin has come! Li Shimin has come!" When Taizong heard all this shouting, his heart shook and his gall quivered. Then he saw a throng of spirits, some with backs broken by the rack, some with severed limbs, and some headless, who barred his way and shouted together, "Give us back our lives! Give us back our lives!" In terror Taizong tried desperately to flee and hide, at the same time crying, "Mr. Cui, save me! Mr. Cui, save me!"

"Your Majesty," said the judge, "these are the spirits of various princes and their underlings, of brigands and robbers from sundry places. Through works of injustice, both theirs and others', they perished and are now cut off from salvation because there is none to receive them or care for them. Since they have no money or belongings, they are ghosts abandoned to hunger and cold. Only if Your Majesty can give them some money will I be able to offer you deliverance." "I came here," said Taizong, "with empty hands. Where can I get money?"

"Your Majesty," said the judge, "there is in the World of the Living a man who has deposited great sums of gold and silver in our Region of Darkness. You can use your name for a loan, and your lowly judge will serve as your voucher; we shall borrow a roomful of money from him and distribute it among the hungry ghosts. You will then be able to get past them." "Who is this man?" asked Taizong. "He's a man from the Kaifeng District in Henan Province," said the judge. "His given name is Liang and his surname is Xiang. He has thirteen rooms of gold and silver down here. If Your Majesty borrows from him, you can repay him when you return to the World of Light." Highly pleased and more than willing to use his name for the loan, Taizong at once signed a note for the judge. He borrowed a roomful of gold and silver, and the grand marshal was asked to distribute the money among the ghosts. The judge also instructed them, saying, "You may divide up these pieces of silver and gold among yourselves and use them accordingly. Let the Great Tang Father pass, for he still has a long time to live. By the solemn word of the Ten Kings I am accompanying him to return to life. When he reaches the world of the living, he has been instructed to hold a Grand Mass of Land and Water for your salvation.[10] So don't start any more trouble." When the ghosts heard these words and received the silver and gold, they obeyed and turned back. The judge ordered the grand marshal to wave the flag for guiding souls, and led Taizong out of the City of the Dead. They set out again on a broad and level path, leaving quickly with light, airy steps.

They traveled for a long time and arrived at the junction of the Sixfold Path of Transmigration. They saw some people who rode the clouds wearing embroidered capes, and some with Daoist amulets of gold fish dangling from their waists; there were in fact monks, nuns, Daoists, and secular persons, and all varieties of beasts and fowls, ghosts and spirits. In an unending stream they all ran beneath the Wheel of Transmigration to enter each into a predestined path. "What is the meaning of this?" asked the Tang emperor. "Your Majesty," said the judge, "as your mind is enlightened to perceive the pervasive immanence of the Buddha-nature in all things, you must remember this and proclaim it in the World of the Living. This is called the Sixfold Path of Transmigration. Those who perform good works will ascend to the way of the immortals; those who remain patriotic to the end will advance to the way of nobility; those who practice filial piety will be born again into the way of blessing; those who are just and honest will enter once more into the way of humans; those who cherish virtue will proceed to the way of riches; those who are vicious and violent will fall back into the way of demons." When the Tang emperor heard this, he nodded his head and sighed, saying,

> "Ah, how truly good is goodness!
> To do good will never bring illness!
> In a good heart always abide.
> On a good way your door fling wide.
> Let no evil thoughts arise,
> And all mischief you must despise.
> Don't say there's no retribution,
> For gods have their disposition."

The judge accompanied the Tang emperor up to the very entrance to the way of nobility before he prostrated himself and called out, "Your Majesty, this is where you must proceed, and here your humble judge will take leave of you. I am asking Grand Marshal Zhu to accompany you a little further." The Tang emperor thanked him, saying, "I'm sorry, sir, that you have had to travel such great distance on my account." "When Your Majesty returns to the World of Light," said the judge, "be very certain that you celebrate the Grand Mass of Land and Water so that those wretched, homeless souls may be delivered. Please do not forget! Only if there is no murmuring for vengeance in the Region of Darkness will there be the prosperity of peace in your World of Light. If there are any wicked ways in your life, you must change them one by one, and you must teach your subjects far and wide to do good. You may be assured then that your empire will be firmly established, and that your fame will go down to posterity." The Tang emperor promised to grant each one of the judge's requests.

Having parted from Judge Cui, he followed Grand Marshal Zhu and entered the gate. The grand marshal saw inside a black-maned bay horse complete with rein and saddle. Lending the emperor assistance from left and right, he quickly helped him mount it. The horse shot forward like an arrow, and soon they reached the bank of the Wei River, where a pair of golden carps could be seen frolicking on top of the waves. Pleased by what he saw, the Tang emperor reined in his horse and stopped to watch. "Your Majesty," said the grand marshal, "let's hurry and get you back into your city while there is still time." But the emperor persisted in his indulgence and refused to go forward. The grand marshal grabbed one of his legs and shouted, "You still won't move? What are you waiting for?" With a loud splash, he was pushed off his horse into the Wei River, and thus he left the Region of Darkness and returned to the World of Light.

We shall now tell you about those who served before the Throne in the Tang dynasty. Xu Mougong, Qin Shubao, Hu Jingde, Duan Zhixian, Ma Sanbao, Cheng Yaojin, Gao Shilian, Li Shiji, Fang Xuanling, Du Ruhui, Xiao Yu,

Fu Yi, Zhang Daoyuan, Zhang Shiheng, and Wang Guei constituted the two groups of civil and military officials. They gathered with the crown prince of the Eastern Palace, the queen, the ladies of the court, and the chief steward in the Hall of the White Tiger for the imperial mourning. At the same time, they discussed issuing the obituary proclamation for the whole empire and crowning the prince as emperor. From one side of the hall, Wei Zheng stepped forward and said, "All of you, please refrain from doing anything hasty. If you alarm the various districts and cities, you may bring about something undesirable and unexpected. Let's wait here for another day, for our lord will surely come back to life."

"What nonsense you are talking, Prime Minister Wei," said Xu Jingzong, coming from below, "for the ancient proverb says, 'Just as spilled water cannot be retrieved, so a dead man can never return!' Why do you mouth such empty words to vex our minds? What reason do you have for this?" "To tell you the truth, Mr. Xu," said Wei Zheng, "I have been instructed since my youth in the arts of immortality. My calculations are most accurate, and I promise you that His Majesty will not die."

As they were talking, they suddenly heard a loud voice crying in the coffin, "You've drowned me! You've drowned me!" It so startled the civil and military officials, and so terrified the queen and the ladies, that every one of them had

> A face brown as autumnal mulberry leaves,
> A body limp as the willow of early spring.
> The legs of the crown prince buckled,
> He could not hold the mourning staff to finish his rites.
> The soul of the steward left him,
> He could not wear the mourning cap to show his grief
> The matrons collapsed;
> The ladies pitched sideways;
> The matrons collapsed
> Like weak hibiscus blasted by savage wind.
> The ladies pitched sideways
> Like lilies overwhelmed by sudden rain.
> The petrified lords—
> Their bones and tendons feeble—
> Trembled and shook,
> All dumb and awestruck.
> The whole White Tiger Hall was like a bridge with broken beams;
> The funeral stage resembled a temple wrecked.

Every person attending the court ran away, and no one dared approach the coffin. Only the upright Xu Mougong, the rational Prime Minister Wei, the courageous Qin Qiong, and the impulsive Jingde came forward and took hold of the coffin. "Your Majesty," they cried, "if there's something bothering you, tell us about it. Don't play ghost and terrify your relatives!"

Then, however, Wei Zheng said, "He's not playing ghost. His Majesty is coming back to life! Get some tools, quick!" They opened the top of the coffin and saw indeed that Taizong was sitting up inside, still shouting, "You've drowned me! Who bailed me out?" Mougong and the rest of them went forward to lift him up, saying, "Don't be afraid, Your Majesty, and wake up. Your subjects are here to protect you." Only then did the Tang emperor open his eyes and say, "How I suffered just now! I barely escaped attack by spiteful demons from the Region of Darkness, only to encounter death by drowning!" "Have no fear, Your Majesty," said the ministers. "What kind of calamity occurred in the water?" "I was riding a horse," the Tang emperor said, "when we came near the Wei River where two fishes were playing. That deceitful Grand Marshal Zhu pushed me off my horse into the river, and I was almost drowned."

"His Majesty is still not entirely free from the influences of the dead," said Wei Zheng. He quickly ordered from the imperial dispensary medicinal broth designed to calm his spirit and fortify his soul. They also prepared some rice gruel, and only after taking such nourishments once or twice did he become his old self again, fully regaining his living senses. A quick calculation revealed that the Tang emperor had been dead for three days and nights and then returned to life to rule again. We have thus a testimonial poem:

> From ancient times how oft the world has changed!
> History is full of kingdoms that rise and fall.
> Countless were the wonders of Zhou, Han, and Jin.
> Which could match King Tang's from death to life recall?

By then it was dusk; the various ministers withdrew after they had seen the emperor retire. The next day, they took off their mourning garb and changed into their court attire: everyone had on his red robe and black cap, his purple sash and gold medal, waiting outside the gate to be summoned to court. We now tell you about Taizong, who, having received the medicine prescribed for calming his spirit and fortifying his soul, and having taken the rice broth several times, was carried into his bedchamber by his attendants. He slept soundly that whole night, and when he arose at dawn, his spirit was fully revived. Look how he was attired:

> He donned a tall, royal cap;
> He wore a dark ocher robe;
> He put on a belt of green jade from Blue Mountain;

He trod a pair of empire-building carefree boots.
His stunning looks
Surpassed anyone in court:
With power to spare
He resumed his reign.
What a great Tang emperor of justice and truth,
The Majestic Li who rose again from the dead!

The Tang emperor went up to the Treasure Hall of the Golden Carriage and gathered together the two groups of civil and military officials, who, after shouting "Long live the emperor" three times, stood in attention according to rank and file. Then they heard this loud announcement: "If there is any business, come forth and make your memorial; if there is no business, you are dismissed from court."

From the east came the row of civil officials and from the west came the row of military officials; they all went forward and prostrated themselves before the steps of white jade. "Your Majesty," they said, "may we inquire how you awoke from your slumber, which lasted so long?"

"On that day, after we had received the letter from Wei Zheng," said Taizong, "we felt that our soul had departed from these halls, having been invited by the imperial guardsmen to join a hunting party. As we were traveling, the men and horses both disappeared, whereupon my father, the former emperor, and my deceased brothers came to hassle us. We would not have been able to escape them had it not been for the arrival of someone in black cap and robe; this man happened to be the judge Cui Jue, who managed to send my deceased brothers away. We handed Wei Zheng's letter over to him, and as he was reading it, some boys in blue came to lead us with flags and banners to the Hall of Darkness, where we were met by the Ten Kings of the Underworld. They told us of the Jing River Dragon, who accused us of having him slain after promising to save him. We in turn explained to them what happened, and they assured us that our case had been jointly reviewed by the Three Tribunes. Then they asked for the Chronicles of Life and Death to examine what was to be our allotted age. Judge Cui presented his books, and King Yama, after checking them, said that Heaven had assigned us a portion of thirty-three years. Since we had ruled for only thirteen years, we were entitled to twenty more years of living. So Grand Marshal Zhu and Judge Cui were ordered to send us back here. We took leave of the Ten Kings and promised to thank them with gifts of melons and other fruits. After our departure from the Hall of Darkness, we encountered in the Underworld all those who were treasonous to the state and disloyal to their parents, those who practiced neither virtue nor righteousness, those who squandered the five grains, those who cheated openly or in secret, those who indulged in unjust weights and measure-ments—in sum, the rapists, the thieves, the liars, the hypocrites, the wan-tons, the deviates, the connivers, and the lawbreakers. They were all suffer-ing from various tortures by grinding, burning, pounding, sawing, frying, boiling, hanging, and skinning. There were tens of thousands of them, and we could not make an end of this ghastly sight. Thereafter we passed by the City of the Dead, filled with the souls of brigands and bandits from all over the Earth, who came to block our path. Fortunately, Judge Cui was willing to vouch for us, and we could then borrow a roomful of gold and silver from Old Man Xiang of Henan to buy off the spirits before we could proceed once more. We finally parted after Judge Cui had repeatedly instructed us that when we returned to the World of Light we were to celebrate a Grand Mass of Land and Water for the salvation of those orphaned spirits. After leaving the Sixfold Path of Transmigration, Grand Marshal Zhu asked us to mount a horse so swift it seemed to be flying, and brought me to the bank of the Wei River. As we were enjoying the sight of two fishes playing in the water, he grabbed our legs and pushed us into the river. Only then did we come back to life." When the various ministers heard these words, they all praised and congratulated the emperor. A notice was also sent out to every town and district in the empire, and all the officials presented gratulatory memorials, which we shall mention no further.

We shall now tell you about Taizong, who proclaimed a general amnesty for the prisoners in the empire. Moreover, he asked for an inventory of those convicted of capital crimes, and the judge from the Board of Justice submitted some four hundred names of those awaiting death by beheading or hanging. Taizong granted them one year's leave to return to their fami-lies, so that they could settle their affairs and put their property in order be-fore going to the marketplace to receive their just deserts. The prisoners all thanked him for such grace before departing. After issuing another edict for the care and welfare of orphans, Taizong also released some three thou-sand court maidens and concubines from the palace and married them off to worthy military officers. From that time on, his reign was truly a virtu-ous one, to which we have a testimonial poem:

Great is the virtue of the Great Tang Ruler!
Surpassing Sage Kings, he makes his people prosper.
Five hundred convicts may now leave the prison;
Three thousand maidens find release from the palace.
The empire's officials all wish him long life.
The ministers at court all give him high praise.
Such good heart, once stirred, the Heavens should bless,
And pass such weal to seventeen generations.

After releasing the court maidens and convicts, Taizong also issued another proclamation to be posted throughout the empire. The proclamation read:

The cosmos, though vast,
Is brightly surveyed by the sun and the moon;
The world, though immense,
Approves not villains in Heaven or on Earth.
If your intent is trickery,
Even this life will bring retribution;
If your giving exceeds receiving,
There's blessing not only in the life hereafter.
A thousand clever designs
Are not as living according to one's duties;
Ten thousand men of violence
Cannot compare with one frugal and content.
If you're bent on good works and mercy,
Need you read the sūtras with diligence?
If you intend to harm others,
Even the learning of Buddha is vain!

From that time on, there was not a single person in the empire who did not practice virtue.

Meanwhile, another notice was posted asking for a volunteer to take the melons and other fruits to the Region of Darkness. At the same time, a roomful of gold and silver from the treasury was sent with the Imperial Duke of Khotan, Hu Jingde, to the Kaifeng District of Henan so that the debt to Xiang Liang could be repaid. After the notice had been posted for some days, a worthy came forth to volunteer his life for the mission. He was originally from Zunzhou; his surname was Liu and his given name Quan, and he belonged to a family of great wealth. The reason he came forward was that his wife, Li Cuilian, happened to have given a gold hairpin from her head, by way of alms, to a monk in front of their house. When Liu Quan chided her for her indiscretion in flaunting herself outside their home, Li became so upset that she promptly hanged herself, leaving behind her a pair of young children, who wept piteously day and night. Liu Quan was so filled with remorse by the sight of them that he was willing to leave life and property to take the melons to hell. He therefore took down the royal notice and came to see the Tang emperor. The emperor ordered him to go to the Lodge of the Golden Pavilion, where a pair of southern melons were put on his head, some money in his sleeve, and some medicine in his mouth.

So Liu Quan died by taking poison. His soul, still bearing the fruits on his head, arrived at the Gate of Spirits. The demon guardian at the door shouted, "Who are you that you dare to come here?" "By the imperial command of the Great Tang Emperor Taizong," said Liu Quan, "I came here especially to present melons and other fruits for the enjoyment of the Ten Kings of the Underworld." The demon guardian received him amiably and led him to the Treasure Hall of Darkness. When he saw King Yama, he presented the melons, saying, "By order of the Tang emperor, I came from afar to present these melons as a token of thanks for the gracious hospitality of the Ten Kings." Highly pleased, King Yama said, "That Emperor Taizong is certainly a man of his word!" He accepted the melons and proceeded to ask the messenger about his name and his home. "Your humble servant," said Liu Quan, "resided originally in Junzhou; my surname is Liu and my given name is Quan. Because my wife hanged herself, leaving no one to care for our children, I decided to leave home and children and sacrifice my life for the country by helping my emperor to take these melons here as a thank offering."

When the Ten Kings heard these words, they asked at once for Li, the wife of Liu Quan; she was brought in by the demon guardian, and wife and husband had a reunion before the Hall of Darkness. They conversed about what had happened and also thanked the Ten Kings for this meeting. King Yama, moreover, examined the Books of Life and Death and found that both husband and wife were supposed to live to a ripe old age. He quickly ordered the demon guardian to take them back to life, but the guardian said, "Since Li Cuilian has been back in the World of Darkness for many days, her body no longer exists. To whom should her soul attach herself?"

"The emperor's sister, Li Yuying," said King Yama, "is destined to die very soon. Borrow her body right away so that this woman can return to life." The demon guardian obeyed the order and led Liu Quan and his wife out of the Region of Darkness to return to life. We do not know how the two of them returned to life; let's listen to the explanation in the next chapter.

TWELVE

The Tang emperor, firmly sincere, convenes a Grand Mass; Guanyin, in epiphany, converts Gold Cicada.

We were telling you about the demon guardian who was leading Liu Quan and his wife out of the Region of Darkness. Accompanied by a swirling dark wind, they went directly back to Chang'an of the great nation. The demon pushed the soul of Liu Quan into the Golden Court Pavilion Lodge, but the soul of Cuilian was brought into the inner court of the royal palace. Just then the Princess Yuying was walking beneath the shadows of flowers along a path covered with green moss. The demon guardian crashed right into her and pushed her to the ground; her living soul was snatched away and the soul of Cuilian was pushed into Yuying's body instead. The demon guardian then returned to the Region of Darkness, and we shall say no more about that.

We now tell you that the maidservants of the palace, both young and old, when they saw that Yuying had fallen and died, ran quickly to the Hall of the Golden Chimes and reported the incident to the queen, saying, "The princess has fallen and died!" Horrified, the queen reported it to Taizong.

When Taizong heard the news, he nodded, sighing, and said, "So this has come to pass indeed! We did ask the King of Darkness whether the old and young of our family would be safe or not. He said, 'They will all be safe, but I fear that your royal sister will not live long.' Now his word is fulfilled." All the inhabitants of the palace came to mourn her, but when they reached the spot where she had fallen, they saw that the princess was breathing.

"Stop weeping! Stop weeping!" said the Tang emperor. "Don't startle her!" He went forward and lifted her head with the royal hand, crying out, "Wake up, royal sister!"

Our princess suddenly turned over and cried, "Husband, walk slowly! Wait for me!" "Sister," said Taizong, "we are all here." Lifting her head and opening her eyes to look around, the princess said, "Who are you that you dare touch me?" "This is your royal brother," said Taizong, "and your sister-in-law."

"Where do I have any royal brother and sister-in-law?" asked the princess. "My family is Li, and my maiden name is Li Cuilian. My husband's surname is Liu and his given name is Quan. Both of us are from Junzhou. Because I pulled a golden hairpin to give to a monk outside our home as alms three months ago, my husband rebuked me for walking indiscreetly out of our doors and thus violating the etiquette appropriate to a woman.

He scolded me, and I became so enraged that I hanged myself with a white silk cord, leaving behind a pair of children who wept night and day. On account of my husband, who was sent by the Tang emperor to the Region of Darkness to present melons, King Yama took pity on us and allowed us both to return to life. He was walking ahead; I could not keep up with him, tripped, and fell. How rude you all are! Not knowing my name, how dare you touch me!" When Taizong heard these words, he said to his attendants, "I suppose my sister was knocked senseless by the fall. She's babbling!" He ordered that Yuying be helped into the palace and medicine be brought in from the court dispensary.

As the Tang emperor went back to the court, one of his assistants came forward to report, saying, "Your Majesty, the man Liu Quan, who went to present the melons, has returned to life. He is now outside the gate, awaiting your order." Greatly startled, the Tang emperor at once gave the order for Liu Quan to be brought in, who then prostrated himself before the red-lacquered courtyard. Taizong asked him, "How did the presentation of melons come off?"

"Your subject," said Liu Quan, "bore the melons on his head and went straight to the Gate of Spirits. I was led to the Hall of Darkness, where I met the Ten Kings of the Underworld. I presented the melons and spoke at length about the sincere gratitude of my lord. King Yama was most delighted, and he complimented Your Majesty profusely, saying, 'That Taizong emperor is indeed a man of virtue and a man of his word!'" "What did you happen to see in the Region of Darkness?" asked the Tang emperor. "Your subject did not travel far," said Liu Quan, "and I did not see much. I only heard King Yama questioning me on my native village and my name. Your subject therefore gave him a full account of how I abandoned home and children because of my wife's suicide and volunteered for the mission. He quickly sent for a demon guardian, who brought in my wife, and we were reunited at the Hall of Darkness. Meanwhile, they also examined the Books of Life and Death and told us that we both should live to a ripe old age. The demon guardian was dispatched to see us back to life. Your subject walked ahead, but my wife fell behind. I am grateful that I am now returned to life, but I do not know where my wife has gone."

Alarmed, the Tang emperor asked, "Did King Yama say anything about your wife?" "He didn't say much," said Liu Quan. "I only heard the demon guardian's exclamation that Li Cuilian had been dead for so long that her body no longer existed. King Yama said, 'The royal sister, Li Yuying, should die shortly. Let Cuilian borrow the body of Yuying so that she may return to life.' Your subject has no knowledge of who that royal sister is and where she resides, nor has he made any attempt to locate her."

When the Tang emperor heard this report, he was filled with delight and said to the many officials around him, "When we took leave of King Yama, we questioned him with regard to the inhabitants of the palace. He said that the old and the young would all be safe, though he feared that our sister would not live long. Just now our sister Yuying fell dying beneath the flowers. When we went to her assistance, she regained her consciousness momentarily, crying, 'Husband, walk slowly! Wait for me!' We thought that her fall had knocked her senseless, as she was babbling like that. But when we questioned her carefully, she said exactly what Liu Quan now tells us."

"If Her Royal Highness passed away momentarily, only to say these things after she regained consciousness," said Wei Zheng, "this means that there is a real possibility that Liu Quan's wife has returned to life by borrowing another person's body. Let us invite the princess to come out, and see what she has to tell us."

"We just asked the court dispensary to send in some medicine," said the Tang emperor, "for we don't know what's happening." Some ladies of the court went to fetch the princess, and they found her inside, screaming, "Why do I need to take any medicine? How could this be my house? Ours is a clean, cool house of tiles, not like this one, yellow as if it had jaundice, and with such gaudy appointments! Let me out! Let me out!" She was still shouting when four or five ladies and two or three eunuchs took hold of her and led her outside to the court.

The Tang emperor said, "Do you recognize your husband?" "What are you talking about?" said Yuying. "The two of us were pledged to each other since childhood as husband and wife. I bore him a boy and a girl. How could I not recognize him?" The Tang emperor asked one of the palatial officials to help her go down from the Treasure Hall. The princess went right before the steps of white jade, and when she saw Liu Quan, she grabbed him, saying, "Husband, where have you been? You didn't even wait for me! I tripped and fell, and then I was surrounded by all these crazy people, talking nonsense! What do you have to say to this?" Liu Quan heard that she was speaking like his wife, but the person he saw certainly did not resemble her, and he dared not acknowledge her to be his own. The Tang emperor said,

"Indeed,
Men have seen mountains cracking, or the gaping of earth;
But none has seen the living exchanged for the dead!"

What a just and kindly ruler! He took his sister's toilet boxes, garments, and jewelry and bestowed them all on Liu Quan; it was as if the man was provided with a dowry. He was, moreover, exempted forever from having to engage in any compulsory service to the Crown, and was told to take the royal sister back to his home. So, husband and wife together expressed their gratitude before the steps and returned happily to their village. We have a testimonial poem:

How long, how short—man has his span of years;
He lives and dies, each foreordained by fate.
Liu Quan presented melons and returned to life;
In someone's body so did Li, his mate.

The two of them took leave of the emperor, went directly back to Junzhou, and saw that both house and children were in good order. They never ceased thereafter to proclaim the rewards of virtue, but we shall speak of them no further.

We now tell you about Yuchi Gong, who took a huge load of gold and silver and went to see Xiang Liang at the Kaifeng District in Henan. It turned out that the man made his living by selling water, while his wife, whose surname was Zhang, sold pottery in front of their home. Whatever money they made, they kept only enough for their subsistence, giving all the rest either as alms to the monks or as gifts to the dead by purchasing paper money and burning it. They thus built up enormous merit; for though they were poor folks in the World of Light, they were, in fact, leading citizens for whom jade and gold were laid up in the other world. When Yuchi Gong came to their door with the gold and silver, Papa Xiang and Mama Xiang were terror-stricken. And when they also saw the district officials with their horses and carriages assembling outside their thatched hut, the aged couple were dumbfounded. They knelt on the floor and kowtowed without ceasing. "Old folks, please arise," said Yuchi Gong. "Though I am an imperial official, I came here with this gold and silver to repay you by order of my king." Shaking and quaking, the man said, "Your lowly servant has never lent money to others. How dare we accept such inexplicable wealth?"

"I have found out," said Yuchi Gong, "that you are indeed a poor fellow. But you have also given alms to feed the monks. Whatever exceeds your necessities you have used to purchase paper money, which you burned in dedication to the Region of Darkness. You have thus accumulated a vast fortune down below. Our emperor, Taizong, returned to life after being dead for three days; he borrowed a roomful of gold and silver from you while he was in the Region of Darkness, and we are returning the exact sum to you. Please count your money accordingly so that we may make our report back to the emperor." Xiang Liang and his wife, however, remained adamant. They raised their hands to Heaven and cried, "If your lowly servants accepted this gold and silver, we should die quickly. We might have been given credit for burning paper cash, but this is a secret unknown to us. Moreover, what evidence do we have that our Father, His Majesty, borrowed our money in some other world? We simply dare not accept this." "His Majesty told us," said Yuchi Gong, "that he received the loan from you because Judge Cui vouched for him, and he could bear testimony. So please accept this." "Even if I were to die," said Xiang Liang, "I could not accept the gift."

Seeing that they persisted in their refusal, Yuchi Gong had no alternative but to send someone back to report to the Throne. When Taizong saw the report and learned that Xiang Liang had refused to accept the gold and silver, he said, "They are truly virtuous elders!" He issued a decree at once that Hu Jingde should use the money to erect a temple, to build a shrine, and to support the religious services that would be performed in them. The old couple, in other words, would be repaid in this manner. The decree went out to Jingde, who, having expressed his gratitude, facing the capital, proclaimed its content for all to know. He used the money to purchase a lot of about fifty acres not needed either by the military authorities or the people. A temple was erected on this piece of land and named the Royal Xiangguo Temple.[1] To the left of it there was also a shrine dedicated to Papa and Mama Xiang, with a stone inscription stating that the buildings were erected under the supervision of Yuchi Gong. This is the Great Xiangguo Temple still standing today.

The work was finished and reported; Taizong was exceedingly pleased. He then gathered many officials together in order that a public notice be issued to invite monks for the celebration of the Grand Mass of Land and Water, so that those orphaned souls in the Region of Darkness might find salvation. The notice went throughout the empire, and officials of all regions were asked to recommend monks illustrious for their holiness to go to Chang'an for the Mass. In less than a month's time, various monks from the empire had arrived. The Tang emperor ordered the court historian, Fu Yi, to select an illustrious priest to take charge of the ceremonies. When Fu Yi received the order, however, he presented a memorial to the Throne that attempted to dispute the worth of Buddha.[2] The memorial said:

The teachings of the Western Territory deny the relations of ruler and subject, of father and son. With the doctrines of the Three Ways[3] and the Six-fold Path,[4] they beguile and seduce the foolish and the simpleminded. They emphasize the sins of the past in order to ensure the felicities of the future. By chanting in Sanskrit, they seek a way of escape. We submit, however, that birth, death, and the length of one's life are ordered by nature; but the conditions of public disgrace or honor are determined by human volition. These phenomena are not, as some philistines would now maintain, ordained by Buddha. The teachings of Buddha did not exist in the time of the Five Thearchs and the Three Kings, and yet those rulers were wise, their subjects loyal, and their reigns long-lasting. It was not until the period of Emperor

Ming in the Han dynasty that the worship of foreign gods was established,[5] but this meant only that priests of the Western Territory were permitted to propagate their faith. The event, in fact, represented a foreign intrusion in China, and the teachings are hardly worthy to be believed.

When Taizong saw the memorial, he had it distributed among the various officials for discussion. At that time the prime minister Xiao Yu came forward and prostrated himself to address the throne, saying, "The teachings of Buddha, which have flourished in several previous dynasties, seek to exalt the good and to restrain what is evil. In this way they are covertly an aid to the nation, and there is no reason why they should be rejected. For Buddha after all is also a sage, and he who spurns a sage is himself lawless. I urge that the dissenter be severely punished."

Taking up the debate with Xiao Yu, Fu Yi contended that propriety had its foundation in service to one's parents and ruler. Yet Buddha forsook his parents and left his family; indeed, he defied the Son of Heaven all by himself, just as he used an inherited body to rebel against his parents. Xiao Yu, Fu Yi went on to say, was not born in the wilds, but by his adherence to this doctrine of parental denial, he confirmed the saying that an unfilial son had in fact no parents. Xiao Yu, however, folded his hands in front of him and declared, "Hell was established precisely for people of this kind." Taizong thereupon called on the Lord High Chamberlain, Zhang Daoyuan, and the President of the Grand Secretariat, Zhang Shiheng, and asked how efficacious the Buddhist exercises were in the procurement of blessings. The two officials replied, "The emphasis of Buddha is on purity, benevolence, compassion, the proper fruits, and the unreality of things. It was Emperor Wu of the Northern Zhou dynasty who set the Three Religions in order.[6] The Chan Master, Da Hui, also had extolled those concepts of the dark and the distant. Generations of people revered such saints as the Fifth Patriarch, who became man,[7] or the Bodhidharma, who appeared in his sacred form; none of them proved to be inconspicuous in grace and power. Moreover, it has been held since antiquity that the Three Religions are most honorable, not to be destroyed or abolished. We beseech, therefore, Your Majesty to exercise your clear and sagacious judgment." Highly pleased, Taizong said, "The words of our worthy subjects are not unreasonable. Anyone who disputes them further will be punished." He thereupon ordered Wei Zheng, Xiao Yu, and Zhang Daoyuan to invite the various Buddhist priests to prepare the site for the Grand Mass and to select from among them someone of great merit and virtue to serve as the altar master. All the officials then bowed their heads to the ground to thank the emperor before withdrawing. From that time also came the law that any person who denounces a monk or Buddhism will have his arms broken.

The next day the three court officials began the process of selection at the Mountain-River Altar, and from among the priests gathered there they chose an illustrious monk of great merit. "Who is this person?" you ask.

Gold Cicada was his former divine name.
As heedless he was of the Buddha's talk,
He had to suffer in this world of dust,
To fall in the net by being born a man.
He met misfortune as he came to Earth,
And evildoers even before his birth.
His father: Chen, a zhuangyuan from Haizhou.
His mother's sire: chief of this dynasty's court.
Fated by his natal star to fall in the stream,
He followed tide and current, chased by mighty waves.
At Gold Mountain, the island, he had great luck,
For the abbot, Qian'an,[8] raised him up.
He met his true mother at age eighteen,
And called on her father at the capital.
A great army was sent by Chief Kaishan
To stamp out at Hongzhou the vivious crew.
The zhuangyuan Guangrui escaped his doom:
Son rejoined sire—how worthy of praise!
They saw the emperor to receive his grace;
Their names resounded in Lingyan Tower.[9]
Declining office, he chose a monk's life
At Hongfu Temple to seek the true Way,
This old Buddha-child, nicknamed River Float,
With a religious name of Chen Xuanzang.

So that very day the multitude selected the priest Xuanzang, a man who had been a monk since childhood, who maintained a vegetarian diet, and who had received the commandments the moment he left his mother's womb. His maternal grandfather was Yin Kaishan, one of the chief army commanders of the present dynasty. His father, Chen Guangrui, had taken the prize of zhuangyuan and was appointed Grand Secretary of the Wen-yuan Chamber. Xuanzang, however, had no love for glory or wealth, being dedicated wholly to the pursuit of Nirvāṇa. Their investigations revealed that he had an excellent family background and the highest moral character. Not one of the thousands of classics and sūtras had he failed to master; none of the Buddhist chants and hymns was unknown to him. The three officials led Xuanzang before the throne. After going through elaborate court ritual, they bowed to report, "Your subjects, in obedience to your holy decree, have selected an illustrious monk by the name of Chen Xuanzang."

Hearing the name, Taizong thought silently for a long time and said, "Can Xuanzang be the son of Grand Secretary Chen Guangrui?" Child River Float kowtowed and replied, "That is indeed your subject." "This is a most appropriate choice," said Taizong, delighted. "You are truly a monk of great virtue and possessing the mind of Chan. We therefore appoint you the Grand Expositor of the Faith, Supreme Vicar of Priests." Xuanzang touched his forehead to the ground to express his gratitude and to receive his appointment. He was given, furthermore, a cassock of knitted gold and five colors, a Vairocana hat,[10] and the instruction diligently to seek out all worthy monks and to rank all these ācāryas[11] in order. They were to follow the imperial decree and proceed to the Temple of Transformation,[12] where they would begin the ritual after selecting a propitious day and hour.

Xuanzang bowed again to receive the decree and left. He went to the Temple of Transformation and gathered many monks together; they made ready the beds, built the platforms, and rehearsed the music. A total of one thousand two hundred worthy monks, young and old, were chosen, who were then further separated into three divisions occupying the rear, middle, and front portions of the hall. All the preparations were completed and everything was put in order before the Buddhas. The third day of the ninth month of that same year was selected as the lucky day, when a Grand Mass of Land and Water lasting forty-nine days (in accordance with the number seven times seven) would begin. A memorial was presented to Taizong, who went with all his relatives and officials, both civil and military, to the Mass on that day to burn incense and listen to the lecture. We have a poem as testimony. The poem says:

> When the year-star of Zhenguan reached thirteen,
> The king called his people to hear the Sacred Books.
> The boundless Law was performed at a plot of truth;
> Cloud, fog, and light filled the Great Promise Hall.
> By grace the king decreed this grand temple's rite;
> Shell-shed Gold Cicada sought wealth of the West.
> He spread wide the good works to save the damned
> And held his faith to preach the Three Modes of Life.[13]

In the thirteenth year of the Zhenguan period, when the year stood at *jisi* and the ninth month at *jiaxu*, on the third day and at the auspicious hour of *gueimao*, Chen Xuanzang, the Great Expositor-Priest, gathered together one thousand two hundred illustrious monks. They met at the Temple of Transformation in the city of Chang'an to expound the various holy sūtras. After holding court early that morning, the emperor led many officials both military and civil and left the Treasure Hall of Golden Chimes by phoenix carriages and dragon chariots. They came to the temple to listen to the lectures and raise incense. How does the imperial cortege appear? Truly it comes with

A sky full of blessed air,
Countless shafts of hallowed light.
The favorable wind blows gently;
The omnific sun shines brightly.
A thousand lords with girdle-jade walk in front and rear.
The many flags of guardsmen stand both left and right.
Those holding gilt bludgeons,
And halberds and axes,
March in pairs and pairs;
The red silk lanterns,
The royal incense urn,
Move in solemnity.
The dragons fly and the phoenixes dance;
The falcons soar and the eagles take wing.
This Son of Heaven's an upright sage;
The righteous ministers are good.
They increase our bliss by a thousand years, surpassing Yu and Shun;
They secure peace of ten thousand ages, rivaling Yao and Tang.
We also see the curve-handled umbrella,
And robes with rolling dragons—
Their glare lighting up each other;
The jade joined-rings,
The phoenix fans,
Waving through holy mist.
Those caps of pearls and belts of jade;
The purple sashes and medals of gold.
A thousand rows of soldiers protect the Throne;
Two lines of marshals uphold the carriage.
This emperor, cleansed and sincere, bows to the Buddha,
Glad to raise incense and seek virtue's fruit.

The grand cortege of the Tang emperor soon arrived in front of the temple. The emperor ordered a halt to the music, left the carriages, and led many officials in the worship of Buddha by taking up burning incense sticks in their hands. After bowing three times holding the incense, they raised their heads and looked around them. This was indeed a splendid religious hall. You see

Dancing flags and banners;
Bright, gleaming sunshades.

Dancing flags and banners
Fill the air with strands of flashing colored mists.
Bright, gleaming sunshades
Glow in the sun as fiery bolts.
Imposing, the gold image of Lokājyeṣṭha;[14]
Most awesome, the jade features of the arhats.
Divine flowers fill the vases.
Sandalwood incense burn in the urns.
The divine flowers filling the vases
Adorn the temple with a brilliant forest of brocade.
The sandalwood incense burning in the urns
Covers the clear sky with waves of fragrant clouds.
Piled high on red trays are fruits in season.
On colored counters, mounds of cakes and sweets rest.
Rows of noble priests chant the holy sūtras
To save from their travails those orphaned souls.

Taizong and his officials each lifted the incense; they also worshipped the golden body of the Buddha and paid homage to the arhats. Thereafter, the Master of the Law, Chen Xuanzang, the Grand Expositor of the Faith, led the various monks to greet the Tang emperor. After the ceremony, they went back to their seats according to their rank and station. The priest then presented Taizong with the proclamation for the deliverance of the orphaned souls. It read:

The supreme virtue is vast and endless, for Buddhism is founded upon Nirvāṇa. The spirit of the pure and the clean circulates freely and flows everywhere in the Three Regions. There are a thousand changes and ten thousand transformations, all regulated by the forces of yin and yang. Boundless and vast indeed are the substance, the function, the true nature, and the permanence of such phenomena. But look at those orphaned souls, how worthy they are of our pity and commiseration! Now by the holy command of Taizong, we have selected and assembled various priests, who will engage in meditation and in the proclamation of the Law. Flinging wide the gates of salvation and setting in motion many vessels of mercy, we would deliver you, the multitudes, from the Sea of Woe and save you from perdition and from the Sixfold Path. You will be led to return to the way of truth and to enjoy the bliss of Heaven. Whether it be by motion, rest, or nonactivity, you will be united with, and become, pure essences. Therefore make use of this noble occasion, for you are invited to the pleasures of the celestial city. Take advantage of our Grand Mass so that you may find release from Hell's confinement, ascend quickly and freely to ultimate bliss, and travel without restraint in the Region of the West.[15]

The poem says:

An urn of immortal incense.
Some scrolls of salvific power.
As we proclaim this boundless Law,
Receive now Heaven's endless grace.
All your guilt and crime abolished,
You lost souls may leave your prison.
May our nation be firmly blessed
With peace long and all-embracing.

Highly pleased by what he read, Taizong said to the monks, "Be firm, all of you, in your devotion, and do not slack in your service to Buddha. After the achievement of merit and after each has received his blessing, we shall reward you handsomely. Be assured that you will not have labored in vain." The twelve hundred monks all touched their foreheads to the ground to express their gratitude. After the three vegetarian meals of the day, the Tang emperor returned to the palace to wait for the formal celebration of the mass seven days hence, when he would again be invited to raise incense. As dusk was about to fall, the various officials all retired. What sort of evening was this? Look at

The long stretch of clear sky as twilight dims,
As specks of jackdaw drop to their perch late.
People grow quiet, the city full of lights:
Now's the time for Chan monks to meditate.

We have told you about the scenery of the night. The next morning the Master of the Law again ascended his seat and gathered the monks to recite their sūtras, but we shall say no more about that.

We shall now tell you about the Bodhisattva Guanyin of the Potalaka Mountain in the South Sea, who, since receiving the command of Tathāgata, was searching in the city of Chang'an for a worthy person to be the seeker of scriptures. For a long time, however, she did not encounter anyone truly virtuous. Then she learned that Taizong was extolling merit and virtue and selecting illustrious monks to hold the Grand Mass. When she discovered, moreover, that the chief priest and celebrant was the monk Child River Float, who was a child of Buddha born from paradise and who happened also to be the very elder whom she had sent to this incarnation, the Bodhisattva was exceedingly pleased. She immediately took the treasures bestowed by Buddha and carried them out with Mokṣa to sell them on the main streets of the city. "What were these treasures?" you ask. They were the embroidered cassock with rare jewels and the nine-ring priestly staff. But she kept hidden the Golden, the Constrictive, and the Prohibitive

Fillets for use in a later time, putting up for sale only the cassock and the priestly staff.

Now in the city of Chang'an there was one of those foolish monks who had not been selected to participate in the Grand Mass but who happened to possess a few strands of pelf. Seeing the Bodhisattva, who had changed herself into a monk covered with scabs and sores, barefooted and bareheaded, dressed in rags, and holding up for sale the glowing cassock, he approached and asked, "You filthy monk, how much do you want for your cassock?" "The price of the cassock," said the Bodhisattva, "is five thousand taels of silver; for the staff, two thousand." The foolish monk laughed and said, "This filthy monk is mad! A lunatic! You want seven thousand taels of silver for two such common articles? They are not worth that much even if wearing them would make you immortal or turn you into a buddha. Take them away! You'll never be able to sell them!" The Bodhisattva did not bother to argue with him; she walked away and proceeded on her journey with Mokṣa.

After a long while, they came to the Eastern Flower Gate and ran right into the chief minister Xiao Yu, who was just returning from court. His outriders were shouting to clear the streets, but the Bodhisattva boldly refused to step aside. She stood on the street holding the cassock and met the chief minister head on. The chief minister pulled in his reins to look at this bright, luminous cassock, and asked his subordinates to inquire about the price of the garment. "I want five thousand taels for the cassock," said the Bodhisattva, "and two thousand for the staff." "What is so good about them," asked Xiao Yu, "that they should be so expensive?" "This cassock," said the Bodhisattva, "has something good about it, and something bad, too. For some people it may be very expensive, but for others it may cost nothing at all."

"What's good about it," asked Xiao Yu, "and what's bad about it?"

"He who wears my cassock," replied the Bodhisattva, "will not fall into perdition, will not suffer in Hell, will not encounter violence, and will not meet tigers and wolves. That's how good it is! But if the person happens to be a foolish monk who relishes pleasures and rejoices in iniquities, or a priest who obeys neither the dietary laws nor the commandments, or a worldly fellow who attacks the sūtras and slanders the Buddha, he will never even get to see my cassock. That's what's bad about it!" The chief minister asked again, "What do you mean, it will be expensive for some and not expensive for others?" "He who does not follow the Law of Buddha," said the Bodhisattva, "or revere the Three Jewels will be required to pay seven thousand taels if he insists on buying my cassock and my staff. That's how expensive it'll be! But if he honors the Three Jewels, rejoices in doing good deeds, and obeys our Buddha, he is a person worthy of these things. I shall willingly give him the cassock and the staff to establish an affinity of goodness with him. That's what I meant when I said that for some it would cost nothing."

When Xiao Yu heard these words, his face could not hide his pleasure, for he knew that this was a good person. He dismounted at once and greeted the Bodhisattva ceremoniously, saying, "Your Holy Eminence, please pardon whatever offense Xiao Yu might have caused. Our Great Tang Emperor is a most religious person, and all the officials of his court are like-minded. In fact, we have just begun a Grand Mass of Land and Water, and this cassock will be most appropriate for the use of Chen Xuanzang, the Grand Expositor of the Faith. Let me go with you to have an audience with the Throne."

The Bodhisattva was happy to comply with the suggestion. They turned around and went into the Eastern Flower Gate. The Custodian of the Yellow Door went inside to make the report, and they were summoned to the Treasure Hall, where Xiao Yu and the two monks covered with scabs and sores stood below the steps. "What does Xiao Yu want to report to us?" asked the Tang emperor. Prostrating himself before the steps, Xiao Yu said, "Your subject going out of the Eastern Flower Gate met by chance these two monks, selling a cassock and a priestly staff. I thought of the priest, Xuanzang, who might wear this garment. For this reason, we asked to have an audience with Your Majesty."

Highly pleased, Taizong asked for the price of the cassock. The Bodhisattva and Mokṣa stood at the foot of the steps but did not bow at all. When asked the price of the cassock, the Bodhisattva replied, "Five thousand taels for the cassock and two thousand for the priestly staff." "What's so good about the cassock," said Taizong, "that it should cost so much?" The Bodhisattva said:

"Of this cassock,
A dragon which wears but one shred
Will miss the woe of being devoured by the great roc;
Or a crane on which one thread is hung
Will transcend this world and reach the place of the gods.
Sit in it:
Ten thousand gods will salute you!
Move with it:
Seven Buddhas will follow you![16]
This cassock was made of silk drawn from ice silkworm[17]
And threads spun by skilled craftsmen.
Immortal girls did the weaving;
Divine maidens helped at the loom.

Bit by bit, the parts were sewn and embroidered.
Stitch by stitch, it arose—a brocade from the heddle,
Its pellucid weave finer than ornate blooms.
Its colors, brilliant, emit precious light.
Wear it, and crimson mist will surround your frame.
Doff it, and see the colored clouds take flight.
Outside the Three Heavens' door its primal light was seen;
Before the Five Mountains its magic aura grew.
Inlaid are layers of lotus from the West,
And hanging pearls shine like planets and stars.
On four corners are pearls that glow at night;
On top stays fastened an emerald.
Though lacking the all-seeing primal form,
It's held by Eight Treasures all aglow.
This cassock
You keep folded at leisure;
You wear it to meet sages.
When it's kept folded at leisure,
Its rainbowlike hues cut through a thousand wrappings.
When you wear it to meet sages,
All Heaven takes fright—both demons and gods!
On top are the ṛddhi pearl,
The māṇi pearl,
The dust-clearing pearl,
The wind-stopping pearl.
There are also the red cornelian,
The purple coral,
The luminescent pearl,[18]
The Śārīputra.
They rob the moon of its whiteness;
They match the sun in its redness.
In waves its divine aura imbues the sky;
In flashes its brightness lifts up its perfection.
In waves its divine aura imbues the sky,
Flooding the Gate of Heaven.
In flashes its brightness lifts up its perfection,
Lighting up the whole world.
Shining upon the mountains and the streams,
It wakens tigers and leopards;
Lighting up the isles and the seas,
It moves dragons and fishes.

Along its edges hang two chains of melted gold,
And joins the collars a ring of snow-white jade.

The poem says:

The august Three Jewels' most noble truths
Judge all Four Creatures on the Sixfold Path.
The mind brightened feeds on God's Law and man's;
The nature perceived transmits the wisdom lamp.
Solemn Vajradhātu[19] *guards one's body*
When a mind's pure like ice in flasks of jade.
Since Buddha caused this cassock to be made,
Which ten thousand kalpas could harm a monk?"

When the Tang emperor, who was up in the Treasure Hall, heard these words, he was highly pleased. "Tell me, priest," he asked again, "What's so good about the nine-ring priestly staff?" "My staff," said the Bodhisattva, "has on it

Nine joined-rings made of iron and set in bronze,
And nine joints of vine immortal ever young.
When held, it scorns the sight of aging bones;
It leaves the mount to return with fleecy clouds.
It roamed through Heaven with the Fifth Patriarch;
It broke Hell's gate where Luo Bo sought his Mom.[20]
Not soiled by the filth of this red-dust world,
It gladly trails the god-monk up Mount Jade."[21]

When the Tang emperor heard these words, he gave the order to have the cassock spread open so that he might examine it carefully from top to bottom. It was indeed a marvelous thing! "Venerable Elder of the Great Law," he said, "we shall not deceive you. At this very moment we have exalted the Religion of Mercy and planted abundantly in the fields of blessing. You may see many priests assembled in the Temple of Transformation to perform the Law and the sūtras. In their midst is a man of great merit and virtue, whose religious name is Xuanzang. We wish, therefore, to purchase these two treasure objects from you to give them to him. How much do you really want for these things?" Hearing these words, the Bodhisattva and Mokṣa folded their hands and gave praise to the Buddha. "If he is a man of virtue and merit," she said to the Throne, bowing, "this humble cleric is willing to give them to him. I shall not accept any money." She finished speaking and turned at once to leave. The Tang emperor quickly asked Xiao Yu to hold her back. Standing up in the Hall, he bowed low before saying, "Previously you claimed that the cassock was worth five thousand taels of silver, and the staff two thousand. Now that you see we want to buy them, you refuse to accept payment. Are you implying that we would bank on our position and take your possession by force? That's absurd! We shall pay you according to the original sum you asked for; please do not refuse it."

Raising her hands for a salutation, the Bodhisattva said, "This humble cleric made a vow before, stating that anyone who reveres the Three Treasures, rejoices in virtue, and submits to our Buddha will be given these treasures free. Since it is clear that Your Majesty is eager to magnify virtue, to rest in excellence, and to honor our Buddhist faith by having an illustrious monk proclaim the Great Law, it is my duty to present these gifts to you. I shall take no money for them. They will be left here and this humble cleric will take leave of you." When the Tang emperor saw that she was so insistent, he was very pleased. He ordered the Court of Banquets to prepare a huge vegetarian feast to thank the Bodhisattva, who firmly declined that also. She left amiably and went back to her hiding place at the Temple of the Local Spirit, which we shall mention no further.

We tell you now about Taizong, who held a noon court and asked Wei Zheng to summon Xuanzang to an audience. That Master of the Law was just leading the monks in chanting sūtras and reciting *geyas*.²² When he heard the emperor's decree, he left the platform immediately and followed Wei Zheng to come before the Throne. "We have greatly troubled our Master," said Taizong, "to render exemplary good works, for which we have hardly anything to offer you in thanks. This morning Xiao Yu came upon two monks who were willing to present us with a brocaded cassock with rare treasures and a nine-ring priestly staff. We therefore call specially for you so that you may receive them for your enjoyment and use." Xuanzang kowtowed to express his thanks.

"If our Master of the Law is willing," said Taizong, "please put the garment on for us to have a look." The priest accordingly shook open the cassock and draped it on his body, holding the staff in his hands. As he stood before the steps, ruler and subjects were all delighted. Here was a true child of Tathāgata! Look at him:

> *His looks imposing, how elegant and fine!*
> *This robe of Buddha fits him like a glove!*
> *Its most lustrous splendor spills o'er the world;*
> *Its bright colors imbue the universe.*
> *Up and down are set rows of shining pearls;*
> *Back and front thread layers of golden cords.*
> *Brocade gilds the robe's edges all around,*

With patterns embroidered most varied and rare.
Shaped like Eight Treasures are the thread-made frogs.
A gold ring joins the collars with velvet loops.
It shows on top and bottom Heaven's ranks,
And stars, great and small, are placed left and right.
Great is the fortune of Xuanzang, the priest,
Now most deserving of this precious thing.
He seems a living arhat from the West,
Or even better than its true elite.
He holds his staff and all its nine rings clang,
Benefic in his Vairocana hat.
A true Buddha-child, it's no idle tale,
He matches the Bodhi and that's no lie!

The various officials, both civil and military, stood before the steps and shouted "Bravo!" Taizong could not have been more pleased, and he told the Master of the Law to keep his cassock on and the staff in his hands. Two regiments of honor guards were ordered to accompany him along with many other officials. They left the gate of the court and proceeded on the main streets toward the temple, and the whole entourage gave the impression that a zhuangyuan was making a tour of the city. The procession was a stirring sight indeed! The merchants and tradesmen in the city of Chang'an, the princes and noblemen, the men of ink and letters, the grown men and the little girls—they all vied to get a good view. Everyone exclaimed, "What a priest! He is truly a living arhat descended to Earth, a live bodhisattva coming to the world!" Xuanzang went right to the temple where he was met by all the monks leaving their seats. The moment they saw him wearing that cassock and holding the staff, they all said that King Kṣitigarbha[23] had arrived! Everyone bowed to him and waited on him left and right. Going up to the main hall, Xuanzang lighted incense to honor the Buddha, after which he spoke of the emperor's favor to the multitude. Thereafter, each went back to his assigned seat, and soon the fiery orb sank westward. So it was

Sunset: mist hid trees and grasses;
The capital's first chimes rang out.
Zheng-zheng they struck thrice, and human traffic ceased;
Streets back and front soon grew quiet.

Though lights burned bright at First Temple,
The lone village was hush and mute.
The monk focused to tend the sūtras still—
Time to smelt demons, to nurse his spirit.[24]

Time went by like the snapping of fingers, and the formal celebration of the Grand Mass on the seventh day was to take place. Xuanzang presented the Tang emperor with a memorial, inviting him to raise the incense. News of these good works was circulating throughout the empire. Upon receiving the notice, Taizong sent for his carriage and led many of his officials, both civil and military, as well as his relatives and the ladies of the court, to the temple. All the people of the city—young and old, nobles and commoners—went along also to hear the preaching. At the same time, the Bodhisattva said to Mokṣa, "Today is the formal celebration of the Grand Mass, the first seventh of seven such occasions. It's about time for you and me to join the crowd. First, we want to see how the mass is going; second, we want to find out whether Gold Cicada is worthy of my treasures; and third, we can discover what division of Buddhism he is preaching about." The two of them thereupon went to the temple; and so it is that

> Affinity will help old comrades meet
> As perfection returns to this holy seat.

As they walked inside the temple to look around, they discovered that such a place in the capital of a great nation indeed surpassed the Ṣaḍ-varṣa,[25] or even the Jetavana Garden of the Śrāvastī.[26] It was truly a lofty temple of Caturdiśgaḥ,[27] resounding with divine music and Buddhist chants. Our Bodhisattva went directly to the side of the platform of many treasures and beheld a form truly resembling the enlightened Gold Cicada. The poem says:

> All things were pure with not a spot of dust.
> Xuanzang of the Great Law sat high onstage.
> Lost souls, redeemed, approached the place unseen;
> The city's highborn came to hear the Law.
> You give when time's ripe: this intent's far-reaching.
> You die as you please, the Canon door's open.
> As they heard him rehearse the Boundless Law,
> Young and old were glad and comforted.

Another poem says:

> Since she made a tour of this holy site,
> She met a friend unlike all other men.
> They spoke of the present and of countless things—
> Of merit and trial in this world of dust.
> The cloud of Law extends to shroud the hills;
> The net of Truth spread wide to fill all space.

Asses your lives and return to good thoughts,
For Heaven's grace is rife as falling blooms.

On the platform, that Master of the Law recited for a while the *Sūtra of Life and Deliverance for the Dead*; he then lectured for a while on the *Heavenly Treasure Chronicle for Peace in the Nation*, after which he preached for a while on the *Scroll on Merit and Self-Cultivation*.[28]

The Bodhisattva drew near and thumped her hands on the platform, calling out in a loud voice, "Hey, monk! You only know how to talk about the teachings of the Little Vehicle. Don't you know anything about the Great Vehicle?" When Xuanzang heard this question, he was filled with delight. He turned and leaped down from the platform, raised his hands and saluted the Bodhisattva, saying, "Venerable Teacher, please pardon your pupil for much disrespect. I only know that the priests who came before me all talk about the teachings of the Little Vehicle. I have no idea what the Great Vehicle teaches." "The doctrines of your Little Vehicle," said the Bodhisattva, "cannot save the damned by leading them up to Heaven; they can only mislead and confuse mortals. I have in my possession Tripiṭaka, three collections of the Great Vehicle Laws of Buddha, which are able to send the lost to Heaven, to deliver the afflicted from their sufferings, to fashion ageless bodies, and to break the cycles of coming and going."

As they were speaking, the officer in charge of incense and the inspection of halls reported to the emperor, "The Master was just in the process of lecturing on the wondrous Law when he was pulled down by two scabby mendicants, babbling some kind of nonsense." The king ordered them to be arrested, and the two monks were taken by many people and pushed into the hall in the rear. When the monk saw Taizong, she neither raised her hands nor made a bow; instead, she lifted her face and said, "What do you want of me, Your Majesty?" Recognizing her, the Tang emperor said, "Aren't you the monk who brought us the cassock the other day?" "I am," said the Bodhisattva. "If you have come to listen to the lecture," said Taizong, "you may as well take some vegetarian food. Why indulge in this wanton discussion with our Master and disturb the lecture hall, delaying our religious service?"

"What that Master of yours was lecturing on," said the Bodhisattva, "happens to be the teachings of the Little Vehicle, which cannot lead the lost up to Heaven. In my possession is the Tripiṭaka, the Great Vehicle Law of Buddha, which is able to save the damned, deliver the afflicted, and fashion the indestructible body." Delighted, Taizong asked eagerly, "Where is your Great Vehicle Law of Buddha?" "At the place of our lord, Tathāgata," said the Bodhisattva, "in the Great Temple of Thunderclap, located in India of the Great Western Heaven. It can untie the knot of a hundred enmities; it can dispel unexpected misfortunes." "Can you remember any of it?" said Taizong. "Certainly," said the Bodhisattva. Taizong was overjoyed and said, "Let the Master lead this monk to the platform to begin a lecture at once."

Our Bodhisattva led Mokṣa and flew up onto the high platform. She then trod on the hallowed clouds to rise up into the air and revealed her true salvific form, holding the pure vase with the willow branch. At her left stood the virile figure of Mokṣa carrying the rod. The Tang emperor was so overcome that he bowed to the sky and worshipped, as civil and military officials all knelt on the ground and burned incense. Throughout the temple, there was not one of the monks, nuns, Daoists, secular persons, scholars, craftsmen, and merchants, who did not bow down and exclaim, "Dear Bodhisattva! Dear Bodhisattva!" We have a song as a testimony. They saw only

Auspicious mist in diffusion
And dharmakāya[29] veiled by holy light.
In the bright air of ninefold Heaven
A lady immortal appeared.
That Bodhisattva
Wore on her head a cap
Fastened by leaves of gold
And set with flowers of jade,
With tassels of dangling pearls,
All aglow with golden light.
On her body she had
A robe of fine blue silk,
Lightly colored
And simply fretted
By circling dragons
And soaring phoenixes.
Down in front was hung
A pair of fragrant girdle-jade,
Which glowed with the moon
And danced with the wind,
Overlaid with precious pearls
And with imperial jade.
Around her waist was tied
An embroidered velvet skirt
Of ice worm silk
And piped in gold,
In which she topped the colored clouds
And crossed the jasper sea.

Before her she led
A cockatoo with red beak and yellow plumes,
Which had roamed the Eastern Ocean
And throughout the world
To foster deeds of mercy and filial piety.
She held in her hands
A grace-dispensing and world-sustaining precious vase,
In which was planted
A twig of pliant willow,
That could moisten the blue sky,
And sweep aside all evil—
All clinging fog and smoke.
Her jade rings joined embroidered loops;
Gold lotus grew beneath her feet.
For three days oft she came and went:
This very Guanshiyin[30] who saves from pain and woe.

So pleased by the vision was Tang Taizong that he forgot about his empire; so enthralled were the civil and military officials that they completely ignored court etiquette. Everyone was chanting, "Namo Bodhisattva Guanshiyin!"[31]

Taizong at once gave the order for a skilled painter to sketch the true form of the Bodhisattva. No sooner had he spoken than a certain Wu Daozi was selected, who could portray gods and sages and was a master of the noble perspective and lofty vision. (This man, in fact, was the one who would later paint the portraits of meritorious officials in the Lingyan Tower.) Immediately he opened up his magnificent brush to record the true form. The hallowed clouds of the Bodhisattva gradually drifted away, and in a little while the golden light disappeared. From midair came floating down a slip of paper on which were plainly written several lines in the style of the *gāthā*:

We greet the great Ruler of Tang
With scripts most sublime of the West.
The way: a hundred and eight thousand miles.
This Mahāyāna seek earnestly.
These Books, when they reach your fair state,
Can redeem damned spirits from Hell.
If someone is willing to go,
He'll become a Buddha of gold.

When Taizong saw the *gāthā*, he said to the various monks: "Let's stop the Mass. Wait until I have sent someone to bring back the scriptures of the Great Vehicle. We shall then renew our sincere effort to cultivate the fruits of virtue." Not one of the officials disagreed with the emperor, who then asked in the temple, "Who is willing to accept our commission to seek scriptures from Buddha in the Western Heaven?" Hardly had he finished speaking when the Master of the Law stepped from the side and saluted him, saying, "Though your poor monk has no talents, he is ready to perform the service of a dog and a horse. I shall seek these true scriptures on behalf of Your Majesty, that the empire of our king may be firm and everlasting." Highly pleased, the Tang emperor went forward to raise up the monk with his royal hands, saying, "If the Master is willing to express his loyalty this way, undaunted by the great distance or by the journey over mountains and streams, we are willing to become bond brothers with you." Xuanzang touched his forehead to the ground to express his gratitude. Being indeed a righteous man, the Tang emperor went at once before Buddha's image in the temple and bowed to Xuanzang four times, addressing him as "our brother and holy monk."

Deeply moved, Xuanzang said, "Your Majesty, what ability and what virtue does your poor monk possess that he should merit such affection from your Heavenly Grace? I shall not spare myself in this journey, but I shall proceed with all diligence until I reach the Western Heaven. If I do not attain my goal, or the true scriptures, I shall not return to our land even if I have to die. I would rather fall into eternal perdition in Hell." He thereupon lifted the incense before Buddha and made that his vow. Highly pleased, the Tang emperor ordered his carriage back to the palace to wait for the auspicious day and hour, when official documents could be issued for the journey to begin. And so the Throne withdrew as everyone dispersed.

Xuanzang also went back to the Temple of Great Blessing. The many monks of that temple and his several disciples, who had heard about the quest for the scriptures, all came to see him. They asked, "Is it true that you have vowed to go to the Western Heaven?" "It is," said Xuanzang. "O Master," one of his disciples said, "I have heard people say that the way to the Western Heaven is long, filled with tigers, leopards, and all kinds of monsters. I fear that there will be departure but no return for you, as it will be difficult to safeguard your life."

"I have already made a great vow and a profound promise," said Xuanzang, "that if I do not acquire the true scriptures, I shall fall into eternal perdition in Hell. Since I have received such grace and favor from the king, I have no alternative but to serve my country to the utmost of my loyalty. It is true, of course, that I have no knowledge of how I shall fare on this journey or whether good or evil awaits me." He said to them again, "My disciples, after I leave, wait for two or three years, or six or seven years. If you see the branches of the pine trees within our gate pointing eastward, you will know that I am about to return. If not, I shall not be coming back." The disciples all committed his words firmly to memory.

The next morning Taizong held court and gathered all the officials together. They wrote up the formal rescript stating the intent to acquire scriptures and stamped it with the seal of free passage. The President of the Imperial Board of Astronomy then came with the report, "Today the positions of the planets are especially favorable for men to make a journey of great length." The Tang emperor was most delighted. Thereafter the Custodian of the Yellow Gate also made a report, saying, "The Master of the Law awaits your pleasure outside the court." The emperor summoned him up to the treasure hall and said, "Royal Brother, today is an auspicious day for the journey, and your rescript for free passage is ready. We also present you with a bowl made of purple gold for you to collect alms on your way. Two attendants have been selected to accompany you, and a horse will be your means of travel. You may begin your journey at once."

Highly pleased, Xuanzang expressed his gratitude and received his gifts, not displaying the least desire to linger. The Tang emperor called for his carriage and led many officials outside the city gate to see him off. The monks in the Temple of Great Blessing and the disciples were already waiting there with Xuanzang's winter and summer clothing. When the emperor saw them, he ordered the bags to be packed on the horses first, and then asked an officer to bring a pitcher of wine. Taizong lifted his cup to toast the pilgrim, saying, "What is the byname of our Royal Brother?" "Your poor monk," said Xuanzang, "is a person who has left the family. He dares not assume a byname." "The Bodhisattva said earlier," said Taizong, "that there were three collections of scriptures in the Western Heaven. Our Brother can take that as a byname and call himself Tripitaka. How about it?" Thanking him, Xuanzang accepted the wine and said, "Your Majesty, wine is the first prohibition of priesthood. Your poor monk has practiced abstinence since birth." "Today's journey," said Taizong, "is not to be compared with any ordinary event. Please drink one cup of this dietary wine, and accept our good wishes that go along with the toast." Xuanzang dared not refuse; he took the wine and was about to drink, when he saw Taizong stoop down to scoop up a handful of dirt with his fingers and sprinkle it in the wine. Tripitaka had no idea what this gesture meant.

"Dear Brother," said Taizong, laughing, "how long will it take you to come back from this trip to the Western Heaven?" "Probably in three years time," said Tripitaka, "I'll be returning to our noble nation." "The years are long and the journey is great," said Taizong. "Drink this, Royal Brother, and remember:

Treasure a handful of dirt from your home,
But love not ten thousand taels of foreign gold."

Then Tripitaka understood the meaning of the handful of dirt sprinkled in his cup; he thanked the emperor once more and drained the cup. He went out of the gate and left, as the Tang emperor returned in his carriage. We do not know what will happen to him on this journey; let's listen to the explanation in the next chapter.

THIRTEEN

In the den of tigers, the Gold Star brings deliverance;
At Double-Fork Ridge, Boqin detains the monk.

The rich Tang ruler issued a decree,
Deputing Xuanzang to seek the source of Chan.
He bent his mind to find the Dragon Den,
With firm resolve to climb the Vulture Peak.[1]
Through how many states did he roam beyond his own?
Through clouds and hills he passed ten thousand times.
He now leaves the throne to go to the West;
He'll keep law and faith to reach the Great Void.

We shall now tell you about Tripitaka, who, on the third day before the fifteenth of the ninth month in the thirteenth year of the period Zhenguan, was sent off by the Tang emperor and many officials from outside the gate of Chang'an. For a couple of days his horse trotted without ceasing, and soon they reached the Temple of the Law Gate. The abbot of that temple led some five hundred monks on both sides to receive him and took him inside. As they met, tea was served, after which a vegetarian meal was presented. Soon after the meal, dusk fell, and thus

Shadows moved to the Star River's nearing pulse;
The moon was bright without a speck of dust.
The wild geese called from the distant sky,
And washing flails beat from nearby homes.
As birds returned to perch on withered trees,
The Chan monks conversed in their Sanskrit tones.
On rush mats placed upon a single bunk,
They sat until halfway through the night.

Beneath the lamps the various monks discussed Buddhist doctrines and the purpose of seeking scriptures in the Western Heaven. Some pointed out that the waters were wide and the mountains very high; others mentioned that the roads were crowded with tigers and leopards; still others maintained that the precipitous peaks were difficult to scale; and another group insisted that the vicious monsters were hard to subdue. Tripitaka, however, kept his mouth shut tightly, but he pointed with his finger to his own heart and nodded his head several times. Not perceiving what he meant, the various monks folded their hands and asked, "Why did the Master of the Law point to his heart and nod his head?"

"When the mind is active," Tripitaka replied, "all kinds of *māra* come into existence; when the mind is extinguished, all kinds of *māra* will be extinguished. This disciple has already made an important vow before Buddha in the Temple of Transformation, and he has no alternative but to fulfill it with his whole heart. If I go, I shall not turn aside until I have reached the Western Heaven, seen Buddha, and acquired the scriptures so that the Wheel of the Law will be turned to us[2] and the kingdom of our lord will be secured forever." When the various monks heard this statement, everyone congratulated and commended him, saying, "A loyal and valiant master!" They praised him unceasingly as they escorted him to bed.

Soon

The bamboos struck down the setting moon[3]
And the cocks crowed to gather the clouds of dawn.

The various monks arose and prepared some tea and the morning meal. Xuanzang put on his cassock and went to worship Buddha in the main hall. "Your disciple, Chen Xuanzang," he said, "is on his way to seek scriptures in the Western Heaven. But my fleshly eyes are dim and unperceptive and do not recognize the true form of the living Buddha. Now I wish to make a vow: that throughout this journey I shall burn incense whenever I come upon a temple, I shall worship Buddha whenever I meet a Buddha, and I shall sweep a pagoda whenever I reach a pagoda. May our Buddha be merciful and soon reveal to me his Diamond Body sixteen feet tall. May he grant me the true scriptures so that they may be preserved in the Land of the East."

He finished his prayer and went back to the hall for the vegetarian meal, after which his two attendants made ready the saddle and urged him to begin his journey. Going out of the temple's gate, Tripitaka took leave of the monks, who grieved to see him go. They accompanied him for ten miles before turning back, tears in their eyes, as Tripitaka proceeded directly toward the West. It was the time of late autumn. You see

Trees growing bare in hamlets as rush petals break;
From every maple column the red leaves fall.
Trekkers through paths of mist and rain are few.
The fair chrysanthemums,
The sharp mountain rocks,
Cold streams and cracked lilies all make one sad.

Snow falls from a frosty sky on rushes and reeds.
One duck at dusk descends in the distant void.
Clouds o'er the wilds move through the gathering gloom.

The swallows depart;
The wild geese appear—
Their cries, though loud, are halting and forlorn.[4]

After traveling for several days, master and disciples arrived at the city of Gongzhou. They were met at once by the various municipal officials of that city, where they spent the night. The next morning they set off again, taking food and drink along the way, resting by night and journeying by day. In two or three days, they arrived at the District of Hezhou, which formed the border of the Great Tang Empire. When the garrison commander of the border as well as the local monks and priests heard that the Master of the Law, a bond brother of the emperor, was on his way to the Western Heaven to see Buddha by royal commission, they received the travelers with due reverence. Some chief priests then invited them to spend the night at Fuyuan Temple, where every resident cleric came to pay respect to the pilgrims. Dinner was served, after which the two attendants were told to feed the horses well, for the Master wanted to leave before dawn. At the first crowing of the cock, he called for his attendants and aroused the monks of that temple. They hastened to prepare tea and breakfast, after which the pilgrims departed from the border.

Because he was somewhat impatient to get going, the Master arose a trifle too early. The fact is that this was late autumn, when cocks crow rather early—at about the time of the fourth watch. Facing the clear frost and the bright moon, the three of them (the horse made up the fourth member of the team) journeyed for some twenty or thirty miles, when they came upon a mountain range. It soon became exceedingly difficult for them to find their way. As they had to poke around in the grass to look for a path, they began to worry that they might be heading in the wrong direction. In that very anxious moment, they suddenly tripped; all three of them as well as the horse tumbled into a deep pit. Tripitaka was terrified; his companions all shook with fear. They were still trembling when they heard voices shouting, "Seize them! Seize them!" A violent wind swept by, and a mob of fifty or sixty ogres appeared, who seized Tripitaka with his companions and hauled them out of the pit. Quivering and shivering, the Master of the Law stole a glance around and saw a ferocious Monster King seated up on high. Truly he had

A figure most awesomely bold,
A face most distinctly fierce.
Light flashed from his lightninglike eyes;
All quaked at his thunderous voice.
His sawlike teeth jutted outward,
Like fangs they emerged from his jaws.

Brocade wrapped his body around,
And coiling stripes covered his spine.
They saw flesh through sparse, steely whiskers.
Keen-edged were his claws like sharp swords.
Even Huang Gong of East Sea would fear[5]
This white-browed King of Mount South.

Tripitaka was so frightened that his spirit left him, while the bones of his followers grew weak and their tendons turned numb.

The Monster King shouted for them to be bound, and the various ogres tied up all three of them with ropes. They were being prepared to be eaten when a clamor was heard outside the camp. Someone came in to report: "The Bear Mountain Lord and the Steer Hermit have arrived." Hearing this, Tripitaka looked up. The first one to come in was a swarthy fellow. "How did he look?" you ask.

He seemed valiant and courageous,
With body both tough and brawny.
His great strength could ford the waters.
He prowled the woods, flaunting his power.
Ever a good omen in dreams,[6]
He showed now his forceful features.
He could break or climb the green trees,
And predicted when winter was near.
Truly he was most clever.
Hence Mountain Lord was his name.

Following behind him was another husky fellow. "How did he look?" you ask.

A cap of twin horns rugged,
And a humpback most majestic.
His green robe showed his calm nature,
He walked with a slumberous gait.
He came from a father named Bull;
His mother's proper name was Cow.
A great boon to people who plowed,
He was thus called the Steer Hermit.

The two of them swaggered in, and the Monster King hurried out to receive them. The Bear Mountain Lord said, "You are in top form, General Yin. Congratulations! Congratulations!" "General Yin looks better than ever," said the Steer Hermit. "It's marvelous! It's marvelous!" "And you two gentlemen, how have you been these days?" asked the Monster King. "Just maintaining my idleness," said the Mountain Lord. "Just keeping up with the times," said the Hermit. After these exchanges, they sat down to chat some more.

Meanwhile, one of Tripitaka's attendants was bound so tightly that he began to moan pitifully. "How did these three get here?" asked the swarthy fellow. "They practically presented themselves at the door!" said the Monster King. "Can they be used for the guests' dinner?" asked the Hermit, laughing. "By all means!" said the Monster King. "Let's not finish them all up," said the Mountain Lord. "We'll dine on two of them and leave one over." The Monster King agreed. He called his subordinates at once to have the attendants eviscerated and their carcasses carved up; their heads, hearts, and livers were to be presented to the guests, the limbs to the host, and the remaining portions of flesh and bone to the rest of the ogres. The moment the order was given, the ogres pounced on the attendants like tigers preying on sheep: munching and crunching, they devoured them in no time at all. The priest nearly died of fear, for this, you see, was his first bitter ordeal since his departure from Chang'an.

As he was nursing his horror, light began to grow in the east. The two monsters did not retire until dawn. Saying, "We're beholden to your generous hospitality today. Permit us to repay in kind in another time," they left together. Soon the sun rose high in the sky, but Tripitaka was still in a stupor, unable to discern which way was north, south, east, or west. In that half-dead condition, he suddenly saw an old man approaching, holding a staff in his hands. Walking up to Tripitaka, the man waved his hands and all the ropes snapped. He then blew on Tripitaka, and the monk began to revive. Falling on the ground, he said, "I thank the aged father for saving the life of this poor monk!" "Get up," the old man said, returning his salute, "have you lost anything?"

"The followers of your poor monk," said Tripitaka, "have been eaten by the monsters. I have no idea where my horse is or my luggage." "Isn't that your horse over there with the two bundles?" asked the old man, pointing with his staff. Tripitaka turned around and discovered that his belongings had indeed remained untouched. Somewhat relieved, he asked the old man, "Aged father, what is this place? How do you happen to be here?" "It is called the Double-Fork Ridge, a place infested with tigers and wolves. How did you manage to get here?" "At the first crow of the cock," said Tripitaka, "your poor monk left the District of Hezhou. Little did I realize that we had risen too early, and we lost our way tramping through fog and dew. We came upon this Monster King so exceedingly ferocious that he captured me and my two followers. There was also a swarthy fellow called the Bear Mountain Lord and a husky fellow called the Steer Hermit. They arrived and addressed the Monster King as General Yin. All three of them devoured my two followers and retired only at dawn. I have no idea where I accrued the fortune and merit that caused the aged father to rescue me here."

"That Steer Hermit," said the old man, "is a wild bull spirit; the Mountain Lord, a bear spirit; and General Yin, a tiger spirit. The various ogres are all demons of mountains and trees, spirits of strange beasts and wolves. Because of the primal purity of your nature, they cannot devour you. Follow me now, and I shall lead you on your way." Tripitaka could not be more thankful. Fastening the bundles on the saddle and leading his horse, he followed the old man out of the pit and walked toward the main road. He tied the horse to the bushes beside the path and turned to thank the aged father. At that moment a gentle breeze swept by, and the old man rose into the air and left, riding on a white crane with a crimson head. As the wind subsided, a slip of paper fluttered down, with four lines of verse written on it:

> I am the Planet Venus from the West,
> Who came to save you by special request,
> Some pupils divine will come to your aid.
> Blame not the scriptures for hardships ahead.

When Tripitaka read this, he bowed toward the sky saying, "I thank the Gold Star for seeing me through this ordeal." After that, he led his horse off again on his lonely and melancholy journey.

On this ridge truly you have

> Cold and soughing, the wind of the rainforest;
> Purling and gurgling, the water of the brooklets;
> Fragrant and musky, wild flowers in bloom;
> In clutters and clumps, rough rocks piled high;
> Chattering and clattering, the apes and the deer;
> In rank and file, the musk and the fallow deer.
> Chirping and cooing, birds frequently call.
> Silent and still, not one man is in sight.
> That master
> Shivers and quivers to his anxious mind.
> This dear horse,
> Scared and nervous, can barely raise his legs.

Ready to abandon his body and sacrifice his life, Tripitaka started up that rugged mountain. He journeyed for half a day, but not a single human being or dwelling was in sight. He was gnawed by hunger and disheartened by the rough road. In that desperate moment, he saw two fierce tigers growling in front of him and several huge snakes circling behind him; vicious creatures appeared on his left and strange beasts on his right. As he was all by himself, Tripitaka had little alternative but to submit himself to the will of Heaven. As if to complete his helplessness, his horse's back was sagging and its legs were buckling; it went to its knees and soon lay prostrate on the ground. He could budge it neither by beating nor by tugging. With hardly an inch of space to stand on, our Master of the Law was in the depths of despair, thinking that certain death would be his fate. We can tell you, however, that though he was in danger, help was on its way. For just as he thought he was about to expire, the vicious creatures began to scatter and the monstrous beasts fled; the fierce tigers vanished and the huge snakes disappeared. When Tripitaka looked further ahead, he saw a man coming over the mountain slope with a steel trident in his hands and bow and arrows at his waist. He was indeed a valiant figure! Look at him:

He had on his head a cap
Of leopard skin, spotted and artemisia white;
He wore on his body a robe
Of lamb's wool with dark silk brocade.
Around his waist was tied a lion king belt,[7]
And on his feet he wore tall boots of suede.
His eyes would bulge like those of someone hung.
His beard curled wildly like a fierce god's!
A bow and poisoned arrows hung on him.
He held a huge trident of finest steel.
His voice like thunder appalled mountain cats,
And wild pheasants quaked at his truculence.

When Tripitaka saw him draw near, he knelt at the side of the path and called out, his hands clasped in front of him, "Great king, save me! Great king, save me!" The fellow came up to Tripitaka and put down his trident. Raising up the monk with his hands, he said, "Don't be afraid, Elder, for I'm not a wicked man. I'm a hunter living in this mountain; my surname is Liu and my given name is Boqin. I also go by the nickname of Senior Guardian of the Mountain. I came here to find some animals to eat, not expecting to run into you. I hope I didn't scare you."

"Your poor monk," said Tripitaka, "is a cleric who has been sent by his Majesty, the Tang emperor, to seek scriptures from Buddha in the Western Heaven. When I arrived here a few moments ago, I was surrounded by tigers, wolves, and snakes, so that I could not proceed. But when the creatures saw you coming they all scattered, and you have thus saved my life. Many thanks! Many thanks!" "Since I live here and my livelihood depends on killing a few tigers and wolves," said Boqin, "or catching a few snakes and reptiles, I usually frighten the wild beasts away. If you have come from the Tang empire, you are actually a native here, for this is still Tang territory and I am a Tang subject. You and I both live off the land belonging to the emperor so that we are in truth citizens of the same nation. Don't be afraid. Follow me. You may rest your horse at my place, and I shall see you off in the morning." Tripitaka was filled with delight when he heard these words, and he led his horse to follow the hunter.

They passed the slope and again heard the howling of the wind. "Sit here, Elder," said Boqin, "and don't move. The sound of that wind tells me that a mountain cat is approaching. I'll take him home so that I can make a meal of him for you." When Tripitaka heard this, his heart hammered and his gall quivered and he became rooted to the ground. Grasping his trident, that Guardian strode forward and came face to face with a great striped tiger. Seeing Boqin, he turned and fled. Like a crack of thunder, the Guardian bellowed, "Cursed beast! Where will you flee?" When the tiger saw him pressing near, he turned with flailing claws to spring at him, only to be met by the Guardian with uplifted trident. Tripitaka was so terrified that he lay paralyzed on the grass. Since leaving his mother's belly, when had he ever witnessed such violent and dangerous goings-on? The Guardian went after that tiger to the foot of the slope, and it was a magnificent battle between man and beast. You see

> Raging resentment,
> And churning whirlwind.
> In raging resentment
> The potent Guardian's hair pushed up his cap;
> Like churning whirlwind
> The striped prince belched dust, displaying his might.
> This one bared its teeth and wielded its paws;
> That one stepped sideways, yet turning to fight.
> The trident reached skyward, reflecting the sun.
> The striped tail stirred up both fog and cloud.
> This one stabbed madly at the breast of his foe;
> That one, facing him would swallow him whole.
> Stay away and you may live out your years.
> Join the fray and you'll meet Yama, the king!
> You hear the roar of the striped prince
> And the harsh cries of the Guardian.
> The roar of the striped prince
> Shook mountains and streams to frighten birds and beasts;
> The harsh cries of the Guardian
> Unlocked the Heavens to make the stars appear.
> The gold eyeballs of this one protruded,
> And wrath burst from the bold heart of that one.
> Lovable was Liu the Mountain Guardian;

Praiseworthy was this king of the wild beasts.
So tiger and man fought, each craving life—
A little slower, and one forfeits his soul!

The two of them fought for about an hour, and as the paws of the tiger began to slow and his torso to slacken, he was downed by the Guardian's trident stabbing him through the chest. A pitiful sight it was! The points of the trident pierced the heart, and at once the ground was covered with blood.

The Guardian then dragged the beast by the ear up the road. What a man! He hardly panted, nor did his face change color. He said to Tripitaka, "We're lucky! We're lucky! This mountain cat should be sufficient for a day's food for the elder." Applauding him unceasingly, Tripitaka said, "The Guardian is truly a mountain god!" "What ability do I have," said Boqin, "that I merit such acclaim? This is really the good fortune of the father. Let's go. I'd like to skin him quickly so that I can cook some of his meat to entertain you." He held the trident in one hand and dragged the tiger with the other, leading the way while Tripitaka followed him with his horse. They walked together past the slope and all at once came upon a mountain village, in front of which were

Old trees soaring skyward,
Roads filled with wild creepers.
In countless canyons the wind was cool;
On many ridges came strange sounds and sights.
One path's wild blooms, their scent clung to one's body;
A few poles of bamboo, what enduring green!
The portal of grass,
The wattle-fenced yard—
A picture to paint or sketch.
The stone-slab bridge,
The white-earth walls—
How charming indeed, and rare!
Now in the wistful face of autumn,
The air was cool and brisk,
By the wayside yellow leaves fell;
Over the peaks the white clouds drifted.
In thinly-grown woods the wild fowls twittered,
And young dogs yelped outside the village gate.

When Boqin reached the door of his house, he threw down the dead tiger and called, "Little ones, where are you?" Out came three or four houseboys, all looking rather unattractive and mean, who hauled the tiger inside. Boqin told them to skin it quickly and prepare it for the guest. He then turned around to welcome Tripitaka into his dwelling, and as they greeted each other, Tripitaka thanked him again for the great favor of saving his life. "We are fellow countrymen," said Boqin, "and there's little need for you to thank me." After they had sat down and drunk tea, an old woman with someone who appeared to be her daughter-in-law came out to greet Tripitaka. "This is my mother, and this my wife," said Boqin. "Pray ask your parent to take the honored seat," said Tripitaka, "and let your poor monk pay his respects." "Father is a guest coming from great distance," said the old woman. "Please relax and don't stand on ceremony." "Mother," said Boqin, "he has been sent by the Tang emperor to seek scriptures from Buddha in the Western Heaven. He met your son just now at the ridge. Since we are fellow countrymen, I invited him to the house to rest his horse. Tomorrow I shall see him on his way."

When she heard these words, the old woman was very pleased. "Good! Good! Good!" she said. "The timing couldn't be better, even if we had planned to invite him. For tomorrow happens to be the anniversary of your late father's death. Let us invite the elder to perform some good deeds and recite an appropriate passage of scripture. We shall see him off day after tomorrow." Although he was a tiger slayer, a so-called "Guardian of the Mountain," our Liu Boqin had a good deal of filial feeling for his mother. When he heard what she said, he immediately wanted to prepare the incense and the paper money, so that Tripitaka might be asked to stay.

As they talked, the sky began to darken. The servants brought chairs and a table and set out several dishes of well-cooked tiger meat, steaming hot. Boqin invited Tripitaka to begin, telling him that rice would follow. "O dear!" said Tripitaka, his hands folded. "To tell you the truth, I have been a monk since leaving my mother's womb, and I have never eaten any meat." Hearing this, Boqin reflected awhile. He then said, "Elder, for generations this humble family has never kept a vegetarian diet. We could, I suppose, find some bamboo shoots and wood ears and prepare some dried vegetables and bean cakes, but they would all be cooked with the fat of deer or tigers. Even our pots and pans are grease-soaked! What am I to do? I must ask the elder's pardon." "Don't fret," said Tripitaka. "Enjoy the food yourself. Even if I were not to eat for three or four days, I could bear the hunger. But I dare not break the dietary commandment." "Suppose you starve to death," said Boqin, "what then?" "I am indebted to the Heavenly kindness of the Guardian," said Tripitaka, "for saving me from the packs of tigers and wolves. Starving to death is better than being food for a tiger."

When Boqin's mother heard this, she cried, "Son, stop such idle talk with the elder. Let me prepare a vegetarian dish to serve him." "Where would you get such a dish?" said Boqin. "Never mind. I'll fix it," said his mother. She asked her daughter-in-law to take down a small cooking pan and heat it until much of the grease had burned off. They washed and scrubbed the pan again and again and then put it back on the stove and boiled some water in it. Taking some elm leaves from the mountain, they made soup with it, after which they cooked some rice with yellow millet mixed with Indian corn. They also prepared two bowls of dried vegetables and brought it all out to the table. "Elder," the aged mother said to Tripitaka, "please have some. This is the cleanest and purest food that my daughter-in-law and I have ever prepared." Tripitaka left his seat to thank her before sitting down again. Boqin removed himself to another place; dishes and bowls full of unsauced and unsalted tiger meat, musk deer meat, serpent meat, fox flesh, rabbit, and strips of cured venison were set before him. To keep Tripitaka company, he sat down and was about to pick up his chopsticks when he saw Tripitaka fold his hands and begin to recite something. Startled, Boqin dared not touch his chopsticks; he jumped up instead and stood to one side. Having uttered no more than a few phrases, Tripitaka said to him, "Please eat." "You are a priest who likes to recite short scriptures," said Boqin. "That was not scripture," said Tripitaka, "only a prayer to be said before meals." "You people who leave your families," said Boqin, "are particular about everything! Even for a meal you have to mumble something!"

They ate their dinner and the dishes and bowls were taken away. Evening was setting in when Boqin led Tripitaka out of the main hall to go for a walk at the back of the dwelling. They passed through a corridor and arrived at a straw shed. Pushing open the door, they walked inside, where they found several heavy bows and some quivers of arrows hanging on the walls. Two pieces of tiger skin, stinking and bloodstained, were draped over the cross beams, and a number of spears, knives, tridents, and rods were stuck into the ground at one corner. There were two seats in the middle of the shed, and Boqin invited Tripitaka to sit for a moment. Seeing that the place was so gruesome and putrid, Tripitaka dared not linger. They soon left the shed and walked further back to a huge garden, where there seemed to be no end of thick clumps of chrysanthemum piling their gold and stands of maple hoisting their crimson. With a loud rustle, more than a dozen fat deer and a large herd of musk deer jumped out. Calm and mild-mannered, they were not at all frightened at the sight of human beings. Tripitaka said, "You must have tamed these animals." "Like the people in your city of Chang'an," said Boqin, "where the affluent store up wealth and treasures and the landlords gather rice and grain, so we hunters must keep some of these wild beasts to prepare against dark days. That's all!" As they walked and conversed, it grew dark, and they returned to the house to rest.

As soon as the members of the family, young and old, arose next morning, they went to prepare vegetarian food to serve to the priest, who was then asked to begin his recitations. Having first washed his hands, the priest went to the ancestral hall with the Guardian to burn incense. Only after he had bowed to the house shrine did Tripitaka beat on his wooden fish and recite first the true sentences for the purification of the mouth, and then the divine formula for the purification of mind and body. He went on to the *Sūtra for the Salvation of the Dead*, after which Boqin requested him to compose in writing a specific prayer for the deliverance of the deceased. He then took up the *Diamond Sūtra* and the *Guanyin Sūtra*, each of which was given a loud and clear recitation. After lunch, he recited several sections from the *Lotus Sūtra* and the *Amitāyus Sūtra*, before finishing with the *Peacock Sūtra* and a brief recounting of the story of Buddha healing a bhikṣu.[8] Soon it was evening again. All kinds of incense were burned together with the various paper horses, images of the deities, and the prayer for the deliverance of the deceased. The Buddhist service was thus completed, and each person retired.

We shall now tell you about the soul of Boqin's father, verily a ghost redeemed from perdition, who came to his own house and appeared to all the members of his family in a dream. "It was difficult," he said, "for me to escape my bitter ordeals in the Region of Darkness, and for a long time I could not attain salvation. Fortunately, the holy monk's recitations have now expiated my sins. King Yama has ordered someone to send me to the rich land of China, where I may assume my next incarnation in a noble family. All of you, therefore, must take care to thank the elder, and see that you are not negligent in any way. Now I leave you." So it is that

> There is, in all things, a solemn purpose:
> To save the dead from perdition and pain.

When the whole family awoke from the dream, the sun was already rising in the east. The wife of Boqin said, "Guardian, I dreamed last night that father came to the house. He said that it was difficult for him to escape his bitter ordeals in the Region of Darkness, and that for a long time he could not attain salvation. Fortunately, the holy monk's recitations have now expiated his sins, and King Yama has ordered someone to send him to the rich land of China where he may assume his next incarnation in a noble family. He told us to take care to thank the elder and not be negligent in any way. After he had finished speaking, he drifted away, despite my plea for him to stay. I woke up and it was all a dream!"

"I had a dream also," said Boqin, "one exactly like yours! Let's get up and talk to mother about this." The two of them were about to do so when they heard the old mother calling, "Boqin, come here. I want to talk to you." They went in and found the mother sitting up in bed. "Son," she said, "I had a happy dream last night. I dreamed that your father came to the house saying that, thanks to the redemptive work of the elder, his sins had been expiated.

He is on his way to the rich land of China, where he will assume his next incarnation in a noble family." Husband and wife laughed uproariously.

Boqin said, "Your daughter-in-law and I both had this dream, and we were just coming to tell you. Little did we expect that mother's call also had to do with this dream." They therefore called on every member of the family to express their gratitude and prepare the monk's horse for travel. They came bowing before the priest and said, "We thank the elder for providing life and deliverance for our deceased father, for which we can never repay you sufficiently." "What has this poor monk accomplished," said Tripitaka, "that merits such gratitude?" Boqin gave a thorough account of the dream that the three of them had, and Tripitaka was also very pleased. A vegetarian meal was again served, and a tael of silver was presented as a token of their gratitude.

Tripitaka refused to accept so much as a penny, though the whole family begged him earnestly. He only said, "If, in compassion, you can escort me on the first part of my way, I shall ever be grateful for such kindness." Boqin and his mother and wife had little alternative but hastily to prepare some biscuits from unrefined flour, which Tripitaka was glad to accept. Boqin was told to escort him as far as possible. Obeying his mother's bidding, the Guardian also ordered several houseboys to join them, each bringing hunting equipment and weapons. They walked to the main road, and there seemed to be no end to the scenic splendor of the mountains and peaks.

When they had traveled for half a day, they came upon a huge mountain so tall and rugged that it truly seemed to touch the blue sky. In a little while the whole company reached the foot of the mountain, and the Guardian began to ascend it as if he were walking on level ground. Halfway up, Boqin turned around and stood still at the side of the road, saying, "Elder, please go on yourself. I must now take leave of you and turn back." When Tripitaka heard these words, he rolled down from his saddle and said, "I beg you to escort me a little further." "You do not realize, Elder," said Boqin, "that this mountain is called the Mountain of Two Frontiers; the eastern half belongs to our Great Tang domain, but the western half is the territory of the Tartars. The tigers and wolves over there are not my subjects, nor should I cross the border. You must proceed by yourself." Tripitaka became fearful; he stretched out his hands and clutched at the sleeves of the hunter, tears pouring from his eyes.

It was at this tender moment of farewell that there came from beneath the mountain a thunderous voice crying, "My master has come! My master has come!" Tripitaka was dumbfounded, and Boqin trembled. We do not know who was crying; let's listen to the explanation in the next chapter.

FOURTEEN

Mind Monkey returns to the Right;
The Six Robbers vanish from sight.[1]

Mind is the Buddha and the Buddha is Mind;
Both Mind and Buddha are important things.
If you perceive there's neither Mind nor Thing,
Yours is the dharmakāya of True Mind.
The dharmakāya
Has no shape or form:
One pearl-like radiance holding myriad things.
The bodiless body is the body true,
And real form is that form which has no form.
There's no form, no void, no no-emptiness;
No coming, no leaving, no pariṇāmanā;[2]
No contrast, no sameness, no being or nonbeing:
No giving, no taking, no hopeful craving.
Light efficacious is in and out the same.
Buddha's whole realm is in a grain of sand.
A grain of sand the chiliocosm holds;
One mind or body's like ten thousand things.
To know this you must grasp the No-mind Spell;
Unclogged and taintless is the karma pure.
Don't do the many acts of good or ill:
This is true submission to Śākyamuni.[3]

We were telling you about Tripitaka and Boqin, who, in fear and alarm, again heard the cry, "My Master has come!" The various houseboys said, "It must be the old ape in that stone box beneath the mountain who is shouting." "It's he! It's he!" said the Guardian. Tripitaka asked, "Who is this old ape?"

"The ancient name of this mountain," said the Guardian, "was the Mountain of Five Phases. It was changed to the Mountain of the Two Frontiers as a result of our Great Tang ruler's western campaigns to secure his empire. A few years ago, I heard from my elders that during the time when Wang Mang usurped the throne of the Han emperor,[4] this mountain fell from Heaven with a divine monkey clamped beneath it. He feared neither heat nor cold, and he took neither food nor drink. He had been watched and guarded by the spirits of the Earth, who fed him iron balls when he was hungry and juices of bronze when he was thirsty. He has lasted from that time until now, surviving both cold and hunger. He must be the one who is making all this noise. Don't be afraid, Elder. Let's go down the mountain to take a look."

Tripitaka had to agree and led his horse down the mountain. They had traveled only a few miles when they came upon a stone box in which there was indeed a monkey who, with his head sticking out, was waving his hands wildly and crying, "Master, why have you taken so long to get here? Welcome! Welcome! Get me out, and I'll protect you on your way to the Western Heaven!" The priest went forward to look more closely at him. "How does he look?" you ask.

A pointed mouth and hollow cheeks;
Two diamond pupils and fiery eyes.
Lichens had piled on his head;
Wisteria grew in his ears.
By his temples was more green grass than hair;
Beneath his chin, moss instead of a beard.
With mud on his brow,
And earth in his nose,
He looked most desperate!
His fingers coarse
And calloused palms
Were caked in filth and dirt!
Luckily, his eyes could still roll about,
And the apish tongue, articulate.
Though in speech he had great ease,
His body he could not move.
He was the Great Sage Sun of five hundred years ago.
Today his ordeal ends, he leaves Heaven's net.

Undeniably a courageous person, that Guardian Liu went up to the creature and pulled away some of the grass at his temples and some of the moss beneath his chin. He asked, "What do you have to say?" "Nothing to you," said the monkey, "but ask that master to come up here. I have a question for him."

"What's your question?" asked Tripitaka. "Are you someone sent by the great king of the Land of the East to go seek scriptures in the Western Heaven?" asked the monkey. "I am," said Tripitaka. "Why do you ask?"

"I am the Great Sage, Equal to Heaven," said the monkey, "who greatly disturbed the Heavenly Palace five hundred years ago. Because of my sin of rebellion and disobedience, I was imprisoned here by the Buddha. Some time ago, a certain Bodhisattva Guanyin had received the decree of Buddha to go to the Land of the East in quest of a scripture pilgrim. I asked her to give me some help, and she persuaded me not to engage again in violence. I was told to believe in the Law of Buddha and faithfully to protect the scripture pilgrim on his way to worship Buddha in the West, for there would be a goodly reward reserved for me when such merit is achieved. I have therefore been maintaining my vigilance night and day, waiting for the Master to come to rescue me. I'm willing to protect you in your quest of scriptures and become your disciple."

When Tripitaka heard these words, he was filled with delight and said, "Though you have this good intention, thanks to the Bodhisattva's instruction, of entering our Buddhist fold, I have neither ax nor drill. How can I free you?" "No need for ax or drill," said the monkey. "If you are willing to rescue me, I'll be able to get out." Tripitaka said, "I'm willing, but how can you get out?" "On top of this mountain," said the monkey, "there is a tag stamped with the golden letters of our Buddha Tathāgata. Go up there and lift up the tag. Then I'll come out." Tripitaka agreed and turned to Boqin, imploring him, "Guardian, come with me up the mountain." "Do you think he's speaking the truth?" asked Boqin. "It's the truth!" the monkey shouted. "I dare not lie!"

Boqin had no choice but to call his houseboys to lead the horses. He himself supported Tripitaka with his hands, and they again started up the tall mountain. Tugging at creepers and vines, they finally arrived at the highest peak, where they beheld ten thousand shafts of golden light and a thousand folds of hallowed air. There was a huge square slab of stone, on which was taped a seal with the golden letters, *Oṁ maṇi padme hūṁ*. Tripitaka approached the stone and knelt down; he looked at the golden letters and kowtowed several times to the stone. Then, facing the West, he prayed: "Your disciple, Chen Xuanzang, was specifically commanded to seek scriptures from you. If it is so ordained that he should be my disciple, let me lift up those golden letters so that the divine monkey may find release and join me at the Spirit Mountain. If he is not predestined to be my disciple, if he is only a cruel monster trying to deceive me and to bring misfortune to our enterprise, let me not lift up this tape." He kowtowed again after he had prayed. Going forward, with the greatest of ease he took down the golden letters. A fragrant wind swept by immediately and blew the tag out of his hands into the air as a voice called out, "I am the prison guard of the Great Sage. Today his ordeal is completed, and my colleagues and I are returning this seal to Tathāgata." Tripitaka, Boqin, and their followers were so terrified that they fell on the ground and bowed toward the sky. They then descended from the tall mountain and came back to the stone box, saying to the monkey, "The tag has been lifted. You may come out." Delighted, the monkey said, "Master, you had better walk away from here so that I can come out. I don't want to frighten you."

When Boqin heard this, he led Tripitaka and the rest of the company to walk back eastward for five or six miles. Again they heard the monkey yelling, "Further still! Further still!" So Tripitaka and the others went still further until they had left the mountain. All at once came a crash so loud that it was as if the mountain was cracking and the earth splitting wide open; everyone was awestruck. The next moment the monkey was already in front of Tripitaka's horse; completely naked, he knelt down and cried, "Master, I'm out!" He bowed four times toward Tripitaka, and then, jumping up, he said to Boqin respectfully, "I thank Elder Brother for taking the trouble of escorting my master. I'm grateful also for your shaving the grass from my face." Having thanked him, he went at once to put the luggage in order so that it could be tied onto the horse's back. When the horse saw him, its torso slackened and its legs stiffened. In fear and trembling, it could hardly stand up. For you see, that monkey had been a BanHorsePlague, who used to look after dragon horses in the celestial stables. His authority was such that horses of this world inevitably would fear him when they saw him.

When Tripitaka saw that the monkey was truly a person of good intentions, someone who truly resembled those who had embraced the Buddhist faith, he called to him, "Disciple, what is your surname?" "My surname is Sun," said the Monkey King. "Let me give you a religious name," said Tripitaka, "so that it will be convenient to address you." "This noble thought of the master is deeply appreciated," said the Monkey King, "but I already have a religious name. I'm called Sun Wukong." "It exactly fits the emphasis of our denomination," said Tripitaka, delighted. "But look at you, you look rather like a little *dhūta*.[5] Let me give you a nickname and call you Pilgrim Sun.[6] How's that?" "Good! Good!" said Wukong. So from then on, he was also called Pilgrim Sun.

When Boqin saw that Pilgrim Sun was definitely preparing to leave, he turned to speak respectfully to Tripitaka, saying, "Elder, you are fortunate to have made an excellent disciple here. Congratulations! This person should be most fit to accompany you. I must take leave of you now." Bowing to thank him, Tripitaka said, "I cannot thank you enough for all your kindness. Please be certain to thank your dear mother and wife when you return to your house. I have caused you all great inconvenience, and I shall thank you again on my way back." Boqin returned his salutation, and they parted.

We shall now tell you about Pilgrim Sun, who asked Tripitaka to mount his horse. He himself, stark naked, carried the luggage on his back and led the way. In a little while, as they were passing the Mountain of Two Frontiers, they saw a fierce tiger approaching, growling and waving its tail. Tripitaka, sitting on his horse, became alarmed, but Pilgrim, walking at the side of the road, was delighted. "Don't be afraid, Master," he said, "for he's here to present me with some clothes." He put down the luggage and took a tiny needle out of his ears. One wave of it facing the wind, and it became an iron rod with the thickness of a rice bowl. He held it in his hands and laughed, saying, "I haven't used this treasure for over five hundred years! Today I'm taking it out to bag a little garment for myself." Look at him! He strode right up to the tiger, crying, "Cursed beast! Where do you think you're going?" Crouching low, the tiger lay prone on the dust and dared not move. Pilgrim Sun aimed the rod at its head, and one stroke caused its brain to burst out like ten thousand red petals of peach blossoms, and the teeth to fly out like so many pieces of white jade. So terrified was our Chen Xuanzang that he fell off his horse. "O God! O God!" he cried, biting his fingers. "When Guardian Liu overcame that striped tiger the other day, he had to do battle with him for almost half a day. But without even fighting today, Sun Wukong reduces the tiger to pulp with one blow of his rod. How true is the saying, 'For the strong, there's always someone stronger!'"

"Master," said Pilgrim as he returned dragging the tiger, "sit down for awhile, and wait till I have stripped him of his clothes. When I put them on, we'll start off again." "Where does he have any clothes?" asked Tripitaka. "Don't mind me, Master," said Pilgrim, "I have my own plan." Dear Monkey King! He pulled off one strand of hair and blew a mouthful of magic breath onto it, crying, "Change!" It changed into a sharp, curved knife, with which he ripped open the tiger's chest. Slitting the skin straight down, he then ripped it off in one piece. He chopped away the paws and the head, cutting the skin into one square piece. He picked it up and tried it for size, and then said, "It's a bit too large; one piece can be made into two." He took the knife and cut it again into two pieces; he put one of these away and wrapped the other around his waist. Ripping off a strand of rattan from the side of the road, he firmly tied on this covering for the lower part of his body. "Master," he said, "let's go! Let's go! When we reach someone's house, we will have sufficient time to borrow some threads and a needle to sew this up." He gave his iron rod a squeeze and it changed back into a tiny needle, which he stored in his ear. Throwing the luggage on his back, he asked his Master to mount the horse.

As they set off, the monk asked him, "Wukong, how is it that the iron rod you used to slay the tiger has disappeared?" "Master," said Pilgrim laughing, "you have no idea what that rod of mine really is. It was acquired originally from the Dragon Palace in the Eastern Ocean. It's called the Precious Divine Iron for Guarding the Heavenly River, and another name of it is the Compliant Golden-Hooped Rod. At the time when I revolted against Heaven, I depended on it a great deal; for it could change into any shape or form, great or small, according to my wish. Just now I had it changed into a tiny embroidery needle, and it's stored that way in my ear. When I need it, I'll take it out." Secretly pleased by what he heard, Tripitaka asked another question: "Why did that tiger become completely motionless when it saw you? How do you explain the fact that it simply let you hit it?" "To tell you the truth," said Wukong, "even a dragon, let alone this tiger, would behave itself if it had seen me! I, old Monkey, possess the ability to subdue dragons and tame tigers, and the power to overturn rivers and stir up oceans. I can look at a person's countenance and discern his character; I can listen merely to sounds and discover the truth. If I want to be big, I can fill the universe; if I want to be small, I can be smaller than a piece of hair. In sum, I have boundless ways of transformation and incalculable means of becoming visible or invisible. What's so strange, then, about my skinning a tiger? Wait till we come to some real difficulties—you'll see my talents then!" When Tripitaka heard these words, he was more relieved than ever and urged his horse forward. So master and disciple, the two of them, chatted as they journeyed, and soon the sun sank in the west. You see

Soft glow of the fading twilight,
And distant clouds slowly returning.
On every hill swells the chorus of birds,
Flocking to shelter in the woods.

The wild beasts in couples and pairs,
In packs and groups they trek homeward.
The new moon, hooklike, breaks the spreading gloom
With ten thousand stars luminous.[7]

Pilgrim said, "Master, let's move along, for it's getting late. There are dense clumps of trees over there, and I suppose there must be a house or village too. Let's hurry over there and ask for lodging." Urging his horse forward, Tripitaka went straight up to a house and dismounted. Pilgrim threw down the bag and went to the door, crying, "Open up! Open up!" An old man came to the door, leaning on a cane. When he pulled open the creaking door, he was panic-stricken by the hideous appearance of Pilgrim, who had the tiger skin around his waist and looked like a thunder god. He began to shout, "A ghost! A ghost!" and other such foolish words. Tripitaka drew near and took hold of him, saying, "Old Patron, don't be afraid. He is my disciple, not a ghost." Only when he looked up and saw the handsome features of Tripitaka did the old man stand still. "Which temple are you from," he asked, "and why are you bringing such a nasty character to my door?"

"I am a poor monk from the Tang court," said Tripitaka, "on my way to seek scriptures from Buddha in the Western Heaven. We were passing through here and it was getting late; that is why we made so bold as to approach your great mansion and beg you for a night's lodging. We plan to leave tomorrow before it's light, and we beseech you not to deny our request."

"Though you may be a Tang man," the old man said, "that nasty charac-ter is certainly no Tang man!" "Old fellow!" cried Wukong in a loud voice, "you really can't see, can you? The Tang man is my master, and I am his disciple. Of course, I'm no sugar man[8] or honey man! I am the Great Sage, Equal to Heaven! The members of your family should recognize me. More-over, I have seen you before."

"Where have you seen me before?" "When you were young," said Wu-kong, "didn't you gather firewood before my eyes? Didn't you haul vege-tables before my face?" The old man said, "That's nonsense! Where did you live? And where was I, that I should have gathered firewood and hauled veg-etables before your eyes?" "Only my son would talk nonsense!" said Wu-kong. "You really don't recognize me! Take a closer look! I am the Great Sage in the stone box of this Mountain of Two Frontiers." "You do look somewhat like him," said the old man, half recognizing the figure before him, "but how did you get out?" Wukong thereupon gave a thorough ac-count of how the Bodhisattva had converted him and how she had asked him to wait for the Tang Monk to lift the tag for his deliverance.

After that, the old man bowed deeply and invited Tripitaka in, call-ing for his aged wife and his children to come out and meet the guests. When he told them what had happened, everyone was delighted. Tea was then served, after which the old man asked Wukong, "How old are you, Great Sage?" "And how old are you?" asked Wukong. "I have lived fool-ishly for one hundred and thirty years!" said the old man. "You are still my great-great-great-great-grandson!" said Pilgrim. "I can't remember when I was born, but I have spent over five hundred years underneath this moun-tain." "Yes, yes," said the old man. "I remember my great-grandfather say-ing that when this mountain dropped from the sky, it had a divine ape clamped underneath it. To think that you should have waited until now for your freedom! When I saw you in my childhood, you had grass on your head and mud on your face, but I wasn't afraid of you then. Now without mud on your face and grass on your head, you seem a bit thinner. And with that huge piece of tiger skin draped around your waist, what great differ-ence is there between you and a demon?"

When the members of his family heard this remark, they all roared with laughter. Being a rather decent fellow, that old man at once ordered a veg-etarian meal to be prepared. Afterwards Wukong said, "What is your fam-ily name?" "Our humble family," said the old man, "goes by the name of Chen." When Tripitaka heard this, he left his seat to salute him, saying, "Old Patron, you and I share the same illustrious clan."[9] "Master," said Pil-grim, "your surname is Tang. How can it be that you and he share the same illustrious ancestors?" Tripitaka said, "The surname of my secular family is also Chen, and I come from the Juxian Village, in the Hongnong District of Haizhou in the Tang domain. My religious name is Chen Xuanzang. Because our Great Tang Emperor Taizong made me his brother by decree, I took the name Tripitaka and used Tang as my surname. Hence I'm called the Tang Monk." The old man was very pleased to hear that they had the same surname.

"Old Chen," said Pilgrim, "I must trouble your family some more, for I haven't taken a bath for five hundred years! Please go and boil some water so that my master and I, his disciple, can wash ourselves. We shall thank you all the more when we leave." The old man at once gave the order for water to be boiled and basins to be brought in with several lamps. As master and disciple sat before the lamps after their baths, Pilgrim said, "Old Chen, I still have one more favor to ask of you. Can you lend me a needle and some thread?" "Of course, of course," replied the old man. One of the amahs was told to fetch the needle and thread, which were then handed over to Pilgrim. Pilgrim, you see, had the keenest sight; he noticed that Tripitaka had taken off a shirt made of white cloth and had not put it on again after his bath. Pilgrim grabbed it and put it on himself. Taking off his tiger skin, he sewed the hems together using a "horse-face fold"[10] and fastened it round his waist again with the strand of rattan. He paraded in front of his master saying, "How does old Monkey look today compared with the way he looked yesterday?" "Very good," said Tripitaka, "very good! Now you do look like a pilgrim! If you don't think that the shirt is too worn or old, you may keep it." "Thanks for the gift!" said Wukong respectfully. He then went out to find some hay to feed the horse, after which master and disciple both retired with the old man and his household.

The next morning Wukong arose and woke up his master to get ready for the journey. Tripitaka dressed himself while Wukong put their luggage in order. They were about to leave when the old man brought in washing water and some vegetarian food, and so they did not set out until after the meal. Tripitaka rode his horse with Pilgrim leading the way; they journeyed by day and rested by night, taking food and drink according to their needs. Soon it was early winter. You see

Frost-blighted maples and the wizened trees;
Few verdant pine and cypress still on the ridge.
Budding plum blossoms spread their gentle scent.
The brief, warm day—
A Little Spring gift![11]
But dying lilies yield to the lush wild tea.

A cold bridge struggles against an old tree's bough,
And gurgling water flows in the winding brook.
Gray clouds, snow-laden, float throughout the sky.

The strong, cold wind
Tears at the sleeve!
How does one bear this chilly might of night?[12]

Master and disciple had traveled for some time when suddenly six men jumped out from the side of the road with much clamor, all holding long spears and short swords, sharp blades and strong bows. "Stop, monk!" they cried. "Leave your horse and drop your bag at once, and we'll let you pass on alive!" Tripitaka was so terrified that his soul left him and his spirit fled; he fell from his horse, unable to utter a word. But Pilgrim lifted him up, saying, "Don't be alarmed, Master. It's nothing really, just some people coming to give us clothes and a travel allowance!" "Wukong," said Tripitaka, "you must be a little hard of hearing! They told us to leave our bag and our horse, and you want to ask them for clothes and a travel allowance?" "You just stay here and watch our belongings," said Pilgrim, "and let old Monkey confront them. We'll see what happens." Tripitaka said, "Even a good punch is no match for a pair of fists, and two fists can't cope with four hands! There are six big fellows over there, and you are such a tiny person. How can you have the nerve to confront them?"

As he always had been audacious, Pilgrim did not wait for further discussion. He walked forward with arms folded and saluted the six men, saying, "Sirs, for what reason are you blocking the path of this poor monk?" "We are kings of the highway," said the men, "philanthropic mountain lords. Our fame has long been known, though you seem to be ignorant of it. Leave your belongings at once, and you will be allowed to pass. If you but utter half a no, you'll be chopped to pieces!" "I have been also a great hereditary king and a mountain lord for centuries," said Pilgrim, "but I have yet to learn of your illustrious names."

"So you really don't know!" one of them said. "Let's tell you then: one of us is named Eye That Sees and Delights; another, Ear That Hears and Rages; another Nose That Smells and Loves; another, Tongue That Tastes and Desires; another, Mind That Perceives and Covets; and another, Body That Bears and Suffers." "You are nothing but six hairy brigands," said Wukong laughing, "who have failed to recognize in me a person who has left the family, your proper master. How dare you bar my way? Bring out the treasures you have stolen so that you and I can divide them into seven portions. I'll spare you then!" Hearing this, the robbers all reacted with rage and amusement, covetousness and fear, desire and anxiety. They rushed forward crying, "You reckless monk! You haven't a thing to offer us, and yet you want us to share our loot with you!" Wielding spears and swords, they surrounded Pilgrim and hacked away at his head seventy or eighty times. Pilgrim stood in their midst and behaved as if nothing were happening.

"What a monk!" said one of the robbers. "He really does have a hard head!" "Passably so!" said Pilgrim, laughing. "But your hands must be getting tired from all that exercise; it's about time for old Monkey to take out his needle for a little entertainment." "This monk must be an acupuncture man in disguise," said the robber. "We're not sick! What's all this about using a needle?" Pilgrim reached into his ear and took out a tiny embroidery needle; one wave of it in the wind and it became an iron rod with the thickness of a rice bowl. He held it in his hands, saying, "Don't run! Let old Monkey try his hand on you with this rod!" The six robbers fled in all directions, but with great strides he caught up with them and rounded all of them up. He beat every one of them to death, stripped them of their clothes, and seized their valuables. Then Pilgrim came back smiling broadly and said, "You may proceed now, Master. Those robbers have been exterminated by old Monkey."

"That's a terrible thing you have done!" said Tripitaka. "They may have been strong men on the highway, but they would not have been sentenced to death even if they had been caught and tried. If you have such abilities, you should have chased them away. Why did you slay them all? How can you be a monk when you take life without cause? We who have left the family should

Keep ants out of harm's way when we sweep the floor,
And put shades on lamps for the love of moths.

How can you kill them just like that, without regard for black or white? You showed no mercy at all! It's a good thing that we are here in the mountains, where any further investigation will be unlikely. But suppose someone offends you when we reach a city and you perpetrate violence again, hitting people indiscriminately with that rod of yours—would I be able to remain innocent and get away scot-free?"

"Master," said Wukong, "if I hadn't killed them, they would have killed you!" Tripitaka said, "As a priest, I would rather die than practice violence. If I were killed, there would be only one of me, but you slaughtered six persons. How can you justify that? If this matter were brought before a judge, and even if your old man were the judge, you certainly would not be able to justify your action." "To tell you the truth, Master," said Pilgrim, "when I, old Monkey, was king on the Flower-Fruit Mountain five hundred years ago, I killed I don't know how many people. I would not have been a Great Sage, Equal to Heaven, if I had lived by what you are saying." "It's precisely because you had neither scruples nor self-control," said Tripitaka, "unleashing your waywardness on Earth and spreading outrage in Heaven, that you had to undergo this ordeal of five hundred years. Now that you have entered the fold of Buddhism, if you still insist on practicing violence and indulge in the taking of life as before, you are not worthy to be a monk, nor can you go to the Western Heaven. You're wicked! You're just too wicked!"

Now this monkey had never in all his life been able to tolerate scolding. When he heard Tripitaka's persistent reprimand, he could not suppress the flames leaping up in his heart. "If that's what you think," he said. "If you think I'm not worthy to be a monk, nor can I go to the Western Heaven, you needn't bother me further with your nagging! I'll leave and go back!" Before Tripitaka had time to reply, Pilgrim was already so enraged that he leaped into the air, crying only, "Old Monkey's off!" Tripitaka quickly raised his head to look, but the monkey had already disappeared, trailed only by a swishing sound fading fast toward the East. Left by himself, the priest could only shake his head and sigh, "That fellow! He's so unwilling to be taught! I only said a few words to him. How could he vanish without a trace and go back just like that? Well, well, well! It must be also that I am destined not to have a disciple or any other companion, for now I couldn't even call him or locate him if I wanted to. I might as well go on by myself!" So, he was prepared to

Lay down his life and go toward the West,
To be his own master and on none rely.

The elder had little alternative but to pack up his bag and put it on the horse, which he did not even bother to mount. Holding his staff in one hand and the reins in the other, he set off sadly toward the West. He had not traveled far when he saw an old woman before him on the mountain road, holding a silk garment and a cap with a floral design. When Tripitaka saw her approach, he hastened to pull his horse aside for her to pass. "Elder, where do you come from," asked the old woman, "and why are you walking here all by yourself?" Tripitaka replied, "Your child was sent by the Great King of the Land of the East to seek true scriptures from the living Buddha in the Western Heaven." "The Buddha of the West," said the old woman, "lives in the Great Temple of Thunderclap in the territory of India, and the journey there is one hundred and eight thousand miles long. You are all by yourself, with neither a companion nor a disciple. How can you possibly think of going there?" "A few days ago," said Tripitaka, "I did pick up a disciple, a rather unruly and headstrong character. I scolded him a little, but he refused to be taught, and disappeared." The old woman said, "I have here a silk shirt and a flower cap inlaid with gold, which used to belong to my son. He had been a monk for only three days when unfortunately he died. I have just finished mourning him at the temple, where I was given these things by his master to be kept in his memory. Father, since you have a disciple, I'll give the shirt and the cap to you." "I'm most grateful for your lavish gifts," said Tripitaka, "but my disciple has left. I dare not take them." "Where did he go?" asked the old woman. Tripitaka replied, "I heard a swishing sound heading toward the east." "My home is not too far away in the east," said the old woman, "and he may be going there. I have a spell which is called the True Words for Controlling the Mind, or the Tight-Fillet Spell. You must memorize it secretly; commit it firmly to your memory, and don't let anyone learn of it. I'll try to catch up with him and persuade him to come back and follow you. When he returns, give him the shirt and the cap to wear; and if he again refuses to obey you, recite the spell silently. He will not dare do violence or leave you again."

On hearing these words, Tripitaka bowed his head to thank her. The old woman changed herself into a shaft of golden light and vanished toward the east. Then Tripitaka realized that it was the Bodhisattva Guanyin who had taught him the True Words; he hurriedly picked up a few pinches of earth with his fingers and scattered them like incense, bowing reverently toward the East. He then took the shirt and the cap and hid them in his bag. Sitting beside the road, he began to recite the True Words for Controlling the Mind. After a few times, he knew it thoroughly by heart, but we shall speak no more of him for the time being.

We now tell you about Wukong, who, having left his master, headed straight toward the Eastern Ocean with a single cloud somersault. He stopped his cloud, opened up a path in the water, and went directly to the Water Crystal Palace. Learning of his arrival, the Dragon King came out to welcome him. After they had exchanged greetings and sat down, the Dragon King said, "I heard recently that the ordeal of the Great Sage had been completed, and I apologize for not having congratulated you yet. I suppose you have again taken occupancy in your immortal mountain and returned to the ancient cave." "I was so inclined," said Wukong, "but I became a monk instead." "What sort of a monk?" asked the Dragon King. "I was indebted to the Bodhisattva of South Sea," said Pilgrim, "who persuaded me to do good and seek the truth. I was to follow the Tang Monk from the Land of the East to go worship Buddha in the West. Since entering the fold of Buddhism, I was given also the name 'Pilgrim.'" "That is indeed praiseworthy!" said the Dragon King. "You have, as we say, left the wrong and followed the right; you have been created anew by setting your mind on goodness. But if that's the case, why are you not going toward the West, but are returning eastward instead?"

Pilgrim laughed and said, "That Tang Monk knows nothing of human nature! There were a few ruffians who wanted to rob us, and I slew them all. But that Tang Monk couldn't stop nagging me, telling me over and over how wrong I was. Can you imagine old Monkey putting up with that sort of tedium? I just left him! I was on my way back to my mountain when I decided to come visit you and ask for a cup of tea." "Thanks for coming! Thanks for coming!" exclaimed the Dragon King. At that moment, the Dragon sons and grandsons presented them with aromatic tea. When they finished the tea, Pilgrim happened to turn around and saw hanging behind him on the wall a painting on the "Presentation of Shoes at Yi Bridge." "What's this all about?" asked Pilgrim. The Dragon King replied, "The incident depicted in the painting took place some time after you were born, and you may not recognize what it was—the threefold presentation of shoes at Yi Bridge." "What do you mean by the threefold presentation of shoes?" asked Pilgrim.

"The immortal in the painting," said the Dragon King, "was named Huang Shigong,[13] and the young man kneeling in front of him was called Zhang Liang.[14] Shigong was sitting on the Yi Bridge when suddenly one of his shoes fell off and dropped under the bridge. He asked Zhang Liang to fetch it, and the young man quickly did so, putting it back on for him as he knelt there. This happened three times. Since Zhang Liang did not display the slightest sign of pride or impatience, he won the affection of Shigong, who imparted to him that night a celestial manual and told him to support the house of Han. Afterwards, Zhang Liang 'made his plans sitting in a military tent to achieve victories a thousand miles away.'[15] When the Han dynasty was established, he left his post and went into the mountains, where he followed the Daoist, Master Red Pine,[16] and became enlightened in the way of immortality. Great Sage, if you do not accompany the Tang Monk, if you are unwilling to exercise diligence or to accept instruction, you will remain a bogus immortal after all. Don't think that you'll ever acquire the Fruits of Truth."

Wukong listened to these words and fell silent for some time. The Dragon King said, "Great Sage, you must make the decision yourself. It's unwise to allow momentary comfort to jeopardize your future." "Not another word!" said Wukong. "Old Monkey will go back to accompany him, that's all!" Delighted, the Dragon King said, "If that's your wish, I dare not detain you. Instead, I ask the Great Sage to show his mercy at once and not permit his master to wait any longer." When Pilgrim heard this exhortation to leave, he bounded right out of the oceanic region; mounting the clouds, he left the Dragon King.

On his way he ran right into the Bodhisattva of South Sea. "Sun Wukong," said the Bodhisattva, "why did you not listen to me and accompany the Tang Monk? What are you doing here?" Pilgrim was so taken aback that he saluted her on top of the clouds. "I'm most grateful for the kind words of the Bodhisattva," he said. "A monk from the Tang court did appear, lifted the seal, and saved my life. I became his disciple, but he blamed me for being too violent. I walked out on him for a little while, but I'm going back right now to accompany him." "Go quickly then," said the Bodhisattva, "before you change your mind again." They finished speaking and each went on his way. In a moment, our Pilgrim saw the Tang Monk sitting dejectedly at the side of the road. He approached him and said, "Master, why are you not on the road? What are you doing here?" "Where have you been?" asked Tripitaka, looking up. "Your absence has forced me to sit here and wait for you, not daring to walk or move." Pilgrim replied, "I just went to the home of the old Dragon King at the Eastern Ocean to ask for some tea."

"Disciple," said Tripitaka, "those who have left the family should not lie. It was less than an hour since you left me, and you claim to have had tea at the home of the Dragon King?" "To tell you the truth," said Pilgrim, laughing, "I know how to cloud somersault, and a single somersault will carry me one hundred and eight thousand miles. That's why I can go and return in no time at all." Tripitaka said, "Because I spoke to you a little sharply, you were offended and left me in a rage. With your ability, you could go and ask for some tea, but a person like me has no other prospect but to sit here and endure hunger. Do you feel comfortable about that?" "Master," said Pilgrim, "if you're hungry, I'll go beg some food for you." "There's no need to beg," said Tripitaka, "for I still have in my bag some dried goods given to me by the mother of Guardian Liu. Fetch me some water in that bowl. I'll eat some food and we can start out again."

Pilgrim went to untie the bag and found some biscuits made of unrefined flour, which he took out and handed over to the master. He then saw light glowing from a silk shirt and a flower cap inlaid with gold. "Did you bring this garment and cap from the Land of the East?" he asked. "I wore these in my childhood," said Tripitaka nonchalantly. "If you wear the hat, you'll know how to recite scriptures without having to learn them; if you put on the garment, you'll know how to perform rituals without having to practice them." "Dear Master," said Pilgrim, "let me put them on." "They may not fit you," said Tripitaka, "but if they do, you may wear them." Pilgrim thereupon took off his old shirt made of white cloth and put on the silk shirt, which seemed to have been made especially for him. Then he put on the cap as well. When Tripitaka saw that he had put on the cap, he stopped eating the dried goods and began to recite the Tight-Fillet Spell silently.

"Oh, my head!" cried Pilgrim. "It hurts! It hurts!" The master went through the recitation several times without ceasing, and the pain was so intense that Pilgrim was rolling on the ground, his hands gripping the flower cap inlaid with gold. Fearing that he might break the gold fillet, Tripitaka stopped reciting and the pain ceased. Pilgrim touched his head with his hand and felt that it was tightly bound by a thin metal band; it could be neither pulled off nor ripped apart, for it had, as it were, taken root on his head. Taking the needle out of his ear, he rammed it inside the fillet and started prying madly. Afraid that he might break the fillet with his pry-ing, Tripitaka started his recitation again, and Pilgrim's head began to hurt once more. It was so painful that he did cartwheels and somersaults. His face and even his ears turned red, his eyes bulged, and his body grew weak. When the master saw his appearance, he was moved to break off his recita-tion, and the pain stopped as before. "My head," said Pilgrim, "the master has put a spell on it." "I was just saying the Tight-Fillet Sūtra," said Tripi-taka. "Since when did I put a spell on you?" "Recite it some more and see what happens," said Pilgrim. Tripitaka accordingly began to recite, and the Pilgrim immediately started to hurt. "Stop! Stop!" he cried. "I hurt the mo-ment you begin to recite. How do you explain that?" "Will you listen now to my instructions?" asked Tripitaka. "Yes, I will," replied Pilgrim. "And never be unruly again?" "I dare not," said Pilgrim.

Although he said that with his mouth, Pilgrim's mind was still devis-ing evil. One wave of the needle and it had the thickness of a rice bowl; he aimed it at the Tang Monk and was about to slam it down on him. The priest was so startled that he went through the recitation two or three more times. Falling to the ground, the monkey threw away the iron rod and could not even raise his hands. "Master," he said, "I've learned my lesson! Stop! Please stop!" "How dare you be so reckless," said Tripitaka, "that you should want to strike me?" "I wouldn't dare strike you," said Pilgrim, "but let me ask you something. Who taught you this magic?" "It was an old woman," said Tripitaka, "who imparted it to me a few moments ago." Growing very angry, Pilgrim said, "You needn't say anything more! The old woman had to be that Guanshiyin! Why did she want me to suffer like this? I'm going to South Sea to beat her up!"

"If she had taught me this magic," said Tripitaka, "she had to know it even before I did. If you go looking for her, and she starts her recitation, won't you be dead?" Pilgrim saw the logic of this and dared not remove himself. Indeed, he had no alternative but to kneel in contrition and plead with Tripitaka, saying, "Master, this is her method of controlling me, al-lowing me no alternative but to follow you to the West. I'll not go to bother her, but you must not regard this spell as a plaything for frequent recita-tion either! I'm willing to accompany you without ever entertaining the thought of leaving again." "If that's so," said Tripitaka, "help me onto the horse and let's get going." At that point, Pilgrim gave up all thoughts of disobedience or rebellion. Eagerly he tugged at his silk shirt and went to gather the luggage together, and they headed again toward the West. We do not know what is to be told after their departure; let's listen to the explana-tion in the next chapter.

FIFTEEN

At Serpent Coil Mountain, the gods give secret protection; At Eagle Grief Stream, the Horse of the Will is reined.

We were telling you about Pilgrim, who ministered to the Tang Monk faithfully as they advanced toward the West. They traveled for several days under the frigid sky of midwinter; a cold wind blew fiercely, and slippery icicles hung everywhere. They traversed

> *A tortuous path of hanging gorges and cliffs,*
> *A parlous range tiered with summits and peaks.*

As Tripitaka was riding along on his horse, his ears caught the distant sound of a torrent. He turned to ask: "Wukong, where is that sound coming from?" Pilgrim said, "The name of this place, I recall, is Serpent Coil Mountain, and there is an Eagle Grief Stream in it. I suppose that's where it's coming from." Before they had finished their conversation, they arrived at the bank of the stream. Tripitaka reined in his horse and looked around. He saw

> *A bubbling cold stream piercing through the clouds,*
> *Its limpid current reddened by the sun.*
> *Its splatter in night rain stirs quiet vales;*
> *Its colors glow at dawn to fill the air.*
> *Wave after wave seems like flying chips of jade,*
> *Their deep roar resonant as the clear wind.*
> *It flows to join one vast stretch of smoke and tide,*
> *Where gulls are lost with egrets but no fishers bide.*

Master and disciple were looking at the stream, when there was a loud splash in midstream and a dragon emerged. Churning the waters, it darted toward the bank and headed straight for the priest. Pilgrim was so startled that he threw away the luggage, hauled the master off his horse, and turned to flee with him at once. The dragon could not catch up with them, but it swallowed the white horse, harness and all, with one gulp before losing itself again in the water. Pilgrim carried his master to high ground and left the priest seated there; then he returned to fetch the horse and the luggage. The load of bags was still there, but the horse was nowhere to be seen. Placing the luggage in front of his master, he said, "Master, there's not a trace of that cursed dragon, which has frightened away our horse." "Disciple," said

Tripitaka, "how can we find the horse again?" "Relax! Relax!" said Pilgrim. "Let me go and have a look!"

He whistled once and leaped up into the air. Shading his fiery eyes and diamond pupils with his hand, he peered in all four directions, but there was not the slightest trace of the horse. Dropping down from the clouds, he made his report, saying, "Master, our horse must have been eaten by that dragon. It's nowhere to be seen!" "Disciple," said Tripitaka, "how big a mouth does that creature have that he can swallow a horse, harness and all? It must have been frightened away instead, probably still running loose somewhere in the valley. Please take another look." Pilgrim said, "You really have no conception of my ability. This pair of eyes of mine in daylight can discern good and evil within a thousand miles; at that distance, I can even see a dragonfly when it spreads its wings. How can I possibly miss something as big as a horse?" "If it has been eaten," said Tripitaka, "how am I to proceed? Pity me! How can I walk through those thousand hills and ten thousand waters?" As he spoke, tears began to fall like rain. When Pilgrim saw him crying, he became infuriated and began to shout: "Master, stop behaving like a namby-pamby! Sit here! Just sit here! Let old Monkey find that creature and ask him to give us back our horse. That'll be the end of the matter." Clutching at him, Tripitaka said, "Disciple, where do you have to go to find him? Wouldn't I be hurt if he should appear from somewhere after you are gone? How would it be then if both man and horse should perish?" At these words, Pilgrim became even more enraged. "You're a weakling! Truly a weakling!" he thundered. "You want a horse to ride on, and yet you won't let me go. You want to sit here and grow old, watching our bags?"

As he was yelling angrily like this, he heard someone calling out in midair: "Great Sage Sun, don't be annoyed. And stop crying, Royal Brother of Tang. We are a band of deities sent by the Bodhisattva Guanyin to give secret protection to the scripture pilgrim." Hearing this, the priest hastily bowed to the ground. "Which divinities are you?" asked Pilgrim. "Tell me your names, so that I can check you off the roll." "We are the Six Gods of Darkness and the Six Gods of Light," they said, "the Guardians of Five Points, the Four Sentinels, and the Eighteen Protectors of Monasteries. Every one of us waits upon you in rotation." "Which one of you will begin today?" asked Pilgrim. "The Gods of Darkness and Light," they said, "to be followed by the Sentinels and the Protectors. We Guardians of Five Points, with the exception of the Golden-Headed Guardian, will be here somewhere night and day." "That being the case," said Pilgrim, "those not on duty may retire, but the first Six Gods of Darkness, the Day Sentinel, and the Guardians should remain to protect my master. Let old Monkey go find that cursed dragon in the stream and ask him for our horse." The various deities obeyed. Only then did Tripitaka feel somewhat relieved as he sat on the cliff and told Pilgrim to be careful. "Just don't worry," said Pilgrim. Dear Monkey King! He tightened the belt around his silk shirt, hitched up his tiger-skin kilt, and went straight toward the gorge of the stream holding the golden-hooped iron rod. Standing halfway between cloud and fog, he cried loudly on top of the water, "Lawless lizard! Return my horse! Return my horse!"

We now tell you about the dragon, who, having eaten the white horse of Tripitaka, was lying on the bottom of the stream, subduing his spirit and nourishing his nature. When he heard someone demanding the horse with abusive language, however, he could not restrain the fire leaping up in his heart and he jumped up quickly. Churning the waves, he darted out of the water, saying, "Who dares to insult me here with his big mouth?" Pilgrim saw him and cried ferociously, "Don't run away! Return my horse!" Wielding his rod, he aimed at the beast's head and struck, while the dragon attacked with open jaws and dancing claws. The battle between the two of them before the stream was indeed fierce. You see

The dragon extending sharp daws:
The monkey lifting his rod.
The whiskers of this one hung like white jade threads;
The eyes of that one shone like red-gold lamps.
The mouth beneath the whiskers of that one belched colored mists:
The iron rod in the hands of this one moved like a fierce wind.
That one was a cursed son who brought his parents grief;
This one was a monster who defied the gods on high.
Both had to suffer because of their plight.
They now want to win, so each displays his might.

Back and forth, round and round, they fought for a long time, until the dragon grew weak and could fight no longer. He turned and darted back into the water; plunging to the bottom of the stream, he refused to come out again. The Monkey King heaped insult upon insult, but the dragon only pretended to be deaf.

Pilgrim had little choice but to return to Tripitaka, saying, "Master, that monster made his appearance as a result of my tongue-lashing. He fought with me for a long time before taking fright and running. He's hiding in the water now and refuses to come out again." "Do you know for certain that it was he who ate my horse?" asked Tripitaka. "Listen to the way you talk!" said Pilgrim. "If he hadn't eaten it, would he be willing to face me and answer me like that?" "The time you killed the tiger," said Tripitaka, "you claimed that you had the ability to tame dragons and subdue tigers. Why can't you subdue this one today?" As the monkey had a rather low tolerance for any kind of provocation, this single taunt of Tripitaka so aroused him that he said, "Not one word more! Let me go and show him who is master!"

With great leaps, our Monkey King bounded right to the edge of the stream. Using his magic of overturning seas and rivers, he transformed the clear, limpid water of the Eagle Grief Stream into the muddy currents of the Yellow River during high tide. The cursed dragon in the depth of the stream could neither sit nor lie still for a single moment. He thought to himself: "Just as 'Blessing never repeats itself, so misfortune never comes singly!' It has been barely a year since I escaped execution by Heaven and came to bide my time here, but now I have to run into this wretched monster who is trying to do me harm." Look at him! The more he thought about the matter, the more irritated he became. Unable to bear it any longer, he gritted his teeth and leaped out of the water, crying, "What kind of monster are you, and where do you come from, that you want to oppress me like this?" "Never mind where I come from," said Pilgrim. "Just return the horse, and I'll spare your life." "I've swallowed your horse into my stomach," said the dragon, "so how am I to throw it up? What are you going to do if I can't return it to you?" Pilgrim said, "If you don't give back the horse, just watch for this rod. Only when your life becomes a payment for my horse will there be an end to this matter!" The two of them again waged a bitter struggle below the mountain ridge. After a few rounds, however, the little dragon just could not hold out any longer; shaking his body, he changed himself into a tiny water snake and wriggled into the marshes.

The Monkey King came rushing up with his rod and parted the grass to look for the snake, but there was not a trace of it. He was so exasperated that the spirits of the Three Worms in his body exploded[1] and smoke began to appear from his seven apertures. He recited a spell beginning with the letter oṃ and summoned the local spirit and the mountain god of that region. The two of them knelt before him, saying, "The local spirit and the mountain god have come to see you."

"Stick out your shanks," said Pilgrim, "and I'll greet each of you with five strokes of my rod just to relieve my feelings."

"Great Sage," they pleaded, "please be more lenient and allow your humble subjects to tell you something." "What have you got to say?" said Pilgrim. "The Great Sage has been in captivity for a long time," said the two deities, "and we had no knowledge of when you were released. That's why we have not been here to receive you, and we beg you to pardon us." "All right," said Pilgrim, "I won't hit you. But let me ask you something. Where did that monstrous dragon in the Eagle Grief Stream come from, and why did he devour my master's white horse?" "We have never known the Great Sage to have a master," the two deities said, "for you have always been a first-rank primordial immortal who submits neither to Heaven nor to Earth. What do you mean by your master's horse?" Pilgrim said, "Of course you didn't know about this. Because of my contemptuous behavior toward Heaven, I had to suffer for this five hundred years. I was converted by the kindly persuasion of Bodhisattva Guanyin, who had the true monk from the Tang court rescue me. As his disciple, I was to follow him to the Western Heaven to seek scriptures from Buddha. We passed through this place, and my master's white horse was lost."

"So, that's how it is!" said the two deities. "There has never been anything evil about this stream, except that it is both broad and deep, and its water is so clear that you can see right to the bottom. Large fowls such as crows or eagles are hesitant to fly over it; for when they see their own reflections in the clear water, they are prone to mistake them for other birds of their own flock and throw themselves into the stream. Hence the name, the Steep Eagle Grief Stream. Some years ago, on her way to look for a scripture pilgrim, Bodhisattva Guanyin rescued a dragon and sent him here. He was told to wait for the scripture pilgrim and was forbidden to do any evil or violence. Only when he is hungry is he permitted to come up to the banks to feed on birds or antelopes. How could he be so ignorant as to offend the Great Sage!"

Pilgrim said, "At first, he wanted to have a contest of strength with me and managed only a few bouts. Afterwards he would not come out even when I abused him. Only when I used the magic of overturning seas and rivers and stirred up the water did he appear again, and then he still wanted to fight. He really had no idea how heavy my rod was! When finally he couldn't hold out any longer, he changed himself into a water snake and wriggled into the grass. I rushed up there to look for him, but there was no trace of him." "You may not know, Great Sage," said the local spirit, "that there are countless holes and crevices along these banks, through which the stream is connected with its many tributaries. The dragon could have crawled into any one of these. But there's no need for the Great Sage to get angry trying to look for him. If you want to capture this creature, all you need do is to ask Guanshiyin to come here; then he'll certainly surrender."

When Pilgrim heard this, he called the mountain god and the local spirit to go with him to see Tripitaka to give an account of what had happened. "If you need to send for the Bodhisattva," said Tripitaka, "when will you be able to return? How can this poor monk endure the cold and hunger?" He had hardly finished speaking when the Golden-Headed Guardian called out from midair, "Great Sage, you needn't leave. Your humble subject will go fetch the Bodhisattva." Pilgrim was very pleased, shouting, "Thanks for taking all that trouble! Go quickly!" The Guardian mounted the clouds swiftly and headed straight for South Sea; Pilgrim asked the mountain god and the local spirit to protect his master and the Day Sentinel to find some vegetarian food, while he himself went back to patrol the stream, and we shall say no more of that.

We now tell you about the Golden-Headed Guardian, who mounted the clouds and soon arrived at South Sea. Descending from the auspicious light, he went straight to the purple bamboo grove of the Potalaka Mountain, where he asked the various deities in golden armor and Mokṣa to announce his arrival. The Bodhisattva said, "What have you come for?" "The Tang Monk lost his horse at the Eagle Grief Stream of the Serpent Coil Mountain," said the Guardian, "and the Great Sage Sun was placed in a terrible dilemma. He questioned the local deities, who claimed that a dragon sent by the Bodhisattva to that stream had eaten it. The Great Sage, therefore, sent me to request the Bodhisattva to go and subdue that cursed dragon, so that he might get back his horse." Hearing this, the Bodhisattva said, "That creature was originally the son of Aorun of the Western Ocean. Because in his carelessness he set fire to the palace and destroyed the luminous pearls hanging there, his father accused him of subversion, and he was condemned to die by the Heavenly Tribunal. It was I who personally sought pardon from the Jade Emperor for him, so that he might serve as a means of transportation for the Tang Monk. I can't understand how he could swallow the monk's horse instead. But if that's what happened, I'll have to get over there myself." The Bodhisattva left her lotus platform and went out of the divine cave. Mounting the auspicious luminosity with the Guardian, she crossed the South Sea. We have a testimonial poem that says:

> Buddha proclaimed the Tripitaka Supreme
> Which the Goddess declared throughout Chang'an:
> Those great, wondrous truths could reach Heaven and Earth;
> Those wise, true words could save the spirits damned.
> They caused Gold Cicada to cast again his shell.
> They moved Xuanzang to mend his ways anew.
> By blocking his path at Eagle Grief Stream,
> A dragon-prince in horse-form returns to the Real.

The Bodhisattva and the Guardian soon arrived at the Serpent Coil Mountain. They stopped the hallowed clouds in midair and saw Pilgrim Sun down below, shouting abuses at the bank of the stream. The Bodhisattva asked the Guardian to fetch him. Lowering his clouds, the Guardian went past Tripitaka and headed straight for the edge of the stream, saying to Pilgrim, "The Bodhisattva has arrived." When Pilgrim heard this, he jumped quickly into the air and yelled at her: "You, so-called Teacher of the Seven Buddhas and the Founder of the Faith of Mercy! Why did you have to use your tricks to harm me?"

"You impudent stableman, ignorant red-buttocks!" said the Bodhisattva. "I went to considerable effort to find a scripture pilgrim, whom I carefully instructed to save your life. Instead of thanking me, you are finding fault with me!" "You saved me all right!" said Pilgrim. "If you truly wanted to deliver me, you should have allowed me to have a little fun with no strings attached. When you met me the other day above the ocean, you could have chastened me with a few words, telling me to serve the Tang Monk with diligence, and that would have been enough. Why did you have to give him a flower cap, and have him deceive me into wearing it so that I would suffer? Now the fillet has taken root on old Monkey's head. And you even taught him this so-called 'Tight-Fillet Spell,' which he recites again and again, causing endless pain in my head! You haven't harmed me, indeed!" The Bodhisattva laughed and said, "O, Monkey! You are neither attentive to admonition nor willing to seek the fruit of truth. If you are not restrained like this, you'll probably mock the authority of Heaven again without regard for good or ill. If you create troubles as you did before, who will be able to control you? It's only through this bit of adversity that you will be willing to enter our gate of Yoga."

"All right," said Pilgrim, "I'll consider the matter my hard luck. But why did you take that condemned dragon and send him here so that he could become a spirit and swallow my master's horse? It's your fault, you know, if you allow an evildoer to perpetrate his villainies some more!" "I went personally to plead with the Jade Emperor," said the Bodhisattva, "to have the dragon stationed here so that he could serve as a means of transportation for the scripture pilgrim. Those mortal horses from the Land of the East, do you think that they could walk through ten thousand waters and a thousand hills? How could they possibly hope to reach the Spirit Mountain, the land of Buddha? Only a dragon-horse could make that journey!" "But right now he's so terribly afraid of me," said Pilgrim, "that he refuses to come out of his hiding place. What can we do?" The Bodhisattva said to the Guardian, "Go to the edge of the stream and say, 'Come out, Third Prince Jade Dragon of the Dragon King Aorun. The Bodhisattva from South Sea is here.' He'll come out then."

The Guardian went at once to the edge of the stream and called out twice. Churning the waters and leaping across the waves, the little dragon appeared and changed at once into the form of a man. He stepped on the clouds and rose up into the air; saluting the Bodhisattva, he said, "I thank the Bodhisattva again for saving my life. I've waited here a long time, but I've heard no news of the scripture pilgrim." Pointing to Pilgrim, the Bodhisattva said, "Isn't he the eldest disciple of the scripture pilgrim?" When he saw him, the little dragon said, "Bodhisattva, he's my adversary. I was hungry yesterday and ate his horse. We fought over that, but he took advantage of his superior strength and defeated me; in fact, he so abused me that I dared not show myself again. But he has never mentioned a word about scripture seeking."

"You didn't bother to ask my name," said Pilgrim. "How did you expect me to tell you anything?" The little dragon said, "Didn't I ask you, 'What kind of a monster are you and where do you come from?' But all you did was shout, 'Never mind where I come from; just return my horse!' Since when did you utter even half the word 'Tang'?" "That monkey," said the Bodhisattva, "is always relying on his own abilities! When has he ever given any credit to other people? When you set off this time, remember that there are others who will join you. So when they ask you, by all means mention first the matter of scripture seeking; they will submit to you without causing you further trouble."

Pilgrim received this word of counsel amiably. The Bodhisattva went up to the little dragon and plucked off the shining pearls hanging around his neck. She then dipped her willow branch into the sweet dew in her vase and sprinkled it all over his body; blowing a mouthful of magic breath on him, she cried, "Change!" The dragon at once changed into a horse with hair of exactly the same color and quality as that of the horse he had swallowed. The Bodhisattva then told him, "You must overcome with utmost diligence all the cursed barriers. When your merit is achieved, you will no longer be an ordinary dragon; you will acquire the true fruit of a golden body." Holding the bit in his mouth, the little dragon humbly accepted the instruction. The Bodhisattva told Wukong to lead him to Tripitaka, saying, "I'm returning across the ocean."

Pilgrim took hold of her and refused to let go, saying, "I'm not going on! I'm not going on! The road to the West is so treacherous! If I have to accompany this mortal monk, when will I ever get there? If I have to endure all these miseries, I may well lose my life. What sort of merit do you think I'll achieve? I'm not going! I'm not going!"

"In years past, before you reached the way of humanity," said the Bodhisattva, "you were most eager to seek enlightenment. Now that you have been delivered from the chastisement of Heaven, how could you become slothful again? The truth of Nirvāṇa in our teaching can never be realized without faith and perseverance. If on your journey you should come across any danger that threatens your life, I give you permission to call on Heaven, and Heaven will respond; to call on Earth, and Earth will prove efficacious. In the event of extreme difficulty, I myself will come to rescue you. Come closer, and I shall endow you with one more means of power." Plucking three leaves from her willow branch, the Bodhisattva placed them at the back of Pilgrim's head, crying, "Change!" They changed at once into three hairs with lifesaving power. She said to him: "When you find yourself in a helpless and hopeless situation, you may use these according to your needs, and they will deliver you from your particular affliction." After Pilgrim had heard all these kind words, he thanked the Bodhisattva of Great Mercy and Compassion. With scented wind and colored mists swirling around her, the Bodhisattva returned to Potalaka.

Lowering the direction of his cloud, Pilgrim tugged at the mane of the horse and led him to Tripitaka, saying, "Master, we have a horse!" Highly pleased by what he saw, Tripitaka said, "Disciple, how is it that the horse has grown a little fatter and stronger than before? Where did you find him?" "Master, you are still dreaming!" said Pilgrim. "Just now the Golden-Headed Guardian managed to bring the Bodhisattva here, and she transformed the dragon of the stream into our white horse. Except for the missing harness, the color and hair are all the same, and old Monkey has pulled him here." "Where is the Bodhisattva?" asked Tripitaka, greatly surprised. "Let me go and thank her." "By this time," said Pilgrim, "the Bodhisattva has probably arrived at South Sea; there's no need to bother about that." Picking up a few pinches of earth with his fingers and scattering them like incense, Tripitaka bowed reverently toward the South. He then got up and prepared to leave again with Pilgrim.

Having dismissed the mountain god and the local spirit and given instructions to the Guardians and the Sentinels, Pilgrim asked his master to mount. Tripitaka said, "How can I ride a horse without harness? Let's find a boat to cross this stream, and then we can decide what to do." "This master of mine is truly impractical!" said Pilgrim. "In the wilds of this mountain, where will you find a boat? Since the horse has lived here for a long time, he must know the water's condition. Just ride him like a boat and we'll cross over." Tripitaka had no choice but to follow his suggestion and climbed onto the barebacked horse; Pilgrim took up the luggage and they arrived at the edge of the stream. Then they saw an old fisherman punting downstream toward them in an old wooden raft. When Pilgrim caught sight of him, he waved his hands and called out: "Old fisherman, come here! Come here! We come from the Land of the East to seek scriptures. It's difficult for my master to cross, so please take us over." Hearing these words, the fisherman quickly punted the raft up to the bank. Asking his master to dismount, Pilgrim helped Tripitaka onto the raft before he embarked the horse and the luggage. That old fisher punted the raft away, and like an arrow in the wind, they crossed the steep Eagle Grief Stream swiftly and landed on the western shore. Tripitaka told Pilgrim to untie a bag and take out a few Tang pennies to give to the old fisherman. With a shove of his pole, the old fisherman pulled away, saying, "I don't want any money." He drifted downstream and soon disappeared from sight. Feeling very much obliged, Tripitaka kept folding his hands to express his gratitude. "Master," said Pilgrim, "you needn't be so solicitous. Don't you recognize him? He is the Water God of this stream. Since he didn't come to pay his respects to old Monkey, he was about to get a beating. It's enough that he is now spared from that. Would he dare take any money!" The Master only half-believed him when he climbed onto the barebacked horse once again; following Pilgrim, he went up to the main road and set off again toward the West. It would be like this that they

> Through the vast Thusness[2] reach the other shore,
> And climb with hearts unfeigned the Spirit Mount.

Master and disciple journeyed on, and soon the fiery sun sank westward as the sky gradually darkened. You see

> Clouds hazy and aimless,
> A mountain moon dim and gloomy.
> The sky, all frosty, builds the cold;
> Howling wind around cuts through you.
> One bird is lost midst the pale, wide sandbars,
> As twilight glows where the distant hills are low.
> A thousand trees roar in sparse woods;
> One ape cries on a barren peak.
> No traveler is seen on this long road
> When boats from afar return for the night.

As Tripitaka, riding his horse, peered into the distance, he suddenly saw something like a hamlet beside the road. "Wukong," he said, "there's a house ahead of us. Let's ask for lodging there and travel again tomorrow." Raising his head to take a look, Pilgrim said, "Master, it's no ordinary house." "Why not?" said Tripitaka. "If it were an ordinary house," said Pilgrim, "there would be no flying fishes or reclining beasts decorating the ridge of its roof. That must be a temple or an abbey." While they were speaking, master and disciple arrived at the gate of the building. Dismounting, Tripitaka saw on top of the gate three large characters: Lishe Shrine. They walked inside, where they were met by an old man with some beads hanging around his neck. He came forward with hands folded, saying, "Master, please take a seat." Tripitaka hastily returned his salutation and then went to the main hall to bow to the holy images. The old man called a youth to serve tea, after which Tripitaka asked him, "Why is this shrine named Lishe?"

The old man said, "This region belongs to the Hamil Kingdom of the western barbarians. There is a village behind the shrine, which was built from the piety of all its families. The 'Li' refers to the land owned by the whole village, and the 'She' is the God of the Soil. During the days of spring sowing, summer plowing, autumn harvesting, and winter storing, each of the families would bring the three beasts,[3] flowers, and fruits to sacrifice at the shrine, so that they might be blessed with good luck in all four seasons, a rich harvest of the five grains, and prosperity in raising the six domestic creatures."[4] When Tripitaka heard these words, he nodded his head to show his approval, saying, "This is truly like the proverb: 'Even three miles from home there are customs entirely distinct.' The families in our region do not practice such good works." Then the old man asked, "Where is the honorable home of the master?" "Your poor monk," said Tripitaka, "happens to have been sent by the royal decree from the Great Tang Nation in the East to go to seek scriptures from Buddha in the Western Heaven. It was getting rather late when I passed your esteemed edifice. I therefore came to your holy shrine to ask for a night's lodging. I'll leave as soon as it gets light." The old man was delighted and kept saying, "Welcome! Welcome!" He called the youth again to prepare a meal, which Tripitaka ate with gratitude.

As usual, Pilgrim was extremely observant. Noticing a rope for hanging laundry tied under the eaves, he walked over to it and pulled at it until it snapped in two. He then used the piece of rope to tie up the horse. "Where did you steal this horse?" asked the old man, laughing. "Old man," said Pilgrim angrily, "watch what you are saying! We are holy monks going to worship Buddha. How could we steal horses?" "If you didn't steal it," laughed the old man, "why is there no saddle or rein, so that you have to rip up my clothesline?"

"This rascal is always so impulsive," said Tripitaka apologetically. "If you wanted to tie up the horse, why didn't you ask the old gentleman properly for a rope? Why did you have to rip up his clothesline? Sir, please don't be angry! Our horse, to tell you the truth, is not a stolen one. When we approached the Eagle Grief Stream yesterday from the east, I had a white horse complete with harness. Little did we anticipate that there was a condemned dragon in the stream who had become a spirit, and who swallowed my horse in one gulp, harness and all. Fortunately, my disciple has some talents, and he was able to bring the Bodhisattva Guanyin to the stream to subdue the dragon. She told him to assume the form of my original white horse, so that he could carry me to worship Buddha in the Western Heaven. It has barely been one day since we crossed the stream and arrived at your holy shrine. We haven't had time to look for a harness."

"Master, you needn't worry," said the old man. "An old man like me loves to tease, but I had no idea your esteemed disciple was so serious about everything! When I was young, I had a little money, and I, too, loved to ride. But over the years I had my share of misfortunes: deaths in the family and fires in the household have not left me much. Thus I am reduced to being a caretaker here in the shrine, looking after the fires and incense, and dependent on the goodwill of the patrons in the village back there for a living. I still have in my possession a harness that I have always cherished, and that even in this poverty I couldn't bear to sell. But since hearing your story, how even the Bodhisattva delivered the divine dragon and made him change into a horse to carry you, I feel that I must not withhold from giving either. I shall bring the harness tomorrow and present it to the master, who, I hope, will be pleased to accept it." When Tripitaka heard this, he thanked him repeatedly. Before long, the youth brought in the evening meal, after which lamps were lit and the beds prepared. Everyone then retired.

Next morning, Pilgrim arose and said, "Master, that old caretaker promised last night to give us the harness. Ask him for it. Don't spare him." He had hardly finished speaking when the old man came in with a saddle, together with pads, reins, and the like. Not a single item needed for riding a horse was lacking. He set them down in the corridor, saying, "Master, I am presenting you with this harness." When Tripitaka saw it, he accepted it with delight and asked Pilgrim to try the saddle on the horse. Going forward, Pilgrim took up the accoutrements and examined them piece by piece. They were indeed some magnificent articles, for which we have a testimonial poem. The poem says:

> The carved saddle shines with studs of silver stars.
> The precious seat glows with bright threads of gold.
> The pads are stacks of fine-spun woolen quilts.
> The reins are three bands of purple cords of silk.
> The bridle's leather straps are shaped like flowers.
> The flaps have gold-etched forms of dancing beasts.
> The rings and bit are made of finest steel.
> Waterproof tassels dangle on both sides.

Secretly pleased, Pilgrim put the saddle on the back of the horse, and it seemed to have been made to measure. Tripitaka bowed to thank the old man, who hastily raised him up, saying, "It's nothing! What do you need to thank me for?" The old man did not ask them to stay any longer; instead, he urged Tripitaka to mount. The priest came out of the gate and climbed into the saddle, while Pilgrim followed, hauling the luggage. The old man then took a whip out from his sleeve, with a handle of rattan wrapped in strips of leather, and the strap knitted with cords made of tiger ligaments. He stood by the side of the road and presented it with hands uplifted, saying, "Holy Monk, I have a whip here that I may as well give you." Tripitaka accepted it on his horse, saying, "Thanks for your donation! Thanks for your donation!"

Even as he was saying this, the old man vanished. The priest turned around to look at the Lishe Shrine, but it had become just a piece of level ground. From the sky came a voice saying, "Holy Monk, I'm sorry not to have given you a better reception! I am the local spirit of Potalaka Mountain, who was sent by the Bodhisattva to present you with the harness. You two must journey to the West with all diligence. Do not be slothful in any moment." Tripitaka was so startled that he fell off his horse and bowed toward the sky, saying, "Your disciple is of fleshly eyes and mortal stock, and he does not recognize the holy visage of the deity. Please forgive me. I beseech you to convey my gratitude to the Bodhisattva." Look at him! All he could do was to kowtow toward the sky without bothering to count how many times! By the side of the road the Great Sage Sun reeled with laughter, the Handsome Monkey King broke up with hilarity. He came up and tugged at his master, saying, "Master, get up! He is long gone! He can't hear you, nor can he see your kowtowing. Why keep up this adoration?" "Disciple," said the priest, "when I kowtowed like that, all you could do was to stand snickering by the side of the road, with not even a bow. Why?" "You wouldn't know, would you?" said Pilgrim. "For playing a game of hide-and-seek like that with us, he really deserves a beating! But for the sake of the Bodhisattva, I'll spare him, and that's something already! You think he dares accept a bow from old Monkey? Old Monkey has been a hero since his youth, and he doesn't know how to bow to people! Even when I saw the Jade Emperor and Laozi, I just gave them my greeting, that's all!" "Blasphemy!" said Tripitaka. "Stop this idle talk! Let's get going without further delay." So the priest got up and prepared to set off again toward the West.

After leaving that place, they had a peaceful journey for two months, for all they met were barbarians, Muslims, tigers, wolves, and leopards. Time went by swiftly, and it was again early spring. You could see jade green gilding the mountain forest, and green sprouts of grass appearing. The plum blossoms were all fallen and the willow-leaves gently budding. As master and disciple were admiring this scenery of spring, they saw the sun sinking westward again. Reining the horse, Tripitaka peered into the distance and saw at the fold of the hill the shadow of buildings and the dark silhouette of towers. "Wukong," said Tripitaka, "look at the buildings over there. What sort of a place is that?" Stretching his neck to look, Pilgrim said, "It has to be either a temple or a monastery. Let's move along and ask for lodging over there." Tripitaka was glad to follow this suggestion and urged his dragon-horse forward. We do not know what took place thereafter; let's listen to the explanation in the next chapter.

SIXTEEN

At Guanyin Hall the monks plot for the treasure;
At Black Wind Mountain a monster steals the cassock.

We were telling you about the disciple and master, who urged the horse forward and arrived at the front gate of the building. They saw that it was indeed a monastery with

> Tiers of towers and turrets,
> And rows of quiet chambers.
> Above the temple gate
> Hung the august panoply of colored nimbus;
> Before the Hall of Five Blessings
> Whirled a thousand strands of bright red mists.
> Two rows of pines and bamboos;
> One grove of juniper and cypress;
> Two rows of pines and bamboos
> Revealed their fair virtue unspoiled by time;
> One grove of juniper and cypress
> Displayed its chaste beauty in comely hues.
> They saw also the tall bell tower,
> The pagoda rugged,
> Monks in silent meditation
> And birds on trees gently cooing.
> A dustless seclusion was the real seclusion,
> For the quiescence of Dao was truly quiescent.

The poem says:

> This temple, like Jetavana, hides in a jade-green grove.
> Its beauty surpasses even the Ṣaḍ-varṣa.[1]
> Pure land among mankind is rare indeed:
> This world's famed mountains are mostly held by monks.

The priest dismounted, and Pilgrim laid down his load. They were about to walk through the gate when a monk came out. "How does he look?" you ask.

> He wore a hat pinned to the left
> And a robe most spotlessly pure.
> Two brass rings hung from his ears;
> A silk sash was wrapped round his waist.

His straw sandals moved sedately;
His hands carried a wooden fish.
His mouth recited constantly
The Wisdom he sought most humbly.

When Tripitaka saw him, he stood waiting by the gate and saluted with his palms pressed together in front of him. The monk returned the greeting at once and said laughing, "I'm sorry, but I don't know you!" He then asked, "Where do you come from? Please come in for some tea." "Your disciple," said Tripitaka, "has been sent by royal decree from the Land of the East to go to seek scriptures from Buddha in the Temple of Thunderclap. It was getting late when we arrived here, and we would like to ask for a night's lodging in your fair temple." "Please take a seat inside," said the monk. Only then did Tripitaka call Pilgrim to lead the horse inside. When the monk caught sight of Pilgrim's face, he became somewhat afraid and asked, "What's that thing leading the horse?" "Speak softly!" said Tripitaka. "He's easily provoked! If he hears you referring to him as a thing, he'll get mad. He happens to be my disciple." With a shiver, the monk bit his finger and said, "Such a hideous creature, and you made him your disciple!" Tripitaka said, "You can't tell by mere appearance. He may be ugly, but he is very useful."

That monk had little choice but to accompany Tripitaka and Pilgrim as they entered the temple gate. Inside, above the main hall's entrance, the words "Guanyin Chan Hall" were written in large letters. Highly pleased, Tripitaka said, "This disciple has repeatedly benefited from the holy grace of the Bodhisattva, though he has had no opportunity to thank her. Now that we are at this Chan hall, it is as if we are meeting the Bodhisattva personally, and it is most proper that I should offer my thanks." When the monk heard this, he told one of the attendants to open wide the door of the hall and invited Tripitaka to worship. Pilgrim tied up the horse, dropped his luggage, and went with Tripitaka up the hall. Stretching his back and then flattening himself on the ground, Tripitaka kowtowed to the golden image as the monk went to beat the drum, and Pilgrim began to strike the bell. Prostrating himself before the seat of the deity, Tripitaka poured out his heart in prayer. When he finished, the monk stopped the drum, but Pilgrim continued to strike the bell without ceasing. Now rapidly, now slowly, he persisted for a long time. The attendant said, "The service is over. Why are you still striking the bell?" Only then did Pilgrim throw away the hammer and say, laughing, "You wouldn't know this! I'm just living by the proverb: 'If you are a monk for a day, strike then the bell for a day!'"[2]

By then, the monks young and old of the monastery and the elders of upper and lower chambers were all aroused by the unruly sound of the bell.

They rushed out together crying, "Who is the maniac fooling with the bell?" Pilgrim leaped out of the hall and shouted, "Your Grandpa Sun sounded it to amuse himself!" The moment the monks saw him, they were so frightened that they tumbled and rolled on the ground. Crawling around, they said, "Father Thunder!" "He's only my great-grandson!" said Pilgrim. "Get up, get up! Don't be afraid. We are noble priests who have come from the Great Tang Nation in the east." The various monks then bowed courteously to him, and when they saw Tripitaka, they were even more reassured. One of the monks, who was the abbot of the monastery, said, "Let the holy fathers come to the living room in the back so that we may offer them some tea." Untying the reins and leading the horse, they picked up the luggage and went past the main hall to the back of the monastery, where they sat down in orderly rows.

After serving tea, the abbot prepared a vegetarian meal, although it was still rather early for dinner. Tripitaka had not finished thanking him when an old monk emerged from the rear, supported by two boys. Look how he was attired:

> He wore on his head a Vairocana hat
> Topped by a precious, shining cat's-eye stone;
> He wore on his body a brocaded woolen frock,
> Piped brilliantly in gold and kingfisher feathers.
> A pair of monk shoes on which Eight Treasures were set,
> And a priestly staff encased with starry gems.
> His face full of wrinkles,
> He looked like the Old Witch of Li Mountain;
> His eyes were dim-sighted,
> Though he seemed a Dragon King of the Eastern Ocean.
> Wind stabbed his mouth for his teeth had fallen,
> And palsy had made crooked his aged back.

The various monks made the announcement: "The Patriarch is here." Tripitaka bowed to receive him, saying, "Old Abbot, your disciple bows to you." The old monk returned the gesture, and they were both seated. "Just now I heard the little ones announcing," said the old monk, "that venerable fathers from the Tang court have arrived from the east. I came out specifically to meet you." "Without knowing any better," said Tripitaka, "we intruded into your esteemed temple. Please pardon us!" "Please, please!" said the old monk. "May I ask the holy father what the distance is between here and the Land of the East?" "Since leaving the outskirts of Chang'an," said Tripitaka, "I traveled for some five thousand miles before passing the Mountain of Two Frontiers, where I picked up a little disciple. Moving on, we passed through the Hamil Kingdom of the western barbarians, and in two months we had traveled another five or six thousand miles. Only then did we arrive at your noble region." "Well, you have covered the distance of ten thousand miles," said the old monk. "This disciple truly has spent his life in vain, for he has not even left the door of the temple. I have, as the saying goes, 'sat in the well to look at the sky.' A veritable piece of dead wood!"

Then Tripitaka asked, "What is the honorable age of the Old Abbot?" "Foolishly I have reached my two hundred and seventieth year," said the old monk. When Pilgrim heard this, he said, "You are only my descendant of the ten-thousandth generation!" "Careful!" said Tripitaka, looking at him sternly. "Don't offend people with your brashness!" "And you, Elder," asked the old monk, "how old are you?" "I dare not tell," said Pilgrim. That old monk thought it was just a foolish remark; he paid no further attention, nor did he ask again. Instead, he called for tea to be served, and a young cleric brought out a tray made of milk-white jade on which there were three cloisonné cups with gold edges. Another youth brought out a white copper pot and poured three cups of scented tea, truly more colorful than camellia buds and more fragrant than cassia flowers. When Tripitaka saw these, he could not cease making compliments, saying, "What marvelous things! What marvelous things! A lovely drink, indeed, and lovely utensils!" "Most disgraceful stuff!" said the old monk. "The holy father resides in the heavenly court of a great nation, and he has witnessed all kinds of rare treasures. Things like these are not worthy of your praise. Since you have come from a noble state, do you have any precious thing you can show me?" "It's pathetic!" said Tripitaka. "We have no precious thing in the Land of the East; and even if we had, I could not bring it with me because of the distance."

From the side, Pilgrim said, "Master, I saw a cassock the other day in our bag. Isn't that a treasure? Why not take it out and show it to him?" When the other monks heard him mentioning a cassock, they all began to snicker. "What are you laughing at?" asked Pilgrim. The abbot said, "To say that a cassock is a treasure, as you just did, is certainly laughable. If you want to talk about cassocks, priests like us would possess more than twenty or thirty such garments. Take the case of our Patriarch, who has been a monk here for some two hundred and fifty years. He has over seven hundred of them!" He then made the suggestion: "Why not take them out for these people to see?" That old monk certainly thought it was his show this time! He asked the attendants to open up the storage room and the dhūtas to bring out the chests. They brought out twelve of them and set them down in the courtyard. The padlocks were unlocked; clothes racks were set up on both sides, and ropes were strung all around. One by one, the cassocks were shaken loose and hung up for Tripitaka to see. It was truly a roomful of embroidery, four walls of exquisite silk!

Glancing at them one by one, Pilgrim saw that they were all pieces of fine silk intricately woven and delicately embroidered, splashed with gold. He laughed and said, "Fine! Fine! Fine! Now pack them up! Let's take ours out for you to look at." Pulling Pilgrim aside, Tripitaka said softly, "Disciple, don't start a contest of wealth with other people. You and I are strangers away from home, and this may be a mistake!" "Just a look at the cassock," said Pilgrim, "how can that be a mistake?" "You haven't considered this," said Tripitaka. "As the ancients declared, 'The rare object of art should not be exposed to the covetous and deceitful person.' For once he sees it, he will be tempted; and once he is tempted, he will plot and scheme. If you are timid, you may end up yielding to his every demand; otherwise, injury and loss of life may result, and that's no small matter." "Relax! Relax!" said Pilgrim. "Old Monkey will assume all responsibility!" Look at him! He did not permit any further discussion! Darting away, he untied the bag, and brilliant rays at once came flashing through the two layers of oil-paper in which the garment was wrapped. He discarded the paper and took out the cassock. As he shook it loose, a crimson light flooded the room and glorious air filled the courtyard. When the various monks saw it, none could suppress the admiration in his heart and the praise on his lips. It was truly a magnificent cassock! It has hanging on it

> Sparkling pearls—marvelous in every way—
> And Buddha's treasures in each aspect rare.
> Up and down spreads grapevine³ weave on gorgeous silk;
> On every side are hems of fine brocade.
> Put it on, and goblins will then be slain.
> Step in it, and demons will flee to Hell.
> It's made by those hands of gods incarnate;
> He who's not a true monk dares not wear it.

When the old monk saw a treasure of such quality, he was indeed moved to villainy. Walking forward, he knelt down before Tripitaka, and tears began to fall from his eyes. "This disciple truly has no luck," he said. "Old Abbot," said Tripitaka, raising him up, "what do you mean?" "It was already getting late," he said, "when the venerable father spread this treasure out. But my eyes are dim and I can't see clearly. Isn't this my misfortune?" "Bring out the lamps," said Tripitaka, "and you can take a better look." The old monk said, "The treasure of the father is already dazzling; if we light the lamps, it will become much too bright for my eyes, and I'll never be able to see it properly." "How would you like to see it?" asked Pilgrim. "If the venerable father is inclined to be gracious," replied the old monk, "please permit me to take it back to my room, where I can spend the night looking at it carefully. Tomorrow I shall return it to you before you continue your journey to the west. How would that be?" Startled, Tripitaka began to complain to Pilgrim, saying, "It's all your doing! It's all your doing!" "What are you afraid of?" said Pilgrim, laughing. "Let me wrap it up and he can take it away. If there's any mishap, old Monkey will take care of it." Tripitaka could not stop him; he handed the cassock over to the monk, saying, "You may look at it, but you must give it back tomorrow morning, just as it is. Don't spoil or damage it in any way!" The old monk was very pleased. After telling the young cleric to take the cassock inside, he gave instructions for the various monks to sweep out the Chan hall in front. Two rattan beds were sent for and the bedding was prepared, so that the two travelers could rest. He gave further instructions for sending them off with breakfast in the morning, after which everyone left. Master and disciple closed up the hall and slept, and we shall say no more of that.

We shall now tell you about the old monk, who had got hold of the cassock by fraud. He took it beneath the lamps in the back room and sat in front of it, bawling. The chief priest of the monastery was so startled that he dared not retire first. The young cleric, not knowing the reason for the weeping, went to report to the other monks, saying, "The aged father has been crying, and it's now the second watch and he still hasn't stopped." Two grand disciples, who were his favorites, went forward to ask him, "Grand master, why are you crying?" "I'm crying over my ill luck," replied the old monk, "for I cannot look at the treasure of the Tang Monk." One of the little monks said, "The aged father is becoming a little senile! The cassock is placed right before you. All you have to do is to untie the package and look at it. Why do you have to cry?" "But I can't look at it for long," said the old monk. "I'm two hundred and seventy years old, and yet I have bargained in vain for those several hundred cassocks. What must I do to acquire that one cassock of his? How can I become the Tang Monk himself?" "The grand master is erring," said the little monk. "The Tang Monk is a mendicant who had to leave his home and country. You are enjoying the benefits of old age here, and that should be sufficient. Why do you want to be a mendicant like him?" The old monk said, "Though I'm relaxing at home and enjoying my declining years, I have no cassock like his to put on. If I can put it on for just one day, I'll die with my eyes shut, for then I shall not have been a monk in vain in this World of Light." "What nonsense!" said another monk. "If you want to put it on, what's so difficult about that? Tomorrow we will ask them to stay for one more day, and you can wear it the whole day; if that's not enough, we'll detain them for ten days so that you can wear the cassock all that time. That will be the end of the matter. Why do you have to cry like this?" "Even if they were to be detained for a whole year," said the old monk, "I would only be able to wear it for one year. That's not long-lasting! The moment they want to leave, we will have to return it. How can we make it last?"

As they were speaking, one of the little monks, whose name was Great Wisdom, spoke up: "Aged Father, if you want it to last, that's easy too!" When the old monk heard that, he brightened up. "My son," he said, "what profound thoughts do you have?" Great Wisdom said, "The Tang Monk and his disciple are travelers and are subjected to a lot of stress and strain. So they are fast asleep now. I suppose a few of us who are strong could take up knives and spears, break open the Chan hall, and kill them. We could bury them in the backyard, and only those of us within the family would know about it. We could also take over the white horse and the luggage, but the cassock could be kept as an heirloom. Now isn't this a plan made to last through posterity?" When the old monk heard this, he was filled with delight. Wiping away his tears, he said, "Good! Good! Good! This plan is absolutely marvelous!" He asked at once for knives and spears.

There was in their midst another little monk, whose name was Big Plan, who was the younger classmate of Great Wisdom. Coming forward, he said, "That plan is no good! If you want to kill them, you must first assess the situation. It's easy to take care of the one with the white face, but the hairy face presents more difficulty. If for some reason you are unable to slay him, you might bring disaster upon yourselves. I have a plan that does not call for knives or spears. How do you feel about this?" "My son," said the old monk, "what sort of plan do you have?" "In the opinion of your little grandson," said Big Plan, "we can call up all the resident heads, both senior and junior, in the eastern wing of this monastery, asking each person and his group to bring a bundle of dried firewood. We'll sacrifice the three rooms of the Chan hall and set fire to them; the people inside will be barred from all exits. Even the horse will be burned with them! If the families who live in front of the temple or behind it should see the fire, we can say that they caused it by their carelessness and burned down our Chan hall. Those two monks will surely be burned to death, but no one will know any better. After that, won't we have the cassock as our heirloom?" When the monks heard this, they were all delighted. "Better! Better! Better! This plan is even more marvelous! More marvelous!" they all said. They sent for the resident heads at once to bring firewood. Alas, this single plan will have the result of

A venerable old monk ending his life,
And the Guanyin Chan Hall reduced to dust.

That monastery, you see, had over seventy suites and some two hundred monks resided there. Hordes of them went to fetch firewood, which they stacked around the Chan hall until it was completely surrounded. They then made plans to light the fire, but we shall say no more of that.

We must now tell you about Tripitaka and his disciple, who had already gone to rest. That Pilgrim, however, was a spiritual monkey; though he lay down, he was only exercising his breath to preserve his spirit, with his eyes half-closed. Suddenly he heard people running around outside and the crackling of firewood in the wind. "This is a time for quietness," he said to himself, his suspicion fully aroused, "so why do I hear people walking about? Could they be thieves plotting against us?" Whirling around, he leaped up, and would have opened the door to look outside, had he not been afraid of waking his master. Look at him display his abilities! With one shake of his body he changed into a bee. Truly he had

A sweet mouth and vicious tail;
A small waist and light body.
He cut through flowers and willow like a dart;
He sought like a meteor the scented pollen.
His light, tiny body could bear much weight.
His thin wings buzzing could ride the wind.
Descending from rafters and beams,
He crawled out to get a clear view.

He then saw that the various monks were hauling hay and carrying firewood; surrounding the Chan hall, they were about to light the fire. "What my master said has really come true!" said Pilgrim, smiling to himself. "Because they wanted to take our lives and rob us of our cassock, they were moved to such treachery. I suppose I could use my rod to attack them, but I'm afraid they wouldn't be able to withstand it. A little beating, and they would all be dead! Then Master would blame me for acting violently again. O, let it be! I shall lead the sheep astray conveniently and meet plot with plot, so that they won't be able to live here anymore." Dear Pilgrim! With a single somersault, he leaped straight up to the South Heaven Gate. He so startled the divine warriors Pang, Liu, Gou, and Bi that they bowed, and so alarmed Ma, Zhao, Wen, and Guan that they bent low. "Good Heavens!" they cried. "That character who disrupted Heaven is here again!" "No need to stand on ceremony, all of you!" said Pilgrim, waving his hand. "And don't be alarmed! I came to find Virūpākṣa, the Broad-Eyed Devarāja."

Before he had finished speaking, the Devarāja arrived and greeted Pilgrim, saying, "It's been a long time! I heard some time ago that the Bodhisattva Guanyin asked the Jade Emperor for the services of the Four Sentinels, the Six Gods of Light and Darkness, and the Guardians to protect the Tang Monk as he goes in quest of scriptures in the Western Heaven. She also said that you had become his disciple. How do you have the leisure to be here today?" "Don't mention leisure!" said Pilgrim. "The Tang Monk met some wicked people on his journey, who are about to have him burned up. It's an extreme emergency, and that's why I've come to borrow your Fire-Repelling Cover to save him. Bring it to me quickly; I'll return it the moment I'm finished with it." "You are wrong," said the Devarāja. "If wicked people are starting a fire, you should go find water to save him. Why do you want the Fire-Repelling Cover?" Pilgrim said, "You have no idea what's behind this. If I find water to save him, the fire won't burn, and that will benefit our enemies instead. I want this cover so that only the Tang Monk will be protected from harm. I don't care about the rest! Let them burn! Quickly! Quickly! A little delay, and it may be too late! You will botch up my affairs down below!" "This monkey is still plotting with an evil mind," said the Devarāja, laughing. "After looking out for himself, he is not worried about other people." "Hurry!" said Pilgrim. "Stop wagging your tongue, or you'll upset my great enterprise!" The Devarāja dared not refuse and gave Pilgrim the cover.

Pilgrim took it and descended through the clouds to the roof of the Chan hall, where he covered up the Tang Monk, the white horse, and the luggage. He himself then went to sit on the roof of the back room occupied by the old monk in order to guard the cassock. As he saw the people lighting the fire, he pressed his fingers together to make a magic sign and recited a spell. Facing the ground to the southwest, he took a deep breath and then blew it out. At once a strong wind arose and whipped the fire into a mighty blaze. What a fire! What a fire! You see

> Rolling black smoke;
> Vaulting red flames.
> With rolling black smoke
> All the stars vanish from the vast sky;
> With vaulting red flames
> The earth's lit up, made crimson for a thousand miles.
> At the beginning,
> What gleaming snakes of gold!
> Soon thereafter,
> What imposing bloody horses!
> The Three Southern Forces display their might.
> The Great God of Fire reveals his power.
> When dried wood burns in such fire intense,
> Why speak of Suiren[4] drilling fire from wood?
> When colored flames shoot out of hot-oiled doors,
> They match even the opened oven of Laozi.

This is how fire rages ruthlessly,
Though no worse than such intended fraud
As not suppressing misdeeds
And abetting violence.
The wind sweeps the fire
And flames fly up for some eight thousand feet;
The fire's helped by the wind,
So ashes burst beyond the Ninefold Heaven.
Ping-ping, pang-pang,
They sound like those firecrackers at year's end.
Po-po, la-la,
They're like the roar of cannons in the camps.
It burns till the Buddha's image cannot flee from the scene,
And the Temple Guardians have no place to hide.
It's like the Red Cliff Campaign in the night,[5]
Surpassing the fire at Epang Palace.[6]

As the saying goes, "One little spark of fire can burn ten thousand acres." In a moment, the strong wind and the raging fire made the entire Guanyin Hall glowing red. Look at all those monks! They began to bring out the chests and carry out the drawers, to grab for tables and snatch up pots. A loud wailing filled the whole courtyard. Pilgrim Sun, however, stood guard at the back while the Fire-Repelling Cover securely screened off the Chan hall at the front. The rest of the place was completely lit up; truly the sky was illuminated by brilliant red flames, and bright gold light shone through the walls.

No one knew, however, that when the fire had begun, it had caught the attention of a mountain monster. For about twenty miles due south of this Guanyin Hall there was a Black Wind Mountain, where there was also a Black Wind Cave. A monster in the cave, who happened to turn over in his sleep, noticed that his windows were lit up. He thought that dawn had broken, but when he arose and took another look, he saw instead the brilliant glow of fire burning in the north. Astonished, the monster said, "Good Heavens! There must be a fire in the Guanyin Hall. Those monks are so careless! Let me see if I can help them a little!" Dear monster! He rose with his cloud and went at once to the place of fire and smoke, where he discovered that the halls front and back were entirely empty while the fire in the corridors on both sides was raging. With great strides he ran inside and was about to call for water when he saw that there was no fire in the back room. Someone, however, was sitting on the roof whipping up the wind. He began to perceive what was happening and ran quickly inside to look around. In the living room of the old monk, he saw on the table colorful radiance emitted by a package wrapped in a blue blanket. He untied it and discovered that it was a cassock of silk brocade, a rare Buddhist treasure. Thus it is how wealth moves the mind of man! He neither attempted to put out the fire nor called for water. Snatching up the cassock, he committed robbery by taking advantage of the confusion and at once turned his cloud back toward the mountain cave.

The fire raged on until the time of the fifth watch before burning itself out. Look at those monks: weeping and wailing, they went with empty hands and naked bodies to rummage about in the ashes, trying desperately to salvage a scrap or two of metal or valuables. Some attempted to erect a temporary shelter along the walls, while others amid the rubble tried to build a makeshift oven so that rice could be cooked. They were all howling and complaining, but we shall say no more about that.

Now we shall tell you about Pilgrim, who, taking the Fire-Repelling Cover, sent it up to the South Heaven Gate with one somersault. He handed it back to the Broad-Eyed Devarāja, saying, "Thanks so much for lending it to me!" The Devarāja took it back and said, "The Great Sage is very honest. I was a little worried that if you did not return my treasure, I would have a hard time finding you. I'm glad you brought it right back." "Do you think that old Monkey is the sort of person who steals openly?" asked Pilgrim. "As the saying goes, 'Return what you borrow, and again you may borrow!'" "I haven't seen you for a long time," said the Devarāja, "and I would like to invite you to spend some time at my palace. How about it?" Pilgrim said, "Old Monkey can't do what he did before, 'squatting on a rotted bench and dispensing lofty discourse.' Now that I have to protect the Tang Monk, I haven't a moment's leisure. Give me a rain check!" He took leave of the Devarāja quickly and dropped down from the clouds. As the sun arose, he arrived at the Chan hall, where with one shake of his body he changed again into a bee. When he flew inside and resumed his original form, he saw that his master was still sleeping soundly.

"Master," cried Pilgrim, "it's dawn. Get up." Only then did Tripitaka awake; he turned around, saying, "Yes, indeed!" Putting on his clothes, he opened the door and went out. As he raised his head, he saw crumbling walls and seared partitions; the towers, the terraces, and the buildings had all disappeared. "Ah!" he cried, greatly shaken. "How is it that the buildings are all gone? Why are there only scorched walls?" "You are still dreaming!" said Pilgrim. "They had a fire here last night." "Why didn't I know about it?" asked Tripitaka. "It's old Monkey who safeguarded the Chan hall," replied Pilgrim. "When I saw that Master was sound asleep, I did not disturb you." "If you had the ability to safeguard the Chan hall," said Tripitaka, "why didn't you put out the fire in the other buildings?" "So that you may learn the truth," said Pilgrim, laughing, "just as you predicted it yesterday. They fell in love with our cassock and made plans to have us burned to death. If old Monkey had been less alert, we would have been reduced to bone and ashes by now!" When Tripitaka heard these words, he was alarmed and asked, "Was it they who set the fire?" "Who else?" said Pilgrim. "Could it be," asked Tripitaka, "that they mistreated you, and you did this?" Pilgrim replied, "Is old Monkey the sort of wretch that would indulge in such sordid business? It really was they who set the fire. When I saw how malicious they were, I admit I did not help them put the fire out. I did, however, manage to provide them with a little wind!"

"My God! My God!" said Tripitaka. "When a fire starts, you should get water. How could you provide wind instead?" "You must have heard," said Pilgrim, "what the ancients said: 'If a man has no desire to harm a tiger, a tiger has no intention of hurting a man.' If they hadn't played with fire, would I have played with wind?" "Where's the cassock?" asked Tripitaka. "Has it been burned?" "Not at all!" replied Pilgrim. "It hasn't been burned, for the fire didn't reach the living quarters of the old monk where the cassock was placed." "I don't care!" exclaimed Tripitaka, his resentment rising. "If there's the slightest damage, I'm going to recite that little something and you'll be dead!" "Master!" cried Pilgrim with alarm, "don't start your recitation! I'll find the cassock and return it to you, and that'll be the end of the matter. Let me go fetch it so that we can start on our journey." Tripitaka led the horse while Pilgrim took up the load of luggage. They left the Chan hall and went to the room at the rear.

We now tell you about the monks, who were still grieving when they suddenly saw master and disciple approaching with the horse and the luggage. Scared out of their wits, they all said, "The wronged souls have come to seek vengeance!" "What wronged souls are seeking vengeance?" shouted Pilgrim. "Give back my cassock quickly!" All the monks fell to their knees at once, saying as they kowtowed, "Holy Fathers! Just as a wrong implies an enemy, so a debt has its proper creditor! If you seek vengeance, please understand that we had nothing to do with this. It was the old monk who plotted with Big Plan against you. Don't make us pay for your lives!" "You damnable beasts!" cried Pilgrim angrily. "Who wants you to pay with your lives? Just give me back the cassock and we'll be going." Two of the monks who were less timid said to him, "Father, you were supposed to be burned to death in the Chan hall, and yet now you come to demand the cassock. Are you indeed a man, or are you a ghost?" "This bunch of accursed creatures!" said Pilgrim, laughing. "Where was the fire? Go to the front and look at the Chan hall. Then you can come back and talk." The monks got up and went to the front to look; not even half an inch of the door, the window, or the screen outside the Chan hall was scorched. One and all were awestruck and became convinced that Tripitaka was a divine monk, and Pilgrim a celestial guardian. They all went forward to kowtow to them, saying, "We have eyes but no pupils, and therefore we did not recognize True Men descending to Earth. Your cassock is at the residence of the old Patriarch at the back." Tripitaka was deeply saddened by the rows of crumbling walls and damaged partitions they went past before arriving at the Patriarch's chambers, which were indeed untouched by fire. The monks dashed in, crying, "Aged Father, the Tang Monk must be a god. He hasn't been burned to death, though we have hurt ourselves. Let's take the cassock quickly and give it back to him."

But the fact of the matter is that the old monk could not find the cassock. In addition, most of the buildings in his monastery had been ruined, and he was, of course, terribly distressed. When he heard the monks calling, how could he have the courage to reply? Feeling utterly helpless and incapable of solving his dilemma, he bent forward, took several great strides, and rammed his head into the wall. How pitiful! The impact made

> *The brain burst, the blood flow, and his soul disperse;*
> *His head stained the sand as his breathing stopped.*

We have a poem as a testimony, which says:

> *So lamentable is this blind old monk!*
> *In vain he lives among men to such old age.*
> *He wants the cassock forever to keep,*
> *Not knowing how uncommon is Buddha's gift.*
> *If you think what endures can come with ease,*
> *Yours will be sure failure and certain grief.*
> *Big Plan, Great Wisdom, of what use are they?*
> *To gain by others' loss—what empty dreams!*

Shocked to tears, the monks cried, "The Patriarch has killed himself. And we can't find the cassock. What shall we do?" "It must have been you who stole it and hid it," said Pilgrim. "Come out, all of you! Give me a complete list of your names and let me check you off the roll one by one." The head residents of all the upper and lower chambers made a thorough accounting of all the monks, the dhūtas, the young novices, and the Daoists in two scrolls, and presented Pilgrim with some two hundred and thirty names. Asking his master to take a seat in the middle, Pilgrim went through the roll and examined the monks one by one. Every person had to loosen his clothes to be searched thoroughly, but there was no cassock. They then went to hunt through the trunks and chests that had been salvaged from the fire, but again there was not the slightest trace of the garment. In dismay, Tripitaka became more and more embittered toward Pilgrim until he began reciting the spell as he sat there. Falling at once to the ground, Pilgrim gripped his head with his hands, hardly able to bear the pain. "Stop the recitation! Stop the recitation!" he cried. "I'll find the cassock." Terrified by what they saw, the various monks went forward and knelt down to plead with Tripitaka, who only then stopped his recitation. Pilgrim leaped straight up and whipped out his rod from his ear. He would have struck at the monks, had not Tripitaka shouted for him to halt, crying, "Monkey! Aren't you afraid of your headache? Do you still want to behave badly? Don't move, and don't hurt people! Let me question them further." The monks kowtowed and begged Tripitaka, saying, "Father, please spare us. Truly we did not see your cassock. It was entirely the fault of that old devil! After he got your cassock last night, he started crying until very late; he didn't even bother to look at it, for all he had on his mind was how he might keep it permanently as an heirloom. That was why he made plans to have you burned to death, but after the fire started, a violent wind arose also. Every one of us was only concerned with putting out the fire and trying to save something. We have no idea where the cassock has gone."

Angrily, Pilgrim walked into the Patriarch's room, pulled out the corpse of the old man rammed to death, and stripped him naked. The body was examined carefully, but the treasure was nowhere to be seen. Even if they had dug up three feet of the ground in that room, there would have been not a trace of it. Pilgrim thought silently for awhile and then asked, "Is there any monster around here who has become a spirit?" "If father hadn't asked," said the abbot, "he would have never known about this. Southeast of us there is a Black Wind Mountain, in which there is a Black Wind Cave. In the cave is a Black Great King, with whom this deceased old fellow of ours used to discuss the Dao frequently. He is the only monster spirit around here." "How far is the mountain from here?" asked Pilgrim. "Only twenty miles," said the abbot. "The peak that you can see right now is where it is." Pilgrim laughed and said, "Relax, Master! No need for further discussion; it must have been stolen by the black monster." "That place is about twenty miles away," said Tripitaka. "How can you be so sure that it was he?" "You didn't see last night's fire," said Pilgrim, "when its light illuminated great distances, and its brightness penetrated the Threefold Heaven. Not just for twenty miles, but for two hundred miles around it could be seen. I have no doubt that he saw the brilliant glow of the fire and used that opportunity to come here secretly. When he saw that our cassock was a treasure, he grabbed it in the confusion and left. Let old Monkey go find him." "Who will care for me while you are gone?" asked Tripitaka. "You can relax," said Pilgrim. "You have in secret the protection of the gods; and in the open, I shall make sure that the monks wait on you." He then called the monks over, saying, "A few of you can go and bury that old devil, while the others can wait on my master and watch our white horse." The monks at once agreed. Pilgrim said again, "Don't give me any casual reply now, only to grow slack in your service after I'm gone. Those who wait on my master must be cheerful and pleasant; those who look after the white horse must take care that water and hay are fed in proper proportions. If there's the slightest mistake, you can count on meeting this rod. Now watch!" He whipped out his rod and aimed it at the seared bricked wall: with one stroke, not only did he pulverize the wall, but the impact was so great that it caused seven or eight more walls to collapse. When the various monks saw this, they were all paralyzed with fear. They knelt to kowtow with tears flowing from their eyes and said, "Father, please be assured that we shall be most diligent in caring for the holy father after you are gone. We wouldn't dream of slacking in any way."

Dear Pilgrim! He swiftly mounted the cloud somersault and went straight to the Black Wind Mountain to look for the cassock. Thus it was that

> Truth-seeking Gold Cicada left Chang'an.[7]
> With gifts he went westward, passing blue-green hills.
> There were wolves and tigers as he walked along,
> Though merchants or scholars were rarely seen.
> One foolish monk's envy abroad he met;
> His refuge solely was the Great Sage's might.
> The fire grew; the wind came and wrecked the Chan hall.
> A Black Bear at night stole the embroidered robe.

We do not know whether Pilgrim found the cassock or not, or whether the outcome of his search was good or bad. Let's listen to the explanation in the next chapter.

SEVENTEEN

Pilgrim Sun greatly disturbs the Black Wind Mountain; Guanshiyin brings to submission the bear monster.

We now tell you that when Pilgrim Sun somersaulted into the air, he so terrified the monks, the dhūtas, the young novices, and the attendants at the Guanyin Hall that every person bowed to the sky, saying, "O, Father! So you are actually an incarnate deity who knows how to ride the fog and sail with the clouds! No wonder fire cannot harm you! That ignorant old carcass of ours—how despicable he was! He used all his intelligence only to bring disaster on his own head." "Please rise, all of you," said Tripitaka. "There's no need for regret. Let's hope that he'll find the cassock, and everything will be all right. But if not, I would fear for your lives; for that disciple of mine has a bad temper, and I'm afraid that none of you will escape him." When the monks heard this, they were all panic-stricken; they pleaded with Heaven for the cassock to be found so that their lives would be preserved, but we shall say no more about them for the moment.

We were telling you about the Great Sage Sun. Having leaped up into the air, he gave one twist of his torso and arrived at once at the Black Wind Mountain. Stopping his cloud, he looked carefully and saw that it was indeed a magnificent mountain, especially in this time of spring. You see

Many streams potently flowing,
Countless cliffs vying for beauty.
The birds call but no man is seen;
Though flowers fall, the tree's yet scented.
The rain passes, the sky's one moist sheet of blue;
The wind comes, the pines rock like screens of jade.
The mountain grass sprouts,
The wild flowers bloom
On hanging cliffs and high ranges.
The wisteria grows,
The handsome trees bud
On rugged peaks and flat plateaus.
You don't even meet a recluse.
Where can you find a woodsman?
By the stream the cranes drink in pairs;
On the rocks wild apes madly play.

Augustly the branches spread their luscious green,
Basking their splendor in bright mountain mist.

Pilgrim was enjoying the scenery when suddenly he heard voices coming from beyond a lovely grass meadow. With light, stealthy steps, he inched forward and hid himself beneath a cliff to have a peep. He saw three monsters sitting on the ground: a swarthy fellow in the middle, a Daoist to the left, and a white-robed scholar to the right. They were in the midst of an animated conversation, discussing how to establish the tripod and the oven, how to knead the cinnabar and refine the mercury, the topics of white snow and yellow sprout,[1] and the esoteric doctrines of heterodox Daoism. As they were speaking, the swarthy fellow said, laughing, "The day after tomorrow will be the date of my mother's labor. Will you two gentlemen pay me a visit?" "Every year we celebrate the Great King's birthday," said the white-robed scholar. "How could we think of not coming this year?" "Last night I came upon a treasure," said the swarthy fellow, "which may be called a brocaded robe of Buddha. It's a most attractive thing, and I think I'm going to use it to enhance my birthday. I plan to give a large banquet, starting tomorrow, and to invite all our Daoist friends of various mountains to celebrate this garment. We shall call the party the Festival of the Buddha Robe. How about that?" "Marvelous! Marvelous!" said the Daoist, laughing. "First I'll come to the banquet tomorrow, and then I'll bring you good wishes on your birthday the day after."

When Pilgrim heard them speaking about a robe of Buddha, he was certain that they were referring to his own treasure. Unable to suppress his anger, he leaped clear of his hiding place and raised high the golden-hooped rod with both hands, shouting, "You larcenous monsters! You stole my cassock. What Festival of the Buddha Robe do you think you are going to have? Give it back to me at once, and don't try to run away!" Wielding his rod, he struck at their heads. In panic, the swarthy fellow fled by riding the wind, and the Daoist escaped by mounting the clouds. The white-robed scholar, however, was killed by one stroke of the rod, and he turned out to be the spirit of a white-spotted snake when Pilgrim pulled his body over for closer examination. He picked up the corpse again and broke it into several pieces before proceeding deep into the mountain to look for the swarthy fellow. Passing pointed peaks and rugged ridges, he found himself in front of a hanging cliff with a cave dwelling below it. You see

Mist and smoke abundant,
Cypress and pine umbrageous.
Mist and smoke abundant, their hues surround the door;
Cypress and pine umbrageous, their green entwines the gate.
Flat, dried wood supports a bridge.

Wisterias coil round the ridge.
Birds carrying red petals reach the cloudy gorge.
And deer tread on florets to comb the rocky flats.
Before that door
The flowers bloom with the season
As the wind wafts their fragrance.
Atop the dyke-shading willows orioles sing;
O'er the bank's sweet peaches butterflies flit.
This rustic spot, though no cause for much praise,
Still rivals the₃ beauty of Mount Penglai.[2]

Pilgrim went to the door and found that the two stone doors were tightly closed. On top of the door was a stone tablet, on which was plainly written in large letters, "Black Wind Mountain, Black Wind Cave." He lifted his rod to beat at the door, crying, "Open the door!" A little demon who stood guard at the door came out and asked, "Who are you, that you dare beat at our immortal cave?" "You damnable beast!" scolded Pilgrim. "What sort of a place is this, that you dare assume the title of 'immortal'? Is the word 'immortal' for you to use? Hurry inside and tell that swarthy fellow to bring out your venerable father's cassock at once. Then I may spare the lives of the whole nest of you." The little demon ran swiftly inside and reported: "Great King! You won't have a Festival of the Buddha Robe. There's a monk with a hairy face and a thunder-god mouth outside demanding the cassock."

That swarthy fellow, after being chased by Pilgrim from the grass meadow, had just managed to reach the cave. He had not even been able to sit down when he again heard this announcement, and he thought to himself: "I wonder where this fellow came from, so arrogant that he dared show up making demands at my door!" He asked for his armor, and, after putting it on, he walked outside holding a lance with black tassels. Pilgrim stood on one side of the gate, holding his iron rod and glaring. The monster indeed cut a formidable figure:

A bowl-like helmet of dark burnished steel;
A black-gold cuirass that shone most bright.
A black silk robe with wide wind-bagging sleeves,
And dark green sashes with long, long tassels.
He held in his hands a black-tasseled lance.
He wore on his feet two black-leather boots.
His eyes' golden pupils like lightning flashed.
He was thus in this mountain the Black Wind King.

"This fellow," said Pilgrim, smiling to himself, "looks exactly like a kiln worker or a coal miner. He must scrub charcoal here for a living! How did he get to be black all over?" The monster called out in a loud voice, "What kind of a monk are you that you dare to be so impudent around here?" Rushing up to him with his iron rod, Pilgrim roared, "No idle conversation! Return the cassock of your venerable grandfather at once!" "What monastery are you from, bonze?" asked the monster, "and where did you lose your cassock that you dare show up at my place and demand its return?" "My cassock," said Pilgrim, "was stored in the back room of the Guanyin Hall due north of here. Because of the fire there, you committed robbery by taking advantage of the confusion; after making off with the garment, you even wanted to start a Festival of the Buddha Robe to celebrate your birthday. Do you deny this? Give it back to me quickly, and I'll spare your life. If you but mutter half a 'no,' I'll overturn the Black Wind Mountain and level the Black Wind Cave. Your whole cave of demons will be pulverized!"

When the monster heard these words, he laughed scornfully and said, "You audacious creature! You yourself set the fire last night, for you were the one who summoned the wind on top of the roof. I took the cassock all right, but what are you going to do about it? Where do you come from, and what is your name? What ability do you have, that you dare mouth such reckless words?" Pilgrim said, "So you don't recognize your venerable grandfather! He is the disciple of the Master of the Law, Tripitaka, who happens to be the brother of the Throne in the Great Tang Nation. My surname is Sun, and my given name is Wukong Pilgrim. If I tell you my abilities, you'll be frightened out of your wits and die right on the spot!" "I won't," said the monster. "Tell me what abilities you have." "My son," said Pilgrim, laughing, "brace yourself! Listen carefully!³

> Great since my youth was my magic power;
> I changed with the wind to display my might.
> Long I trained my nature and practiced Truth
> To flee the wheel of karma with my life.
> With mind sincere I always sought the Way;
> Seedlings of herbs I plucked on Mount Lingtai.⁴
> There was in that mountain an old immortal.
> His age: one hundred and eight thousand years!
> He became my master most solemnly
> And showed me the way to longevity,
> Saying that in my body were physic and pills
> Which one would work in vain to seek outside.
> He gave me those high secrets of the gods;
> With no foundation I would have been lost.
> My inner light relumed, I sat in peace
> As sun and moon mated within myself.⁵

I thought of nothing—all my desires gone,
My body strengthened, my six senses cleansed.
From age back to youth was an easy boon;
To join transcendents was no distant goal.
Three years without leaks[6] made a godlike frame,
Immune to sufferings known to mortal men.
Playing through the Ten Islets and Three Isles,
I made the rounds at Heaven's very edge.
I lived like that for some three hundred years,
Though not yet ascended to the Ninefold Heaven.
Taming sea dragons brought me treasure true:
The golden-hooped rod I did find below.
As field marshal at the Flower-Fruit Mount,
Monsters I gathered at Water-Curtain Cave.
Then the Jade Emperor gave to me the name,
Equal to Heaven—such, the rank most high.
Thrice I caused havoc in Divine Mists Hall;
Once I stole peaches from the Mother Queen.
Thus came a hundred thousand men divine
To curb me with their rows of spears and swords.
The Devarāja was beaten back to Heaven,
While Naṭa in pain led his troops and fled.
Xiansheng Master[7] knew transformations well;
With him I waged a contest and I fell.
Laozi, Guanyin, and the Jade Emperor
All watched the battle at South Heaven Gate.
When Laozi decided to lend his help,
Erlang brought me to Heaven's magistrate.
To the monster-routing pillar I was tied;
The gods were told to have my head cut off.
Failing to harm me with either sledge or sword,
They would blast and burn me with thunderclaps.
What skills indeed did this old Monkey have,
Who was not even half a whit afraid!
Into Laozi's brazier they sent me next,
To have me slowly cooked by fire divine.
The day the lid was opened I jumped out
And ran through Heaven brandishing a rod.
Back and forth I prowled with none to stop me,
Making havoc through all thirty-six Heavens.
Then Tathāgata revealed his power:
Under Mount Five Phases he had me clamped,

And there I squirmed for a full five hundred years
Till by luck Tripitaka left the Tang court.
Now I go West, having yielded to Truth,
To see Jade Eyebrows at Great Thunderclap.[8]
Go and ask in the four corners of the universe:
You'll learn I'm the famous ranking daimon of all time!"

When the monster heard these words, he laughed and said, "So you are the BanHorsePlague who disturbed the Celestial Palace?" What most annoyed Pilgrim was when people called him BanHorsePlague. The moment he heard that name, he lost his temper. "You monstrous rogue!" he shouted. "You would not return the cassock you stole, and yet you dare insult this holy monk. Don't run away! Watch this rod!" The swarthy fellow jumped aside to dodge the blow; wielding his long lance, he went forward to meet his opponent. That was some battle between the two of them:

The compliant rod,
The black-tasseled lance.
Two men display their power before the cave:
Stabbing at the heart and face;
Striking at the head and arm.
This one proves handy with a death-dealing rod;
That one tilts the lance for swift, triple jabs.
The "white tiger climbing the mountain" extends his paws;
The "yellow dragon lying on the road"[9] turns his back.
With colored mists flying
And bright flashes of light,
Two monster-gods' strength is yet to be tried.
One's the truth-seeking, Equal-to-Heaven Sage;
One's the Great Black King who's now a spirit.
Why wage this battle in the mountain still?
The cassock, for which each would aim to kill!

That monster fought with Pilgrim for more than ten rounds until about noon, but the battle was a draw. Using his lance to halt the rod for a moment, the swarthy fellow said, "Pilgrim Sun, let us put away our weapons for the time being. Let me have some lunch first, and then I'll wage a further contest with you." "Accursed beast!" said Pilgrim. "You want to be a hero? Which hero wants to eat after fighting for merely half a day? Consider old Monkey, who was imprisoned beneath the mountain for altogether five hundred years and he hadn't even tasted a drop of water. So, what's this about being hungry? Don't give me any excuses and don't run away! Give me back my cassock, and I'll allow you to go and eat." But that monster only managed to throw one more feeble thrust with his lance before dashing into the cave and shutting his stone doors. He dismissed his little demons and made preparations for the banquet, writing out invitation cards to the monster kings of various mountains, but we shall say no more about that.

We must tell you that Pilgrim had no success in breaking down the door and so had to return to the Guanyin Hall. The clerics of that monastery had already buried the old monk, and they were all gathered in the back room to minister to the Tang Monk, serving him lunch soon after he had finished breakfast. As they were scurrying about fetching soup and hauling water, Pilgrim was seen descending from the sky. The monks bowed courteously and received him into the back room to see Tripitaka. "Wukong," said Tripitaka, "so you've returned. How is the cassock?" "At least I found the real culprit," said Pilgrim. "It was a good thing that we did not punish these monks, for the monster of Black Wind Mountain did steal it. I went secretly looking for him, and saw him seated on a beautiful grass meadow having a conversation with a white-robed scholar and an old Daoist. He was, in a sense, making a confession without being tortured, saying something about the day after tomorrow being his birthday, when he would invite all the other griffins for the occasion. He also mentioned that he had found an embroidered Buddha robe last night, in celebration of which he was planning to throw a large banquet, calling it the Festival of the Buddha Robe. Old Monkey rushed up to them and struck out with his rod; the swarthy fellow changed into the wind and left, and the Daoist also disappeared. The white-robed scholar, however, was killed, and he turned out to be a white-spotted snake who had become a spirit. I quickly chased the swarthy fellow to his cave and demanded that he come out to fight. He had already admitted that he took the cassock, but we fought to a draw after half a day of battle. The monster returned to his cave because he wanted to eat; he closed his stone doors tightly and refused to fight anymore. I came back to see how you were and to make this report to you. Since I know the whereabouts of the cassock, I'm not worried about his unwillingness to give it back to me."

When the various monks heard this, some of them folded their hands while others kowtowed, all chanting, "Namo Amitābha! Now that the whereabouts of the cassock is known, we have a claim to our lives again."

"Don't celebrate yet," said Pilgrim, "for I have not yet recovered it, nor has my master left. Wait until we have the cassock so that my master can walk peacefully out of this door before you start cheering. If there's the slightest mishap, old Monkey is no customer to be provoked, is he? Have you served some good things to my master? Have you given our horse plenty of hay?"

"We have, we have, we have!" cried the monks hastily. "Our service to the holy monk has not slackened in the least!" "You were gone only half a day," said Tripitaka, "and I have been served tea three times and have had two vegetarian meals. They didn't dare slight me. You should therefore make a great effort to get back the cassock." "Don't rush!" said Pilgrim. "Since I know where he is, I shall certainly capture this fellow and return the garment to you. Relax! Relax!"

As they were speaking, the abbot brought in some more vegetarian dainties to serve to the holy monk Sun. Pilgrim ate some and left at once on the hallowed cloud to search for the monster. As he was traveling, he saw a little demon approaching from the main road, who had a box made of pear tree wood wedged between his left arm and his body. Suspecting that something important was inside the box, Pilgrim raised his rod and brought it down hard on the demon's head. Alas, the demon could not take such a blow! He was instantly reduced to a meat patty, which Pilgrim tossed to the side of the road. When he opened the box, there was indeed an invitation slip, on which was written:

> Your student-servant, the Bear, most humbly addresses the Exalted Aged Dean of the Golden Pool. For the gracious gifts you have bestowed on me on several occasions I am profoundly grateful. I regret that I was unable to assist you last night when you were visited by the God of Fire, but I suppose that Your Holy Eminence has not been adversely affected in any way. Your student by chance has acquired a Buddha robe, and this occasion calls for a festive celebration. I have therefore prepared with care some fine wine for your enjoyment, with the sincere hope that Your Holy Eminence will be pleased to give us a visit. This invitation is respectfully submitted two days in advance.

When Pilgrim saw this, he roared with laughter, saying, "That old carcass! He didn't lose anything by his death! So he belonged to a monster's gang! Small wonder that he lived to his two hundred and seventieth year! That monster, I suppose, must have taught him some little magic like ingesting his breath,[10] and that was how he enjoyed such longevity. I can still remember how he looked. Let me change myself into that monk and go to the cave to see where my cassock is located. If I can manage it, I'll take it back without wasting my energy."

Dear Great Sage! He recited a spell, faced the wind, and changed at once into an exact semblance of that old monk. Putting away his iron rod, he strode to the cave, crying, "Open the door!" When the little demon who stood at the door saw such a figure, he quickly made his report inside: "Great King, the Elder of the Golden Pool has arrived." Greatly surprised, the monster said, "I just sent a little one to deliver an invitation to him, but he could not possibly have reached his destination even at this moment. How could the old monk arrive so quickly? I suppose the little one did not run into him on the way, but Pilgrim Sun must have asked him to come here for the cassock. You, steward, hide the cassock! Don't let him see it!"

Walking through the front door, Pilgrim saw in the courtyard pines and bamboos sharing their green, peaches and plums competing in their glamour; flowers were blooming everywhere, and the air was heavy with the scent of orchids. It was quite a grotto-heaven. He saw, moreover, a parallel couplet mounted on both sides of the second doorway that read:

A deep mountain retreat without worldly cares.
A divine cave secluded—what joy serene.

Pilgrim said to himself, "This fellow is also one who withdraws from dirt and dust, a fiendish creature who knows his fate."[11] He walked through the door and proceeded further; when he passed through the third doorway, he saw carved beams with elaborate ornaments and large windows brightly decorated. Then the swarthy fellow appeared, wearing a casual jacket made of fine dark-green silk, topped by a crow-green cape of figured damask; he wore a head-wrap of black cloth and was shod in a pair of black suede boots. When he saw Pilgrim entering, he tidied his clothes and went down the steps to receive him, saying, "Golden Pool, old friend, we haven't seen each other for days. Please take a seat! Please take a seat!" Pilgrim greeted him ceremoniously, after which they sat down and drank tea.

After tea, the monster bowed low and said, "I just sent you a brief note, humbly inviting you to visit me the day after tomorrow. Why does my old friend grant me that pleasure today, already?" "I was just coming to pay my respects," said Pilgrim, "and I did not anticipate meeting your kind messenger. When I saw that there was going to be a Festival of the Buddha Robe, I came hurriedly, hoping to see the garment." "My old friend may be mistaken," said the monster, laughing. "This cassock originally belonged to the Tang Monk, who was staying at your place. Why would you want to look at it here, since you must surely have seen it before?" "Your poor monk," answered Pilgrim, "did borrow it, but he did not have the opportunity last night to examine it before it was taken by the Great King. Moreover, our monastery, including all our belongings, was destroyed by fire, and the disciple of that Tang Monk was rather bellicose about the matter. In all that confusion, I couldn't find the cassock anywhere, not knowing that the Great King in his good fortune found it. That is why I came specially to see it."

As they were speaking, one of the little demons out on patrol came back to report: "Great King, disaster! The junior officer who went to deliver the invitation was beaten to death by Pilgrim Sun and left by the wayside. Our enemy followed the clue and changed himself into the Golden Pool Elder so that he could obtain the Buddha robe by fraud." When the monster heard that, he said to himself, "I was wondering already why he came today, and in such a hurried manner too! So, it's really he!" Leaping up, he grabbed his lance and aimed it at Pilgrim. Whipping out the rod from his ear, Pilgrim assumed his original form and parried the lance. They rushed from the living room to the front courtyard, and from there they fought their way out to the front door. The monsters in the cave were frightened out of their wits; young and old in that household were horror-stricken. This fierce contest before the mountain was even unlike the last one. What a fight!

> This Monkey King boldly posed as a monk;
> That swarthy chap wisely concealed the robe.
> Back and forth went their clever repartee,
> Adapting to each instant perfectly.
> He would see the cassock but had no means:
> This runic treasure's a mystery indeed!
> The small imp on patrol announced mishap;
> The old fiend in anger showed his power.
> They fought their way out of the Black Wind Cave,
> The rod and the lance forced a trial by might.
> The rod checked the lance, their noise resounding;
> The lance met the rod, causing sparks to fly.
> The changes of Wukong, all unknown to men;
> The monster's magic skills, so rare on earth.
> This one wanted for his birthday fete a Buddha robe.
> Would that one with no cassock go home in peace?
> The bitter fight this time seemed without end.
> Even a live Buddha descending could not break them up!

From the entrance of the cave the two of them fought up to the peak of the mountain, and from the peak of the mountain they fought their way up to the clouds. Belching wind and fog, kicking up sand and rocks, they fought until the red sun sank toward the west, but neither of them could gain the upper hand. The monster said, "Hey, Sun! Stop for a moment! It's getting too late to fight any more. Go away! Come back tomorrow morning, and we'll decide your fate." "Don't run away, my son," cried Pilgrim. "If you want to fight, act like a fighter! Don't give me the excuse that it's getting late." With his rod, he rained blows indiscriminately on his opponent's head and face, but the swarthy fellow changed once more into a clear breeze and went back to his cave. Tightly bolting his stone doors, he refused to come out.

Pilgrim had no alternative except to go back to the Guanyin Hall. Dropping down from the clouds, he said, "Master." Tripitaka, who was waiting for him with bulging eyes, was delighted to see him; but when he did not see the cassock, he became frightened again. "How is it that you still have not brought back the cassock?" he asked. Pilgrim took out from his sleeve the invitation slip and handed it over to Tripitaka, saying, "Master, the monster and that old carcass used to be friends. He sent a little demon here with this invitation for him to go to a Festival of the Buddha Robe. I killed the little demon and changed into the form of the old monk to get inside the cave. I managed to trick him into giving me a cup of tea, but when I asked for the cassock, he refused to show it to me. As we were sitting there, my identity was leaked by someone on patrol in the mountain, and we began to fight. The battle lasted until this early evening and ended in a draw. When the monster saw that it was late, he slipped back into the cave and tightly bolted up his stone door. Old Monkey had no choice but to return here for the moment."

"How's your skill as a fighter when compared with his?" asked Tripitaka. "Not much better," said Pilgrim. "We are quite evenly matched." Tripitaka then read the invitation slip and handed it to the abbot, saying, "Could it be that your master was also a monster-spirit?" Falling to his knees, the abbot said, "Old Father, my master is human. Because that Great Black King attained the way of humanity through self-cultivation, he frequently came to the monastery to discuss religious texts with my master. He imparted to my master a little of the magic of nourishing one's spirit and ingesting breath; hence they address each other as friends."

"This bunch of monks here," said Pilgrim, "don't have the aura of monsters: each one has a round head pointing to the sky and a pair of feet set flat on the earth. They are a little taller and heavier than old Monkey, but they are no monsters. Look at what's written on the slip: 'your student-servant, the Bear.' This creature must be a black bear who has become a spirit." Tripitaka said, "I have heard from the ancients that the bear and the ape are of the same kind. They are all beasts, in other words. How can this bear become a spirit?" "Old Monkey is also a beast," said Pilgrim, laughing, "but I became the Great Sage, Equal to Heaven. Is he any different? All the creatures of this world who possess the nine apertures can become immortals through the art of self-cultivation." "You just said that the two of you were evenly matched," said Tripitaka again. "How can you defeat him and recover my cassock?" "Lay off! Lay off!" said Pilgrim. "I know what to do." As they were discussing the matter, the monks brought in the evening meal for master and disciple. Afterwards, Tripitaka asked for lamps to go to the Chan hall in front to rest. The rest of the monks reclined against the walls beneath some temporary awnings and slept, while the back rooms were given to accommodate the senior and junior abbots. It was now late. You see

The Silver Stream aglow;
The air perfectly pure;

The sky full of bright and twinkling stars;
The river marked by receding tide.
All sounds are hushed;
All hills emptied of birds.
The fisherman's fire dies by the brook;
The lamps grow faint on the pagoda.
Last night ācāryas sounded drums and bells.
Only weeping is heard throughout this night!

So they spent the night in the Chan hall, but Tripitaka was thinking about the cassock. How could he possibly sleep well? As he tossed and turned, he suddenly saw the windows growing bright. He arose at once and called: "Wukong, it's morning. Go find the cassock quickly." Pilgrim leaped up with a bound and saw that the monks were bringing in washing water. "All of you," said Pilgrim, "take care to minister to my master. Old Monkey is leaving." Getting up from his bed, Tripitaka clutched at him, asking, "Where are you going?" "Come to think of it," said Pilgrim, "this whole affair reveals the irresponsibility of the Bodhisattva Guanyin. She has a Chan hall here where she has enjoyed the incense and worship of all the local people, and yet she can permit a monster-spirit to be her neighbor. I'm leaving for the South Sea to find her for a little conversation. I'm going to ask her to come here and demand that the monster return the cassock to us." "When will you be back?" asked Tripitaka. "Probably right after breakfast," answered Pilgrim. "At the latest, I should be back around noon, when everything should be taken care of. All of you monks must take care to wait on my master. Old Monkey is leaving."

He said he was leaving, and the next instant he was already out of sight. In a moment, he arrived at the South Sea, where he stopped his cloud to look around. He saw

A vast expanse of ocean,
Where water and sky seemed to merge.
Auspicious light shrouded the earth;
Hallowed air brightened the world.
Endless snow-capped waves surged up to Heaven;
Layers of misty billows washed out the sun.
Water flying everywhere;
Waves churning all around.
Water flying everywhere rolled like thunderclaps;
Waves churning all around boomed like cannonade.
Speak not merely of water;
Let's look more at the center.
The treasure-filled mountain of five dazzling colors:

Red, yellow, green, deep purple, and blue.
If this be Guanyin's scenic region true,
Look further at Potalaka of South Sea.
What a splendid place!
The tall mountain peak
Cut through airy space.
In its midst were thousands of rare flowers,
A hundred kinds of divine herbs.
The wind stirred the precious trees;
The sun shone on the golden lotus.
Glazed tiles covered the Guanyin Hall;
Tortoiseshell spread before the Tidal-Sound Cave.
In the shades of green willow the parrot spoke;
Within the bamboo grove the peacock sang.
On rocks with grains like fingerprints,
The guardians fierce and solemn.
Before the cornelian foreshore,
Mokṣa strong and heroic.

Pilgrim, who could hardly take his eyes off the marvelous scenery, lowered his cloud and went straight to the bamboo grove. The various deities were there to receive him, saying, "The Bodhisattva told us some time ago about the conversion of the Great Sage, for whom she had nothing but praise. You are supposed to be accompanying the Tang Monk at this moment. How do you have the time to come here?" "Because I am accompanying the Tang Monk," said Pilgrim, "I had an incident on our journey about which I must see the Bodhisattva. Please announce my arrival." The deities went to the mouth of the cave to make the announcement, and the Bodhisattva asked him to enter. Obeying the summons, Pilgrim went before the bejeweled lotus platform and knelt down.

"What are you doing here?" asked the Bodhisattva. "On his journey my master came across one of your Chan halls," said Pilgrim, "where you receive the services of fire and incense from the local people. But you also permitted a Black Bear Spirit to live nearby and to steal the cassock of my master. Several times I tried to get it back but without success. I have come specifically to ask you for it." The Bodhisattva said, "This monkey still speaks insolently! If the Bear Spirit stole your cassock, why did you come to ask me for it? It was all because you had the presumption, you wretched ape, to show off your treasure to sinister people. Moreover, you had your share of evildoing when you called for the wind to intensify the fire, which burned down one of my way stations down below. And yet you still want to be rowdy around here?" When Pilgrim heard the Bodhisattva speaking like that, he realized that she had knowledge of past and future events. Hurriedly he bowed with humility and said, "Bodhisattva, please pardon the offense of your disciple. It was as you said. But I'm upset by the monster's refusal to give us back our cassock, and my master is threatening to recite that spell of his at any moment. I can't bear the headache, and that's why I have come to cause you inconvenience. I beseech the Bodhisattva to have mercy on me and help me capture that monster, so that we may recover the garment and proceed toward the West."

"That monster has great magical power," said the Bodhisattva, "really just as strong as yours. All right! For the sake of the Tang Monk, I'll go with you this time." When Pilgrim heard this, he bowed again in gratitude and asked the Bodhisattva to leave at once. They mounted the blessed clouds and soon arrived on the Black Wind Mountain. Dropping down from the clouds, they followed a path to look for the cave.

As they were walking, they saw a Daoist coming down the mountain slope, holding a glass tray on which there were two magic pills. Pilgrim ran right into him, whipped out his rod, and brought it down squarely on his head, with one blow causing the brains to burst and blood to shoot out from the neck. Completely stunned, the Bodhisattva said, "Monkey, you are still so reckless! He didn't steal your cassock; he neither knew nor wronged you. Why did you kill him with one blow?"

"Bodhisattva," said Pilgrim, "you may not recognize him, but he is a friend of the Black Bear Spirit. Yesterday he was having a conversation with a white-robed scholar on the grass meadow. Since they were invited to the cave of the Black Bear Spirit, who was going to give a Festival of the Buddha Robe to celebrate his birthday, this Daoist said that he would first go to celebrate his friend's birthday today and then attend the festival tomorrow. That's how I recognized him. He must have been on his way to celebrate the monster's birthday." "If that's how it is, all right," said the Bodhisattva. Pilgrim then went to pick up the Daoist and discovered that he was a gray wolf. The tray, which had fallen to one side, had an inscription on the bottom: "Made by Master Transcending Void."

When Pilgrim saw this, he laughed and said, "What luck! What luck! Old Monkey will benefit; the Bodhisattva will save some energy. This monster may be said to have made a confession without torture, while the other monster may be destined to perish today." "What are you saying, Wukong?" said the Bodhisattva. "Bodhisattva," said Pilgrim, "I, Wukong, have a saying: plot should be met with plot. I don't know whether you will listen to me or not." "Speak up!" said the Bodhisattva.

"Look, Bodhisattva!" said Pilgrim. "There are two magic pills on this little tray, and they are introductory gifts that we shall present to the monster. Beneath the tray is the five-word inscription 'Made by Master Transcending Void,' and this shall serve as our contact with the monster. If you will listen to me, I'll give you a plan that will dispense with weapons and do away with combat. In a moment, the monster will meet pestilence; in the twinkling of an eye, the Buddha robe will reappear. If you do not follow my suggestion, you may go back to the West, and I, Wukong, will return to the East; the Buddha robe will be counted as lost, while Tripitaka Tang will have journeyed in vain."

"This monkey is pretty clever with his tongue!" said the Bodhisattva, laughing. "Hardly!" said Pilgrim. "But it is a small plan!" "What's your plan?" asked the Bodhisattva. "Since the tray has this inscription beneath it," said Pilgrim, "the Daoist himself must be this Master Transcending Void. If you agree with me, Bodhisattva, you can change yourself into this Daoist. I'll take one of the pills and then change myself into another pill— a slightly bigger one, that is. Take this tray with the two magic pills and present them to the monster as his birthday gift. Let the monster swallow the bigger pill, and old Monkey will accomplish the rest. If he is unwilling to return the Buddha robe, old Monkey will make one—even if I have to weave it with his guts!"

The Bodhisattva could not think of a better plan and she had to nod her head to show her approval. "Well?" said Pilgrim, laughing. Immediately the Bodhisattva exercised her great mercy and boundless power. With her infinite capacity for transformation, her mind moved in perfect accord with her will, and her will with her body: in one blurry instant, she changed into the form of the immortal Master Transcending Void.

> Her crane-down cloak swept by the wind,
> With airy steps she'd pace the void.
> Her face, aged like cypress and pine,
> Shows fair, fresh features never seen.
> She moves with freedom without end,
> A special self-sustaining Thus!
> In sum all return to one Form,
> But from bodies perverse set free.

When Pilgrim saw the transformation, he cried, "Marvelous, Marvelous! Is the monster the Bodhisattva, or is the Bodhisattva the monster?" The Bodhisattva smiled and said, "Wukong, the Bodhisattva and the monster— they both exist in a single thought. Considered in terms of their origin, they are all nothing." Immediately enlightened, Pilgrim turned around and changed at once into a magic pill:

> A rolling-pan steadying pearl—
> Round, bright, of no known recipe.

Fused "three time three"[12] *at Mount Goulou;*[13]
Forged "six times six," with Shao Weng's[14] *help.*
Like glazed tiles and yellow gold flames
It shines with sun and mani's light.
Its coat of mercury and lead
Has power not with ease assessed.

The pill into which Pilgrim had changed was slightly larger than the other one. Making a mental note of it, the Bodhisattva took the glass tray and went straight to the entrance of the monster's cave. She paused to look around and saw

Deep gorges, parlous cliffs,
Clouds rising from the peaks;
Green pines and cypresses,
And wind rustling in the woods.
Deep gorges, parlous cliffs:
A place truly made for monsters and not for man!
But green pines and cypresses
Might seem fit for pious recluse to seek the Way.
The mountain has a stream,
And the stream has water,
Its current murmurs lightly as a lute
Worthy to cleanse your ears.
The cliff has deers,
The woods have cranes,
Where softly hums the music of the spheres
To lift your spirit.
So it was the bogus immortal's luck that Bodhi came:
To vouchsafe boundless mercy was her vow.

After looking over the place, the Bodhisattva was secretly pleased and said to herself, "If this cursed beast could occupy such a mountain, it might be that he is destined to attain the Way." Thus she was already inclined to be merciful.

When she walked up to the cave's entrance, some of the little demons standing guard there recognized her, saying, "Immortal Transcending Void has arrived." Some went to announce her arrival, while others greeted her. Just then, the monster came bowing out the door, saying, "Transcending Void, you honor my humble abode with your divine presence!" "This humble Daoist," said the Bodhisattva, "respectfully submits an elixir pill as a birthday gift." After the two of them had bowed to each other, they were seated. The incidents of the day before were mentioned, but the Bodhisattva made no reply. Instead, she took up the tray and said, "Great King, please accept the humble regard of this little Daoist." She chose the large pill and pushed it over to the monster, saying, "May the Great King live for a thousand years!" The monster then pushed the other pill over to the Bodhisattva, saying, "I wish to share this with Master Transcending Void." After this ceremonial presentation, the monster was about to swallow it, but the pill rolled by itself right down his throat. It changed back into its original form and began to do physical exercises! The monster fell to the ground, while the Bodhisattva revealed her true form and recovered the Buddha Robe from the monster. Pilgrim then left the monster's body through his nose, but fearing that the monster might still be truculent, the Bodhisattva threw a fillet on his head. As he arose, the monster did indeed pick up his lance to thrust at Pilgrim. The Bodhisattva, however, rose into the air and began reciting her spell. The spell worked, and the monster felt excruciating pain on his head; throwing away the lance, he rolled wildly all over the ground. In midair, the Handsome Monkey King nearly collapsed with laughter; down below the Black Bear Monster almost rolled himself to death on the ground.

"Cursed beast." said the Bodhisattva, "will you now surrender?" "I surrender," said the monster without any hesitation, "please spare my life!" Fearing that too much effort would have been wasted, Pilgrim wanted to strike at once. Quickly stopping him, the Bodhisattva said, "Don't hurt him; I have some use for him." Pilgrim said, "Why not destroy a monster like him, for of what use can he be?" "There's no one guarding the rear of my Potalaka Mountain," said the Bodhisattva, "and I want to take him back there to be a Great Mountain-Guardian God." "Truly a salvific and merciful goddess," said Pilgrim, laughing, "who will not hurt a single sentient being. If old Monkey knew a spell like that, he'd recite it a thousand times. That would finish off as many black bears as there are around here!"

So, we shall tell you about the monster, who regained consciousness after a long time. Convinced by the unbearable pain, he had no choice but to fall on his knees and beg: "Spare my life, for I'm willing to submit to Truth!" Dropping down from the blessed luminosity, the Bodhisattva then touched his head and gave him the commandments, telling him to wait on her, holding the lance. So it was with the Black Bear:

Today his vaulting ambition is checked;
This time his boundless license has been curbed.

"You may return now, Wukong," instructed the Bodhisattva, "and serve the Tang Monk attentively. Don't start any more trouble with your carelessness." "I'm grateful that the Bodhisattva was willing to come this far to help," said Pilgrim, "and it is my duty as disciple to see you back." "You may

be excused," said the Bodhisattva. Holding the cassock, Pilgrim then kowtowed to her and left, while the Bodhisattva led the bear and returned to the
great ocean. We have a testimonial poem:

> Auspicious light surrounds the golden form:
> What maze of colors so worthy of praise!
> She shows great mercy to succor mankind,
> To reveal gold lotus as she scans the world.
> She comes all because of scripture seeking;
> Then she withdraws, as ever chaste and pure.
> The fiend converted, she leaves for the sea;
> A Buddhist regains a brocade-cassock.

We do not know what happened afterwards; let's listen to the explanation
in the next chapter.

EIGHTEEN

At Guanyin Hall the Tang Monk leaves his ordeal;
At Gao Village the Great Sage casts out the monster.

Pilgrim took leave of the Bodhisattva. Lowering the direction of his cloud, he hung the cassock on one of the fragrant cedars nearby. He took out his rod and fought his way into the Black Wind Cave. But where could he find even a single little demon inside? The fact of the matter was that when they saw the Bodhisattva's epiphany, causing the old monster to roll all over the ground, they all scattered. Pilgrim, however, was not to be stopped; he piled dried wood around the several doorways in the cave and started a fire in the front and in the back. The whole Black Wind Cave was reduced to a "Red Wind Cave"! Picking up the cassock, Pilgrim then mounted the auspicious luminosity and went north.

We now tell you about Tripitaka, who was impatiently waiting for Pilgrim's return and wondering whether Bodhisattva had consented to come and help, or whether Pilgrim on some pretext had left him. He was filled with such foolish thoughts and wild speculations when he saw bright, rose-colored clouds approaching in the sky. Dropping at the foot of the steps and kneeling, Pilgrim said, "Master, the cassock is here!"

Tripitaka was most delighted, and not one of the monks could hide his pleasure. "Good! Good!" they cried. "Now we've found our lives again!" Taking the cassock, Tripitaka said, "Wukong, when you left in the morning, you promised to come back either after breakfast or sometime around noon. Why do you return so late, when the sun is already setting?" Pilgrim then gave a thorough account of how he went to ask for the Bodhisattva's help, and how she in her transformation had subdued the monster. When Tripitaka heard the account, he prepared an incense table at once and worshipped, facing south. Then he said, "Disciple, since we have the Buddha robe, let us pack up and leave." "No need to rush like that," said Pilgrim. "It's getting late, hardly the time to travel. Let's wait until tomorrow morning before we leave." All the monks knelt down and said, "Elder Sun is right. It is getting late, and, moreover, we have a vow to fulfill. Now that we are all saved and the treasure has been recovered, we must redeem our vow and ask the venerable elders to distribute the blessing.[1] Tomorrow we shall see you off to the West."

"Yes, yes, that's very good!" said Pilgrim. Look at those monks! They all emptied their pockets and presented all the valuables they had managed to salvage from the fire. Everyone made some contribution. They prepared some vegetarian offerings, burned paper money to request perpetual peace, and recited several scrolls of scriptures for the prevention of calamities and deliverance from evil. The service lasted until late in the evening. The next morning they saddled the horse and took up the luggage, while the monks accompanied their guests for a great distance before turning back. As Pilgrim led the way forward, it was the happiest time of spring. You see

The horse making light tracks on grassy turfs;
Gold threads of willow swaying with fresh dew.
Peaches and apricots fill the forest gay.
Creepers grow with vigor along the way.
Pairs of sun-warmed ducks rest on sandy hanks;
The brook's fragrant flowers tame the butterflies.
Thus autumn goes, winter fades, and spring's half gone;
When will merit be made and the True Writ found?

Master and disciple traveled for some six or seven days in the wilderness. One day, when it was getting late, they saw a village in the distance. "Wukong," said Tripitaka, "look! There's a village over there. How about asking for lodging for the night before we travel again tomorrow?" "Let's wait until I have determined whether it is a good or bad place before we decide," said Pilgrim. The master pulled in the reins as Pilgrim stared intently at the village. Truly there were

Dense rows of bamboo fences;
Thick clusters of thatched huts.
Skyscraping wild trees faced the doorways;
The winding brooklet reflected the houses.
Willows by the path unfurled their lovely green;
Fragrant were the flowers blooming in the yard.
At this time of twilight fast fading,
The birds chattered everywhere in the woods.
As kitchen smoke arose,
Cattle returned on every lane and path,
You saw, too, well-fed pigs and chickens sleeping by the house's edge,
And the old, sotted neighbor coming with a song.

After surveying the area, Pilgrim said, "Master, you may proceed. It appears to be a village of good families, where it will be appropriate for us to seek shelter."

The priest urged the white horse on, and they arrived at the beginning of a lane heading into the village, where they saw a young man wearing a cotton head-wrap and a blue jacket. He had an umbrella in his hand and a bundle on his back; his trousers were rolled up, and he had on his feet a pair of straw sandals with three loops. He was striding along the street in a resolute manner when Pilgrim grabbed him, saying, "Where are you going? I have a question for you: what is this place?" Struggling to break free, the man protested, "Isn't there anyone else here in the village? Why must you pick me for your question?" "Patron," said Pilgrim genially, "don't get upset. 'Helping others is in truth helping yourself.' What's so bad about your telling me the name of this place? Perhaps I can help you with your problems." Unable to break out of Pilgrim's grip, the man was so infuriated that he jumped about wildly. "Jinxed! I'm jinxed!" he cried. "No end to the grievances I have suffered at the hands of my family elders and I still have to run into this baldheaded fellow and suffer such indignity from him!"

"If you have the ability to pry open my hand," said Pilgrim, "I'll let you go." The man twisted left and right without any success: it was as if he had been clamped tight with a pair of iron tongs. He became so enraged that he threw away his bundle and his umbrella; with both hands, he rained blows and scratches on Pilgrim. With one hand steadying his luggage, Pilgrim held off the man with the other, and no matter how hard the man tried, he could not scratch or even touch Pilgrim at all. The more he fought, the firmer was Pilgrim's grip, so that the man was utterly exasperated.

"Wukong," said Tripitaka, "isn't someone coming over there? You can ask someone else. Why hang onto him like that? Let the man go." "Master, you don't understand," said Pilgrim, laughing. "If I ask someone else, all the fun will be gone. I have to ask him if, as the saying goes, 'there's going to be any business'!" Seeing that it was fruitless to struggle any more, the man said finally, "This place is called the Mr. Gao Village in the territory of the Kingdom of Qoco. Most of the families here in the village are surnamed Gao, and that's why the village is so called. Now please let me go." "You are hardly dressed for a stroll in the neighborhood," said Pilgrim, "so tell me the truth. Where are you going, and what are you doing anyway? Then I'll let you go."

The man had little alternative but to speak the truth. "I'm a member of the family of old Mr. Gao, and my name is Gao Cai. Old Mr. Gao has a daughter, his youngest, in fact, who is twenty years old and not yet betrothed. Three years ago, however, a monster-spirit seized her and kept her as his wife. Having a monster as his son-in-law bothered old Mr. Gao terribly. He said, 'My daughter having a monster as her spouse can hardly be a lasting arrangement. First, my family's reputation is ruined, and second, I don't even have any in-laws with whom we can be friends.' All that time he wanted to have this marriage annulled, but the monster absolutely refused; he locked the daughter up instead in the rear building and would not permit her to see her family for nearly half a year. The old man, therefore, gave me several taels of silver and told me to find an exorcist to capture the monster. Since then, I have hardly rested my feet; I managed to turn up three or four persons, all worthless monks and impotent Daoists. None of them could subdue the monster. A short while ago I received a severe scolding for my incompetence, and with only half an ounce more of silver as a travel allowance, I was told to find a capable exorcist this time. I didn't expect to run into you, my unlucky star, and now my journey is delayed. That's what I meant by the grievances I had suffered in and out of the family, and that's why I was protesting just now. I didn't know you had this trick of holding people, which I couldn't overcome. Now that I have told you the truth, please let me go."

"It's really your luck," said Pilgrim, "coupled with my vocation: they fit like the numbers four and six when you throw the dice! You needn't travel far, nor need you waste your money. We are not worthless monks or impotent Daoists, for we really do have some abilities; we are most experienced, in fact, in capturing monsters. As the saying goes, 'You have now not only a caring physician, but now you have cured your eyes as well!' Please take the trouble of returning to the head of your family and tell him that we are holy monks sent by the Throne in the Land of the East to go worship Buddha in the Western Heaven and acquire scriptures. We are most capable of seizing monsters and binding fiends." "Don't mislead me," said Gao Cai, "for I've had it up to here! If you are deceiving me and really don't have the ability to take the monster, you will only cause me more grievances." Pilgrim said, "I guarantee that you won't be harmed in any way. Lead me to the door of your house." The man could not think of a better alternative; he picked up his bundle and umbrella and turned to lead master and disciple to the door of his house. "You two elders," he said, "please rest yourselves for a moment against the hitching posts here. I'll go in to report to my master." Only then did Pilgrim release him. Putting down the luggage and dismounting from the horse, master and disciple stood and waited outside the door.

Gao Cai walked through the main gate and went straight to the main hall in the center, but it just so happened that he ran right into old Mr. Gao. "You thick-skinned beast!" railed Mr. Gao. "Why aren't you out looking for an exorcist? What are you doing back here?" Putting down his bundle and umbrella, Gao Cai said, "Let me humbly inform my lord. Your servant just reached the end of the street and ran into two monks: one riding a horse and the other hauling a load. They caught hold of me and refused to let go, asking where I was going. At first I absolutely refused to tell them, but they were most insistent and I had no means of freeing myself. It was only then that I gave them a detailed account of my lord's affairs. The one who was holding me was delighted, saying that he would arrest the monster for us." "Where did they come from?" asked old Mr. Gao. "He claimed to be a holy monk, the brother of the emperor," said Gao Cai, "who was sent from the Land of the East to go worship Buddha in the Western Heaven and acquire scriptures." "If they are monks who have come from such a great distance," said old Mr. Gao, "they may indeed have some abilities. Where are they now?" "Waiting outside the front door," said Gao Cai.

Old Mr. Gao quickly changed his clothes and came out with Gao Cai to extend his welcome, crying, "Your Grace!" When Tripitaka heard this, he turned quickly, and his host was already standing in front of him. That old man had on his head a dark silk wrap; he wore a robe of Sichuan silk brocade in spring-onion white with a dark green sash, and a pair of boots made of rough steer hide. Smiling affably, he addressed them, saying, "Honored Priests, please accept my bow!" Tripitaka returned his greeting, but Pilgrim stood there unmoved. When the old man saw how hideous he looked, he did not bow to him. "Why don't you say hello to me?" demanded Pilgrim. Somewhat alarmed, the old man said to Gao Cai: "Young man! You have really done me in, haven't you? There is already an ugly monster in the house that we can't drive away. Now you have to fetch this thunder-spirit to cause me more troubles!"

"Old Gao," said Pilgrim, "it's in vain that you have reached such old age, for you have hardly any discernment! If you want to judge people by appearances, you are utterly wrong! I, old Monkey, may be ugly, but I have some abilities. I'll capture the monster for your family, exorcise the fiend, apprehend that son-in-law of yours, and get your daughter back. Will that be good enough? Why all these mutterings about appearances!" When the old man heard this, he trembled with fear, but he managed to pull himself together sufficiently to say, "Please come in!" At this invitation, Pilgrim led the white horse and asked Gao Cai to pick up their luggage so that Tripitaka could go in with them. With no regard for manners, he tethered the horse on one of the pillars and drew up a weather-beaten lacquered chair for his master to be seated. He pulled over another chair and sat down on one side. "This little priest," said old Mr. Gao, "really knows how to make himself at home!" "If you are willing to keep me here for half a year," said Pilgrim, "then I'll truly feel at home!"

After they were seated, old Mr. Gao asked, "Just now my little one said that you two honored priests came from the Land of the East?" "Yes," replied Tripitaka. "Your poor monk was commissioned by the court to go to the Western Heaven to seek scriptures for Buddha. Since we have reached your village, we would like to ask for lodging for the night. We plan to leave early tomorrow morning." "So the two of you wanted lodging?" said old Mr. Gao. "Then why did you say you could catch monsters?" "Since we are asking for a place to stay," said Pilgrim, "we thought we might as well catch a few monsters, just for fun! May we ask how many monsters there are in your house?" "My God!" exclaimed old Mr. Gao, "How many monsters could we feed? There's only this one son-in-law, and we have suffered enough from him!" "Tell me everything about the monster," said Pilgrim, "how he came to this place, what sort of power he has, and so forth. Start from the beginning and don't leave out any details. Then I can catch him for you."

"From ancient times," said old Mr. Gao, "this village of ours has never had any troubles with ghosts, goblins, or fiends; in fact, my sole misfortune consists of not having a son. I had three daughters born to me: the eldest is named Fragrant Orchid; the second one, Jade Orchid; and the third, Green Orchid. The first two since their youth had been promised to people belonging to this same village, but I had hoped that the youngest would take a husband who would stay with our family and consent to have his children bear our name. Since I have no son, he would in fact become my heir and look after me in my old age. Little did I expect that about three years ago, a fellow would turn up who was passably good-looking. He said that he came from the Fuling Mountain and that his surname was Zhu (Hog). Since he had neither parents nor brothers, he was willing to be taken in as a son-in-law, and I accepted him, thinking that someone with no other family attachment was exactly the right sort of person. When he first came into our family, he was, I must confess, fairly industrious and well-behaved. He worked hard to loosen the earth and plow the fields without even using a buffalo; and when he harvested the grains, he did the reaping without sickle or staff. He came home late in the evening and started early again in the morning, and to tell you the truth, we were quite happy with him. The only trouble was that his appearance began to change."

"In what way?" asked Pilgrim. "Well," said old Mr. Gao, "when he first came, he was a stout, swarthy fellow, but afterwards he turned into an idiot with huge ears and a long snout, with a great tuft of bristles behind his head. His body became horribly coarse and hulking. In short, his whole appearance was that of a hog! And what an enormous appetite! For a single meal, he has to have three to five bushels of rice: a little snack in the morning means over a hundred biscuits or rolls. It's a good thing he keeps a vegetarian diet; if he liked meat and wine, the property and estate of this old man would be consumed in half a year!" "Perhaps it's because he's a good worker," said Tripitaka, "that he has such a good appetite." "Even that appetite is a small problem!" said old Mr. Gao. "What is most disturbing is that he likes to come riding the wind and disappears again astride the fog; he kicks up stones and dirt so frequently that my household and my neighbors have not had a moment's peace. Then he locked up my little girl, Green Orchid, in the back building, and we haven't seen her for half a year and don't know whether she's dead or alive. We are certain now that he is

a monster, and that's why we want to get an exorcist to drive him away."
"There's nothing difficult about that," said Pilgrim. "Relax, old man! Tonight I'll catch him for you, and I'll demand that he sign a document of an-
nulment and return your daughter. How's that?" Immensely pleased, old
Mr. Gao said, "My taking him in was a small thing, when you consider how
he has ruined my good reputation and how many relatives of ours he had
alienated! Just catch him for me. Why bother about a document? Please,
just get rid of him for me." Pilgrim said, "It's simple! When night falls, you'll
see the result!"

The old man was delighted; he asked at once for tables to be set and a
vegetarian feast to be prepared. When they had finished the meal, evening
was setting in. The old man asked, "What sort of weapons and how many
people do you need? We'd better prepare soon." "I have my own weapon,"
replied Pilgrim. The old man said, "The only thing the two of you have
is that priestly staff, hardly something you can use to battle the monster,"
whereupon Pilgrim took an embroidery needle out of his ear, held it in his
hands, and waving it once in the wind, changed it into a golden-hooped rod
with the thickness of a rice bowl. "Look at this rod," he said to old Mr. Gao.
"How does it compare with your weapons? Think it'll do for the monster?"
"Since you have a weapon," said old Mr. Gao again, "do you need some attendants?" "No need for any attendants," said Pilgrim. "All I ask for is some
decent elderly persons to keep my master company and talk with him, so
that I may feel free to leave him for a while. I'll catch the monster for you
and make him promise publicly to leave, so that you will be rid of him for
good." The old man at once asked his houseboy to send for several intimate
friends and relatives, who soon arrived. After they were introduced, Pilgrim said, "Master, you may feel quite safe sitting here. Old Monkey is off!"

Look at him! Lifting high his iron rod, he dragged old Mr. Gao along,
saying, "Lead me to the back building where the monster is staying so that
I may have a look." The old man indeed took him to the door of the building in the rear. "Get a key quickly!" said Pilgrim. "Take a look yourself," said
old Mr. Gao. "If I could use a key on this lock, I wouldn't need you." Pilgrim
laughed and said, "Dear old man! Though you are quite old, you can't even
recognize a joke! I was just teasing you a little, and you took my words literally." He went forward and touched the lock: it was solidly welded with
liquid copper. Annoyed, Pilgrim smashed open the door with one terrific
blow of his rod and found it was pitch black inside. "Old Gao," said Pilgrim, "go give your daughter a call and see if she is there inside." Summoning up his courage, the old man cried, "Miss Three!" Recognizing her father's voice, the girl replied faintly, "Papa! I'm over here!" His golden pupils
ablaze, Pilgrim peered into the dark shadows. "How does she look?" you
ask. You see that

Her cloudlike hair is unkempt and unbrushed;
Her jadelike face is grimy and unwashed.
Though her nature refined is unchanged,
Her lovely image is weary and wan.
Her cherry lips seem completely bloodless,
And her body is both crooked and bent.
Knitted in sorrow
The moth-brows²are pallid;
Weakened by weight loss,
The speaking voice is faint.

She came forward, and when she saw that it was old Mr. Gao, she clutched at him and began to wail.

"Stop crying! Stop crying!" said Pilgrim. "Let me ask you: where is the monster?" "I don't know where he has gone," said the girl. "Nowadays he leaves in the morning and comes back only after nightfall. Surrounded by cloud and fog, he comes and goes without ever letting me know where he is. Since he has learned that father is trying to drive him away, he takes frequent precautions; that's why he comes only at night and leaves in the morning." "No need to talk anymore," Pilgrim said. "Old Man! Take your beloved daughter to the building in front, and then you can spend all the time you want with her. Old Monkey will be here waiting for him; if the monster doesn't show up, don't blame me. But if he comes at all, I'll pull out the weeds of your troubles by the roots!" With great joy, old Mr. Gao led his daughter to the front building. Exercising his magic might, Pilgrim shook his body and changed at once into the form of that girl, sitting all by herself to wait for the monster. In a little while, a gust of wind swept by, kicking up dust and stones. What a wind!

At first it was a breeze gentle and light.
Thereafter it became gusty and strong.
A light, gentle breeze that could fill the world!
A strong, gusty wind that nothing else could stop!
Flowers and willow snapped like shaken hemp;
Trees and plants were felled like uprooted crops.
It stirred up streams and seas, cowing ghosts and gods.
It fractured rocks and mountains, awing Heaven and Earth.
Flower-nibbling deer lost their homeward trail.
Fruit-picking monkeys all were gone astray.
The seven-tiered pagoda crashed on Buddha's head.
Flags on eight sides damaged the temple's top.
Gold beams and jade pillars were rooted up.
Like flocks of swallow flew the roofing tiles.

The boatman lifted his oars to make a vow,
Eager to have his livestock sacrificed.
The local spirit abandoned his shrine.
Dragon kings from four seas made humble bows.
At sea the ship of yakṣa ran aground,
While half of Great Wall's rampart was blown down.

When the violent gust of wind had gone by, there appeared in midair a monster who was ugly indeed. With his black face covered with short, stubby hair, his long snout and huge ears, he wore a cotton shirt that was neither quite green nor quite blue. A sort of spotted cotton handkerchief was tied round his head. Said Pilgrim, smiling to himself, "So, I have to do business with a thing like this!" Dear Pilgrim! He neither greeted the monster, nor did he speak to him; he lay on the bed instead and pretended to be sick, moaning all the time. Unable to tell the true from the false, the monster walked into the room and, grabbing his "spouse," he at once demanded a kiss. "He really wants to sport with old Monkey!" said Pilgrim, smiling to himself. Using a holding trick, he caught the long snout of that monster and gave it a sudden, violent twist, sending him crashing to the floor with a loud thud. Picking himself up, the monster supported himself on the side of the bed and said, "Sister, how is it that you seem somewhat annoyed with me today? Because I'm late, perhaps?" "I'm not annoyed!" said Pilgrim. "If not," said that monster, "why did you give me such a fall?" "How can you be so boorish," said Pilgrim, "grabbing me like that and wanting to kiss me? I don't feel very well today; under normal conditions I would have been up waiting for you and would have opened the door myself. You may take off your clothes and go to sleep."

The fiend did not suspect anything and took off his clothes. Pilgrim jumped up and sat on the chamber pot, while the fiend climbed into bed. Groping around, he could not feel anyone and called out, "Sister, where have you gone? Please take off your clothes and go to sleep." "You go to sleep first," said Pilgrim, "for I have to wait until I've dropped my load." The fiend indeed loosened his clothes and stayed in bed. Suddenly Pilgrim gave out a sigh, saying, "My luck's pretty low!" "What's bothering you?" said the monster. "What do you mean, your luck's pretty low? It's true that I have consumed quite a bit of food and drink since I entered your family, but I certainly did not take them as free meals. Look at the things I did for your family: sweeping the grounds and draining the ditches, hauling bricks and carrying tiles, building walls and pounding mortar, plowing the fields and raking the earth, planting seedlings of rice and wheat—in short, I took care of your entire estate. Now what you have on your body happens to be brocade, and what you wear as ornaments happens to be gold. You enjoy the flowers and fruits of four seasons, and you have fresh vegetables for the table in all eight periods. Whatever makes you so dissatisfied that you have to sigh and lament, saying your luck's pretty low?"

"It isn't quite as you say," said Pilgrim. "Today my parents gave me a severe scolding over the partition wall, throwing bricks and tiles into this place." "What were they scolding you for?" asked the monster. Pilgrim said, "They said that since we have become husband and wife, you are in fact a son-in-law in their family but one who is completely without manners. A person as ugly as you is unpresentable: you can't meet your brothers-in-law, nor can you greet the other relatives. Since you come with the clouds and leave with the fog, we really don't know what family you belong to and what your true name is. In fact, you have ruined our family's reputation and defiled our legacy. That was what they rebuked me for, and that's why I'm upset." "Though I am somewhat homely," said the monster, "it's no great problem if they insist on my being more handsome. We discussed these matters before when I came here, and I entered your family fully with your father's consent. Why did they bring it up again today? My family is located in the Cloudy Paths Cave of Fuling Mountain; my surname is based on my appearance. Hence I am called Zhu (Hog), and my official name is Ganglie (Stiff Bristles). If they ever ask you again, tell them what I have told you."

"This monster is quite honest," said Pilgrim to himself, secretly pleased. "Without torture, he has already made a plain confession; with his name and location clearly known, he will certainly be caught, regardless of what may happen." Pilgrim then said to him, "My parents are trying to get an exorcist here to arrest you." "Go to sleep! Go to sleep!" said the monster, laughing. "Don't mind them at all! I know as many transformations as the number of stars in the Heavenly Ladle,[3] and I own a nine-pronged muckrake. Why should I fear any exorcist, monk, or Daoist priest? Even if your old man were pious enough to be able to get the Monster-Routing Patriarch to come down from the Ninefold Heaven, I could still claim to have been an old acquaintance of his. And he wouldn't dare do anything to me."

"But they were saying that they hoped to invite someone by the name of Sun," said Pilgrim, "the so-called Great Sage, Equal to Heaven, who caused havoc in the Celestial Palace five hundred years ago. They were going to ask him to come catch you." When the monster heard this name, he became rather alarmed. "If that's true," he said, "I'm leaving. We can't live as a couple anymore!" "Why do you have to leave so suddenly?" asked Pilgrim. "You may not know," said the monster, "that that BanHorsePlague who caused such turmoil in Heaven has some real abilities. I fear that I am no match for him, and losing my reputation is not my form!"

When he had finished speaking, he slipped on his clothes, opened the door, and walked right out. Pilgrim grabbed him, and with one wipe of his own face he assumed his original form, shouting: "Monster, where do you think you're going? Take a good look and see who I am!" The monster turned around and saw the protruding teeth, the gaping mouth, the fiery eyes, the golden pupils, the pointed head, and the hairy face of Pilgrim— virtually a living thunder god! He was so horrified that his hands became numb and his feet grew weak. With a loud ripping sound, he tore open his shirt and broke free of Pilgrim's clutch by changing into a violent wind. Pilgrim rushed forward and struck mightily at the wind with his iron rod; the monster at once transformed himself into myriad shafts of flaming light and fled toward his own mountain. Mounting the clouds, Pilgrim pursued him, crying, "Where are you running to? If you ascend to Heaven, I'll chase you to the Palace of the Polestar, and if you go down into the Earth, I'll follow you into the heart of Hell!" Good Heavens! We do not know where the chase took them to or what was the outcome of the fight. Let's listen to the explanation in the next chapter.

NINETEEN

At Cloudy Paths Cave, Wukong takes in Eight Rules;
At Pagoda Mountain, Tripitaka receives the Heart Sūtra.

We were telling you about the flaming light of the monster, who was fleeing, while the Great Sage riding the rosy clouds followed right behind. As they were thus proceeding, they came upon a tall mountain, where the monster gathered together the fiery shafts of light and resumed his original form. Racing into a cave, he took out a nine-pronged muckrake to fight. "Lawless monster!" shouted Pilgrim. "What region are you from, fiend, and how do you know old Monkey's names? What abilities do you have? Make a full confession quickly and your life may be spared!" "So you don't know my powers!" said that monster. "Come up here and brace yourself! I'll tell you!

> *My mind was dim since the time of youth;*
> *Always I loved my indolence and sloth.*
> *Neither nursing nature nor seeking the Real,*[1]
> *I passed my days deluded and confused.*
> *I met a true immortal suddenly*
> *Who sat and spoke to me of cold and heat.*[2]
> *'Repent,' he said, 'and cease your worldly way:*
> *From taking life accrues a boundless curse.*
> *One day when the Great Limit ends your lot,*
> *For eight woes and three ways*[3] *you'll grieve too late!'*
> *I listened and turned my will to mend my ways:*
> *I heard, repented, and sought the wondrous rune.*
> *By fate my teacher he became at once,*
> *Pointing out passes keyed to Heav'n and Earth.*
> *Taught to forge the Great Pill Nine Times Reversed,*[4]
> *I worked without pause through day and night*[5]
> *To reach Mud-Pill Palace*[6] *topping my skull*
> *And Jetting-Spring Points*[7] *on soles of my feet.*
> *With kidney brine flooding the Floral Pool,*[8]
> *My Cinnabar Field*[9] *was thus warmly nursed.*
> *Baby and Fair Girl*[10] *mated as yin and yang;*
> *Lead and mercury mixed as sun and moon.*
> *In concord Li-dragon and Kan-tiger*[11] *used,*
> *The spirit turtle sucked dry the gold crow's blood.*[12]
> *'Three flowers joined on top,'*[13] *the root reclaimed;*

'Five breaths faced their source'[14] and all freely flowed.
My merit done, I ascended on high,
Met by pairs of immortals from the sky.
Radiant pink clouds arose beneath my feet;
With light, sound frame I faced the Golden Arch.
The Jade Emperor gave a banquet for gods
Who sat in rows according to their ranks.
Made a marshal of the Celestial Stream,
I took command of both sailors and ships.
Because Queen Mother gave the Peaches Feast—
When she met her guests at the Jasper Pool—
My mind turned hazy for I got dead drunk,
A shameless rowdy reeling left and right.
Boldly I barged into Vast Cold Palace[15]
Where the charming fairy received me in.
When I saw her face that would snare one's soul,
My carnal itch of old could not be stopped!
Without regard for manners or for rank,
I grabbed Miss Chang'e[16] asking her to bed.
For three or four times she rejected me:
Hiding east and west, she was sore annoyed.
My passion sky-high I roared like thunder,
Almost toppling the arch of Heaven's gate.
Inspector General[17] told the Emperor Jade;
I was destined that day to meet my fate.
The Vast Cold completely enclosed airtight
Left me no way to run or to escape.
Then I was caught by the various gods,
Undaunted still, for wine was in my heart.
Bound and taken to see the Emperor Jade,
By law I should have been condemned to death.
It was Venus the Gold Star, Mr. Li,
Who left the ranks and knelt to beg for me.
My punishment changed to two thousand blows,
My flesh was torn; my bones did almost crack.
Alive! I was banished from Heaven's gate
To make my home beneath the Fuling Mount.
An errant womb's my sinful destination:
Stiff-Bristle Hog's my worldly appellation!"

When Pilgrim heard this, he said, "So you are actually the Water God of
the Heavenly Reeds, who came to earth. Small wonder you knew old Mon-

key's name." "Curses!" cried the monster. "You Heaven-defying BanHorse-Plague! When you caused such turmoil that year in Heaven, you had no idea how many of us had to suffer because of you. And here you are again to make life miserable for others! Don't give me any lip! Have a taste of my rake!" Pilgrim, of course, was unwilling to be tolerant; lifting high his rod, he struck at the monster's head. The two of them thus began a battle in the middle of the mountain, in the middle of the night. What a fight!

> Pilgrim's gold pupils blazed like lightning;
> The monster's round eyes flashed like silver blooms.
> This one spat out colored fog:
> That one spouted crimson mist.
> The spouted crimson mist lit up the dark;
> The colored fog spat out made bright the night.
> The golden-hooped rod;
> The nine-pronged muckrake.
> Two true heroes most worthy of acclaim:
> One was the Great Sage descended to earth;
> One was a Marshal who came from Heaven.
> That one, for indecorum, became a monster;
> This one, to flee his ordeal, bowed to a monk.
> The rake lunged like a dragon wielding his claws:
> The rod came like a phoenix darting through flowers.
> That one said: "Your breaking up a marriage is like patricide!"
> This one said: "You should be arrested for raping a young girl!"
> Such idle words!
> Such wild clamor!
> Back and forth the rod blocked the rake.
> They fought till dawn was about to break,
> When the monster's two arms felt sore and numb.

From the time of the second watch, the two of them fought until it was growing light in the east. That monster could hold out no longer and fled in defeat. He changed once more into a violent gust of wind and went straight back to his cave, shutting the doors tightly and refusing to come out. Outside the cave, Pilgrim saw a large stone tablet, which had on it the inscription, "Cloudy Paths Cave." By now, it was completely light. Realizing that the monster was not going to come out, Pilgrim thought to himself, "I fear that Master may be anxiously waiting for me. I may as well go back and see him before returning here to catch the monster." Mounting the clouds, he soon arrived at Old Gao village.

We shall now tell you about Tripitaka, who chatted about past and present with the other elders and did not sleep all night. He was just wondering why Pilgrim had not shown up, when suddenly the latter dropped down into the courtyard. Straightening out his clothes and putting away his rod, Pilgrim went up to the hall, crying, "Master! I've returned!" The various elders hurriedly bowed low, saying, "Thank you for all the trouble you have been to!" "Wukong, you were gone all night," said Tripitaka. "If you captured the monster, where is he now?" "Master," said Pilgrim, "that monster is no fiend of this world, nor is he a strange beast of the mountains. He is actually the incarnation of the Marshal of the Heavenly Reeds. Because he took the wrong path of rebirth, his appearance assumed the form of a wild hog: but actually his spiritual nature has not been extinguished. He said that he derived his surname from his appearance, and he went by the name of Zhu Ganglie. When I attacked him with my rod in the rear building, he tried to escape by changing into a violent gust of wind; I then struck at the wind, and he changed into shafts of flaming light and retreated to his mountain cave. There he took out a nine-pronged muckrake to do battle with old Monkey for a whole night. Just now when it grew light, he could fight no longer and fled into the cave, shutting the doors tightly and not coming out any more. I wanted to break down the door to finish him off, but I was afraid that you might be waiting here anxiously. That's why I came back first to give you some news."

When he had finished speaking, old Mr. Gao came forward and knelt down, saying, "Honored Priest, I have no alternative but to say this. Though you have chased him away, he might come back here after you leave. What should we do then? I may as well ask you to do us the favor of apprehending him, so that we shall not have any further worries. This old man, I assure you, will not be ungrateful or unkind; there will be a generous reward for you. I shall ask my relatives and friends to witness the drawing up of a document, whereby I shall divide my possessions and my property equally with you. All I want is to pluck up the trouble by the root, so that the pure virtue of our Gao family will not be tainted."

"Aren't you being rather demanding, old man?" said Pilgrim, laughing. "That monster did tell me that, although he has an enormous appetite and has consumed a good deal of food and drink from your family, he has also done a lot of good work for you. Much of what you were able to accumulate these last few years you owe to his strength, so that he really hasn't taken any free meals from you. Why ever do you want to have him driven away? According to him, he is a god who has come down to earth and who has helped your family earn a living. Moreover, he has not harmed your daughter in any way. Such a son-in-law, I should think, would be a good match for your daughter and your family. So, what's all this about ruining your family's reputation and damaging your standing in the community? Why not really accept him as he is?"

"Honored Priest," said old Mr. Gao, "though this matter may not offend public morals, it does leave us with a bad name. Like it or not, people will say, 'The Gao family has taken in a monster as a son-in-law!' How can one stand remarks of that kind?" "Wukong," said Tripitaka, "if you have worked for him all this while, you might as well see him through to a satisfactory conclusion." Pilgrim said, "I was testing him a little, just for fun. This time when I go, I'll apprehend the monster for certain and bring him back for you all to see. Don't worry, old Gao! Take good care of my master. I'm off!"

He said he was off, and the next instant he was completely out of sight. Bounding up that mountain, he arrived at the cave's entrance; a few strokes of the iron rod reduced the doors to dust. "You overstuffed coolie!" he shouted, "Come out quickly and fight with old Monkey!" Huffing and puffing, the monster was lying in the cave and trying to catch his breath. When he heard his doors being struck down and heard himself called "an overstuffed coolie," he could not control his wrath. Dragging his rake, he pulled himself together and ran out. "A BanHorsePlague like you," he yelled, "is an absolute pest! What have I done to you that you have to break my doors to pieces? Go and take a look at the law: a man who breaks someone's door and enters without permission may be guilty of trespassing, a crime punishable by death!" "Idiot!" said Pilgrim, laughing. "I may have broken down the door, but my case is still a defensible one. But you, you took a girl from her family by force—without using the proper matchmakers and witnesses, without presenting the proper gifts of money and wine. If you ask me, you are the one guilty of a capital crime!" "Enough of this idle talk," said the monster, "and watch out for old Hog's rake!" Parrying the rake with his rod, Pilgrim said, "Isn't that rake of yours just something you use as a regular farmhand to plow the fields or plant vegetables for the Gao family? Why on earth should I fear you?"

"You have made a mistake!" said the monster. "Is this rake a thing of this world? Just listen to my recital:

This is divine ice steel greatly refined,
Polished so highly that it glows and shines.
Laozi wielded the large hammer and tong;
Mars himself added charcoals piece by piece.
Five Kings of Five Quarters applied their schemes;
Twelve Gods of Time expended all their skills.
They made nine prongs like dangling teeth of jade,
And brass rings were cast with dropping gold leaves.
Decked with five stars and six brightnesses,
Its frame conformed to eight spans and four climes.
Its whole length set to match the cosmic scheme

Accorded with yin yang, with the sun and moon:
Six-Diagram Gods etched as Heaven ruled;[18]
Eight-Trigram Stars stood in ranks and files.
They named this the High Treasure Golden Rake,
A gift for Jade Emperor to guard his court.
Since I learned to be a great immortal,
Becoming someone with longevity,
I was made Marshal of the Heavenly Reeds
And given this rake, a sign of royal grace.
When it's held high, there'll be bright flames and light;
When it's brought low, strong wind blows down white snow.
The warriors of Heaven all fear it;
The Ten Kings of Hell all shrink from it.
Are there such weapons among mankind?
In this wide world there's no such fine steel.
It changes its form after my own wish,
Rising and falling after my command.
I've kept it with me for several years,
A daily comrade I never parted from.
I've stayed with it right through the day's three meals,
Nor left it when I went to sleep at night.
I brought it along to the Peaches Feast,
And with it I attended Heaven's court.
Since I wrought evil relying on wine,
Since trusting my strength I displayed my fraud,
Heaven sent me down to this world of dust,
Where in my next life I would sin some more.
With wicked mind I ate men in my cave,
Pleased to be married at the Gao Village.
This rake can overturn sea dragons' and turtles' lairs
And rake up mountain dens of tigers and wolves.
All other weapons there's no need to name,
Only my rake is of most fitting fame.
To win in battle? Why, it's no hard thing!
And making merit? It need not be said!
You may have a bronze head, an iron brain, and a full steel frame.
I'll rake till your soul melts and your spirit leaks!"

When Pilgrim heard these words, he put away his iron rod and said, "Don't brag too much, Idiot! Old Monkey will stretch out his head right here, and you can give him a blow. See if his soul melts and his spirit leaks!" The monster did indeed raise his rake high and bring it down with all his might; with a loud bang, the rake made sparks as it bounced back up. But the blow did not make so much as a scratch on Pilgrim's head. The monster was so astounded that his hands turned numb and his feet grew weak. He mumbled, "What a head! What a head!" "You didn't know about this, did you?" said Pilgrim. "When I caused such turmoil in Heaven by stealing the magic pills, the immortal peaches, and the imperial wine, I was captured by the Little Sage Erlang and taken to the Polestar Palace. The various celestial beings chopped me with an ax, pounded me with a bludgeon, cut me with a scimitar, jabbed me with a sword, burned me with fire, and struck me with thunder—all this could not hurt me one whit. Then I was taken by Laozi and placed in his eight-trigram brazier, in which I was refined by divine fire until I had fiery eyes and diamond pupils, a bronze head and iron arms. If you don't believe me, give me some more blows and see whether it hurts me at all."

"Monkey," said the monster, "I remember that at the time you were causing trouble in Heaven, you lived in the Water-Curtain Cave of the Flower-Fruit Mountain, in the Aolai Country of the East Pūrvavideha Continent. Your name hasn't been heard of for a long time. How is it that you suddenly turn up at this place to oppress me? Could my father-in-law have gone all that way to ask you to come here?" "Your father-in-law did not go to fetch me," said Pilgrim. "It's old Monkey who turned from wrong to right, who left the Daoist to follow the Buddhist. I am now accompanying the royal brother of the Great Tang Emperor in the Land of the East, whose name is Tripitaka, Master of the Law. He is on his way to the Western Heaven to seek scriptures from Buddha. We passed through the Gao Village and asked for lodging; old man Gao then brought up the subject of his daughter and asked me to rescue her and to apprehend you, you overstuffed coolie!"

Hearing this, the monster threw away his muckrake and said with great affability, "Where is the scripture pilgrim? Please take the trouble of introducing me to him." "Why do you want to see him?" asked Pilgrim. The monster said, "I was a convert of the Bodhisattva Guanshiyin, who commanded me to keep a vegetarian diet here and to wait for the scripture pilgrim. I was to follow him to the Western Heaven to seek scriptures from the Buddha, so that I might atone for my sins with my merit and regain the fruits of Truth. I have been waiting for a number of years without receiving any further news. Since you have been made his disciple, why didn't you mention the search for scriptures in the first place? Why did you have to unleash your violence and attack me right at my own door?"

"Don't try to soften me with deception," said Pilgrim, "thinking that you can escape that way. If you are truly sincere about accompanying the Tang Monk, you must face Heaven and swear that you are telling the truth. Then I'll take you to see my master." At once the monster knelt down and kowtowed as rapidly as if he were pounding rice with his head. "Amitābha," he cried, "Namo Buddha! If I am not speaking the truth in all sincerity, let me be punished as one who has offended Heaven—let me be hewn to pieces!"

Hearing him swear such an oath, Pilgrim said, "All right! You light a fire and burn up this place of yours; then I'll take you with me." The monster accordingly dragged in bunches of rushweed and thorns and lighted the fire; the Cloudy Paths Cave soon looked like a derelict potter's kiln. "I have no other attachment," he said to Pilgrim. "You can take me away." "Give me your muckrake and let me hold it," said Pilgrim, and our monster at once handed it over. Yanking out a piece of hair, Pilgrim blew onto it and cried, "Change!" It changed into a three-ply hemp rope with which he prepared to tie up the monster's hands. Putting his arms behind his back, the monster did nothing to stop himself from being bound. Then Pilgrim took hold of his ear and dragged him along, crying, "Hurry! Hurry!"

"Gently, please!" pleaded the monster. "You are holding me so roughly, and my ear is hurting!" "I can't be any gentler," said Pilgrim, "for I can't worry about you now. As the saying goes, 'The nicer the pig, the nastier the grip!' After you have seen my master and proved your worth, I'll let you go." Rising up to a distance halfway between cloud and fog, they headed straight for the Gao Family Village. We have a poem as a testimony:[19]

> Strong is metal's nature to vanquish wood:
> Mind Monkey has the Wood Dragon subdued.
> With metal and wood both obedient as one,
> All their love and virtue will grow and show.
> One guest and one host[20] there's nothing between;
> Three matings, three unions—there's great mystery![21]
> Nature and feelings gladly fused as Last and First:[22]
> Both will surely be enlightened in the West.

In a moment they had arrived at the village. Grasping the rake and pulling at the monster's ear, Pilgrim said, "Look at the one sitting in a most dignified manner up there in the main hall: that's my master." When old Mr. Gao and his relatives suddenly saw Pilgrim dragging by the ear a monster who had his hands bound behind his back, they all gladly left their seats to meet them in the courtyard. The old man cried, "Honored Priest! There's that son-in-law of mine." Our monster went forward and fell on his knees, kowtowing to Tripitaka and saying, "Master, your disciple apologizes for not coming to meet you. If I had known earlier that my master was staying in my father-in-law's house, I would have come at once to pay my respects, and none of these troubles would have befallen me." "Wukong," said Tripitaka, "how did you manage to get him here to see me?" Only then did Pilgrim release his hold. Using the handle of the rake to give the monster a whack, he shouted, "Idiot! Say something!" The monster gave a full account of how the Bodhisattva had converted him.

Greatly pleased, Tripitaka said at once, "Mr. Gao, may I borrow your incense table?" Old Mr. Gao took it out immediately, and Tripitaka lighted the incense after purifying his hands. He bowed toward the south, saying, "I thank the Bodhisattva for her holy grace!" The other elders all joined in the worship by adding incense, after which Tripitaka resumed his seat in the main hall and asked Wukong to untie the monster. Pilgrim shook his body to retrieve his hair, and the rope fell off by itself. Once more the monster bowed to Tripitaka, declaring his intention to follow him to the West, and then bowed also to Pilgrim, addressing him as "elder brother" because he was the senior disciple.

"Since you have entered my fold and have decided to become my disciple," said Tripitaka, "let me give you a religious name so that I may address you properly." "Master," said the monster, "the Bodhisattva already laid hands on my head and gave me the commandments and a religious name, which is Zhu Wuneng (Awake to Power)." "Good! Good!" said Tripitaka, laughing. "Your elder brother is named Wukong and you are called Wuneng; your names are well in accord with the emphasis of our denomination." "Master," said Wuneng, "since I received the commandments from the Bodhisattva, I was completely cut off from the five forbidden viands and the three undesirable foods. I maintained a strict vegetarian diet in my father-in-law's house, never touching any forbidden food. Now that I have met my master today, let me be released from my vegetarian vow." "No, no!" said Tripitaka. "Since you have not eaten the five forbidden viands and the three undesirable foods, let me give you another name. Let me call you Eight Rules."[23] Delighted, Idiot said, "I shall obey my master." For this reason, he was also called Zhu Eight Rules.

When old Mr. Gao saw the happy ending of this whole affair, he was more delighted than ever. He ordered his houseboys immediately to prepare a feast to thank the Tang Monk. Eight Rules went forward and tugged at him, saying, "Papa, please ask my humble wife to come out and greet the granddads and uncles. How about it?" "Worthy brother!" said Pilgrim, laughing. "Since you have embraced Buddhism and become a monk, please don't ever mention 'your humble wife' again. There may be a married Daoist in this world, but there's no such monk, is there? Let's sit down, rather, and have a nice vegetarian meal. We'll have to start off soon for the West."

Old Mr. Gao set the tables in order and invited Tripitaka to take the honored seat in the middle: Pilgrim and Eight Rules sat on both sides while the relatives took the remaining seats below. Mr. Gao opened a bottle of dietary wine and filled a glass: he sprinkled a little of the wine on the ground to thank Heaven and Earth before presenting the glass to Tripitaka. "To tell you the truth, aged sir," said Tripitaka, "this poor monk has been a vegetarian from birth. I have not touched any kind of forbidden food since childhood." "I know the reverend teacher is chaste and pure," said old Mr. Gao, "and I did not dare bring forth any forbidden foodstuff. This wine is made for those who maintain a vegetarian diet: there's no harm in your taking a glass." "I just don't dare use wine," said Tripitaka. "for the prohibition of strong drink is a monk's first commandment." Alarmed, Wuneng said, "Master, though I kept a vegetarian diet, I didn't cut out wine." "Though my capacity is not great," said Wukong, "and I'm not able to handle more than a crock or so, I haven't discontinued the use of wine either." "In that case," said Tripitaka, "you two brothers may take some of this pure wine. But you are not permitted to get drunk and cause trouble." So the two of them took the first round before taking their seats again to enjoy the feast. We cannot tell you in full what a richly laden table that was, and what varieties of delicacies were presented.

After master and disciples had been feted, old Mr. Gao took out a red lacquered tray bearing some two hundred taels of gold and silver in small pieces, which were to be presented to the three priests for travel expenses. There were, moreover, three outer garments made of fine silk. Tripitaka said, "We are mendicants who beg for food and drink from village to village. How could we accept gold, silver, and precious clothing?"

Coming forward and stretching out his hand, Pilgrim took a handful of the money, saying, "Gao Cai, yesterday you took the trouble to bring my master here, with the result that we made a disciple today. We have nothing to thank you with. Take this as remuneration for being a guide; perhaps you can use it to buy a few pairs of straw sandals. If there are any more monsters, turn them over to me and I'll truly be grateful to you." Gao Cai took the money and kowtowed to thank Pilgrim for his reward. Old Mr. Gao then said, "If the masters do not want the silver and gold, please accept at least these three simple garments, which are but small tokens of our goodwill." "If those of us who have left the family," said Tripitaka again, "accept the bribe of a single strand of silk, we may fall into ten thousand kalpas from which we may never recover. It is quite sufficient that we take along the leftovers from the table as provisions on our way." Eight Rules spoke up from the side: "Master, Elder Brother, you may not want these things. But I was a son-in-law in this household for several years, and the payment for my services should be worth more than three stones of rice! Father, my shirt was torn by Elder Brother last night; please give me a cassock of blue silk. My shoes are worn also, so please give me a good pair of new shoes." When old Mr. Gao heard that, he dared not refuse; a new pair of shoes and a cassock were purchased at once so that Eight Rules could dispose of the old attire.

Swaggering around, our Eight Rules spoke amiably to old Mr. Gao, saying, "Please convey my humble sentiments to my mother-in-law, my great-aunt, my second aunt, and my uncle-in-law, and all my other relatives. Today I am going away as a monk, and please do not blame me if I cannot take leave of them in person. Father, do take care of my better half. If we fail in our quest for scriptures, I'll return to secular life and live with you again as your son-in-law." "Coolie!" shouted Pilgrim. "Stop babbling nonsense!" "It's not nonsense," said Eight Rules. "Sometimes I fear that things may go wrong, and then I could end up unable either to be a monk or to take a wife, losing out on both counts." "Less of this idle conversation!" said Tripitaka. "We must hurry up and leave." They packed their luggage, and Eight Rules was told to carry the load with a pole. Tripitaka rode on the white horse, while Pilgrim led the way with the iron rod across his shoulders. The three of them took leave of old Mr. Gao and his relatives and headed toward the West. We have a poem as testimony:

> The earth's mist-shrouded, the trees appear tall.
> The Buddha-son of Tang court ever toils.
> He eats in need rice begged from many homes;
> He wears when cold a robe patched a thousandfold.
> Holdfast at the breast the Horse of the Will!
> The Mind-Monkey is sly—let him not wail!
> Nature one with feelings, causes all joined[24]—
> The moon's full of gold light when hair is shorn.[25]

The three of them proceeded toward the West, and for about a month it was an uneventful journey. When they crossed the boundary of Qoco, they looked up and saw a tall mountain. Tripitaka reined in his horse and said, "Wukong, Wuneng, there's a tall mountain ahead. We must approach it with care." "It's nothing!" said Eight Rules. "This mountain is called the Pagoda Mountain and a Crow's Nest Chan Master lives there, practicing austerities. Old Hog has met him before." "What's his business?" said Tripitaka. "He's fairly accomplished in the Way," said Eight Rules, "and he once asked me to practice austerities with him. But I didn't go, and that was the end of the matter."

As master and disciple conversed, they soon arrived at the mountain. What a splendid mountain! You see

> South of it, blue pines, jade-green junipers;
> North of it, green willows, red peach trees.
> A clamorous din:
> The mountain fowls are conversing.
> A fluttering dance:

Immortal cranes unite in flying.
A dense fragrance:
The flowers in a thousand colors.
A manifold green:
Diverse plants in forms exotic.
In the stream green water flows bubbling;
Before the cliff float petals of hallowed cloud.
Truly a place of rare beauty, a well-secluded spot;
Silence is all, not a man to be seen.

As the master sat on his horse, peering into the distance, he saw on top of the fragrant juniper tree a nest made of dried wood and grass. To the left, musk deer carried flowers in their mouths; to the right, mountain monkeys were presenting fruits. At the top of the tree, blue and pink phoenixes sang together, soon to be joined by a congregation of black cranes and brightly colored pheasants. "Isn't that the Crow's Nest Chan Master?" asked Eight Rules, pointing. Tripitaka urged on his horse and rode up to the tree.

We now tell you about that Chan Master, who, seeing the three of them approach, left his nest and jumped down from the tree. Tripitaka dismounted and prostrated himself. Raising him up with his hand, the Chan Master said, "Holy Monk, please arise! Pardon me for not coming to meet you." "Old Chan Master," said Eight Rules, "please receive my bow!" "Aren't you the Zhu Ganglie of the Fuling Mountain?" asked the Chan Master, startled. "How did you have the good fortune to journey with the holy monk?" "A few years back," said Eight Rules, "I was beholden to the Bodhisattva Guanyin for persuading me to follow him as a disciple." "Good! Good! Good!" said the Chan Master, greatly pleased. Then he pointed to Pilgrim and asked, "Who is this person?" "How is it that the old Chan recognizes him," said Pilgrim, laughing, "and not me?" "Because I haven't had the pleasure of meeting you," said the Chan Master. Tripitaka said, "He is my eldest disciple, Sun Wukong." Smiling amiably, the Chan Master said, "How impolite of me!"

Tripitaka bowed again and asked about the distance to the Great Thunderclap Temple of the Western Heaven. "It's very far away! Very far away!" said the Chan Master. "What's more, the road is a difficult one, filled with tigers and leopards." With great earnestness, Tripitaka asked again, "Just how far is it?" "Though it may be very far," answered the Chan Master, "you will arrive there one day. But all those *māra* hindrances along the way are hard to dispel. I have a Heart Sūtra here in this scroll; it has fifty-four sentences containing two hundred and seventy characters. When you meet these *māra* hindrances, recite the sūtra and you will not suffer any injury or harm." Tripitaka prostrated himself on the ground and begged to receive it, whereupon the Chan Master imparted the sūtra by reciting it orally. The sūtra said:

HEART SŪTRA OF THE GREAT PERFECTION OF WISDOM

When the Bodhisattva Guanzizai[26] was moving in the deep course of the Perfection of Wisdom, she saw that the five heaps[27] were but emptiness, and she transcended all sufferings. Śāriputra, form is no different from emptiness, emptiness no different from form; form is emptiness, and emptiness is form. Of sensations, perceptions, volition, and consciousness, the same is also true. Śāriputra, it is thus that all dharmas are but empty appearances, neither produced nor destroyed, neither defiled nor pure, neither increasing nor decreasing. This is why in emptiness there are no forms and no sensations, perceptions, volition, or consciousness; no eye, ear, nose, tongue, body, or mind; no form, sound, smell, taste, touch, or object of mind. There is no realm of sight [and so forth], until we reach the realm of no mind-consciousness; there is no ignorance, nor is there extinction of ignorance [and so forth], until we reach the stage where there is no old age and death, nor is there the extinction of old age and death; there is no suffering, annihilation, or way; there is no cognition or attainment. Because there is nothing to be attained, the mind of the Bodhisattva, by virtue of reliance upon the Perfection of Wisdom, has no hindrances: no hindrances, and therefore, no terror or fear; he is far removed from error and delusion, and finally reaches Nirvāṇa. All the Buddhas of the three worlds[28] rely on the Perfection of Wisdom, and that is why they attain the ultimate and complete enlightenment. Know, therefore, that the Perfection of Wisdom is a great divine spell, a spell of great illumination, a spell without superior, and a spell without equal. It can do away with all sufferings—such is the unvarnished truth. Therefore, when the Spell of the Perfection of Wisdom is to be spoken, say this spell: "Gate! Gate! Pāragate! Pārasaṃgate! Bodhisvāhā!"[29]

Now because that master of the law from the Tang court was spiritually prepared, he could remember the Heart Sūtra after hearing it only once. Through him, it has come down to us this day. It is the comprehensive classic for the cultivation of Perfection, the very gateway to becoming a Buddha.

After the transmission of the sūtra, the Chan Master trod on the cloudy luminosity and was about to return to his crow's nest. Tripitaka, however, held him back and earnestly questioned him again about the condition of the road to the West. The Chan Master laughed and said:

"The way is not too hard to walk;
Try listening to what I say.

A thousand hills and waters deep;
Places full of goblins and snags;
When you reach those sky-touching cliffs,
Fear not and put your mind at rest.
Crossing the Rub Ear Precipice,
You must walk with steps placed sideways.
Take care in the Black Pine Forest;
Fox-spirits will likely bar your way.
Griffins will fill the capitals;
Monsters all mountains populate;
Old tigers sit as magistrates;
Graying wolves act as registrars.
Lions, elephants—all called kings!
Leopards, tigers are coachmen all!
A wild pig totes a hauling pole;
You'll meet ahead a water sprite.
An old stone ape of many years
Now nurses over there his spite!
Just ask that acquaintance of yours:
Well he knows the way to the West."

Hearing this, Pilgrim laughed with scorn and said, "Let's go. Don't ask him, ask me! That's enough!" Tripitaka did not perceive what he meant. The Chan Master, changing into a beam of golden light, went straight up to his crow's nest, while the priest bowed toward him to express his gratitude. Enraged, Pilgrim lifted his iron rod and thrust it upward violently, but garlands of blooming lotus flowers were seen together with a thousand-layered shield of auspicious clouds. Though Pilgrim might have the strength to overturn rivers and seas, he could not catch hold of even one strand of the crow's nest. When Tripitaka saw this, he pulled Pilgrim back, saying, "Wukong, why are you jabbing at the nest of a bodhisattva like him?" "For leaving like that after abusing both my brother and me," said Pilgrim. "He was speaking of the way to the Western Heaven," said Tripitaka. "Since when did he abuse you?"

"Didn't you get it?" asked Pilgrim. "He said, 'A wild pig totes a hauling pole,' and insulted Eight Rules. 'An old stone ape of many years' ridiculed old Monkey. How else would you explain that?" "Elder Brother," said Eight Rules, "don't be angry. This Chan Master does know the events of past and future. Let's see if his statement, 'You'll meet ahead a water sprite,' will be fulfilled or not. Let's spare him and leave." Pilgrim saw the lotus flowers and auspicious fog near the nest, and he had little alternative than to ask his

master to mount so that they could descend from the mountain and proceed toward the West. Lo, their journey

Thus shows that in man's world pure leisure is rare,
But evils and ogres are rife in the hills!

We really do not know what took place in the journey ahead; let's listen to
the explanation in the next chapter.

TWENTY

At Yellow Wind Ridge the Tang Monk meets adversity; In mid-mountain, Eight Rules strives to be first.

> *The dharma is born through the mind;*
> *It'll be destroyed, too, through the mind.*
> *By whom it is destroyed or born,*
> *That you must determine yourself.*
> *If it is through your own mind,*
> *Why do others need to tell you?*
> *All that you need is your hard work*
> *To draw blood out of iron ore.*
> *Let a silk cord puncture your nose*
> *To tie a firm knot on the void;*
> *Fasten that to the no-work tree,*[1]
> *That you'd not be vicious and wild.*
> *Regard not the thief as your son,*
> *And forget all dharma and mind.*
> *Let not the Other deceive me:*
> *With one big punch strike him out first.*
> *The manifest mind's also no mind;*
> *Manifest Law is law that's stopped.*
> *When both Bull*[2] *and Man disappear,*
> *The jade-green sky is bright and clear.*
> *Any autumn moon's just as round:*
> *You can't tell one from the other.*

This enigmatic *gāthā* was composed by Xuanzang, master of the law, after he had thoroughly mastered the *Heart Sūtra*, which had, in fact, broken through the gate of his understanding. He recited it frequently, and the beam of spiritual light penetrated by itself to his innermost being.

We turn now to tell you about the three travelers, who dined on the wind and rested by the waters, who clothed themselves with the moon and cloaked themselves with the stars on their journey. Soon, it was the scene of summer again, beneath a torrid sky. They saw

> *Flowers gone, and butterflies cared not to linger;*
> *On tall trees the cicada chirp turned brazen.*
> *Wild worms made their cocoons, fair pomegranates their fire,*
> *As new lilies in the ponds appeared.*[3]

As they were traveling one day, it was growing late again when they saw a hamlet beside the mountain road. "Wukong," said Tripitaka, "look at that sun setting behind the mountain, hiding its fiery orb, and the moon rising on the eastern sea, revealing an icy wheel. It's a good thing that a family lives by the road up there. Let us ask for lodging for the night and proceed tomorrow." "You are right!" said Eight Rules. "Old Hog is rather hungry, too! Let's go and beg for some food at the house. Then I can regain my strength to pole the luggage."

"This family-hugging devil!" said Pilgrim. "You only left the family a few days ago, and you are already beginning to complain." "Elder Brother," said Eight Rules, "I'm not like you—I can't imbibe the wind and exhale the mist. Since I began following our master a few days ago, I've been half hungry all the time. Did you know that?" Hearing this, Tripitaka said, "Wuneng, if your heart still clings to the family, you are not the kind of person who wants to leave it. You may as well turn back!" Idiot was so taken aback that he fell on his knees and said, "Master, please do not listen to the words of Elder Brother. He loves to put blame on others: I haven't made any complaint, but he said that I was complaining. I'm only an honest moron, who said that I was hungry so that we could find some household to beg for food. Immediately he called me a family-hugging devil! Master, I received the commandments from the Bodhisattva and mercy from you, and that was why I was determined to serve you and go to the Western Heaven. I vow that I have no regrets. This is, in fact, what they call the practice of strict austerities. What do you mean, I'm not willing to leave the family?" "In that case," said Tripitaka, "you may get up."

Leaping up with a bound, Idiot was still muttering something as he picked up the pole with the luggage. He had no choice but to follow his companions with complete determination up to the door of the house by the wayside. Tripitaka dismounted, Pilgrim took the reins, and Eight Rules put down the luggage, all standing still beneath the shade of a large tree. Holding his nine-ringed priestly staff and pressing down his rain hat woven of straw and rattan, Tripitaka went to the door first. He saw inside an old man reclining on a bamboo bed and softly reciting the name of Buddha. Tripitaka dared not speak loudly; instead, he said very slowly and quietly, "Patron, salutations!" The old man jumped up and at once began to straighten out his attire. He walked out of the door to return the greeting, saying, "Honored Priest, pardon me for not coming to meet you. Where did you come from? What are you doing at my humble abode?" "This poor monk," said Tripitaka, "happens to be a priest from the Great Tang in the Land of the East. In obedience to an imperial decree, I am journeying to the Great Thunderclap Temple to seek scriptures from the Buddha. It was getting late when I arrived in your esteemed region, and I would beg for shelter for one night in your fine mansion. I beseech you to grant me this favor." "You can't go there," said the old man, shaking his head and waving his hand, "it's exceedingly difficult to bring scriptures back from the Western Heaven. If you want to do that, you might as well go the Eastern Heaven!" Tripitaka fell silent, thinking to himself, "The Bodhisattva clearly told me to go to the West. Why does this old man now say that I should head for the East instead? Where in the East would there be any scriptures?" Terribly flustered and embarrassed, he could not make any reply for a long time.

We now tell you about Pilgrim, who had always been impulsive and mischievous. Unable to restrain himself, he went forward and said in a loud voice, "Old man! Though you are of such great age, you don't have much common sense. We monks have traveled a great distance to come and ask you for shelter, and here you are trying to intimidate us with discouraging words. If your house is too small and there's not enough space for us to sleep, we'll sit beneath the trees for the night and not disturb you." "Master!" said the old man, taking hold of Tipitaka, "you don't say anything. But that disciple of yours with a pointed chin, shriveled cheeks, a thunder-god mouth, and blood-red eyes—he looks like a demon with a bad case of consumption—how dare he offend an aged person like me!"

"An old fellow like you," said Pilgrim with a laugh, "really has very little discernment! Those who are handsome may be good for their looks only! A person like me, old Monkey, may be small but tough, like the skin around a ball of ligaments!" "I suppose you must have some abilities," said the old man. "I won't boast," said Pilgrim, "but they are passable." "Where did you used to live?" asked the old man, "and why did you shave your hair to become a monk?" "The ancestral home of old Monkey," said Pilgrim, "is at the Water-Curtain Cave in the Flower-Fruit Mountain, in the Aolai Country of the East Pūrvavideha Continent. I learned to be a monster-spirit in my youth, assuming the name of Wukong, and with my abilities I finally became the Great Sage, Equal to Heaven. Because I did not receive any acceptable appointment in Heaven, I caused great turmoil in the Celestial Palace, and incurred great calamities for myself. I was, however, delivered from my ordeals and have turned to Buddhism instead to seek the fruits of Truth. As a guardian of my master, who is in the service of the Tang court, I am journeying to the Western Heaven to worship Buddha. Why should I fear tall mountains, treacherous roads, wide waters, and wild waves? I, old Monkey, can apprehend monsters, subdue demons, tame tigers, capture dragons— in sum, I know a little about all the matters that a person needs to know to go up to Heaven or to descend into Earth. If by chance your household is suffering from some such disturbances as flying bricks and dancing tiles, or talking pots and doors opening by themselves, old Monkey can quiet things down for you."

When that old man heard this lengthy speech, he roared with laughter and said, "So you are really a garrulous monk who begs for alms from place to place!" "Only your son is garrulous!" said Pilgrim. "I'm not very talkative these days, because following my master on his journey is quite tiring." "If you were not tired," said that old man, "and if you were in the mood to chatter, you would probably talk me to death! Since you have such abilities, I suppose you can go to the West successfully. How many of you are there? You may rest in my thatched hut." "We thank the old patron for not sending us away," said Tripitaka; "there are three of us altogether." "Where is the third member of your party?" asked the old man. "Your eyes must be somewhat dim, old man," said Pilgrim. "Isn't he over there standing in the shade?" The old man did indeed have poor sight; he raised his head and stared intently. The moment he saw Eight Rules with his strange face and mouth, he became so terrified that he started to rush back into the house, tripping at every step. "Shut the door! Shut the door!" he cried. "A monster is coming!" Pilgrim caught hold of him, saying, "Don't be afraid, old man! He's no monster; he's my younger brother." "Fine! Fine! Fine!" said the old man, shaking all over. "One monk uglier than another!"

Eight Rules approached him and said, "You are really mistaken, Aged Sir, if you judge people by their looks. We may be ugly, but we are all useful." As the old man was speaking with the three monks in front of his house, two young men appeared to the south of the village, leading an old woman and several young children. All of them had their clothes rolled up and were walking barefoot, for they were returning after a day's planting of young shoots of grain. When they saw the white horse, the luggage, and the goings-on in front of their house, they all ran forward, asking, "What are you people doing here?" Turning his head, Eight Rules flapped his ears a couple of times and stuck out his long snout once, so frightening the people that they fell down right and left, madly scattering in every direction. Tripitaka, alarmed, kept saying, "Don't be afraid! Don't be afraid! We are not bad people! We are monks in quest of scriptures." Coming out of his house, the old man helped the old woman up, saying, "Mama, get up! Calm yourself. This master came from the Tang court. His disciples may look hideous, but they are really good people with ugly faces. Take the boys and girls back into the house." Clutching at the old man, the old woman walked inside with the two young men and their children.

Sitting on the bamboo bed in their house, Tripitaka began to protest, saying, "Disciples! The two of you are not only ugly in appearance, but you are also rude in your language. You have scared this family badly, and you are causing me to sin." "To tell you the truth, Master," said Eight Rules, "since I started accompanying you, I have become a lot better behaved. At the time when I was living in Old Gao Village, all I needed to do was to pout and flap my ears once, and scores of people would be frightened to death!" "Stop talking rubbish, Idiot," said Pilgrim, "and fix your ugliness." "Look at the way Wukong talks," said Tripitaka. "Your appearance comes with your birth. How can you tell him to fix it?" "Take that rakelike snout," said Pilgrim, "put it in your bosom, and don't take it out. And stick your rush-leaf-fan ears to the back of your head, and don't shake them. That's fixing it." Eight Rules did indeed hide his snout and stick his ears to the back of his head; with his hands folded in front of him to hide his head, he stood on one side of his master. Pilgrim took the luggage inside the main door, and tied the white horse to one of the posts in the courtyard.

The old man then brought a young man in to present three cups of tea placed on a wooden tray. After the tea, he ordered a vegetarian meal to be prepared. Then the young man took an old, unvarnished table full of holes and several stools with broken legs, and placed them in the courtyard for the three of them to sit where it was cool. Only then did Tripitaka ask, "Old patron, what is your noble surname?" "Your humble servant goes by the surname of Wang," said the old man. "And how many heirs do you have?" asked Tripitaka. "I have two sons and three grandchildren," said the old man. "Congratulations! Congratulations!" said Tripitaka. "And what is your age?" "I have foolishly lived till my sixty-first year," the old man said. "Good! Good! Good!" said Pilgrim. "You have just begun a new sexagenary cycle." "Old patron," said Tripitaka again, "you said when we first came that the scriptures in the Western Heaven were difficult to get. Why?" "The scriptures are not hard to get," said the old man, "but the journey there is filled with hazards and difficulties. Some thirty miles west of us there is a mountain called the Yellow Wind Ridge of Eight Hundred Miles. Monsters infest that mountain, and that's what I meant by difficulties. Since this little priest claims that he has many abilities, however, you may perhaps proceed after all." "No fear! No fear!" said Pilgrim. "With old Monkey and his younger brother around, we'll never be touched, no matter what kind of monster we meet."

While they spoke, one of the sons brought out some rice and placed it on the table, saying, "Please eat." Tripitaka immediately folded his hands to begin his grace, but Eight Rules had already swallowed a whole bowl of rice. Before the priest could say the few sentences, Idiot had devoured three more bowlfuls. "Look at the glutton!" said Pilgrim. "It's like we've met a *preta*!" Old Wang was a sensitive person. When he saw how fast Eight Rules was eating, he said, "This honored priest must be really hungry! Quick, bring more rice!" Idiot in truth had an enormous appetite. Look at him! Without lifting his head once, he finished over ten bowls, while Tripitaka and Pilgrim could hardly finish two. Idiot refused to stop and wanted to eat still more. "In our haste we have not prepared any dainty viands," said old

Wang, "and I dare not press you too much. Please take at least one more helping." Both Tripitaka and Pilgrim said, "We have had enough." "Old man," said Eight Rules, "what are you mumbling about? Who's having a game of divination with you? Why mention all that about the fifth *yao* and the sixth *yao*?[4] If you have rice, just bring more of it, that's all!" So Idiot in one meal finished all the rice in that household, and then he said he was only half full! The tables and dishes were cleared away, and after bedding had been placed on the bamboo bed and on some wooden boards, the travelers rested.

The next morning, Pilgrim went to saddle the horse, while Eight Rules put their luggage in order. Old Wang asked his wife to prepare some refreshments and drinks to serve them, after which the three of them expressed their thanks and took leave of their host. The old man said, "If there is any mishap on your journey after you leave here, you must feel free to return to our house." "Old man," said Pilgrim, "don't speak such disconcerting words. Those of us who have left the family never retrace our steps!" They then urged on the horse, picked up the luggage, and proceeded toward the West. Alas! What this journey means for them is that

There's no safe way which leads to the Western Realm;
There'll be great disasters brought by demons vile.

Before the three of them had traveled for half a day, they did indeed come upon a tall mountain, exceedingly rugged. Tripitaka rode right up to the hanging cliff and looked around, sitting sideways on his saddle. Truly

Tall was the mountain;
Rugged, the peak;
Steep, the precipice;
Deep, the canyon;
Gurgling, the stream;
And fresh were the flowers.
This mountain, whether tall or not,
Its top reached the blue sky;
This stream, whether deep or not,
Its floor opened to Hell below.
Before the mountain,
White clouds rose in continuous rings
And boulders in shapes grotesque.
Countless the soul-rending cliffs ten thousand yards deep;
Behind them, winding, twisting, dragon-hiding caves,
Where water dripped from ledges drop by drop.
He also saw some deer with zigzag horns;

Dull and dumbly staring antelopes;
Winding and coiling red-scaled pythons;
Silly and foolish white-faced apes;
Tigers that climbed the hills to seek their dens at night;
Dragons that churned the waves to leave their lairs at dawn.
If one stepped before a cave's entrance,
The dead leaves crackled;
The fowls in the grass
Darted up with wings loudly beating;
The beasts in the forest
Walked with paws noisily scratching.
Suddenly wild creatures hurried by,
Making hearts beat with fear.
Thus it was that the Due-to-Fall Cave duly faced the Due-to-Fall Cave,[5]
The Cave duly facing the Due-to-Fall Cave duly faced the mount.
One blue bill dyed like a thousand yards of jade,
Mist-veiled like countless mounds of jade-green gauze.

The master rode forward very slowly, while the Great Sage Sun also walked at a slower pace and Zhu Wuneng proceeded leisurely with the load. As all of them were looking at the mountain, a great whirlwind suddenly arose. Alarmed, Tripitaka said, "Wukong, the wind is rising!" "Why fear the wind?" said Pilgrim. "This is the breath of Heaven in the four seasons, nothing to be afraid of." "But this is a terribly violent wind, unlike the kind that comes from Heaven," said Tripitaka. "How so?" said Pilgrim. Tripitaka said, "Look at this wind!

Augustly it blows in a blusterous key,
An immense force leaving the jade-green sky.
It passes the ridge, just hear the trees roar.
It moves in the wood, just see the poles quake.
Willows by the banks are rocked to the roots;
Blown garden flowers now soar with their leaves.
Fishing boats, nets drawn, make their hawsers taut;
Vessels with sails down have their anchors cast.
Trekkers in mid-journey have lost their way;
Woodsmen in the hills cannot hold their loads.
From woods with fruits divine the apes disperse;
From clumps of rare flowers the small fawns flee.
Before the cliff cypress fall one by one;
Downstream bamboo and pine die leaf by leaf.
Earth and dust are scattered while sand explodes;
Rivers and seas overturned, waves churn and roll."

Eight Rules went forward and tugged at Pilgrim, saying, "Elder Brother, the wind is too strong! Let's find shelter until it dies down." "You are too soft, Brother," said Pilgrim, laughing, "when you want to hide the moment the wind gets strong. What would happen to you if you were to meet a monster-spirit face to face?" "Elder Brother," said Eight Rules, "you probably haven't heard of the proverb,

> Flee the fair sex like a foe;
> Flee the wind like an arrow!

We suffer no loss if we take shelter just for a little while."

"Stop talking," said Pilgrim, "and let me seize the wind and smell it." "You are fibbing again, Elder Brother," said Eight Rules, with a laugh, "for how can the wind be seized for you to smell? Even if you manage to catch hold of it, it will slip past you at once." "Brother," said Pilgrim, "you didn't know that I have the magic to 'seize the wind.'" Dear Great Sage! He allowed the head of the wind to move past but he caught hold of its tail and sniffed at it. Finding it somewhat fetid, he said, "This is indeed not a very good wind, for it smells like a tiger or else like a monster; there's something definitely strange about it."

Hardly had he finished speaking when from over a hump of the mountain a fierce striped tiger with a whiplike tail and powerful limbs appeared. Tripitaka was so horrified that he could no longer sit on the saddle; he fell head over heels from the white horse and lay beside the road, half out of his wits. Throwing down the luggage, Eight Rules took up his muckrake and rushed past Pilgrim. "Cursed beast!" he shouted. "Where are you going?" He lunged forward and struck at the beast's head. That tiger stood straight up on his hind legs and, raising his left paw, punctured his own breast with one jab. Then, gripping the skin, he tore downward with a loud rending noise and he became completely stripped of his own hide as he stood there by the side of the road. Look how abominable he appears! Oh! That hideous form:

> All smeared with blood, the naked body;
> Most sickly red, the warped legs and feet;
> Like shooting flames, wild hair by the temples;
> Bristlingly hard, two eyebrows pointing upward;
> Hellishly white, four steel-like fangs;
> With light aglow, a pair of gold eyes;
> Imposing of mien, he mightily roared;
> With power fierce, he cried aloud.

"Slow down! Slow down!" he shouted. "I am not any other person. I am the vanguard of the forces commanded by the Great King Yellow Wind. I have received the Great King's strict order to patrol this mountain and to catch a few mortals to be used as hors d'oeuvres for him. Where did you monks come from that you dare reach for your weapons to harm me?" "Cursed beast that you are!" cried Eight Rules. "So you don't recognize me! We are no mortals who just happen to be passing by; we are the disciples of Tripitaka, the royal brother of the Great Tang Emperor in the Land of the East, who by imperial decree is journeying to the Western Heaven to seek scriptures from the Buddha. You better stand aside quickly for us to pass, and don't alarm my master. Then I'll spare your life. But if you are impudent as before, there will be no clemency when this rake is lifted up!"

That monster-spirit would not permit any further discussion. He quickly drew near, assumed a fighting pose, and clawed at Eight Rules's face. Dodging the blow, Eight Rules struck at once with his rake. Since the monster had no weapons in his hands, he turned and fled, with Eight Rules hard on his heels. Racing to the slope below, the monster took out from beneath a clump of rocks a pair of bronze scimitars, with which he turned to face his pursuer. So the two of them clashed right in front of the mountain slope, closing in again and again. Meanwhile, Pilgrim lifted up the Tang Monk and said, "Master, don't be afraid. Sit here and let old Monkey go help Eight Rules strike down that monster so that we can leave." Only then did Tripitaka manage to sit up; trembling all over, he began to recite the *Heart Sūtra*, but we shall say no more of that.

Whipping out the iron rod, Pilgrim shouted, "Catch him!" Eight Rules at once attacked with even greater ferocity, and the monster fled in defeat. "Don't spare him," yelled Pilgrim. "We must catch him!" Wielding rod and rake, the two of them gave chase down the mountain. In panic, the monster resorted to the trick of the gold cicada casting its shell: he rolled on the ground and changed back into the form of a tiger. Pilgrim and Eight Rules would not let up. Closing in on the tiger, they intended to dispose of him once and for all. When the monster saw them approaching, he again stripped himself of his own hide and threw the skin over a large piece of rock, while his true form changed into a violent gust of wind heading back the way he had come. Suddenly noticing the master of the law sitting by the road and reciting the *Heart Sūtra*, he caught hold of him and hauled him away by mounting the wind. O, pity that Tripitaka,

The River Float fated to suffer oft!
It's hard to make merit in Buddha's gate!

Having taken the Tang Monk back to the door of his cave, the monster stopped the wind and said to the one standing guard at the door, "Go report to the Great King and say that the Tiger Vanguard has captured a monk. He awaits his order outside the door." The Cave Master gave the order for him to enter. The Tiger Vanguard, with the two bronze scimitars hanging from his waist, lifted up the Tang Monk in his hands. He went forward and knelt down, saying, "Great King! Though your humble officer is not talented, he thanks you for granting him the honored command of doing patrol in the mountain. I encountered a monk who is Tripitaka, master of the law and brother to the Throne of the Great Tang in the Land of the East. While he was on his way to seek scriptures from Buddha, I captured him to present to you here for your culinary pleasure." When the Cave Master heard this, he was a little startled. "I have heard some rumor," he said, "that the master of the law Tripitaka is a divine monk who is going in search of scriptures by imperial decree of the Great Tang. He has under him a disciple whose name is Pilgrim Sun and who possesses tremendous magical power and prodigious intelligence. How did you manage to catch him and bring him here?"

"He has, in fact, two disciples," said the Vanguard. "The one who appeared first used a nine-pronged muckrake, and he had a long snout and huge ears. Another one used a golden-hooped iron rod, and he had fiery eyes and diamond pupils. As they were chasing me to attack me, I used the trick of the gold cicada casting its shell and succeeded not only in eluding them but also in catching this monk. I now respectfully present him to the Great King as a meal." "Let's not eat him yet," said the Cave Master.

"Great King," said the Vanguard, "only a worthless horse turns away ready feed!" "You haven't considered this," said the Cave Master. "There's nothing wrong with eating him, but I'm afraid his two disciples may come to our door and argue with us. Let's tie him instead to one of the posts in the rear garden and wait for three or four days. If those two don't show up to disturb us, then we can enjoy the double benefit of having his body cleaned and not having to bicker with our tongues. Then we can do what we want with him, whether we wish him boiled, steamed, fried, or sautéed; we can take our time to enjoy him." Highly pleased, the Vanguard said, "The Great King is full of wisdom and foresight, and what he says is most reasonable. Little ones, take the priest inside."

Seven or eight demons rushed up from the sides and took the Tang Monk away; like hawks catching sparrows, they bound him firmly with ropes. This is how that

Ill-fated River Float on Pilgrim broods;
The god-monk in pain calls Wuneng to mind.

"Disciples," he said, "I don't know in what mountain you are catching monsters, or in what region you are subduing goblins. But I have been captured by this demon from whom I have to suffer great injury. When shall we see each other again? Oh, what misery! If you two can come here quickly, you may be able to save my life. But if you tarry, I shall never survive!" As he lamented and sighed, his tears fell like rain.

We now tell you about Pilgrim and Eight Rules, who, having chased the tiger down the slope of the mountain, saw him fall and collapse at the foot of the cliff. Lifting his rod, Pilgrim brought it down on the tiger with all his might, but the rod bounced back up and his hands were stung by the impact. Eight Rules, too, gave a blow with his muckrake, and its prongs also rebounded. They then discovered that it was nothing but a piece of tigerskin covering a large slab of stone. Greatly startled, Pilgrim said, "Oh, no! Oh, no! He's tricked us!" "What trick?" asked Eight Rules. Pilgrim replied, "This is called the trick of the gold cicada casting its shell. He left his skin covering the stone here to fool us, but he himself has escaped. Let's go back at once to take a look at Master. Let's hope that he has not been hurt." They retreated hurriedly, but Tripitaka had long vanished. Bellowing like thunder, Pilgrim cried, "What shall we do? He has taken Master away." "Heavens! Heavens!" wailed Eight Rules, leading the horse, as tears fell from his eyes, "where shall we go to look for him?" With head held high, Pilgrim said, "Don't cry! Don't cry! The moment you cry, you already feel defeated. They have to be somewhere in this mountain. Let's go and search for them."

The two of them indeed rushed up the mountain, passing the ridges and scaling the heights. After traveling for a long time, they suddenly beheld a cave dwelling emerging from beneath a cliff. Pausing to take a careful look around, they saw that it was indeed a formidable place. You see

A pointed peak fortresslike;
An old path ever winding;
Blue pines and fresh bamboos;
Green willows and verdant wu-trees;[6]
Strange rocks in twos below the cliff;
Rare fowls in pairs within the woods.
A stream flowing far away spills over a wall of stones;
The mountain brook reaches the sandy banks in small drops.
Wasteland clouds in clusters;
And grass as green as jade.
The sly vixen and hare scamper wildly about;
Horned deer and musk deer lock to contest their strength.
Slanted across the cliff dangles an aged vine;
Half down the gorge an ancient cedar hangs.
August and grand, this place surpasses Mount Hua;[7]
The falling blooms and singing birds rival Tiantai's.

"Worthy Brother," said Pilgrim, "you may leave the luggage in the fold of the mountain, where it will be protected from the wind. Then you can graze the horse nearby and you need not come out. Let old Monkey go fight with him at his door. That monster has to be caught before our master can be rescued." "No need for instructions," said Eight Rules. "Go quickly!" Pulling down his shirt and tightening his belt on the tiger-skin skirt, Pilgrim grasped his rod and rushed up to the cave, where he saw six words in large letters above the door: "Yellow Wind Cave, Yellow Wind Peak." He at once poised himself for battle, with legs apart and one foot slightly ahead of the other. Holding his rod high, he cried, "Monster! Send out my master at once, lest I overturn your den and level your dwelling!"

When the little demons heard this, every one of them was panic-stricken and ran inside to make the report, "Great King, disaster!" The Yellow Wind Monster, who was sitting there, asked, "What's the matter?" "Outside the cave door there's a monk with a thunder-god mouth and hairy face," said one of the little demons, "holding in his hands a huge, thick, iron rod and demanding the return of his master." Somewhat fearful, the Cave Master said to the Tiger Vanguard, "I asked you to patrol the mountain, and you should merely have caught a few mountain buffalo, wild boar, fat deer, or wild goats. Why did you have to bring back a Tang Monk? Now we have provoked his disciple to come here to create all sorts of disturbance. What shall we do?" "Don't be anxious, Great King," said the Vanguard, "and put your worries to rest. Though this junior officer is untalented, he is willing to lead fifty soldiers out there and bring in that so-called Pilgrim Sun as a condiment for your meal." "In addition to the various officers here," said the Cave Master, "we have some seven hundred regulars. You may pick as many of them as you want. Only if that Pilgrim is caught will we be able to enjoy a piece of that monk's flesh with any comfort. And if that happens, I'm willing to become your bond brother. But I fear that if you can't catch him, you may even get hurt. You mustn't blame me then!"

"Relax! Relax! Let me go now!" said the Tiger Monster. He checked off the roll fifty of the toughest little demons, who began beating drums and waving banners. He himself took up the two bronze scimitars and leaped out of the cave, crying with a loud voice, "Where did you come from, you monkey-monk, that you dare make such a racket here?!" "You skin-flaying beast!" shouted Pilgrim. "You were the one who used that shell-casting trick to take away my master. Why do you question me instead? You better send out my master immediately, or I'll not spare your life." "I took your master," said the Tiger Monster, "so that he could be served to my Great King as meat for his rice. If you know what's good for you, get away from here. If not, I'll catch you too, and you'll be eaten along with him. It will be like 'one free piece of merchandise with every purchase!'" When he heard this, Pilgrim was filled with anger. With grinding teeth and fiery eyes all ablaze, he lifted his iron rod and yelled, "What great ability do you have, that you dare talk like that? Don't move! Watch this rod!" Wielding his scimitars swiftly, the Vanguard turned to meet him. It was truly some battle as the two of them let loose their power. What a fight!

> *That monster is truly a goose's egg,*
> *But Wukong is a goose-egg stone no less!*
> *When bronze swords fight Handsome Monkey King,*
> *It's like eggs coming to strike at stones.*
> *How can sparrows quarrel with the phoenix?*
> *Dare pigeons oppose the eagles and hawks?*
> *The monster belches wind—the mount's filled with dust;*
> *Wukong spits out fog and clouds hide the sun.*
> *They fight for no more than four or five rounds;*
> *The Vanguard grows weak, having no strength left.*
> *He turns in defeat to flee for his life,*
> *Hard pressed by Wukong, who seeks his death.*

Not able to hold out any longer, the monster turned and fled. But since he had boasted in front of the Cave Master, he dared not go back to the cave; instead, he fled toward the mountain slope. Pilgrim, of course, would not let him go; holding his rod, he gave chase relentlessly, shouting and crying along the way. As they reached the fold of the mountain, which formed a wind break, he happened to look up, and there was Eight Rules grazing the horse. Hearing all the shouts and clamor, Eight Rules turned around and saw that it was Pilgrim chasing a defeated Tiger Monster. Abandoning the horse, Eight Rules lifted his rake and approaching from one side brought it down hard on the monster's head. Pity that Vanguard!

> *He hoped to leap clear of the brown-rope net,*
> *Not knowing he would meet the fisher's coop.*

One blow from Eight Rules's rake produced nine holes, from which fresh blood spurted out, and the brains of the monster's whole head ran dry! We have a poem as a testimony for Eight Rules, which says:

> *Returning to True Teaching some years ago,*
> *He kept a chaste diet to realize the Real Void.*
> *To serve Tripitaka is his pious wish:*
> *This, a new Buddhist convert's first merit.*

Idiot put his foot on the monster's spine and brought down the rake on him once more. When Pilgrim saw that, he was very pleased, saying, "That's right, Brother! He was audacious enough to lead scores of little de-mons against me, but he was defeated. Instead of fleeing back to the cave, he came here seeking death. It's a good thing you are here, or else he would have escaped again." "Is he the one who took our master with the wind?" asked Eight Rules. "Yes! Yes!" said Pilgrim. "Did you ask him the where-abouts of our master?" said Eight Rules. "This monster brought Master to the cave," said Pilgrim, "to be served to some blackguard of a Great King as meat for his rice. I was enraged, fought with him, and chased him here for you to finish him off. Brother, this is your merit! You can remain here guarding the horse and luggage, and let me drag this dead monster back to the mouth of the cave to provoke battle again. We must capture the old monster before we can rescue Master." "You are right, Elder Brother," said Eight Rules. "Go, go now! If you beat that old monster, chase him here and let old Hog intercept and kill him." Dear Pilgrim! Holding the iron rod in one hand and dragging the dead tiger with the other, he went back to the mouth of the cave. So it was that

> The dharma-master met monsters in his ordeal;
> Feeling and nature in peace wild demons subdued.

We do not know whether he managed this time to overcome the mon-ster and rescue the Tang Monk; let's listen to the explanation in the next chapter.

TWENTY-ONE

The Vihārapālas¹ prepare lodging for the Great Sage; Lingji of Sumeru crushes the wind demon.

We shall now tell about those fifty defeated little demons, who rushed into the cave carrying their broken drums and torn banners. "Great King," they cried, "the Tiger Vanguard was no match for the hairy-faced monk. That monk chased him down the eastern slope until the Vanguard disappeared." When the old monster heard this, he was terribly upset. As he bowed his head in silent deliberation, another little demon who stood guard at the door came to report, "Great King, the Tiger Vanguard was beaten to death by the hairy-faced monk and dragged up to our door to provoke battle." Hearing this, the old monster became even angrier."This fellow does not know when to stop!" he said. "I have not eaten his master, but he has killed our Vanguard instead. How insolent!" Whereupon he bellowed, "Bring me my armor. I have heard only rumors about this Pilgrim Sun, and I'm going out there to find out what sort of monk he really is. Even if he has nine heads and eight tails, I'm going to take him in here to pay for the life of my Tiger Vanguard!" The little demons quickly brought out the armor. After having been properly buckled and laced, the old monster took a steel trident and leaped out of the cave, leading the rest of the demons. Standing in front of the door, the Great Sage watched the monster emerge with a truly aggressive appearance. Look how he is attired. You see

Gold helmet reflecting the sun;
Gold cuirass gleaming with light.
A pheasant-tail tassel flies from the helmet;
A light yellow silk robe topped by the cuirass,
Tied with a dragonlike sash of brilliant hues.
His breastplate emits eye-dazzling light.
His boots of suede
Are dyed by locust flowers.
His embroidered kilt
Is decked with willow leaves.
Holding a sharp trident in his hands,
He seems almost the Erlang² Boy of old!

When he had come out, the old monster shouted, "Who is Pilgrim Sun?" With one foot on the carcass of the Tiger Monster and the compliant iron rod in his hands, Pilgrim replied: "Your Grandpa Sun is here! Send my master out!" The old monster took a careful look and saw the diminutive figure of Pilgrim—less than four feet, in fact—and his sallow cheeks. He said with a laugh: "Too bad! Too bad! I thought you were some kind of invincible hero. But you are only a sickly ghost, with nothing more than your skeleton left!"

"Child," said Pilgrim laughing, "how you lack perception! Your grandpa may be somewhat small in size, but if you have the courage to hit me on the head with the handle of your trident, I'll grow six feet at once." "Harden your head," said the monster, "and have a taste of my handle!" Our Great Sage was not in the least frightened. When the monster struck him once, he stretched his waist and at once grew more than six feet, attaining the height of ten feet altogether. The monster was so alarmed that he tried to use his trident to hold him down, shouting, "Pilgrim Sun, how dare you stand at my door, displaying this paltry magic of body protection! Stop using tricks! Come up here and let's measure our real abilities!" "My dear son," said Pilgrim with laughter, "the proverb says: 'Mercy should be shown before the hand is raised!' Your grandpa is pretty heavy-handed, and he fears that you won't be able to bear even one stroke of this rod!" Refusing to listen to any such discussion, the monster turned his trident around and stabbed at Pilgrim's chest. The Great Sage, of course, was not at all perturbed, for as the saying goes, the expert is never exercised. He raised his rod and, using the movement of the "black dragon sweeping the ground" to parry the trident, struck at the monster's head. The two of them thus began a fierce battle before that Yellow Wind Cave:

> The Monster King became enraged;
> The Great Sage released his might.
> The Monster King became enraged,
> Wishing to seize Pilgrim to pay for his Vanguard.
> The Great Sage released his might
> To capture this spirit and to save the priest.
> The trident arrived, blocked by the rod;
> The rod went forth, met by the trident.
> This one, a mountain-ruling captain of his hosts.
> That one, the Handsome Monkey King who defends the Law.
> At first they fought on the dusty earth;
> Then each arose midway to the sky.
> The fine steel trident;
> Pointed, sharp, and brilliant.
> The compliant rod:
> Body black and yellow hoops.
> Stabbed by them, your soul goes back to darkness!

Struck by them, you'll face King Yama!
You must rely on quick arms and keen sight.
You must have a tough frame and great strength.
The two fought without regard for life or death;
We know not who will be safe or who will be hurt.

The old monster and the Great Sage fought for thirty rounds, but neither could gain the upper hand. Pressing for a quick victory, Pilgrim decided to use the trick of "the body beyond the body." He tore from himself a handful of hairs that he chewed to pieces in his mouth. Spitting them out, he cried, "Change!" They changed at once into more than a hundred Pilgrims: all having the same appearance and all holding an iron rod, they surrounded the monster in midair. Somewhat alarmed, the monster also resorted to his special talent. He turned to face the ground to the southwest and opened his mouth three times to blow out some air. Suddenly a mighty yellow wind arose in the sky. Dear wind! It was indeed powerful.

Cold and whistling, it changed Heaven and Earth,
As yellow sand whirled without form or shape.
It cut through woods and hills to break pines and plums;
It tossed up dirt and dust, cracking crags and cliffs.
Waves churned in Yellow River to cloud its floor;
Tide and current swelled up at River Xiang.
The Polestar Palace in the blue sky shook;
The Hall of Darkness was almost blown down;
The Five Hundred Arhats all yelled and screamed;
The Eight Guards of Akṣobhya all cried and shrieked.
Mañjuśrī's green-haired lion ran away;
Viśvabhadra lost his white elephant.[3]
Snake and turtle of Zhenwu left their fold;[4]
Aflutter were the saddle-flaps of Zitong's[5] *mule.*
Traveling merchants sent their cries to Heaven,
And boatmen bowed to make their many vows—
Their mistlike lives awash in rolling waves;
Their names, their fortunes, adrift in the tide!
Caves on genie mountains were black as pitch;
The isle of Penglai[6] *was gloomy and dark.*
Laozi could not tend his elixir oven;
Age Star folded his fan of grapevine leaves.
As Queen Mother went to the Peaches Feast,
The wind blew her skirt and pins awry.
Erlang lost his way to the Guanzhou town;
Naṭa found it hard to pull out his sword.

Li Jing missed the pagoda in his hand;
Lu Ban⁷ dropped his golden-headed drill.
While three stories of Thunderclap fell down,
The stone bridge at Zhaozhou broke in twain.
The orb of the red sun had little light;
The stars of all Heaven grew obscure and faint.
Birds of south mountains flew to northern hills;
Water of east lakes spilled over to the west.
Fowls with mates broke up, they ceased their calls;
Mothers and sons parted, their cries turned mute.
Dragon Kings sought yakṣas all over the sea;
Thunder gods hunted lightnings everywhere.
Ten Kings of Yama tried to find their judge;
In Hell, Bull-Head ran after Horse-Face.
This wind blew down the Potalaka Mount
And whipped up one scroll of Guanyin's verse.
White lotus-blooms, cut down, flew beside the sea;
Twelve halls of the Bodhisattva were blown down.
From Pan Gu till this time since wind was known,
There never was wind with such ferocity.
Hu-la-la!
The universe did almost split apart!
The whole world was one mighty trembling mass!

This violent wind called up by the monster blew away all those little Pilgrims formed by the Great Sage's hairs and sent them reeling through the air like so many spinning wheels. Unable even to wield their rods, how could they possibly hope to draw near to fight? Pilgrim was so alarmed that he shook his body and retrieved his hairs. He then lifted the iron rod and tried to attack the monster all by himself, only to be met by a mouthful of yellow wind right on his face. Those two fiery eyes with diamond pupils of his were so blasted that they shut tightly and could not be opened. No longer able to use his rod, he fled in defeat while the monster retrieved the wind, which we shall mention no further.

We tell you now about Zhu Eight Rules, who, when he saw the violent yellow windstorm arriving and the whole of Heaven and Earth growing dim, led the horse and took the luggage to the fold of the mountain. There he crouched on the ground and refused to open his eyes or raise his head, his mouth incessantly calling on the name of Buddha and making vows. As he was wondering how Pilgrim was faring in his battle and whether his master was dead or alive, the wind stopped and the sky brightened again. He looked up and peered toward the entrance of the cave, but he could neither see any movement of weapons nor hear the sound of gongs and drums. Idiot dared not approach the cave, since there was no one else to guard the horse and the luggage. Deeply distressed and not knowing what to do, he suddenly heard the Great Sage approaching from the west, grunting and snorting as he came. Bowing to meet his companion, he said, "Elder Brother, what a mighty wind! Where did you come from?"

With a wave of his hand, Pilgrim said, "Formidable! It's truly formidable! Since I, old Monkey, was born, I have never witnessed such a violent wind! That old monster fought me with a steel trident, and we battled for over thirty rounds. It was then that I used the magic of the body beyond the body and had him surrounded. He panicked and called up this wind, which was ferocious indeed. Its force was so overwhelming that I had to suspend my operation and flee instead. Whew! What a wind! Whew! What a wind! Old Monkey also knows how to call up the wind and how to summon the rain, but it's hardly as vicious as the wind of this monster-spirit!" "Elder Brother," said Eight Rules, "how is the martial technique of that monster?" "It's presentable," said Pilgrim, "and he knows how to use the trident! He is, in fact, just about the equal of old Monkey. But that wind of his is vicious, and that makes it difficult to defeat him." "In that case," said Eight Rules, "how are we going to rescue Master?"

Pilgrim said, "We'll have to wait to rescue Master. I wonder if there is any eye doctor around here who can take a look at my eyes." "What's the matter with your eyes?" asked Eight Rules. Pilgrim replied, "That monster blew a mouthful of wind on my face, and my eyes were so sorely blasted that they are now watering constantly." "Elder Brother," said Eight Rules, "we are in the middle of a mountain, and it's getting late. Let's not talk about eye doctors; we don't even have a place to stay." "It won't be difficult to find lodging," said Pilgrim. "I doubt that the monster has the gall to harm our master. Let's find our way back to the main road and see whether we can stay with a family. After spending the night, we can return to subdue the monster tomorrow when it's light." "Exactly, exactly," agreed Eight Rules.

Leading the horse and carrying up the luggage, they left the fold of the mountain and went up the road. Dusk was setting in, and as they walked, they heard the sound of barking dogs toward the south of the mountain slope. Stopping to look, they saw a small cottage with flickering lamplights. Not bothering to look for a path, the two of them walked through the grass and arrived at the door of that household. They saw

Dark clumps of purplish fungi;
Greyish piles of white stones;
Dark clumps of purplish fungi with much green grass;
Greyish piles of white stones half grown with moss:

A few specks of fireflies, their faint light aglow;
A forest of wild woods stand in dense rows;
Orchids ever fragrant;
Bamboos newly planted;
A clear stream flows a winding course;
Old cedars lean o'er a deep cliff.
A secluded place where no travelers come:
Only wild flowers bloom before the door.

Not daring to enter without permission, they both called out: "Open the door! Open the door!" An old man inside appeared with several young farmers, all holding rakes, pitchforks, and brooms. "Who are you? Who are you?" they asked. With a bow, Pilgrim said, "We are disciples of a holy monk from the Great Tang in the Land of the East. We were on our way to seek scriptures from the Buddha in the Western Heaven when we passed through this mountain, and our master was captured by the Yellow Wind Great King. We have yet to rescue him. Since it is getting late, we have come to ask for lodging for one night at your house. We beg you for this means of convenience." Returning the bow, the old man said, "Pardon me for not coming to greet you. This is a place where clouds are more numerous than people, and when we heard you calling at the door just now, we were afraid that it might be someone like a wily fox, a tiger, or a bandit from the mountain. That's why my little ones might have offended you by their rather brusque manner. Please come in. Please come in."

The two brothers led the horse and hauled the luggage inside; after tying up the animal and putting down the load, they exchanged greetings again with the old man of the cottage before taking their seats. An old manservant then came forward to present tea, after which several bowls of sesame seed rice were brought out.[8] After they had finished the rice, the old man asked for bedding to be laid out for them to sleep. Pilgrim said, "We don't need to sleep just yet. May I ask the good man whether there is in your region someone who sells eye medicine?"

"Which one of you elders has eye disease?" asked the old man. Pilgrim said, "To tell you the truth, Venerable Sir, we who have left the family rarely become ill. In fact, I have never known any disease of the eye." "If you are not suffering from an eye disease," said the old man, "why do you want medicine?" "We were trying to rescue our master at the entrance of the Yellow Wind Cave today," said Pilgrim. "Unexpectedly that monster blew a mouthful of wind at me, causing my eyes to hurt and smart. At the moment, I'm weeping constantly, and that's why I want to find eye medicine."

"My goodness! My goodness!" said the old man. "A young priest like you, why do you lie? The wind of that Great King Yellow Wind is most fearsome, not comparable with any spring-autumn wind, pine-and-bamboo wind, or the wind coming from the four quarters."

"I suppose," said Eight Rules, "it must be brain-bursting wind, goat-ear wind, leprous wind, or migrainous wind!" "No, no!" said the old man. "His is called the Divine Wind of Samādhi." "What's it like?" asked Pilgrim. The old man said, "That wind

> Can blow to dim Heaven and Earth,
> And sadden both ghosts and gods.
> So savage it breaks rocks and stones,
> A man will die when he's blown!

If you had encountered that wind of his, you think you would still be alive? Only if you were an immortal could you remain unharmed."

"Indeed!" said Pilgrim. "I may not be an immortal (for they belong to the younger generation, as far as I am concerned), but it will take some doing to finish me off! That wind, however, did cause my eyeballs to hurt and smart."

"If you can say that," said the old man, "you must be a person with some background. Our humble region has no one who sells eye medicine. But I myself suffer from watery eyes when the wind blows in my face, and I met an extraordinary person once who gave me a prescription. It's called the three-flowers and nine-seeds ointment, capable of curing all wind-induced eye maladies." When Pilgrim heard these words, he bowed his head and said humbly, "I'm willing to ask you for some and try it on myself." The old man consented and went into the inner chamber. He took out a little cornelian vase and pulled off the stopper; using a small jade pin to scoop out some ointment, he dabbed it onto Pilgrim's eyes, telling him to close his eyes and rest quietly, for he would be well by morning. After doing this, the old man took the vase and retired with his attendants. Eight Rules untied the bags, took out the bedding, and asked Pilgrim to lie down. As Pilgrim groped about confusedly with his eyes closed, Eight Rules laughed and said, "Sir, where's your seeing-eye cane?" "You overstuffed idiot!" said Pilgrim. "You want to take care of me as a blind man?" Giggling to himself, Idiot fell asleep, but Pilgrim sat on the mattress and did exercises to cultivate his magic power. Only after the third watch did he sleep.

Soon it was the fifth watch and dawn was about to break. Wiping his face, Pilgrim opened his eyes, saying, "It's really marvelous medicine! I can see a hundred times better than before!" He then turned his head to look around. Ah! There were neither buildings nor halls, only some old locust trees and tall willows. The brothers were actually lying on a green grass meadow. Just then, Eight Rules began to stir, saying, "Elder Brother, why are you making all these noises?" "Open your eyes and take a look," said Pilgrim. Raising his head, Idiot discovered that the house had disappeared. He was so startled that he scrambled up at once, crying, "Where's my horse?" "Isn't it over there, tied to a tree?" said Pilgrim. "And the luggage?" asked Eight Rules.

"Isn't it there by your head?" said Pilgrim. "This family is rather shifty!" said Eight Rules. "If they have moved, why didn't they give us a call? If they had let old Hog know about it, they might have received some farewell gifts of tea and fruits. Well, I suppose they must be trying to hide from something and are afraid that the county sheriff may get wind of it; so they moved out in the night. Good Heavens! We must have been dead to the world! How could we not have heard anything when they dismantled the whole house?" "Idiot, stop babbling!" said Pilgrim, chuckling. "Take a look on that tree and see what kind of paper slip is there." Eight Rules took it down. It was a four-line poem that read:

This humble abode's no mortal abode:
A cottage devised⁹ by the Guardians of Law,
Who gave the wondrous balm to heal your sore.
Fret not and do your best to quell the fiend.

Pilgrim said, "A bunch of roguish deities! Since we changed to the dragon-horse, I had not taken a roll call of them. Now they are playing tricks on me instead!"

"Elder Brother," said Eight Rules, "stop putting on such airs! How would they ever let you check them off the roll?" "Brother," said Pilgrim, "you don't know about this. These Eighteen Protectors of Monasteries, the Six Gods of Darkness and Six Gods of Light, the Guardians of Five Points, and the Four Sentinels all have been ordered by the Bodhisattva to give secret protection to Master. The other day they reported their names to me, but since you have been with us, I have not made use of them. That's why I haven't made a roll call." "Elder Brother," said Eight Rules, "if they were ordered to give secret protection to Master, they had reason not to reveal themselves. That's why they had to devise this cottage here, and you shouldn't blame them. After all, they did put ointment on your eyes for you yesterday, and they did take care of us for one meal. You can say that they have done their duty. Don't blame them. Let's go and rescue Master." "Brother, you are right," said Pilgrim. "This place is not far from the Yellow Wind Cave. You had better stay here and look after the horse and luggage in the woods. Let old Monkey go into the cave to make some inquiry after the condition of Master. Then we can do battle with the monster again." "Exactly," said Eight Rules. "You should find out whether Master is dead or alive; if he's dead, each one of us can tend to our own business; if he's not, we can do our best to discharge our responsibility." Pilgrim said, "Stop talking nonsense! I'm off!"

With one leap he arrived at the entrance of the cave and found the door still shut and the inhabitants sound asleep. Pilgrim neither made any noise nor disturbed the monsters; making the magic sign and reciting the spell, he shook his body and changed at once into a spotted-leg mosquito. It was tiny and delicate, for which we have a testimonial poem:

> A pesky small shape with sharp sting;
> His tiny voice can hum like thunder!
> Adept at piercing gauze nets and orchid rooms,
> He likes the warm, sultry climate.
>
> He fears incense and swatting fans,
> But dearly loves bright lights and lamps.
> Airy, agile, all too clever and fast,
> He flies into the fiend's cave.[10]

The little demon who was supposed to guard the door was lying there asleep, snoring. Pilgrim gave him a bite on his face, causing the little demon to roll over half awakened. "O my father!" he said. "What a big mosquito! One bite and I already have a big lump." He then opened his eyes and said, "Why, it's dawn!" Just then, the second door inside opened with a creak, and Pilgrim immediately flew in. The old monster was giving orders to all his subordinates to be especially careful in guarding the various entrances while they made ready their weapons. "If the wind yesterday did not kill that Pilgrim Sun," he said, "he will certainly come back today. When he comes, we'll finish him off."

Hearing this, Pilgrim flew past the main hall and arrived at the rear of the cave, where he found another door tightly shut. Crawling through a crack in the door, he discovered a large garden, in the middle of which, bound by ropes to a pole, was the Tang Monk. That master was shedding tears profusely, constantly wondering where Wukong and Wuneng were to be found. Pilgrim stopped his flight and alighted on his bald head, saying, "Master!" Recognizing his voice, the Elder said, "Wukong, I nearly died thinking of you! Where are you calling from?" "Master," said Pilgrim, "I'm on your head. Calm yourself and stop worrying. We must first capture the monster before we can rescue you. "Disciple," said the Tang Monk, "when will you be able to capture the monster?" "The Tiger Monster who took you," said Pilgrim, "has already been slain by Eight Rules. But the wind of the old monster is a powerful weapon. I suspect we should be able to capture him today. Relax and stop crying. I'm leaving."

Having said that, he flew at once to the front, where the old monster was seated aloft, making a roll call of all the commanders of his troops. A little demon suddenly appeared, waving the command flag. He dashed up to the hall, crying, "Great King, this little one was on patrol in the mountain when he ran into a monk with a long snout and huge ears sitting in the woods not far from our entrance. If I hadn't run away quickly, he would have caught me. But I didn't see that hairy-faced monk who came here yesterday." "If Pilgrim Sun is absent," said the old monster, "it may mean that he's been killed by the wind. Or, he may have gone to try to find help." "Great King," said one of the demons, "it would be our good fortune if he had been killed. But suppose he's not dead? If he succeeds in bringing with him some divine warriors, what shall we do then?" The old monster said, "Who's afraid of any divine warrior? Only the Bodhisattva Lingji can overcome the power of my wind; no one else can do us any harm."

That Pilgrim resting on one of the beams above him was delighted by this one statement. He flew out of the cave at once and, changing back into his original form, arrived at the woods. "Brother!" he cried. Eight Rules asked, "Elder Brother, where have you been? Just now a monster with a command flag came by, and I chased him away." "Thank you! Thank you!" said Pilgrim, laughing. "Old Monkey changed into a mosquito to enter the cave to see how Master was doing. I found him tied to a post in the garden, weeping. After telling him not to cry, I flew around the roof to spy on them some more. That was when the fellow who held the command flag came in panting, saying that you had chased him. He also said that he had not seen me. The old monster made some wild speculations about my having been killed by the wind, or else having gone to find help. Then, without being prompted, he suddenly mentioned someone else. It's marvelous, simply marvelous!" "Whom did he mention?" asked Eight Rules. "He said that he wasn't afraid of any divine warrior," said Pilgrim, "for no one else could overpower his wind save the Bodhisattva Lingji. The only trouble is that I don't know where this Lingji lives." As they were thus conversing, they suddenly saw an aged man walking by the side of the main road. Look at his appearance:

> Strong, he uses no cane to walk,
> With flowing snowlike hair and beard.
> Though wit and eyes are quite dim and blurry,
> Thin bones and sinews are still tough.
>
> Back and head bent he walked slowly,
> With thick brows and a pink face, childlike.
> Look at his features and they seem human,
> Though he's like Long-Life Star no less![11]

Highly pleased when he caught sight of him, Eight Rules said, "Elder Brother, the proverb says:

You want to know the way,
Hear what the tourist say.

Why don't you approach him and ask?"

The Great Sage put away his iron rod and straightened out his clothes. Approaching the old man, he said, "Aged Sir, receive my bow." Somewhat reluctantly, the old man returned his greeting, saying, "What region are you from, monk? What are you doing here in this wilderness?" "We are holy monks on our way to seek scriptures," said Pilgrim. "Yesterday we lost our master here, and so I'm approaching you to ask where the Bodhisattva Lingji lives." "Lingji lives south of here," said the old man, "about three thousand miles away. There is a mountain called the Little Sumeru Mountain, which has within it a Land of the Way, the Chan hall where the Bodhisattva lectures on sūtras. I suppose you are trying to obtain scriptures from him." "Not from him," said Pilgrim, "but I have something that requires his attention. Will you please show me the way?" Pointing with his hand toward the south, the old man said, "Follow that winding path." The Great Sage Sun was tricked into turning his head to look at the path, when the old man changed himself into a gentle breeze and vanished. A small slip of paper was left beside the road, on which was written this quatrain:

To tell the Equal to Heaven Great Sage,
The old man is in truth one Long Life Li!
On Sumeru's the Flying-Dragon Staff.
Lingji in years past received this Buddhist arm.

Pilgrim took up the slip and went back down the road. "Elder Brother," said Eight Rules, "our luck must have been rather bad lately. For two days we saw ghosts in broad daylight. Who is that old man who left after changing into a breeze?" Pilgrim gave Eight Rules the slip of paper. "Who is this Long-Life Li?" asked Eight Rules, when he had read the verse. "It's the name of the Planet Venus from the West," said Pilgrim. Eight Rules hurriedly bowed toward the sky, crying, "Benefactor! Benefactor! Had it not been for the Gold Star, who personally begged the Jade Emperor to be merciful, I don't know what would have become of old Hog!" "Elder Brother," said Pilgrim, "you do have a sense of gratitude. But don't expose yourself. Take cover deep in the woods and carefully guard the luggage and the horse. Let old Monkey find the Sumeru Mountain and seek help from the Bodhisattva." "I know, I know!" said Eight Rules. "Hurry up and go! Old Hog has mastered the law of the turtle: withdraw your head when you needn't stick it out!"

The Great Sage Sun leaped into the air; mounting the cloud-somersault, he headed straight south. He was fast, indeed! With a nod of his head, he covered three thousand miles; just a twist of his torso carried him over eight hundred! In a moment he saw a tall mountain with auspicious clouds hanging halfway up its slopes and holy mists gathered around it. In the fold of the mountain there was indeed a temple. He could hear the melodious sounds of the bells and sonorous stones[12] and could see the swirling smoke of incense. As he approached the door, the Great Sage saw a Daoist with a string of beads around his neck, who was reciting the name of Buddha. Pilgrim said, "Daoist, please accept my bow." The Daoist at once bowed in return, saying, "Where did the venerable father come from?" "Is this where the Bodhisattva Lingji expounds the scriptures?" asked Pilgrim. "Indeed it is," said the Daoist. "Do you wish to speak to someone?"

"May I trouble you, sir, to make this announcement for me," said Pilgrim. "I am the disciple of the master of the Law, Tripitaka, who is the royal brother of the Great Tang Emperor in the Land of the East; I am the Great Sage, Equal to Heaven, Sun Wukong, also named Pilgrim. I have a matter that requires me to have an audience with the Bodhisattva." The Daoist laughed and said, "The venerable father has given me a long announcement! I can't quite remember all those words." "Just say that Sun Wukong, the disciple of the Tang Monk, has arrived," said Pilgrim.[13]

The Daoist agreed and made that announcement in the lecture hall, whereupon the Bodhisattva at once put on his cassock and asked for more incense to be burned to welcome the visitor. Then the Great Sage walked in the door and peered inside. He saw

A hall full of brocade and silk;
A house most solemn and grand;
Pupils reciting the Lotus Sūtra;
An old leader tapping the golden gong.
Set before the Buddha
Were all immortal fruits and flowers.
Spread out on the altars
Were vegetarian dainties and viands.
The bright, precious candles,
Their golden flames shot up like rainbows;
The fragrant true incense,
Its jadelike smoke flew up as colored mists.
So it was that, after the lecture one would calmly meditate,
When white-cloud flakes circled the tips of pines.
The wisdom sword retired, for Māra snapped
In this space of Prajñā-pāramitā.

The Bodhisattva straightened out his attire to receive Pilgrim, who entered the hall and took the seat of the guest. Tea was offered, but Pilgrim said, "No need for you to bother about tea. My master faces peril at the Yellow Wind Mountain, and I beseech the Bodhisattva to exercise his great dharma power to defeat the monster and rescue him." "I did receive the command of Tathāgata," said the Bodhisattva, "to keep the Yellow Wind Monster here in submission. Tathāgata also gave me a Wind-Stopping Pearl and a Flying-Dragon Precious Staff. At the time when I captured him, I spared the monster his life only on condition that he would retire in the mountain and abstain from the sin of taking life. I did not know that he would want to harm your esteemed teacher and transgress the Law. That is my fault." The Bodhisattva would have liked to prepare some vegetarian food to entertain Pilgrim, but Pilgrim insisted on leaving. So he took the Flying-Dragon Staff and mounted the clouds with the Great Sage.

In a little while they reached the Yellow Wind Mountain. "Great Sage," said the Bodhisattva, "this monster is rather afraid of me. I will stand here at the edge of the clouds while you go down there to provoke battle. Entice him to come out so that I may exercise my power." Pilgrim followed his suggestion and lowered his cloud.

Without waiting for further announcement, he whipped out his iron rod and smashed the door of the cave, crying, "Monster, give me back my Master!" Those little demons standing guard at the door were so terrified that they ran to make the report. "This lawless ape," said the monster, "is truly ill-behaved! He would not defer to kindness, and now he has even broken my door! This time when I go out, I'm going to use that divine wind to blow him to death." He put on his armor as before, and took up the steel trident. Walking out of the door and seeing Pilgrim, he did not utter a word before aiming the trident at Pilgrim's chest. The Great Sage stepped aside to dodge this blow and then faced him with uplifted rod. Before they had fought for a few rounds, the monster turned his head toward the ground in the southwest and was about to open his mouth to summon the wind. From midair, the Bodhisattva threw down the Flying-Dragon Precious Staff as he recited some kind of spell. It was instantly transformed into a golden dragon with eight claws, two of which caught hold of that monster's head and threw him two or three times against the boulders beside the mountain cliff. The monster changed back into his original form and became a mink with yellow fur.

Pilgrim ran up and was about to strike with his rod, but he was stopped by the Bodhisattva, who said to him, "Great Sage, do not harm him. I have to take him back to see Tathāgata. Originally he was a rodent at the foot of the Spirit Mountain who had acquired the Way. Because he stole some of the pure oil in the crystal chalice, he fled for fear that the vajra attendants would seize him. Tathāgata thought that he was not guilty of death, and that is why I was asked to capture him in the first place and banish him to this region. But now he has offended the Great Sage and has attempted to harm the Tang Monk. Therefore I must take him to see Tathāgata so that his guilt may be clearly established. Only then will this merit be completed." When Pilgrim heard this, he thanked the Bodhisattva, who left for the West, and we shall say no more of that.

We now tell you about Zhu Eight Rules, who was thinking about Pilgrim in the woods when he heard someone calling down by the slope, "Brother Wuneng, bring the horse and the luggage here." Recognizing Pilgrim's voice, Idiot quickly ran out of the woods and said to Pilgrim, "Elder Brother, how did everything go?" "I invited the Bodhisattva Lingji to come here," said Pilgrim, "to use his Flying-Dragon Staff to capture the monster. He was a mink with yellow fur who became a spirit and has now been taken by the Bodhisattva to Spirit Mountain to face Tathāgata. Let's go into the cave to rescue Master." Idiot was delighted. The two of them smashed their way into the cave and with their rake and rod slaughtered all the wily hares, the vixen, the musk deer, and the horned deer. Then they went to the garden in the back to rescue their master, who, after coming out, asked, "How did you two manage to catch the monster so that you could rescue me?" Pilgrim gave a thorough account of how he went to seek the Bodhisattva's help to subdue the monster, and the master thanked him profusely. Then the two brothers found some vegetarian food in the cave, which they prepared along with some tea and rice. After eating, they left and again found the road to the West. We do not know what took place hereafter; let's listen to the explanation in the next chapter.

TWENTY-TWO

Eight Rules fights fiercely at the Flowing-Sand River; Mokṣa by order receives Wujing's submission.

Now we tell you about the Tang Monk and his disciples, the three travelers, who were delivered from their ordeal. In less than a day they passed the Yellow Wind Mountain and proceeded toward the West through a vast level plain. Time went by swiftly, and summer yielded to the arrival of autumn. All they saw were some

> Cold cicadas sing on dying willows
> As the Great Fire rolls toward the West.

As they proceeded, they came upon a huge and turbulent river, its waves surging and splashing. "Disciples," exclaimed Tripitaka, "look at that vast expanse of water in front of us. Why are there no boats in sight? How can we get across?" Taking a close look, Eight Rules said, "It's very turbulent, too rough for any boat!" Pilgrim leaped into the air and peered into the distance, shading his eyes with his hand. Even he became somewhat frightened and said, "Master, it's truly hard! Truly hard! If old Monkey wishes to cross this river, he need only make one twist of his body and he will reach the other shore. But for you, Master, it's a thousand times more difficult, for you can't traverse it even in ten thousand years!"

"I can't even see the other shore from here," said Tripitaka. "Really, how wide is it?"

"It's just about eight hundred miles wide," said Pilgrim. "Elder Brother," said Eight Rules, "how could you determine its width just like that?"

"To tell you the truth, Worthy Brother," said Pilgrim, "these eyes of mine can determine good or evil up to a thousand miles away in daylight. Just now when I was up in the air, I could not tell how long the river was, but I could make out its width to be at least eight hundred miles."

Sighing anxiously, the elder pulled back his horse and suddenly discovered on the shore a slab of stone. When the three of them drew closer to have a look, they saw three words written in seal-script ("Flowing-Sand River") below which there were also four lines written in regular style. It read:

> These Flowing-Sand metes, eight hundred wide;
> These Weak Waters, three thousand deep.

A goose feather cannot stay afloat;
A rush petal will sink to the bottom.

As master and disciples were reading the inscription, the waves in the river suddenly rose like tall mountains, and with a loud splash from the midst of the waters a monster sprang out. Looking most savage and hideous, he had

A head full of tousled and flame-like hair;
A pair of bright, round eyes which shone like lamps;
An indigo face, neither black nor green;
An old dragon's voice like thunderclap or drum.
He wore a cape of light yellow goose down.
Two strands of white reeds tied around his waist.
Beneath his chin nine skulls were strung and hung;
His hands held an awesome priestly staff.

Like a cyclone, the fiend rushed up to the shore and went straight for the Tang Monk. Pilgrim was so taken aback that he grabbed his master and dashed for high ground to make the escape. Putting down the pole, Eight Rules whipped out his rake and brought it down hard on the monster. The fiend used his staff to parry the blow, and so the two of them began to unleash their power on the bank of the Flowing-Sand River. This was some battle!

The nine-pronged rake;
The fiend-routing staff;
These two met in battle on the river shore.
This one was the Marshal of Heavenly Reeds:
That one was the Curtain-Raising Captain by the Throne.
In years past they met in Divine Mists Hall;
Today they fought and waged a test of might.
From this one the rake went out like a dragon stretching its claws;
From that one the staff blocked the way like a sharp-tusked elephant.
They stood with their limbs outstretched;
Each struck at the other's rib cage.
This one raked madly, heedless of head or face;
That one struck wildly without pause or rest.
This one was a cannibal spirit, long a lord of Flowing-Sand;
That one was a Way-seeking fighter upholding Law and Faith.

Closing in again and again, the two of them fought for twenty rounds, but neither emerged the victor.

The Great Sage meanwhile was standing there to protect the Tang Monk. As he held the horse and guarded the luggage, he became so aroused by the sight of Eight Rules engaging that fiend that he ground his teeth and rubbed his hands vehemently. Finally he could not restrain himself—whipping out the rod, he said, "Master, sit here and don't be afraid. Let old Monkey go play with him a little." The master begged in vain for him to stay, and with a loud whoop he leaped forward. The monster, you see, was just having a grand time fighting with Eight Rules, the two of them so tightly locked in combat that nothing seemed able to part them. Pilgrim, however, rushed up to the monster and delivered a terrific blow at his head with his iron rod. The monster was so shaken that he jumped aside: turning around he dove straight into the Flowing-Sand River and disappeared. Eight Rules was so upset that he leaped about wildly, crying, "Elder Brother! Who asked you to come? The monster was gradually weakening and was finding it difficult to parry my rake. Another four or five rounds and I would have captured him. But when he saw how fierce you were, he fled in defeat. Now, what shall we do?" "Brother," said Pilgrim laughing, "to tell you the truth, since defeating the Yellow Wind Fiend a month ago, I have not played with my rod all this time after leaving the mountain.[1] When I saw how delicious your fight with him was, I couldn't stand the itch beneath my feet! That's why I jumped up here to have some fun with him. That monster doesn't know how to play, and I suppose that's the reason for his departure."

Holding hands and teasing each other, the two of them returned to the Tang Monk. "Did you catch the monster?" asked the Tang Monk. "He didn't last out the fight," said Pilgrim, "and he scrambled back to the water in defeat." "Disciple," said Tripitaka, "since this monster has probably lived here a long time, he ought to know the deep and the shallow parts of the river. After all, such a boundless body of weak water, and not a boat in sight—we need someone who is familiar with the region to lead us across." "Exactly!" said Pilgrim. "As the proverb says,

> He who's near cinnabar turns red;
> He who's near ink becomes black.

The monster living here must have a good knowledge of the water. When we catch him, we should not slay him, but just make him take Master across the river before we dispose of him." "Elder Brother," said Eight Rules, "no need for further delay. You go ahead and catch him, while old Hog guards our master."

"Worthy Brother," said Pilgrim with a laugh, "in this case I've really nothing to brag about, for I'm just not comfortable doing business in water. If all I do is walk around down there, I still have to make the magic sign and recite the water-repelling spell before I can move anywhere. Or else I have to change into a water creature like a fish, shrimp, crab, or turtle before going in. If it were a matter of matching wits in the high mountains or up in the clouds, I know enough to deal with the strangest and most difficult situation. But doing business in water somewhat cramps my style!"

"When I was Marshal of the Heavenly River in former years," said Eight Rules, "I commanded a naval force of eighty thousand men, and I acquired some knowledge of that element. But I fear that that monster may have a few relatives down there in his den, and I won't be able to withstand him if his seventh and eighth cousins all come out. What will happen to me then if they grab me?" "If you go into the water to fight him," said Pilgrim, "don't tarry. Make sure, in fact, that you feign defeat and entice him out here. Then old Monkey will help you." "Right you are," said Eight Rules. "I'm off!" He took off his blue silk shirt and his shoes; holding the rake with both hands, he divided the waters to make a path for himself. Using the ability he had developed in bygone years, he leaped through billows and waves and headed for the bottom of the river.

We now tell you about that monster, who went back to his home in defeat. He had barely caught his breath when he heard someone pushing water, and as he rose to take a look, he saw Eight Rules pushing his way through with his rake. That monster lifted his staff and met him face to face, crying, "Monk, watch where you are going or you'll receive a blow from this!" Using the rake to block the blow, Eight Rules said, "What sort of a monster are you that you dare to bar our way?" "So you don't recognize me," said the monster. "I'm no demon or fiend, nor do I lack a name or surname." "If you are no demon or fiend," said Eight Rules, "why do you stay here and take human lives? Tell me your name and surname, and I'll spare your life." The monster said:

"My spirit was strong since the time of birth.
I once made a tour of the universe,
Where my fame as a hero became well-known—
A gallant type for all to emulate.
Through countless nations I went as I pleased;
Over lakes and seas I did freely roam.
To learn the Way I strayed to Heaven's edge;
To find a teacher I stumped this great earth.
For years my clothes and alms bowl went with me:
Not for one day did my spirit turn lax.
For scores of times I cruised cloudlike the earth
And walked to all places a hundred times.
Only then a true immortal I did meet,
Who showed me the Great Path of Golden Light.
I took back Baby Boy and Fair Girl first;[2]
Then released Wood Mother and Squire of Gold.[3]

Bright Hall's[4] kidney-brine flooded Floral Pool;[5]
The Tower's[6] liver-fire plunged to the heart.
Three thousand merits done, I saw Heaven's face
And solemnly worshipped the Point of Light.
Then the Jade Emperor exalted me;
The Curtain-Raising Captain he made me.
An honored one in South Heaven Gate,
I was much esteemed at Divine Mists Hall.
I hung at my waist the Tiger-Headed Shield:
I held in my hands the Fiend-Routing Staff.
Just like the sunlight my gold helmet shone;
My body's armor flashed like radiant mists.
I was chief of the guardians of the Throne:
I was first as attendant of the court.
When Queen Mother gave the Festival of Peach—
She served her guests at Jasper Pool a feast—
I dropped and broke a glass-like cup of jade,
And souls from all the hosts of Heaven fled.
Jade Emperor grew mightily enraged;
Hands clasped, he faced his counsel on the left.
Stripped of my hat, my armor, and my rank,
I had my whole body pushed to the block.
Only the Great Immortal, Naked Feet,
Came from the ranks and begged to have me freed.
Pardoned from death and with my sentence stayed,
I was sent to the shores of Flowing-Sand.
Sated, I lie wearily in the stream;
Famished, I churn the waves to find my feed.
The woodsman sees me and his life is gone;
The fishers face me and they soon perish.
From first to last I've eaten many men;
Over and over I took human lives.
Since you dare to work violence at my door,
My stomach this day has its fondest hopes!
Don't say you're too coarse to be eaten now.
I'll catch you, and look, that's my minced meat sauce!"

Infuriated by what he heard, Eight Rules shouted, "You brazen thing! You haven't the slightest perception! Old Hog is tempting enough to make people's mouths water, and you dare say that I'm coarse, that I'm to be chopped up for a chopped meat sauce! Come to think of it, you would like to consider me a piece of tough old bacon! Watch your manners and swallow this rake of your ancestor!" When the monster saw the rake coming, he used the style of "the phoenix nodding its head" to dodge the blow. The two of them thus fought to the surface of the water, each one treading the waters and waves. This conflict was somewhat different from the one before. Look at

The Curtain-Raising Captain,
The Marshal of Heavenly Reeds:
Each showing most nicely his magic might.
This one waved above his head the fiend-routing staff:
That one moved the rake as swiftly as his hand.
The vaulting waves rocked hills and streams;
The surging tide the cosmos dimmed.
Savage like Jupiter wielding banners and flags!
Fierce like Hell's envoy upsetting sacred tops!
This one guarded the Tang Monk devotedly;
That one, a water fiend, perpetrated his crimes.
The rake's one stroke would leave nine red marks:
The staff's one blow would dissolve man's soul.
They strove to win the fight;
They struggled to prevail.
All in all for the scripture pilgrim's sake,
They vented their fury without restraint.
They brawled till carps and perches lost their newborn scales,
And all turtles damaged their tender shells.
Red shrimps and purple crabs all lost their lives,
And sundry water gods all upward bowed!
You heard only the waves rolled and crashed like thunderclaps.
The world amazed saw sun and moon grow dark!

The two of them fought for two hours, and neither prevailed. It was like

A brass pan meeting an iron broom,
A jade gong facing a golden bell.

We now tell you about the Great Sage, who was standing guard beside the Tang Monk. With bulging eyes he watched them fighting on the water, but he dared not lift his hands. Finally, Eight Rules made a half-hearted blow with his rake and, feigning defeat, turned to flee toward the eastern shore. The monster gave chase and was about to reach the river bank when our Pilgrim could no longer restrain himself. He abandoned his master, whipped out the iron rod, leaped to the riverside and struck at the monster's head. Fearing to face him, the monster swiftly dove back into the river. "You Ban-HorsePlague!" shouted Eight Rules. "You impulsive ape! Can't you be a bit more patient? You could have waited until I led him up to high ground and then blocked his path to the river. We would have caught him then. Now he has gone back in, and when do you think he'll come out again?" "Idiot," said Pilgrim laughing, "stop shouting! Let's go talk to Master first."

Eight Rules went with Pilgrim back to high ground to Tripitaka. "Disciple," said Tripitaka, bowing, "you must be tired!" "I won't complain about my fatigue," said Eight Rules. "Let's subdue the monster and take you across the river. Only that plan is perfect!" Tripitaka said, "How did the battle go with the monster just now?" "He was just about my equal," said Eight Rules, "and we fought to a draw. But then I feigned defeat and he chased me up to the bank. When he saw Elder Brother lifting his rod, however, he fled." "So what are we going to do?" asked Tripitaka. "Master, relax!" said Pilgrim. "Let's not worry now, for it's getting late. You sit here on the cliff and let old Monkey go beg some vegetarian food. Take some rest after you eat, and we'll find a solution tomorrow." "You are right," said Eight Rules. "Go, and come back quickly."

Pilgrim swiftly mounted the clouds and went north to beg a bowl of vegetarian food from a family to present to his master. When the master saw him return so soon, he said, "Wukong, let us go to that household which gave us the food and ask them how we may cross this river. Isn't this better than fighting the monster?" With a laugh, Pilgrim said, "That household is quite far from here, about six or seven thousand miles, no less! How could the people there know about the water? What's the use of asking them?" "You are fibbing again, Elder Brother!" said Eight Rules. "Six or seven thousand miles, how could you cover that distance so quickly?" "You have no idea," said Pilgrim, "about the capacity of my cloud somersault, which with one leap can cover one hundred and eight thousand miles. For the six or seven thousand here, all I have to do is to nod my head and stretch my waist, and that's a round trip already! What's so hard about that?"

"Elder Brother," said Eight Rules, "if it's so easy, all you need to do is to carry Master on your back: nod your head, stretch your waist, and jump across. Why continue to fight this monster?" "Don't you know how to ride the clouds?" asked Pilgrim. "Can't you carry him across the river?"

"The mortal nature and worldly bones of Master are as heavy as the Tai Mountain," Eight Rules said. "How could my cloud soaring bear him up? It has to be your cloud somersault." "My cloud somersault is essentially like cloud soaring," said Pilgrim, "the only difference being that I can cover greater distances more rapidly. If you can't carry him, what makes you think I can? There's an old proverb that says:

Move Mount Tai: it's light as mustard seeds.
Lift a man and you won't leave the red dust!

Take this monster here: he can use spells and call upon the wind, pushing and pulling a little, but he can't carry a human into the air. And if it's this kind of magic, old Monkey knows every trick well, including becoming invisible and making distances shorter. But it is required of Master to go through all these strange territories before he finds deliverance from the sea of sorrows; hence even one step turns out to be difficult. You and I are only his protective companions, guarding his body and life, but we cannot exempt him from these woes, nor can we obtain the scriptures all by ourselves. Even if we had the ability to go and see Buddha first, he would not bestow the scriptures on you and me. Remember the adage:

> What's easily gotten
> Is soon forgotten."

When Idiot heard these words, he accepted them amiably as instruction. Master and disciples ate some of the simply prepared vegetarian food before resting on the eastern shore of the Flowing-Sand River.

The next morning, Tripitaka said, "Wukong, what are we going to do today?" "Not much," said Pilgrim, "except that Eight Rules must go into the water again." "Elder Brother," said Eight Rules, "you only want to stay clean, but you have no hesitation making me go into the water." "Worthy Brother," said Pilgrim, "this time I'll try not to be impulsive. I'll let you trick him into coming up here, and then I'll block his retreat along the river bank. We must capture him." Dear Eight Rules! Wiping his face, he pulled himself together. Holding the rake in both hands, he walked to the edge of the river, opened up a path in the water, and went to the monster's home as before. The monster had just wakened from his sleep when he heard the sound of water. Turning quickly to look, he saw Eight Rules approaching with the rake. He leaped out at once and barred the way, shouting, "Slow down! Watch out for my staff!" Eight Rules lifted his rake to parry the blow, saying, "What sort of mourning staff do you have there that you dare ask your ancestor to watch out for it?" "A fellow like you," said the monster, "wouldn't recognize this!

> For years my staff has enjoyed great fame,
> At first an evergreen tree in the moon.
> Wu Gang[7] cut down from it one huge limb:
> Lu Ban then made it, using all his skills.
> Within the hub's one solid piece of gold:
> Outside it's wrapped by countless pearly threads.
> It's called the treasure staff for crushing fiends,
> E'er placed in Divine Mists to quell the ogres.
> Since I had made a mighty general's rank,

Jade Emperor put it always by my side.
It lengthens or shortens after my desire;
It grows thick or thin with my command.
It went to guard the Throne at the Peaches Feast:
It served at court in Heaven's world above.
On duty it saw the many sages bowed,
And immortals, too, when the screen rolled up.
Of numinous power one arm divine,
It's no worldly weapon of humankind.
Since I was banished from the gate of Heav'n,
It roamed with me at will beyond the seas.
Perhaps it is not right for me to boast,
But swords and spears of man can't match this staff.
Look at that old, rusted muckrake of yours:
Fit only for hoeing fields and raking herbs!"

"You unchastened brazen thing!" said Eight Rules, laughing. "Never mind whether it's fit for hoeing fields! One little touch and you won't even know how to begin putting bandages or ointment on nine bleeding holes! Even if you are not killed, you will grow old with chronic infection!" The monster raised his hands and again fought with Eight Rules from the bottom of the river up to the surface of the water. This battle was even more different from the first one. Look at them

Wielding the treasure staff.
Striking with muckrake;
They would not speak as if they were estranged.
Since Wood Mother constrained the Spatula,[8]
That caused the two to fight most fiercely.
No win or loss;
With no regret.
They churned up waves and billows with no peace.
How could this one control his bitter rage;
That one found unbearable his pain.
Rake and staff went back and forth to show their might;
The water rotted like poison in Flowing-Sand.
They huffed and puffed!
They worked and toiled!
All because Tripitaka would face the West.
The muckrake so ferocious!
The staff so nimbly used!
This one made a grab to pull him up the shore;
That one sought to seize and drown him in the stream.

They roared like thunder, stirring dragon and fish.
Gods and ghosts cowered as the Heavens grew dim.

This time they fought back and forth for thirty rounds, and neither one proved to be the stronger. Again Eight Rules pretended to be defeated and fled, dragging his rake. Kicking up the waves, the monster gave chase and they reached the edge of the river. "Wretch!" cried Eight Rules. "Come up here! We can fight better on solid ground up here." "You are just trying to trick me into going up there," scolded the monster, "so that you can bring out your assistant. You come down here, and we can fight in the water." The monster, you see, had become wise; he refused to go up to the bank and remained near the edge of the water to argue with Eight Rules.

When Pilgrim saw that the monster refused to leave the water, he became highly irritated, and all he could think of was to catch him at once. "Master," he said, "you sit here. Let me give him a taste of the 'ravenous eagle seizing his prey.'" He somersaulted into the air and then swooped down onto the monster, who was still bickering with Eight Rules. When he heard the sound of the wind, he turned quickly and discovered Pilgrim hurtling down from the clouds. Putting away his staff, he dove into the water and disappeared. Pilgrim stood on the shore and said to Eight Rules, "Brother, that monster is catching on! He refuses to come up now. What shall we do?" "It's hard, terribly hard!" said Eight Rules. "I just can't beat him—even when I summoned up the strength of my milk-drinking days! We are evenly matched!" "Let's go talk to Master," said Pilgrim.

The two of them went up again to high ground and told the Tang Monk everything. "If it's so difficult," said the Elder, tears welling up in his eyes, "how can we ever get across?" "Master, please don't worry," said Pilgrim. "It is hard for us to cross with this monster hiding deep in the river. So, don't fight with him any more, Eight Rules; just stay here and protect Master. I'm going to make a trip up to South Sea." "Elder Brother," said Eight Rules, "what do you want to do at South Sea?" Pilgrim said, "This business of seeking scriptures originated from the Bodhisattva Guanyin; the one who delivered us from our ordeals was also the Bodhisattva Guanyin. Today our path is blocked at this Flowing-Sand River and we can't proceed. Without her, how can we ever solve our problem? Let me go ask her to help us: it's much better than doing battle with this monster." "You have a point there, Elder Brother," said Eight Rules. "When you get there, please convey my gratitude to her for her kindly instructions in the past." "Wukong," said Tripitaka, "if you want to go see the Bodhisattva, you needn't delay. Go, and hurry back."

Pilgrim catapulted into the air with his cloud somersault and headed for the South Sea. Ah! It did not even take him half an hour before he saw the scenery of the Potalaka Mountain. In a moment, he dropped down from his somersault and arrived at the edge of the purple bamboo grove, where he was met by the Spirits of the Twenty-Four Ways. They said to him, "Great Sage, what brings you here?" "My master faces an ordeal," said Pilgrim, "which brings me here specially to see the Bodhisattva." "Please take a seat," said the spirits, "and allow us to make the announcement." One of the spirits who was on duty went to the entrance of the Tidal-Sound Cave, announcing, "Sun Wukong wishes to have an audience with you." The Bodhisattva was leaning on the rails by the Treasure Lotus Pool, looking at the flowers with the Pearl-Bearing Dragon Princess. When she heard the announcement, she went back to the cave, opened the door, and asked that he be shown in. With great solemnity, the Great Sage prostrated himself before her.

"Why are you not accompanying the Tang Monk?" asked the Bodhisattva. "For what reason did you want to see me again?" "Bodhisattva," said Pilgrim, looking up at her, "my master took another disciple at the Gao Village, to whom you had given the religious name of Wuneng. After crossing the Yellow Wind Ridge, we have now arrived at the Flowing-Sand River eight hundred miles wide, a body of weak water, which is difficult for Master to get across. There is, moreover, a monster in the river who is quite accomplished in the martial arts. We are grateful to Wuneng, who fought in the water with him three times but could not beat him. The monster is, in fact, blocking our path and we cannot get across. That is why I have come to see you, hoping you will take pity and grant us deliverance."

"Monkey," said the Bodhisattva, "are you still acting so smug and self-sufficient that you refuse to disclose the fact that you are in the service of the Tang Monk?" "All we had intended to do," said Pilgrim, "was to catch the monster and make him take Master across the river. I am not too good at doing business in the water, so Wuneng went down alone to his lair to look for him, and they had some conversation. I presume the matter of scripture seeking was not mentioned."

"That monster in the Flowing-Sand River," said the Bodhisattva, "happens to be the incarnate Curtain-Raising Captain, who was also brought into the faith by my persuasion when I told him to accompany those on their way to acquire scriptures. Had you been willing to mention that you were a scripture pilgrim from the Land of the East, he would not have fought you; he would have yielded instead." Pilgrim said, "That monster is afraid to fight now; he refuses to come up to the shore and is hiding deep in the water. How can we bring him to submission? How can my master get across this body of weak water?"

The Bodhisattva immediately called for Hui'an. Taking a little red gourd from her sleeves, she handed it over to him, saying, "Take this gourd and go with Sun Wukong to the Flowing-Sand River. Call 'Wujing,' and he'll come out at once. You must first take him to submit to the Tang Monk. Next, string together those nine skulls of his and arrange them according to the position of the Nine Palaces. Put this gourd in the center, and you will have a dharma vessel ready to ferry the Tang Monk across the boundary formed by the Flowing-Sand River." Obeying the instructions of his master, Hui'an left the Tidal-Sound Cave with the Great Sage carrying the gourd. As they departed the purple bamboo grove in compliance with the holy command, we have a testimonial poem:

> The Five Phases well matched as Heaven's truth,
> His former master he can recognize.
> Refine the self as base for wondrous use;
> Good and bad discerned will reveal the cause.
> Metal returns to nature—the same kind are both.
> Wood begs for favor: they'll all be redeemed.
> Two-Earths[9] completes merit to reach the void:
> Water and fire blended, dustless and clean.

In a little while the two of them lowered their clouds and arrived at the Flowing-Sand River. Recognizing the disciple Mokṣa, Zhu Eight Rules led his master to receive him. After bowing to Tripitaka, Mokṣa then greeted Eight Rules, who said, "I was grateful to be instructed by Your Reverence so that I could meet the Bodhisattva. I have indeed obeyed the Law, and I am happy recently to have entered the gate of Buddhism. Since we have been constantly on the road, I have yet to thank you. Please forgive me." "Let's forget about these fancy conversations," said Pilgrim. "We must go and call that fellow." "Call whom?" asked Tripitaka. Pilgrim replied, "Old Monkey saw the Bodhisattva and gave her an account of what happened. The Bodhisattva told me that this monster in the Flowing-Sand River happened to be the incarnation of the Curtain-Raising Captain. Because he had sinned in Heaven, he was banished to this river and became a monster. But he was converted by the Bodhisattva, who had told him to accompany you to the Western Heaven. Since we did not mention the matter of seeking scriptures, he fought us bitterly. Now the Bodhisattva has sent Mokṣa with this gourd, which that fellow will turn into a dharma vessel to take you across the river." When Tripitaka heard these words, he bowed repeatedly to Mokṣa, saying, "I beseech Your Reverence to act quickly." Holding the gourd and treading half on cloud and half on fog, Mokṣa moved directly above the surface of the Flowing-Sand River. He cried with a loud voice, "Wujing! Wujing! The scripture pilgrim has been here for a long time. Why have you not submitted?"

We now tell you about that monster who, fearful of the Monkey King, had gone back to the bottom of the river to rest in his den. When he heard someone call him by his religious name, he knew that it had to be the Bodhisattva Guanyin. And when he heard, moreover, that the scripture pilgrim had arrived, he no longer feared the ax or the halberd. Swiftly he leaped out of the waves and saw that it was the disciple Mokṣa. Look at him! All smiles, he went forward and bowed, saying, "Your Reverence, forgive me for not coming to meet you. Where is the Bodhisattva?" "My teacher did not come," said Mokṣa, "but she sent me to tell you to become the disciple of the Tang Monk without delay. You are to take the skulls around your neck and this gourd, and to fashion with them a dharma vessel according to the position of the Nine Palaces so that he may be taken across this body of weak water." "Where is the scripture pilgrim?" asked Wujing. Pointing with his finger, Mokṣa said, "Isn't he the one sitting on the eastern shore?"

Wujing caught sight of Eight Rules and said, "I don't know where that lawless creature came from! He fought with me for two whole days, never once saying a word about seeking scriptures." When he saw Pilgrim, he said again. "That customer is his assistant, and a formidable one, too! I'm not going over there!" "That is Zhu Eight Rules," said Mokṣa, "and that other one is Pilgrim Sun, both disciples of the Tang Monk and both converted by the Bodhisattva. Why fear them? I'll escort you to the Tang Monk." Only then did Wujing put away his precious staff and straighten his yellow silk shirt.

He jumped ashore and knelt before Tripitaka, saying, "Master, your disciple has eyes but no pupils, and he failed to recognize your noble features. I have greatly offended you, and I beg you to pardon me." "You bum!" said Eight Rules. "Why did you not submit in the first place? Why did you only want to fight with me? What do you have to say for yourself?" "Brother," said Pilgrim, laughing, "don't berate him. It's really our fault for not mentioning that we were seeking scriptures, and we didn't tell him our names." "Are you truly willing to embrace our faith?" said the elder. "Your disciple was converted by the Bodhisattva," said Wujing. "Deriving my surname from the river, she gave me the religious name Sha Wujing. How could I be unwilling to take you as my master?" "In that case," said Tripitaka, "Wukong may bring over the sacred razor and shave off his hair." The Great Sage indeed took the razor and shaved Wujing's head, after which he came again to pay homage to Tripitaka, Pilgrim, and Eight Rules, thus becoming the youngest disciple of the Tang Monk. When Tripitaka saw that he comported himself very much like a monk, he gave him the nickname of Sha Monk. "Since you have embraced the faith," said Mokṣa, "there's no need for further delay. You must build the dharma vessel at once."

Not daring to delay, Wujing took off the skulls around his neck and strung them up with a rope after the design of the Nine Palaces, placing the gourd in the middle. He then asked his master to leave the shore, and our elder thus embarked on the dharma vessel. As he sat in the center, he found it to be as sturdy as a little boat. He was, moreover, supported by Eight Rules on his left and Wujing on his right, while Pilgrim Sun, leading the dragon-horse, followed in the rear, treading half on cloud and half on fog. Above their heads Mokṣa also took up his post to give them added protection. In this way our master of the Law was safely ferried across the boundary of the Flowing-Sand River: with the wind calm and waves quiet he crossed the weak water. It was truly as fast as flying or riding an arrow, for in a little while he reached the other shore, having been delivered from the mighty waves. He did not drag up mud or water, and happily both his hands and feet remained dry. In sum, he was pure and clean without engaging in any activity. When master and disciples reached solid ground again, Mokṣa descended from the auspicious clouds. As he took back his gourd, the nine skulls changed into nine curls of dark wind and vanished. Tripitaka bowed to thank Mokṣa and also gave thanks to the Bodhisattva. So it was that Mokṣa went straight back to the South Sea, while Tripitaka mounted his horse to go to the West. We do not know how long it took them to achieve the right fruit of scripture acquisition; let's listen to the explanation in the next chapter.

TWENTY-THREE

Tripitaka does not forget his origin;
The Four Sages test the priestly mind.

A long journey westward is his decree,
As frosted blooms fall in autumn's mild breeze.
Tie up the sly ape, don't loosen the ropes!
Hold back the mean horse, and don't use the whip!
Wood Mother was once fused with Metal Squire;
Yellow Dame and Naked Son ne'er did differ.[1]
Bite open the iron ball—there's mystery true:
Perfection of wisdom will come to you.

The principal aim of this chapter is to make clear that the way to acquire scriptures is no different from the way of attending to the fundamentals in one's life.

We now tell you about master and disciples, the four of them, who, having awakened to the suchness of all things, broke free from the fetters of dust. Leaping clear from the sea of nature's flowing sand, they were completely rid of any hindrance and proceeded westward on the main road. They passed through countless green hills and blue waters; they saw wild grass and untended flowers in endless arrays. Time was swift indeed and soon it was autumn again. You see

Maple leaves redden the mountain;
Yellow blooms endure the night-wind.
Old cicada's song turns languid;
Sad crickets ever voice their plaint.
Cracked lotus leaves like green silk fans;
Fragrant oranges like gold balls.
Lovely, those rows of wild geese,
In dots they spread to distant sky.

As they journeyed, it was getting late again. "Disciples," said Tripitaka, "it's getting late. Where shall we go to spend the night?" "Master," said Pilgrim, "what you said is not quite right. Those who have left home dine on the winds and rest beside the waters; they sleep beneath the moon and lie on the frost; in short, any place can be their home. Why ask where we should spend the night?" "Elder Brother," said Zhu Eight Rules, "all you seem to care about is making progress on the journey, and you've no concern for the burdens of others. Since crossing the Flowing-Sand River, we have been doing nothing but scaling mountains and peaks, and hauling this heavy load is becoming rather hard on me. Wouldn't it be much more reasonable to look for a house where we can ask for some tea and rice, and try to regain our strength?"

"Idiot," said Pilgrim, "your words sound as if you begrudge this whole enterprise. If you think that you are still back in the Gao Village, where you can enjoy the comfort that comes to you without your exerting yourself, then you won't make it! If you have truly embraced the faith of Buddhism, you must be willing to endure pain and suffering; only then will you be a true disciple." "Elder Brother," said Eight Rules, "how heavy do you think this load of luggage is?" Pilgrim said, "Brother, since you and Sha Monk joined us, I haven't had a chance to pole it. How would I know its weight?" "Ah! Elder Brother," said Eight Rules, "just count the things here:

> Four yellow rattan mats;
> Long and short, eight ropes in all.
> To guard against dampness and rain,
> There are blankets—three, four layers!
> The flat pole's too slippery, perhaps?
> You add nails on nails at both ends!
> Cast in iron and copper, the nine-ringed priestly staff.
> Made of bamboo and rattan, the long, large cloak.

With all this luggage, you should pity old Hog, who has to walk all day carrying it! You only are the disciple of our master: I've been made into a long-term laborer!"

"Idiot!" said Pilgrim with a laugh, "to whom are you protesting?" "To you, Elder Brother," said Eight Rules. "If you're protesting to me," said Pilgrim, "you've made a mistake! Old Monkey is solely concerned with Master's safety, whereas you and Sha Monk have the special responsibility of looking after the luggage and the horse. If you ever slack off, you'll get a good whipping in the shanks from this huge rod!" "Elder Brother," said Eight Rules, "don't mention whipping, for that only means taking advantage of others by brute force. I realize that you have a proud and haughty nature, and you are not about to pole the luggage. But look how fat and strong the horse is that Master is riding: he's only carrying one old monk. Make him take a few pieces of luggage, for the sake of fraternal sentiment!" "So you think he's a horse!" said Pilgrim. "He's no earthly horse, for he is originally the son of Aorun, the Dragon King of the Western Ocean. Because he set fire to the palace and destroyed some of its pearls, his father charged him with disobedience and he was condemned by Heaven. He was fortunate to have the Bodhisattva Guanyin save his life, and he was placed in the Eagle Grief Stream to await Master's arrival. At the appropriate time, the Bodhisattva also appeared personally to take off his scales and horns and to remove the pearls around his neck. It was then that he changed into this horse to carry Master to worship Buddha in the Western Heaven. This is a matter of achieving merit for each one of us individually, and you shouldn't bother him."

When Sha Monk heard these words, he asked, "Elder Brother, is he really a dragon?" "Yes," replied Pilgrim. Eight Rules said, "Elder Brother, I have heard an ancient saying that a dragon can breathe out clouds and mists, kick up dust and dirt, and he even has the ability to leap over mountains and peaks, the divine power to stir up rivers and seas. How is it that he is walking so slowly at the moment?" "You want him to move swiftly?" said Pilgrim. "I'll make him do that. Look!" Dear Great Sage! He shook his golden-hooped rod once, and there were ten thousand shafts of colorful lights! When that horse saw the rod, he was so afraid that he might be struck by it that he moved his four legs like lightning and darted away. As his hands were weak, the master could not restrain the horse from this display of its mean nature. The horse ran all the way up a mountain cliff before slowing down to a trot. The master finally caught his breath, and that was when he discovered in the distance several stately buildings beneath some pine trees. He saw

Doors draped by hanging cedars:
Houses beside a green hill;
Pine trees fresh and straight.
And some poles of mottled bamboo.
By the fence wild chrysanthemums glow with the frost:
By the bridge orchid reflections redden the stream.
Walls of white plaster;
And fences brick-laid.
A great hall, how noble and august:
A tall house, so peaceful and clean.
No oxen or sheep are seen, nor hens or dogs.
After autumn's harvest farm chores must be light.

As the master held on to the saddle and slowly surveyed the scenery, Wukong and his brothers arrived. "Master," said Wukong, "you didn't fall off the horse?" "You brazen ape!" scolded the elder. "You were the one who frightened the horse! It's a good thing I managed to stay on him!" Attempting to placate him with a smile, Pilgrim said, "Master, please don't scold me. It all began when Zhu Eight Rules said that the horse was moving too slowly: so I made him hurry a little." Because he tried to catch up with the horse, Idiot ran till he was all out of breath, mumbling to himself, "I'm done, done! Look at this belly of mine, and the slack torso! Already the pole is so heavy that I can hardly carry it. Now I'm given the additional bustle and toil of running after this horse!" "Disciples," said the elder, "look over there. There's a small village where we may perhaps ask for lodging." When Pilgrim heard these words, he looked up and saw that it was covered by auspicious clouds and hallowed mists. He knew then that this place had to be a creation of buddhas or immortals, but he dared not reveal the Heavenly secret. He only said, "Fine! Fine! Let's go ask for shelter."

Quickly dismounting, the elder discovered that the towered entrance gate was decorated with carved lotus designs and looped slits in the woodwork; its pillars were carved and its beams gilded. Sha Monk put down the luggage, while Eight Rules led the horse, saying, "This must be a family of considerable wealth!" Pilgrim would have gone in at once, but Tripitaka said, "No, you and I are priests, and we should behave with circumspection. Don't ever enter a house without permission. Let's wait until someone comes out, and then we may request lodging politely." Eight Rules tied up the horse and sat down, leaning against the wall. Tripitaka sat on one of the stone drums while Pilgrim and Sha Monk seated themselves at the foot of the gate. They waited for a long time, but no one came out. Impatient by nature, Pilgrim leaped up after a while and ran inside the gate to have a look. There were, in fact, three large halls facing south, each with its curtains drawn up highly. Above the door screen hung a horizontal scroll painting with motifs of long life and rich blessings. And pasted on the gold lacquered pillars on either side was this new year couplet written on bright red paper:

Frail willows float like gossamer, the low bridge at dusk:
Snow dots the fragrant plums, a small yard in the spring.

In the center hall, there was a small black lacquered table, its luster half gone, bearing an old bronze urn in the shape of a beast. There were six straight-backed chairs in the main hall, while hanging screens were mounted on the walls east and west just below the roof.

As Pilgrim was glancing at all this furtively, the sound of footsteps suddenly came from behind the door to the rear, and out walked a middle-aged woman who asked in a seductive voice, "Who are you, that you dare enter a widow's home without permission?" The Great Sage was so taken aback that he could only murmur his reply: "This humble monk came from the Great Tang in the Land of the East, having received the royal decree to seek scriptures from Buddha in the West. There are four of us altogether. As we reached your noble region, it became late, and we therefore approached the sacred abode of the old Bodhisattva to seek shelter for the night." Smiling amiably, the woman said, "Elder, where are your other three companions?

Please invite them to come in." "Master," shouted Pilgrim in a loud voice, "you are invited to come in." Only then did Tripitaka enter with Eight Rules and Sha Monk, who was leading the horse and carrying the luggage as well. The woman walked out of the hall to greet them, where she was met by the furtive, wanton glances of Eight Rules. "How did she look?" you ask.

She wore a gown of mandarin green and silk brocade,
Topped by a light pink vest,
To which was fastened a light yellow embroidered skirt;
Her high-heeled, patterned shoes glinted beneath.
A black lace covered her stylish coiffure,
Nicely matching the twin-colored braids like dragons coiled.
Her ivory palace-comb, gleaming red and halcyon-blue,
Supported two gold hair-pins set aslant.
Her half-grey tresses swept up like phoenix wings;
Her dangling earrings had rows of precious pearls.
Still lovely even without powder or rouge,
She had charm and beauty like one fair youth.

When the woman saw the three of them, she became even more amiable and invited them with great politeness into the main hall. After they had exchanged greetings one after the other, the pilgrims were told to be seated for tea to be served. From behind the screen a young maid with two tufts of flowing locks appeared, holding a golden tray with several white-jade cups. There were

Fragrant tea wafting warm air,
Strange fruits spreading fine aroma.

That lady rolled up her colorful sleeves and revealed long, delicate fingers like the stalks of spring onions; holding high the jade cups, she passed the tea to each one of them, bowing as she made the presentation. After the tea, she gave instructions for vegetarian food to be prepared. "Old Bodhisattva," said Tripitaka bowing, "what is your noble surname? And what is the name of your esteemed region?" The woman said, "This belongs to the West Aparagodānīya Continent. My maiden surname is Jia (Unreal), and the surname of my husband's family is Mo (Nonexisting). Unfortunately, my in-laws died prematurely, and my husband and I inherited our ancestral fortune, which amounted to more than ten thousand taels of silver and over fifteen thousand acres of prime land. It was fated, however, that we should have no son, having given birth only to three daughters. The year before last, it was my great misfortune to lose my husband also, and I was left a widow. This year my mourning period is completed, but we have no other relatives beside mother and daughters to inherit our vast property and land. I would have liked to marry again, but I find it difficult to give up such wealth. We are delighted, therefore, that the four of you have arrived, for we four, mother and daughters, would like very much to ask you to become our spouses. I do not know what you will think of this proposal."

When Tripitaka heard these words, he turned deaf and dumb; shutting his eyes to quiet his mind, he fell silent and gave no reply. The woman said, "We own over three hundred acres of paddies, over four hundred and sixty acres of dried fields, and over four hundred and sixty acres of orchards and forests. We have over a thousand head of yellow water buffalo, herds of mules and horses, countless pigs and sheep. In all four quarters, there are over seventy barns and haystacks. In this household there is grain enough to feed you for more than eight or nine years, silk that you could not wear out in a decade, gold and silver that you might spend for a lifetime. What could be more delightful than our silk sheets and curtains, which can render spring eternal? Not to mention those who wear golden hairpins standing in rows! If all of you, master and disciples, are willing to change your minds and enter the family of your wives, you will be most comfortable, having all these riches to enjoy. Will that not be better than the toil of the journey to the West?" Like a mute and stupid person, Tripitaka refused to utter a word.

The woman said, "I was born in the hour of the Cock, on the third day of the third month, in the year Dinghai. As my deceased husband was three years my senior, I am now forty-five years old. My eldest daughter, named Zhenzhen, is twenty; my second daughter, Aiai, is eighteen; and my youngest daughter, Lianlian, is sixteen.[2] None of them has been betrothed to anyone. Though I am rather homely, my daughters fortunately are rather good-looking. Moreover, each of them is well trained in needlework and the feminine arts. And because we had no son, my late husband brought them up as if they were boys, teaching them some of the Confucian classics when they were young as well as the art of writing verse and couplets. So, although they reside in a mountain home, they are not vulgar or uncouth persons; they would make suitable matches, I dare say, for all of you. If you elders can put away your inhibitions and let your hair grow again, you can at once become masters of this household. Are not the silk and brocade that you will wear infinitely better than the porcelain almsbowl and black robes, the straw sandals and grass hats?"

Sitting aloft in the seat of honor, Tripitaka was like a child struck by lightning, a frog smitten by rain. With eyes bulging and rolling upward, he could barely keep himself from keeling over in his chair. But Eight Rules, hearing of such wealth and such beauty, could hardly quell the unbearable itch in his heart! Sitting on his chair, he kept turning and twisting as if a needle were pricking him in the ass. Finally he could restrain himself no longer. Walking forward, he tugged at his master, saying, "Master! How can you completely ignore what the lady has been saying to you? You must try to pay some attention." Jerking back his head, the priest gave such a hostile shout that Eight Rules backed away hurriedly. "You cursed beast!" he bellowed. "We are people who have left home. How can we possibly allow ourselves anymore to be moved by riches and tempted by beauty?"

Giggling, the woman said, "Oh dear, dear! Tell me, what's so good about those who leave home?" "Lady Bodhisattva," said Tripitaka, "tell me what is so good about those of you who remain at home?" "Please take a seat, elder," said the woman, "and let me tell you the benefits in the life of those of us who remain at home. If you ask what they are, this poem will make them abundantly clear.

> When spring fashions appear I wear new silk;
> Pleased to watch summer lilies I change to lace.
> Autumn brings fragrant rice-wine newly brewed.
> In winter's heated rooms my face glows with wine.
> I may enjoy the fruits of all four climes
> And every dainty of eight seasons, too.
> The silk sheets and quilts of the bridal eve
> Best the mendicant's life of Buddhist chants."

Tripitaka said, "Lady Bodhisattva, you who remain in the home can enjoy riches and glory; you have things to eat, clothes to wear, and children by your side. That is undeniably a good life, but you do not know that there are some benefits in the life of those of us who have left home. If you ask what they are, this poem will make them abundantly clear.

> The will to leave home is no common thing:
> You must tear down the old stronghold of love!
> No cares without, tongue and mouth are at peace;
> Your body within has good yin and yang.
> When merit's done, you face the Golden Arch
> And go back, mind enlightened, to your Home.
> It beats the life of lust for household meat:
> You rot with age, one stinking bag of flesh!"

When the woman heard these words, she grew terribly angry, saying, "How dare you to be so insolent, you brazen monk! If I had had no regard for the fact that you have come from the Land of the East, I would have sent you away at once. Now, I was trying to ask you, with all sincerity, to enter our family and share our wealth, and you insult me instead. Even though you have received the commandments and made the vow never to return to secular life, at least one of your followers could become a member of our family. Why are you being so legalistic?"

Seeing how angry she had become, Tripitaka was intimidated and said, "Wukong, why don't you stay here." Pilgrim said, "I've been completely ignorant in such matters since the time I was young. Let Eight Rules stay." "Elder Brother," said Eight Rules, "don't play tricks on people. Let's all have some further discussion." "If neither of you is willing," said Tripitaka, "I'll ask Wujing to stay." "Listen to the way Master is speaking!" said Sha Monk. "Since I was converted by the Bodhisattva and received the commandments from her, I've been waiting for you. It has been scarcely two months since you took me as your disciple and gave me your teachings, and I have yet to acquire even half an inch of merit. You think I would dare seek such riches! I will journey to the Western Heaven even if it means my death! I'll never engage in such perfidious activities!" When the woman saw them refusing to remain, she quickly walked behind the screen and slammed the door to the rear. Master and disciples were left outside, and no one came out again to present tea or rice.

Exasperated, Eight Rules began to find fault with the Tang Monk, saying, "Master, you really don't know how to handle these matters! In fact, you have ruined all our chances by the way you spoke! You could have been more flexible and given her a vague reply so that she would at least have given us a meal. We would at least have enjoyed a pleasant evening, and whether we would be willing to stay tomorrow or not would have been for us to decide. Now the door is shut and no one is going to come out. How are we going to last through the night in the midst of these empty ashes and cold stoves?"

"Second Brother," said Wujing, "why don't you stay here and become her son-in-law?" Eight Rules said, "Brother, don't play tricks on people. Let's discuss the matter further." "What's there to discuss?" said Pilgrim. "If you are willing, Master and that woman will become in-laws, and you will be the son-in-law who lives in the girl's home. With such riches and such treasures in this family, you will no doubt be given a huge dowry and a nice banquet to greet the kinsfolk, which all of us can also enjoy. Your return to secular life here will in fact benefit both parties concerned." "You can say that all right," said Eight Rules, "but for me it's a matter of fleeing the secular life only to return to secular life, of leaving my wife only to take another wife."

"So, Second Brother already has a wife?" said Sha Monk. "You didn't realize," Pilgrim said, "that originally he was the son-in-law of Mr. Gao of the Old Gao Village, in the Kingdom of Qoco. Since I defeated him, and since he had earlier received the commandments from the Bodhisattva, he had little choice but to follow the priestly vocation. That's the reason he abandoned his former wife to follow Master and to go worship Buddha in the Western Heaven. I suppose he has felt the separation keenly and has been brooding on it for some time. Just now, when marriage was mentioned, he must have been sorely tempted. Idiot, why don't you become the son-in-law of this household? Just make sure that you make a few extra bows to old Monkey, and you won't be reprimanded!" "Nonsense! Nonsense!" said Idiot. "Each one of us is tempted, but you only want old Hog to be embarrassed. The proverb says, 'A monk is the preta of sensuality,' and which one of us can truly say that he doesn't want this? But you have to put on a show, and your histrionics have ruined a good thing. Now we can't even get a drop of tea or water, and no one is tending the lamps or fires. We may last through the night, but I doubt that the horse can: he has to carry someone tomorrow and walk again, you know. If he goes hungry for a night, he might be reduced to a skeleton. You people sit here, while old Hog goes to graze the horse." Hastily, Idiot untied the reins and pulled the horse outside. "Sha Monk," said Pilgrim, "you stay here and keep Master company. I'll follow him and see where he is going to graze the horse." "Wukong," said Tripitaka, "you may go and see where he's going, but don't ridicule him." "I know," said Pilgrim. The Great Sage walked out of the main hall, and with one shake of his body he changed into a red dragonfly. He flew out of the front gate and caught up with Eight Rules.

Idiot pulled the horse out to where there was grass, but he did not graze him there. Shouting and whooping, he chased the horse instead to the rear of the house, where he found the woman standing outside the door with three girls, enjoying the sight of some chrysanthemums. When mother and daughters saw Eight Rules approaching, the three girls slipped inside the house at once, but the woman stood still beside the door and said, "little elder, where are you going?" Our Idiot threw away the reins and went up to greet her with a most friendly "Hello!" Then he said, "Mama, I came to graze the horse." "Your master is much too squeamish," said the woman. "If he took a wife in our family, he would be much better off, wouldn't he, than being a mendicant trudging to the West?" "Well, they all have received the command of the Tang emperor," said Eight Rules, with a laugh, "and they haven't the courage to disobey the ruler's decree. That's why they are unwilling to do this thing. Just now they were all trying to play tricks on me in the front hall, and I was somewhat embarrassed because I was afraid that Mama would find my long snout and large ears too offensive." "I don't, really." said the woman. "And since we have no master of the house, it's better to take one than none at all. But I do fear that my daughters may find you somewhat unattractive." "Mama," said Eight Rules, "please instruct your noble daughters not to choose their men that way. Others may be more handsome, but they usually turn out to be quite useless. Though I may be ugly, I do live by certain principles." "And what are they?" asked the woman. Eight Rules replied,

> "Though I may be somewhat ugly,
> I can work quite diligently.
> A thousand acres of land, you say?
> No need for oxen to plow it.
> I'll go over it once with my rake,
> And the seeds will grow in season.
> When there's no rain I can make rain.
> When there's no wind I'll call for wind.
> If the house is not tall enough,
> I'll build you a few stories more.
> If the grounds are not swept I'll give them a sweep.
> If the gutter's not drained I'll draw it for you.
> All things both great and small around the house
> I am able to do most readily."

"If you can work around the house," said the woman, "you should discuss the matter again with your master. If there's no great inconvenience, we'll take you." "No need for further discussion," said Eight Rules, "for he's no genuine parent of mine. Whether I want to do this or not is for me to decide." "All right, all right," said the woman. "Let me talk to my girls first." She slipped back inside immediately and slammed the rear door shut. Eight Rules did not graze the horse there either, but led it back to the front. Little did he realize, however, that Great Sage Sun had heard everything. With wings outstretched, the Great Sage flew back to see the Tang Monk, changing back into his original form. "Master," he said, "Wuneng is leading the horse back here." "Of course he's leading the horse," said the Tang Monk, "for if he doesn't, it may run away in a fit of mischief." Pilgrim started to laugh and gave a thorough account of what the woman and Eight Rules had said, but Tripitaka did not know whether to believe him or not.

In a little while Idiot arrived and tied up the horse. "Have you grazed him?" asked the elder. "There's not much good grass around here," said Eight Rules, "so it's really no place to graze a horse." "It may not be a place to graze the horse," said Pilgrim, "but is it a place to lead a horse?"[3] When Idiot heard this question, he knew that his secret was known. He lowered his head and turned it to one side; with pouting lips and wrinkled brows, he remained silent for a long time. Just then, they heard the side door open with a creak, and out came a pair of red lanterns and a pair of portable incense burners. There were swirling clouds of fragrance and the sounds of tinkling girdle-jade when the woman walked out leading her three daughters. Zhenzhen, Aiai, and Lianlian were told to bow to the scripture pilgrims, and as they did so, standing in a row at the main hall, they appeared to be most beautiful indeed. Look at them!

Each mothlike eyebrow painted halcyon-blue:
Each pretty face aglow with springlike hues.
What beguiling, empire-shaking beauty!
What ravishing, heart-jolting charm!
Their filigreed headgears enhance their grace;
Silk sashes afloat, they seem wholly divine.
Like ripe cherries their lips part, half-smiling,
As they walk slowly and spread their orchid-scent.
Their heads full of pearls and jade
Atop countless hairpins slightly trembling.
Their bodies full of delicate aroma,
Shrouded by exquisite robes of fine golden thread.
Why speak of lovely ladies of the South,
Or the good looks of Xizi?[4]
They look like the fairy ladies descending from the Ninefold Heaven,
Or the Princess Change leaving her Vast Cold Palace.

When he saw them, Tripitaka lowered his head and folded his hands in front of him, while the Great Sage became mute and Sha Monk turned away completely. But look at that Zhu Eight Rules! With eyes unblinking, a mind filled with lust, and passion fast rising, he murmured huskily, "What an honor it is to have the presence of you immortal ladies! Mama, please ask these dear sisters to leave." The three girls went behind the screen, leaving the pair of lanterns behind.

The woman said, "Have you four elders made up your mind which one of you shall be betrothed to my daughters?" "We have discussed the matter," said Wujing, "and we have decided that the one whose surname is Zhu shall enter your family."

"Brother," said Eight Rules, "please don't play any tricks on me. Let's discuss the matter further."

"What's there to discuss?" said Pilgrim. "You have already made all the arrangements with her at the back door, and even call her 'Mama.' What's there to discuss anymore? Master can be the in-law for the groom while this woman here will give away the bride; old Monkey will be the witness, and Sha Monk the go-between. There's no need even to consult the almanac, for today happens to be the most auspicious and lucky day. You come here and bow to Master, and then you can go inside and become her son-in-law." "Nothing doing! Nothing doing!" said Eight Rules. "How can I engage in this kind of business?"

"Idiot!" said Pilgrim. "Stop this fakery! You have addressed her as 'Mama' for countless times already! What do you mean by 'nothing doing'? Agree to this at once, so that we may have the pleasure of enjoying some wine at the wedding." He caught hold of Eight Rules with one hand and pulled at the woman with the other, saying, "Mother-in-law, take your son-in-law inside." Somewhat hesitantly, Idiot started to shuffle inside, while the woman gave instructions to a houseboy, saying, "Take out some tables and chairs and wipe them clean. Prepare a vegetarian dinner to serve these three relatives of ours. I'm leading our new master inside." She further gave instructions for the cook to begin preparation for a wedding banquet to be held the next morning. The houseboys then left to tell the cook. After the three pilgrims had eaten their meal, they retired to the guest rooms, and we shall say no more of them for the moment.

We now tell you about Eight Rules, who followed his mother-in-law and walked inside. There were row upon row of doorways and chambers with tall thresholds, causing him constantly to stumble and fall. "Mama," said Idiot, "please walk more slowly. I'm not familiar with the way here, so you must guide me a little." The woman said, "These are all the storerooms, the treasuries, the rooms where the flour is ground. We have yet to reach the kitchen." "What a huge house!" said Eight Rules. Stumbling along a winding course, he walked for a long time before finally reaching the inner chamber of the house. "Son-in-law," said the woman, "since your brother said that today is a most auspicious and lucky day, I have taken you in. In all this hurry, we have not had the chance of consulting an astrologer, nor have we been prepared for the proper wedding ceremony of worshiping Heaven and Earth and of spreading grains and fruits on the bridal bed. Right now, why don't you kowtow eight times toward the sky?" "You are right, Mama," said Eight Rules. "You take the upper seat also, and let me bow to you a few times. We'll consider that my worship of Heaven and Earth as well as my gesture of gratitude to you. Doing these two things at once will save me some trouble." "All right, all right," said his mother-in-law, laughing. "You are indeed a son-in-law who knows how to fulfill your household duties with the least effort. I'll sit down, and you can make your bows."

The candles on silver candlesticks were shining brightly throughout the hall as Idiot made his bows. Afterwards he said, "Mama, which one of the dear sisters do you plan to give me?"

"That's my dilemma," said his mother-in-law. "I was going to give you my eldest daughter, but I was afraid of offending my second daughter. I was going to give you my second daughter, but I was afraid then of offending my third daughter. And if I were to give you my third daughter, I fear that my eldest daughter may be offended. That's why I cannot make up my mind."

"Mama," said Eight Rules, "if you want to prevent strife, why not give them all to me? That way, you will spare yourself a lot of bickering that can destroy the harmony of the family."

"Nonsense!" said his mother-in-law. "You mean you alone want to take all three of my daughters?"

"Listen to what you're saying, Mama!" said Eight Rules. "Who doesn't have three or four concubines nowadays? Even if you have a few more daughters, I'll gladly take them all. When I was young, I learned how to be long-lasting in the arts of love. You can be assured that I'll render satisfactory service to every one of them."

"That's no good! That's no good!" said the woman. "I have a large handkerchief here, with which you can cover your head, blindfold yourself, and determine your fated marriage that way. I'm going to ask my daughters to walk past you, and the one you can catch with your hands will be betrothed to you." Idiot accepted her suggestion and covered his head with his handkerchief. We have a testimonial poem that says:

> The fool knows not the true causes of things;
> Beauty's sword can in secret wound the self.
> The Duke of Zhou of old had fixed the rites.
> But a bridegroom today still veils his head!

After Idiot had tied himself up properly, he said, "Mama, ask the dear sisters to come out." "Zhenzhen, Aiai, Lianlian," cried his mother-in-law, "you all come out and determine your fated marriage, so that one of you may be given to this man."

With the sounds of girdle-jade and the fragrance of orchids, it seemed that some immortal ladies had suddenly appeared. Idiot indeed stretched forth his hands to try to catch hold of one of the girls, but though he darted about madly this way and that, he could not lay hands on anyone on either side of him. It seemed to him, to be sure, that the girls were making all kinds of movement around him, but he could not grab a single one of them. He lunged toward the east and wrapped his arms around a pillar; he made a dive toward the west and slammed into a wooden partition. Growing faint from rushing about like that, he began to stumble and fall all over the place—tripping on the threshold in front of him, smashing into the brick wall behind him! Fumbling and tumbling around, he ended up sitting on the floor with a bruised head and a swollen mouth.

"Mama," he cried, panting heavily, "you have a bunch of slippery daughters! I can't catch a single one of them! What am I to do? What am I to do?" Taking off his blindfold, the woman said, "Son-in-law, it's not that my daughters are slippery; it's just that they are all very modest. Each defers to the other so that she may take you."

"If they are unwilling to take me, Mama," said Eight Rules, "why don't you take me instead?"

"Dear son-in-law," said the woman, "you really have no regard for age or youth, when you even want your mother-in-law! My three daughters are really quite talented, for each one of them has woven a silk undershirt studded with pearls. Try them on, and the one whose shirt fits you will take you in."

"Fine! Fine! Fine!" said Eight Rules. "Bring out all three undershirts and let me try them on. If all fit me, they can all have me." The woman went inside and took out one undershirt, which she handed over to Eight Rules. Taking off his blue silk shirt, Idiot took up the undergarment and draped it over his body at once. Before he had managed to tie the strings, however, he suddenly fell to the floor. The undershirt, you see, had changed into several pieces of rope which had him tightly bound. As he lay there in unbearable pain, the women vanished.

We now tell you about Tripitaka, Pilgrim, and Sha Monk, who woke up when it began to grow light in the East. As they opened their eyes, they discovered that all the noble halls and buildings had vanished. There were neither carved beams nor gilded pillars, for the truth of the matter was that they had all been sleeping in a forest of pines and cedars. In a panic, the elder began to shout for Pilgrim, and Sha Monk also cried, "Elder Brother, we are finished! We have met some ghosts!" The Great Sage Sun, however, realized fully what had happened. Smiling gently, he said, "What are you talking about?"

"Look where we've been sleeping!" cried the elder.

"It's pleasant enough in this pine forest," said Pilgrim, "but I wonder where that Idiot is going through his ordeal."

"Who is going through an ordeal?" asked the elder.

Pilgrim answered with a laugh. "The women of that household happened to be some bodhisattvas from somewhere, who had waited for us to teach us a lesson. They must have left during the night, but unfortunately Zhu Eight Rules has to suffer." When Tripitaka heard this, he quickly folded his hands to make a bow. Then they saw a slip of paper hanging on an old cedar tree, fluttering in the wind. Sha Monk quickly took it down for his master to read. On it was written the following eight-line poem:

Though the old Dame of Li Shan[5] had no desire,
Guanyin invited her to leave the mount.
Mañjuśri and Viśvabhadra, too, were guests
Who took in the woods the form of maidens fair.
The holy monk's virtuous and truly chaste,
But Eight Rules's profane, loving things mundane.

Henceforth he must repent with quiet heart,
For if he's slothful, the way will be hard.

As the elder, Pilgrim, and Sha Monk recited this poem aloud, they heard a loud call from deep in the woods: "Master, the ropes are killing me! Save me, please! I'll never dare do this again!"

"Wukong," said Tripitaka, "is it Wuneng who is calling us?"

"Yes," said Sha Monk. "Brother," said Pilgrim, "don't bother about him. Let us leave now."

"Though Idiot is stupid and mischievous," said Tripitaka, "he is at least fairly honest, and he has arms strong enough to carry the luggage. Let's have some regard for the Bodhisattva's earlier intention, let's rescue him so that he may continue to follow us. I doubt that he'll ever dare do this again." Sha Monk thereupon rolled up the bedding and put the luggage in order, after which Great Sage Sun untied the horse to lead the Tang Monk into the woods to see what had happened. Ah! So it is that

You must take care in the pursuit of truth
To purge desires, and you'll enter the Real.

We do not know what sort of good or evil was in store for the Idiot; let's listen to the explanation in the next chapter.

TWENTY-FOUR

At Long Life Mountain the Great Immortal detains his old friend;
At Five Villages Abbey, Pilgrim steals the ginseng[1] fruit.

We shall tell you about the three of them who, on entering the forest, found Idiot tied to a tree. He was screaming continuously because of the unbearable pain. Pilgrim approached and said to him, laughing, "Dear son-in-law! It's getting rather late, and you still haven't got around to performing the proper ceremony of thanking your parents or announcing your marriage to Master. You are still having a grand old time playing games here! Hey! Where's your mama? Where's your wife? What a dear son-in-law, all bound and beaten!" When Idiot heard such ridicule, he was so mortified that he clenched his teeth to try to endure the pain without making any more noise. Sha Monk, however, could not bear to look at him; he put down the luggage and went forward to untie the ropes. After he was freed, Idiot could only drop to his knees and kowtow toward the sky, for he was filled with shame. For him we have as a testimony this lyric to the tune of "Moon Over West River":

> Eros is a sword injurious:
> Live by it and you will be slain.
> The lady so fair and lovely at sixteen
> Is more vicious than a yakṣa!

> You have but one principal sum;
> You can't add profit to your purse.
> Guard and keep well your precious capital,
> Which you must not squander and waste.

Scooping up some dirt and scattering it like incense, Eight Rules bowed to the sky. "Did you recognize those bodhisattvas at all?" asked Pilgrim. "I was in a stupor, about to faint," replied Eight Rules. "How could I recognize anyone?" Pilgrim then handed him the slip of paper. When Eight Rules saw the *gāthā*, he was more embarrassed than ever. "Second Brother does have all the luck," said Sha Monk with a laugh, "for you have attracted these four bodhisattvas here to become your wives!" "Brother," said Eight Rules, "let's not ever mention that again! It's blasphemy! From now on, I'll never dare do such foolish things again. Even if it breaks my bones, I'll carry the pole and luggage to follow Master to the West." "You are finally speaking sensibly," said Tripitaka.

Pilgrim then led his master up the main road, and after journeying for a long time, they suddenly came upon a tall mountain. Pulling in the reins, Tripitaka said, "Disciples, let's be careful as we travel up this mountain before us, for there may be monsters seeking to harm us." "Ahead of your horse you have the three of us," said Pilgrim. "Why fear the monsters?" Reassured by these words, the elder proceeded. That mountain is truly a magnificent mountain:

> A tall mountain most rugged,
> Its shape both lofty and grand.
> Its root joins the Kunlun² ranges;
> Its top reaches to the sky.
> White cranes come oft to perch on junipers;
> Black apes hang frequently on the vines.
> As the sun lights up the forest,
> Strands upon strands of red mist are circling;
> As wind rises from dark gorges,
> Ten thousand pink cloud pieces soar and fly.
> Hidden birds sing madly in green bamboos;
> Pheasants do battle amidst wildflowers.
> You see that Thousand-Year Peak,
> That Five-Blessings³ Peak,
> And the Hibiscus Peak—
> They all glow and shimmer most awesomely;
> That Ageless Rock,
> That Tiger-Tooth Rock,
> And that Three-Heaven Rock—
> Where auspicious air rises endlessly.
> Below the cliff, delicate grass;
> Atop the ridge, fragrant plum.
> The thorns and briars are thick;
> The orchids are pale and pure.
> The deep woods's phoenix musters a thousand fowls;
> An old cave's unicorn rules countless beasts.
> Even the brook seems caring:
> She twists and turns as if looking back.
> The peaks are continuous:
> Row upon row circling all around.
> You also see those green locust trees,⁴
> Those mottled bamboos,
> And those verdant pines—

Rivals ever fresh in their dense lushness;
Those pears milk-white,
Those peaches red,
And those willows green—
All competing in their Triple-Spring hues.
Dragons sing and tigers roar;
The cranes dance and the apes wail;
The musk deer from flowers walk out;
The phoenix cries facing the sun.
It's a mount divine, land of true blessings,
The same as Penglai, wondrous fairyland.
See those flowers blooming and dying—this mountain scene,
Where clouds draw near or leave the soaring peaks.

With great delight, Tripitaka said as he rode along, "Disciples, since I began this journey to the West, I have passed through many regions, all rather treacherous and difficult to traverse. None of the other places has scenery like this mountain, which is extraordinarily beautiful. Perhaps we are not far from Thunderclap, and, if so, we should prepare in a dignified and solemn manner to meet the World's Honored One."

"It's early, much too early!" said Pilgrim, laughing. "We are nowhere near!"

"Elder Brother," said Sha Monk, "how far is it for us to reach Thunderclap?"

"One hundred and eight thousand miles," said Pilgrim, "and we have not even covered one-tenth of the distance."

"Elder Brother," said Eight Rules, "how many years do we have to travel before we get there?"

"If we were talking about you two, my worthy brothers," said Pilgrim, "this journey would take some ten days. If we were talking about me, I could probably make about fifty round trips in a day and there would still be sunlight. But if we are talking about Master, then don't even think about it!"

"Wukong," said the Tang Monk, "tell us when we shall be able to reach our destination."

Pilgrim said, "You can walk from the time of your youth till the time you grow old, and after that, till you become youthful again; and even after going through such a cycle a thousand times, you may still find it difficult to reach the place you want to go to. But when you perceive, by the resoluteness of your will, the Buddha-nature in all things, and when every one of your thoughts goes back to its very source in your memory, that will be the time you arrive at the Spirit Mountain."

"Elder Brother," said Sha Monk, "even though this is not the region of

Thunderclap, a place of such scenic splendor must be the residence of a good man." "That's an appropriate observation," said Pilgrim, "for this can hardly be a place for demons or goblins; rather, it must be the home of a holy monk or an immortal. We can walk leisurely and enjoy the scenery." We shall say no more about them for the time being.

We now tell you about this mountain, which had the name of the Long Life Mountain. In the mountain there was a Daoist Abbey called the Five Villages Abbey; it was the abode of an immortal whose Daoist style was Master Zhenyuan[5] and whose nickname was Lord, Equal to Earth. There was, moreover, a strange treasure grown in this temple, a spiritual root that was formed just after chaos had been parted and the nebula had been established prior to the division of Heaven and Earth. Throughout the four great continents of the world, it could be found in only the Five Villages Abbey in the West Aparagodānīya Continent. This treasure was called grass of the reverted cinnabar,[6] or the ginseng fruit. It took three thousand years for the plant to bloom, another three thousand years to bear fruit, and still another three thousand years before they ripened. All in all, it would be nearly ten thousand years before they could be eaten, and even after such a long time, there would be only thirty such fruits. The shape of the fruit was exactly that of a newborn infant not yet three days old, complete with the four limbs and the five senses. If a man had the good fortune of even smelling the fruit, he would live for three hundred and sixty years; if he ate one, he would reach his forty-seven thousandth year.

That day, the Great Zhenyuan Immortal happened to have received a card from the Celestial Worthy of Original Commencement, who invited him to the Miluo Palace in the Heaven of Highest Clarity to listen to the discourse on "The Daoist Fruit of the Chaotic Origin." That Great Immortal, you see, had already trained countless disciples to become immortals; even now he had with him some forty-eight disciples, all Daoists of the Quanzhen Order who had acquired the Way. When he went up to the region above to listen to the lecture that day, he took forty-six disciples along with him, leaving behind two of the youngest ones to look after the temple. One was called Clear Breeze, and the other was named Bright Moon. Clear Breeze was only one thousand two hundred and twenty years old, while Bright Moon had just passed his one thousand two hundredth birthday. Before his departure, Master Zhenyuan gave instructions to the two young lads, saying, "I cannot refuse the invitation of the Great Honorable Divine, and I'm leaving for the Miluo Palace to attend a lecture. You two must be watchful, for an old friend of mine will be passing by here any day. Don't fail to treat him kindly: you may, in fact, strike down from the tree two of the ginseng fruits for him to eat as a token of our past friendship."

"Who is this friend of yours, Master?" asked one of the lads. "Tell us, so that we may take good care of him." "He is a holy monk serving the Great Tang Emperor in the land of the East," said the Great Immortal, "and his religious name is Tripitaka. He is now on his way to the Western Heaven to acquire scriptures from Buddha."

"According to Confucius," said one of the lads, laughing, " 'One does not take counsel with those who follow a different Way.'[7] We belong to the Mysterious Fold of the Great Monad. Why should we associate with a Buddhist monk?"

"You should know," said the Great Immortal, "that that monk happens to be the incarnate Gold Cicada, the second disciple of Tathāgata, the Aged Sage of the West. Five hundred years ago, I became acquainted with him during the Feast of the Ullambana Bowl, when he presented me tea with his own hands as the various sons of Buddha paid me their respect. That's why I consider him an old friend." When the two immortal lads heard these words, they accepted them as the instruction of their master. As the Great Immortal was about to leave, he cautioned them again, saying, "Those fruits of mine are all numbered. You may give him two, but no more." "When the garden was opened to the public," said Clear Breeze, "we shared and ate two of the fruits; there should be still twenty-eight of them on the tree. We wouldn't think of using any more than you have told us to." The Great Immortal said, "Though Tripitaka Tang is an old friend, his disciples, I fear, may be somewhat rowdy. It's best not to let them know about the fruits." After he had finished giving these instructions to the two lads, the Great Immortal ascended to the region of Heaven with all his disciples.

We tell you now about the Tang Monk and his three companions, who were making a tour of the mountain. Looking up, they suddenly discovered several tall buildings by a cluster of pines and bamboos. "Wukong," said the Tang Monk, "what sort of place do you think that is over there?" After taking a look at it, Pilgrim said, "It's either a Daoist abbey or a Buddhist monastery. Let's move along, and we'll find out more about it when we get there." They soon arrived at the gate, and they saw

> A pine knoll cool and serene;
> A bamboo path dark and secluded;
> White cranes coming and leaving with clouds afloat;
> And apes climbing up and down to hand out fruits.
> Before the gate, the pond's wide and trees cast long shadows;
> The rocks crack, breaking the moss's growth.
> Palatial halls dark and tall as the purple Heaven;
> And towers aloft from which bright red mists descend.
> Truly a blessed region, a spiritual place
> Like the cloudy cave of Penglai:

Quiet, untouched by the affairs of man;
Tranquil, fit to nurse the mind of Dao.
Bluebirds may bring at times a Queen Mother's note;
A phoenix oft arrives with a Laozi scroll.
There's no end to the sight of this noble Daoist scene:
It's the spacious home of immortals indeed!

As the Tang Monk dismounted, he saw on the left a huge stone tablet, on which the following inscription was written in large letters:

The Blessed Land of the Long Life Mountain.
The Cave Heaven of the Five Villages Abbey.

"Disciples," said the Elder, "it's indeed a Daoist abbey." "Master," said Sha Monk, "with such splendid scenery, there must be a good man living in this temple. Let us go in and take a look. When we return to the East after completing our merits, this may be the place for another visit because of its marvelous scenery." "Well spoken," said Pilgrim, and they all went inside. On both sides of the second gate they saw this New Year couplet:

Long-living and ever young, this immortal house.
Of the same age as Heaven, this Daoist home.

Pilgrim said with a snicker, "This Daoist is mouthing big words just to intimidate people! When I, old Monkey, caused disturbance in the Heavenly Palace five hundred years ago, I did not encounter such words even on the door of Laozi!" "Never mind him!" said Eight Rules. "Let's go inside! Let's go inside! You never know, maybe this Daoist does possess some virtuous accomplishment."

When they passed through the second gate, they were met by two young lads who were hurrying out. Look how they appear:

Healthy in bone and spirit with visage fair,
On their heads were short bundled tufts of hair.
Their Daoist gowns, free falling, seemed wrapped in mists;
Their feathered robes, more quaint, for the wind-blown sleeves.
Dragon-heads had their sashes knotted tight;
Silk cords laced lightly their sandals of straw.
Such uncommon looks were of no worldly-born;
They were Clear Breeze and Bright Moon, two lads divine.

The two young lads came out to meet them, bowing and saying, "Old Master, forgive us for not coming to meet you. Please take a seat." Delighted, the elder followed the two lads to the main hall to look around. There were altogether five huge chambers facing south, separated by floor-length windows that had carved panes and were translucent at the top and solid at the bottom. Pushing open one of these, the two immortal lads invited the Tang Monk into the central chamber, with a panel hanging on the middle wall on which two large characters—"Heaven, Earth"—were embroidered in five colors. Beneath the panel was a cinnabar-red lacquered incense table, on which there was an urn of yellow gold. Conveniently placed beside the urn were several sticks of incense.

The Tang Monk went forward and with his left hand, took up some incense to put into the urn. He then prostrated himself three times before the table, after which he turned around and said, "Immortal lads, your Five Villages Abbey is in truth a godly region of the West. But why is it that you do not worship the Three Pure Ones, the Thearchs of Four Quarters, or the many Lords of High Heaven? Why is it that you merely put up these two words of Heaven and Earth to receive the oblation of fire and incense?" Smiling, one of the lads said, "To tell you the truth, Master, putting these two words up is an act of flattery on the part of our teacher, for of these two words, the one on top,[8] may deserve our reverence, but the one below is hardly worthy of our fire and incense." "What do you mean by an act of flattery?" asked Tripitaka. The lad replied, "The Three Pure Ones are friends of our teacher; the Four Thearchs, his old acquaintances; the Nine Luminaries, his junior colleagues; and the God of the New Year, his unwanted guest!"

When Pilgrim heard this remark, he laughed so hard that he could barely stand up. "Elder Brother," said Eight Rules, "why are you laughing?" "Talk about the shenanigans of old Monkey!" said Pilgrim. "Just listen to the flimflam of this Daoist kid!" "Where is your honorable teacher?" asked Tripitaka. "Our teacher," said the lad, "had been invited by the Honorable Divine of the Origin to attend a lecture on 'The Daoist Fruit of the Chaotic Origin' at the Miluo Palace in the Heaven of Highest Clarity. He's not home."

No longer able to restrain himself after hearing these words, Pilgrim shouted: "You stinking young Daoists! You can't even recognize people! Whom are you trying to hoodwink? What kind of taradiddle is this? Who is that Heavenly Immortal in the Miluo Palace who wanted to invite this wild bull shank of yours? And what sort of lecture is he going to give?" When Tripitaka saw how aroused Pilgrim was, he feared that the lads might give some reply that would lead to real trouble. So he said, "Wukong, stop being quarrelsome. If we leave this place the moment after we arrive, it is hardly a friendly gesture. The proverb says, 'The egrets do not devour the egret's flesh.' If their teacher is not here, why bother them? You go to graze the horse outside the temple gate; let Sha Monk look after the luggage and Eight Rules fetch some grain from our bags. Let's borrow their pans and stove to prepare a meal for ourselves. When we are done, we can pay them a few pennies for firewood and that will be the end of the matter. Attend to your business, each of you, and let me rest here for a while. After the meal, we'll leave." The three of them duly went about their business.

Clear Breeze and Bright Moon, filled with admiration, said softly to each other: "What a monk! Truly the incarnation of a lovable sage of the West, whose true origin is not at all obscured! Well, our master did tell us to take care of the Tang Monk and to serve him some ginseng fruits as a token of past friendship. He also cautioned us about the rowdiness of his disciples, and he couldn't have been more correct. It's a good thing that those three, so fierce in their looks and so churlish in their manners, were sent away. For had they remained, they would certainly have to see the ginseng fruits." Then Clear Breeze said, "Brother, we are still not quite certain whether that monk is really an old acquaintance of Master. We had better ask him and not make a mistake." The two lads therefore went forward again and said, "May we ask the old master whether he is Tripitaka Tang from the Great Tang Empire, who is on his way to fetch scriptures from the Western Heaven?" Returning their bows, the elder said, "I am, indeed. How is it that the immortal youths know my vulgar name?" "Before our master's departure," said one of them," he gave us instructions that we should go some distance to meet you. We did not expect your arrival to be so soon, and thus we failed in the proper etiquette of greeting you. Please take a seat, Master, and allow us to serve you tea." "I hardly deserve that," said Tripitaka, but Bright Moon went quickly back to his room and brought back a cup of fragrant tea to present to the elder. After Tripitaka had drunk the tea, Clear Breeze said, "Brother, we must not disobey our master's command. Let's go and bring back the fruit."

The two lads took leave of Tripitaka and went back to their room, where one of them took out a gold mallet and the other a wooden tray for carrying elixir. They also spread out several silk handkerchiefs on the tray before going to the Ginseng Garden. Clear Breeze then climbed on the tree to strike at the fruits with the mallet, while Bright Moon waited below, holding the tray. In a moment, two of the fruits dropped down and fell onto the tray. The young lads returned to the main hall and presented the fruits to the Tang Monk, saying, "Master Tang, our Five Villages Abbey is situated in the midst of wild and desolate country. There's not much that we can offer you except these two fruits, our local products. Please use them to relieve your thirst." When the elder saw the fruits, he trembled all over and backed away three feet, saying, "Goodness! Goodness! The harvest seems to be plentiful this year! But why is this abbey so destitute that they have to practice cannibalism here? These are newborn infants not yet three days old! How could you serve them to me to relieve my thirst?"

"This monk," said Clear Breeze quietly to himself, "has been so corrupted by the fields of mouths and tongues, by the sea of strife and envy, that all he possesses are but two fleshly eyes and a worldly mind. That's why he can't recognize the strange treasures of our divine abode!" Bright Moon then drew near and said, "Master, this thing is called ginseng fruit. It's perfectly all right for you to eat one." "Nonsense! Nonsense!" said Tripitaka. "Their parents went through who knows how much suffering before they brought them to birth! How could you serve them as fruits when they are less than three days old?" Clear Breeze said, "Honestly, they were formed on a tree." "Rubbish! Rubbish!" said the elder. "How can people grow on trees? Take them away! This is blasphemy!" When the young lads saw that he absolutely refused to eat them, they had no choice but to take the tray back to their own room. The fruit, you see, is peculiar: if it is kept too long, it will become stiff and inedible. So, when the two of them reached their room, they each took one of the fruits and began to eat them, sitting on the edge of their beds.

Alas, now this is what has to happen! That chamber of theirs, you see, was immediately adjacent to the kitchen; joined, in fact, by a common wall. Even the whispered words from one room could be heard in the other, and Eight Rules was busily cooking rice in the kitchen. All that talk, moments before, about taking the golden mallet and the elixir tray had already caught his attention. Then, when he heard how the Tang Monk could not recognize ginseng fruits that were served him, and how they had to be eaten by the young lads in their own room, he could not stop his mouth watering, and said to himself, "How can I try one myself?" Since he himself was reluctant to do anything, he decided to wait for Pilgrim's arrival so that they could plan something together. Completely distracted by now from tending the fire in the stove, he kept sticking his head out of the door to watch for Pilgrim. In a little while, he saw Pilgrim arrive, leading the horse. Having tied the horse to a locust tree, Pilgrim started to walk toward the rear, when Idiot waved to him madly with his hands, crying, "Come this way! Come this way!" Pilgrim turned around and went to the door of the kitchen, saying, "Idiot, why are you yelling? Not enough rice, perhaps? Let the old monk have his fill first, and we can beg more rice from some big household along our way."

"Come in," said Eight Rules. "This has nothing to do with the amount of rice we have. There's a treasure in this Daoist temple. Did you know that?"

"What kind of treasure?" asked Pilgrim.

"I can tell you," said Eight Rules with a laugh, "but you have never seen it; I can put it before you, but you won't recognize it." "You must be joking, Idiot," said Pilgrim. "Five hundred years ago, when I, old Monkey, searched for the Way of Immortality, I went all the way to the corner of the ocean and the edge of the sky. What can there be that I have never seen?"

"Elder Brother," said Eight Rules, "have you ever seen the ginseng fruit?" Somewhat startled, Pilgrim said, "That I really have never seen! But I have heard that ginseng fruit is the grass of the reverted cinnabar. When a man eats it, his life will be prolonged. But where can one get ahold of it?" "They have it here," said Eight Rules. "The two lads brought two of these fruits for Master to eat, but that old monk could not recognize them for what they were. He said that they were infants not yet three days old and dared not eat them. The lads themselves were quite disobliging; if Master would not eat, they should have given them to us. Instead, they hid them from us. Just now in the room next door, each had a fruit to himself and finished it with great relish. I got so excited that I was drooling, wondering how I could have a taste of this fruit. I know you are quite tricky. How about going to their garden and stealing a few for us to have a taste of them?"

"That's easy," said Pilgrim. "Old Monkey will go, and they will be at the reach of his hands!" He turned quickly and began to walk to the front. Eight Rules caught hold of him and said, "Elder Brother, I heard them talking in the room, and they mentioned something about using a gold mallet to knock down the fruits. You must do it properly, and without being detected." "I know! I know!" exclaimed Pilgrim.

Our Great Sage used the magic of body concealment and stole into the Daoist chamber. The two Daoist lads, you see, were not in the room, for they had gone back to the main hall to speak to the Tang Monk after they had finished eating the fruits. Pilgrim looked everywhere for the gold mallet and discovered a stick of red gold hanging on the window pane: it was about two feet long and as thick as a finger. At the lower end there was a knob about the size of a clove of garlic, while the upper end had a hole through which a green woolen thread was fastened. He said to himself: "This must be the thing called the gold mallet." Taking it down, he left the Daoist chamber, went to the rear, and pushed through a double-leaf door to have a look. Ah, it was a garden! You see

Vermilion fences and carved railings;
Artificial hills ruggedly built.
Strange flowers rival the sun in brightness;
Bamboos match well the clear sky in blueness.
Beyond the flowing-cup pavilion,
One curvate band of willows like mists outspread;
Before the moon-gazing terrace,
Bands of choice pines like spilled indigo.

Shining red,
Pomegranates with brocade-like sacs;
Fresh, tender green,
Grass by the ornamental stools;
Luxuriant blue,
Sand-orchids like jade;
Limpid and smooth,
The water in the brook.
The cassia glows with the wutong by the golden well;[9]
The locust trees stand near the red fences and marble steps.
Some red and some white: peaches with a thousand leaves;
Some fragrant and some yellow: chrysanthemums of late fall.
The rush-flower supports
Complement the peony pavilion;
The hibiscus terrace
Connects with the peony plot.
There are countless princely bamboos that mock the frost,
And noble pines that defy the snow.
There are, moreover, crane hamlets and deer homes,
The square pool and the round pond.
The stream spills chips of jade;
The ground sprouts mounds of gold.
The winter wind cracks and whitens the plum blossoms;
A touch of spring breaks open the begonia's red.
Truly it may be called the best fairyland on Earth,
The finest floral site of the West.

Pilgrim could not take his eyes off this marvelous place. He came upon another door that he pushed open and found inside a vegetable garden,

Planted with the herbs of all four seasons:
Spinach, celery, mare's tail,[10] beet, ginger, and seaweed;
Bamboo shoot, melon, squash, and watercress;
Chive, garlic, coriander, leek, and scallion;

Hollow water-lotus, young celery, and bitter su;[11]
The gourd and the eggplant that must be trimmed;
Green turnip, white turnip, and taro deep in the earth;
Red spinach, green cabbage, and purple mustard plant.[12]

Pilgrim smiled to himself and said, "So he's a Daoist who eats his home-grown food!"

He walked past the vegetable garden and found another door, which he pushed open also. Ah! There was a huge tree right in the middle of the garden, with long, healthy branches and luxuriant green leaves that some-what resembled those of the plantain. Soaring straight up, the tree was over a thousand feet tall, and its base must have measured sixty or seventy feet around. Leaning on the tree, Pilgrim looked up and found one gin-seng fruit sticking out on one of the branches pointing southward. It cer-tainly had the appearance of an infant with a tail-like peduncle. Look at it dangling from the end of the branch, with limbs moving wildly and head bobbing madly! It seemed to make sounds as it swung in the breeze. Filled with admiration and delight, Pilgrim said to himself, "What a marvelous thing! It's rarely seen! It's rarely seen!" With a swish, he vaulted up the tree.

The monkey, you see, was an expert in climbing trees and stealing fruits. He took the gold mallet and struck lightly at the fruit, which dropped at once from the branch. Pilgrim leaped down after it but the fruit was no-where to be seen. Though he searched for it all over the grass, there was not a trace of it. "Strange! Strange!" said Pilgrim. "I suppose it could walk with its legs, but even so, it could hardly have jumped across the wall. I know! It must be the local spirit of this garden who will not allow me to steal the fruit; he must have taken it." Making the magic sign and reciting a spell that began with the letter *om*, he summoned the local spirit of the garden, who came bowing to Pilgrim and said, "Great Sage, what sort of instruc-tions do you have for this humble deity?"

"Don't you know," said Pilgrim, "that old Monkey happens to be the world's most famous thief? When I stole the immortal peaches, the impe-rial wine, and the efficacious pills that year, there was no one brave enough to share the spoils with me. How is it, therefore, when I steal just one of their fruits today, that you have the gall to snatch away the prime portion? Since these fruits are formed on a tree, I suppose even the fowls of the air may partake of them. What's wrong with my eating one of them? How dare you grab it the moment I knock it down?" "Great Sage," said the local spirit, "you have made a mistake in blaming me. This treasure is something that belongs to an earthbound immortal, whereas I am only a ghost immor-tal.[13] Would I dare take it? I don't even have the good fortune to smell it!"

"If you hadn't snatched it," said Pilgrim, "why did it disappear the mo-ment it fell?" "You may know only about its power to prolong life, Great Sage," said the local spirit, "but you don't know its background."

"What do you mean by background?" said Pilgrim. "This treasure," said the local spirit, "will bloom only once in three thousand years; it will bear fruit after another three thousand years; and the fruit won't ripen for yet another three thousand years. All in all, one must wait for almost ten thou-sand years before there are thirty of these fruits. A person lucky enough to smell it once will live for three hundred and sixty years; if he eats one, he will live for forty-seven thousand years. However, the fruit is resistant to the Five Phases." "What do you mean by resistant to the Five Phases?" asked Pilgrim. The local spirit replied, "This fruit will fall when it encounters gold; it will wither when it encounters wood; it will melt when it encounters water; it will dry up if it encounters fire; and it will be assimilated if it encounters earth. That is why one has to use an instrument of gold to knock it down, but when it falls, it has to be held by a tray cushioned with silk handkerchiefs. The moment it touches wood, it will wither and will not prolong life even if it's eaten. When it is eaten, it should be held in a porcelain container and should be dissolved with water. Again, fire will dry it up and it will be useless. Finally, what is meant by its assimilation into earth may be illustrated by what happened just now, for when you knocked it down, it at once crawled into the ground. This part of the garden will last for at least forty-seven thousand years. Even a steel pick will not be able to bore through it, for it is three or four times harder than raw iron. That is why a man will live long if he eats one of the fruits. If you don't believe me, Great Sage, strike at the ground and see for yourself." Whipping out his golden-hooped rod, Pilgrim gave the ground a terrific blow. The rod rebounded at once, but there was not the slightest mark on the ground. "Indeed! Indeed!" said Pilgrim. "This rod of mine can turn a boulder into powder; it will leave its mark even on raw iron. How is it that there's not even a scratch on the ground? Well, in that case, I have made a mistake in blaming you. You may go back."[14] The local spirit thus went back to his own shrine.

The Great Sage, however, had his own plan: after climbing up on the tree, he held the golden mallet in one hand and, with the other, pulled up the front of his silk shirt to make a little sack. Parting the leaves and branches, he knocked three of the fruits into the sack. He jumped down from the tree and ran straight to the kitchen. "Elder Brother," said Eight Rules smiling, "do you have them?" "Aren't these the ones?" said Pilgrim. "I reached and took, that's all! But we shouldn't let Sha Monk pass up the chance of tasting this fruit. You call him." Eight Rules waved his hands and cried, "Wujing, come!" Setting down the luggage, Sha Monk ran into the kitchen and said, "Elder Brother, why did you call me?" Opening the sack, Pilgrim said, "Brother, take a look. What are these?" When Sha Monk saw them, he said, "Ginseng fruits." "Fine!" said Pilgrim. "So, you recognize them! Where did you taste them before?" "I have never tasted the fruit before," said Sha Monk. "But when I was the Curtain-Raising Captain, I waited on the Throne to attend the Festival of Immortal Peaches, and I once saw many immortals from beyond the sea presenting this fruit to the Lady Queen Mother as a birthday gift. So I have seen it, but I have never tasted it. Elder Brother, will you let me try a little?" "No need to say anymore," said Pilgrim. "There's one for each of us brothers."

The three of them took the fruits and began to enjoy them. That Eight Rules, of course, had a huge appetite and a huge mouth. When he heard the conversation of the young lads earlier, he already felt ravenous. The moment he saw the fruit, therefore, he grabbed it and, with one gulp, swallowed it whole. Then he rolled up his eyes and said in a roguish manner to Pilgrim and Sha Monk, "What are you two eating?" "Ginseng fruit," said Sha Monk. "How does it taste?" asked Eight Rules. "Wujing," said Pilgrim, "don't listen to him. He ate it first. Why all these questions now?" "Elder Brother," said Eight Rules, "I ate it somewhat too hurriedly, not as the two of you are doing, mincing and munching little by little to discover its taste. I swallowed it without even knowing whether it had a pit or not! Elder Brother, if you are helping someone, help him to the end. You have roused the worms in my stomach! Please fetch me another fruit so that I can take time to enjoy it." "Brother," said Pilgrim, "you really don't know when to stop! This thing here is not like rice or noodles, food to stuff yourself with. There are only thirty such fruits in ten thousand years! It's our great fortune to have eaten one already, and you should not regard this lightly. Stop now! It's enough." He stretched himself and threw the gold mallet into the adjacent room through a little hole on the window paper without saying anything more to Eight Rules.

Idiot, however, kept muttering and mumbling to himself. When the two Daoist lads unexpectedly came back to the room to fetch some tea for the Tang Monk, they heard Eight Rules complaining about "not enjoying my ginseng fruit," and saying that it would be much better if he could have a taste of another one. Hearing this, Clear Breeze grew suspicious and said, "Bright Moon, listen to that monk with the long snout; he said he wanted to eat another ginseng fruit. Before our master's departure, he told us to be wary of their mischief. Could it be that they have stolen our treasures?" Turning around, Bright Moon said, "Elder Brother, it looks bad, very bad! Why has the golden mallet fallen to the ground? Let's go into the garden to take a look." They ran hastily to the back and found the door to the flower garden open. "I closed this door myself," said Clear Breeze. "Why is it open?" They ran past the flower garden and saw that the door to the vegetable garden was also open. They dashed into the ginseng garden; running up to the tree, they started to count, staring upward. Back and forth they counted, but they could find only twenty-two of the fruits. "You know how to do accounting?" asked Bright Moon. "I do," said Clear Breeze, "give me the figures!" "There were originally thirty fruits," said Bright Moon. "When Master opened the garden to the public, he divided two of them for all of us, so that twenty-eight fruits were left. Just now we knocked down two more for the Tang Monk, leaving twenty-six behind. Now we have only twenty-two left. Doesn't that mean that four are missing? No need for further explanation; they must have been stolen by that bunch of rogues. Let's go and chide the Tang Monk."

The two of them went out of the garden gate and came directly back to the main hall. Pointing their fingers at the Tang Monk, they berated him with all kinds of foul and abusive language, accusing him of being a larcenous baldhead and a thievish rat. They went on like this for a long time, until finally the Tang Monk could not endure it any longer. "Divine lads," he said, "why are you making all this fuss? Be quiet a moment. If you have something to say, say it slowly, but don't use such nonsensical language." "Are you deaf?" asked Clear Breeze. "Am I speaking in a barbarian tongue that you can't understand? You stole and ate our ginseng fruits. Do you now forbid me to say so?" "What is a ginseng fruit like?" asked the Tang Monk. "Like an infant," said Bright Moon, "as you said when we brought two of them for you to eat just now." "Amitābha Buddha!" exclaimed the Tang Monk. "I only had to take one look at that thing and I trembled all over! You think I would dare steal one and eat it? Even if I had a case of bulimia, I would not dare indulge in such thievery. Don't blame the wrong person." "You might not have eaten them," said Clear Breeze, "but your followers wanted to steal them and eat them." "Perhaps you are right," said Tripitaka, "but there's no need for you to shout. Let me ask them. If they have stolen them, I will ask them to repay you."

"Repay!" said Bright Moon. "You couldn't buy these fruits even if you had the money!"

"If they can't buy them with money," said Tripitaka, "they can at least offer you an apology, for as the proverb says, 'Righteousness is worth a thousand pieces of gold.' That should be sufficient. Moreover, we are still not sure whether it is my disciples who took your fruits." "What do you mean, not sure?" said Bright Moon. "They were arguing among themselves, saying something about the portions not being equally divided."

"Disciples," cried Tripitaka, "come, all of you." When Sha Monk heard this, he said, "It's terrible! We've been discovered! Old master is calling us, and the Daoist lads are making all this racket. They must have found out!" "It is extremely embarrassing!" said Pilgrim. "This is just a matter of food and drink. But if we say so, that means we are stealing for our mouths! Let's not admit it." "Yes! Yes!" said Eight Rules. "Let's deny it!" The three of them had no choice, however, but to leave the kitchen for the main hall. Alas, we do not know how they would be able to deny the charges; let's listen to the explanation in the next chapter.

TWENTY-FIVE

The Zhenyuan Immortal gives chase to catch the
  scripture monk;
Pilgrim Sun greatly disturbs Five Villages Abbey.

We were telling you about the three brothers, who went to the main hall and said to their master, "The rice is almost done. Why did you call us?" "Disciples," said Tripitaka, "I didn't want to ask you about the rice. They have something called the ginseng fruit in this Abbey, which looks like a newborn infant. Which one of you stole it and ate it?" "Honestly," said Eight Rules, "I don't know anything about it, and I haven't seen it." "It's the one who is laughing! It's the one who is laughing!" said Clear Breeze. "I was born with a laughing face!" snapped Pilgrim. "Don't think because you have lost some kind of a fruit that you can keep me from laughing!" "Disciple, don't get angry," said Tripitaka. "Those of us who have left the family should not lie, nor should we enjoy stolen food. If you have in truth eaten it, you owe them an apology. Why deny it so vehemently?" When Pilgrim perceived how reasonable this advice of his master was, he said truthfully, "Master, it's not my fault. It was Eight Rules who overheard those two Daoist lads eating some sort of ginseng fruit. He wanted to try one to see how it tasted and told me to knock down three of the fruits; each of us brothers had one. It's true that we have eaten them. What's to be done about that?" "He stole four of the fruits," said Bright Moon, "and still this monk could claim that he's not a thief!" "Amitābha Buddha!" said Eight Rules. "If you stole four of them, why did you only bring out three for us to divide among ourselves? Didn't you skim something off the top already?" So saying, Idiot began to make a fuss again.

When the immortal lads found out the truth, they became even more abusive in their language; the Great Sage became so enraged that he ground his steel-like teeth audibly and opened wide his fiery eyes. He gripped his golden-hooped rod again and again, struggling to restrain himself and saying to himself, "These malicious youths! They certainly know how to give people a lashing with their tongues! All right, so I have to take such abuse from them. Let me offer them in return 'a plan for eliminating posterity,' and none of them will have any more fruit to eat!" Dear Pilgrim! He pulled off a strand of hair behind his head and blew on it with his magic breath, crying "Change!" It changed at once into a specious Pilgrim, standing by the Tang Monk, Wujing, and Wuneng to receive the scolding from the Daoist lads. His true spirit rose into the clouds, and with one leap he arrived at the ginseng garden. Whipping out his golden-hooped rod, he gave the tree a terrific blow, after which he used that mountain-moving divine strength of his to give it a mighty shove. Alas,

> Leaves fell, limbs cracked, and roots became exposed;
> The Daoists lost their grass of reverted cinnabar.

After the Great Sage had pushed down the tree, he tried to look for the fruits on the branches but he could not find even half a fruit. The treasure, you see, would fall when it met with gold, and both ends of his rod were wrapped in gold. Moreover, iron is also one of the five metallic elements. The blow of the rod, therefore, shook loose all the fruits from the tree, and when they fell, they became assimilated to the earth once they touched the ground, so that there was not a single fruit left on the tree. "Fine! Fine!" he said. "Now all of us can scram!" He put away his iron rod and went back to the front. With a shake of his body he retrieved his hair, but the rest of the people, like those of fleshly eyes and mortal stock, could not perceive what had taken place.

We now tell you about the two immortal lads, who ranted at the pilgrims for a long time. Clear Breeze said, "Bright Moon, these monks do take our reproach quite well. We have been upbraiding them as if they were chickens all this time, but not once have they even attempted to answer us. Could it be that they really did not steal the fruits? With the tree so tall and the leaves so dense, we could have made a mistake in our tallying, and we might have chided them unjustly. We should go and investigate further." "You are right," said Bright Moon, and the two of them accordingly went back to the garden. But what they saw was only a tree on the ground with broken boughs and fallen leaves, without so much as a single fruit on it. Clear Breeze was so aghast that his legs gave way and he fell to the ground; Bright Moon shook so violently that he could hardly stand up. Both of them were scared out of their wits! We have, as testimony, this poem:

> Tripitaka went westward to the Long Life Mount;
> Wukong cut down the grass of reverted cinnabar.
> Boughs broken and leaves fallen, the divine root exposed:
> Clear Breeze and Bright Moon were horrified!

The two of them lay on the ground, hardly able to speak coherently. They could only blurt out, "What shall we do? What shall we do? The magic root of our Five Villages Abbey is severed! The seed of this divine house of ours is cut off! When our master returns, what shall we tell him?" Then Bright Moon said, "Elder Brother, stop hollering! Let's pull ourselves together and not alarm those monks. There's no one else here; it has to be that fellow with a hairy face and a thundergod beak who used magic unseen to ruin our treasure. If we try to talk to him, he will probably deny it, and further argument may well lead to actual combat. In the event of a fight, how do you suppose the two of us could stand up to the four of them? It would be better if we deceived them now by saying that the fruits were not missing, and that since we made a mistake in our counting, we were offering them our own apology. Their rice is almost cooked. When they eat, we shall even present them with a few side dishes. When each of them is holding a bowl, you stand on the left of the door and I'll stand on the right, and we'll slam the door shut together. We'll lock it and all the other doors of this Abbey too, so that they will not be able to escape. We can then wait for Master to return and let him do with them what he wills. Since the Tang Monk is an old acquaintance of Master, he might decide to forgive them, and that would be his act of kindness. Should he decide not to, however, we have at least managed to catch the thieves, for which we ourselves might be forgiven." When he heard these words, Clear Breeze said, "You are right! You are right!"

The two of them forced themselves to look cheerful as they walked back to the main hall from the rear garden. Bowing to the Tang Monk, they said, "Master, our coarse and vulgar language just now must have offended you. Please pardon us!" "What are you saying?" asked Tripitaka. "The fruits were not missing," said Clear Breeze, "but we couldn't see them clearly because of the dense foliage. We went back again to have a second look and we found the original number."

Hearing this, Eight Rules chimed in at once. "You lads, you are young and impulsive, quick to condemn before you even know the truth of the matter. You throw out your castigations at random, and you have accused us unjustly. It's blasphemy!" Pilgrim, however, understood what was going on; though he did not say anything, he thought to himself, "It's a lie! It's a lie! The fruits were done with! Why do they say such things? Could it be that they have the magic of revivification?" Meanwhile, Tripitaka said to his disciples, "In that case, bring us some rice. We'll eat and leave."

Eight Rules went at once to fetch the rice, while Sha Monk set the table and chairs. The two lads brought out seven or eight side dishes, including pickles, pickled eggplants, radishes in wine sauce, string beans in vinegar, salted lotus roots, and blanched mustard plants for master and disciples to eat with their rice. They also brought out a pot of fine tea and two mugs, and stood on either side of the table to wait on them. As soon as the four of them had taken up their bowls, however, the lads, one on each side, took hold of the door and slammed it tightly shut. They then bolted it with a double-shackle brass lock. "You lads made a mistake," said Eight Rules with a laugh, "or else your custom here is rather strange. Why do you shut the door before you eat?" "Indeed!" said Bright Moon. "For good or ill, we will not open the door until after we have eaten." Then Clear Breeze lashed out at them, saying, "You bulimic and gluttonous bald thieves! You stole and ate our divine fruits, and you were thus already guilty of eating the produce of someone's garden without permission. Now you have even knocked over our divine tree and destroyed this immortal root of our of Five Villages Abbey. And you still dare to speak to us defiantly? If you think you can reach the Western Heaven to behold the face of Buddha, you will have to ride the Wheel of Transmigration and do it in the next incarnation!" When Tripitaka heard these words, he threw down his rice bowl and sat there weighed down as if by a huge boulder on his heart. The lads then went to lock both the front gate and the second gate before returning to the main hall to revile them once more with the most abusive language. Calling them thieves again and again, the two lads assailed them until it was late, when they then left to eat. After the meal, the lads went back to their own room.

The Tang Monk began to complain at Pilgrim, saying, "You mischievous ape! Every time it's you who cause trouble! If you stole and ate their fruits, you should have been more forbearing to their reproach. Why did you have to knock down even their tree? If you were brought into court, even if your old man were the judge, you would not be able to defend yourself when you behave like that!" "Don't scold me, Master," said Pilgrim. "If those lads have gone to sleep, let them sleep. We'll leave tonight." "Elder Brother," said Sha Monk, "all the doors have been locked securely. How can we leave?" Pilgrim said with a laugh, "Never mind! Never mind! Old Monkey will find a way!" "You have a way, all right!" said Eight Rules. "All you need to do is to change into some sort of an insect, and you can fly out through a hole or a crack in the window. But what about those of us who don't know how to change into these tiny things? We have to stay and take the blame for you." "If he does something like that," said the Tang Monk, "and leaves us behind, I'll recite that *Old-Time Sūtra* and see whether he can take it!" When he heard this, Eight Rules did not know whether to laugh or not. "Master," he said, "what are you saying? I have only heard the *Śūraṅgama Sūtra*, the *Lotus Sūtra*, the *Peacock Sūtra*, the *Guanyin Sūtra*, and the *Diamond Sūtra* in Buddhism, but I have never heard of anything called the *Old-Time Sūtra*."

"You don't know about this, Brother," said Pilgrim. "This fillet that I wear on my head was given to Master by the Bodhisattva Guanyin. Master deceived me into wearing it, and it took root, as it were, on my head so that it could never be removed. There is, moreover, the Tight-Fillet Spell or the Tight-Fillet Sūtra. The moment he recites that, I'll have a terrible headache, for it's the magic trick designed to give me a hard time. Master, don't recite it. I won't betray you. No matter what happens, all of us will leave together."

As they spoke, it grew dark and the moon rose in the East. Pilgrim said, "When all is quiet and the crystal orb is bright, this is the time for us to steal away." "Elder Brother," said Eight Rules, "stop this hocus-pocus. The doors are all locked. Where are we going to go?" "Watch my power!" said Pilgrim. He seized his golden-hooped rod and exercised the lock-opening magic; he pointed the rod at the door and all the locks fell down with a loud pop as the several doors immediately sprung open. "What talent!" said Eight Rules, laughing. "Even if a little smith were to use a lock pick, he wouldn't be able to do this so nimbly." Pilgrim said, "This door is nothing! Even the South Heaven Gate would immediately fly open if I pointed this at it!" They asked their master to go outside and mount the horse; Eight Rules poled the luggage and Sha Monk led the way toward the West. "Walk slowly, all of you," said Pilgrim. "Let me go and see to it that the Daoist lads will sleep for a month." "Disciple," said Tripitaka, "don't harm them, or you will be guilty of murder as well as robbery." "I won't harm them," said Pilgrim.

Going inside again, he went to the door of the room where the lads were sleeping. He still had around his waist a few sleep-inducing insects, which he had won from the Devarāja Virūpākṣa when they had played a game of guess-fingers at the East Heaven Gate. Taking out two of these insects, he filliped them through a hole in the window. They headed straight for the faces of the lads who fell at once into a sleep so deep that it seemed nothing could arouse them. Then Pilgrim turned around and caught up with the Tang Monk, and all of them fled, following the main road to the West.

Throughout that whole night, the horse did not pause to rest, and they journeyed until it was almost dawn. "Monkey," said the Tang Monk, "you have just about killed me! Because of your mouth, I've had to spend a sleepless night." "Stop this complaining!" said Pilgrim. "It's dawn now, and you may as well take some rest in the forest here by the road. After you have regained a little strength, we'll move on." All that elder could do was to dismount and use a pine root as his couch. As soon as he put down the luggage, Sha Monk dozed off, while Eight Rules fell asleep with a rock as his pillow. The Great Sage Sun, however, had other interests. Just look at him! Climbing the trees and leaping from branch to branch, he had a grand time playing. We shall leave them resting and make no further mention of them now.

We now tell you about the Great Immortal, who left the Tushita Palace with the lesser immortals after the lecture was over. Descending from the Green Jasper Heaven and dropping down from the auspicious clouds, they arrived before the Five Villages Abbey at the Long Life Mountain, where they found the gates wide open and the grounds neat and clean. "Well," said the Great Immortal, "Clear Breeze and Bright Moon are not that useless after all! Ordinarily, they don't even bestir themselves when the sun is high, but today when we are away, they are willing to rise early to open the gates and sweep the grounds." All the lesser immortals were delighted, but when they reached the main hall, they discovered neither fire and incense nor any trace of a human person. Clear Breeze and Bright Moon were simply nowhere to be seen!

"Because of our absence, the two of them must have stolen away with our things," said the rest of the immortals. "Nonsense!" said the Great Immortal. "How could those who seek the way of immortality dare to engage in such wickedness? They must have forgotten to close the gates last night and gone to sleep. They are probably not yet awake this morning." When they all reached the door of the Daoist lads, they found the door tightly shut and heard heavy snoring from within. They pounded on the door and attempted to rouse them, but the lads could not be wakened by all that clamor. Finally, the immortals managed to pry open the door and pull the lads off their beds; even then they did not wake up. "Dear immortal lads!" said the Great Immortal, laughing. "Those who have attained immortality should not be so desirous of sleep, for their spirits are full. Why are they so fatigued? Could it be that someone has played a trick on them? Quickly, bring me some water!" One of the lads brought half a cup of water to the Great Immortal, who recited a spell before spitting a mouthful of water on the lads' faces. The Sleep Demon was thus exorcised.

Both lads woke up, and as they opened their eyes and wiped their faces, they suddenly saw all the familiar faces of their teacher, Lord, Equal to Earth, and the other immortals. Clear Breeze and Bright Moon were so startled that they knelt down at once and kowtowed, saying, "Master, your old friends, the monks who came from the East, were a bunch of vicious thieves!" "Don't be afraid!" said the Great Immortal, smiling. "Take your time and tell me about them."

"Master," said Clear Breeze, "Shortly after you left that day, a Tang Monk from the Land of the East did indeed arrive with three other monks and a horse. In obedience to your command, your disciples, having ascertained their origin, took two of the ginseng fruits and served them. That elder, however, had worldly eyes and a foolish mind, for he could not recognize the treasures of our immortal house. He insisted that they were newborn infants not yet three days old and absolutely refused to eat them. For this reason, each of us ate one of the fruits instead. We didn't expect, however, that one of his three disciples, a fellow whose surname was Sun and whose given name was Wukong Pilgrim, would steal and eat four of the fruits. When we discovered the theft, we tried to reason with him, speaking rather forthrightly to that monk. But he refused to listen to us and instead used the magic of the spirit leaving the body to—oh, this is painful!" When the two lads reached this point in their discourse, they could not hold back their tears. "Did that monk strike you?" asked the rest of the immortals. "He did not hit us," said Bright Moon, "but he struck down our ginseng tree."

When the Great Immortal heard this, he was not angry. Instead, he said, "Don't cry! Don't cry! What you don't know is that the fellow with the name of Sun is also a minor immortal of the Great Monad; he has great magic power and has caused much disturbance in Heaven. If our treasure tree is struck down, all I want to know is whether you will be able to recognize these monks if you see them again." "Certainly," said Clear Breeze. "In that case," said the Great Immortal, "follow me. The rest of you disciples can prepare the instruments of punishment. When I return, they shall be whipped."

The various immortals took this instruction, while the Great Immortal mounted the auspicious luminosity with Clear Breeze and Bright Moon to give chase to Tripitaka. In a moment they had covered a thousand miles, but when the Great Immortal looked toward the West at the tip of the cloud, he could not see the Tang Monk anywhere. When he turned around and stared eastward instead, he found that he had overtaken the pilgrims by some nine hundred miles, for that elder, even with his horse galloping nonstop all night, had managed to travel only one hundred and twenty miles. Reversing the direction of his cloud, the Great Immortal made the trip back in an instant. "Master," said one of the lads, "that's the Tang Monk sitting beneath a tree by the road." "I see him," said the Great Immortal. "You two go back and prepare the ropes. Let me capture them by myself." Clear Breeze and Bright Moon went back to the Abbey at once.

Dropping down from the clouds, the Great Immortal changed himself into a mendicant Daoist[1] with one shake of his body. "How was he dressed?" you ask.

A priestly robe patched a hundred times
And a sash in the style of Mr. Lü.[2]
His hands waved a yak's-tail
And lightly tapped a fish-drum.
Straw sandals with three loops shod his feet;
A sinuous turban wrapped around his head.
With wind-filled sleeves all aflutter,
He sang of the rising moon.

He came straight to the tree and said in a loud voice to the Tang Monk, "Elder, this poor Daoist raises his hands!" Hastily returning the salutation, the elder said, "Pardon me for not paying respects to you first." "Where did the elder come from," asked the Great Immortal, "and why is he sitting in meditation here beside the road?" Tripitaka said, "I am a scripture seeker sent by the Great Tang of the Land of the East to the Western Heaven." Feigning surprise, the Great Immortal said, "When you came from the East, did you pass through my humble mountain abode?" "Which precious mountain is the abode of the venerable immortal?" asked the elder. The Great Immortal said, "The Five Villages Abbey in the Long Life Mountain is where I reside."

The moment he heard this, Pilgrim, having something very much on his mind, replied, "No! No! We came by another route up there." Pointing a finger firmly at him, the Great Immortal said with a laugh, "Brazen ape! Who are you trying to fool? You struck down my ginseng fruit tree in my Abbey, and then you fled here in the night. You dare deny this? Why try to cover up? Don't run away! Go quickly and bring back another tree for me!" When Pilgrim heard this, he grew angry and whipped out his iron rod; without waiting for further discussion, he struck at the head of the Great Immortal. Stepping aside to dodge the blow, the Great Immortal trod on the auspicious luminosity and rose into the air, closely followed by Pilgrim, who also mounted the clouds. The Great Immortal changed back into his true form in midair, and this was how he appeared:

> He wore a cap of purple gold,
> And a carefree gown trimmed with crane's down.
> He had on his feet a pair of shoes;
> A silk sash was tied round his waist.
> His body seemed that of a lad
> His face, that of a lady fair,
> But with flowing moustaches and beard.
> Some crow feathers adorned his hair.
> He faced Pilgrim but without a weapon,
> Save a jade yak's-tail[3] which he twirled in his hand.

Above and below, Pilgrim struck wildly with his rod, only to be parried again and again by the Great Immortal wielding his jade yak's tail. After two or three rounds of fighting, the Great Immortal displayed his magic of the cosmos in the sleeve. Standing on the tip of a cloud and facing the wind, he gently flipped open the wide sleeve of his gown and sent it toward the earth in a sweeping motion. All four of the monks and the horse were at once scooped up into the sleeve. "This is dreadful!" said Eight Rules. "We have been placed in a clothes bag!" "It isn't a clothes bag, Idiot!" said Pilgrim. "We've been scooped up into his sleeve." "In that case," said Eight Rules, "it shouldn't be too difficult! Let me use my rake and make a hole in his gown. When we make our escape, we can claim that he was careless and didn't hold us securely, so that we fell out of his sleeve." Idiot started to dig into the garment madly with his rake, but all to no avail: although the material was soft to the touch, it was harder than steel when it came into contact with the rake.

Turning around the direction of his auspicious cloud, the Great Immortal went back to the Five Villages Abbey and sat down, ordering his disciples to fetch some ropes. As the little immortals went about their business, he fished out the pilgrims one by one like puppets from his sleeve: first he brought out the Tang Monk and had him bound to one of the large pillars in the main hall. Then he took out the three disciples and had them tied to three other pillars. Finally he took out the horse and had it tied up in the courtyard; it was given some hay while the luggage was thrown into one of the corridors. "Disciples," said the Great Immortal, "these monks are persons who have left home, and they should not be harmed by knives or spears, hatchets or battle-axes. Bring out my leather whip instead and give them a beating—as an act of vengeance for my ginseng fruit!" Some of the immortals went quickly to fetch the whip—not the sort made of cow hide, sheep hide, suede, or buffalo hide. It was, rather, a whip of seven thongs made of dragon hide. After soaking it in water for a while, one of the more robust little immortals took it up and asked, "Master, which one shall be flogged first?" The Great Immortal replied, "Tripitaka Tang is the unworthy senior member of his party. Beat him first."

When Pilgrim heard what he said, he thought to himself, "That old monk of mine cannot stand such flogging. If he's destroyed by the whip, wouldn't that be my sin?" Unable to remain silent any longer, he said, "Sir, you are mistaken! It was I who stole the fruits, and it was I who ate the fruits. Moreover, I also pushed down the tree. Why don't you flog me first? Why do you have to whip him?" "This brazen ape," said the Great Immortal, laughing, "does know how to speak courageously! All right, let's flog him first." "How many lashes?" asked the little immortal. "As many as the original number of the fruits," said the Great Immortal. "Thirty lashes." Lifting high the whip, the little immortal was about to strike. Fearing that this weapon of an immortal's house might be a formidable one, Pilgrim opened his eyes wide to see where he was going to be struck and found that the little immortal was about to flog his legs. With a twist of his torso, Pilgrim said, "Change!" and his two legs became hard as steel, all ready to be flogged. With measured strokes, the little immortal gave him thirty lashes before putting down the whip.

It was already almost noon when the Great Immortal said again, "We should now give Tripitaka a flogging, since he did not know how to discipline his mischievous disciples and permitted them to indulge in unruly behavior." As the immortal took up the whip again, Pilgrim said, "You are again mistaken, sir. When the fruits were stolen, my master was conversing in this hall with the two lads; he had no knowledge whatever of what we brothers had perpetrated. Though he might be guilty of not being strict enough in his discipline of us, those of us who are his disciples should receive the punishment for him. Flog me again." "This lawless ape!" said the Great Immortal. "Though he is sly and devious, he does possess some filial sentiments! In that case, let's flog him again." The little immortal again gave him thirty lashes. When Pilgrim lowered his head to take a look, he saw that his two legs had been beaten until they were shining like mirrors, though he had no sensation whatever, either of pain or of itching. By this time it was getting late, and the Great Immortal said, "Soak the whip in water. Wait until tomorrow, and then we shall punish them again." The little immortals retrieved the whip and placed it in water, after which everyone retired to his own chamber. When they had finished their evening meal, all went away to sleep, and we shall say no more of them now.

With tears flowing from his eyes, the elder began to complain bitterly to his three disciples, saying, "You all have caused this trouble, but I have to suffer with you in this place. What are you going to do about it?" "Stop this complaining," said Pilgrim. "They flogged me first, and you haven't even had a taste of it yet. Why do you have to grumble like that?" "Though I have not been flogged," said the Tang Monk, "this rope is causing me to ache all over." "Master," said Sha Monk, "there are others here who are your companions in bondage!" "Stop this racket, all of you!" said Pilgrim. "In a little while, we'll all be on our way again."

"Elder Brother," said Eight Rules, "you are fibbing again. We are tightly bound now in hemp ropes sprayed with water. They are not like the locks on those doors that you opened so easily with your magic!"

"This is no exaggeration," said Pilgrim, "but I'm not afraid of a three-ply hemp rope sprayed with water. Even if it were a coir cord as thick as a small bowl, I would consider it as insubstantial as the autumn wind!" Hardly had he finished speaking when it became completely quiet everywhere. Dear Pilgrim! He contracted his body and at once freed himself from the ropes, saying, "Let's go, Master!"

"Elder Brother," said a startled Sha Monk, "save us, too!" "Speak softly! Speak softly!" said Pilgrim. He untied Tripitaka, Sha Monk, and Eight Rules; they put on their clothes, saddled the horse, and picked up the luggage from the corridor. As they walked out of the Abbey gate, Pilgrim said to Eight Rules, "Go to the edge of the cliff there and bring back four willow trees." "What do you want them for?" asked Eight Rules. "I have use for them. Bring them quickly."

Idiot did possess some sort of brutish strength. He did as he was told, and with one shove of his snout he felled one of the willow trees. Knocking down three more, he gathered them up into a bundle and hauled them back. Pilgrim stripped the branches off the trunks, and the two of them carried the trunks inside, where they fastened them to the pillars with the ropes with which they had earlier been tied up themselves. Then the Great Sage recited a spell; biting the tip of his own tongue, he spat some blood on the trees and cried, "Change!" One of them changed into the elder, another changed into a figure like himself, and the two other trees changed into Sha Monk and Eight Rules. They all seemed to look exactly alike; when questioned, they knew how to make replies; when their names were called, they knew how to answer. Only then did the two of them run back out and catch up with their master. As before, the horse did not pause to rest for that whole night as they fled the Five Villages Abbey. When morning arrived, however, the elder was nodding on the horse, hardly able to remain in the saddle. When Pilgrim saw him like that, he called out, "Master, you are terribly soft! How is it that a person who has left home like yourself has so little endurance? If I, old Monkey, went without sleep even for a thousand nights, I still would not feel fatigue. Well, you had better get off the horse, so that travelers won't see your condition and laugh at you. Let's find a temporary shelter beneath the mountain slope and rest awhile before we move on again."

We shall not tell you any more now about master and disciples resting by the way; we shall tell you instead of the Great Immortal, who rose at the crack of dawn and went out at once to the main hall after taking his morning meal. He said, "Bring out the whip. It's Tripitaka's turn today to be flogged." The little immortal wielded the whip and said to the Tang Monk, "I'm going to beat you." "Go ahead," said the willow tree, and he was given thirty lashes. Changing the direction of his whip, the little immortal said to Eight Rules, "I'm going to flog you." "Go ahead," said the other willow tree, and the one that was changed into the form of Sha Monk gave the same reply when it was his turn. By the time they reached Pilgrim, the real Pilgrim, resting by the wayside, was suddenly sent into a violent shudder. "Something's wrong!" he exclaimed. "What do you mean?" asked Tripitaka. Pilgrim said, "I transformed four willow trees into the four of us, thinking that since they flogged me twice yesterday, they would not beat me again today. But they are giving my transformed body a beating, and that's why my true body is shivering. I had better stop the magic." Hastily, Pilgrim recited a spell to suspend the magic.

Look at those frightened Daoist lads! The one who was doing the flogging threw away the whip and ran to report, saying, "Master, at first I was beating the Great Tang Monk, but now I am only striking at some willow roots!" When the Great Immortal heard these words, he laughed bitterly, saying, "Pilgrim Sun! Truly a marvelous Monkey King! It was rumored that when he caused great disturbance in Heaven, even the cosmic nets that the gods set up could not hold him. I suppose there must be some truth to that! So, you escaped! But why did you have to tie up these willow trees here to impersonate you and your companions? I'm not going to spare you! I'll pursue you!" Saying this, the Great Immortal at once rose into the clouds; he peered toward the West and saw the monks fleeing, poling the load of luggage and riding the horse. The Great Immortal dropped down from the clouds, crying, "Pilgrim Sun! Where are you running to? Give me back my ginseng tree!" Hearing this, Eight Rules said, "We're finished! Our foe is here again!" "Master," said Pilgrim, "let's pack up that little word 'Kindness' for the moment. Allow us to indulge in a little violence and finish him off so that we can make our escape." When the Tang Monk heard these words, he trembled all over, hardly able to reply. Without even waiting for his answer, however, Sha Monk lifted his precious staff, Eight Rules brought out his muck-rake, and the Great Sage wielded his iron rod. They all rushed forward to surround the Great Immortal in midair and began to strike at him furiously. For this vicious battle, we have the following poem as testimony:

> Wukong knew not that Zhenyuan Immortal—
> Lord, Equal to Earth—was wondrous and strange.
> Though three weapons divine showed forth their might,
> One yak's-tail flew up with natural ease
> To parry the thrusts on the left and right,
> To block the blows struck at the front and back.
> Night passed, day came, still they could not escape!
> How long would it take them to reach the West?

The three brothers all raised their divine weapons and attacked the immortal together, but the Great Immortal had only the fly brush with which to meet his adversaries. The battle, however, had not lasted for half an hour when the Great Immortal spread open his sleeve and with one scoop, recaptured the four monks, the horse, and their luggage. Reversing the direction of his cloud, he went back to his Abbey, where he was greeted by the other immortals. The Master Immortal took a seat in the main hall and again took out the pilgrims one by one from his sleeve. The Tang Monk was bound to a short locust tree in the courtyard, while Sha Monk and Eight Rules were fastened to two other trees, one on each side. Pilgrim, however, was tightly bound but left on the ground. "I suppose," thought Pilgrim to himself, "they are going to interrogate me." After the immortals had finished tying up the captives, they were told to bring out ten large bales of cloth. "Eight Rules," said Pilgrim with a laugh, "this gentleman must have the good intention of making us some clothes! He might as well be more economical and just cut us a few monks' bells!"[4] After the little immortals had brought out the homespun cloth, the Great Immortal said, "Wrap up Tripitaka Tang, Zhu Eight Rules, and Sha Monk entirely in the cloth." The little immortals obeyed and wrapped the three of them completely. "Fine! Fine! Fine!" said Pilgrim, laughing. "We are prepared to be buried alive!" After they were wrapped, the Daoists brought out some lacquer that they had made themselves, and the Great Immortal gave the order that the wrappings of the pilgrims be completely coated with the varnish. Only their faces were left uncovered. "Sir," said Eight Rules, "I'm all right on top, but leave me a hole down below so that I can unburden myself!"

The Great Immortal next gave the order that a huge frying pan be brought out. "Eight Rules, we are lucky!" said Pilgrim, laughing. "If they are hauling out a pan, they must want to cook some rice for us to eat." "That's all right with me," said Eight Rules. "If they let us eat some rice, we'll be well-fed ghosts even if we die!" The various immortals duly brought out a huge pan, which they set up before the steps of the main hall. After giving the order that a big fire be built with plenty of dry firewood, the Great Immortal said, "Fill the pan with clear oil. When it boils, dump Pilgrim Sun into the pan and fry him! That'll be his payment for my ginseng tree!"

When Pilgrim heard this, he was secretly pleased, saying to himself, "This is exactly what I want! I haven't had a bath for some time and my skin is so dry that it's getting itchy. For good or ill, I'll enjoy a little scorching and be most grateful for it." In a moment, the oil was about to boil. The Great Sage, however, was quite cautious; fearing that this might be some form of formidable divine magic that would be difficult for him to handle once he was in the pan, he looked around quickly. In the east he saw a little terrace with a sundial on top, but to the west he discovered a stone lion. With a bound, Pilgrim rolled himself toward the west; biting the tip of his tongue, he spat a mouthful of blood on the stone lion, crying, "Change!" It changed into a figure just like himself, all tied up in a bundle. His true spirit rose into the clouds, from where he lowered his head to stare at the Daoists.

Just then, one of the little immortals gave this report, "Master, the oil is sizzling in the pan." "Pick up Pilgrim Sun and throw him in!" said the Great Immortal. Four of the divine lads went to carry him, but they could not lift him up; eight more joined them, but they had no success either. They added four more, and still they could not even budge him. "This monkey loves the earth so much that he can't be moved!" said one of the immortals. "Though he may be rather small, he's quite tough!" Finally, twenty little immortals managed to lift him up and hurl him into the pan; there was a loud splash, big drops of boiling oil flew out in every direction, and the faces of those little Daoists were covered with blisters. Then they heard the lad who was tending the fire crying, "The pan's leaking! The pan's leaking!" Hardly had he uttered these words when all the oil was gone. What they saw in the pan with its bottom punctured was a stone lion.

Enraged, the Great Immortal said, "That wretched ape! He's wicked indeed! And I've allowed him to show off right in front of my nose! So, he wanted to escape, but why did he have to ruin my pan? I suppose it's exceedingly difficult to catch the wretched ape, and even if one does catch him, trying to hold him is like trying to grasp sand or handle mercury, to catch a shadow or seize the wind! All right! All right! Let him go. Untie Tripitaka Tang and bring out a new pan. We'll fry him instead in order to avenge my ginseng tree." The various little immortals accordingly went to untie the lacquer cloth, but Pilgrim, who heard this clearly in the air, thought to himself, "Master is utterly helpless! If he arrives in the pan, the first boiling bubble will kill him and the second will burn him up; by the time the oil sizzles three or four times, he'll be a messy monk! I had better go and save him!" Dear Great Sage! He lowered the direction of his cloud and went back to the main hall. With his hands at his waist, he said, "Don't untie the lacquer wrapping to fry my master. Let me go into the pan of boiling oil instead."

"You wretched ape!" cried a somewhat startled Great Immortal. "How dare you display such tricks to wreck my stove?"[5] "If you have the misfortune of meeting me," said Pilgrim, laughing, "your stove deserves to be overturned! Why blame me? Just now, I was about to receive your kind hospitality in the form of oily soup, but I suddenly had the urge to relieve myself. If I opened up right in the pan, I was afraid that I might spoil your hot oil so that it could not be used for cooking. Now that I'm completely relieved, I feel quite good about going into the pan. Don't fry my master; fry me instead." When the Great Immortal heard these words, he laughed menacingly and ran out of the hall to catch hold of Pilgrim. We do not know what sort of things he has to say to him, or whether Pilgrim manages to escape again. Let's listen to the explanation in the next chapter.

Notes

PREFACE TO THE REVISED EDITION

1. Inspired by David Hawkes and John Minford in *The Story of the Stone*, and by Andre Lévy in *Wu cheng'en La Pérégrination vers l'Ouest*, I have emulated some of their examples of name translation.

PREFACE TO THE FIRST EDITION

1. A. Rogačev and V. Kolokolov, trans., *Wu Ch'êng-ên: Putešestvije na zapad*, 4 vols. (Moscow, 1959). See Z. Novotná's note in *Revue bibliographique de sinologie* 5 (1959): 304, for a brief descriptive review. I have not been able to obtain a copy of this edition for examination.

2. *Si yeou ki, ou le voyage en occident*, trans. Louis Avenol (Paris, 1957).

3. *The Monkey King*, ed. Zdena Novotná and trans. George Theiner (London, 1964).

4. (London, 1943). This book is currently available in a paper edition by Grove Press.

INTRODUCTION

1. See Liang Qichao 梁啟超, "Zhongguo Yindu zhi jiaotong 中國印度之交通," in *Foxue yanjiu shiba pian* 佛學研究十八篇 (1936; reprint Taipei, 1966); Ven Dongchu 釋東初, *Zhong-Yin Fojiao jiaotong shi* 中印佛教交通史 (Taipei, 1968), pp. 166-222.

2. See "Tang shangdu Zhangjing si Wukong zhuan 唐上都章敬寺悟空傳," in *Song Gaoseng zhuan* 宋高僧傳, j 3 (#722, T 50: 2061); Sylvan Lévi and Édouard Chavannes, "L'itinéraire d'Ou-k'ong," *JA*, 9th ser. 6 (1895): 341-85.

3. The dates of the monk's birth, departure for India, and death have been topics of endless controversy in modern Chinese scholarship. Just the date of birth alone has been placed in 596, 600, or 602. For the earliest date, I follow the conclusion reached by Liang Qichao, "Zhina neixueyuan jingjiaoben Xuanzang shuhou 支那內學院精校本玄奘傳書後," in *Foxue yanjiu*; Luo Xianglin 羅香林, "Jiu Tangshu Xuanzang zhuan jiangshu 舊唐書玄奘傳講疏," in *Jinian Xuanzang dashi linggu guiguo feng'an zhuanji* 記念玄奘大師靈骨歸國奉安專輯 (Taipei, 1957), pp. 66-67. Their views are followed more recently by Master Yinshun 印順 and by Ōta, 1993, p. 7. The studies by Liang, Luo, and Yinshun have been collected in two volumes of modern essays devoted to the pilgrim. See *Xuanzang dashi yanjiu* 玄奘大師研究, in *Xiandai foxue congkan* 現代佛學叢刊, ed., Zhang Mantao 張曼濤 (Taipei, 1977), vols. 8 and 16. More debates on these dates are included in volume 16. The problem with the early date is that it contradicts Xuanzang's own statement in his memorial to Emperor Taizong during the final stage of his return journey: "In the fourth month of the third year of the Zhenguan reign period [i.e., 630], braving the transgression of the articles of law, I departed for India on my own authority." The memorial, most likely genuine, is preserved in book 5, the first half of his biography compiled by his disciples Huili 慧立 and Yanzong 彥悰, generally regarded as the work's most reliable section. The biography known as *Da Tang Da Ci'ensi Sanzang*

Fashi zhuan 大唐大慈恩寺三藏法師傳, found in #2052, T 50, has a modern critical edition gathered with a huge collection of the most important historical documents concerning the pilgrim's life and work and conveniently printed in a massive single volume: see SZZSHB. The discrepancy between the traditional date and the reconstructed one is usually explained on the basis of calligraphic similarity between the graph for original/first (*yuan* 元), as in the "first year of the Zhenguan period," and the graph for three/third (*san* 三), thereby inducing mistranscription or misreading.

4. See the FSZ, *j* 1 in SZZSHB. Some English accounts of Xuanzang's life and exploits include Arthur Waley, *The Real Tripitaka and Other Pieces* (London, 1952), pp. 11-130; René Grousset, *In the Footsteps of the Buddha*, trans. J. A. Underwood (New York, 1971); Richard Bernstein, *Ultimate Journey: Retracing the Path of an Ancient Buddhist Monk Who Crossed Asia in Search of Enlightenment* (New York, 2001); Ch'en Mei-Chin, *The Eminent Chinese Monk Hsuan-Tsang: His Contribution to Buddhist Scripture Translation and to the Propagation of Buddhism in China* (Ann Arbor, 2002); and Sally Hovey Wriggins, *The Silk Road Journey with Xuanzang* (Boulder, CO, 2004).

5. Arthur F. Wright, "The Formation of Sui Ideology, 581-604," in *Chinese Thought and Institutions*, ed. John K. Fairbank (Chicago, 1957), p. 71.

6. See Huang Shengfu 黃聲孚, *Tangdai Fojiao dui zhengzhi zhi yingxiang* 唐代佛教對政治之影響 (Hong Kong, 1959); Arthur F. Wright, "Tang T'tai-tsung and Buddhism," and Stanley Weinstein, "Imperial Patronage in the Formation of T'ang Buddhism," in *Perspectives on the T'ang*, eds. Arthur F. Wright and Denis Twitchett (New Haven, 1973), pp. 239-64 and pp. 265-306; and Stanley Weinstein, *Buddhism Under the T'ang* (Cambridge, 1987), esp. part one.

7. Kenneth Ch'en, *Buddhism in China: A Historical Survey* (Princeton, 1964), pp. 117-18. For a discussion of the various interpretations of this sūtra prior to the time of Xuanzang, see Tang Yongtong 湯用彤, *Han Wei Liang-Jin Nanbei Chao Fojiao shi* 漢魏兩晉南北朝佛教史, 2 vols. (Shanghai, 1937), 1: 284-87, 2: 134-39, 189-218.

8. For the text and Xuanzang's translation of the commentary by Vasubandhu, see T 31: 97-450, #s 1592, 1593, 1595, 1596, 1597, and 1598. For a modern commentary on this śāstra, see Yinshun, *She dacheng lun jiangji* 攝大乘論講記 (1946; reprint Taipei, 1972).

9. FSZ, *j* 3. See also Ren Jiyu 任繼愈, *Han-Tang Fojiao sixiang lunji* 汉唐佛教思想论集 (Beijing, 1963), pp. 61-62.

10. This was the famous Incident of the Xuanwu Gate 玄武門事變. See CHC 3/1 (1979): 182-87, 190-93.

11. For the accounts of Xuanzang's perilous departure from Tang territory through several of the fortified passes, see my essay, "The Real Tripitaka Revisited: International Religion and National Politics," in CJ, pp. 188-203. Most scholars follow the biography and set the date of Xuanzang's departure in 629. I have, however, found Liang Qichao's argument for the earlier date to be more persuasive, and his conclusion is further supported by Luo Xianglin's additional research. See Luo (note 3), pp. 66-67.

12. The apology was tendered first in the form of a written memorial and then allegedly repeated orally to the emperor during the monk's audience with his ruler. See the accounts in FSZ, *j* 5 and 6 in SZZSHB, p. 126 and p. 132.

13. For the textual account by the *Jiu Tangshu*, *j* 191, see SZZSHB, pp. 837-38.

14. See Isobe, pp. 53-65, and further important analysis and summary in Cao

Bingjian 曹炳建, "Xin faxian de *Xiyouji* ziliao jiqi jiedu 新发现的《西游记》资料及其解读," *Nanjing Shida Xuebao* 南京师大学报 1 (January 2009): 132-37. Earlier twentieth-century recoveries of much-studied material artifacts associated with Xuanzang's pilgrimage (see XYJYJZL, unnumbered pages fronting volume) would include six Dunhuang wall murals generally dating to the Xixia 西夏 period of 1038-1227 (a Tibetan-speaking state composed of Tangut tribes in modern Gansu and Shaanxi provinces, it began as a tributary state of the Song and later claimed independent sovereignty); a depiction of the human pilgrim and his novelistic disciples on a sculptured relief (*fudiao* 浮雕) at a cave's entrance on Hangzhou's famous Feilai Mountain 飛來峰 (dating controversial, as some scholars had argued that the relief could have been influenced by the 1592 novel); a likely Yuan porcelain pillow with etchings of human pilgrim and disciples now collected in Guangdong Museum; and possibly another wall mural in the Blue Dragon Monastery 青龍寺 located at Mount Ji 稷山 in the modern province of Shanxi 山西. The most spectacular recent find seems to be the discovery in Japan of a large collection of thirty-two paintings of the pilgrimage, first introduced to the world and studied by Tanaka Isse 田仲一成 and Toda Teisuke 戶田禎佑 in 1992. The paintings were published in facsimile duplications in 2001 as a two-volume album titled *Tōsō Shukyō Zusatsu* 唐僧取經圖冊 (Painting Album on the Tang Monk Acquiring Scriptures) by Nigensha 二玄社 of Kabushiki Kaisha 株式會社 (not seen by the present translator). Several Japanese scholars have contributed essays to the album, including the XYJ specialist Isobe Akira and the Chinese art historian Iwakura Masaaki 板倉聖哲. Although Tanaka and Toda in their essays thought that the paintings originally could have been the work of the Yuan painter Wang Zhenpeng 王振朋 (1280?-1329?), they also argued that the scenes depicted reflected direct linkage to episodes in the 1592 novel. Their studies have been discussed, in turn, by Isobe Akira in two essays of his own, disputing the current form of the album as a confused collation of different segments of a story divergent from the novelistic narrative and suggesting that there could have been more than one painter. See "'Tōsō Shukyō Zusatsu' ni ukagau Saiyūki monogatari—Daitō shukkai kara Saitenjiku nyukoku e—『唐僧取経圖冊』に窺ら「西游記」物語," *Toyama Daigaku Jinbun Gakubu Kiyō* 富山大学人文学部紀要 24 (1996): 338-25 [Arabic numbers in reverse; in Japanese numbering, pp. 1-14]; and "'Tōsō Shukyō Zusatsu' ni ken miru Saiyūki monogatari—Daitōkoku shukkyo madeo chūshin ni—『唐僧取経圖冊』に見る西游記物語—大唐國出境までを中心に—," *Tōhōgaku Ronshū,* Eastern Studies Fiftieth Anniversary Volume (The Tōhō Gakkai, 1997), pp. 169-86. On pp. 325-26 of the 1996 essay, two photographs of porcelain vases featuring some of the paintings were reproduced, but these vases were identified as those made in the Jiajing era (1522-1566) of the Ming. As far as I know, the album has caught the attention of only two Chinese scholars and they, in turn, have provided a summary report supported by some astute analysis and a minor corrective reading of an "old style" poetic inscription on one of the paintings. See Cao Bingjian 曹炳建 and Huang Lin 黄霖, "Tang Seng qujing tuce tankao《唐僧取经图冊》探考" *Shanghai Shifan Daxie Xuebao* 上海师范大学学报 37/6 (November 2008): 72-82. The paintings as a whole seem to indicate a great many story fragments and episodes unknown to the extant full-length or abridged versions of the novel named *Xiyouji.*

15. See *Antecedents* in the abbreviations for full citation.

16. This Buddhist text, though one of the shortest, has long been venerated as one

of the religion's most succinct articulations of emptiness in relation to Buddha's understanding of perfect wisdom. It is also a text that had elicited more commentaries in Asia than any other sūtra. For a study of its philosophical treatments and ritual uses in India, Tibet, and the West, see Donald S. Lopez Jr., *Elaborations on Emptiness: Uses of the Heart Sūtra* (Princeton, 1996).

17. *Ouyang Wenzhong ji* 歐陽文忠集, *j* 125, 4b (SBBY): "惟藏院畫玄奘取經一壁獨在尤為絕筆."

18. The *qujingji* was examined in 1916 by Luo Zhenyu 羅振玉, who published a photographic facsimile of it in his *Jishi'an congshu* 吉石盦叢書 with his own postface 跋. The poetic tale or *shihua* was examined by both Wang Guowei 王國維 and Luo in 1911, who also published it in 1916 with postfaces by himself (dated 1916) and by Wang (dated 1915). Modern editions of the *shihua* include the 1925 edition by the Commercial Press of Shanghai, and a 1954 edition by the Zhongguo gudian wenxue chubanshe 中國古典文學出版社 of Shanghai. All future references in this translation are to the 1954 edition. More recent modern reprints of the *shihua* text can be found conveniently in XYJZLHB, pp. 39-58, and in XYJYJZL, pp. 154-73. For a recent translated version of the poetic tale, see CATCL, pp. 1181-207.

19. Hu Shiying 胡士瑩, *Huaben xiaoshuo gailun* 话本小说概论 (2 vols., Beijing, 1980), 1: 199.

20. On the importance of the Deep Sand God (*shensha shen* 深沙神), see Hu Shi (1923), pp. 364-65; for the possible earlier sources of this deity, see *Antecedents*, pp. 18-21.

21. In the dramatic version of the story, Guizimu became the mother of Red Boy 紅孩兒, and both of them were subdued by Guanyin. Dudbridge, in *Antecedents*, p. 18, note 2, points out that the name Guizimu appears only incidentally in the hundred-chapter novel, but it is nonetheless significant that its appearance occurs in the very episode of the Red Boy. See XYJ, chapter 42, p. 485.

22. See *Houcun xiansheng daquan ji* 後村先生大全集, *j* 43, 18b. The additional reference to a monkey acolyte in *j* 24, 2a, only mentions an ugly face of such a figure without any overt relation to the theme of the quest for scriptures. See *Antecedents*, pp. 45-47, for a discussion of these two poetic passages.

23. G. Ecke and P. Demiéville, *The Twin Pagodas of Zayton*, Harvard-Yenching Institute Monograph Series, 11 (Cambridge, MA, 1935), p. 35.

24. Ōta and Torii in the "Kaisetsu 解說" of the translated *Saiyūki*, 1: 432, have challenged Ecke and Demiéville's interpretation of the carving by pointing out that the figure at the upper right-hand corner should be thought of simply as a figure of Buddha and not of Xuanzang, which Monkey will become on success of bringing the scriptures. It may be added that Sun Wukong of the novel did use a sword or scimitar (cf. JW, chapters 2 and 3) prior to acquiring his famous rod. None of the scholars consulted here sees fit to discuss the significance of what seems to be a headband worn by the carved figure.

25. The story, which appears in the third volume of the fragment from the *Qingping shantang huaben* 清平山堂話本, also exists in slightly revised form in the anthology *Gujin xiaoshuo* 古今小說, *j* 20. For the possible date of this story, see Patrick Hanan, *The Chinese Short Story* (Cambridge, MA, 1973), pp. 116, 137-38.

26. So dated by Dudbridge in *Antecedents*, p. 133.

27. Ibid., p. 128.

28. Dudbridge's arguments (pp. 126-27) against any connection between the white ape legend and Sun Wukong of the full-length XYJ do not seem to me to be entirely convincing. Already conceding that the Sun Xingzhe of the twenty-four-act drama is explicitly represented as an abductor of women, Dudbridge insists that this may not be part of the "authentic" tradition because of (1) "the liberties taken with the materials to the cause of dramatic expediency," and (2) the Kōzanji version, "earliest and, in its own way, most genuine of the sources, [which] shows no trace of any such characterization in its monkey-hero." To these arguments, it may be pointed out (1) that there is no reason why the Kōzanji version, just because it is the earliest text, should contain every significant element of a *developing* tradition; (2) that the name Great Sage (Dasheng, though without the qualifying Qitian or Equal-to-Heaven), already found in the Song poetic tale (section 17), has been used frequently in popular fiction and drama such as those canvassed by Dudbridge to name a variety of animal demons or spirits; and (3) that the Sun Wukong of the novel, though less ribald in speech and manner than his dramatic counterpart, is no stranger to sexual play when it is called for (cf. XYJ, chapter 60, p. 694; chapter 81, pp. 927-28). For a more recent essay on pictorial accounts as ancient as the latter Han depicting the female abduction by an ape and the battles of animal warriors, see Wu Hung, "The Earliest Pictorial Representations of Ape Tales: An Inter-disciplinary Study of Early Chinese Narrative Art," *TP* 73, 1-3 (1987): 86-112.

29. See Hu Shi 1923, pp. 368-70; Lu Xun 魯迅, *Zhongguo xiaoshuo de lishi de bianqian* 中國小說的歷史的變遷 (Lectures originally given in 1924; reprint Hong Kong, 1957), p. 19; Huang Zhigang 黃芝崗, *Zhongguo de shuishen* 中國的水神 (Shanghai, 1934), p. 178; Wolfram Eberhard, *Die chinesische Novelle des. 17-19. Jahrhunderts*, suppl. 9 to *Artibus Asiae* (Ascona, Switzerland, 1948), p. 127; Wu Xiaoling 吳曉鈴, "*Xiyouji yu Lomoyan shu* 西游記與羅摩延書," *Wenxue yanjiu* 文學研究, 2 (1958), 168; and Ishiada Eiichirō, "The Kappa Legend," *Folklore Studies* (Peking) 9 (1950): 125-26.

30. *Antecedents*, p. 148.

31. See Hu Shi (1923), pp. 370-72. After Hu's essay, the Indian prototype of the monkey hero was advocated by various scholars. They include Chen Yinque 陳寅恪, "*Xiyouji Xuanzang dizi gushi de yanbian* 西游記玄奘弟子的演變", *LSYYCK* 2 (1930): 157-60; Zheng Zhenduo 鄭振鐸, "*Xiyouji de yanhua* 西游記的演化," first published 1933, reprinted in *Zhongguo wenxue yanjiu* 中國文學研究 (3 vols., Beijing, 1957), 1:291-92; and more recently Huang Mengwen 黃孟文, *Songdai baihua xiaoshuo yanjiu* 宋代白話小說研究 (Singapore, 1971), pp. 177-78.

32. The translated edition refers to *The Rāmāyaṇa of Vālmīki: An Epic of Ancient India*. I (Bālakāṇḍa), trans. Robert P. Goldman (Princeton, 1984); II (Ayodhyākāṇḍa), trans. Sheldon I. Pollock (Princeton, 1986); III (Āraṇyakāṇḍa), trans. Sheldon I. Pollock (Princeton, 1991); IV (Kiskindhākāṇḍa), trans. Rosalind Lefeber (Princeton, 1994); and V (Sundarakāṇḍa), trans. Robert P. Goldman (Princeton, 1994).

33. Wu, pp. 168-69.

34. *Antecedents*, p. 162.

35. See the informative study by Meir Shahar, "The Lingyin Si Monkey Disciples and the Origins of Sun Wukong," *HJAS* 52 (June 1992): 193-224.

36. "Many Shaiva family portraits include the pets. Skanda has his peacock, Ganesha his bandicoot, Shiva his bull, and Parvati her lion. For this is another way, in ad-

dition to full-life avatars and periodic theophanies, in which the Hindu gods become present in our world. Most gods and goddesses (apart from the animal, or animal from the waist or neck down, or animal from the waist or neck up forms of the deities) are accompanied by a vehicle (*vahana*), an animal that serves the deity as a mount. In contrast with the Vedic gods who rode on animals you could ride on (Surya driving his fiery chariot horses, Indra on his elephant Airavata or driving his bay horses), the sectarian Hindu gods sit cross-legged on their animals or ride sidesaddle, with the animals under them presented in profile and the gods full face. Sometimes the animal merely stands beside the deity, both of them stationary." Thus observes Wendy Doniger keenly in her recent and magisterial study, *The Hindus: An Alternative History* (New York, 2009), pp. 398-99. For more accounts of animals and religion, see pp. 233-45, 255-56, 315-16, and 436-38.

37. One has to think only of the *Fengshen yanyi* 封神演義 (Investiture of the Gods), a novel published possibly at about the same time as the full-length XYJ, to recall how many animals—including strange beasts and mythical marine creatures—serve as appointed beasts of burden for different deities of a multitudinous and largely Daoist pantheon.

38. R. H. Van Gulik, *The Gibbon in China: An Essay in Chinese Animal Lore* (Leiden, 1967), pp. 18-75.

39. According to Zhang Jinchi 张锦池, "*Xiyouji*" *kaolun* 西游记考论 (Harbin, 1997) p. 116, note 1, of the twenty-five entries on "monkeys *yuanhou*" in the TPGJ, *j* 444-46, eleven of these are colored by Daoist elements and four by Buddhist.

40. *Antecedents*, p. 159, and this point is repeated in his more recent article "The *His-yu Chi* Monkey and the Fruits of the Last Ten Years," *Hanxue yanjiu* 漢學研究, 6/1 (1988): 474-75.

41. *Antecedents*, p. 159.

42. Isobe Akira 磯部彰, "Gempon *Saiyūki* ni okeru Son gyōsha no keisei—Ko gyōsha kara Son gyōsha e'『元本西游記』ねおけゐ孫行者の形成—猴行者から孫行者へ," *Shūkan tōyō gaku* 集刊東洋學 38 (1977): 103-27, incorporated as chapter 7, "Son Gokū zō no keisei to sono hatten 孫悟空像の形成とその發展," in Isobe, pp. 215-47. The story cited by Dudbridge from the *Yijianzhi* in *j* 6 (4 vols., Beijing, 1981), 1: 47 is titled "Zongyan's Disposition of the Monkey Monster 宗演去猴妖," but the name changes to "The Record of the Monkey-King God of Fuzhou 福州猴王神記" in such other Song story collections as the *Songren baijia xiaoshuo* 宋人百家小說 and the *Zhandeng conghua* 剪燈叢話. As a further linkage to the XYJ evolving tradition, Isobe (p. 247) cites another story found in the *Fuzhou County Gazette* 福州縣志, *j* 10, that refers to a Monkey King receiving cultic worship in the Nengren Temple 能仁寺 as a "Guardian of the Law." The creature's considerable magic powers nonetheless eventually cause the chief abbot to exorcise its efficacy and epiphany by inscribing (most likely a passage of Buddhist scripture) on the back of its image.

43. Translations of the name of this Daoist order include: "Completely Sublimated" (Arthur Waley), "Perfect Realization" (Holmes Welch), "Complete Truth" (Kristofer Schipper), "Complete Perfection" (Nathan Sivin), "Complete Reality" (Thomas Cleary), "Integrating Perfection" (Russell Kirkland, drawing on Igor de Rachewiltz's translation of *quan*), and "Completion of Authenticity" (Vincent Goossaert and Paul Katz). No one name is sufficient to match the polysemy conveyed in the evolving writings by the or-

der's patriarchs and disciples, because the term implies at once conditions and processes—a state of primal authenticity and a condition of restored perfection attained through ascesis formulated through deliberate syncretism. Schipper's decision in TC 2: 1127ff. to render it as "Complete Truth" might have stemmed in part from the tradition's self-understanding as a reform movement aimed at purifying the different doctrines flourishing in other orders or sects of Daoism. A stele text in the Yuan (erected by Li Ding 李鼎 in 1263), made this claim: "At the beginning of the Jin's Dading reign period (1161-90), the Patriarch [Wang] Chongyang appeared, using the knowledge of the Way, Virtue, Nature, and Life/Destiny for proclamation as Complete Truth, to purge the spreading defects of a hundred lineages and continue the ultimate knowledge of millennia 金大定初，重陽祖師出焉，以道德性命之學唱為全真，洗百家之流弊，紹千載之絕學." See the "Da Yuan chongxiu gu louguan Zongshenggong ji" bei《大元重修古樓觀宗聖宮記》碑 cited in Guo Wu 郭武, Quanzhen Daozu Wang Chongyan zhuan 全真道祖王重陽傳 (Hong Kong, 2001), p. 78. The irony is that the whole thrust of the order's doctrinal development from Song-Yuan times to subsequent centuries is built on a self-conscious effort to integrate and harmonize the Three Religions (of Confucianism, Daoism, and Buddhism). See Schipper, TC 2: 1127ff.

44. See "Xiuzhen shishu Wuzhenpian 修真十書悟真篇," j 30 (the juan or chapter is entitled "Songs and Odes to the Lineage of Chan 禪宗歌頌," in DZ 263, 4: 746. This ode apparently enjoyed such popularity that it has been used frequently as an "independent" composition to express the notion of Buddhist and Daoist enlightenment attained through one's own mind and self-knowledge. The popularity extends well into the mid-Qing period and beyond. For its printing as an interlinear commentary of the Heart Sūtra, see Zhu Di 朱棣, annot., Jin'gang boruo Boluomi jing jizhu 金剛般若波羅蜜經集注 (Shanghai, 1984), pp. 172-73. My thanks are due Professor Qiancheng Li for identifying this last particular use of the ode. The first line of Zhang's ode, in fact, uses verbatim a sentence that has filled the pages of many volumes of Buddhist scriptures from different lineages, and it is one particularly favored by Chan Buddhism. The sentence is the celebrated assertion—"jixin jifo 即心即佛," and the rhetoric's punning repetition may be translated as "This Mind That's Buddha"—that appears repeatedly in such texts as the Jingde chuandeng lu 景德傳燈錄, #2076, T 51: 0253b and 0457a; the Fayan Chanshi yulu 法演禪師語錄, #1905, T 47: 0651a; and especially in the pages of Lizu dashi fabao tanjing 六祖大師法寶壇經, #2008, T 48: 0355a, where the assertion is further glossed by the Patriarch Huineng thus: "Where no forethought is begotten is the mind; where afterthought is not extinguished is Buddha 前念不生即心, 後念不滅即佛." This doctrine of the complete reciprocity of Mind and Buddha, however, is not universally affirmed in Chinese Buddhism. For an astute analysis of its historical development and contestation in Chan Buddhism, see Ge Zhaoguang 葛兆光, Zhongguo chan sixiangshi—cong 6 shiji dao 9 shiji 中國禪思想史—从6世纪到9世纪 (Beijing, 1995), pp. 315-32. The interesting phenomenon in the DZ—the Daoist Zhang Boduan composing what he called doctrinal lyrics to celebrate the Chan lineage—should indicate the explicit syncretism of the Quanzhen Order already in the eleventh century.

45. Antecedents, p. 162.

46. Ji Xianlin, Luomoyan'na chutan 罗摩衍那初探 (7 vols., Beijing, 1979), p. 136. See also his study, "The Rāmāyaṇa in China《罗摩衍那》在中国," in his Fojiao yu Zhong-

Yin wenhua jiaoliu shi 佛教与中印文化交流史 (Nanchang, Jiangxi, 1990), pp. 78-118, which is a much lengthier essay supporting and complementing Victor Mair's essay cited in note 47. Another important study charting the possible Tibetan transmission of the Indian story to China is found in Liu Ts'un-yan [Cunren] 柳存仁, "Zangben *Luomoyan'na* benshi sijian 藏本羅摩衍那本事私箋," in *Daojia yu Daoshu, Hefengtang wenji xubian* 道家與道術,和風堂文集續編 (Shanghai, 1999), pp. 154-93. For Ji's translation of the epic, see *Luomoyan'na* 羅摩衍那 (Beijing, 1980-84). Other previous selective translations of the Indian epic include "*Luomoyan'na*" yu "*Mahapalada*" 罗摩衍那 与玛哈帕腊达, trans. Sun Yong 孙用译 (Beijing, 1962), and the pioneering version by Mi Wenkai 糜文開, *Gu Yindu liangda shishi* 古印度兩大史詩 (Hong Kong, 1951; reprint Taipei, 1967).

47. Victor Mair, "Suen Wu-kung = Hanumat? The Progress of a Scholarly Debate," in *Proceedings on the Second International Conference on Sinology, Academia Sinica* (Taipei, June 1989): 659-752.

48. On the varying means of disseminating the Indian epic and the consequential modifications of the plot and form of "the Rāma story," see A. K. Ramanujan, "Three Hundred Rāmāyaṇas: Five Examples and Three Thoughts on Translation," originally presented to the Conference on Comparison of Civilization (Pittsburgh, 1987); reprint in Vinay Dharwadker, ed., *The Collected Essays of A. K. Ramanujan* (New Delhi, 1999), pp. 131-60; and Philip Lutgendorf, *Hanuman's Tale: The Messages of a Divine Monkey* (Oxford, 2007), esp. chapter 4. For further studies of Chinese and Indian literary relations, see the informative entries in *Zhong-Yin wenxue guanxi yuanliu* 中印文学关系源流, ed. Yu Longyu 郁龙余 (Changsha, Hunan, 1986).

49. Mair, 675.

50. Ibid., 679.

51. The story's title, as Mi Wenkai pointed out in the preface to his selective translation of the Indian epics, may have been a mistranslation, confusing Daśaratha ("Ten Chariots," the real name of Rāma's father) with Daśarata ("Ten Luxuries or Excesses"). The point is repeated in Mair.

52. Mair, 682-83.

53. Ramnath Subbaraman, "Beyond the Question of the Monkey Imposter: Indian Influence on the Chinese Novel, *The Journey to the West*," *Sino-Platonic Papers* 114 (March 2002): 26. For discussion of the parallels between R and the novel's Scarlet-Purple Kingdom episode, see pp. 18-25; XYJTY, 1: 194-204; Mair, 724-25.

54. Surviving remnants of encyclopedia have been published in fascimile by Beijing's Zhonghua shuju (1960). For the Chinese text of the particular section under discussion, see Zheng Chenduo, 1: 270-72.

55. *Antecedents*, p. 63; see also pp. 179-88 for the Chinese text and translation.

56. See ibid, pp. 73-74 for a detailed listing. The Korean reader repeatedly mentions a text named "Tripitaka Tang's Record of the Journey to the West, *Tang Sanzang Xiyouji* 唐三藏西游記," which is described, moreover, as a first-class "plain or commentarial narrative, *pinghua* 平話." See XYJYJZL, pp. 248-54. Most contemporary Chinese scholars now assume that a lost text that may well be characterized as a *Xiyouji pinghua* was in wide circulation in early Ming, the contents of which closely resemble parts of the twenty-four act drama and the full-length novel of 1592.

57. *Antecedents*, pp. 73-74.

58. Originally in *Shibun* 斯文 9, 1-10, 3. I use here the text included in the *Yuanquxuan waibian* 元曲選外編, ed. Sui Shusen 隋樹森 (3 vols., Beijing, 1959), 2: 633-94.

59. See Sun Kaidi 孫楷第, "Wu Cheng'en yu zaju *Xiyouji* 吳承恩與雜劇西游記," first published 1939, reprinted in *Cangzhouji* 滄州集 (2 vols., Beijing, 1965), 2: 366-98; Yan Dunyi 嚴敦易, "*Xiyouji* he gudian xiqu di guanxi 西游記和古典戲曲的關係," first published 1954, reprinted in LWJ, pp. 142-52; and *Antecedents*, pp. 76-80.

60. See "*Xiyouji* zubenkao de zai shangque 西游記祖本考的再商榷," *Xinya xuebao* 新亞學報 6 (1964): 4977-518; and "The Hundred-Chapter *Hsi-yu chi* and its Early Versions," *Asia Major*, n.s. 14 (1969): 141-91, hereafter cited as "Early Versions." Important studies more recently include XTYTY, 1: 4-164; Plaks, pp. 189-202; Isobe, pp. 145-214, 273-338; Ōta, passim; Liu Ts'un-yan, "Lun Ming-Qing Zhongguo tongsu xiaoshuo zhi banben 論明清中國通俗小說之版本," and "*Siyouji* de Ming keben 四游記的明刻本," in HFTWJ, 2: 1095-166, 3: 1260-318; and Li Shiren 李时人, *Xiyouji kaolun* 西游记考论 (Hangzhou, Zhejiang, 1991), pp. 123-86.

61. "Early Versions," 155-57; XYJTY 1: 117-18.

62. See XYJTY 1:51; Li Shiren, pp. 124-28.

63. "Early Versions," p. 151.

64. The printing house Shidetang was located in Nanjing, a crucial city of flourishing printing houses and book trade that complemented the commercial and literary activities found in the northern Fujian area of Jianyang 建陽. Shidetang was an established enterprise well known for its various publications of literati drama, full-length prose fictions, and even scripts of civil service examinations. For its activities and a few other noted Jiangnan printing houses, see *Xiaoshuo shufanglu* 小说书坊录, eds. Wang Qingyuan 王清原 et al. (Beijing, 2002) p. 15; Robert Hegel, *Reading Illustrated Fiction in Late Imperial China* (Stanford, 1998), chapter 3, esp. pp. 140-52; Lucille Chia, *Printing for Profit: The Commercial Publishers of Jianyang, Fujian (11th-17th Centuries)* (Cambridge, MA, 2002), chapter 5, esp. pp. 171-74; and also "Of three Mountains Street: The Commercial Publishers of Ming Nanjing," in *Printing and Book Culture in Later Imperial China*, ed. Cynthia J. Brokaw and Kai-wing Chow (Berkeley, CA, 2005), pp. 107-51; Zhang Xiumin 張秀民, *Zhongguo yinshua shi* 中国印刷史 (Shanghai, 1989), pp. 340-53; and Miao Yonghe 缪咏禾, *Mingdai chuban shigao* 明代出版史稿 (Nanjing, 2000), pp. 72-74, where it is noted that there might have been two publishing houses by the same name of Shidetang run by household or lineage related family members with the name of Tang 唐. As Dudbridge has detailed for us, the Shidetang stemma actually consists of three distinct versions thus far known to us: (1) the "Huayang" editions because of the text's repeated reference to the Huayang Grotto-Heaven Master "checking" the text, and all bearing the name of *Xinke chuxiang guanban dazi Xiyouji* 新刻出像官板大字西游記 [A newly engraved, illustrated *Journey to the West* set with the large characters of official blocks]; (2) the edition titled *Dingqie jingben quanxiang Tangseng qujing Xiyouji* 鼎鍥京本全像唐僧取經西游記 [A newly engraved, capital edition of the *Tang Monk's Journey to the West to Fetch Scriptures*, completely illustrated], with title-page identification of Yang Minzhai 陽閩齋 as printer and publisher, and the Qingbaitang 清白堂 as the publishing house, and its earliest date may be set at 1603; and (3), the *Erke guanban Tang Sanzang Xiyouji* 二刻官版唐三藏西游記 [A second engraving or printing of the official edition of *Tripitaka Tang's Journey to the West*], with publisher named as Zhu Jiyuan 朱繼源 and dating possibly to 1631. Extant versions of the 1592 edition include

one preserved in the National Beijing Library's rare book department (transferred to Taiwan's National Palace Museum after 1949), one in the collection of Japan's Tenri Library, and one in microfilm at the Library of Congress.

65. "Early Versions," p. 184. Belonging to the same textual stemma of this edition was another group of extant editions appearing during the subsequent three and a half decades, all bearing the title of *Li Zhuowu xiansheng piping Xiyouji* 李卓吾先生批評 西游記, many copies of which have been preserved in either institutional or personal collections scattered in Japan, Taiwan, and the British Museum, with two microfilmed versions deposited at the libraries of Yale University and the University of Chicago. The language of this edition follows fairly closely that of the Shidetang's narrative, but it lacks both the important preface by Chen Yuanzhi which we shall discuss later and, like the 1592 version, the "Chen Guangrui story" as well. Recent critical editions of the work include Wu Cheng'en, *Xiyouji jiaozhu* 西游記校注, ed. Xu Shaozhi 徐少知, and annotated by Zhou Zhongming 周中明 and Zhu Tong 朱彤 (Taipei, 1996); and *Li Zhuowu xiansheng piping Xiyouji* 李卓吾先生批評西游記, eds. Chen Hong 陈宏 and Yang Bo 杨 波 (2 vols., Changsha, Hunan, 2006).

66. Plaks, p. 190.

67. See Jerome J. McGann, *The Textual Condition* (Princeton, 1991); McGann, ed., *Textual Criticism and Literary Interpretation* (Chicago, 1985); Anne E. McLaren, "Ming Audiences and Vernacular Hermeneutics: The Uses of *The Romance of the Three Kingdoms*," *TP* 81 (1995): 51-80; McLaren, "Constructing New Reading Publics in Late Ming China," in Brokaw and Chow, eds., *Printing and Book Culture*, pp. 152-83; and Robert Hegel, *Reading Illustrated Fiction*, pp. 290-326.

68. See XYJ, pp. 1-7. The six other editions utilized by the Beijing publisher include:

Xinjuan chuxiang guben Xiyou Zhengdaoshu 新鐫出像古本西游證道書, 100 chapters but slightly abridged. Dated to 1662, this edition has two distinguishing features: it contains the controversial "chapter 9 on the Chen Guangrui story," and it has a preface attributed to Yu Ji 虞集 (1272-1348), a major scholar of the Southern Song. Named editors are identified as Huang Taihong and Wang Xiangxu.

Xiyou zhenquan 西游真詮, ed. Chen Shibin 陳士斌 (styled Wuyizi 悟一子), with a preface dated to 1694 and another preface dated to 1696 by the noted Qing poet, essayist, and dramatist You Tong 尤侗 (1618-1704); 100 chapters but slightly abridged; contains "the Chen Guangrui story."

Xinshuo Xiyouji 新說西游記, ed. Zhang Shushen 張書紳, with two extant unabridged hundred-chapter versions dated similarly to 1749. It has one-hundred chapters based on the Shidetang text, with comprehensive commentary noted for its advocacy of Neo-Confucianism.

Xiyou yuanzhi 西游原旨, ed. Liu Yiming 劉一明 (1734-1821). His original preface is dated to 1798, but the extant earliest printed edition bears the date of 1810. It has one-hundred chapters but is somewhat abridged. Liu was also a fairly well-known Daoist and a practicing physiological alchemist. Commentary indicates direct descent from the tradition of Quanzhen doctrines, further enhanced by various tenets advanced by the Three-Religions-in-One movement. See ET 1: 690-91. For this edition of the XYJ, Liu wrote a prefatorial "Dufa 讀法, A Guide to Reading," which has been translated into

English by Anthony C. Yu, with further annotations by David Rolston. See *How to Read the Chinese Novel*, ed. David L. Rolston (Princeton, 1990), pp. 295-315.

Tongyi Xiyou zhengzhi 通易西游正旨, one-hundred chapters with anonymous preface and postface, 1839.

Xiyouji pingzhu 西游記評注, its commentator identified as Hanjingzi 含晶子, with preface dated to 1891. It has one-hundred chapters but likely it is a reduced version of the *Xiyou yuanzhi*. For a detailed listing of the premodern editions of XYJ along with modern Chinese printed versions (commercial and academic) and selected foreign translations (up to the mid-1970s), see XYJTY 1:41-71.

69. See my "Narrative Structure and the Problem of Chapter Nine in the *Xiyouji*," *JAS* 34 (1975): 295-311, reprinted in CJ, pp. 108-28.

70. Guanglu is likely not a real name of Mr. Tang but the professional title or rank of office. According to Professor Cao Bingjian, "Xin faxian de *Xiyouji* ziliao . . . ," p. 135, citing, in turn, the preface in Huang Yongnian 黃永年 and Huang Zhouxing 黃周星, *Huang Zhouxing Dingben "Xiyouji"* 黃周星定本《西游記》(Beijing, 1998), it may well have referred to the office of Chief Minister (*qing* 卿) belonging to the Court of Imperial Entertainments, Guanglu si 光祿寺, "in charge of catering for the imperial household, court officials, and imperial banquets honoring foreign envoys and other dignitaries." See Hucker, # 3348, p. 288. If this is the case, Tang Guanglu might have been a nomenclature similar to something like "Secretary Clinton."

71. See *Wu Cheng'en shiwenji* 吳承恩詩文集, ed. Liu Xiuye 劉修業 (Beijing, 1958); and Liu Ts'un-yan, "Wu Ch'êng-ên: His Life and Career," TP 53, reprinted in Liu Ts'un-yan, *Selected Papers from the Hall of Harmonious Wind* (Leiden, 1976), pp. 259-355.

72. See *Tianqi Huai'an Fuzhi* 天啟淮安府志, j 19, 3b.

73. Miao Yonghe, *Mingdai*, pp. 23-25.

74. Excerpts of these texts are readily available in XYJYJZL, p. 9; XYJZLHB, pp. 180-81.

75. See *Three Kingdoms: A Historical Novel*, attr. Luo Guanzhong; trans. Moss Roberts (Berkeley, CA, 1991), pp. 937-38, 946-47.

76. Quoted in Hu Shi (1923), p. 378. Reprints of the entire relevant passage, including some poems by Wu Cheng'en, are readily available in WCESWJ, pp. 196-99; XYJYJZL, pp. 8-9; XYJZLHB, pp. 168-71.

77. See Zhang Peiheng 章培恒, "Baihuiben *Xiyouji* shifou Wu Cheng'en suozuo 百回本《西游記》是否吳承恩所作?" *Shehui kexue zhanxian* 社会科学战线 4 (1983): 295-305.

78. Tanaka Iwao 田中巖, "*Saiyuki no sakusha* 西游記の作者," *Shibun* 斯文, n.s. 8 (1953): 37.

79. See ibid., 33-34, for some samples of Li's annotations.

80. Liu Ts'un-yan, "Life and Career," pp. 17-20.

81. See C. K. Hsiao, "An Iconoclast of the Sixteenth Century," *Tien Hsia Monthly* 6 (1938): 317-41; Guo Shaoyu 郭紹虞, *Zhongguo wenxue pipingshi* 中國文學批評史 (2 vols., Shanghai, 1947), 2: 242-46; Wu Ze 吳澤, *Rujiao pantu Li Zhuowu* 儒教叛徒李卓吾 (Shanghai, 1949), pp. 59-228; Rong Zhaozu 容肇祖, *Li Zhuowu pingzhuan* 李卓吾評傳 (Shanghai, 1936), pp. 69-106; Jean-François Billeter, *Li Zhi, philosophe maudit (1527-1602): contribution à une sociologie du mandarinat chinois de la fin des Ming* (Genève, 1979); Chen Qinghui 陳清輝, *Li Zhuowu shengping ji qi sixiang yanjiu* 李卓吾生

平及其思想研究 (Taipei, 1993); Xu Sumin 许苏民, *Li Zhi de zhen yu qi* 李贽的真与奇 (Nanjing, 1998); Xu Jianping 许建平, *Li Zhuowu zhuan* 李卓吾传 (Beijing, 2004); Xu Jianping, *Li Zhi sixiang yanbianshi* 李贽思想演变史 (Beijing, 2005); Fu Xiaofan 傅小凡, *Li Zhi zhexue sixiang yanjiu* 李贽哲学思想研究 (Fuzhou, Fujian, 2007); and Fu Qiutao 傅秋涛, *Li Zhuowu zhuan* 李卓吾传 (Changsha, Hunan, 2007).

82. Hu Shi's translation in the Preface to *Monkey*, p. 1, text slightly emended; for the Chinese text, see WCESWJ, p. 62.

83. Edward L. Schafer, "*Yu-yang tsa-tsu* 酉陽雜俎," in IC, pp. 940-41.

84. This group of persons, enigmatically named (the word *gong* 公 is translated as "sire" in Robert Campany's book listed in the abbreviations section), has motivated polemical exchanges among contemporary XYJ critics. Li An'gang 李安纲, "Zailun Wu Cheng'en bushi Xiyouji de zuozhe 再论吴承恩不是西游记的作者," *Tangdu xuekan* 唐都学刊, 4 (2001): 81-82, has argued from a reference to the TPGJ's entry on the Prince Liu An 劉安 to assert that these were eight immortals or transcendents 神仙 coming to visit Liu. The prince, grandson of the founder of the Han dynasty, Liu Bang, was appointed King of Huainan in 164 BCE and died in 122 BCE. He was credited with a number of esoteric writings, the most well-known of which was the *Inner Book* 內書 that eventually became the *Huainanzi* 淮南子, preserved in DZ 1176. For the book's formation and textual history, see Harold D. Roth, *The Textual History of the 'Huai-nan Tzu'* (Ann Arbor, 1992). Cai Tieying 蔡铁鹰, in "*Xiyouji"de dansheng*《西游记》的诞生 (Beijing, 2007), pp. 238-39, on the other hand, has countered with citations from the *Shiji* and other post-Han sources to maintain that the Eight Squires were merely courtiers of King Huainan's assumed "secular" court. Neither critic bothered to check other available sources, for the early Daoist alchemist Ge Hong 葛洪 (283-343) had already mentioned these persons as "eight transcendent squires 仙人八公." See the *Baopuzi*, Inner 11: 9b, where it is written: "Previously eight transcendent squires each had ingested one item [this chapter of the book is about ingesting organic and inorganic matter to attain longevity] so as to attain the condition of land transcendent. Several hundred years thereafter, each of them united with the divine elixir's golden liquid and thereby ascended to the realm of the Grand Purity 昔仙人八公各服一物以得陸仙, 各數百年, 乃合神丹金液而升太清耳." In his other famous treatise, *Shenxianzhuan*, Ge had more to say about the Eight Squires and their visitation of Prince Liu. For the Chinese text of the story, see "Huainan Wang 淮南王" in the *Liexianzhuan Shenxianzhuan* 列仙传神仙传, trans. and anno. Teng Xiuzhan 滕修展 et al. (Tianjin, 1996), pp. 285-88. For the reconstructed text in English, see the translation and discussion in Campany, pp. 234-38.

85. The Chinese clause is characteristically ambiguous, because it can mean "an older edition" (so construed by some Chinese scholars because the phrase *jiu you xu* could have been an abbreviated form of *jiuben you xu*) or "previously, there was a preface [which is now absent from the present printing]." The official title of the 1592 edition, however, displays prominently the description of it being "newly printed or engraved, *xinke*." Whether this conventional tag simply represents a habitual mode of rhetoric used for advertising, for issuing "the assurance that the reader had not seen *this particular* edition previously," according to the perceptive generalization of Robert Hegel's *Reading Illustrated Fiction*, p. 304, on books published in the Wanli era, is worth pondering. But that possibility is only one among other options, which may include,

in fact, the following: that there was an older edition of XYJ, whether in printed or manuscript form; that it was printed at Shidetang also or by another publishing house called Rongshoutang 榮壽堂 (the name of which was written onto the margins of several *juan*-segment divisions of the 1592 edition); and that this notation indicates that the two publishing houses shared printing blocks for the production of one or another edition of the 1592 text. See the detailed and authoritative discussion in Cao Bingjian 曹炳建 , "*Xiyouji* Shidetang ben yanjiu erti《西游记》世德堂本研究二题," *Dongnan Daxue Xuebao* 东南大学学报, 11/2 (March 2009): 112-16.

86. 1592, 1: 2-5. As a foundational term in Buddhism, *zang* relates to the religion's perennial grappling with the philosophical paradox of how fundamental nature or reality can be both real and unreal, substantial and insubstantial, distinct and nondistinct in its attributes by being used to translate the Sanskrit term, *Garbhadhātu* 胎藏界. According to Soothill, p. 312a-b, it is "the womb treasury, the universal source from which all things are produced; the matrix; the embryo; likened to a womb in which all of a child is conceived—its body, mind, etc. It is container and content; it covers and nourishes, and is the source of all supply. It represents the 理性 fundamental nature, both material elements and pure bodhi, or wisdom in essence or purity." As Andrew Rawlinson has observed, however, because *garbha* . . . is translated by *ts'ang* [*sic, zang*], "a certain vacuum was created in the Chinese vocabulary which the terms *fo-hsing* [*foxing* 佛性] and *fo-hsin* [*foxin*] 佛心 (=*buddha-citta*) neatly filled." See "the Ambiguity of the Buddha-nature Concept in India and China," in *Early Ch'an in China and Tibet*, eds. Whalen Lai and Lewis R. Lancaster (Berkeley, 1983), p. 260. The tangled web of meaning woven by multiple Sanskrit terms representing the nature of Buddha in Mahāyāna Buddhism extends outward when some of the Chinese terms used in translation are exploited by other traditions like Neo-Confucianism and Quanzhen Daoism. As we shall see, the terms *xin* and *xing* are crucial for reading a novel like XYJ.

87. *Xiyou zhengdao shu* 西游證道書, fasc. reprint of 1662 edition in *Guben xiaoshuo jicheng* 古本小說集成, 437-440 (4 vols., Shanghai, 1990), 1: 2-6.

88. See "Quanzhen jiao he xiaoshuo Xiyouji 全真教和小說西游記," in HFTWJ, 3: 1331-33. The importance of Feng for the full-length novel is to be found in the fact that two of his compositions, a lyric to the tune of "Su Wu in Slow Pace or *Suwu man* 蘇武慢" and a ritual text named "Script for Ascending the Hall or *Shengtang wen* 升堂文" are both structured into the novel—the lyric for chapter 8 and the prose text for chapter 12. The lyric is preserved in *Minghe yuyin*, DZ, 744, *j* 2, 2; the ritual text in *j* 9, 13-14.

89. For the Chinese text of this *Xiyouji*, see *Qiu Chuji ji* 邱处机集, ed. Zhao Weidong 赵卫东 (Jinan, 2005), pp. 201-39; DZ 34: 480-501. For an English translation, see Arthur Waley, *Travels of an Alchemist* (London, 1931). More recent studies include Igor de Rachewiltz and Terence Russel, "Ch'iu Ch'u-chi (1148-1227)," *Papers on Far Eastern History* 29 (1984): 1-27; Tao-chung Yao, "Ch'iu Ch'u-chi and Chinggis Khan," *HJAS* 46 (1986): 201-19; Florian C. Reiter, "Ch'iu Chu-chi, ein Alchemist im China des frühen 13. Jahrhunderts. Neue Gesichtspunkte für eine historische Bewertung," *Zeitschrift der Deutschen Morgenländischen Gesellschaft* 139 (1989): 184-207; and Vincent Goossaert, "Qiu Chuji," in ET 2: 808-11, with additional bibliography.

90. Plaks, p. 197, note 33. The poetic lines cited come from *Qiuzu quanshu jieji* 邱祖全書節輯, p. 256, collected in the *Daozang jinghua* 道藏精華, 5/2 (Taipei, 1960).

91. See Chen Zhibin 陳志濱, "Xiyouji de zuozhe shi Wu Cheng'en mo 西游記的作

者是吳承恩麼?" in *Xiyouji shiyi* 西游記釋義, annotated by Chen Dunfu 陳敦甫 (Taipei, 1976). This edition of the novel is an official publication printed by the Quanzhen Publishing House in Taiwan. Chen Dunfu is a well-known leader of Taiwan's Quanzhen Order.

92. I cite only some representative pieces from academic journals since the publication of Plaks's book in 1987. See Li Angang 李安綱, "*Xingming guizh shi Xiyouji de wenhua yuanxing* 《性命主旨》是《西游記》的文化原形," *Shanxi Daxue Xuebao* 山西大學學報, 4 (1996): 27-35 (Li has published many other essays on the novel and a completely new edition thereof, boldly identifying the author as Anonymous 无名氏 and annotating the fiction meticulously with the conceptualities and terms of the noncanonical Daoist text mentioned in this essay's title—see Li in the list of abbreviations); Huang Lin 黃霖, "*Guanyu Xiyouji de zuozhe he zhuyao jingshen* 关于《西游記》的作者和主要精神," *Fudan Xuebao* 复旦学报, 2 (1998): 78-83; Liao Xiangdong 廖向东, "*Shi dafu wenhua jingshen de zhigui—Xiyouji 'sanjiao heyi' xinlun* 士大夫文化精神的指归—《西游记》「三教合一」新論," *Zhejiang Shifan Daxue Xuebao* 浙江师范大学学报, 27/2 (2002): 31-36; Hu Yicheng 胡义成, "*Xiyouji shouyao zuozhe shi Yuan-Ming liangdai Quanzhen jiaotu* 《西游记》首要作者是元明两代全真教徒," *Yuncheng Gaodeng Zhuanke Xuexiao Xuebao* 运城高等专科学校学报, 20/2 (April 2002): 5-14; Cao Bingjian 曹炳建, "*Huimou Xiyouji zuozhe yanjiu ji wojian* 回眸《西游记》作者研究及我见," *Liaoning Shifan Daxue Xuebao* 辽宁师范大学学报, 25/5 (September 2002): 82-86; Guo Jian 郭健, "*Xiyouji yu 'jindan dadao'* 《西游记》与 '金丹大道'," *Huazhong Keji Daxue Xuebao* 华中科技大学学报, 6 (2002): 81-83; Chen Hong, Chen Hong 陈洪, 陈宏, "*Lun Xiyouji yu Quanzhenjiao zhi yuan* 论《西游记》与全真教之缘," *Wenxue yichan* 文学遗产, 6 (2003); Huang Yi 黄毅, Xu Jianping 许建平 "*Bainian Xiyouji zuozhe yanjiu de huigu yu fanxing* 百年《西游记》作者研究的回顾与反省," *Yunnan Shehui Kexue* 云南社会科学, 2 (2004): 114-20; Wang Qizhou 王齐洲, "*Lun Mingren dui Xiyouji de renshi* 论明人对《西游记》的认识," *Shehui Kexue Yanjiu* 社会科学研究, 1 (2004): 135-39; and Hu Xiaowei 胡小伟, "*Cong Zhiyuan bianwei lu dao Xiyouji* 从《至元辩伪录》到《西游记》," *Henan Daxue Xuebao* 河南大学学报, 44/1 (January 2004): 68-73.

93. Liu, "Quanzhenjiao," in HFTWJ 3: 1376, 1381-82. Liu's long essay (pp. 1319-91) is indispensable reading on the subject for any serious student.

94. Plaks's point is made on p. 199, but again, the serious student should read all of the chapter in Plaks, pp. 183-276.

95. Ren Bantang 任半塘, *Tangxinong* 唐戲弄 (2 vols., Beijing, 1958), 2: 876-88.

96. Maurice Winternitz, *A History of Indian Literature*, trans. S. Ktkar and H. Kohn (2 vols., Calcutta, 1933), 2: 91.

97. Winternitz, ibid., p. 115, cites the *Saddharma-puṇḍarīka sūtra* to point out that "Buddhha teaches by means of sūtras, gāthās, legends, and jātakas."

98. See the "*Miaofalianhua jing* jiangwen 妙法蓮華經講文," and the "*Weimojie jing* jiangwen 維摩詰經講文," in *Dunhuang bianwenji* 敦煌變文集, ed. Wang Zhongmin 王重民 et al. (2 vols., Beijing, 1957), 2: 501-645. Older critical studies of the genre relative to Chinese literature have been conveniently collected in *Dunhuang bianwen lunwen lu* 敦煌變文論文錄, eds. Zhou Shaoliang 周紹良 and Bai Huawen 白化文 (2 vols., Shanghai, 1982). For more recent Western scholarship, see Victor Mair, *T'ang Transformation Texts: A Study of the Buddhist Contribution to the Rise of Vernacular Fiction and Drama in China* (Cambridge, MA, 1989); and also "The Contribution of T'ang and Five Dynasties

Transformation Texts (pien-wen) to Later Chinese Popular Literature," *Sino-Platonic Papers* 12 (1989), pp. 1-71.

99. Hu Shi, *Baihua wenxue shi* 白話文學史 (Shanghai, 1928; reprint Taipei, 1957), pp. 204-10.

100. See James I. Crump, "The Conventions and Craft of Yuan Drama," *JAOS* 91 (1971): 14-24; "The Elements of Yuan Opera," *JAS* 17 (1958): 425-26; Cyril Birch, "Some Formal Characteristics of the *hua-pen* Story," *BSOAS* 17 (1955): 348, 357; Jaroslav Průšek, "The Creative Methods of Chinese Medieval Story-Tellers," in *Chinese History and Literature* (Dordrecht, Holland, 1970), pp. 367-68; Patrick Hanan, "The Early Chinese Short Story: A Critical Theory in Outline," *HJAS* 27 (1969): 174; Hanan, "Sources of the *Chin P'ing Mei*," *Asia Major*, n.s. 10 (1963): 28; Hanan, "The *Yün-men Chuan*: From Chantefable to Short Story," *BSOAS* 36 (1973): 302-03; and Hu Shiying, *Huaben xiaoshuo gailun*, 1, pp. 27-37, and especially chapters 3 and 4.

101. See *The Plum in the Golden Vase or, Chin P'ing Mei*, trans. David Tod Roy (Princeton, 1993), 1: xlv.

102. Apart from full or partial quotations from known sources that we shall discuss in part IV of this introduction and record in the chapters' annotations, there are thirty-two poems in XYJ which may also be found, with minor variations, in the *Fengshen yanyi* 封神演義 (Investiture of the Gods), a work whose date and authorship are by no means firmly established, though it is generally regarded as approximately of the same period as the 1592 XYJ. The following table will make clear the location of these poems in the two narratives.

Poem	XYJ	Fengshen yanyi (All references are to the 1960 edition, published in Hong Kong by Zhonghua shuju)
1.	Chapter 1, p. 2	Chapter 43, p. 401
2.	Chapter 1, p. 8	Chapter 38, pp. 348-49
3.	Chapter 1, p. 9	Chapter 37, p. 335
5.	Chapter 4, p. 37	Chapter 12, p. 116
6.	Chapter 5, p. 51	Chapter 45, p. 419
7.	Chapter 7, p. 70	Chapter 78, p. 765
8.	Chapter 7, p. 76	Chapter 78, p. 764
9.	Chapter 16, p. 185	Chapter 64, p. 621
10.	Chapter 17, p. 191	Chapter 49, p. 465
11.	Chapter 18, p. 204	Chapter 52, p. 494
12.	Chapter 28, p. 318	Chapter 55, p. 520
13.	Chapter 28, p. 315	Chapter 66, p. 641
14.	Chapter 36, p. 411	Chapter 55, p. 518
15.	Chapter 37, p. 421	Chapter 54, p. 514
16.	Chapter 41, p. 472	Chapter 71, p. 694
17.	Chapter 41, p. 476	Chapter 64, p. 623
18.	Chapter 42, p. 486	Chapter 83, p. 819
19.	Chapter 47, p. 555	Chapter 88, p. 879
20.	Chapter 48, p. 555	Chapter 88, p. 879
21.	Chapter 48, p. 555	Chapter 89, p. 889

22.	Chapter 50, p. 575	Chapter 45, p. 426
23.	Chapter 56, p. 643	Chapter 59, p. 567
24.	Chapter 65, p. 742	Chapter 63, p. 613
25.	Chapter 66, p. 751	Chapter 58, p. 559
26.	Chapter 70, p. 796	Chapter 63, p. 606
27.	Chapter 84, p. 953	Chapter 62, p. 595
28.	Chapter 85, p. 966	Chapter 61, pp. 583-84
29.	Chapter 86, p. 976	Chapter 62, p. 601
30.	Chapter 96, p. 1080	Chapter 85, p. 841
31.	Chapter 98, p. 1103	Chapter 71, p. 687
32.	Chapter 98, p. 1106	Chapter 65, pp. 628-29

Liu Ts'un-yan in *Buddhist and Taoist Influences on Chinese Novels, vol. I: The Authorship of the "Fêng Shên Yen I"* (Wiesbade, 1962), pp. 204-42, and Wei Juxian 衛聚賢 in "*Fengshenbang*" *gushi tanyuan* 封神榜故事探源 (private edition; Hong Kong, 1960), II: 207-09, have both claimed that the *Fengshen* novel might have been the source for XYJ. On the basis of variations in diction, syntax, meter, rhyme, and the probable changes induced by different contexts, Nicholas Koss has reached an opposite conclusion: it is the author of the *Fengshen* who has deliberately borrowed from XYJ. See "The Relationship of Hsi-yu Chi and Feng-shen Yen-I: An Analysis of Poems Found in Both Novels," *TP*, LXV/4-5 (1979): 143-65.

103. *Classic Chinese Novel*, p. 120.

104. For example, C. H. Wang, "Towards Defining a Chinese Heroism," *JAOS* 95 (1975): 26.

105. See also Arai ken 荒井健, "*Saiyūki no naka no Saiyūki* 西游記のなかの西游記," *Tōhō Gappō* 東方學報 36 (1964): 591-96, for some suggestive comments on this point.

106. Průšek, pp. 386 and 393.

107. Eric Auerbach, *Dante: Poet of the Secular World*, trans. Ralph Manheim (Chicago, 1961), p. 95.

108. In folk wisdom of the Chinese, open wounds and sores, when exposed to sunlight, would dry up and thus heal more quickly. But a dried scab, a sign of near complete recovery, would render the sunlight superfluous, and the line thus suggests that the entire effort by the villagers and the priest to get rid of the monster is useless.

109. C. M. Bowra, *Heroic Poetry* (London, 1952), p. 31.

110. *Sibu gudian xiaoshuo pinglun* 四部古典小说评论 (Beijing, 1973), p. 31.

111. Lu Xun 鲁迅, "Zhongguo xiaoshuo shilue 中國小說史略," in *Lu Xun quanji* 鲁迅全集 (16 vols., Beijing, 1981), 9: 154-78.

112. See the commentary at the end of the first chapter of the *Xiyou zhenquan*.

113. *Xinshuo Xiyouji* 新說西游記, annot. Zhang Shushen 張書紳. Facs. reprint of Qiyoutang 其有堂 edition (1749) in *Guben xiaoshuo jicheng*, vols. 111-116 (6 vols., Shanghai, 1990), 1: 1.

114. Hu Shi (1923), pp. 383, 390.

115. *Monkey*, p. 5.

116. Hu Shi (1923), p. 390: "西游記被這三四百年來的無數道士和尚秀才弄壞了. 道士說, 這部書是一部金丹妙訣. 和尚說, 這部書是禪門心法. 秀才說, 這部書是一部正心誠意的理學書. 這些解說都是西游記的大仇敵."

117. Lu Xun, "Xiaoshuo shilue" in *Quanji*, 9: 166: "作者雖是儒生, 此書則實出於遊戲, 亦非語道, 故全書僅偶見五行生克之常談, 尤未學佛."

118. Tanaka Kenji 田中謙二 and Arai Ken 荒井健, "*Saiyūki no Bungaku* 西游記の文學," in *Chūgoku no Hachi-Dai Shōsetsu* 中國の八大小說 (Tokyo, 1965), p. 193.

119. Hsia, *Introduction*, p. 138.

120. As noted before, the bibliography of Andrew Plaks's book of 1987 has an unrivalled plenitude of coverage of titles in European and Asian languages. For a comprehensive checklist of twentieth-century Japanese scholarship (with some Chinese references) on the novel up to 1990, see Isobe Akira 磯部彰, "*Saiyūki kenkyū sencho runbun mokuroku* 西游記研究專著論文目錄," in *Toyama daigaku jinbun gakubu kiyō* 富山大學人文學部紀要 16 (1990), pp. 53–87. Publications since 1987 pertinent to our discussion will be mentioned and cited accordingly.

121. *Da Tang gu Sanzang Xuanzang Fashi xingzhuang* 大唐三藏玄奘法師行狀, in SZZSHB, p. 289. The account of this episode in FSZ mentions the barbarian as one converted to Buddhism by Xuanzang and having received the five prohibitions from the Master himself, thus adding poignance to the later incident of threatened killing and warning of the pilgrim. See SZZSHB, pp. 9–10.

122. *Shihua*, p. 1 and p. 31. The English translation of the Tang Monk's first statement in CATCL, p. 1182—"This humble monk has a mission"—completely misses the accurate force of the word *chi* 敕, which in postimperial literary usage can only mean an order from the emperor or the imperial court. The translation of the pilgrim's repeated declaration on p. 1199 has to follow the text's added specificity by rendering it as "a command from the Emperor of T'ang." Misreading of this important word can lead even a seasoned specialist like Isobe Akira to label part of the painting albums with the title, "The Imperial Decree for Acquiring Scriptures in the Western Heaven 西天取经的敕命." The title, in turn, has elicited a justifiable correction by Cao Bingjian and Huang Lin in "tankao," 74: "the Tang Monk owed the acquisition of scriptures not to any imperial decree, for it should still be regarded as a personal act of going illegally abroad 唐僧取经并非奉了敕命, 仍应为个人偷越出境的行为." The word *chi*, it should be noted, is also used extensively in Daoist rituals and should be translated in both its verbal and nominal sense as "authoritative(ly) command." As virtually all scholars of Daoism recognize, the religion's rituals largely emulate or appropriate those of the early imperial state.

123. History locates Xuanzang's burial site in Fanchuan 樊川, about forty miles south of the capital Chang'an. In 880 CE, when the city fell to the forces of the rebel Huang Chao 黃巢 (see CHC, 3/1: 745-50), the tomb was destroyed but somehow parts of the monk's skeletal remains (a skull and other fragments) were discovered by the Abbot Kezhi 可致法師 at the Zige Monastery 紫閣寺 on Mount Zhongnan 終南山 in 1027, during the Tiansheng 天聖 era of the Song Emperor Renzong. The abbot accompanied their transfer all the way southeast to Jinling 金陵 (the modern Nanjing), where the remains were reburied. Discovered by Japanese occupation troops in 1942, the remains were first brought to Japan and then flown back to Taiwan in 1955. See SZZSHB, pp. 842-59, and the special volume, *Jinian Xuanzang dashi linggu guiguo feng'an zhuanji* 記念玄奘大師靈骨歸國奉安專輯 (Taipei, 1977) for detailed accounts by both Chinese and Japanese scholars. The burial site's distant relocation, if true, would shed light on how the Xuanzang legend since the Northern Song had received its diverse

and divergent elaborations, connecting it to different geographical areas. Sometimes, there would be the report (e.g., in the dramatic version) on his birthplace and rearing near China's southeastern coast; another account (e.g., the Korean reader; see XYJYJZL, p. 248) would mention the Shaanxi origin.

124. The monk or abbot has different names in different accounts in the evolution of Xuanzang's personal history, one of which is Faming 法明. Chinese and Japanese scholars concentrating on "evidential scholarship 考證學" endlessly speculate on the origin or reason for such variations, including possibly the fear of incurring the taboo of one nominal graph violating imperial names or titles. The scholarship shows little interest in understanding the fictional development of the story complex, in which the principal characters (both Xuanzang and his disciples) all have had a multiplicity of names in different accounts and texts, where also different deities may perform the same roles or functions (e.g., whether it was Guanyin or the South Pole Star God 南極 仙翁 who sent the prenatal Xuanzang to his mother as a divine gift).

125. In developing the significant theme of transcendent motivation for seeking scripture, the play also differs from the full-length novel. Throughout the *zaju*, the Buddha himself is never seen, though his presence is presumed. Concerning the scripture enterprise, Guanyin's spoken soliloquy that opens the play ascribes the desire to impart scriptures to the Land of the East to the assembled disciples beneath Buddha's throne. Their discussion (諸佛議論), in fact, results in their selection of the human priest and gives his preincarnate identity as Variocana Buddha (reading 毘盧伽 尊者 as 毘盧舍耶). See *Xiyouji zaju*, p. 623. The identity is noteworthy because it affirms the venerable association of the human priest with the Chan (Zen) lineage of Buddhism in the popular imagination, an association that, in turn, might have found easy acceptance and further exploitation in Quanzhen Daoism. Vairocana, after all, is the leader of the Five Dhyāna lineage or Chanzong 禪宗, founded upon the core emphasis of Dhyāna, meditation or *chanding* 禪定. The selection of the scripture pilgrim by the general assembly is also significant to the extent that it seems to indicate a decision reached by a peer group. Chapter 8 of the full-length novel, on the other hand, changed this decision to that of the Buddha's sovereign compassion alone. When he then queried the silent assembly as to who would be willing to undertake a journey to the Land of the East to find the appropriate pilgrim, Guanyin answered the call with words and forthrightness not unlike the episode on the prophet's commission in Isaiah 6 of the Tanakh.

126. So Henry Y. H. Zhao, "Historiography and Fiction in Chinese Culture," in Franco Moretti, ed., *The Novel, Volume 1: History, Geography, and Culture* (Princeton, 2006), pp. 69-83.

127. The historical Xuanzang's own words on when and how he left China are as follows: "in the fourth month of the third year of the Zhenguan 貞觀 reign period (630 CE), braving the transgression of the articles of law, I departed for India on my own authority" (FSZ in SZZSHB, p. 126). Perhaps applying in confusion this year to the legend, the dramatic version of the Chen Guangrui story announces that Xuanzang was born on the fifteenth of the tenth month of Zhenguan 3 (*Xiyouji zaju*, p. 639), but this would mean that Xuanzang's selection as the scripture pilgrim at age eighteen or older would have to take place in Zhenguan 21 or later. Historically, most scholars agreed that by Zhenguan 19 (645), Xuanzang had already returned to Tang territory after his long pil-

grimage. With respect to the novel, the chapter 9 paragraph opening common to both the spurious and the Shidetang versions, however, dates the pilgrim's selection to year 13, and this is reconfirmed in chapter 100 of all full-length versions, when the emperor's own words record his date of reunion with his commissioned priest as Zhenguan 27 (XYJ, p. 1126). The impossible chronology of the controversial chapter 9 would have made the pilgrim's selection in the same year that his father was appointed *zhuangyuan* prior to his conception.

128. Chapter 12: 取經文牒.... 通行寶印. In subsequent chapters, the rescript is always referred to as the *tongguan wendie* 通關文牒 (literally, the rescript for going through a pass) that, in the overall emplotment of the novel, has immense political and religious significance yet to be studied.

129. For what might well have been regard for harmonizing numerical symbolism in the text, in this particular instance having to do with Buddhism, the novel reduces the length of the pilgrimage to fourteen years, making the number of days on the journey 5,040 days (i.e., 360 x 14). At the story's very end, the Buddha added eight more days (see the Patriarch's words at the end of chapter 98) for the pilgrims's return from India to Chang'an and then back again to India under divine escorts, making the grand total of 5,048 days to correspond exactly to the canonical number of "scrolls, *juan*" first identified with the *Kaiyuan shijiao lu* 開元釋教錄 compiled by Zhisheng 智昇 in 730 CE.

130. A conclusion also reached by Cao Bingjian, "'Chun Ru' renge de fasi yu pipan—Tang seng xinlun '醇儒'人格的反思与批判—唐僧新论," *Zhongzhou Xuekan* 中州学刊 4 (July 1999): 109-11. See esp. Cao's citations (p. 110) of the Tang Monk's use of Confucian rhetoric and ideals in his discourse in chapters 24, 27, 36, 47, and 80 of the novel.

131. Kenneth Ch'en, *Buddhism in China*, p. 321. As a representative text of this lineage, see Vasubandhu 世親, *Wei Shih Er Shi Lun* 唯識二十論, or "The Treatise in Twenty Stanzas on Representation-only" (New Haven, AOS, 1938).

132. Ch'en, *Buddhism in China*, pp. 322-25.

133. This is a virtual paraphrase of a line from the *Mahāparinirvāṇa sūtra* 大般涅盤 經, #374, in T 12: 488b: "all sentient beings possess the nature of Buddha 一切眾生悉 有佛性." The assertion is repeated endlessly throughout this lengthy scripture. As will be seen in what follows immediately, whether all beings indeed could be so predicated and in what way(s) could one realize Buddha's nature in oneself became the cardinal points of debate in Chan Buddhism. This line of teaching had an enormous impact on Song Neo-Confucianism, and it was readily picked up and elaborated further by Quanzhen patriarchs from the time of Zhang Boduan in the tenth century.

134. For example, apart from the two famous poems (by the priest Shenxiu 神秀 and answered by the acolyte Huineng 慧能) on the metaphor of the mind as mirror and on whether its clarity depends on its original purity or constant cleaning in *Tanjing*, chapter 1, and *The Platform Scripture*, section 6, numerous other such verse dialogues and disputations appear in all the subsequent segments of the text. The canonical name of the scripture is *Liuzu Dashi Fabao Tanjing* 六祖法師法寶壇經 in #2008, T 48: 435b ff. Among the thirty-plus versions of this scripture in four stemmas, the Dunhuang text of the sūtra in manuscript form and discovered in the first half of the twentieth century is acknowledged to be the earliest, dating possibly to the eighth century. For the Dunhuang text, I use *The Platform Scripture*, trans. Wing-tsit Chan (New York, 1963). For

the received text, I use *Liuzu Tanjing* 六祖壇經, (Taipei, 1997), a modern critical edition with vernacular translation and annotation by Li Zhonghua 李中華.

135. This difference in the enlightenment process further divided the lineage into the Northern and Southern Schools. A succinct summary of the schools's divergent views may be found in Wing-tsit Chan's introduction to his translation of *The Platform Scripture*, pp. 14-16. See also John R. McRae, *The Northern School and the Formation of Early Ch'an Buddhism* (Honolulu, 1986); and Ge Zhaoguang, *Zhongguo Chan sixiangshi*, pp. 46-112. Ma Tianxiang 麻天祥 in *Zhongguo Chanzong sixiang fazhan shi* 中国禅宗思想发展史, rev. ed. (Wuhan, 2007), p. 19, has this observation: "sudden enlightenment is the transcendence of linguistic signs and the severance of thinking by ordinary logic. Directly, it grasps the totality of an indivisible principle 顿悟就是超乎言象, 斩断通常的逻辑思维, 直接, 整体把握不可分隔的理." A revisionist study exerting an enormous impact on Western scholarship on Chan in the last two decades is Bernard Faure, *The Rhetoric of Immediacy: A Cultural Critique of Chan/Zen Buddhism* (Princeton, 1991). For some astute analysis of the topoi of means and media in the tradition, see esp. chapters 2 and 3.

136. Martina Darga, "Xingming guizhi," in ET 2: 1106. Joseph Needham, in SCC, V/5 (1983): 229-30, dates it to the end of the sixteenth century because the first edition appeared in 1615. This would place the text's production less than twenty years after the first publication of XYJ.

137. The two parallel sentences are found verbatim in the following: "大乘起信論廣釋," in #2814, T85: 1136c; "六祖大師法寶壇經," in # 2008, T48: 032a; "景德傳燈錄," in #2076, T51: 0236b; "鎮州臨濟慧照禪師語錄" in #1985, T47: 0502b; "大明高僧傳," in #2062, T50: 0920a.

138. See Wang Shouren, "Chongxiu Shanyin xian xueji 重修山陰縣學記," in *Wang Wengcheng Gong quanshu* 王文成公全書, eds. Wu Guang 吳光, et al. (2 vols. Shanghai, 1992), 1: 257.

139. See note 43.

140. For some examples of the familiar metaphors of "the Monkey of the Mind" and "the Horse of the Will" studding Buddhist texts, see *Zhengfa nianchu jing* 正法念處經 in #721, T 17: 0024a: "是心猿猴, 此心猿猴"; *Nianfo jing* 念佛經 in #1966, T 47: 0132c: "制護心猿無放逸"; *Fayuan zhulin* 法宛珠林 in #2122, T 53: 0653b: "識馬易奔心猿難制"; *Lebang wenlei* 樂邦文類 in #1969A, T 47: 0220a: " 心猿意馬尚顛狂." For examples in Quanzhen writings, see Wang Chongyang 王重陽, *Chongyang quanzhen ji* 重陽全真集, in DZ 1153, 25: 694: "心猿緊縛無邪染 / 意馬牢擒不夜巡"; juan 3, 17a: "修身爭似修心"; 25: 716: "如要修持 / 先把心猿鎖"; 25: 740: "不得意馬外遊 / 不得心猿內動."

141. Although my interpretation here does not wholly follow the thesis, fully and astutely articulated by Ping Shao, in "Huineng, Subhūti, and Monkey's Religion in *Xiyou ji*," *JAS* 65/4 (November 2006): 713-40, I have learned greatly from this splendid study. Professor Shao not only has documented quite thoroughly the Chan concepts and scriptures surfacing in the novel (pp. 713-20), but he also argued that parallels between the novel and Chan writings may lead one to conclude that "Monkey is Huineng reincarnate in terms of his enhanced spiritual nature" (p. 721). Shao next uses incisively the ideas of Zhang Boduan to orient both the pilgrims—and by extension, the attentive readers—to understand the integrative (or syncretistic) movement from strict Buddhism to a Daoist ideal of utilizing Buddhist language, especially that of Chan. In

Shao's view, with which I agree, "Zhang may have accepted Chan philosophy, but he was far from having become a Buddhist. His reliance on the Buddha-nature concept [*mingxin jianxing*] was simply the highlight of continuous efforts made by the Taoists to bring their own thinking up to date" (p. 731). For further analysis of why Zhang insisted on the cultivation of "golden elixir" requires "intuitive apprehension of Buddhist principles 了悟佛理," see Zhuang Hongyi 莊宏誼, "Bei Song Daoshi Zhang Boduan famo ji qi jindan sixiang 北宋道士張伯端法脈及其金丹思想," in *Daojiao yanjiu yu Zhongguo zongjiao wenhua* 道教研究與中國文化, ed. Li Zhitian 黎志添 (Hong Kong, 2003), pp. 217-50.

Quanzhen's Northern patriarch Wang Zhe 王喆 or Wang Chongyang (1113-1170) and his followers less than a century later continued this aggressive appropriation of certain key notions of Chan for their own use in internal alchemy. It is noteworthy that one of the earliest stele inscriptions erected for Wang by a Jin Daoist cleric official began with these lines: "Now, therefore, each of the Three Religions has its ultimate words and wondrous principles. The person in Buddhism who acquired the mind of Buddha was Bodhidharma, and his religion was named Chan. In the Confucian religion, the person who transmitted the familial learning of Confucius was Zisi, whose book was named *The Doctrine of the Mean*. The ultimate principles of the Daoist religion encompassing five thousand words were transmitted without utterance and appeared without action. 夫三教各有至言妙理. 釋教得佛之心者, 達摩也, 其教名之曰禪. 儒教傳孔子之家學者, 子思也, 其書名之曰中庸. 道教通五千言之至理, 不言而傳, 不行而至." See "Zhongnanshan shenxian Chongyang Wang Zhenren Quanzhen Jiaozhu bei 終南山神仙重陽王真人全真教主碑," in *Daojia jinshi lue* 道家金石略, comp. Chen Yuan 陳垣 (Beijing, 1988), p. 450. To claim that Bodhidharma alone captured Buddha's mind (or approbation, an alternative translation of *dexin*) would likely be met with stiff objections from other Buddhist lineages. But this emhpasis of the Daoist order helps explain the prominent and ubiquitous presence of Chan in the XYJ text. The Quanzhen patriarchs emulated precedents supposedly set by Chan masters that they did not wish to "establish doctrines with language 不立文字," but that reservation did not discourage the Daoist leaders from poetic compositions. Abundant examples from Wang Chongyang's corpora reveal his understanding of how the extolled unity of the Three Religions, far from being a neatly settled condition, can be affirmed only from the point of view of a dynamic and assertive Quanzhen hermeneutic. In the first four lines of a full-length regulated verse, "When Squire Ren inquired about the Three Religions 任公問三教," Wang writes: "The Way passes through Confucian gate and Buddhist house, / For the Three Religions from one ancestor descend. / Awakened wholly, you'd know the ins and outs; / Comprehension permits you feel its breadth and length 儒門釋戶道相通, 三教從來一祖風, 悟徹便令知出入, 曉明應許覺寬洪" (in *Chongyang quanzhen ji* 重陽全真集, DZ 1153, 25: 693). In another poem, "When asked about Buddhism and Daoism 問禪道者為何," Wang becomes slightly more polemical by insisting that his bluntly partisan perspective makes a difference in understanding another tradition. "The Dao in Buddhism is ever seen as powerless, / But to know Buddhism in Daoism will end love or hate [i.e., conflict]. / Perfecting both Dao and Chan is the lofty student; / Once Daoist-Chan is acquired you'll be a true monk 禪中見道總無能, 道裏通禪絕愛憎, 禪道兩全為上士 [an allusion to *Daodejing* 41: 'When the lofty or superior student hears the Dao, he will be diligent to practice it 上士聞道, 勤而行之'], 道

禪一得自真僧" (DZ 1153, 25: 694). Still, in a third and final example ("A reply to Squire Zhan on the temporal priority of Buddhism over Daoism 答戰公問釋後道"), Wang seeks to help his reader realize that the claim of unity stems from his Order's particular view of the Three Religions: "Buddhists and Daoists have always been one household, / With two kinds of features but their truths don't differ. / Knowing the mind to see one's nature is Quanzhen's consciousness; / Understanding mercury and lead yields virtuous sprouts 釋道從來是一家, 兩般形貌理無差, 識心見性全真覺, 知汞通鉛結善芽" (DZ 1153, 25: 691).

142. See Franciscus Verellen, "The Dynamic Design: Ritual and Contemplative Graphics in Daoist Scriptures," in *Daoism in History: Essays in Honour of Liu Ts'un-yan*, ed. Benjamin Penny (London and New York, 2006), pp. 175-76.

143. *Yuanqu xuan* 元曲選 (3 vols., SBBY), 3: 2 (page numbers in accordance with individual plays).

144. For a penetrating examination of the problem of mind-and-heart cultivation and its ironic allegorization in the novel, see Lam Ling Hon, "Cannibalizing the Heart: The Politics of Allegory and *The Journey to the West*," in *Literature, Religion, and East/West Comparison*, ed. Eric Ziolkowski (Newark, 2004), pp. 162-180. The so-called sixth-ear macaque, *liuer mihou* 六耳獼猴 of this episode is indeed a secret double of Sun Wukong. The name, meaning metonymically a third pair of ears, signifies a furtive and illegitimate intruder, the uncanny other of the divided self that may also be recalcitrant and subversive. Its very identity is already foreshadowed back in chapter 2 (XYJ, p. 16), when Monkey begged Subodhi to impart to him the formula for immortality: "There is no 'sixth-ear' [i.e., a third person] here except your disciple."

145. The irony here is that the doctrine of no mind or the avoidance of two minds as a metaphor for mental discrimination is only too familiar to Chan Buddhism. In the *Laṅkāvatāra Sūtra*, another foundational text favored by the sect, of which there were four known translations in Chinese, this teaching was also pervasive. See *juan* 4 of the translation by Bodhiruci, *Dasheng ru lengqie jing* 大乘入楞伽經, #672, T 16: 614b: "凡愚見有二 / 不了唯心現 / 故起二分別 / 若知但是心 / 分別則不生." One can also see why so many Chan followers, rightly or wrongly, found Zhuangzi's thought on ultimate nondiscrimination to be so genial.

146. Extensive discussion of the motion or movement of the mind is found in *Mencius* 2A, 2. Mao Zedong declared his unperturbed courage while being surrounded by enemy troops in a 1928 lyric to the tune of "Moon Over West River": "Enemy troops surround me in ten thousand layers, / But I remain aloof and unmoved 敵軍圍困萬千重, 我自巋然不動." See *Mao Zhuxi shici* 毛主席詩詞 (Beijing, 1974), p. 2a.

147. See Ren Bantang, 1: 393-412.

148. Examples of these metaphors are virtually endless in the Canon. See the small collection of poems devoted to the subject in *Zhizhenzi longhu huandan shi* 至真子龍虎還丹詩, in DZ 269, 4: 913-15.

149. Even a brief and selected citation of some of the most important publications in this area cannot ignore the pioneering works of the past. See Henri Maspero, "Methods of 'Nourishing the Vital Principle' in the Ancient Taoist Religion," in *Taoism and Chinese Religion*, trans. Frank A. Kireman Jr. (Amherst, MA, 1981), pp. 443-554; and Nathan Sivin, *Chinese Alchemy: Preliminary Studies* (Cambridge, MA, 1968). Because the technical rhetoric and terminology of internal alchemy (*neidan*) frequently employ

the same vocabulary in physical or external alchemy (*waidan*), the classic monographs of Chen Guofu 陳國符, *Daozang yuanliu kao* 道藏源流考, rev. ed. (Taipei, 1975), and *Daozang yuanliu xukao* 道藏源流續考 (Taipei, 1983) are indispensable references. Other important publications include Isabelle Robinet, *Meditation Taoïste* (Paris, 1979); Robinet, *Introduction à l'alchimie intérieure taoïste: De l'unité et de la multiplicité* (Paris, 1995); SCC, V/5 (1983), with invaluable and extensive classified bibliographies in several languages; Farzeen Baldrian-Hussein, *Procédés Secrets du Joyau Magique: Traité d'Alchimie Taoïste du XIe siècle* (Paris, 1984); Catherine Despeux, *Taoïsme et corps humain*, Le Xiuzhen Tu (Paris, 1994); Stephen Eskildsen, *The Teachings and Practices of the Early Quanzhen Taoist Masters* (Albany, 2004); Fabrizio Pregardio, *Great Clarity and Alchemy in Early Medieval China* (Stanford, 2006); Louis Komjathy, *Cultivating Perfection: Mysticism and Self-Transformation in Early Quanzhen Daoism* (Leiden, 2007); and relevant sections of DH and ET. Chinese books on the subject are legion, but one must sift through a huge amount of publications in diverse fields (e.g., on medicine, athletics, *qigong*, and religion) to determine which are the useful titles. For the ongoing work of interpreting and annotating the present translation, I have learned from Zhang Rongming 張榮明, *Zhongguo gudai qigong yu xian-Qin zhexue* 中國古代气功与先秦哲学 (Shanghai, 1987); Tian Chengyang 田诚阳, *Xianxue xiangshu* 仙學详述 (Beijing, 1999); Hao Qin 郝勤, *Longhu dandao* 龙虎丹道 (Chengdu, 1994); Lu Guolong 卢国龙, *Daojiao zhexue* 道教哲学 (Beijing, 1997); Zhang Guangbao 张广保, *Tang-Song neidan daojia* 唐宋内丹道家 (Shanghai, 2001); and Ge Guolong 戈國龍, *Daojiao neidanxue shuyuan* 道教內丹學溯源 (Taipei, 2004).

150. FSZ 1, in SZZSHB, p. 12. See also *Antecedents*, pp. 18-21, and Hu Shi (1923), 358.

151. On this important theme of banished gods as characters in Chinese fiction, see Li Fengmao 李豐楙, *Liuchao Sui-Tang xiandaolei xiaoshuo yanjiu* 六朝隋唐仙道類小說研究 (Taipei, 1986); Li Fengmao, *Wuru yu zhejiang* 誤入與謫降 (Taipei, 1996). Deities (human or nonhuman figures) incurring reincarnation through banishment or seduction by the human world (*wuru*) provide a frequent motif for late imperial fiction ranging from the *Sanguozhi pinghua* 三國志平話 (fourteenth century), the *Outlaws of the Marshes* (sixteenth-century recension), the *Shuoyue quanzhuan* 說岳全傳 (eighteenth century), to, of course, *The Story of the Stone* (also eighteenth century). Just as XYJ makes this popular motif central to its narrative action, so, too, the text of the *Stone* exploits it for charting the tragic fate of the two teenage lovers. From the first chapter of this last Qing novel's earliest manuscript (1754), the quatrain *gātha* ends the episode of the protagonist-stone's origin and human incarnation with the familiar lines: "With no talents could one repair the azure sky? / Wrongly he entered the red-dust world for these few years 無材可去補蒼天，枉入紅塵若許年." In sound and sense, the phrase "wrong entrance (*wuru* 誤入, or entrance by mistake)," potently resonates with "futile or wrongful entrance (*wangru* 枉入)," for banished incarnation can result from either personal fault or judicial injustice.

152. Arthur F. Wright, "Fu I and the Rejection of Buddhism," *Journal of the History of Ideas* 12 (1951): 33-47.

153. See the essays collected in the LWJ and Sa Mengwu 薩孟武, *Xiyouji yu Zhongguo gudai zhengzhi* 西游記與中國古代政治 (Taipei, 1969).

154. See Chun-fang Yü, *Kuan-yin: The Chinese Transformation of Avalokiteśvara* (New York, 2001).

155. A small, spoonlike instrument used as a dry measure for small amounts of powdered medicine, it is also frequently employed as a metonym for Sha Wujing in the narrative (e.g., chapter 22). Because the second graph in the term *daogui* 刀圭 may be anagrammatically separated into two identical individual graphs (i.e., *tu* 土), another name often used by the novel's narrator to designate Sha Monk is "Double Earth, *ertu,* 二土."

156. See Wolfram Eberhard, "Beiträge zur kosmologischen Spekulation Chinas in der Han-Zeit," *Baessler Archiv* 16 (1933): 1-100; SCC 2 (1970), pp. 253-65; Manfred Porkert, *The Theoretical Foundations of Chinese Medicine: Systems of Correspondence,* MIT East Asian Science Series, 3 (Cambridge, MA, 1974), pp. 43-54. For one of the most detailed attempted accounts of how alchemical, Five phases, and *Yijing* (Classic of Change) terminologies, together with Buddhist numerology, are integrated to provide different forms of correlative schematization for the five pilgrims, see Nakano Miyoko 中野美代子, *Saiyūki no himitsu* 西游記の秘密 (Tokyo, 1984), section II, pp. 71-170.

157. At the height of a fierce battle ranging the powerful Bull Demon King (Niu mowang) against Wukong, Wuneng, and other deities coming to the pilgrims' assistance in chapter 61, the Pig, echoing Monkey's self-exegetical commentarial poem, adds these lines of another similar poem: "Wood's born at *hai,* the hog's its proper mate, / Who'll lead back the Bull to return to earth. / Monkey's the one who is born under the *shen:* / Harmless, docile, how harmonious it is!" The correlation of horary stems and symbolic animals should be self-evident.

158. See DZ 1098, 24: 248-49. The term Yellow Dame is frequently glossed as meaning a person's will or intention (i.e, *yi* 意; so ET 2: 1158), but in the rhetoric of internal alchemy, the psychological acquires further the physiological meaning as the "secretion of the spleen. The secretion's name is true earth 脾中之涎.涎者,名真土." This definition clarifies the multiple correlations with Sha Monk. It should be noted here as well that this form of relating the viscera to mental or psychological faculties did not originate with the Daoist religion. As early as *The Classic of Difficult Issues* 難經, a medical text compiled in the first century CE, we encounter already such description: "The heart weighs twelve ounces. It has seven holes and three hairs. It is filled with three ko of essential sap. It masters the haboring of the spirit. The spleen weighs two catties and three ounces. Its flat width is three inches. Its length is five inches. It has a half catty of dispersed fat. It masters the containment of the blood and supplies the five depots with warmth. It masters the harboring of the sentiments.... The kidneys consist of two [separate] entities; they weigh one catty and one ounce. The master harboring of the mind 心重十二兩, 中有七孔三毛, 盛精汁三合, 主藏神.脾重二斤三兩, 扁廣三寸, 長五寸,有散膏半斤,主裏血,溫五藏,主藏意....腎有兩枚,重一斤一兩,主藏志." See *Nan-Ching: The Classic of Difficult Issues,* trans. and annotated Paul U. Unschuld (Berkeley, Los Angeles, and London, 1986), pp. 416-17.

159. See Liu Ts'un-yan, "Lin Chao-ên (15170-1598), the Master of the Three Teachings," in *Selected Papers from the Hall of Harmonious Wind* (Leiden: E. J. Brill, 1976), pp. 149-74; Judith A. Berling, *The Syncretic Religion of Lin Chao-en* (New York: Columbia University Press, 1980); Chün-fang Yü, *The Renewal of Buddhism in China: Chu-hung and the Late Ming Synthesis* (New York: Columbia University Press, 1981); and Timothy Brook, "Rethinking Syncretism: The Unity of the Three Teachings and their Joint Worship in Late-Imperial China," *Journal of Chinese Religions* 21 (Fall 1993): 14-44. In

early imperial Chinese history from the late Han down to the Tang, the Three Religions (*sanjiao*) were often used interchangeably as the Three Daos or Three Ways (*sandao*). See Robert Ford Campany, "On the Very Idea of Religions (in the Modern West and in Early Medieval China)," *HR* 42/4 (May 2003): 287-319, and the important essays gathered in *Sankyō kōshō ronsō* 三教交涉論叢, comp. Mugitani Kunio 麥谷邦夫 (Kyōto-shi, 2005). Comparative discussions of the Three Religions might have begun as early as the Late Han; see the "Lihuo lun 理惑論," attributed to Mou Rong 牟融 and collected in the *Hongming ji* 弘明集, j 1, 1a-22b, SBCK, if it were written indeed by the person recorded in the canonical *Hou Hanshu* 後漢書, j 56. Scholarly opinion, however, thinks that the essay's content is no earlier than the Six Dynasties; so CHC, 1 (1986): 854. The *Hongming ji*, nonetheless, contains many disputative essays by clerics and court officials on the merits and defects of two or three religions together. With the Yuan official Chen Yi 陳謐 and his major treatise, *Sanjiao pingxin lun* 三教平心論, we may discern a new polemical tactic in harmonizing or integrating through interpretation the diverse emphases and terminologies of the Three Religions. As he said in the preface, "The rise of the Three Religions has had a noble past. Operating in a parallel manner in the world, they transform and perfect the empire. When we examine them from their histories, they certainly were not all the same. When we analyze them from their principles, they could not be entirely different. One becomes three; three also becomes one. You cannot receive them while favoring one or the other 三教之興, 其來尚矣. 并行於世, 化成天下, 以跡議之, 而未始不異, 以理推之, 而未始不同. 一而三, 三而一, 不可得而親疏焉." The essay is collected in #2117, T 52, but I use another modern edition (Shanghai, 1935), bearing the Qing emperor Yongzheng's 1734's edict and affirming the value of the piece, because "the principles by which the Three Religions have enlightened the people of our domain have all emerged from the same origin 三教之覺民於海內也, 理同出於一原." Chen's writing might well have further funded the syncretistic tendencies in Quanzhen hermeneutics back in the Yuan, but there were also apparent differences in emphasis. The call to treat all Three Religions with the same respect because their doctrines could ultimately be seen as belonging to the same source had found an undeniable echo across the centuries from the 1592 XYJ text, for this message formed Sun Wukong's very words when he counseled the ruler of the Cart Slow Kingdom after his domain was purged of three monsters masquerading as Daoist clergy in persecution of Buddhists (see the beginning of JW 2, chapter 47). On the other hand, as we have seen previously in note 158, this sloganized ideal did not prevent the Daoists or Buddhists or Confucians from claiming that their particular take of the Three Religions was the most authentic or useful one in forging homogeneity from religious plurality.

160. The illustration is found in XMGZ, 9: 526, and in XMGZ-Taipei, p. 114. The illustration is taken from the clearer reproduction in SCC, V/5 (1983): 49.

161. For the Buddhists' rehearsal of their sufferings and persecutions in the hands of the Daoists that included beatings, forced migrations, hard labor as slaves, exposure, confinement, and pictured warrants for escapees that led to mass suicide, see XYJ, chapter 44, pp. 508-10.

162. See my "Religion and Literature in China: The 'Obscure Way' in *The Journey to the West*," in CJ, pp. 169; see also Franciscus Verellen, "Luo Gongyuan, Légende et culte d'un saint taoïste," JA 275 (1987): 283-332.

163. Preserved in the *Song Gaoseng zhuan* 宋高僧傳 (#2061, T 50: 712-14).

164. How this phrase should be translated in different periods of Chinese medical and religious history requires brief discussion. The phrase is found in the writings by Ge Hong 葛洪 (283-343); see the *Baopuzi* 抱朴子, *neipian* 8, 2b SBBY. But much earlier than Ge, the phrase was already used in a line of a classical poem by the famed Cao Zhi 曹植 (192-232) and titled "Feilong pian 飛龍篇, The Dragon in Flight." It is preserved in one version of a poem of a journey to Mount Tai that resulted in encounters with immortals. The narrator received divine drugs that would "restore my essence, augment my brain." The translation here by Stephen Owen in *The Making of Early Chinese Classical Poetry*, Harvard East Asian Monographs 261 (Cambridge, 2006), p. 142, shows exemplary caution by separating the drug's efficacy into two separate participial phrases without any necessary connection: that is, the drug would do X and it would do Y with the recipient's body. Because the poet's era was one in which the *Scripture of Great Clarity* (*Taiqing jing* 太清經) and related texts were in circulation to promote external alchemy (*waidan*), Owen's translation would comport with the understanding that our phrase might point to the physical or chemical "ingredients of the elixir [being] transmuted, or 'reverted' (*huan*) into their 'essence' (*jing*), which coagulates itself under the upper part of the crucible." The *jing* in coagulation thus gathered from the physical instrument might then be construed as a drug possessive of restorative efficacy when ingested. See Fabrizio Pregadio, *Great Clarity*, p. 10. By the time of the novel's formative period in the Ming or even earlier, however, the discourse of external alchemy had long been displaced by that of internal alchemy, wherein "the adept nourishes himself and his gods not through the ingestion of external substances, but through components of his own inner body; he finds the vital ingredients within himself, and their ingestion takes place internally" (Pregadio, p. 209). In the full-length novel, in other words, there is similarly a causal relation: the adept sends the essence up to the brain in order to nourish and replenish the body.

165. For the meaning of River-Carts and illustrations, see SCC, V/5: 254-55. According to DJDCD, p. 405, the cart can refer to the "vehicle" or the cargo therein transported. For the specific references to the three named carts, see, for example, "Sanji zhiming quanti 三極致命筌蹄," DZ 275, the different texts gathered under the general title of "Xiuzhen shishu 修真十書," DZ 263, and the "Chongyang Zhenren jinguan yusuo jue 重陽真人金關玉鎖訣," DZ 1156. For discussion, see Franzeen Baldrian-Hussein, *Proécédes secret du Joyau magique* (Paris, 1984), pp. 171-83; Jennifer Oldstone-Moore, "Alchemy and *Journey to the West*: The Cart-slow Kingdom Episode," *JCR* 26 (1998): 51-66; and Liu Ts'un-yan, "Quanzhen jiao he xiaoshuo Xiyouji," HFTWJ 3: 1270-72. It should be noted that the ox cart of the Daoist treatises has been transformed into the Tiger Strength Immortal in the novel. Drawings of the carts are abundant in the Daoist canon, and for easily visible reproductions, see the picture titled "Les trois chariots" in Baldrian-Hussein, p.173, and in SCC V/5: 177. Baldrian-Hussein's enlarged reproduction is used here. It should also be noted that some Daoist texts seemed to distinguish between river carts and the three carts drawn by three beasts, the original source of the last type likely to have come from the *Lotus Sūtra* (see JW 4, chapter 100, note 19). See also the discussion in Louis Komjathy, *Cultivating Perfection: Mysticism and Self-Transformation in Early Quanzhen Daoism* (Leiden, 2007), pp. 208-11; p. 297, note 44.

166. A diagram of these two pulse conduits may be found in SCC V/5: 256.

167. See Wang Guoguang 王国光, "*Xiyouji*" *bielun* 西游记别论 (Shanghai: Xue-lin chubanshe, 1990); Wang Gang 王崗, "*Xiyouji*—Yige wanzheng di Daojiao neidan xiulian guocheng 西游記——一個完整的道教內丹修煉過程," 清華學報 n.s., 25 (1995): 51-86.

168. *Chongyang zhenren jinguan yusuo jue*, DZ 1156, 25: 800.

169. See Dai Yuanchang 戴源長, *Xianxue cidian* 仙學詞典 (Taipei, 1962), p. 35.

170. *Jinguan yusuo jue*, DZ 25: 801; translation of *xue* 穴 follows SCC, V/6: 61.

171. For more illustrations of the Double Pass or *shuang guan* 雙, see *Shangyangzi jin-dan tayao tu* 上陽子金丹大要圖, DZ 1068, 2b, reproduced in SCC V/5: 105.

172. DZ 1072, 6b-7a. My translation follows Needham's suggestion in SCC V/5: 220; see 219-26 and 240-43 for his informative report on the use of figurative language in alchemical writings. This understanding of symbols based on illustrative analogy per-vades all writings on inner alchemy. One commentator of the Tang treatise "Ruyao jing 入药镜" preserved in *Daoshu* 道樞, *j* 37, in DZ 20: 807-12, observes similarly: "Yellow Dame, Baby Boy, Fair Girl are not truly existent. It is a description by analogous sym-bolism, and they do not refer to any three things other than the body, the mind, and the intention 黄婆, 嬰兒, 姹女, 非真有也. 乃譬喻之說, 無出乎身心意三者而已." The com-ment is cited in He Qin 郝勤, *Longhu dandao—Daojiao neidanshu* 龙虎丹道——道教内丹术 (Chengdu, 1994), p. 175.

173. The most comprehensive study I know of on the use of *pi* as part of religious rhetoric is Li Sher-shiueh [Shixue] 李奭學, "*Zhushu duo geyan*: Lun Gao Yizhi *Pixue* ji qi yu Zhongxi xiucixue chuantong di guanxi 《著書多格言》:論高一志《譬學》及其與中西修辭學傳統的關係," *Renwen Zhongguo xuebao* 人文中國學報 / *Sino-Humanities* 13 (2007): 55-116.

174. *Qianlong Jiaxuben Zhiyanzhai chongping Shitouji* 乾隆甲戌本脂硯齋重評石頭記 (Taipei: Hu Shi(h) jinianguan, 1961), *j* 1, 1.

175. This irony is described thus by Professor Liu Ts'un-yan in HFTWJ 3: 1350-51: "Look at the name and thinking about its meaning, a story that describes Xuanzang's story of scripture-seeking fundamentally should be one devoted to promote Buddhist doctrine and spirit." However, he and many other contemporary scholars have pointed out how the rhetoric and diction of canonical and noncanonical Daoism have per-vaded the novel's text. For another view of the language of politics and irony in the novel, see Qiu Jiahui 邱加輝, "Houhua Xiyou/houhua Xiyou 候话《西游》/ 后话《西游》," in Song Geng 宋耕, ed., *Chongdu chuantong—kua wenhua yuedu xin shiye*《重读传统——跨文化阅读新视野》(Beijing, 2005), pp. 236-60.

176. Yu, "Two Literary Examples of Religious Pilgrimage," in CJ, p. 149.

177. *Xue* when outside the body is blood, but within the body it is the relatively yin portion of the pneumatic vitalities, *qi*. See Nathan Sivin, *Traditional Medicine in Contem-porary China* (Ann Arbor, 1987), pp. 156-61.

178. For the text of the scroll, see *Baojuan* 寶卷 ed., Zhang Xishun 張希舜, et al. (40 vols., Taiyuan, 1994), 14: 37-38. This scroll's publication is dated to 1562 (Jiajing 41) or thirty years prior to the publication of XYJ, according to Zhang Jinchi, *Xiyouji kaolun*, p. 213. Andrew Plaks's argument for a "sixteenth-century" milieu for the production of the full-length novel is impressively on target.

179. See his *Blindness and Insight: Essays in the Rhetoric of Contemporary Criticism*, 2nd ed., rev. (Minneapolis, 1983), p. 35. Original French lines may be found in *The Flowers*

of Evil & Paris Spleen: Poems by Charles Baudelaire, trans. William H. Crosby (Brookport, NY, 1991), p. 164.

180. *The Taoist Body,* trans. Karen C. Duval (Berkeley, 1993), pp. 100-01.

181. *Baopuzi, neipian* 18, 3a. SBBY.

182. See *Taoism and the Arts of China,* ed. Stephen Little (Chicago, 2000), and its reproductions of the "Diagram of Reverted Illumination 反照圖" and "The Diagram of Comprehensive Illumination 普照圖," p. 348.

183. Cited by de Man, *Blindness and Insight,* p. 35. For the German original of Benjamin's observation, see his *Ursprung des deutschen Trauerspiels,* in *Gesammelte Schriften* (7 vols., Frankfurt am Main, 1972-89), 1: 406: "'Min Weinen streuten wir den Samen in den Brachen / und gingen traurig aus.' Leer also geht die Allegorie. Das schlechthin Böse, das als bleibende Tiefe sir hegte, existiert nur in ihr, ist *einzig und allein Allegorie, bedeutet etwas anderes als es ist. Und zwar bedeutet es genau das Nichtsein dessen, was es vorstellt*" (emphasis mine). I am grateful to Haun Saussy, University Professor of Comparative Literature, the University of Chicago, for tracking down the German passage for me. The English translation is found in Walter Benjamin, *The Origin of German Tragic Drama,* trans. John Osborne (London, 1977), p. 233: "'Weeping we scattered the seed on the fallow ground / and sadly we went away.' Allegory goes away empty-handed. Evil as such, which it cherished as enduring profundity, *exists only in allegory, is nothing other than allegory, and means something different from what it is. It means precisely the nonexistence of what it presents*" (emphasis mine).

184. *Monkey,* pp. 7-8.

185. Joyce Carol Oates, *The Edge of Impossibility: Tragic Forms in Literature* (New York, 1972), p. 5.

CHAPTER ONE

1. In Chinese legend, Pan Gu was said to be the first human, born from the union of the yin and yang forces. See the *Wuyun linian ji* 五運歷年記 and the *Shuyi ji* 述異記. He also assisted in the formation of the universe.

2. This is likely a reference to a shorter or abridged version of the Tripitaka story, compiled by Zhu Dingchen of Canton and published in the late sixteenth century, during the reign of Wanli by a Fujian bookseller, Liu Qiumao. See the present volume's introduction II for further discussion of the text in relation to JW.

3. This is Shao Yong 邵雍 (1011-1077), a Song scholar and an expert in the *Classic of Change*.

4. The Three August Ones and the Five Thearchs 三皇五帝 refer to the legendary sage rulers at the dawn of Chinese civilization. There has been no agreement on who the Three August Ones or the Five Thearchs were, and ancient Chinese texts present several varied combinations.

5. These four continents forming the world belong to the geography of Indian Buddhism.

6. These islets and islands were famous abodes of gods or immortals.

7. The twenty-four solar terms are seasonal divisions of a year established in the Han. They are: *lichun* (Spring begins), *yushui* (rain water), *jingzhi* (excited insects), *chunfen* (vernal equinox), *qingming* (clear and bright), *guyu* (grain rains), *lixia* (summer begins), *xiaoman* (grain fills), *mangzhong* (grain in ear), *xiazhi* (summer solstice), *xiaoshu* (slight

heat), *dashu* (great heat), *liqiu* (autumn begins), *chushu* (limit of heat), *bailu* (white dew)
qiufen (autumnal equinox), *hanlu* (cold dew), *shuangjiang* (hoar frost descends), *lidong*
(winter begins), *xiaoxue* (slight snow), *daxue* (great snow), *dongzhi* (winter solstice), *xiao-
han* (slight cold), and *dahan* (great cold).

8. A quotation of two lines of a Tang poem.

9. "Blessed Land and Cave/Grotto Heaven," 洞天福地, common Daoist metaphors
to indicate their place of residence, urban or in the wilds and mountains. See ET, 1:
368-73.

10. Confucius, *Analects*, 2. 22.

11. "Loanname . . .": literally, through a borrowed name. The term *jiaming* 假名 in
the poem points to the important concepts of "entering the provisional (*rujia* 入假)"
by Zhiyi 智顗 (538-597 CE) and of *prañapti* in Buddhism developed by Nāgājuna. *Jia*
means to borrow, to pretend, to assume, and to hypothesize, and *jiaming* thus means
false, provisional, or unreal names. In the Buddhist doctrine of *upāya*, however, unre-
alities can provide the very means to think about the real, because the illusory or phenomenal can reveal and teach what is true. *Jiaming* thus resonates with the Daoist philosophy of language and signs and their massive exploitation of symbols, tropes, and
metaphors (*piyu*) discussed in introduction IV. See also the perceptive analysis of the
novel in relations to *prajñapti* in Qiancheng Li's pioneering monograph, *Fictions of Enlightenment: Journey to the West, Tower of Myriad Mirrors, and Dream of the Red Chamber*
(Honolulu, 2004), pp. 35-46. *Jiaming* in a literary context is thus another marvelous
synonym for fiction.

12. Yellow-sperm (*Polygonatum gigantum* var. *thumbergii*): a small plant the roots of
which are often used for medicinal purposes by the Chinese.

13. According to ancient Chinese taxonomy, the five divisions of living creatures are:
the winged creatures, the hairy creatures, the armored creatures, the scaly creatures,
and the naked creatures (i.e., humans).

14. The dragon's pulse is one of the magnetic currents recognized by geomancers.

15. The rotted ax handle (*lanke*) alludes to a mountain by such a name (Lankeshan)
in the province of Zhejiang, south of Juzhou. According to the *Shuyiji* 述異記, a certain Wang Zhi (王質) of the Jin (晉) period went to this mountain to gather wood. Two
youths whom he saw playing chess gave him a fruit to eat shaped like the pit of a nut,
after which he felt no hunger at all. When at last the game was finished, one of the
youths pointed to his ax and said, "Your handle has rotted!" When Wang returned to
his home, a century had elapsed. There is also a chess classic in Chinese named *Lanke
jing*; see JW, chapter 10.

16. Double Three: *sansan* 三三 can mean quite a few things in Chinese. First, it can
be an abbreviated term for three times three, which means the number 9, a symbol of
perfection in both Buddhism and Daoism, as we will see throughout the novel. Second,
it may likely allude to the Buddhist doctrine of the three samādhis (also accepted by
some Quanzhen patriarchs), the meditation on three subjcsts, which are (1) *kong*, or
emptiness, purging the mind of all ideas and illusions; (2) *wuxiang*, or no appearance,
purging the mind of all phenomena and external forms; and (3) *wuyuan*, or no desire,
purging the mind of all desires. The Double Three is the advanced type of meditation,
which term of each is doubled (e.g., *kongkong*, etc.).

17. A pun on the words "surname" and "temper," both of which are pronounced *xing*,

but are written with a different radical to the left of the Chinese graphs. The Patriarch asked for Monkey's surname, but Monkey heard it as a remark about his "temper." See further discussion in introduction IV. The dialogue here between the Patriarch Subodhi and Monkey with puns on "name" and "temper [the graph has a third important meaning of nature]" seems most likely to have been derived from a conversation between the Fourth Chan (Zen) Patriarch Daoxin 道信 (530-651) and a young boy of exceptionally attractive features whom he met while traveling to Yellow Plum County (the youth later to be canonized as the Fifth Patriarch Hongren 弘忍 [602-675]). "The Patriarch asked: 'Son, what's your name (姓)?' The child replied, 'It's the nature (性) of Buddha.' The Patriarch said, 'So, you don't have a name!' The boy said, 'It's because my nature is empty/void (姓空故).' Recognizing him to be a vessel of the Dharma, the Patriarch ordered his attendant to go the boy's home to beg parental permission for the youth to leave the family [i.e., to become a Buddhist]. The parents regarded this as predestined affinity and offered no objection; they gave him up as a disciple to be named Hongren (profound forbearance)." The story is preserved in the classic of Chan genealogy, Jingde chuandeng lu 景德傳燈錄 (A Record of the Transmission of the Lamp in the Jingde era), compiled by the monk Daoyuan 道原 in 1004. See # 2076 in T51: 0222b.

CHAPTER TWO

1. In Buddhism, *māra* has the meaning of the Destroyer, the Evil One, and the Hinderer. The Chinese term *mo* traditionally used to translate it also has the meaning of demon. "Primal or primordial or original spirit, *yuanshen* 元神" is a term favored by Ming alchemical texts. According to Martina Darga's entry on "Shengtai or Holy Embryo," "comparing the development of the embryo to the revelation of Buddhahood is typical of *neidan* texts of the Ming period. For instance, the XMGZ . . . uses Body of the Law (*fashen* 法身, *dharmakāya*) as a synonym for *shengtai*. The birth of the embryo represents the appearance of the original spirit (*yuanshen* 元神) or Buddhahood and is understood as enlightenment." See ET 2: 884. This understanding is consistently presumed in the text of XYJ.

2. Possibly a reference to Buddhism here, but it is Buddhism as seen through the understanding of Ming syncretism. The three vehicles (*sansheng, triyāna*) are the conveyances that carry living beings across mortality to the shores of *Nirvāṇa*. They are generally divided into the categories of great, medium, and small.

3. The tail of the yak or deer was adopted by the great conversationalists of antiquity as a ceremonious instrument. Used sometimes as a fly-brush or duster, it became inseparably associated with the Daoist or Buddhist recluse and served as a symbol of his purity and detachment.

4. "Three Parties, *sanjia* 三家": see the discussion of the possible different meanings of the term in introduction IV.

5. I have not been able to determine the meaning of the metaphor "treading the arrow," though it may refer to some practice (possibly sexual) in physiological alchemy. Other practices, such as "taking red lead (*hongqian*), making autumn stone (*qiushi*)," mentioned by the Patriarch, echo a similar portion of XMGZ that reviews various techniques and practices of alchemists. See the chapter, "On Deviancy and Orthodoxy, Xiezheng shuo 邪正說," in XMGZ-Taipei, pp. 55-56. "Red mercury" is the

name for a virgin's menstrual discharge, while "autumn stone" refers to the urine of a virgin boy.

6. The period from 11:00 p.m. to 1:00 a.m.

7. A symbol of perfection and a symbol for brazier in alchemy, the moon, as we have seen in the name of the Patriarch's cave, may also refer to the heart in alchemical discourse.

8. In this line, the moon, the rabbit, the sun, and the crow may all refer to various parts of the viscera inside the human adept's body.

9. "Tortoise and snake": an allusion to the Perfected Warrior or Zhenwu (also known as the Dark Warrior, Xuanwu), "a divinity known for his powers of healing and exorcism. In Han dynasty cosmology, the Dark Warrior was one of the four animals corresponding to the cardinal directions. . . . Usually depicted as a serpent coiled around a tortoise." The allusion here uses the figure to symbolize the state of achieved immortality. Citation from entry in ET 2: 1266.

10. According to the literature of internal alchemy, there are five forces in the human body that correspond to the Five Phases: *jing* (sperm or essence, water); *shen* (spirit, fire); *hun* (soul, wood); *po* (vigor, metal or gold); *yi* (intent or will, earth). If the forces are allowed to follow their natural course, then the fluids become blood, and the blood becomes vital discharges (sperm, menstruation, vaginal fluids, and saliva) which may flow out of the body. The advocacy of reversing the five forces aims at retaining them within the body, and eventually, reversing their flow with the help of harnassing the body's pneumatic vitality (*qi*), so as to prevent decline and decay.

11. The period from 11:00 a.m. to 1:00 p.m.

12. "Nine apertures": eyes, nostrils, ears, mouth, and urinal and anal passages.

13. Oxen made of cast iron were placed in streams or fields; farmers used them as a charm to prevent floods.

14. "Eight epochs": the first days of spring, summer, autumn, and winter, the two equinoxes, and the solstices.

15. "Three Regions": the Buddhist division of the world into the three realms of desire, form, and pure spirit. Hence the term frequently means the world or the universe.

16. "Five Phases": *wuxing* 五行; they are metal, wood, water, fire, and earth. For the precise meaning of the term, Five Evolutive Phases, see Manfred Porkert, *The Theoretical Foundations of Chinese Medicine: Systems of Correspondence* (Cambridge), 1974), pp. 43‒54.

17. An inconsistency in the text.

CHAPTER THREE

1. "Ten species": the five kinds of beings (ecclesiastical, earthly, human, divine, and demonic) and the five divisions of living creatures (see chapter 1, note 13). The Hell of Ninefold Darkness (*jiuyou* 九幽) is a Daoist hell.

2. A *yakṣa* is generally thought of in Indian religions as a demon in the earth, the air, or the lower heavens. They can be violent and malignant, but in this novel, they seem to be associated much more with the oceans.

3. Heavenly River is the Chinese name for the Milky Way.

4. The Great Yu was the putative founder of the Xia dynasty (ca. 2205 BCE) and the mythic conqueror of the Flood in China.

5. The accepted understanding in Chinese historical culture is that the transcendence of the Five Phases (i.e., to be beyond the control of their dynamics) is to have attained de facto the state of immortality.

6. For the translation of these ten kings, I follow Arthur Waley. See his discussion in *A Catalogue of Paintings Recovered from Tun-Huang by Sir Aurel Stein* (London, 1931), pp. xxvi-xxx. For more recent scholarship, see Stephen F. Teiser, *The Scripture on the Ten Kings and the Making of Purgatory in Medieval Chinese Buddhism* (Honolulu, 1994).

7. The identity of this divinity, 邱弘濟, is intriguing, as he appears quite often in the entire novel—chapters 3, 6, 31, 51, 58, 83, and 87—and holding no less another exalted title of Celestial Master (*tianshi* 天師). For a brief but illuminating discussion that the person might be the apotheosized Qiu Chuji, see "Quanzhen jiao," in HFTWJ, 3: 1381-82.

8. This is likely the apotheosized Ge Hong.

9. As noted in the introduction, these are the stock metaphors, often in pairs, of internal or physiological alchemy.

CHAPTER FOUR

1. The verse here is alluding to the Indra heaven with its thirty-three summits (*trayastriṁśās*) and to the six heavens of desire (*devalokas*). The first of these heavens is situated halfway up Mount Sumeru, where Indra is said to rule over his thirty-two devas. For descriptions of the Heavens, see the *Dazhidu lun* 大智度論 (the śastra ascribed to Nāgārjuna on the greater *Prajñā-pāramitā sūtra*, translated by Kumārajīva), and *Jushe lun* 俱舍論 (the *Abhidharma-kośa śāstra*), translated into Chinese by Paramārtha and the historical Xuanzang.

2. The Star of Long Life in Chinese mythology.

3. Special judges in the Underworld, traditionally robed in red, blue, and green.

4. "Jade rabbit, gold crow": Daoist metaphors for the sun and the moon. The lunar rabbit or hare, according to some scholars, may also have been a myth derived from Indian sources.

5. In Chinese folklore, the monkey is said to be able to ward off sickness from horses. This title is a pun on the words *bi* (to avoid, to keep off), *ma* (horse), and *wen* (pestilence, plague).

6. In this poem, which is exceedingly difficult to translate, the author has made use of numerous lists of horses associated with the emperors Zhou Muwang (ca. 1001-942 BCE), Qin Shi Huangdi (221-209 BCE), and Han Wendi (179-157 BCE). To construct the poem, some names are used merely for their tonal effects (e.g., *chizhi* and *yaoniao*), while others have ostensible meanings as well. My translation attempts to approximate the original. Those interested in famous and legendary horses in Chinese lore should consult the relevant sections on horses in the TPYL, *j* 9.

7. The modern Khokand, where the best horses are said to be raised.

8. This is the legendary character Zhang Daoling 張道陵, widely celebrated as the founder of the Daoist religion and also intimately associated with the the Way of the Celestial Masters or Tianshi Dao 天師道. See respective entries on Zhang and "Tianshi" in ET 2: 1222-23, 979-81.

9. Li Jing 李靖, the god here, is actually the Indian deity Vaiśravaṇa. For a detailed study of the lineage and pedigree of this deity and his family in Chinese literary and

religious history, see Liu Ts'un-yan, "Pishamen tianwang fuzi yu Zhongguo xiaoshuo zhi guanxi 毘沙門天王父子與中國小說之關係," in HFTWJ, 2: 1045–94.

10. The Three Platforms (*santai*) or terraces are the offices of Daoist Star Spirits (i.e., three pairs of stars in *Ursa Major*), which are said to correspond to the Three Officials (*sangong*) in imperial government. See the "Tianwenzhi 天文志," in *Jinshu* 晉書, *j* 13; entries "Taiyi" and "Taishang ganying pian" in ET 2: 958 and 949.

11. This is the Bull Monster King, who will reappear in the Red Boy episode, chapters 40–42, and in the episode of the Mountain of Flames, chapters 59–61.

12. "Star Spirits of Five Poles": *wudou xingjun* 五斗, literally, Lords of the Five Dippers, they are Daoist deities.

CHAPTER FIVE

1. The highest gods of the Daoist Pantheon. They are: the Jade-Pure Celestial Worthy of Original Commencement (Yuqing yuanshi tianzun), the Exalted-Pure Celestial Worthy of Numinous Treasures (Shangqing lingbao tianzun), and the Primal-Pure Celestial Worthy of the Way and Virtue (Taiqing daode tianzun, also named Taiqing taishang laojun). The last one is the name of the deified Laozi.

2. "Four Thearchs": the *sidi* 四帝 of early Chinese mythology firmly embraced by later Daoism are divided according to directional orientations and colors—green (east), white (west), red (south), and black (north). The Center's Yellow Thearch or Yellow Emperor, when added, makes up the Five Thearchs, a group different from legendary figures in documents of history, possibly alluded to in the beginning of chapter 1.

3. Nine Luminaries: Āditya (the sun), Sōma (the moon), Aṅgāraka (Mars, also in Chinese, the Planet of Fire), Budha (Mercury, the Planet of Water), Bṛhaspati (Jupiter, the Planet of Wood), Sukra (Venus, the Planet of Gold), Śanaiścara (Saturn, the Planet of Earth), Rāhu (the spirit that causes eclipses), and Ketu, a comet.

4. The Generals of the Five Quarters are the five powerful Bodhisattvas who are guardians of the four quarters and the center. The Constellations or Star Lodges (*xu* 宿) are the twenty-eight *nakṣatras*, divided into four mansions (east-spring, south-summer, west-autumn, and north-winter), each of which has seven members.

5. These four are the external protectors of Indra, each living on a side of Mount Meru. They defend the world against the attack of evil spirits or asuras; hence the name of The Four Devarājas, Guardians of the World. They are: Dhṛtarāṣṭra, Upholder of the Kingdom; Virūḍhaka, King of Growth; Virūpākṣa, the Broad-eyed Deva King; and Vaiśravaṇa, the God of Great Learning. Kuvera, the God of Wealth, is also a member of this group.

6. They are: Zi (Rat, 11:00 p.m.–1:00 a.m.), Chou (Ox, 1:00–3:00 a.m.), Yin (Tiger, 3:00–5:00 a.m.), Mao (Hare, 5:00–7:00 a.m.), Chen (Dragon, 7:00–9:00 a.m.), Si (Serpent, 9:00–11:00 a.m.), Wu (Horse, 11:00 a.m.–1:00 p.m.), Wei (Sheep, 1:00–3:00 p.m.), Shen (Monkey, 3:00–5:00 p.m.), You (Cock, 5:00–7:00 p.m.), Xu (Dog, 7:00–9:00 p.m.), Hai (Boar, 9:00–11:00 p.m.).

7. Five Elders: these deities of the Daoist Pantheon represent the essences (*jing*) of the Five Phases.

8. All of these are deities of the Daoist Pantheon, developed and expanded from the early medieval period down to the time of the Ming. The various deities are a syncretic assembly of those appropriated from Indic Buddhism and of those local and transre-

gional figures in territorial China. Some of those figures antedated the rise of organized Daoism in the second century CE.

9. This is Xu Sun 許遜 (trad. 239-374), a figure celebrated in cultic religious lore as
healer, exorcist, dragon-slayer, and a highly filial son. His several biographies and portraits are found in the DZ. See entry on name in ET 2: 1124-26.

10. Sometimes called the Lady Queen Mother (Wangmu niangniang), or the Queen
Mother of the West (Xi Wangmu), she is the highest goddess of Daoism. Her official
residence is the Palace of the Jasper Pool on Mount Kunlun in Tibet. She has been studied extensively in international scholarship. See entry in ET 2: 1119-20 and relevant
bibliography.

11. Five-colored clouds: these clouds are always considered auspicious symbols and
symptoms of a hallowed region, inhabited by gods or transcendents.

12. Naked Feet: A Song book of anecdotes by one Wang Mingqing 王明清 told the
story of how the mother of the crown prince, Zhaoling 昭陵, was summoned to attend
the emperor because she dreamt that an immortal (yushi 羽士) with bare feet revealed
to her that he was to be her son. Zhaoling, who later became the Emperor Renzong, was
fond of taking off shoes and socks as a boy. Because of Renzong's known devotion to the
Daoist religion, he was later nicknamed the Immortal of Naked Feet, a distinguished
honor because the title was also used first to designate Laozi.

13. "Dragon livers, phoenix marrow, bear paws, lips of apes": four of the eight dainties (see the wine makers's complaint later in this chapter) in traditional grand cuisine
of historical Chinese culture, the rest being rabbit embryo, carp tail, broiled asprey,
and koumiss.

14. According to the chapter "On Golden Elixir, Jindan 金丹," in Baopuzi, neipian, j
4, attributed to the alchemist Ge Hong (283-343), the classification of the efficacy of
the elixir is as follows: "The elixir of one turn, if taken, will enable a man to become an
immortal in three years; that of two turns, if taken, will enable a man to become an immortal in two years. . . ." And so on, until one reaches the elixir of nine reverted [cylin-
drical] turns (jiuzhuan jindan 九轉金丹 or huandan 還丹), which, if taken, "will enable
a man to become an immortal in three days." The "turn" apparently refers to the process of cyclical chemical or physical manipualtions of the elixir ingredients: hence the
greater the number of turns, the more powerful the elixir. See Nathan Sivin, Chinese Alchemy: Preliminary Studies (Cambridge, MA, 1968), pp. 36-52; SCC, 5/2: 62-71.

15. Fearless Guards: these are custodians of the Law.

16. Temporal Guardians: they are the guardians of the year, the month, the day, and
the hour.

17. Five Mountains and Four Rivers: the moutains are Tai (east), Hua (west), Heng
(south), Heng (north), and Song (central). The four rivers are the Yangzi, the Huanghe
(Yellow River), the Huai, and the Zhi.

18. Five Plagues: possibly a reference to the five epidemics in Vaiśālī during Buddha's
lifetime: eye-bleeding, nose-bleeding, pus from the ears, lockjaw, and foul taste of all food.

19. All the names in the following five lines of verse are the members of the Twenty-
Eight Constellations.

20. In Buddhism, the ten evil things (Daśākuśala) are: killing, stealing, adultery, lying, double-tongue, deceitful language, filthy language, covetousness, anger, and per-
verted thoughts.

CHAPTER SIX

1. The Potalaka Mountain, located southeast of Malakūta, is the home of Avalokiteśvara. In the Chinese tradition of popular Buddhism, the equivalent place is the Putuo Mountain, east of the port city of Ningbo in Zhejiang Province, where it is the center of the cult of Guanyin.

2. In Chinese religions, the Immortal Master Erlang has been variously identified with Zhao Yu 趙昱 of the Sui, with Li Bing 李冰 of Sichuan, and with a certain Yang Jian 楊戩, the powerful magician and warrior in the *Investiture of the Gods*. For further discussions, see Huang Zhigang 黃芝崗, *Zhongguo di shuishen* 中國的水神 (Shanghai, 1934), pp. 7–84; *Antecedents*, pp. 146–54; Li Sichun 李思純, "Guankoushi shen kao 灌口氏神考," and Liu Dexing 劉德馨, "Du Guankoushi shen kao di shangque 讀灌口氏神考的商榷," in *Jiangcun shilun* 江村十論 (Shanghai, 1957), pp. 63–74, 75–78; and more recently, Ho Kin Chung, "Métamorphoses d'une figure mythologique: Erlang Shen," in *Hommage à Kwong Hing Foon: études d'histoire culturelle de la Chine*, ed. Jean-Pierre Diény (Paris, 1995), pp. 215–38.

3. In Buddhism, the eight emblems would refer to the eight marks of good fortune on the sole of Buddha's foot—wheel, conch shell, umbrella, canopy, lots flower, jar, pair of fishes, and mystic signs—which, in turn, were symbols of the organs in Buddha's body. On the other hand, the emblems (literally, treasures) may refer to the magic weapons of the Eight Immortals of Daoism: sword, fan, flower basket, lotus flower, flute, gourd, castanet, and a stringed musical instrument.

4. Chi City: 赤城, likely a reference to the Prefecture of Guanzhou in Sichuan Province, since the Erlang cult was supposed to have originated from the region.

5. This aspect of Erlang's lineage, an important one in the god's legend, alludes again to the theme of the banished immortal for transgressive behavior. The cultic belief is that Erlang is the second son of the Jade Emperor's sister (hence the name, Erlang 二郎 or Second Son), who was exiled to this world for adultery and her son's illegitimate birth. Erlang's subsequent act of rescuing his mother from her imprisonment beneath the Peach Mountain is thus a filial act that redeems both mother and son.

6. In traditional depiction, Erlang always appears as a god with a third, vertical almond-shaped eye in the center of his forehead.

CHAPTER SEVEN

1. The phrase, "the Monkey of the Mind and the Horse of the Will" (*xinyuan yima*) is made up of metaphors commonly used in Buddhist writings. See discussion in introduction IV. Echoing the titular couplet here, the fourth poem of the chapter expands and clarifies the metaphor of *xinyuan*. The term appears repeatedly in the titles of chapters 14, 30, 35, 36, and 41.

2. Possibly a reference to the Sun God, although "Lord of the East or Dongjun" in classical Chinese poetry may refer to the East wind that refreshes and revives in spring time.

3. Samādhi fire: the fire that is said to consume the body of Buddha when he enters Nirvāṇa. But in the syncretic religious milieu of vernacular fiction, this fire is possessed by many fighters or warriors who have attained immortality (including a Daoist deity like Erlang), and it is often used as a weapon.

4. In Daoism, seven is regarded as a sacred number; a perfected cycle often is calculated on the basis of seven times seven. The symbolic signifance may also have derived from Buddhist understanding that after death, a human can attain the proper "reformation" for transmigration proper after seven cycles of seven days of dissolution and formation. See FXDCD, p. 48b, for various entries on "Seven times Seven 七七."

5. This line explicitly rejects any interpretation of the Monkey figure in terms of physical or external alchemy (*waidan*), even though his symbolic significance will be troped and correlated with several metaphors often used in physiological or internal alchemy.

6. "Three refuges (*triśaraṇa*)" refer to three kinds of surrender: to Buddha as master, to the Law (*Dharma*) as medicine, and to the community of monks (*Saṅgha*) as friends. The "five commandments (*pañca veramaṇī*)" are prohibitions against killing, stealing, adultery, lying, and intoxicating beverages.

7. The twin Sāl trees in the grove in which Śākyamuni entered Nirvāṇa.

8. Numinous Officer Wang: Wang Numinous Officer 王靈官, a familiar guardian deity of Daoist temples. For attributed name and legends, see entry in ET 2: 1013-14.

9. Known for its luster, this pearl is said to give sight to the blind.

10. The progress to transcendence is clear and specific in the novel: magic, immortality, and Buddhahood may be attained by disciplined morality and askesis, but lapses and backsliding can reverse the process. For an animal figure like Monkey, he can revert back to his "original form (*yuanxing* 原形)," just like many monsters and even celestial gods can do so throughout the novel.

11. This is the Daoist celestial officer who happens to be the pre-incarnate Pig or Zhu Wuneng (nicknamed Eight Rules), the second disciple of the novel's human pilgrim. The reference here anticipates Eight Rules' words later in chapter 19 berating Monkey: "When you caused such turmoil that year in Heaven, you had no idea how many of us had to suffer because of you."

12. According to the *Suishu* 隋書, the Six Women Officials were established in the Han dynasty. They were in charge of palace upkeep, palatial protocol, court attire, food and medicine, and the various artisans of the court. See *j* 36 in *Ershiwushi* 3: 24-57a.

13. For the translation of the names of the Daoist "Trinity," I follow more recent scholarship. See the entry on "*sanqing*: Three Clarities; Three Purities; Three Pure Ones" in ET 2: 840-44.

14. Pinning of corsages: supposedly a custom of the Song. After offering sacrifices at the imperial family's ancestral shrine, the emperor and his subjects would pin flowers on their clothes and their caps.

15. Wuling: a prefecture located in the town of Changde in modern Hunan province. Its fame rests on the "Peach-Blossom Spring" poems written by Tao Qian (365-427) and later by Wang Wei (655-759). The spring is near the town.

16. "Sun and moon . . . vase": a metaphoric expression for the alchemical process that accelerates time to accomplish the desired transformation of the substances deposited therein.

17. Ten Islets: mythical places for the home of immortals or transcendents.

18. The three wains are the three vehicles (*triyāna*) drawn by a goat, a deer, and an ox to convey the living across the cycles of births and deaths (*saṁsāra*) to the shores of

Nirvāṇa. The vehicles may well have prefigured the later metaphors of the three chariots or carts (*sanche* 三車) adopted in the discourse of internal alchemy. See discussion of JW, chapters 44-46, in introduction IV.

19. "Nine-grade" refers to the nine classes or grades of rewards in the Pure Land.

20. The Mādhyamika or Sanlun School advocates the doctrine of formless or nothingness (*animitta, nirābhāsa*).

21. "Form is emptiness and the very emptiness is form" is the celebrated assertion of the *Heart Sūtra* (the *Prajñāpāramitāhrdaya*). See a full translation in JW, chapter 19, and also *Buddhist Texts through the Ages*, trans. and ed. Edward Conze, et al. (New York, 1964), p. 152.

22. Buddha's transformed (deified) body is said to be sixteen feet tall, the same height as his earthly body.

23. Good stock: (善根, *kuśala-mula*), the Buddhist idea of the good seeds sown by a virtuous life that will bring future rewards.

CHAPTER EIGHT

1. One of the two capitals of the Tang (618-906), renamed Xi'an in modern times, it is located in Shaanxi Province.

2. "Polishing . . . foodstuff": metaphors for useless labor, here used as a slightly polemical ridicule of Chan Buddhist rituals.

3. The mustard seed, or *sarṣapa*, is considered in Buddhist lore to be the smallest grain, whereas the Sumeru is the central mountain range of the Buddhist cosmos. Hence these two lines refer to the paradox that the smallest may contain the greatest.

4. One of Śākyamuni's principal disciples who was also chief of the ascetics before the enlightenment, with another and more familiar name of Mahākāśyapa. The reference alludes to a famous tale of how only one disciple of the Buddha understood his esoteric teaching on Chan (Zen) principles by smiling at Buddha's gift of a single flower. Twenty-eight generations later, the mystery passed down by this disciple allegedly reached China as this division of Buddhism so named.

5. Ten stops or stages (*daśabhūmi*): part of the different stages taught by different schools of Buddhism on the process of how a bodhisattva might develop into a Buddha.

6. Three wains or vehicles (*sansheng* 三乘; Skt. *Triyāna*): differently explained by various exponents, the three vehicles usually refer to the three means of conveyance that carry sentient beings across the cycles of birth and death or mortality to reach the shores of Ultimate Bliss or Nirvāṇa. In different scriptures, the vehicles or carts are usually drawn by a goat, a deer, and an ox or a bull, and these three images also appear in Quanzhen writings, as we have seen in introduction IV. In the literature on internal or physiological alchemy, moreover, the term refers to three levels of accomplishment (sometimes named *sancheng* 三成), comprising the process of refining (or "smelting") essence into pneumatic vitality (*lianjing huaqi* 煉精化氣), refining pneumatic vitality into spirit (*lianqi huashen* 煉氣化神), and refining spirit and reverting to emptiness (*lianshen huanxu* 煉神還虛). See the entry on "Neidan" in ET 2: 764-66. Some commentators of the XYJ understand different episodes of the novel as illustrative representations of part of these processes.

7. The four creatures, according to Buddhist understanding, are those born of the

womb or stomach (*jarāyuja, viviparous*), as are mammals; those born of eggs (*aṇḍaja, oviparous*), as are birds; those born of moisture (*saṁsvedaja*, i.e., worms and fishes); and those which evolve or metamorphose in different forms (*aupapāduka*, i.e., insects). The six ways point to the sixfold path of reincarnation or transmigration, which are: that of hell (*nāraka-gati*), that of hungry ghosts (*preta-gati*), that of malevolent spirits (*asura-gati*), that of animals (*tiryagyoni-gati*), that of man (*manuṣya-gati*), and that of heavenly beings (*deva-gati*).

8. A stream in Guangdong Province where, in the Tang, the Sixth Patriarch of Chan Huineng taught.

9. A place said to be frequented by the Buddha, and where the *Lotus sūtra* was preached. The full name is Spirit Vulture Peak (Lingjiu feng 靈鷲峰; Skt., Gṛdhra-kūṭa).

10. Three jewels or three treasures (*sanbao* 三寶) : a reference to the Buddha, the Dharma, and the Saṅgha.

11. As noted in introduction III, item 3, this poem, except for the concluding three lines, is a near verbatim citation of a lyric to the same tune by one Feng Zunshi, collected in a volume of the Daoist Canon.

12. Wisdom and understanding.

13. Three realms: *sanjie* 三界, the Buddhist analogs to the triple world of Brahmanic cosmology. They are the earth, atmosphere, and heaven.

14. *Sārī* or *satrīra* is usually associated with the relics of Buddha.

15. The permanent reality underlying all phenomena.

16. Tianzhu: the traditional Chinese name for India.

17. That is, the Mādhyamika School.

18. A park near Śrāvastī, said to be a favorite resort of Śākyamuni. The park and the region are mentioned again in chapter 93.

19. The "Ghost Festival" or "Feast of All Souls," celebrated in China by both Daoists and Buddhists. For an earlier study of this and other "masses" for the dead, see K. L. Reichelt, *Truth and Tradition in Chinese Buddhism: A Study of Chinese Mahayana Buddhism* (Shanghai, 1927), pp. 77–126. For a more recent and authoritative treatment of the festival, see Stephen F. Teiser, *The Ghost Festival in Medieval China* (Princeton, 1988).

20. The name means "the most venerable one of the world," an epithet for Buddha.

21. A reference to the five substances or components of an intelligent being like a human. They are form (*rūpa*), reception (*vendanā*, i.e., sensation and feeling), thought (*sañyñā*, i.e., discernment), action (*saṁskāra*), and cognition (*vijñāna*).

22. They differ according to different traditions. In Confucianism, they refer to filial piety, fraternal submission, fidelity, and trustworthiness (*xiao, di, zhong, xin*). In Buddhism, according to a text like the *Mahāyāna-Nirvāṇa Sūtra*, they refer to permanence, joy, the reality of the self, and purity.

23. A kind of sandalwood from southern India.

24. Weak Water (*ruoshui*) is a river located in northwestern China (now Kansu Province), and the entire region has the name of Flowing Sand (*liusha*). See Albert Herrmann, *An Historical Atlas of China*, new ed. (Chicago, 1966), maps 4 and 5.

25. "Wuyi" refers to Wuyishanli, or Arachosia. See Herrmann, map 16, A4.

26. It was Buddha's custom to lay his hand on top of his disciple's head while teaching him.

27. *Sha* means sand, and *Wujing* means "he who awakes to purity."

28. A pun on his religious name, as the Gate of Sand refers to the sand of the River Ganges: hence Buddhism.

29. Marshal of the Heavenly Reeds (Tianpeng yuanshuai) is one of the Four Sages (*sisheng*) in the Daoist pantheon, high-ranking aides to the Jade Emperor.

30. Goddess of the Moon is named Chang'e, wife of the famous legendary archer, Hou Yi, who was said to have obtained drugs of immortality from the Lady Queen Mother of the West. Chang'e stole them and fled to the moon to take up residence in the Vast Cold Palace (Guanghan gong, referred to again in chapter 19). For the story of the goddess, see the end of the Lecture on "Viewing the Dark (*lanming*)," *Huainanzi*, 6.

31. A colloquialism of the Huai'an region, referring to a man living in the woman's house after marriage.

32. The monster here is quoting the words of Confucius in *Analects* 3.13.

33. *Zhu* means pig or hog, and *Wuneng* means "he who awakes to power."

34. According to various Buddhist teachings, the five forbidden viands may refer to spices (leeks, garlic, onion, green onion, and scallion) or to kinds of meat (the flesh of horse, dog, bullock, goose, and pigeon). The three undesirable foods, prohibited by Daoism, are wild goose, dog, and black fish.

35. In vernacular Chinese literature, the mendicant monk with scabby sores or leprosy is frequently a holy man in disguise.

CHAPTER NINE

1. The eight rivers are those and their tributaries in Shaanxi Province: Wei, Jing, Ba, Liao, Ju, Hao, Li, and Chan.

2. Taizong was the second emperor of the Tang dynasty, reigning from 627 to 649 CE.

3. The cyclical name of a year is derived from combining the Ten Celestial Stems with the Twelve Branches or Horary Characters.

4. Wei Zheng 魏徵 was a great statesman of the early Tang period, highly respected by the emperor. He had the reputation of being a fearless remonstrant to the throne. He was also appointed as one of the editors and compilers of the official dynastic histories of the Zhou, Sui, and Northern Qi, three dynasties preceding the Tang. See Howard J. Wechsler, *Mirror to the Son of Heaven: Wei Cheng at the Court of T'ang T'ai-tsung* (New Haven, 1974); CHC 3/1 (1979): 193-211.

5. "The three sessions of examination": a slightly imprecise designation by the novelistic author. Historically, the Tang established two fundamental levels of scrutiny in the examination system—students at the local schools and graduates from the capital's state schools. Beyond them were the candidates for the most advanced level (*jinshi* 進士), and these were permitted to choose one of twelve subjects (e.g., the classics, law, mathematics, and calligraphy) in which they were to be examined. Eventually, the nomenclature *jinshi* became the highest degree that students taking such civil service examinations could attain. By 658, however, the first palace examination took place, "organized by the emperor's order for specified candidates" (see CHC 3/1: 277). Empress Wu Zetian (r. 690-705) also "in 689 . . . initiated the personal examination of candidates by the ruler" and made it her practice to appoint the most successful candidates to the highest court offices (ibid., 311, 14). It was in the time of the Song that the so-called palace examination (*dianshi* 殿試) was regularized, thereby completing "the three-level examination process: the emperors personally administered this fi-

nal tier of the examination series. In 1066, the government decided that the examinations would be given once every three years. . ."; by 1069, the subject was reduced to only one. The student attaining the highest "grade" in the palace examination was named a *zhuangyuan* 狀元 (literally, the head or source) of the [examination] proclamation." This was the honor attained by the character Chen Guangrui of this chapter. See Thomas H. C. Lee, *Education in Traditional China, A History* (Leiden, 2000), pp. 132-40.

6. "Baby name": literally, a nursing name 乳名, which means that the name is bestowed as a nickname of an infant, subject to change in appropriate circumstance.

7. Since the time of the Song, the most urgent military matters or documents of official pardon were sent by tablets with gold-colored inscriptions or characters. See the *Songshi, Yufuzhi* 宋史, 輿服志.

8. *Cintāmaṇi*, the magic pearl that is capable of responding to every wish and is produced by the ocean's Dragon King.

9. In the *Xu Bowuzhi* 續博物志, it is recorded that there are nine grades of pearls from Vietnam, the second largest kind named "rolling pearl 走珠." But the name "rolling-pan 走盤" may allude to the term used in an essay of Su Dongpo, which reads, "there are four scrolls of *Lengjia* [i.e., the *Laṅkāvatāra sūtra*]," which can stabilize the heart . . . as pearls roll on the pan." See the *Dongpo qiji* 東坡七集, *j* 49: 8, SBBY.

10. *Jiaoxiao* 絞綃: raw silk spun and sold by mermaids, according to Chinese mythology. A bale here (*duan*) is eighteen Chinese feet in length.

CHAPTER TEN

1. The following section is adapted from the encyclopedic chronicle *Yongle dadian* 永樂大典, compiled in 1403-1408 under the commission of the Ming emperor Chengzu. For the Chinese text, see the facsimile version published by Beijing's Zhonghua shuju, 1960; for a translation of this particular episode, see *Antecedents*, pp. 177-79. On the poetic dialogues between the fisherman and the woodcutter, C. T. Hsia in his *Introduction*, p. 347, note 13, has called attention to its parallel to a similar episode in the well-known seventeenth-century novel, *Fengshen yanyi*, or *Investiture of the Gods* (chapter 23), and written that "the Chinese have traditionally associated fishermen and woodcutters with an idyllic life of contemplation detached from worldly cares. The phrase *yü ch'iao* occurs frequently in T'ang poetry. The Northern Sung philosopher Shao Yung wrote a short dialogue between a fisherman and a woodcutter entitled *Yü-ch'iao wên-ta*." Illustrations in the older editions (e.g., the 1592 Shidetang's version) bear the explicit title *Yuchao wenda*.

2. Lyric: now a conventionalized term to translate a genre of premodern Chinese verse named *ci* 詞, which developed toward the end of the Tang period (907). Originally appearing as popular songs and ballads from the teahouses and brothels, the poems were further influenced by musical modes from central and northern Asia. Their tonal patterns and rhyme schemes followed the established patterns of tonal juxtapositions of the Tang regulated verse (*lüshi*), but these patterns became much more varied and complex when each "tune" eventually came to possess its own distinctive scheme or set metrical form for tones, length of lines, and rhymes. Most tunes consist of two halves, generally—but not invariably—of matching patterns, of which the lyrics of this chapter offer some ready examples. Later in the Song, longer lyrics developed

occasionally with three segments. The segments are named "pieces, or *pian* 片," in Chinese prosody, but they should not be confused with stanzaic constructions of poetry from other languages.

3. "Chicken heads": seeds of *Euryale-ferox*, so named because of their shape.

4. *Chun* leaves: *Cedrela sinensio* or *Cedrela odorata*. *Lian* sprouts: *Melia japonica*.

5. This poem is adapted primarily from lines of the first half of another lyric to the tune of "A Courtful of Blossoms, *Mantingfang* 满庭芳," by the Song poet Qin Guan 秦觀 (1049-1100). The pertinent lines read: "Dense flowers of red smartweeds; / Tousled leaves of yellow rushes / . . . The blue sky empty and wide, / Light clouds and a clear Chu River / . . . . With a small golden hook / And a line slowly drawn / I stir a pool of stars 红蓼花繁, / 黄蘆葉亂, / . . . 齊天空闊, / 雲淡楚江清. / . . . . 金钩细, / 絲編慢捲, / 牽動一潭星." See QSC 1: 458.

6. Circling chess: the game of Go or *weiqi* 圍棋.

7. This is a quotation from the last two lines of the first of two poems on "Small plum blossoms in a mountain garden 山園小梅" by the early Song poet, Lin Bu 林逋 (967-1028), better known as Lin Hejing 林和靖.

8. The linking-verse is generally a long poem composed by two or more persons, each offering alternate lines. To test the skill of the participants, often regarded as contestants, one particular rhyme scheme will be mandated for use for the entire composition.

9. The writing of the Chinese text here is a bit ambiguous. The first line of the poem would be spoken presumably by Zhang Shao, the fisherman, to be followed in the next line by the woodcutter, and so on.

10. Longmen: a place in Shaanxi Province famous for the carp making its annual ascent up the rapids of the Yellow River.

11. "Frost Descends . . . Double Ninth": one of the twenty-four solar terms, Frost Descends is approximately 23 October in the calendar. The ninth day of the ninth lunar month is also called Double Yang, a much celebrated festival. For the legends associated with the day, see A. R. Davis, "The Double Ninth Festival in Chinese Poetry: A Study of Variations Upon a Theme," in *Wen-lin: Studies in the Chinese Humanities*, ed. Chow Tsetsung (Madison, Milwaukee, and London, 1968), pp. 45-64.

12. Three Dukes refer to the three chief officials of state (*sangong* 三公), traditionally understood to be the Taishi (Grand Turtor), the Taifu (Grand Preceptor), and the Taibao (Grand Guardian or Protector) of the Zhou. For critical reconstruction of the various governmental officers and agencies, see Herlee G. Creel, *The Origins of Statecraft in China*, Vol. 1 (Chicago and London, 1970), pp. 101-32. For more recent discussion of the term's usages in imperial China, see Hucker, # 4871, p. 399. My translation here follows Hucker.

13. These two lines quote from the famous conversation between the strategist Zhuge Liang and his rival of another state, Zhou Yu, before the battle of Red Cliff against the vastly superior forces of Cao Cao, the third contender for the throne of Han. See *The Three Kingdoms*, chapter 49.

14. The four proper names mentioned in these two lines refer to Confucius (Kong Qiu), Mencius (Meng Ke), the Duke of Zhou (Zhou Gong), and King Wen (putative founder of the Zhou dynasty).

15. Unlike the Arabic numeral one, the Chinese graph for one is a single horizon-

tal stroke. Thus the headwrap is quite flat as used in the traditional attire of a student or scholar.

16. Dragon . . . Tiger: references to the astronomical signs as zodiac animals under which these people were born.

17. An incense burner.

18. Guigu or Guiguzi (Master of the Ghostly Valley) was a legendary strategist and expert diviner of antiquity.

19. Duanxi, a stream in Guangdong Province famous for its stones that can be turned into fine ink slabs.

20. Famous poet of the Jin (265-419 CE) who was also known to be a master occultist. There is a typographical error in the Chinese text here, as the personal name Pu 璞 is given as 模.

21. The hours of Dragon, Serpent, Horse, and Sheep are 7:00-9:00 a.m., 9:00-11:00 a.m., 11:00 a.m.-1:00 p.m., and 1:00-3:00 p.m.

22. The hour of the Monkey is 3:00-5:00 p.m.

23. Silver stream is a metaphor for the Milky Way.

24. Time float: a clepsydra or water clock. In this device, water drips from a large jar, and the receding liquid is measured by a bamboo index. By the time the water falls to a certain marking, it will be the first watch.

25. An allusion to *Zhuangzi* 2, where the narrator dreams that is transformed into a butterfly.

26. The hour of the Rat is 11:00 p.m.-1:00 a.m.

27. Royal flags and banners are decorated with the feathers of kingfishers or halcyons.

28. Yao and Shun: the legendary sage emperors, two of the five thearchs of antiquity. Shun was said to have served Yao with complete loyalty and obedience before succeeding the latter as ruler.

29. Mountain-river (*shanhe*) is usually a metaphor for the world or empire.

30. The three signs: the sun, the moon, and the stars.

31. The Chess Immortal is literally the immortal with the rotted ax handle, the allusion used in chapter 1; see note 15.

32. Jingde: frequently the name of Yuchi Gong in vernacular Chinese fiction. He was a famous general serving at the Tang court.

33. The last lines of the poem and the immediately following episode of the novel provide a bit of satirical etiology for the origin of the popular practice of having portraits of these two generals pasted on either side of a house's main entrance as guardian spirits.

34. Shen Shu 神荼 and Yu Lü 鬱壘 are also guardian deities of the home, their portraits similarly pasted on either side of the main entrance. See Derk Bodde, *Festivals in Classical China* (Princeton and Hong Kong, 1975), pp. 127-38.

35. The poem is actually a lyric to the tune of "Moon Over West River."

36. In a famous episode of "The Three Kingdoms," chapter 85, the dying emperor, Liu Bei, entrusts the affairs of state to his prime minister and strategist, Zhuge Liang. To the faithful and able subject who has served him for nearly three decades, the emperor says, "If my heir can be helped, then help him. But if he turns out to be worthless, then take the throne yourself at Chengdu."

CHAPTER ELEVEN

1. As noted in introduction III, item 4, this regulated poem is actually a poetic paraphrase and partial adaption of a prose ritual text titled, "Shengtang wen 昇堂文 (Proclamation upon the ascension of the Main Hall)" by one Qin Zhenren 秦真人, in Minghe yuyin, DZ 1100, 24: 308-09.

2. "Termites disband": an allusion to the Tang short story Nankeji 南柯记 (Story of the Southern Branch), or the Nanke taishou zhuan 南柯太守傳 (The Magistrate of the Southern Branch). A certain man who had a huge locust tree (sophora japonica) in his garden dreamed of journeying to a distant country, where he married the princess and stayed for two decades before returning. When he awoke, he discovered a huge ant hill beneath the tree in his own garden, and close examination revealed that its structure was a miniature replica of the places he had visited in his dream. The sight made the man realize the brevity and vanity of human life, and he became thereafter a Daoist. The story in Chinese literature has been regarded as one of the classic treatments of sic gloria mundi transit.

3. The cuckoo's sound is said to imitate the Chinese phrase burugui, which may be translated, "Why not go back?"

4. Court regalia of officials in different periods generally had a stiff, loose belt worn with hornlike buckles.

5. Emperor Taizong's full Chinese name is Li Shimin 李世民.

6. The Chinese characters for thirteen appear thus: 十三. Adding two more strokes to the first graph (meaning ten) should make its appearance thus: 卅, meaning thirty. The two graphs together thus lengthen the emperor's allotted life to thirty-three.

7. Eastern melon is actually winter melon, or white gourd, the name here being a pun since east and winter (dong) are homonyms. Western and southern melons are watermelons and pumpkins, respectively.

8. Shu, historical name for the region that is the modern Sichuan Province, known for its rugged mountains. Lu in the next line refers to another famous mountain in modern Jiangsi Province.

9. The lowest and deepest of the eight hot hells in Buddhism. See the study by Daigan and Alicia Matsunaga, The Buddhist Concept of Hell (New York, 1972).

10. The Mass or Assembly, which offered food for both water and land spirits, was a Buddhist ritual said to have been inaugurated by Emperor Wu of the Liang (r. 502-49), but its liturgical popularity arose much later. According to Stephen F. Teiser, The Ghost Festival in Medieval China (Princeton, 1988), p. 108: "the Sung dynasties saw the growth of a liturgical tradition centering on the 'Assembly of Water and Land' (shui-lu hui), a kind of mass dedicated to wandering spirits. Offerings to spirits haunting waterways were dumped into streams and rivers, while presents destined for souls suffering recompense in the hells were thrown onto the ground. This ritual too was practiced at irregular intervals throughout the year, including the fifteenth day of the seventh month." A specific text on this ritual event may be found in Chishengguang daochang niansong yi 熾盛光道場念誦儀, written by Zunshi 遵式 (964-1032), and collected as #1951, in T. For treatment of Ming revival of the ritual by Zhuhong, see Chün-fang Yü, The Renewal of Buddhism in China: Chu-hung and the Late Ming Synthesis (New York, 1981), pp. 184-85.

CHAPTER TWELVE

1. Royal Xiangguo Temple: 敕建相國寺 literally means "the Xiangguo Temple Built by Imperial Commission." *Xiangguo* means "prime minister." The author of the XYJ apparently invented this episode, constantly punning on the sounds of the two syllables, which could refer to 相果, the fruits of Xiang. The temple of this name allegedly was built in the Kaifeng district of the modern Henan Province during the period of the Warring States (403-222 BCE). Destroyed repeatedly, it was finally rebuilt by the Tang emperor, Ruizong (684 CE).

2. Historically, Fu Yi 傅奕 was one of the most ardent critics of Buddhis. See Arthur F. Wright, "Fu I and the Rejection of Buddhism," *Journal of the History of Ideas* 12 (1951): 33-47; Stanley Weinstein, *Buddhism Under the Tang* (Cambridge and New York, 1987), pp. 7-9.

3. Three Ways: the three unhappy *gati* or paths of evildoers that lead to (1) the hell that burns with fire; (2) the hell of blood where, as animals, they mutually devour themselves; and (3) the hell of swords, where even leaves and plants are actually sharp blades.

4. Sixfold Path: the six directions or paths of reincarnation. They consist of (1) the way to hell, *naraka-gati*; (2) the way to that of hungry ghosts, *preta-gati*; (3) the way to that of beasts, *tiryagyoni-gati*; (4) the way to that of malevolent spirits, *assura-gati*; (5) the way to that of humans, *manuṣya-gati*; and (6) the way to that of celestial beings, *deva-gati*.

5. Emperor Ming or Mingdi (58-76 CE) ruled during the Later or Eastern Han.

6. Wudi of the Northern Zhou ruled during the period 561-78 CE, and he personally sponsored court debates on the merits of the Three Religions.

7. The Fifth Patriarch of the Chan Order was Hongren (601-74 CE). It is said that when his mother was carrying him, their whole house was illuminated by divine light night and day for over a month. At his birth, he was covered by a strange fragrance. See the *Song Gaosengzhuan* 宋高僧傳, *j* 2, in #2061, T 50: 719 ff., and the *Jingde Chuandenglu* 景德傳燈錄, *j* 3, in #2076, T 51: 216 ff.

8. The abbot's name here contradicts the Abbot Faming named in chapter 9; it is another textual detail suggesting that the former chapter might have been a composition alien to the 1592 version.

9. In the Tang period, this tower was established as a sort of national Valhalla, where portraits of meritorious officials were displayed.

10. A hat with the picture of the Vairocana Buddha on its brim.

11. A spiritual master or preceptor, used frequently in Chinese writings as a synonym for a Buddhist priest.

12. *Anpapādaka*, meaning direct metamorphosis or birth by transformation.

13. That is, the past, the present, and the future lives.

14. The most honorable one of the world.

15. As noted in introduction III, item 12, this proclamation is a modified version of another "Shengtang wen" by Feng Zunshi, collected in the *Minghe yuyin*, DZ 1100, 24: 308.

16. Seven Buddhas: they are seven ancient buddhas or Sapta Buddha, including Vipaśyin, Śikhui, Viśvabhū, Krakucchanda, Kanakmuni, Kāśyapa, and Śākyamuni.

17. That is, silkworms white as ice.

18. A pearl that glows at night.

19. The golden or diamond element in the universe, signifying the indestructible and active wisdom of Vairocana.

20. Luo Bo: the Chinese name for Mahāmaudgalyāyana, one of the chief disciples of Śākyamuni, who was famous for his journey to Hell to save his mother from the marauding hungry ghosts.

21. Another abode of the Lady Queen Mother of the West.

22. A metrical piece, one of the twelve classes of sūtras in Hīnayāna Buddhism.

23. The name of the guardian of the Earth, one of the eight Dhyāni-Bodhisattvas who, with Yama, rule as Ten Kings of the Underworld.

24. This poem is another lyric to the tune of "Moon Over West River."

25. The sexennial assembly of Buddha's disciples.

26. See chapter 8, note 18.

27. Name of a famous Buddhist monastery.

28. These three texts seem to be the inventions of the novel's author.

29. The true, spiritual form or "body"; the embodiment of essential Buddha-hood.

30. The full name of Guanyin, meaning in popular understanding, "she who hearkens to the voices of the world."

31. "Namo": I yield to or submit to.

CHAPTER THIRTEEN

1. Vulture Peak: Gṛdhrakūṭa, a place supposedly frequented by the Buddha and where the Lotus sūtra was preached. The full name of the mountain is Spirit Vulture Mountain.

2. The Wheel of the Law is *dharmacakra*, the truth of Buddha able to vanquish all evil and all resistance. It rolls on from man to man and from age to age.

3. Bamboo sticks were struck by the watchman as he announced the time.

4. This is a lyric to the tune of "Celestial Immortal."

5. Huang Gong, a man of the Han period and a native of Donghai (in modern Jiangsu Province), was reputedly a tamer of tigers. See the *Xijing zaji* 西京雜记, *j* 3.

6. From antiquity, the dream of a bear had been interpreted by the Chinese as a sign of the imminent birth of a male child. See the "Xiaoya 小雅" segment of the *Classic of Poetry*.

7. The lion king, or *shiman* 獅蠻, was supposedly a pastry decoration made of flour and shaped like a barbarian king with a lion head. This ornament also appeared on belt buckles; hence the name.

8. A mendicant monk. The story is actually named "Bichu Purged from Evil Karma 芯蒭洗業," which tells of Buddha's encountering an ascetic practicing austerities northeast of a stūpa in the Jetavana Garden. When asked why he looked so sad by the patriarch, the man replied that he was ill and had no one to care for him. Whereupon Buddha stretched out his hand and touched the man, who was healed at once. Taking him out of his hut, Buddha bathed and clothed him before urging him to be even more diligent in his religious devotion.

CHAPTER FOURTEEN

1. The six robbers or *cauras* refer to the six senses of the body, which impede enlightenment: hence they appear in this chapter's allegory as bandits.

2. The term literally means to turn toward. It also refers to the bestowal of merit by one being on another.

3. As discussed in introduction I and III, this poem is an adaptation of an ode by the Song Quanzhen Daoist, Zhang Boduan. For documentation, see the end of introduction III, item 6.

4. Wang Mang 王莽 (45 BCE-23 CE) was a prime minister during the Early Han who usurped the emperor's throne. He was, however, also known as a reformer.

5. Literally, the word means shaken, shaken off, or cleansed. It points to the practice of asceticism as an antidote to worldly attachments. Hence it is also used in the Chinese vernacular as a name for any mendicant.

6. Literally, the Chinese term *xingzhe* means a novice who practices austerities or asceticism, and who is also a mendicant.

7. This is another lyric to the tune of "Moon Over West River."

8. A pun: sugar in Chinese is also expressed by the phoneme *tang*.

9. "The same illustrious clan": Tripitaka's remark here is based on the principle articulated in the *Records of Rites*, which states, "those of the same patrilineal name belong to the same clan 同姓從宗." See *Liji, j* 39 in SSJZS 2: 1507.

10. "Horse-face fold": a colloquialism in the southern dialects that refers to the making of a folded lining. The term is still in use in Cantonese.

11. The tenth month of the lunar year is often referred to as Little Spring.

12. This is another lyric to the tune of "Celestial Immortal."

13. Huang Shigong (黄石公, Squire of the Yellow Stone): a legendary figure who became an immortal. He was also the putative author of the *Sushu* 素書, an extra-canonical Daoist text.

14. Zhang Liang 張良 (d. 187 BCE), legendary Daoist tactician who assisted Liu Bang in securing the Han empire.

15. "Made his plans . . . away": a quotation from the *Shiji* 史記, *j* 8, "Gaozu benji 高祖本紀." It was Liu Bang's own compliment to Zhang Liang, then used subsequently as a hyperbole for the achievements of any military strategist.

16. Master Red Pine (Chisong zi 赤松子), a legendary immortal of high antiquity. For stories and texts associated with him, see the entries in ET 1: 271-73.

CHAPTER FIFTEEN

1. According to the Daoist religion, the Three Corpses are spirits resident in different parts of the human body as parasites: the head, the chest, and the abdomen (in certain texts, the feet are mentioned as a variant location). They thus also have the name of the Three Worms (*sanchong* 三蟲), able to "cause disease, invite other disease-causing agents into the body, and report their host's transgressions to heaven so as to shorten his life span." These spirit-worms are regarded as variously connected to human appetites and desires and thus must be subdued through ritual and the practice of austerities. See entry on "*sanshi* and *jiuchong* (three corpses and nine worms)" in ET 2: 844-46. For a scriptural account, see the *Taiqing zhonghuang zhenjing* 太清中黄真經 in DZ 817, 18: 386.

2. "Thusness": that is, *zhenru* 真如 or *bhūtatathatā*, thus always, eternally so, hence the Real.

3. The cow, the sheep, and the pig.

4. The cow, the sheep, the pig, the dog, the chicken, and the horse.

CHAPTER SIXTEEN

1. This is the sexennial assembly of Buddha's disciples.

2. Monkey is mocking the proverb by literalizing the saying, which usually is employed to mean, "if you live and work as a monk, you might as well do the work for the duration."

3. Grapevine: literally, dragon whiskers (*Juncus effusus*), a kind of rush used for weaving mats.

4. Suiren: the legendary Chinese Prometheus, who was said to have invented fire by rubbing sticks of wood together.

5. Red Cliff Campaign: the famous episode in *The Three Kingdoms* (chapters 48-50) when Cao Cao was defeated by the combined tactics of Zhuge Liang and Zhou Yu, who attacked Cao's larger fleet with burning boats.

6. A palace built in the capital, Xianyang, in Shaanxi, by Shihuangdi (221-209 BCE) of the Qin. It was razed by the warrior and contender for the throne, Xiang Yu, and the fire was said to have lasted for three months.

7. The Chinese text here had Beijing, 京畿, which was impossible. This was probably an inconsistency or a deliberate use of the late Ming capital's name as a metaphor caused by the constraint of rhyme in the regulated poem.

CHAPTER SEVENTEEN

1. The tripod and the oven may refer to the utensils of external alchemy, or they may be metaphors for different parts of the viscera in the human body. White snow and yellow sprout are metaphors for mercury and lead, but such chemical substances also may be used as metaphors for physiological elements within the body.

2. Mount Penglai is one of the three famous mythical mountains in the Eastern Sea or Ocean, where immortals live.

3. This is the first of three long regulated poems (*pailü*) articulating part of the autobiography of each of the human-like disciples of Xuanzang in the novel (see chapters 19 and 22 for similar declarations from the other two disciples). The dragon-horse was not given this privilege. Each poem details the initial stage and attainment in terms of the disciple's religious pedigree, making clear that the person had succeeded in distilling the inner elixir of alchemy to become an immortal before further transgression banished him to suffer again in the human world.

4. Mount Lingtai: that is, the Mountain of Spirit Platform or Heart and Mind (see chapter 1). Notice that Monkey's verse here is reaffirming that the residence of his teacher, Master Subhodi, is squarely located in a mountain which can be interpreted as the Heart and Mind. Thus the entire narrative episode, in view of such double meanings, may suggest that all those entertaining events of "seeking and learning the Way (*fangdao* 訪道 and *candao* 參道)" are only allegorical depictions of mental or psychic experiences.

5. Literally, "sun and moon copulated as male and female (*li, kan*) in my body." According to the discourse of internal alchemy, the sun and the moon may be the metaphors for the heart and the kidneys, respectively, which in turn are further correlated with the male and female symbols (*li* 離 and *kan* 坎) in the eight trigram lore of the *Classic of Change*. When the pneumatic vitality (i.e., *qi* 氣) of the heart and the kidneys are in proper balance or restored to their primordial condition, the internal elixir (*neidan*) is formed and immortality is achieved.

6. "Without leaks": *wulou* 無漏 or *loujin* 漏盡, "cessation of overflow," a Daoist adaptation of the Sanskrit *āsravakṣaya* for describing part of the process taught in what was called the "Greater Celestial Circuit (*da zhoutian* 大周天)" process of internal alchemy. See ET 1: 688-89.

7. Xiansheng: that is, the Immortal Master of Illustrious Sagacity, the God Erlang (see chapter 6).

8. The Buddha is said to have luminous eyebrows the color of white jade.

9. The references to the tiger and dragon in these two lines are likely descriptive metaphors for postures or movements (*zhao* 招) in Chinese martial art.

10. "Ingesting . . . breath": *fuqi* 服氣. Internal or physiological alchemy places great emphasis on the manipulation of pneumatic vitality (*qi*) in the human body for retention, circulation, and refinement. See SCC V/5: 142-51, and the entry on "Nourishing Life, *yangsheng* 養生," in ET 2: 1148-50.

11. "Knowing one's destiny or life (*zhiming* 知命)" is a venerable concept in the Chinese history of ideas, though the term also has accrued a variety of meanings down through the centuries. Beginning with Confucius' declaration in *Analects* 2. 4, that "at fifty [he] understood the will of Heaven or the fate ordained by Heaven (*wushi er zhi tianming* 五十而知天命)," the phrase *zhiming* signals different notions in different traditions, including all three major religions. Monkey's description of the monster is intentionally ironic in a twofold manner. As a fiendish creature (*guaiwu* 怪物), his foe is not supposed to entertain such a lofty sense of self-understanding, but the oxymoron (no less than the cave-dwelling's refined beauty) may also indicate Monkey's dawning recognition of the monster's resemblance to himself, the perception of which is further validated by the subsequent conversation between Monkey and his master, and by the monster's submission to Guanyin later in the chapter.

12. The numbers, "three times three" and "six times six" likely refer to the lines of the *Qian* Hexagram (three unbroken lines on top and three on the bottom) and the *Kun* Hexagram (six lines on the left, and six on the right, with a space in between), as found in the *Classic of Change*. They are not only regarded as the parental *gua* of all the sixty-four hexagrams, but they are also the definitive symbols of male and female; hence, of the yin and the yang. For a translation of the received text, see *The I Ching or Book of Changes*, the Richard Wilhelm Translation rendered into English by Cary F. Baynes, with a preface by Hellmut Wilhelm (1967), Bollingen Series 19 (Princeton, 1971), pp. 3-20. For a translation of an older text more recently discovered, see *I Ching: The Classic of Changes*, trans. Edward L. Shaughnessy (New York, 1996), pp. 38-39, 102-03.

13. The Goulou (勾漏 = 句漏, also articulated as Julou) may refer to a mountain in northern Guangxi Province. It is so named because it has many caves or grottoes which are joined to one another. Legend has it that the famed alchemist Ge Hong (283-343) did some of his work here.

14. Shao Weng 少翁 was supposed to be some kind of magician from the state of Qi. See the *Shiji, j* 12 and 28. See *Ershiwishi* 1: 0043b-c, 0116c.

CHAPTER EIGHTEEN

1. After rites involving sacrificial offerings, the sacrifical meats and fruits are then distributed among the celebrants. Hence the name "blessing."

2. Moth-brows (i.e., mothlike eyebrows) is a common term describing a woman's delicately painted and curved eyebrows.

3. That is, thirty-six (see chapter 2). The Heavenly Ladle is the name for the thirty-six stars of the Big Dipper revolving around the North Star.

CHAPTER NINETEEN

1. Seeking the Real: literally, cultivating authenticity or immortality (xiuzhen).

2. Cold and heat (hanwen 寒溫): a phrase usually glossed (e.g., XYJCD, p. 121) as a reference to the weather used in conventional greetings (hanxuan 寒喧). This is erroneous, for the context here, unlike that in Outlaws of the Marshes, chapter 81, suggests an actual reference to alchemical processes inside or outside the body. Its source may be found precisely in a relatively early text (the received version established probably no later than the sixth century CE), ZhouYi cantongqi 周易參同契, in DZ 999, 20: 78. The two lines of verse therein ("Add caution to watch periodically;/Inspect to adjust cold and heat 候視加謹慎, 審察調寒溫) may allude to both chemical processes external to the body and physiological activities as developed in later theories of internal alchemy.

3. The eight woes (banan 八難) refer to eight conditions or states of being (the state of hells; the state of animals; the state of hungry ghosts; the states of being deaf, blind, and dumb; the state of no affliction; and the state of the intermediate period between a Buddha and his successor) that make it difficult for one to see Buddha or hear his law. The three ways (santu 三途) are that of fire, where one is burned in hell; of blood, which is the realm of predatory animals; and of the sword, with which hungry ghosts are tortured.

4. The term, jiuzhuan huandan 九轉還丹 means the "Reverted Cinnabar/Elixir of Nine Cycles," and its production has been discussed in many texts of the Daoist Canon of different periods and practices. Joseph Needham's explanation for the basic concern in Daoist alchemy for "reversion, regeneration, and return" is succinct: "For the proto-chemical alchemist the term huan tan meant an elixir or part of an elixir prepared by cyclical transformation, such as may be brought about by repeated separation and sublimatory re-combination of mercury and sulphur, reducing cinnabar and re-forming mercuric sulphide. If this were accomplished nine times it could be the [Reverted Cinnabar of Nine Cycles] described in many of the books. On the other hand, the phrase huan tan was applied by the 'physiological alchemists' . . . to a chhi [qi, pneumatic vitality, breath] or substance generated by techniques purposefully within the human body which would bring about a reversion of the tissues from an ageing state to an infantile state." See SCC V/5: 25.

5. What follows in the next eight lines are allusions to the various techniques and stages in the process of internal or physiological alchemy. To understand the process, students will need to consult not only the relevant Daoist texts but also the important illustrations or diagrams (tu 圖) scattered throughout these texts that have served to assist visualization of internal or invisible realities, to pictorialize the frequently and variously used didactic device of analogous symbolism (piyu 譬喻). For overviews of Daoist anatomy and physiology related to the alchemical process, the best reproductions of several Ming and Qing diagrams (untranslated) may be found in Taoism and the Arts of China, eds. Stephen Little and Shawn Eichman (Art Institute of Chicago, 2000), pp. 348-51. Catherine Despeux's Taoïsme et corps humain, Le xiuzhen tu (Paris, 1994), provides an excellent discussion of this "Diagram for Cultivating Immortality."

For another similar study of the "Diagram of Internal Pathways, *Neijing tu* 內境圖," see the essays by Louis Komjathy, "Mapping the Daoist Body, Part One," in *Journal of Daoist Studies* 1 (2008): 67-92, and "Part Two" in *Journal of Daoist Studies* 2 (2009): 64-108.

6. Mud-Pill Palace: *niwan gong* 泥丸宮, a term used by the Daoists to refer to the upper part of the head or, in Joseph Needham's words, "the Daoist brain." The term is controversial since the same phonemes (as construed by historical phonology and not modern Mandarin) are used in Buddhist writings, but the orthography therein is often changed to 泥洹. See brief discussion in SCC V/5: 38.

7. Jetting-Spring Points: *yongquan xue* 湧泉穴, a term referring to two points at the center of the soles. The *xue* is the name for the sensitive nodal points spread out in the entire human body for connecting and conducting the circulation of vital energetics or pneumatic vitalities. As such, they form the crucial "relay stations," so to speak, in the sinarteriology discursively constructed in Chinese *materia medica* and supplemented in Daoist anatomy. See Manfred Porkert, *The Theoretical Foundations of Chinese Medicine: Systems of Correspondence* (Cambridge, 1972), pp. 197-345. "The hole [associated with] the kidneys is located in the center of the sole of the foot," and it is sometimes written as *yongquan* 涌泉. See *Nan-Ching: The Classic of Difficult Issues*, trans. Paul U. Unschuld (Berkeley, CA, 1986), p. 462.

8. The Floral Pool, *huachi* 華池, refers to the spot beneath the tongue in the mouth, where saliva supposedly originates. The idea is that the energetics refined in the renal system (which corresponds to the phase Water, *shui* 水, of the Five Phases) flows throughout the body and can be directed to a specific spot or area by alchemical action. See Porkert, *Theoretical Foundations*, pp. 140-46, 162-63.

9. One of the most important terminologies in both traditional Chinese medical theories and Daoist physiology, the name *dantian* 丹田 is often translated as Cinnabar Field. The English rendering, however, fails inevitably to convey the doubleness of meaning inherent in the Chinese nomenclature, which refers to both the imagined features of the inner abdominal region of the alchemist and the imagined space where the elixir (also called *dan*, the same Chinese graph) is forged. As Needham rightly points out, the visual and physical properties of *dan* are construed as scarlet red (hence the use of cinnabar for translation because of the mineral's color) and harboring fiery warmth. See SCC V/5: 38. These characteristics reflect, in turn, the physiological alchemist's venerable analogy drawn between zones of the human body and the material vessels of oven or furnace and cauldron or tripod (*lu, ding*) employed in the earlier practice of physical or proto-chemical alchemy. In the internal alchemist discourse, furthermore, *dantian* is an imagined abdominal space "devoid of material counterparts," additionally classified into different levels or parts, and indispensable for the production of the elixir. Thus its name also has the meaning of the "elixir field." See the entry on *"dantian"* for more detailed elaboration in ET 1: 302-03.

10. Baby and Fair Girl: *ying'er* 嬰兒 *chanü* 姹女. As noted in the introduction to this volume, the term "baby boy" often means the state of realized immortality in Daoist discourse. But in the huge corpora of writings authored by internal alchemists, the terms acquire further symbolical meanings in different schemes of correlation and correspondence. As annotators have pointed out, "baby boy" here may point to lead and "fair girl" to mercury, but these chemical elements, in turn, may symbolize energetics or pneumatic vitalities (*qi*) harnassed from different anatomical regions.

11. As explained in chapter 17, footnote 5, *Li* 離 and *Kan* 坎 are names of two trigrams (掛) developed in the *Classic of Change* to symbolize the male and female. In different schemes of correspondence elaborated in alchemy texts, they also acquire further correlative significance with symbolic animals, of which the dragon and the tiger are a prominent pair. Along with the turtle and the snake, they form the characteristic creatures indicating opposite but complementary signs of physiological functions and potencies.

12. Spirit turtle, gold crow: *linggui* 靈龜 and *jinwu* 金烏, both names of somatic elements in alchemy. The spirit turtle here may be another name for the dark liquid of the kidneys, while the gold crow indicates the sun or the heart. The line refers to the union of yin and yang through the absorption of yang energy by yin.

13. Literally, three flowers (or florescences) congregate on top (*sanhua juding* 三花= 華聚頂). It refers to the completion of the process whereby the three vital elements of the body (spermal essence, *jing*; pneumatic vitality, *qi*; and spirit or energy, *shen*) are brought back (reverted) to the top of one's head. The elixir so distilled would be regarded as the "fruition (*jiezi* 結子)" of the union of the three "flowers." For scriptural source, see, for example, the "Taiqingjing Huangting jing 太清境黃庭經," in *Taishang sanshiliu bu zunjing* 太上三十六部尊經, DZ 8, 1: 606, and the *Jindan sibai zi* 金丹四百字, DZ 1081, 24: 161. This second text's author was Zhang Boduan, the founding patriarch of the Southern Order of Quanzhen Daoism, discussed in our introduction.

14. Five breaths … *wuqi chaoyuan* 五氣朝元, refers to the pneumatic vitality, *qi*, of the five viscera (heart, liver, spleen, lungs, and kidneys) in harmonious balance. See also the *Jindan sibai zi*, loc. cit. There are several variations of the sources for these five pneumatic elements, and one of them, for example, may select and schematize the psychological or mental part of the body (e.g., the mind, the emotions), as we have in XMGZ-Taipei, p. 135.

15. A poetic name for the mythic palace on the moon.

16. Chang'e: the immortal goddess who resides in the moon.

17. Inspector General: same as Numinous Officer Wang.

18. Deities may be hypostatized from the trigrams and hexagrams of the *Classic of Change*. The idea of these two lines here, however, is that the symbols of these divinities are engraved or etched on different parts of the rake.

19. This poem is the first of the novel's many passages in which the relations of the pilgrims to each other are depicted allegorically by the terms of the Five Phases (*wuxing*), further correlated with other pertinent symbols like Monkey and Dragon.

20. In alchemical lore, lead is sometimes regarded as host (*zhu*) and mercury as the guest (*ke* or *bin*), and vice versa. In the process when metal "attacks" or "vanquishes (*fa, ke*)" wood, lead will act as host and mercury as guest.

21. According to *yin yang* theorists, three matings (*sanjiao* 三交) refer to the intercourse of pneumatics (*qi*) of the *yin* (darkness, female), the *yang* (light, male), and *tian* (Heaven, sky); nothing can be created if one is lacking. Later, the idea is expanded to the correlation of the Five Phases with the cycles of the year, the month, and the day, which is also thus called three unions (*sanhe* 三合).

22. Last and First: literally, *zhen* 貞 (to determine, divine) and *yuan* 元 (the primary, the initial), two of the four "attributes" assigned to the first hexagram (乾 *qian or jian*) that opens the text of the *Classic of Change*, with which the author/redactor of a later

text like the *ZhouYi cantongqi* would further correlate with the affective faculties of the human. Thus the combination in this line may point again to the conjoining of opposites, an idea fundamental to alchemical theories.

23. Eight Rules: that is, eight proscriptions. These are the first eight of the ten commandments in Buddhism forbidding killing, stealing, sexual immorality, lying, the use of cosmetics and other personal comforts (e.g., a fine bed), strong drink, the use of dancing and music, and eating out of regulation hours. The last two deal with specific forbidden foods and the rule for fasting.

24. Causes all joined: literally, the various causes are fused (*zhuyuan he* 諸緣合), a probable reference to the harmonious working of the cycle of twelve *nidānas*.

25. Hair shorn: the phrase refers to a story in which one Old Man Wang (Wang Weng 黃翁) attained physical longevity in stages. At the last, when since his time of birth he went through five times during which his hair was shorn or fell off and apparently grew back again, he realized immortality. See the *Hanwu dongming ji* 漢武洞冥記, *j* 1.

26. Guanzizai: Guanyin, the Onlooking Lord.

27. *Pañcaskandha*: the five aggregates or elements constitutive of the human person: they are (1) *rūpa*, physical phenomena related to the five senses; (2) *verdanā*, sensation or reception from stimuli from events and things; (3) *sañjñā*, discernment or perception; (4) *saṃskāra*, decision or volition; and (5) *vijñāna*, cognition and consciousness.

28. Three worlds: the past, present, and future ones.

29. The quotation says: "Gone, gone, gone beyond, completely gone beyond! O what an awakening! All hail!"

CHAPTER TWENTY

1. No-work tree: the tree of passivity, nonactivity, spontaneity, and noncausality.

2. The Buddha is sometimes referred to as the king of bulls, possibly because his name, Gautama, is thought to be a derivative of *gaus*, or bull. For possible Daoist source for this particular line of the verse, see Item 7 near the end of introduction III of this volume.

3. In form, this poem seems like the first section of a lyric to the tune of "Moon Over West River."

4. A pun on the words *yao* 爻 and *yao* 殽. The first refers to lines in a hexagram of the *Classic of Change*, and the second means cuisine or fine food.

5. These two lines represent a tour de force of punning hard to replicate in another language.

6. *Wu*, short for *wutong* 梧桐, *Sterculia platanifolia*, sometimes translated as the pawlownia.

7. Mount Hua and Tiantai Mountain are famous mountains located in Shaanxi and Anhui provinces, respectively. For a good description of these mountains and their significance in the history of Chinese religions, see Mary Augusta Mullikin and Anna M. Hotchkis, *The Nine Sacred Mountains of China* (Hong Kong, 1973).

CHAPTER TWENTY-ONE

1. These are the guardian spirits of a monastery.

2. Erlang, who customarily uses a lance-like weapon with three points and two blades, sometimes also would wield a trident.

3. These two Indian figures are frequently depicted as the two disciples appearing on the left and right of Tathāgata: the former rides a green lion and the latter a white elephant. For a discussion of these two disciples as idealizations of Śāriputra and Maudagalyāyana, see Yinshun 印順, "Wenxu yu Puxian 文殊與普賢," in *Fojiao shidi kaolun* 佛教史地考論 (Taipei, 1973), pp. 233-44.

4. See chapter 2, note 9.

5. Zitong 梓橦: the god of a northern Sichuanese cult who is freqently depicted as a riding a mule. See Terry F. Kleeman, *A God's Own Tale: The Book of Transformations of Wenchang, the Divine Lord of Zitong* (Albany, 1999), and the entry on "Wenchang" in ET 2: 1033-34.

6. Penglai: one of the three famous legendary mountainous islands in the eastern ocean where divine immortals made their residences.

7. Lu Ban 魯班: reputedly a craftsman of marvelous skills in the Spring and Autumn period, Lu was subsequently venerated by carpenters and builders as their patron deity. In his own poetic autobiography of chapter 19, Eight Rules claimed that Lu had a hand in making his rake.

8. Sesame seed rice: an allusion to the often told story of Liu Chen 劉晨 and Ruan Zhao 阮肇, who went to gather herbs on Tiantai Mountain and met immortals there. They were fed peaches and rice with sesame seeds.

9. Devised: the Chinese phrase, *dianhua* 點化, is a technical term for understanding the nature and use of illusion. For Buddhism, it can be a means of deception (as illusory entrapments devised by monsters and demons mentioned in chapter 50) or a form of convenience in assistance or instruction (i.e., *upāya*). In Daoism, especially in the discourse on alchemy, the term has the developed meaning of using "a particle" of Primordial Breath (*yuanqi*) to facilitate the formation of the elixir. See entry on "*dianhua*" in ET 1: 357-58.

10. This poem is another lyric to the tune of "Moon Over West River."

11. This lyric is set to the same tune as the previous poem's.

12. Sonorous stones: the *qing* 磬, a small gong-like stone with the inside hollowed out, to be struck in religious services.

13. This little piece of conversation virtually repeats the episode in another novel, when the contender for the throne of Han, Liu Bei, visited the master strategist, Zhuge Liang, at his thatched hut to request assistance. See *Three Kingdoms, A Historical Novel,* chapter 37, 284.

CHAPTER TWENTY-TWO

1. The sentence here in Pilgrim's statement also presents a subtle satire, on the part of the narrator, of the familiar sight of monkeys doing tricks with sticks and poles in vaudeville shows popular in certain regions of China.

2. As in Eight Rules's previous verse autobiography (chapter 19), the monster here recounts his experience of self-cultivation by means of physiological alchemy. For "Baby Boy" and "Fair Girl," see note 10 of that chapter.

3. In the discourse of internal alchemy, "Wood Mother" is one of several metaphors of mercury. Correlating with the Twelve Temporal Branches or Horary Characters is the belief that "true mercury is born at the hour of Hai 真汞生亥." Because the animal symbolizing the hour is boar or pig (*hai shu zhu* 亥屬豬), our disciple Eight Rules is

nicknamed later in the narrative as Wood Mother. Lead, on the other hand, is named metaphorically as the Squire of Gold or Squire of Metal (*jingong* 金公, *jinweng* 金翁). The first Chinese term may have been an anagrammatic reading of the Chinese graph for lead or *qian* 鉛, which may be broken up into the two graphs of *jin* and *gong*. I owe this suggestion to Professor Nathan Sivin. Gold or metal is further correlated with the Horary Character of *shen* 申, the symbolic animal of which is a monkey. Thus another nickname for Sun Wukong throughout the narrative is Metal Squire.

4. Bright Hall or Hall of Light: *mingtang* 明堂, one of the most famous nomenclatures for a palatial building consecrated for imperial rituals in antiquity, it is internalized as a metaphor of anatomical space by the discourse on internal alchemy. The spot varies in different texts, but generally, the name is regarded as a spot one inch inside the skull, between the eyebrows. See entry on "*mintang*" in ET 2: 751–52.

5. Floral Pool: see chapter 19, note 8.

6. Tower or *chonglou* refers to the windpipe or the trachea. Since the medical theorists and the alchemists thought that it had twelve sections, the full name of this part of the body is named the Twelve-Tiered Tower (*shier chonglou* 十二重樓).

7. Wu Gang: 吳剛, an immortal of the Han period, according to the *Yuyang zazu* 酉陽雜俎, who took up residence in the moon. There he tried frequently to cut down a cassia tree, only to have it grow again once it was felled.

8. Spatula: *daoguei* 刀圭, the spatula or knifelike instrument that both medical herbalists and the physical alchemists use to separate or measure their chemicals or herbs. For the internal alchemists, the term can refer further to refined saliva in the last stage of elixir formation. *Daogui* in the novel is also used as a metaphor for this monster who will soon become Xuanzang's third disciple, Sha Wujing.

9. Two-Earths: an anagrammatic pun on the graph *gui* 圭, used for spatula. *Gui* is made up of two graphs, earth or *tu* 土, one on top of the other.

CHAPTER TWENTY-THREE

1. Yellow Dame: this is what the secretion of the spleen in internal alchemy is called (*huangpo*), and it is considered vital to the nourishment of the other viscera. In the narrative, the term is frequently used to designate Sha Monk. Red child or red boy (*chizi*) in literary Chinese usually refers to the newborn infant because of its color, but its meaning varies greatly in different traditions. In classical Confucian teachings, the term seems to indicate the seminal capacity for moral attainment if one takes *Mencius* 4B. 12 as an example ("A great man is one who does not lose the heart/mind of the new-born babe"). In Laozi's *Daodejing*, chapter 55, the red child exemplifies the paragon of virtuous power resident in complete peaceableness and gentleness. In internal alchemy, however, the formation of the baby can refer to the state of achieved physical immortality, and it is in this sense that the term is occasionally and proleptically used in the narrative to identify Tripitaka.

2. The names of the three daughters make up the Chinese phrase, *zhen ai lian*, which may be translated as "truly [worthy to be] loved and adored."

3. "To lead a horse": a Chinese metaphor for a marriage go-between.

4. Xizi: the legendary beauty and concubine of King Fucha of the ancient kingdom of Wu.

5. Dame of Li Shan: Lishan Laomu 黎山老母, or the Old Dame of Li Mountain,

seems to have been originally a river demon (as interpreted by Dudbridge in *Antecedents*, pp. 144-46), but in quite a few works of late imperial and early modern Chinese popular fiction, she emerged as a powerful goddess similar to her role in this chapter.

CHAPTER TWENTY-FOUR

1. Ginseng: 人参, *panax schinseng*, a plant highly treasured in traditional Chinese medicine both as an aphrodisiac and as a longevity herb.

2. Kunlun: the largest mountain range in China, beginning in Tibet and extending eastward to form three ranges in North, Central, and South China. Commonly regarded as the most important sacred mountain of Daoism, it is the legendary home of the Lady Queen Mother of the West and the Jade-Pure Honorable Divine of the Origin (Yuqing yuanshi tianzun).

3. Five blessings: they are long life, wealth, health, love of virtue, and a natural death.

4. Locust trees: *Sophora japonica*.

5. Zhenyuan literally means "one who has pacified his origin."

6. For the possible origin of the phrase "reverted cinnabar or elixir" (*huandan* 還丹), see the *Baopuzi* 抱朴子, SBCK, 4. 3a and 7b; and also *Alchemy, Medicine, and Religion in the China of A.D. 320: The "Nei P'ien" of Ko Hung*, trans. James R. Ware (Cambridge, MA, 1966), pp. 70 and 77.

7. A citation from *Analects* 15.40.

8. "The one on top": i.e., the word Heaven or *tian*.

9. The railings on top of a well in wealthy households are frequently painted gold; hence the frequent references to a "golden well" in classical Chinese verse.

10. Mare's tail: *Hippuris*, a plant used primarily to feed goldfish.

11. *Su: Dipsacus asper.*

12. The poem is another lyric to the tune of "Moon Over West River."

13. Immortals or, as in recent translations, transcendents (*xian*, 仙), are strictly humans who by practice and action—whether medicinal or physiological—attain immortality or physical longevity, a belief held since antiquity in China. By early medieval times, they are often classified into three broad categories: celestial, earthbound, and demon or ghost (i.e., those consigned to service in the underworld after attaining *xian*-ship)—*tianxian, dixian, guixian*. For discussion, see SCC, V/2 (1974): 11-12; 92-113. For Ge Hong's contribution to the subject's theory and practice, see Campany, pp. 13-128.

14. This entertaining anecdote on the fictive ginseng's potency indicates the same part of the belief that physical longevity induced by alchemy manifests in hardened bodily parts as evidential symptoms of fortification and renewal. Thus, the loss of body hairs was construed as a sign of returning youth. As the magic fruit strengthens the ground, so ingested substances in external alchemy, according to long-held notions, would empower the body. See the death of the character Jia Jing 賈敬, a devoted practitioner of Daoist alchemy in the Qing masterwork fiction, *Hongloumeng*. The description of his death by prolonged swallowing of mercuric elixir and other chemical substances in chapter 63 of the novel is both vivid and comparatively instructive. Jia died with a "purple face and cracked and shrivelled lips" and an "iron-hard abdomen (腹中堅硬似鐵, 面皮嘴唇燒的紫絳皺裂)." For English translation of the episode, see *The Story of the Stone*, 5 vols., Cao Xueqin and Gao E, trans. David Hawkes and John Minford (Hammondsworth, 1073-86), 3: 240.

CHAPTER TWENTY-FIVE

1. Mendicant Daoist: "*xingjiao* Quanzhen 行脚全真," literally, a Quanzhen [Daoist] with walking legs! As in several instances in the novel, the name of the Order may be used as a metaphor for a general Daoist of whatever sect or lineage.

2. Mr. Lü: this is Lü Dongbin 呂洞賓, a semilegendary figure of the late Tang and early Song who had attained lasting fame as an immortal and ranked among the equally famous Eight Immortals (*baxian*) populating Chinese literature, art, architecture, and popular cultural artifacts. Subject of several hagiographies, Lü also was credited with attributed poems and lyrics, and during the Song and later, several conversion plays were written about his life and religious activities, including his ardent attempt to convert the Tang Confucian literati official Han Yu. He was also a highly popular and venerated patriarch of the Quanzhen Order. See the entry on his name in ET 1: 712-14.

3. A jade yak's-tail: that is, a yak's-tail duster with a jade handle.

4. The monk's robe is sometimes nicknamed a bell (as in chapter 46 of this novel during Monkey's contest of magic with three Daoist monsters) because it is shaped like one—tight and narrow on top, loose and wide at the bottom.

5. Stove: *zao* 灶, the mud or clay furnace in most traditional Chinese kitchens for cooking. To overturn or ruin a stove (*duzao* 倒 or 搗灶), however, is to inflict bad luck.

Index

Boldface type denotes volume number. This index is principally one of proper names and places along with titles of some scriptural texts referenced in the novel. The names, nicknames, and allegorical nomenclatures of the Five Pilgrims are too numerous to be included.

40712249R00340

Made in the USA
Middletown, DE
21 February 2017